1/05

THE
SCIENCE FICTION
HALL OF FAME
Volume Two A

THE
SCIENCE FICTION
HALL OF FAME

Volume Two A

The Greatest Science Fiction Novellas of All Time
Chosen by the Members of
The Science Fiction Writers of America

Edited by Ben Bova

TOR®

A TOM DOHERTY ASSOCIATES BOOK
NEW YORK

THE SCIENCE FICTION HALL OF FAME, VOLUME TWO A: THE GREATEST
SCIENCE FICTION NOVELLAS OF ALL TIME, CHOSEN BY THE MEMBERS OF
THE SCIENCE FICTION WRITERS OF AMERICA

This book is printed on acid-free paper.

A Tor Book
Published by Tom Doherty Associates, LLC
175 Fifth Avenue
New York, NY 10010

www.tor.com

Tor® is a registered trademark of Tom Doherty Associates, LLC.

ISBN 0-765-30534-8
EAN 978-0765-30534-3

First Tor Edition: December 2004

Printed in the United States of America

0 9 8 7 6 5 4 3 2 1

ACKNOWLEDGMENTS

Call Me Joe, by Poul Anderson, copyright © 1957 by Street & Smith Publications, Inc. All rights reserved. Reprinted by permission of the author and his agent, Robert P. Mills.

Who Goes There?, by John W. Campbell, Jr., copyright © 1938 by Street & Smith Publications, Inc. (renewed 1966 by The Condé-Nast Publications, Inc.). All rights reserved. Reprinted by permission of the author's agents, Scott Meredith Literary Agency, Inc.

Nerves, by Lester del Rey, copyright © 1942 by Street & Smith Publications, Inc. (renewed 1970 by The Condé-Nast Publications, Inc.). All rights reserved. Reprinted by permission of the author's agents, Scott Meredith Literary Agency, Inc.

Universe, by Robert A. Heinlein, copyright © 1941 by Street & Smith Publications, Inc. (renewed 1969 by The Condé-Nast Publications, Inc.). All rights reserved. Reprinted by permission of the author and his agent, Lurton Blassingame.

The Marching Morons, by C. M. Kornbluth, copyright © 1951 by Galaxy Publishing Corporation. Reprinted by permission of Robert P. Mills on behalf of the author's estate.

Vintage Season, by Henry Kuttner and C. L. Moore (as Lawrence O'Donnell), copyright © 1946 by Street & Smith Publications, Inc., in the U.S.A. and Great Britain. All rights reserved. Reprinted by permission of the authors' agent, the Harold Matson Company, Inc.

. . . And Then There Were None, by Eric Frank Russell, copyright © 1951 by Street & Smith Publications, Inc. All rights reserved.

The Ballad of Lost C'mell, by Cordwainer Smith, copyright © 1962 by Galaxy Publishing Corporation. Reprinted by permission of the author's estate and their agents, Scott Meredith Literary Agency, Inc.

Baby Is Three, by Theodore Sturgeon, copyright © 1952 by Galaxy Publishing Corporation.

The Time Machine, by H. G. Wells, copyright © 1934 by Alfred A. Knopf, Inc. Reprinted by permission of Collins-Knowlton-Wing, Inc., on behalf of the author's estate.

With Folded Hands, by Jack Williamson, copyright © 1954 by Street & Smith Publications, Inc. All rights reserved. Reprinted by permission of the author's agents, Scott Meredith Literary Agency, Inc.

CONTENTS

INTRODUCTION

This two-book set is the second volume of the Science Fiction Hall of Fame, and consists of stories of longer lengths than those published in the highly acclaimed Volume One.

These stories have been selected by the members of The Science Fiction Writers of America (SFWA), the organization of some four hundred professional science fiction writers. Thus, the Science Fiction Hall of Fame is the definitive anthology in this field, the collective choice of the practitioners of the science fiction art themselves.

Founded in 1965, each year since 1966 SFWA has given achievement awards for the best stories of the year. The awards are called Nebulas, and are chosen on the basis of a vote by SFWA's members. The purpose of the Science Fiction Hall of Fame anthologies is to bestow a similar recognition on stories that were published prior to 1966, and thus never had a chance to earn a Nebula.

Like the annual Nebula awards themselves, election to the Hall of Fame anthology is based on a poll of SFWA's members. Volume One was restricted to short stories; Volume Two is devoted to novelets and novellas.

The voting procedure began with recommendations. For nearly a full year, SFWA members sent in suggestions for stories that were worthy of inclusion in the Hall of Fame. As editor, I quickly began to see that it was going to be a heartbreaking job to rule out *any* of these fine tales. Almost every title recommended brought back a powerful memory of the first time I had read that particular piece. And the authors! H. G. Wells, John W. Campbell, Jr., Robert Heinlein, Cyril Kornbluth . . . how could any of them be ruled out?

A ballot was finally prepared, consisting of seventy-six recommended stories. The SFWA members were asked to vote for ten stories out of the seventy-six. Since many authors had more than one story on the ballot, and we didn't want any individual author to be represented more than once in the anthology, the members were further asked to vote for only one story per author.

Many of the ballots came back with screams of despair and frustration scribbled over them. "How can I pick only ten of 'em?" was the typical cry. Most of the members wanted most of the recommended stories to go into the final anthology.

When the votes were counted, the top ten stories were:

WHO GOES THERE? by John W. Campbell, Jr.
A CANTICLE FOR LEIBOWITZ by Walter M. Miller, Jr.
WITH FOLDED HANDS by Jack Williamson
THE TIME MACHINE by H. G. Wells
BABY IS THREE by Theodore Sturgeon
VINTAGE SEASON by Henry Kuttner and C. L. Moore
THE MARCHING MORONS by C. M. Kornbluth
UNIVERSE by Robert A. Heinlein
BY HIS BOOTSTRAPS by Robert A. Heinlein
NERVES by Lester del Rey

Since several authors had more than one story on the ballot, and thus were in the unhappy position of competing with themselves, I sliced the pie in the other direction, too, and looked for the ten most popular authors:

Robert A. Heinlein
Theodore Sturgeon
John W. Campbell, Jr.
Walter M. Miller, Jr.
Lester del Rey
C. M. Kornbluth
Jack Williamson
H. G. Wells
Poul Anderson
Henry Kuttner and C. L. Moore

The procedure for picking the stories to go into the anthology, then, was fairly straightforward, since most of the top authors were also represented among the most popular stories. I prepared a list of stories that included the highest vote-getters among the stories and the most popular authors. For any individual author, I picked the story of his that had received the most votes.

It was much easier to start the list than end it. There was always the temptation to sneak in just one more story—after all, I would tell myself, *this one's* really too good to be left out. I ended with a list of twenty-two stories, totalling more than 400,000 words. Far too much for a single book.

I took my problem to Larry Ashmead, the editorial mastermind who presides over Doubleday's science fiction publications. It was a shameful dereliction of duty, but I didn't have the heart to cut out any of those twenty-two stories. Thankfully, neither did Larry. After one look at the list, he suggested making a two-book set so that all the stories could be included.

Unfortunately, two of the stories—Miller's *A Canticle for Leibo-witz,* and Ray Bradbury's *The Fireman*—were unavailable for this anthology. Both are currently available in book form, however.

So here is the second volume of the Science Fiction Hall of Fame, with stories ranging from H. G. Wells's *The Time Machine* (published 1895) to Cordwainer Smith's *The Ballad of Lost C'mell* (1962). It represents the best that science fiction has to offer, by some of the best writers working in this or any field of literature.

One final note of acknowledgment and thanks. Much of the onerous work of tracking down publication dates and magazines, toting up wordage lengths, and finding copies of the original stories, was done by Anthony R. Lewis. Without his aid, this volume might still be little more than an unfulfilled promise.

THE
SCIENCE FICTION
HALL OF FAME
Volume Two A

CALL ME JOE
by Poul Anderson

The wind came whooping out of eastern darkness, driving a lash of ammonia dust before it. In minutes, Edward Anglesey was blinded. He clawed all four feet into the broken shards which were soil, hunched down and groped for his little smelter. The wind was an idiot bassoon in his skull. Something whipped across his back, drawing blood, a tree yanked up by the roots and spat a hundred miles. Lightning cracked, immensely far overhead where clouds boiled with night.

As if to reply, thunder toned in the ice mountains and a red gout of flame jumped and a hillside came booming down, spilling itself across the valley. The earth shivered.

Sodium explosion, thought Anglesey in the drumbeat noise. The fire and the lightning gave him enough illumination to find his apparatus. He picked up tools in muscular hands, his tail gripped the trough, and he battered his way to the tunnel and thus to his dugout.

It had walls and roof of water, frozen by sun-remoteness and compressed by tons of atmosphere jammed onto every square inch. Ventilated by a tiny smoke hole, a lamp of tree oil burning in hydrogen made a dull light for the single room.

Anglesey sprawled his slate-blue form on the floor, panting. It was no use to swear at the storm. These ammonia gales often came at sunset, and there was nothing to do but wait them out. He was tired, anyway.

It would be morning in five hours or so. He had hoped to cast an axhead, his first, this evening, but maybe it was better to do the job by daylight.

He pulled a dekapod body off a shelf and ate the meat raw, pausing for long gulps of liquid methane from a jug. Things would improve once he had proper tools; so far, everything had been painfully grubbed and hacked to shape with teeth, claws, chance icicles, and what detestably weak and crumbling fragments remained of the spaceship. Give him a few years and he'd be living as a man should.

He sighed, stretched, and lay down to sleep.

Somewhat more than one hundred and twelve thousand miles away, Edward Anglesey took off his helmet.

He looked around, blinking. After the Jovian surface, it was always a little unreal to find himself here again, in the clean, quiet orderliness of the control room.

His muscles ached. They shouldn't. He had not really been fighting a gale of several hundred miles an hour, under three gravities and a temperature of 140 absolute. He had been here, in the almost nonexistent pull of Jupiter V, breathing oxynitrogen. It was Joe who lived down there and filled his lungs with hydrogen and helium at a pressure which could still only be estimated, because it broke aneroids and deranged piezoelectrics.

Nevertheless, his body felt worn and beaten. Tension, no doubt—psychosomatics. After all, for a good many hours now he had, in a sense, been Joe, and Joe had been working hard.

With the helmet off, Anglesey held only a thread of identification. The esprojector was still tuned to Joe's brain but no longer focused on his own. Somewhere in the back of his mind, he knew an indescribable feeling of sleep. Now and then, vague forms or colors drifted in the soft black—dreams? Not impossible that Joe's brain should dream a little when Anglesey's mind wasn't using it.

A light flickered red on the esprojector panel, and a bell whined electronic fear. Anglesey cursed. Thin fingers danced over the controls of his chair, he slewed around and shot across to the bank of dials. Yes, there—K tube oscillating again! The circuit blew out. He wrenched the face plate off with one hand and fumbled in a drawer with the other.

Inside his mind, he could feel the contact with Joe fading. If he once lost it entirely, he wasn't sure he could regain it. And Joe was an investment of several million dollars and quite a few highly skilled man-years.

Anglesey pulled the offending K tube from its socket and threw it on the floor. Glass exploded. It eased his temper a bit, just enough so he could find a replacement, plug it in, switch on the current again.

As the machine warmed up, once again amplifying, the Joeness in the back alleys of his brain strengthened.

Slowly, then, the man in the electric wheel chair rolled out of the room, into the hall. Let somebody else sweep up the broken tube. To hell with it. To hell with everybody.

Jan Cornelius had never been farther from Earth than some comfortable Lunar resort. He felt much put upon that the Psionics Corporation should tap him for a thirteen-month exile. The fact that he knew as much about esprojectors and their cranky innards as any other man alive was no excuse. Why send anyone at all? Who cared?

Obviously the Federation Science Authority did. It had seemingly given those bearded hermits a blank check on the taxpayer's account.

Thus did Cornelius grumble to himself, all the long hyperbolic path to Jupiter. Then the shifting accelerations of approach to its tiny inner satellite left him too wretched for further complaint. And when he finally, just prior to disembarkation, went up to the greenhouse for a look at Jupiter, he said not a word. Nobody does, the first time.

Arne Viken waited patiently while Cornelius stared. *It still gets me too,* he remembered. *By the throat. Sometimes I'm afraid to look.*

At length Cornelius turned around. He had a faintly Jovian appearance himself, being a large man with an imposing girth. "I had no idea," he whispered. "I never thought . . . I had seen pictures, but . . ."

Viken nodded. "Sure, Dr. Cornelius. Pictures don't convey it."

Where they stood, they could see the dark broken rock of the satellite, jumbled for a short way beyond the landing slip and then chopped off sheer. This moon was scarcely even a platform, it seemed, and cold constellations went streaming past it, around it. Jupiter lay across a fifth of that sky, softly ambrous, banded with colors, spotted with the shadows of planet-sized moons and with whirlwinds as broad as Earth. If there had been any gravity to speak of, Cornelius would have thought, instinctively, that the great planet was falling on him. As it was, he felt as if sucked upward, his hands were still sore where he had grabbed a rail to hold on.

"You live here . . . all alone . . . with this?" He spoke feebly.

"Oh, well, there are some fifty of us all told, pretty congenial," said Viken. "It's not so bad. You sign up for four-cycle hitches—four ship arrivals—and believe it or not, Dr. Cornelius, this is my third enlistment."

The newcomer forbore to inquire more deeply. There was something not quite understandable about the men on Jupiter V. They were mostly bearded, though otherwise careful to remain neat; their low-gravity movements were somehow dreamlike to watch; they hoarded their conversation, as if to stretch it through the year and a month between ships. Their monkish existence had changed them—or did they take what amounted to vows of poverty, chastity, and obedience because they had never felt quite at home on green Earth?

Thirteen months! Cornelius shuddered. It was going to be a long, cold wait, and the pay and bonuses accumulating for him were scant comfort now, four hundred and eighty million miles from the sun.

"Wonderful place to do research," continued Viken. "All the facilities, hand-picked colleagues, no distractions—and, of course . . ." He jerked his thumb at the planet and turned to leave.

Cornelius followed, wallowing awkwardly. "It is very interesting, no doubt," he puffed. "Fascinating. But really, Dr. Viken, to drag me way out here and make me spend a year-plus waiting for the next ship—to do a job which may take me a few weeks . . ."

"Are you sure it's that simple?" asked Viken gently. His face swiveled around, and there was something in his eyes that silenced Cornelius. "After all my time here, I've yet to see any problem, however complicated, which when you looked at it the right way didn't become still more complicated."

They went through the ship's air lock and the tube joining it to the station entrance. Nearly everything was underground. Rooms, laboratories, even halls, had a degree of luxuriousness—why, there was a fireplace with a real fire in the common room! God alone knew what *that* cost! Thinking of the huge chill emptiness where the king planet laired, and of his own year's sentence, Cornelius decided that such luxuries were, in truth, biological necessities.

Viken showed him to a pleasantly furnished chamber which would be his own. "We'll fetch your luggage soon, and unload your psionic stuff. Right now, everybody's either talking to the ship's crew or reading his mail."

Cornelius nodded absently and sat down. The chair, like all low-gee furniture, was a mere spidery skeleton, but it held his bulk comfortably enough. He felt in his tunic, hoping to bribe the other man into keeping him company for a while. "Cigar? I brought some from Amsterdam."

"Thanks." Viken accepted with disappointing casualness, crossed long, thin legs and blew grayish clouds.

"Ah . . . are you in charge here?"

"Not exactly. No one is. We do have one administrator, the cook, to handle what little work of that type may come up. Don't forget, this is a research station, first, last, and always."

"What is your field, then?"

Viken frowned. "Don't question anyone else so bluntly, Dr. Cornelius," he warned. "They'd rather spin the gossip out as long as possible with each newcomer. It's a rare treat to have someone whose every last conceivable reaction hasn't been—no, no apologies to me. 'S all right. I'm a physicist, specializing in the solid state at ultra-high pressures." He nodded at the wall. "Plenty of it to be observed— there!"

"I see." Cornelius smoked quietly for a while. Then: "I'm supposed to be the psionics expert, but, frankly, at present I've no idea why your machine should misbehave as reported."

"You mean those, uh, K tubes have a stable output on Earth?"

"And on Luna, Mars, Venus—everywhere, apparently, but here." Cornelius shrugged. "Of course, psibeams are always persnickety, and sometimes you get an unwanted feedback when—no. I'll get the facts before I theorize. Who are your psimen?"

"Just Anglesey, who's not a formally trained esman at all. But he took it up after he was crippled, and showed such a natural aptitude that he was shipped out here when he volunteered. It's so hard to get anyone for Jupiter V that we aren't fussy about degrees. At that, Ed seems to be operating Joe as well as a Ps.D. could."

"Ah, yes. Your pseudojovian. I'll have to examine that angle pretty carefully, too," said Cornelius. In spite of himself, he was getting interested. "Maybe the trouble comes from something in Joe's biochemistry. Who knows? I'll let you into a carefully guarded little secret, Dr. Viken: psionics is not an exact science."

"Neither is physics," grinned the other man. After a moment, he added more soberly: "Not my brand of physics, anyway. I hope to make it exact. That's why I'm here, you know. It's the reason we're all here."

Edward Anglesey was a bit of a shock the first time. He was a head, a pair of arms, and a disconcertingly intense blue stare. The rest of him was mere detail, enclosed in a wheeled machine.

"Biophysicist originally," Viken had told Cornelius. "Studying atmospheric spores at Earth Station when he was still a young man—accident, crushed him up, nothing below his chest will ever work again. Snappish type, you have to go slow with him."

Seated on a wisp of stool in the esprojector control room, Cornelius realized that Viken had been soft-pedaling the truth.

Anglesey ate as he talked, gracelessly, letting the chair's tentacles wipe up after him. "Got to," he explained. "This stupid place is officially on Earth time, GMT. Jupiter isn't. I've got to be here whenever Joe wakes, ready to take him over."

"Couldn't you have someone spell you?" asked Cornelius.

"Bah!" Anglesey stabbed a piece of prot and waggled it at the other man. Since it was native to him, he could spit out English, the common language of the station, with unmeasured ferocity. "Look here. You ever done therapeutic esping? Not just listening in, or even communication, but actual pedagogic control?"

"No, not I. It requires a certain natural talent, like yours." Cornelius smiled. His ingratiating little phrase was swallowed without being noticed by the scored face opposite him. "I take it you mean cases like, oh, re-educating the nervous system of a palsied child?"

"Yes, yes. Good enough example. Has anyone ever tried to suppress the child's personality, take him over in the most literal sense?"

"Good God, no!"

"Even as a scientific experiment?" Anglesey grinned. "Has any esprojector operative ever poured on the juice and swamped the child's brain with his own thoughts? Come on, Cornelius, I won't snitch on you."

"Well . . . it's out of my line, you understand." The psionicist looked carefully away, found a bland meter face and screwed his eyes to that. "I have, uh, heard something about . . . Well, yes, there were attempts made in some pathological cases to, uh, bull through . . . break down the patient's delusions by sheer force—"

"And it didn't work," said Anglesey. He laughed. "It *can't* work, not even on a child, let alone an adult with a fully developed personality. Why, it took a decade of refinement, didn't it, before the machine was debugged to the point where a psychiatrist could even 'listen in' without the normal variation between his pattern of thought and the patient's—without that variation setting up an interference scrambling the very thing he wanted to study. The machine has to make automatic compensations for the differences between individuals. We still can't bridge the differences between species.

"If someone else is willing to cooperate, you can very gently guide his thinking. And that's all. If you try to seize control of another brain, a brain with its own background of experience, its own ego, you risk your very sanity. The other brain will fight back instinctively. A fully developed, matured, hardened human personality is just too complex for outside control. It has too many resources, too much hell the subconscious can call to its defense if its integrity is threatened. Blazes, man, we can't even master our own minds, let alone anyone else's!"

Anglesey's cracked-voice tirade broke off. He sat brooding at the instrument panel, tapping the console of his mechanical mother.

"Well?" said Cornelius after a while.

He should not, perhaps, have spoken. But he found it hard to remain mute. There was too much silence—half a billion miles of it, from here to the sun. If you closed your mouth five minutes at a time, the silence began creeping in like fog.

"Well," gibed Anglesey. "So our pseudojovian, Joe, has a physically adult brain. The only reason I can control him is that his brain has never been given a chance to develop its own ego. I *am* Joe. From the moment he was 'born' into consciousness, I have been there. The psibeam sends me all his sense data and sends him back my motor-nerve impulses. Nevertheless, he has that excellent brain, and its cells are recording every trace of experience, even as yours and mine; his synapses have assumed the topography which is my 'personality pattern.'

"Anyone else, taking him over from me, would find it was like an attempt to oust me myself from my own brain. It couldn't be done. To be sure, he doubtless has only a rudimentary set of Anglesey-memories—I do not, for instance, repeat trigonometric theorems while controlling him—but he has enough to be, potentially, a distinct personality.

"As a matter of fact, whenever he wakes up from sleep—there's usually a lag of a few minutes, while I sense the change through my normal psi faculties and get the amplifying helmet adjusted—I have a bit of a struggle. I feel almost a . . . a resistance until I've brought his mental currents completely into phase with mine. Merely dreaming has been enough of a different experience to . . ." Anglesey didn't bother to finish the sentence.

"I see," murmured Cornelius. "Yes, it's clear enough. In fact, it's astonishing that you can have such total contact with a being of such alien metabolism."

"I won't for much longer," said the esman sarcastically, "unless you can correct whatever is burning out those K tubes. I don't have an unlimited supply of spares."

"I have some working hypotheses," said Cornelius, "but there's so little known about psibeam transmission—is the velocity infinite or merely very great, is the beam strength actually independent of distance? How about the possible effects of transmission—oh, through the degenerate matter in the Jovian core? Good Lord, a planet where water is a heavy mineral and hydrogen is a metal! What do we know?"

"We're supposed to find out," snapped Anglesey. "That's what this whole project is for. Knowledge. Bull!" Almost, he spat on the floor. "Apparently what little we have learned doesn't even get through to people. Hydrogen is still a gas where Joe lives. He'd have to dig down a few miles to reach the solid phase. And I'm expected to make a scientific analysis of Jovian conditions!"

Cornelius waited it out, letting Anglesey storm on while he himself turned over the problem of K-tube oscillation.

"They don't understand back on Earth. Even here they don't. Sometimes I think they refuse to understand. Joe's down there without much more than his bare hands. He, I, we started with no more knowledge than that he could probably eat the local life. He has to spend nearly all his time hunting for food. It's a miracle he's come as far as he has in these few weeks—made a shelter, grown familiar with the immediate region, begun on metallurgy, hydrurgy, whatever you want to call it. What more do they want me to do, for crying in the beer?"

"Yes, yes," mumbled Cornelius. "Yes, I . . ."

Anglesey raised his white bony face. Something filmed over in his eyes.

"What—" began Cornelius.

"Shut up!" Anglesey whipped the chair around, groped for the helmet, slapped it down over his skull. "Joe's waking. Get out of here."

"But if you'll let me work only while he sleeps, how can I—"

Anglesey snarled and threw a wrench at him. It was a feeble toss, even in low gee. Cornelius backed toward the door. Anglesey was tuning in the esprojector. Suddenly he jerked.

"Cornelius!"

"Whatisit?" The psionicist tried to run back, overdid it, and skidded in a heap to end up against the panel.

"K tube again." Anglesey yanked off the helmet. It must have hurt like blazes, having a mental squeal build up uncontrolled and amplified in your own brain, but he said merely: "Change it for me. Fast. And then get out and leave me alone. Joe didn't wake up of himself. Something crawled into the dugout with me—I'm in trouble down there!"

It had been a hard day's work, and Joe slept heavily. He did not wake until the hands closed on his throat.

For a moment then he knew only a crazy smothering wave of panic. He thought he was back on Earth Station, floating in null gee at the end of a cable while a thousand frosty stars haloed the planet before him. He thought the great I beam had broken from its moorings and started toward him, slowly, but with all the inertia of its cold tons, spinning and shimmering in the Earthlight, and the only sound himself screaming and screaming in his helmet trying to break from the cable the beam nudged him ever so gently but it kept on moving he moved with it he was crushed against the station wall nuzzled into it his mangled suit frothed as it tried to seal its wounded self there was blood mingled with the foam his blood *Joe roared*.

His convulsive reaction tore the hands off his neck and sent a black shape spinning across the dugout. It struck the wall, thunderously, and the lamp fell to the floor and went out.

Joe stood in darkness, breathing hard, aware in a vague fashion that the wind had died from a shriek to a low snarling while he slept.

The thing he had tossed away mumbled in pain and crawled along the wall. Joe felt through lightlessness after his club.

Something else scrabbled. The tunnel! They were coming through the tunnel! Joe groped blind to meet them. His heart drummed thickly and his nose drank an alien stench.

The thing that emerged, as Joe's hands closed on it, was only about half his size, but it had six monstrously taloned feet and a pair of three-fingered hands that reached after his eyes. Joe cursed, lifted it while it writhed, and dashed it to the floor. It screamed, and he heard bones splinter.

"Come on, then!" Joe arched his back and spat at them, like a tiger menaced by giant caterpillars.

They flowed through his tunnel and into the room, a dozen of them entered while he wrestled one that had curled itself around his shoulders and anchored its sinuous body with claws. They pulled at his legs, trying to crawl up on his back. He struck out with claws of his own, with his tail, rolled over and went down beneath a heap of them and stood up with the heap still clinging to him.

They swayed in darkness. The legged seething of them struck the dugout wall. It shivered, a rafter cracked, the roof came down. Anglesey stood in a pit, among broken ice plates, under the wan light of a sinking Ganymede.

He could see now that the monsters were black in color and that they had heads big enough to accommodate some brain, less than human but probably more than apes. There were a score of them or so, they struggled from beneath the wreckage and flowed at him with the same shrieking malice.

Why?

Baboon reaction, thought Anglesey somewhere in the back of himself. See the stranger, fear the stranger, hate the stranger, kill the stranger. His chest heaved, pumping air through a raw throat. He yanked a whole rafter to him, snapped it in half, and twirled the iron-hard wood.

The nearest creature got its head bashed in. The next had its back broken. The third was hurled with shattered ribs into a fourth, they went down together. Joe began to laugh. It was getting to be fun.

"Yee-ow! Ti-i-i-iger!" He ran across the icy ground, toward the pack. They scattered, howling. He hunted them until the last one had vanished into the forest.

Panting, Joe looked at the dead. He himself was bleeding, he ached, he was cold and hungry and his shelter had been wrecked—but he'd whipped them! He had a sudden impulse to beat his chest and howl. For a moment he hesitated. Why not? Anglesey threw back his head and bayed victory at the dim shield of Ganymede.

Thereafter he went to work. First build a fire, in the lee of the spaceship—which was little more by now than a hill of corrosion. The monster pack cried in darkness and the broken ground, they had not given up on him, they would return.

He tore a haunch off one of the slain and took a bite. Pretty good. Better yet if properly cooked. Heh! They'd made a big mistake in calling his attention to their existence! He finished breakfast while Ganymede slipped under the western ice mountains. It would be morning soon. The air was almost still, and a flock of pancake-shaped sky-skimmers, as Anglesey called them, went overhead, burnished copper color in the first pale dawn streaks.

Joe rummaged in the ruins of his hut until he had recovered the water-smelting equipment. It wasn't harmed. That was the first order of business, melt some ice and cast it in the molds of ax, knife, saw, hammer he had painfully prepared. Under Jovian conditions, methane was a liquid that you drank and water was a dense hard mineral. It would make good tools. Later on he would try alloying it with other materials.

Next—yes. To hell with the dugout, he could sleep in the open again for a while. Make a bow, set traps, be ready to massacre the black caterpillars when they attacked him again. There was a chasm not far from here, going down a long way toward the bitter cold of the metallic-hydrogen strata: a natural icebox, a place to store the several weeks' worth of meat his enemies would supply. This would give him leisure to— Oh, a hell of a lot!

Joe laughed exultantly and lay down to watch the sunrise.

It struck him afresh how lovely a place this was. See how the small brilliant spark of the sun swam up out of eastern fog banks colored dusky purple and veined with rose and gold; see how the light strengthened until the great hollow arch of the sky became one shout of radiance; see how the light spilled warm and living over a broad fair land, the million square miles of rustling low forests and wave-blinking lakes and feather-plumed hydrogen geysers; and see, see, see how the ice mountains of the west flashed like blued steel!

Anglesey drew the wild morning wind deep into his lungs and shouted with a boy's joy.

"I'm not a biologist myself," said Viken carefully. "But maybe for that reason I can better give you the general picture. Then Lopez or Matsumoto can answer any questions of detail."

"Excellent." Cornelius nodded. "Why don't you assume I am totally ignorant of this project? I very nearly am, you know."

"If you wish," laughed Viken.

They stood in an outer office of the xenobiology section. No one else was around, for the station's clocks said 1730 GMT and there was only one shift. No point in having more, until Anglesey's half of the enterprise had actually begun gathering quantitative data.

The physicist bent over and took a paperweight off a desk. "One of the boys made this for fun," he said, "but it's a pretty good model of Joe. He stands about five feet tall at the head."

Cornelius turned the plastic image over in his hands. If you could imagine such a thing as a feline centaur with a thick prehensile tail . . . The torso was squat, long-armed, immensely muscular; the hairless head was round, wide-nosed, with big deep-set eyes and heavy jaws, but it was really quite a human face. The over-all color was bluish gray.

"Male, I see," he remarked.

"Of course. Perhaps you don't understand. Joe is the complete pseudojovian—as far as we can tell, the final model, with all the bugs worked out. He's the answer to a research question that took fifty years to ask." Viken looked sidewise at Cornelius. "So you realize the importance of your job, don't you?"

"I'll do my best," said the psionicist. "But if . . . well, let's say that tube failure or something causes you to lose Joe before I've solved the oscillation problem. You do have other pseudos in reserve, don't you?"

"Oh, yes," said Viken moodily. "But the cost . . . We're not on an unlimited budget. We do go through a lot of money, because it's expensive to stand up and sneeze this far from Earth. But for that same reason our margin is slim."

He jammed hands in pockets and slouched toward the inner door, the laboratories, head down and talking in a low, hurried voice. "Perhaps you don't realize what a nightmare planet Jupiter is. Not just the surface gravity—a shade under three gees, what's that?—but the gravitational potential, ten times Earth's. The temperature. The pressure. Above all, the atmosphere, and the storms, and the darkness!

"When a spaceship goes down to the Jovian surface, it's a radio-controlled job; it leaks like a sieve, to equalize pressure, but otherwise it's the sturdiest, most utterly powerful model ever designed; it's loaded with every instrument, every servomechanism, every safety device the human mind has yet thought up to protect a million-dollar hunk of precision equipment. And what happens? Half the ships never reach the surface at all. A storm snatches them and throws them away, or they collide with a floating chunk of Ice Seven—small version of the Red Spot—or, so help me, what passes for a flock of *birds* rams one and stoves it in! As for the fifty per cent which do land, it's a one-way trip. We don't even try to bring them back. If the stresses coming down haven't sprung something, the corrosion has doomed them anyway. Hydrogen at Jovian pressure does funny things to metals.

"It cost a total of about five million dollars to set Joe, one pseudo, down there. Each pseudo to follow will cost, if we're lucky, a couple of million more."

Viken kicked open the door and led the way through. Beyond was a big room, low-ceilinged, coldly lit and murmurous with ventilators. It reminded Cornelius of a nucleonics lab; for a moment he wasn't sure why, then he recognized the intricacies of remote control, remote observation, walls enclosing forces which could destroy the entire moon.

"These are required by the pressure, of course," said Viken, pointing to a row of shields. "And the cold. And the hydrogen itself, as a minor hazard. We have units here duplicating conditions in the Jovian, uh, stratosphere. This is where the whole project really began."

"I've heard something about that. Didn't you scoop up airborne spores?"

"Not I." Viken chuckled. "Totti's crew did, about fifty years ago. Proved there was life on Jupiter. A life using liquid methane as its basic solvent, solid ammonia as a starting point for nitrate synthesis: the plants use solar energy to build unsaturated carbon compounds, releasing hydrogen; the animals eat the plants and reduce those compounds again to the saturated form. There is even an equivalent of combustion. The reactions involve complex enzymes and—well, it's out of my line."

"Jovian biochemistry is pretty well understood, then."

"Oh, yes. Even in Totti's day they had a highly developed biotic technology: Earth bacteria had already been synthesized and most gene structures pretty well mapped. The only reason it took so long to diagram Jovian life processes was the technical difficulty, high pressure and so on."

"When did you actually get a look at Jupiter's surface?"

"Gray managed that, about thirty years ago. Set a televisor ship down, a ship that lasted long enough to flash him quite a series of pictures. Since then, the technique has improved. We know that Jupiter is crawling with its own weird kind of life, probably more fertile than Earth. Extrapolating from the airborne micro-organisms, our team made trial syntheses of metazoans and—"

Viken sighed. "Damn it, if only there were intelligent native life! Think what they could tell us, Cornelius, the data, the—just think back how far we've gone since Lavoisier, with the low-pressure chemistry of Earth. Here's a chance to learn a high-pressure chemistry and physics at least as rich with possibilities!"

After a moment, Cornelius murmured slyly, "Are you certain there *aren't* any Jovians?"

"Oh, sure, there could be several billion of them." Viken shrugged. "Cities, empires, anything you like. Jupiter has the surface area of a hundred Earths, and we've only seen maybe a dozen small regions. But we do know there aren't any Jovians using radio. Considering their atmosphere, it's unlikely they ever would invent it for themselves—imagine how thick a vacuum tube has to be, how strong a pump you need! So it was finally decided we'd better make our own Jovians."

Cornelius followed him through the lab into another room. This was less cluttered, it had a more finished appearance; the experimenter's haywire rig had yielded to the assured precision of an engineer.

Viken went over to one of the panels which lined the walls and looked at its gauges. "Beyond this lies another pseudo," he said. "Female, in this instance. She's at a pressure of two hundred atmospheres and a temperature of 194 absolute. There's a . . . an umbilical arrangement, I guess you'd call it, to keep her alive. She was grown to adulthood in this, uh, fetal stage—we patterned our Jovians after the terrestrial mammal. She's never been conscious, she won't ever be till she's 'born.' We have a total of twenty males and sixty females waiting here. We can count on about half reaching the surface. More can be created as required. It isn't the pseudos that are so expensive, it's their transportation. So Joe is down there alone till we're sure that his kind *can* survive."

"I take it you experimented with lower forms first," said Cornelius.

"Of course. It took twenty years, even with forced-catalysis techniques, to work from an artificial airborne spore to Joe. We've used the psibeam to control everything from pseudo insects on up. Interspecies control is possible, you know, if your puppet's nervous system is deliberately designed for it and isn't given a chance to grow into a pattern different from the esman's."

"And Joe is the first specimen who's given trouble?"

"Yes."

"Scratch one hypothesis." Cornelius sat down on a workbench, dangling thick legs and running a hand through thin sandy hair. "I thought maybe some physical effect of Jupiter was responsible. Now it looks as if the difficulty is with Joe himself."

"We've all suspected that much," said Viken. He struck a cigarette and sucked in his cheeks around the smoke. His eyes were gloomy. "Hard to see how. The biotics engineers tell me *Pseudocentaurus sapiens* has been more carefully designed than any product of natural evolution."

"Even the brain?"

"Yes. It's patterned directly on the human, to make psibeam control possible, but there are improvements—greater stability."

"There are still the psychological aspects, though," said Cornelius. "In spite of all our amplifiers and other fancy gadgets, psi is essentially a branch of psychology, even today—or maybe it's the other way around. Let's consider traumatic experiences. I take it the . . . the adult Jovian fetus has a rough trip going down?"

"The ship does," said Viken. "Not the pseudo itself, which is wrapped up in fluid just like you were before birth."

"Nevertheless," said Cornelius, "the two-hundred-atmospheres pressure here is not the same as whatever unthinkable pressure exists down on Jupiter. Could the change be injurious?"

Viken gave him a look of respect. "Not likely," he answered. "I told you the J ships are designed leaky. External pressure is transmitted to the, uh, uterine mechanism through a series of diaphragms, in a gradual fashion. It takes hours to make the descent, you realize."

"Well, what happens next?" went on Cornelius. "The ship lands, the uterine mechanism opens, the umbilical connection disengages, and Joe is, shall we say, born. But he has an adult brain. He is not protected by the only half-developed infant brain from the shock of sudden awareness."

"We thought of that," said Viken. "Anglesey was on the psibeam, in phase with Joe, when the ship left this moon. So it wasn't really Joe who emerged, who perceived. Joe has never been much more than a biological waldo. He can only suffer mental shock to the extent that Ed does, because it *is* Ed down there!"

"As you will," said Cornelius. "Still, you didn't plan for a race of puppets, did you?"

"Oh, heavens, no," said Viken. "Out of the question. Once we know Joe is well established, we'll import a few more esmen and get him some assistance in the form of other pseudos. Eventually fe-

males will be sent down, and uncontrolled males, to be educated by
the puppets. A new generation will be born normally—well, anyhow,
the ultimate aim is a small civilization of Jovians. There will be hunt-
ers, miners, artisans, farmers, housewives, the works. They will support a few key members, a kind of priesthood. And that priesthood
will be esp-controlled, as Joe is. It will exist solely to make instruments, take readings, perform experiments, and tell us what we want
to know!"

Cornelius nodded. In a general way, this was the Jovian project as
he had understood it. He could appreciate the importance of his own
assignment.

Only, he still had no clue to the cause of that positive feedback in
the K tubes.

And what could he do about it?

His hands were still bruised. *Oh God,* he thought with a groan, for
the hundredth time, *does it affect me that much? While Joe was fighting down there, did I really hammer my fists on metal up here?*

His eyes smoldered across the room, to the bench where Cornelius
worked. He didn't like Cornelius, fat cigar-sucking slob, interminably
talking and talking. He had about given up trying to be civil to the
Earthworm.

The psionicist laid down a screwdriver and flexed cramped fingers.
"Whuff!" He smiled. "I'm going to take a break."

The half-assembled esprojector made a gaunt backdrop for his
wide soft body, where it squatted toad fashion on the bench. Anglesey
detested the whole idea of anyone sharing this room, even for a few
hours a day. Of late he had been demanding his meals brought here,
left outside the door of his adjoining bedroom-bath. He had not gone
beyond for quite some time now.

And why should I?

"Couldn't you hurry it up a little?" snapped Anglesey.

Cornelius flushed. "If you'd had an assembled spare machine, instead of loose parts—" he began. Shrugging, he took out a cigar stub
and relit it carefully; his supply had to last a long time. Anglesey wondered if those stinking clouds were blown from his mouth of malicious
purpose. *I don't like you, Mr. Earthman Cornelius, and it is doubtless
quite mutual.*

"There was no obvious need for one, until the other esmen arrive," said Anglesey in a sullen voice. "And the testing instruments report this one in perfectly good order."

"Nevertheless," said Cornelius, "at irregular intervals it goes into wild oscillations which burn out the K tube. The problem is why. I'll have you try out this new machine as soon as it is ready, but, frankly, I don't believe the trouble lies in electronic failure at all—or even in unsuspected physical effects."

"Where, then?" Anglesey felt more at ease as the discussion grew purely technical.

"Well, look. What exactly is the K tube? It's the heart of the esprojector. It amplifies your natural psionic pulses, uses them to modulate the carrier wave, and shoots the whole beam down at Joe. It also picks up Joe's resonating impulses and amplifies them for your benefit. Everything else is auxiliary to the K tube."

"Spare me the lecture," snarled Anglesey.

"I was only rehearsing the obvious," said Cornelius, "because every now and then it is the obvious answer which is hardest to see. Maybe it isn't the K tube which is misbehaving. Maybe it is you."

"What?" The white face gaped at him. A dawning rage crept across its thin bones.

"Nothing personal intended," said Cornelius hastily. "But you know what a tricky beast the subconscious is. Suppose, just as a working hypothesis, that way down underneath, you don't *want* to be on Jupiter. I imagine it is a rather terrifying environment. Or there may be some obscure Freudian element involved. Or, quite simply and naturally, your subconscious may fail to understand that Joe's death does not entail your own."

"Um-m-m." *Mirabile dictu,* Anglesey remained calm. He rubbed his chin with one skeletal hand. "Can you be more explicit?"

"Only in a rough way," replied Cornelius. "Your conscious mind sends a motor impulse along the psibeam to Joe. Simultaneously, your subconscious mind, being scared of the whole business, emits the glandular-vascular-cardiac-visceral impulses associated with fear. These react on Joe, whose tension is transmitted back along the beam. Feeling Joe's somatic fear symptoms, your subconscious gets still more worried, thereby increasing the symptoms. Get it? It's exactly similar to ordinary neurasthenia, with this exception, that since there is a powerful amplifier, the K tube, involved, the oscillations can build up uncontrollably within a second or two. You should be thankful the tube does burn out—otherwise your brain might do so!"

For a moment Anglesey was quiet. Then he laughed. It was a hard, barbaric laughter. Cornelius started as it struck his eardrums.

"Nice idea," said the esman. "But I'm afraid it won't fit all the data. You see, I like it down there. I like being Joe."

He paused for a while, then continued in a dry impersonal tone: "Don't judge the environment from my notes. They're just idiotic things like estimates of wind velocity, temperature variations, mineral properties—insignificant. What I can't put in is how Jupiter looks through a Jovian's infrared-seeing eyes."

"Different, I should think," ventured Cornelius after a minute's clumsy silence.

"Yes and no. It's hard to put into language. Some of it I can't, because man hasn't got the concepts. But . . . oh, I can't describe it. Shakespeare himself couldn't. Just remember that everything about Jupiter which is cold and poisonous and gloomy to us is *right* for Joe."

Anglesey's tone grew remote, as if he spoke to himself. "Imagine walking under a glowing violet sky, where great flashing clouds sweep the earth with shadow and rain strides beneath them. Imagine walking on the slopes of a mountain like polished metal, with a clean red flame exploding above you and thunder laughing in the ground. Imagine a cool wild stream, and low trees with dark coppery flowers, and a waterfall—methanefall, whatever you like—leaping off a cliff, and the strong live wind shakes its mane full of rainbows! Imagine a whole forest, dark and breathing, and here and there you glimpse a pale-red wavering will-o'-the-wisp, which is the life radiation of some fleet, shy animal, and . . . and . . ."

Anglesey croaked into silence. He stared down at his clenched fists, then he closed his eyes tight and tears ran out between the lids. "Imagine being *strong!*"

Suddenly he snatched up the helmet, crammed it on his head and twirled the control knobs. Joe had been sleeping, down in the night, but Joe was about to wake up and—roar under the four great moons till all the forest feared him?

Cornelius slipped quietly out of the room.

In the long brazen sunset light, beneath dusky cloud banks brooding storm, he strode up the hill slope with a sense of day's work done.

Across his back, two woven baskets balanced each other, one laden with the pungent black fruit of the thorn tree and one with cable-thick creepers to be used as rope. The ax on his shoulder caught the waning sunlight and tossed it blindingly back.

It had not been hard labor, but weariness dragged at his mind and he did not relish the household chores yet to be performed, cooking and cleaning and all the rest. Why couldn't they hurry up and get him some helpers?

His eyes sought the sky resentfully. Moon Five was hidden; down here, at the bottom of the air ocean, you saw nothing but the sun and the four Galilean satellites. He wasn't even sure where Five was just now, in relation to himself. *Wait a minute, it's sunset here, but if I went out to the viewdome I'd see Jupiter in the last quarter, or would I, oh, hell, it only takes us half an Earth day to swing around the planet anyhow—*

Joe shook his head. After all this time, it was still damnably hard, now and then, to keep his thoughts straight. *I, the essential I, am up in heaven, riding Jupiter Five between cold stars. Remember that. Open your eyes, if you will, and see the dead control room super-imposed on a living hillside.*

He didn't, though. Instead, he regarded the boulders strewn wind-blasted gray over the tough mossy vegetation of the slope. They were not much like Earth rocks, nor was the soil beneath his feet like ter-restrial humus.

For a moment Anglesey speculated on the origin of the silicates, aluminates, and other stony compounds. Theoretically, all such ma-terials should be inaccessibly locked in the Jovian core, down where the pressure got vast enough for atoms to buckle and collapse. Above the core should lie thousands of miles of allotropic ice, and then the metallic-hydrogen layer. There should not be complex minerals this far up, but there were.

Well, possibly Jupiter had formed according to theory, but had thereafter sucked enough cosmic dust, meteors, gases and vapors down its great throat of gravitation to form a crust several miles thick. Or more likely the theory was altogether wrong. What did they know, what *could* they know, the soft pale worms of Earth?

Anglesey stuck his—Joe's—fingers in his mouth and whistled. A baying sounded in the brush, and two midnight forms leaped toward him. He grinned and stroked their heads; training was progressing faster than he'd hoped, with these pups of the black caterpillar beasts he had taken. They would make guardians for him, herders, servants.

On the crest of the hill, Joe was building himself a home. He had logged off an acre of ground and erected a stockade. Within the grounds there now stood a lean-to for himself and his stores, a methane well, and the beginnings of a large, comfortable cabin.

But there was too much work for one being. Even with the half-intelligent caterpillars to help, and with cold storage for meat, most of his time would still go to hunting. The game wouldn't last forever, either; he had to start agriculture within the next year or so—Jupiter year, twelve Earth years, thought Anglesey. There was the cabin to finish and furnish; he wanted to put a waterwheel, no, methane wheel, in the river to turn any of a dozen machines he had in mind, he wanted to experiment with alloyed ice and—

And, quite apart from his need of help, why should he remain alone, the single thinking creature on an entire planet? He was a male in this body, with male instincts—in the long run, his health was bound to suffer if he remained a hermit, and right now the whole project depended on Joe's health.

It wasn't right!

But I am not alone. There are fifty men on the satellite with me. I can talk to any of them, anytime I wish. It's only that I seldom wish it, these days. I would rather be Joe.

Nevertheless . . . I, the cripple, feel all the tiredness, anger, hurt, frustration, of that wonderful biological machine called Joe. The others don't understand. When the ammonia gale flays open his skin, it is I who bleed.

Joe lay down on the ground, sighing. Fangs flashed in the mouth of the black beast which humped over to lick his face. His belly growled with hunger, but he was too tired to fix a meal. Once he had the dogs trained . . .

Another pseudo would be so much more rewarding to educate.

He could almost see it, in the weary darkening of his brain. Down there, in the valley below the hill, fire and thunder as the ship came to rest. And the steel egg would crack open, the steel arms—already crumbling, puny work of worms!—lift out the shape within and lay it on the earth.

She would stir, shrieking in her first lungful of air, looking about with blank mindless eyes. And Joe would come and carry her home. And he would feed her, care for her, show her how to walk—it wouldn't take long, an adult body would learn those things very fast.

In a few weeks she would even be talking, be an individual, a soul.

Did you ever think, Edward Anglesey, in the days when you also walked, that your wife would be a gray four-legged monster?

Never mind that. The important thing was to get others of his kind down here, female *and* male. The station's niggling little plan would have him wait two more Earth years, and then send him only another dummy like himself, a contemptible human mind looking through eyes which belonged rightfully to a Jovian. It was not to be tolerated!

If he weren't so tired . . .

Joe sat up. Sleep drained from him as the realization entered. *He* wasn't tired, not to speak of. Anglesey was. Anglesey, the human side of him, who for months had slept only in cat naps, whose rest had lately been interrupted by Cornelius—it was the human body which drooped, gave up, and sent wave after soft wave of sleep down the psibeam to Joe.

Somatic tension traveled skyward; Anglesey jerked awake.

He swore. As he sat there beneath the helmet, the vividness of Jupiter faded with his scattering concentration, as if it grew transparent; the steel prison which was his laboratory strengthened behind it. He was losing contact. Rapidly, with the skill of experience, he brought himself back into phase with the neural currents of the other brain. He willed sleepiness on Joe, exactly as a man wills it on himself.

And, like any other insomniac, he failed. The Joe body was too hungry. It got up and walked across the compound toward its shack.

The K tube went wild and blew itself out.

The night before the ships left, Viken and Cornelius sat up late.

It was not truly a night, of course. In twelve hours the tiny moon was hurled clear around Jupiter, from darkness back to darkness, and there might well be a pallid little sun over its crags when the clocks said witches were abroad in Greenwich. But most of the personnel were asleep at this hour.

Viken scowled. "I don't like it," he said. "Too sudden a change of plans. Too big a gamble."

"You are only risking—how many?—three male and a dozen female pseudos," Cornelius replied.

"And fifteen J ships. All we have. If Anglesey's notion doesn't work, it will be months, a year or more, till we can have others built and resume aerial survey."

"But if it does work," said Cornelius, "you won't need any J ships, except to carry down more pseudos. You will be too busy evaluating data from the surface to piddle around in the upper atmosphere."

"Of course. But we never expected it so soon. We were going to bring more esmen out here, to operate some more pseudos—"

"But they aren't *needed*," said Cornelius. He struck a cigar to life and took a long pull on it, while his mind sought carefully for words. "Not for a while, anyhow. Joe has reached a point where, given help, he can leap several thousand years of history—he may even have a radio of sorts operating in the fairly near future, which would eliminate the necessity of much of your esping. But without help, he'll just have to mark time. And it's stupid to make a highly trained human esman perform manual labor, which is all that the other pseudos are needed for at this moment. Once the Jovian settlement is well established, certainly, then you can send down more puppets."

"The question is, though," persisted Viken, "can Anglesey himself educate all those pseudos at once? They'll be helpless as infants for days. It will be weeks before they really start thinking and acting for themselves. Can Joe take care of them meanwhile?"

"He has food and fuel stored for months ahead," said Cornelius. "As for what Joe's capabilities are—well, hm-m-m, we just have to take Anglesey's judgment. He has the only inside information."

"And once those Jovians do become personalities," worried Viken, "are they necessarily going to string along with Joe? Don't forget, the pseudos are not carbon copies of each other. The uncertainty principle assures each one a unique set of genes. If there is only one human mind on Jupiter, among all those aliens—"

"One *human* mind?" It was barely audible. Viken opened his mouth inquiringly. The other man hurried on.

"Oh, I'm sure Anglesey can continue to dominate them," said Cornelius. "His own personality is rather—tremendous."

Viken looked startled. "You really think so?"

The psionicist nodded. "Yes. I've seen more of him in the past weeks than anyone else. And my profession naturally orients me more toward a man's psychology than his body or his habits. You see a waspish cripple. I see a mind which has reacted to its physical handicaps by developing such a hellish energy, such an inhuman power of concentration, that it almost frightens me. Give that mind a sound body for its use and nothing is impossible to it."

"You may be right, at that," murmured Viken after a pause. "Not that it matters. The decision is taken, the rockets go down tomorrow. I hope it all works out."

He waited for another while. The whirring of ventilators in his little room seemed unnaturally loud, the colors of a girlie picture on the wall shockingly garish. Then he said slowly, "You've been rather close-mouthed yourself, Jan. When do you expect to finish your own esprojector and start making the tests?"

Cornelius looked around. The door stood open to an empty hallway, but he reached out and closed it before he answered with a slight grin, "It's been ready for the past few days. But don't tell anyone."

"How's that?" Viken started. The movement, in low gee, took him out of his chair and halfway across the table between the men. He shoved himself back and waited.

"I have been making meaningless tinkering motions," said Cornelius, "but what I waited for was a highly emotional moment, a time when I can be sure Anglesey's entire attention will be focused on Joe. This business tomorrow is exactly what I need."

"*Why?*"

"You see, I have pretty well convinced myself that the trouble in the machine is psychological, not physical. I think that for some reason, buried in his subconscious, Anglesey doesn't want to experience Jupiter. A conflict of that type might well set a psionic-amplifier circuit oscillating."

"Hm-m-m." Viken rubbed his chin. "Could be. Lately Ed has been changing more and more. When he first came here, he was peppery enough, and he would at least play an occasional game of poker. Now he's pulled so far into his shell you can't even see him. I never thought of it before, but . . . yes, by God, Jupiter must be having some effect on him."

"Hm-m-m." Cornelius nodded. He did not elaborate—did not, for instance, mention that one altogether uncharacteristic episode when Anglesey had tried to describe what it was like to be a Jovian.

"Of course," said Viken thoughtfully, "the previous men were not affected especially. Nor was Ed at first, while he was still controlling lower-type pseudos. It's only since Joe went down to the surface that he's become so different."

"Yes, yes," said Cornelius hastily. "I've learned that much. But enough shop talk—"

"No. Wait a minute." Viken spoke in a low, hurried tone, looking past him. "For the first time, I'm starting to think clearly about this. Never really stopped to analyze it before, just accepted a bad situation. There *is* something peculiar about Joe. It can't very well involve his physical structure, or the environment, because lower forms didn't give this trouble. Could it be the fact that Joe is the first puppet in all history with a potentially human intelligence?"

"We speculate in a vacuum," said Cornelius. "Tomorrow, maybe, I can tell you. Now I know nothing."

Viken sat up straight. His pale eyes focused on the other man and stayed there, unblinking. "One minute," he said.

"Yes?" Cornelius shifted, half rising. "Quickly, please. It is past my bedtime."

"You know a good deal more than you've admitted," said Viken. "Don't you?"

"What makes you think that?"

"You aren't the most gifted liar in the universe. And then, you argued very strongly for Anglesey's scheme, this sending down the other pseudos. More strongly than a newcomer should."

"I told you, I want his attention focused elsewhere when—"

"Do you want it that badly?" snapped Viken.

Cornelius was still for a minute. Then he sighed and leaned back. "All right," he said. "I shall have to trust your discretion. I wasn't sure, you see, how any of you old-time station personnel would react. So I didn't want to blabber out my speculations, which may be wrong. The confirmed facts, yes, I will tell them; but I don't wish to attack a man's religion with a mere theory."

Viken scowled. "What the devil do you mean?"

Cornelius puffed hard on his cigar; its tip waxed and waned like a miniature red demon star. "This Jupiter Five is more than a research station," he said gently. "It is a way of life, is it not? No one would come here for even one hitch unless the work was important to him. Those who re-enlist, they must find something in the work, something which Earth with all her riches cannot offer them. No?"

"Yes," answered Viken. It was almost a whisper. "I didn't think you would understand so well. But what of it?"

"Well, I don't want to tell you, unless I can prove it, that maybe this has all gone for nothing. Maybe you have wasted your lives and a lot of money, and will have to pack up and go home."

Viken's long face did not flicker a muscle. It seemed to have congealed. But he said calmly enough, "Why?"

"Consider Joe," said Cornelius. "His brain has as much capacity as any adult human's. It has been recording every sense datum that came to it, from the moment of 'birth'—making a record in itself, in its own cells, not merely in Anglesey's physical memory bank up here. Also, you know, a thought is a sense datum, too. And thoughts are not separated into neat little railway tracks; they form a continuous field. Every time Anglesey is in rapport with Joe, and thinks, the thought goes through Joe's synapses as well as his own—and every thought carries its own associations, and every associated memory is recorded. Like if Joe is building a hut, the shape of the logs might remind Anglesey of some geometric figure, which in turn would remind him of the Pythagorean theorem—"

"I get the idea," said Viken in a cautious way. "Given time, Joe's brain will have stored everything that ever was in Ed's."

"Correct. Now, a functioning nervous system with an engrammatic pattern of experience, in this case a *nonhuman* nervous system—isn't that a pretty good definition of a personality?"

"I suppose so, Good Lord!" Viken jumped. "You mean Joe is—taking over?"

"In a way. A subtle, automatic, unconscious way." Cornelius drew a deep breath and plunged into it. "The pseudojovian is so nearly perfect a life-form: your biologists engineered into it all the experience gained from nature's mistakes in designing *us*. At first, Joe was only a remote-controlled biological machine. Then Anglesey and Joe became two facets of a single personality. Then, oh, very slowly, the stronger, healthier body . . . more amplitude to its thoughts . . . do you see? Joe is becoming the dominant side. Like this business of sending down the other pseudos—Anglesey only thinks he has logical reasons for wanting it done. Actually, his 'reasons' are mere rationalizations for the instinctive desires of the Joe facet.

"Anglesey's subconscious must comprehend the situation, in a dim reactive way; it must feel his human ego gradually being submerged by the steamroller force of *Joe's* instincts and *Joe's* wishes. It tries to defend its own identity, and is swatted down by the superior force of Joe's own nascent subconscious.

"I put it crudely," he finished in an apologetic tone, "but it will account for that oscillation in the K tubes."

Viken nodded, slowly, like an old man. "Yes, I see it," he answered. "The alien environment down there . . . the different brain structure. . . . Good God! Ed's being swallowed up in Joe! The puppet master is becoming the puppet!" He looked ill.

"Only speculation on my part," said Cornelius. All at once, he felt very tired. It was not pleasant to do this to Viken, whom he liked. "But you see the dilemma, no? If I am right, then any esman will gradually become a Jovian—a monster with two bodies, of which the human body is the unimportant auxiliary one. This means no esman will ever agree to control a pseudo—therefore, the end of your project."

He stood up. "I'm sorry, Arne. You made me tell you what I think, and now you will lie awake worrying, and I am maybe quite wrong and you worry for nothing."

"It's all right," mumbled Viken. "Maybe you're not wrong."

"I don't know." Cornelius drifted toward the door. "I am going to try to find some answers tomorrow. Good night."

The moon-shaking thunder of the rockets, crash, crash, crash, leaping from their cradles, was long past. Now the fleet glided on metal wings, with straining secondary ram-jets, through the rage of the Jovian sky.

As Cornelius opened the control-room door, he looked at his telltale board. Elsewhere a voice tolled the word to all the stations, *One ship wrecked, two ships wrecked,* but Anglesey would let no sound enter his presence when he wore the helmet. An obliging technician had haywired a panel of fifteen red and fifteen blue lights above Cornelius' esprojector, to keep him informed, too. Ostensibly, of course, they were only there for Anglesey's benefit, though the esman had insisted he wouldn't be looking at them.

Four of the red bulbs were dark and thus four blue ones would not shine for a safe landing. A whirlwind, a thunderbolt, a floating ice meteor, a flock of mantalike birds with flesh as dense and hard as iron—there could be a hundred things which had crumpled four ships and tossed them tattered across the poison forests.

Four ships, hell! Think of four living creatures, with an excellence of brain to rival your own, damned first to years in unconscious night and then, never awakening save for one uncomprehending instant, dashed in bloody splinters against an ice mountain. The wasteful callousness of it was a cold knot in Cornelius' belly. It had to be done, no doubt, if there was to be any thinking life on Jupiter at all; but then let it be done quickly and minimally, he thought, so that the next generation could be begotten by love and not by machines!

He closed the door behind him and waited for a breathless moment. Anglesey was a wheel chair and a coppery curve of helmet, facing the opposite wall. No movement, no awareness whatsoever. Good! It would be awkward, perhaps ruinous, if Anglesey learned of this most intimate peering. But he needn't, ever. He was blindfolded and ear-plugged by his own concentration.

Nevertheless, the psionicist moved his bulky form with care, across the room to the new esprojector. He did not much like his snooper's role, he would not have assumed it at all if he had seen any other hope. But neither did it make him feel especially guilty. If what he suspected was true, then Anglesey was all unawares being twisted into something not human; to spy on him might be to save him.

Gently, Cornelius activated the meters and started his tubes warming up. The oscilloscope built into Anglesey's machine gave him the other man's exact alpha rhythm, his basic biological clock. First you adjusted to that, then you discovered the subtler elements by feel, and when your set was fully in phase you could probe undetected and—

Find out what was wrong. Read Anglesey's tortured subconscious and see what there was on Jupiter that both drew and terrified him.

Five ships wrecked.

But it must be very nearly time for them to land. Maybe only five would be lost in all. Maybe ten would get through. Ten comrades for—Joe?

Cornelius sighed. He looked at the cripple, seated blind and deaf to the human world which had crippled him, and felt a pity and an anger. It wasn't fair, none of it was.

Not even to Joe. Joe wasn't any kind of soul-eating devil. He did not even realize, as yet, that he *was* Joe, that Anglesey was becoming a mere appendage. He hadn't asked to be created, and to withdraw his human counterpart from him would very likely be to destroy him.

Somehow, there were always penalties for everybody when men exceeded the decent limits.

Cornelius swore at himself, voicelessly. Work to do. He sat down and fitted the helmet on his own head. The carrier wave made a faint pulse, inaudible, the trembling of neurones low in his awareness. You couldn't describe it.

Reaching up, he turned to Anglesey's alpha. His own had a somewhat lower frequency, it was necessary to carry the signals through a heterodyning process. Still no reception. Well, of course he had to find the exact wave form, timbre was as basic to thought as to music. He adjusted the dials slowly, with enormous care.

Something flashed through his consciousness, a vision of clouds roiled in a violet-red sky, a wind that galloped across horizonless immensity—he lost it. His fingers shook as he turned back.

The psibeam between Joe and Anglesey broadened. It took Cornelius into the circuit. He looked through Joe's eyes, he stood on a hill and stared into the sky above the ice mountains, straining for sign of the first rocket; and simultaneously he was still Jan Cornelius, blurrily seeing the meters, probing about for emotions, symbols, any key to the locked terror in Anglesey's soul.

The terror rose up and struck him in the face.

Psionic detection is not a matter of passive listening in. Much as a radio receiver is necessarily also a weak transmitter, the nervous system in resonance with a source of psionic-spectrum energy is itself emitting. Normally, of course, this effect is unimportant; but when you pass the impulses, either way, through a set of heterodyning and amplifying units, with a high negative feedback . . .

In the early days, psionic psychotherapy vitiated itself because the amplified thoughts of one man, entering the brain of another, would combine with the latter's own neural cycles according to the ordinary vector laws. The result was that both men felt the new beat frequencies as a nightmarish fluttering of their very thoughts. An analyst, trained into self-control, could ignore it; his patient could not, and reacted violently.

But eventually the basic human wave timbres were measured, and psionic therapy resumed. The modern esprojector analyzed an incoming signal and shifted its characteristics over to the "listener's" pattern. The *really* different pulses of the transmitting brain, those which could not possibly be mapped onto the pattern of the receiving neurones—as an exponential signal cannot very practicably be mapped onto a sinusoid—those were filtered out.

Thus compensated, the other thought could be apprehended as comfortably as one's own. If the patient were on a psibeam circuit, a skilled operator could tune in without the patient being necessarily aware of it. The operator could either probe the other man's thoughts or implant thoughts of his own.

Cornelius' plan, an obvious one to any psionicist, had depended on this. He would receive from an unwitting Anglesey-Joe. If his theory was right and the esman's personality was being distorted into that of a monster, his thinking would be too alien to come through the filters. Cornelius would receive spottily or not at all. If his theory was wrong, and Anglesey was still Anglesey, he would receive only a normal human stream of consciousness and could probe for other troublemaking factors.

His brain roared!

What's happening to me?

For a moment, the interference which turned his thoughts to saw-toothed gibberish struck him down with panic. He gulped for breath, there in the Jovian wind, and his dreadful dogs sensed the alienness in him and whined.

Then, recognition, remembrance, and a blaze of anger so great that it left no room for fear. Joe filled his lungs and shouted it aloud, the hillside boomed with echoes:

"Get out of my mind!"

He felt Cornelius spiral down toward unconsciousness. The over-whelming force of his own mental blow had been too much. He laughed, it was more like a snarl, and eased the pressure.

Above him, between thunderous clouds, winked the first thin de-scending rocket flare.

Cornelius' mind groped back toward the light. It broke a watery surface, the man's mouth snapped after air and his hands reached for the dials, to turn his machine off and escape.

"Not so fast, you." Grimly, Joe drove home a command that locked Cornelius' muscles rigid. "I want to know the meaning of this. Hold still and let me look!" He smashed home an impulse which could be rendered, perhaps, as an incandescent question mark. Re-membrance exploded in shards through the psionicist's forebrain.

"So. That's all there is? You thought I was afraid to come down here and be Joe, and wanted to know why? But I *told* you I wasn't!"

I should have believed, whispered Cornelius.

"Well, get out of the circuit, then." Joe continued growling it vo-cally. "And don't ever come back in the control room, understand? K tubes or no, I don't want to see you again. And I may be a cripple, but I can still take you apart cell by cell. Now sign off—leave me alone. The first ship will be landing in minutes."

You a cripple—you, Joe Anglesey?

"What?" The great gray being on the hill lifted his barbaric head as if to sudden trumpets. "What do you mean?"

Don't you understand? said the weak, dragging thought. *You know how the esprojector works. You know I could have probed Anglesey's mind in Anglesey's brain without making enough interference to be noticed. And I could not have probed a wholly nonhuman mind at all, nor could it have been aware of me. The filters would not have passed such a signal. Yet you felt me in the first fractional second. It can only mean a human mind in a nonhuman brain.*

You are not the half-corpse on Jupiter Five any longer. You're Joe—Joe Anglesey.

"Well, I'll be damned," said Joe. "You're right."

He turned Anglesey off, kicked Cornelius out of his mind with a single brutal impulse, and ran down the hill to meet the spaceship.

Cornelius woke up minutes afterward. His skull felt ready to split apart. He groped for the main switch before him, clashed it down, ripped the helmet off his head and threw it clanging on the floor. But it took a little while to gather the strength to do the same for Anglesey. The other man was not able to do anything for himself.

They sat outside sick bay and waited. It was a harshly lit barrenness of metal and plastic, smelling of antiseptics—down near the heart of the satellite, with miles of rock to hide the terrible face of Jupiter.

Only Viken and Cornelius were in that cramped little room. The rest of the station went about its business mechanically, filling in the time till it could learn what had happened. Beyond the door, three biotechnicians, who were also the station's medical staff, fought with death's angel for the thing which had been Edward Anglesey.

"Nine ships got down," said Viken dully. "Two males, seven females. It's enough to start a colony."

"It would be genetically desirable to have more," pointed out Cornelius. He kept his own voice low, in spite of its underlying cheerfulness. There was a certain awesome quality to all this.

"I still don't understand," said Viken.

"Oh, it's clear enough—now. I should have guessed it before, maybe. We had all the facts, it was only that we couldn't make the simple, obvious interpretation of them. No, we had to conjure up Frankenstein's monster."

"Well," Viken's words grated, "we have played Frankenstein, haven't we? Ed is dying in there."

"It depends on how you define death." Cornelius drew hard on his cigar, needing anything that might steady him. His tone grew purposely dry of emotion.

"Look here. Consider the data. Joe, now: a creature with a brain of human capacity, but without a mind—a perfect Lockean *tabula rasa* for Anglesey's psibeam to write on. We deduced, correctly enough—if very belatedly—that when enough had been written, there would be a personality. But the question was, whose? Because, I suppose, of normal human fear of the unknown, we assumed that any personality in so alien a body had to be monstrous. Therefore it must be hostile to Anglesey, must be swamping him—"

The door opened. Both men jerked to their feet.

The chief surgeon shook his head. "No use. Typical deep-shock traumata, close to terminus now. If we had better facilities, maybe . . ."

"No," said Cornelius. "You cannot save a man who has decided not to live any more."

"I know." The doctor removed his mask. "I need a cigarette. Who's got one?" His hands shook a little as he accepted it from Viken.

"But how could he—decide—anything?" choked the physicist. "He's been unconscious ever since Jan pulled him away from that . . . that thing."

"It was decided before then," said Cornelius. "As a matter of fact, that hulk in there on the operating table no longer has a mind. I know. I was there." He shuddered a little. A stiff shot of tranquilizer was all that held nightmare away from him. Later he would have to have that memory exorcised.

The doctor took a long drag of smoke, held it in his lungs a moment, and exhaled gustily. "I guess this winds up the project," he said. "We'll never get another esman."

"I'll say we won't." Viken's tone sounded rusty. "I'm going to smash that devil's engine myself."

"Hold on a minute!" exclaimed Cornelius. "Don't you understand? This isn't the end. It's the beginning!"

"I'd better get back," said the doctor. He stubbed out his cigarette and went through the door. It closed behind him with a deathlike quietness.

"What do you mean?" Viken said it as if erecting a barrier.

"*Won't* you understand?" roared Cornelius. "Joe has all Anglesey's habits, thoughts, memories, prejudices, interests. Oh, yes, the different body and the different environment—they do cause some changes, but no more than any man might undergo on Earth. If you were suddenly cured of a wasting disease, wouldn't you maybe get a little boisterous and rough? There is nothing abnormal in it. Nor is it abnormal to want to stay healthy—no? Do you see?"

Viken sat down. He spent a while without speaking.

Then, enormously slow and careful: "Do you mean Joe is Ed?"

"Or Ed is Joe. Whatever you like. He calls himself Joe now, I think—as a symbol of freedom—but he is still himself. What *is* the ego but continuity of existence?

"He himself did not fully understand this. He only knew—he told me, and I should have believed him—that on Jupiter he was strong and happy. Why did the K tube oscillate? A hysterical symptom! Anglesey's subconscious was not afraid to stay on Jupiter—it was afraid to come back!

"And then, today, I listened in. By now, his whole self was focused on Joe. That is, the primary source of libido was Joe's virile body, not Anglesey's sick one. This meant a different pattern of impulses— not too alien to pass the filters, but alien enough to set up interference. So he felt my presence. And he saw the truth, just as I did.

"Do you know the last emotion I felt as Joe threw me out of his mind? Not anger any more. He plays rough, him, but all he had room to feel was joy.

"I *knew* how strong a personality Anglesey has! Whatever made me think an overgrown child brain like Joe's could override it? In there, the doctors—bah! They're trying to salvage a hulk which has been shed because it is useless!"

Cornelius stopped. His throat was quite raw from talking. He paced the floor, rolled cigar smoke around his mouth but did not draw it any farther in.

When a few minutes had passed, Viken said cautiously, "All right. You should know—as you said, you were there. But what do we do now? How do we get in touch with Ed? Will he even be interested in contacting us?"

"Oh, yes, of course," said Cornelius. "He is still himself, remember. Now that he has none of the cripple's frustrations, he should be more amiable. When the novelty of his new friends wears off, he will want someone who can talk to him as an equal."

"And precisely who will operate another pseudo?" asked Viken sarcastically. "I'm quite happy with this skinny frame of mine, thank you!"

"Was Anglesey the only hopeless cripple on Earth?" asked Cornelius quietly.

Viken gaped at him.

"And there are aging men, too," went on the psionicist, half to himself. "Someday, my friend, when you and I feel the years close in, and so much we would like to learn—maybe we too would enjoy an extra lifetime in a Jovian body." He nodded at his cigar. "A hard, lusty, stormy kind of life, granted—dangerous, brawling, violent—but life as no human, perhaps, has lived it since the days of Elizabeth the First. Oh, yes, there will be small trouble finding Jovians."

He turned his head as the surgeon came out again.

"Well?" croaked Viken.

The doctor sat down. "It's finished," he said.

They waited for a moment, awkwardly.

"Odd," said the doctor. He groped after a cigarette he didn't have. Silently, Viken offered him one. "Odd. I've seen these cases before. People who simply resign from life. This is the first one I ever saw that went out smiling—smiling all the time."

WHO GOES THERE?
by John W. Campbell, Jr. (as Don A. Stuart)

The place stank. A queer, mingled stench that only the ice-buried cabins of an Antarctic camp know, compounded of reeking human sweat, and the heavy, fish-oil stench of melted seal blubber. An overtone of liniment combated the musty smell of sweat-and-snow-drenched furs. The acrid odor of burnt cooking fat, and the animal, not-unpleasant smell of dogs, diluted by time, hung in the air.

Lingering odors of machine oil contrasted sharply with the taint of harness dressing and leather. Yet, somehow, through all that reek of human beings and their associates—dogs, machines and cooking—came another taint. It was a queer, neck-ruffling thing, a faintest suggestion of an odor alien among the smells of industry and life. And it was a lifesmell. But it came from the thing that lay bound with cord and tarpaulin on the table, dripping slowly, methodically onto the heavy planks, dank and gaunt under the unshielded glare of the electric light.

Blair, the little bald-pated biologist of the expedition, twitched nervously at the wrappings, exposing clear, dark ice beneath and then pulling the tarpaulin back into place restlessly. His little birdlike motions of suppressed eagerness danced his shadow across the fringe of dingy gray underwear hanging from the low ceiling, the equatorial fringe of stiff, graying hair around his naked skull a comical halo about the shadow's head.

Commander Garry brushed aside the lax legs of a suit of underwear, and stepped toward the table. Slowly his eyes traced around the rings of men sardined into the Administration Building. His tall, stiff body straightened finally, and he nodded. "Thirty-seven. All here." His voice was low, yet carried the clear authority of the commander by nature, as well as by title.

"You know the outline of the story back of that find of the Secondary Pole Expedition. I have been conferring with Second-in-

Command McReady, and Norris, as well as Blair and Dr. Copper. There is a difference of opinion, and because it involves the entire group, it is only just that the entire Expedition personnel act on it.

"I am going to ask McReady to give you the details of the story, because each of you has been too busy with his own work to follow closely the endeavors of the others. McReady?"

Moving from the smoke-blued background, McReady was a figure from some forgotten myth, a looming, bronze statue that held life, and walked. Six-feet-four inches he stood as he halted beside the table, and, with a characteristic glance upward to assure himself of room under the low ceiling beams, straightened. His rough, clashingly orange windproof jacket he still had on, yet on his huge frame it did not seem misplaced. Even here, four feet beneath the drift-wind that droned across the Antarctic waste above the ceiling, the cold of the frozen continent leaked in, and gave meaning to the harshness of the man. And he was bronze—his great red-bronze beard, the heavy hair that matched it. The gnarled, corded hands gripping, relaxing, gripping and relaxing on the table planks were bronze. Even the deep-sunken eyes beneath heavy brows were bronzed.

Age-resisting endurance of the metal spoke in the cragged heavy outlines of his face, and the mellow tones of the heavy voice. "Norris and Blair agree on one thing; that animal we found was not—terrestrial in origin. Norris fears there may be danger in that; Blair says there is none.

"But I'll go back to how, and why, we found it. To all that was known before we came here, it appeared that this point was exactly over the South Magnetic Pole of Earth. The compass does point straight down here, as you all know. The more delicate instruments of the physicists, instruments especially designed for this expedition and its study of the magnetic pole, detected a secondary effect, a secondary, less powerful magnetic influence about 80 miles southwest of here.

"The Secondary Magnetic Expedition went out to investigate it. There is no need for details. We found it, but it was not the huge meteorite or magnetic mountain Norris had expected to find. Iron ore is magnetic, of course; iron more so—and certain special steels even more magnetic. From the surface indications, the secondary pole we found was small, so small that the magnetic effect it had was preposterous. No magnetic material conceivable could have that effect.

Soundings through the ice indicated it was within one hundred feet of the glacier surface.

"I think you should know the structure of the place. There is a broad plateau, a level sweep that runs more than 150 miles due south from the Secondary station, Van Wall says. He didn't have time or fuel to fly farther, but it was running smoothly due south then. Right there, where that buried thing was, there is an ice-drowned mountain ridge, a granite wall of unshakable strength that has dammed back the ice creeping from the south.

"And four hundred miles due south is the South Polar Plateau. You have asked me at various times why it gets warmer here when the wind rises, and most of you know. As a meteorologist I'd have staked my word that no wind could blow at −70 degrees—that no more than a 5-mile wind could blow at −50—without causing warming due to friction with ground, snow and ice and the air itself.

"We camped there on the lip of that ice-drowned mountain range for twelve days. We dug our camp into the blue ice that formed the surface, and escaped most of it. But for twelve consecutive days the wind blew at 45 miles an hour. It went as high as 48, and fell to 41 at times. The temperature was −63 degrees. It rose to −60 and fell to −68. It was meteorologically impossible, and it went on uninterruptedly for twelve days and twelve nights.

"Somewhere to the south, the frozen air of South Polar Plateau slides down from that 18,000-foot bowl, down a mountain pass, over a glacier, and starts north. There must be a funneling mountain chain that directs it, and sweeps it away for four hundred miles to hit that bald plateau where we found the secondary pole, and 350 miles farther north reaches the Antarctic Ocean.

"It's been frozen there since Antarctica froze twenty million years ago. There never has been a thaw there.

"Twenty million years ago Antarctica was beginning to freeze. We've investigated, thought and built speculations. What we believe happened was about like this.

"Something came down out of space, a ship. We saw it there in the blue ice, a thing like a submarine without a conning tower or directive vanes, 280 feet long and 45 feet in diameter at its thickest.

"Eh, Van Wall? Space? Yes, but I'll explain that better later." McReady's steady voice went on.

"It came down from space, driven and lifted by forces men haven't discovered yet, and somehow—perhaps something went wrong then—it tangled with Earth's magnetic field. It came south here, out of control probably, circling the magnetic pole. That's a savage country there, but when Antarctica was still freezing it must have been a thousand times more savage. There must have been blizzard snow, as well as drift, new snow falling as the continent glaciated. The swirl there must have been particularly bad, the wind hurling a solid blanket of white over the lip of that now-buried mountain.

"The ship struck solid granite head-on, and cracked up. Not every one of the passengers in it was killed, but the ship must have been ruined, her driving mechanism locked. It tangled with Earth's field, Norris believes. No thing made by intelligent beings can tangle with the dead immensity of a planet's natural forces and survive.

"One of its passengers stepped out. The wind we saw there never fell below 41, and the temperature never rose above —60. Then—the wind must have been stronger. And there was drift falling in a solid sheet. The *thing* was lost completely in ten paces." He paused for a moment, the deep, steady voice giving way to the drone of wind overhead, and the uneasy, malicious gurgling in the pipe of the galley stove.

Drift—a drift-wind was sweeping by overhead. Right now the snow picked up by the mumbling wind fled in level, blinding lines across the face of the buried camp. If a man stepped out of the tunnels that connected each of the camp buildings beneath the surface, he'd be lost in ten paces. Out there, the slim, black finger of the radio mast lifted 300 feet into the air, and at its peak was the clear night sky. A sky of thin, whining wind rushing steadily from beyond to another beyond under the licking, curling mantle of the aurora. And off north, the horizon flamed with queer, angry colors of the midnight twilight. That was spring 300 feet above Antarctica.

At the surface—it was white death. Death of a needle-fingered cold driven before the wind, sucking heat from any warm thing. Cold—and white mist of endless, everlasting drift, the fine, fine particles of licking snow that obscured all things.

Kinner, the little, scar-faced cook, winced. Five days ago he had stepped out to the surface to reach a cache of frozen beef. He had reached it, started back—and the drift-wind leapt out of the south. Cold, white death that streamed across the ground blinded him in twenty seconds. He stumbled on wildly in circles. It was half an hour before rope-guided men from below found him in the impenetrable murk.

It was easy for man—or *thing*—to get lost in ten paces.

"And the drift-wind then was probably more impenetrable than we know." McReady's voice snapped Kinner's mind back. Back to welcome, dank warmth of the Ad Building. "The passenger of the ship wasn't prepared either, it appears. It froze within ten feet of the ship.

"We dug down to find the ship, and our tunnel happened to find the frozen—animal. Barclay's ice-ax struck its skull.

"When we saw what it was, Barclay went back to the tractor, started the fire up and when the steam pressure built, sent a call for Blair and Dr. Copper. Barclay himself was sick then. Stayed sick for three days, as a matter of fact.

"When Blair and Copper came, we cut out the animal in a block of ice, as you see, wrapped it and loaded it on the tractor for return here. We wanted to get into that ship.

"We reached the side and found the metal was something we didn't know. Our beryllium-bronze, non-magnetic tools wouldn't touch it. Barclay had some tool-steel on the tractor, and that wouldn't scratch it either. We made reasonable tests—even tried some acid from the batteries with no results.

"They must have had a passivating process to make magnesium metal resist acid that way, and the alloy must have been at least 95 per cent magnesium. But we had no way of guessing that, so when we spotted the barely opened lock door, we cut around it. There was clear, hard ice inside the lock, where we couldn't reach it. Through the little crack we could look in and see that only metal and tools were in there, so we decided to loosen the ice with a bomb.

"We had decanite bombs and thermite. Thermite is the ice-softener; decanite might have shattered valuable things, where the thermite's heat would just loosen the ice. Dr. Copper, Norris and I placed a 25-pound thermite bomb, wired it, and took the connector up the tunnel to the surface, where Blair had the steam tractor waiting. A hundred yards the other side of that granite wall we set off the thermite bomb.

"The magnesium metal of the ship caught, of course. The glow of the bomb flared and died, then it began to flare again. We ran back to the tractor, and gradually the glare built up. From where we were we could see the whole ice-field illuminated from beneath with an unbearable light; the ship's shadow was a great, dark cone reaching off toward the north, where the twilight was just about gone. For a moment it lasted, and we counted three other shadow-things that might have been other—passengers—frozen there. Then the ice was crashing down and against the ship.

"That's why I told you about that place. The wind sweeping down from the Pole was at our backs. Steam and hydrogen flame were torn away in white ice-fog; the flaming heat under the ice there was yanked away toward the Antarctic Ocean before it touched us. Otherwise we wouldn't have come back, even with the shelter of that granite ridge that stopped the light.

"Somehow in the blinding inferno we could see great hunched things, black bulks glowing, even so. They shed even the furious incandescence of the magnesium for a time. Those must have been the engines, we knew. Secrets going in blazing glory—secrets that might have given Man the planets. Mysterious things that could lift and hurl that ship—and had soaked in the force of the Earth's magnetic field. I saw Norris' mouth move, and ducked. I couldn't hear him.

"Insulation—something—gave way. All Earth's field they'd soaked up twenty million years before broke loose. The aurora in the sky above licked down, and the whole plateau there was bathed in cold fire that blanketed vision. The ice-ax in my hand got red hot, and hissed on the ice. Metal buttons on my clothes burned into me. And a flash of electric blue seared upward from beyond the granite wall.

"Then the walls of ice crashed down on it. For an instant it squealed the way dry-ice does when it's pressed between metal.

"We were blind and groping in the dark for hours while our eyes recovered. We found every coil within a mile was fused rubbish, the dynamo and every radio set, the earphones and speakers. If we hadn't had the steam tractor, we wouldn't have gotten over to the Secondary Camp.

"Van Wall flew in from Big Magnet at sun-up, as you know. We came home as soon as possible. That is the history of—that." McReady's great bronze beard gestured toward the thing on the table.

II

Blair stirred uneasily, his little, bony fingers wriggling under the harsh light. Little brown freckles on his knuckles slid back and forth as the tendons under the skin twitched. He pulled aside a bit of the tarpaulin and looked impatiently at the dark ice-bound thing inside.

McReady's big body straightened somewhat. He'd ridden the rocking, jarring steam tractor forty miles that day, pushing on to Big Magnet here. Even his calm will had been pressed by the anxiety to mix again with humans. It was lone and quiet out there in Secondary Camp, where a wolf-wind howled down from the Pole. Wolf-wind howling in his sleep—winds droning and the evil, unspeakable face of that monster leering up as he'd first seen it through clear, blue ice, with a bronze ice-ax buried in its skull.

The giant meteorologist spoke again. "The problem is this. Blair wants to examine the thing. Thaw it out and make micro slides of its tissues and so forth. Norris doesn't believe that is safe, and Blair does. Dr. Copper agrees pretty much with Blair. Norris is a physicist, of course, not a biologist. But he makes a point I think we should all hear. Blair has described the microscopic life-forms biologists find living, even in this cold and inhospitable place. They freeze every winter, and thaw every summer—for three months—and live.

"The point Norris makes is—they thaw, and live again. There must have been microscopic life associated with this creature. There is with every living thing we know. And Norris is afraid that we may release a plague—some germ disease unknown to Earth—if we thaw those microscopic things that have been frozen there for twenty million years.

"Blair admits that such micro-life might retain the power of living. Such unorganized things as individual cells can retain life for unknown periods, when solidly frozen. The beast itself is as dead as those frozen mammoths they find in Siberia. Organized, highly developed life-forms can't stand that treatment.

"But micro-life could. Norris suggests that we may release some disease-form that man, never having met it before, will be utterly defenseless against.

"Blair's answer is that there may be such still-living germs, but that Norris has the case reversed. They are utterly non-immune to man. Our life-chemistry probably——"

"Probably!" The little biologist's head lifted in a quick, birdlike motion. The halo of gray hair about his bald head ruffled as though angry. "Heh. One look——"

"I know," McReady acknowledged. "The thing is not Earthly. It does not seem likely that it can have a life-chemistry sufficiently like ours to make cross-infection remotely possible. I would say that there is no danger."

McReady looked toward Dr. Copper. The physician shook his head slowly. "None whatever," he asserted confidently. "Man cannot infect or be infected by germs that live in such comparatively close relatives as the snakes. And they are, I assure you," his clean-shaven face grimaced uneasily, "*much* nearer to us than—*that.*"

Vance Norris moved angrily. He was comparatively short in this gathering of big men, some five-feet-eight, and his stocky, powerful build tended to make him seem shorter. His black hair was crisp and hard, like short, steel wires, and his eyes were the gray of fractured steel. If McReady was a man of bronze, Norris was all steel. His movements, his thoughts, his whole bearing had the quick, hard impulse of steel spring. His nerves were steel—hard, quick-acting—swift corroding.

He was decided on his point now, and he lashed out in its defense with a characteristic quick, clipped flow of words. "Different chemistry be damned. That thing may be dead—or, by God, it may not—but I don't like it. Damn it, Blair, let them see the monstrosity you are petting over there. Let them see the foul thing and decide for themselves whether they want that thing thawed out in this camp.

"Thawed out, by the way. That's got to be thawed out in one of the shacks tonight, if it is thawed out. Somebody—who's watchman tonight? Magnetic—oh, Connant. Cosmic rays tonight. Well, you get to sit up with that twenty-million-year-old mummy of his.

"Unwrap it, Blair. How the hell can they tell what they are buying if they can't see it? It may have a different chemistry. I don't know what else it has, but I know it has something I don't want. If you can judge by the look on its face—it isn't human so maybe you can't—it was annoyed when it froze. Annoyed, in fact, is just about as close an approximation of the way it felt as crazy, mad, insane hatred. Neither one touches the subject.

"How the hell can these birds tell what they are voting on? They haven't seen those three red eyes, and that blue hair like crawling worms. Crawling—damn, it's crawling there in the ice right now!

"Nothing Earth ever spawned had the unutterable sublimation of devastating wrath that thing let loose in its face when it looked around this frozen desolation twenty million years ago. Mad? It was mad clear through—searing, blistering mad!

"Hell, I've had bad dreams ever since I looked at those three red eyes. Nightmares. Dreaming the thing thawed out and came to life—that it wasn't dead, or even wholly unconscious all those twenty million years, but just slowed, waiting—waiting. You'll dream, too, while that damned thing that Earth wouldn't own is dripping, dripping in the Cosmos House tonight.

"And, Connant," Norris whipped toward the cosmic ray specialist, "won't you have fun sitting up all night in the quiet. Wind whining above—and that thing dripping——" He stopped for a moment, and looked around.

"I know. That's not science. But this is, it's psychology. You'll have nightmares for a year to come. Every night since I looked at that thing I've had 'em. That's why I hate it—sure I do—and don't want it around. Put it back where it came from and let it freeze for another twenty million years. I had some swell nightmares—that it wasn't made like we are—which is obvious—but of a different kind of flesh that it can really control. That it can change its shape, and look like a man—and wait to kill and eat——

"That's not a logical argument. I know it isn't. The thing isn't Earth-logic anyway.

"Maybe it has an alien body-chemistry, and maybe its bugs do have a different body-chemistry. A germ might not stand that, but, Blair and Copper, how about a virus? That's just an enzyme molecule, you've said. That wouldn't need anything but a protein molecule of any body to work on.

"And how are you so sure that, of the million varieties of microscopic life it may have, *none* of them are dangerous? How about diseases like hydrophobia—rabies—that attacks any warm-blooded creature, whatever its body-chemistry may be? And parrot fever? Have you a body like a parrot, Blair? And plain rot—gangrene—necrosis, do you want? *That* isn't choosy about body-chemistry!"

Blair looked up from his puttering long enough to meet Norris' angry, gray eyes for an instant. "So far the only thing you have said this thing gave off that was catching was dreams. I'll go so far as to admit that." An impish, slightly malignant grin crossed the little man's seamed face. "I had some, too. So. It's dream-infectious. No doubt an exceedingly dangerous malady.

"So far as your other things go, you have a badly mistaken idea about viruses. In the first place, nobody has shown that the enzyme-molecule theory, and that alone, explains them. And in the second place, when you catch tobacco mosaic or wheat rust, let me know. A wheat plant is a lot nearer your body-chemistry than this other-world creature is.

"And your rabies is limited, strictly limited. You can't get it from, nor give it to, a wheat plant or a fish—which is a collateral descendant of a common ancestor of yours. Which this, Norris, is not." Blair nodded pleasantly toward the tarpaulined bulk on the table.

"Well, thaw the damned thing in a tub of formalin if you must thaw it. I've suggested that——"

"And I've said there would be no sense in it. You can't compromise. Why did you and Commander Garry come down here to study magnetism? Why weren't you content to stay at home? There's magnetic force enough in New York. I could no more study the life this thing once had from a formalin-pickled sample than you could get the information you wanted back in New York. And—if this one is so treated, *never in all time to come can there be a duplicate!* The race it came from must have passed away in the twenty million years it lay frozen, so that even if it came from Mars then, we'd never find its like. And—the ship is gone.

"There's only one way to do this—and that is the best possible way. It must be thawed slowly, carefully, and not in formalin."

Commander Garry stood forward again, and Norris stepped back muttering angrily. "I think Blair is right, gentlemen. What do you say?"

Connant grunted. "It sounds right to us, I think—only perhaps he ought to stand watch over it while it's thawing." He grinned ruefully, brushing a stray lock of ripe-cherry hair back from his forehead. "Swell idea, in fact—if he sits up with his jolly little corpse."

Garry smiled slightly. A general chuckle of agreement rippled over the group. "I should think any ghost it may have had would have starved to death if it hung around here that long, Connant," Garry suggested. "And you look capable of taking care of it. 'Ironman' Connant ought to be able to take out any opposing players, still."

Connant shook himself uneasily. "I'm not worrying about ghosts. Let's see that thing. I——"

Eagerly Blair was stripping back the ropes. A single throw of the tarpaulin revealed the thing. The ice had melted somewhat in the heat of the room, and it was clear and blue as thick, good glass. It shone wet and sleek under the harsh light of the unshielded globe above.

The room stiffened abruptly. It was face up there on the plain, greasy planks of the table. The broken half of the bronze ice-ax was still buried in the queer skull. Three mad, hate-filled eyes blazed up with a living fire, bright as fresh-spilled blood, from a face ringed with a writhing, loathsome nest of worms, blue, mobile worms that crawled where hair should grow——

Van Wall, six feet and 200 pounds of ice-nerved pilot, gave a queer, strangled gasp and butted, stumbled his way out to the corridor. Half the company broke for the doors. The others stumbled away from the table.

McReady stood at one end of the table watching them, his great body planted solid on his powerful legs. Norris from the opposite end glowered at the thing with smouldering hate. Outside the door, Garry was talking with half a dozen of the men at once.

Blair had a tack hammer. The ice that cased the thing *schluffed* crisply under its steel claw as it peeled from the thing it had cased for twenty thousand thousand years——

III

"I know you don't like the thing, Connant, but it just has to be thawed out right. You say leave it as it is till we get back to civilization. All right, I'll admit your argument that we could do a better and more complete job there is sound. But—how are we going to get this across the Line? We have to take this through one temperate zone, the equatorial zone, and half way through the other temperate zone before we get it to New York. You don't want to sit with it one night, but you suggest, then, that I hang its corpse in the freezer with the beef?" Blair looked up from his cautious chipping, his bald, freckled skull nodding triumphantly.

Kinner, the stocky, scar-faced cook, saved Connant the trouble of answering. "Hey, you listen, mister. You put that thing in the box with the meat, and by all the gods there ever were, I'll put you in to keep it company. You birds have brought everything movable in this camp in onto my mess tables here already, and I had to stand for that. But you go putting things like that in my meat box or even my meat cache here, and you cook your own damn grub."

"But, Kinner, this is the only table in Big Magnet that's big enough to work on," Blair objected. "Everybody's explained that."

"Yeah, and everybody's brought everything in here. Clark brings his dogs every time there's a fight and sews them up on that table.

Ralsen brings in his sledges. Hell, the only thing you haven't had on that table is the Boeing. And you'd 'a' had that in if you coulda figured a way to get it through the tunnels."

Commander Garry chuckled and grinned at Van Wall, the huge Chief Pilot. Van Wall's great blond beard twitched suspiciously as he nodded gravely to Kinner. "You're right, Kinner. The aviation department is the only one that treats you right."

"It does get crowded, Kinner," Garry acknowledged. "But I'm afraid we all find it that way at times. Not much privacy in an Antarctic camp."

"Privacy? What the hell's that? You know, the thing that really made me weep, was when I saw Barclay marchin' through here chantin' 'The last lumber in the camp! The last lumber in the camp!' and carryin' it out to build that house on his tractor. Damn it, I missed that moon cut in the door he carried out more'n I missed the sun when it set. That wasn't just the last lumber Barclay was walkin' off with. He was carryin' off the last bit of privacy in this blasted place."

A grin rode even on Connant's heavy face as Kinner's perennial good-natured grouch came up again. But it died away quickly as his dark, deep-set eyes turned again to the red-eyed thing Blair was chipping from its cocoon of ice. A big hand ruffed his shoulder-length hair, and tugged at a twisted lock that fell behind his ear in a familiar gesture. "I know that cosmic ray shack's going to be too crowded if I have to sit up with that thing," he growled. "Why can't you go on chipping the ice away from around it—you can do that without anybody butting in, I assure you—and then hang the thing up over the power-plant boiler? That's warm enough. It'll thaw out a chicken, even a whole side of beef, in a few hours."

"I know." Blair protested, dropping the tack hammer to gesture more effectively with his bony, freckled fingers, his small body tense with eagerness, "but this is too important to take any chances. There never was a find like this; there never can be again. It's the only chance men will ever have, and it has to be done exactly right.

"Look, you know how the fish we caught down near the Ross Sea would freeze almost as soon as we got them on deck, and come to life again if we thawed them gently? Low forms of life aren't killed by quick freezing and slow thawing. We have——"

"Hey, for the love of Heaven—you mean that damned thing will come to life!" Connant yelled. "You get the damned thing—— Let me at it! That's going to be in so many pieces——"

"NO! *No,* you fool—" Blair jumped in front of Connant to protect his precious find. "No. Just *low* forms of life. For Pete's sake let me finish. You can't thaw higher forms of life and have them come to. Wait a moment now—hold it! A fish can come to after freezing because it's so low a form of life that the individual cells of its body can revive, and that alone is enough to re-establish life. Any higher forms thawed out that way are dead. Though the individual cells revive, they die because there must be organization and cooperative effort to live. That cooperation cannot be re-established. There is a sort of potential life in any uninjured, quick-frozen animal. But it can't—can't under any circumstances—become active life in higher animals. The higher animals are too complex, too delicate. This is an intelligent creature as high in its evolution as we are in ours. Perhaps higher. It is as dead as a frozen man would be."

"How do you know?" demanded Connant, hefting the ice-ax he had seized a moment before.

Commander Garry laid a restraining hand on his heavy shoulder. "Wait a minute, Connant. I want to get this straight. I agree that there is going to be no thawing of this thing if there is the remotest chance of its revival. I quite agree it is much too unpleasant to have alive, but I had no idea there was the remotest possibility."

Dr. Copper pulled his pipe from between his teeth and heaved his stocky, dark body from the bunk he had been sitting in. "Blair's being technical. That's dead. As dead as the mammoths they find frozen in Siberia. Potential life is like atomic energy—there, but nobody can get it out, and it certainly won't release itself except in rare cases, as rare as radium in the chemical analogy. We have all sorts of proof that things don't live after being frozen—not even fish, generally speaking —and no proof that higher animal life can under any circumstances. What's the point, Blair?"

The little biologist shook himself. The little ruff of hair standing out around his bald pate waved in righteous anger. "The point is," he said in an injured tone, "that the individual cells might show the characteristics they had in life, if it is properly thawed. A man's muscle cells live many hours after he has died. Just because they live, and a few things like hair and fingernail cells still live, you wouldn't accuse a corpse of being a Zombie, or something.

"Now if I thaw this right, I may have a chance to determine what sort of world it's native to. We don't, and can't know by any other means, whether it came from Earth or Mars or Venus or from beyond the stars.

"And just because it looks unlike men, you don't have to accuse it of being evil, or vicious or something. Maybe that expression on its face is its equivalent to a resignation to fate. White is the color of mourning to the Chinese. If men can have different customs, why can't a so-different race have different understandings of facial expressions?"

Connant laughed softly, mirthlessly. "Peaceful resignation! If that is the best it could do in the way of resignation, I should exceedingly dislike seeing it when it was looking mad. That face was never designed to express peace. It just didn't have any philosophical thoughts like peace in its make-up.

"I know it's your pet—but be sane about it. That thing grew up on evil, adolesced slowly roasting alive the local equivalent of kittens, and amused itself through maturity on new and ingenious torture."

"You haven't the slightest right to say that," snapped Blair. "How do you know the first thing about the meaning of a facial expression inherently inhuman? It may well have no human equivalent whatever. That is just a different development of Nature, another example of Nature's wonderful adaptability. Growing on another, perhaps harsher world, it has different form and features. But it is just as much a legitimate child of Nature as you are. You are displaying the childish human weakness of hating the different. On its own world it would probably class you as a fish-belly, white monstrosity with an insufficient number of eyes and a fungoid body pale and bloated with gas.

"Just because its nature is different, you haven't any right to say it's necessarily evil."

Norris burst out a single, explosive, "Haw!" He looked down at the thing. "May be that things from other worlds don't *have* to be evil just because they're different. But that thing *was!* Child of Nature, eh? Well, it was a hell of an evil Nature."

"Aw, will you mugs cut crabbing at each other and get the damned thing off my table?" Kinner growled. "And put a canvas over it. It looks indecent."

"Kinner's gone modest," jeered Connant.

Kinner slanted his eyes up to the big physicist. The scarred cheek twisted to join the line of his tight lips in a twisted grin. "All right, big boy, and what were you grousing about a minute ago? We can set the thing in a chair next to you tonight, if you want."

"I'm not afraid of its face," Connant snapped. "I don't like keeping a wake over its corpse particularly, but I'm going to do it."

Kinner's grin spread. "Uh-huh." He went off to the galley stove and shook down ashes vigorously, drowning the brittle chipping of the ice as Blair fell to work again.

IV

"*Cluck,*" reported the cosmic ray counter, "*cluck-brrrp-cluck.*" Connant started and dropped his pencil.

"Damnation." The physicist looked toward the far corner, back at the Geiger counter on the table near that corner, and crawled under the desk at which he had been working to retrieve the pencil. He sat down at his work again, trying to make his writing more even. It tended to have jerks and quavers in it, in time with the abrupt proud-hen noises of the Geiger counter. The muted whoosh of the pressure lamp he was using for illumination, the mingled gargles and bugle calls of a dozen men sleeping down the corridor in Paradise House formed the background sounds for the irregular, clucking noises of the counter, the occasional rustle of falling coal in the copper-bellied stove. And a soft, steady *drip-drip-drip* from the thing in the corner.

Connant jerked a pack of cigarettes from his pocket, snapped it so that a cigarette protruded and jabbed the cylinder into his mouth. The lighter failed to function, and he pawed angrily through the pile of papers in search of a match. He scratched the wheel of the lighter several times, dropped it with a curse and got up to pluck a hot coal from the stove with the coal tongs.

The lighter functioned instantly when he tried it on returning to the desk. The counter ripped out a series of chucking guffaws as a burst of cosmic rays struck through to it. Connant turned to glower at it, and tried to concentrate on the interpretation of data collected during the past week. The weekly summary——

He gave up and yielded to curiosity, or nervousness. He lifted the pressure lamp from the desk and carried it over to the table in the corner. Then he returned to the stove and picked up the coal tongs. The beast had been thawing for nearly 18 hours now. He poked at it with an unconscious caution; the flesh was no longer hard as armor plate, but had assumed a rubbery texture. It looked like wet, blue rubber glistening under droplets of water like little round jewels in the glare of the gasoline pressure lantern. Connant felt an unreasoning desire to pour the contents of the lamp's reservoir over the thing in its box and drop the cigarette into it. The three red eyes glared up at him sightlessly, the ruby eyeballs reflecting murky, smoky rays of light.

He realized vaguely that he had been looking at them for a very long time, even vaguely understood that they were no longer sightless. But it did not seem of importance, of no more importance than the labored, slow motion of the tentacular things that sprouted from the base of the scrawny, slowly pulsing neck.

Connant picked up the pressure lamp and returned to his chair. He sat down, staring at the pages of mathematics before him. The clucking of the counter was strangely less disturbing, the rustle of the coals in the stove no longer distracting.

The creak of the floorboards behind him didn't interrupt his thoughts as he went about his weekly report in an automatic manner, filling in columns of data and making brief, summarizing notes.

The creak of the floorboards sounded nearer.

V

Blair came up from the nightmare-haunted depths of sleep abruptly. Connant's face floated vaguely above him; for a moment it seemed a continuance of the wild horror of the dream. But Connant's face was angry, and a little frightened. "Blair—Blair you damned log, wake up."

"Uh-eh?" The little biologist rubbed his eyes, his bony, freckled fingers crooked to a mutilated child-fist. From surrounding bunks other faces lifted to stare down at them.

Connant straightened up. "Get up—and get a lift on. Your damned animal's escaped."

"Escaped—what!" Chief Pilot Van Wall's bull voice roared out with a volume that shook the walls. Down the communication tunnels other voices yelled suddenly. The dozen inhabitants of Paradise House tumbled in abruptly, Barclay, stocky and bulbous in long woolen underwear, carrying a fire extinguisher.

"What the hell's the matter?" Barclay demanded.

"Your damned beast got loose. I fell asleep about twenty minutes ago, and when I woke up, the thing was gone. Hey, Doc, the hell you say those things can't come to life. Blair's blasted potential life developed a hell of a lot of potential and walked out on us."

Copper stared blankly. "It wasn't—Earthly," he sighed suddenly. "I—I guess Earthly laws don't apply."

"Well, it applied for leave of absence and took it. We've got to find it and capture it somehow." Connant swore bitterly, his deep-set black eyes sullen and angry. "It's a wonder the hellish creature didn't eat me in my sleep."

Blair stared back, his pale eyes suddenly fear-struck. "Maybe it di—er—uh—we'll have to find it."

"You find it. It's your pet. I've had all I want to do with it, sitting there for seven hours with the counter clucking every few seconds, and you birds in here singing night-music. It's a wonder I got to sleep. I'm going through to the Ad Building."

Commander Garry ducked through the doorway, pulling his belt tight. "You won't have to. Van's roar sounded like the Boeing taking off down wind. So it wasn't dead?"

"I didn't carry it off in my arms, I assure you," Connant snapped. "The last I saw, that split skull was oozing green goo, like a squashed caterpillar. Doc just said our laws don't work—it's unearthly. Well, it's an unearthly monster, with an unearthly disposition, judging by the face, wandering around with a split skull and brains oozing out."

Norris and McReady appeared in the doorway, a doorway filling with other shivering men. "Has anybody seen it coming over here?" Norris asked innocently. "About four feet tall—three red eyes—brains oozing—— Hey, has anybody checked to make sure this isn't a cracked idea of humor? If it is, I think we'll unite in tying Blair's pet around Connant's neck like the Ancient Mariner's albatross."

"It's no humor," Connant shivered. "Lord, I wish it were. I'd rather wear——" He stopped. A wild, weird howl shrieked through the corridors. The men stiffened abruptly, and half turned.

"I think it's been located," Connant finished. His dark eyes shifted with a queer unease. He darted back to his bunk in Paradise House, to return almost immediately with a heavy .45 revolver and an ice-ax. He hefted both gently as he started for the corridor toward Dogtown. "It blundered down the wrong corridor—and landed among the huskies. Listen—the dogs have broken their chains——"

The half-terrorized howl of the dog pack changed to a wild hunting melee. The voices of the dogs thundered in the narrow corridors, and through them came a low rippling snarl of distilled hate. A shrill of pain, a dozen snarling yelps.

Connant broke for the door. Close behind him, McReady, then Barclay and Commander Garry came. Other men broke for the Ad Building, and weapons—the sledge house. Pomroy, in charge of Big Magnet's five cows, started down the corridor in the opposite direction—he had a six-foot-handled, long-tined pitchfork in mind.

Barclay slid to a halt, as McReady's giant bulk turned abruptly away from the tunnel leading to Dogtown, and vanished off at an angle. Uncertainly, the mechanician wavered a moment, the fire extinguisher in his hands, hesitating from one side to the other. Then he was racing after Connant's broad back. Whatever McReady had in mind, he could be trusted to make it work.

Connant stopped at the bend in the corridor. His breath hissed suddenly through his throat. "Great God——" The revolver exploded thunderously; three numbing, palpable waves of sound crashed through the confined corridors. Two more. The revolver dropped to the hard-packed snow of the trail, and Barclay saw the ice-ax shift into defensive position. Connant's powerful body blocked his vision, but beyond he heard something mewing, and, insanely, chuckling. The dogs were quieter; there was a deadly seriousness in their low snarls. Taloned feet scratched at hard-packed snow, broken chains were clinking and tangling.

Connant shifted abruptly, and Barclay could see what lay beyond. For a second he stood frozen, then his breath went out in a gusty curse. The Thing launched itself at Connant, the powerful arms of the man swung the ice-ax flatside first at what might have been a hand. It scrunched horribly, and the tattered flesh, ripped by a half-dozen savage huskies, leapt to its feet again. The red eyes blazed with an unearthly hatred, an unearthly, unkillable vitality.

Barclay turned the fire extinguisher on it; the blinding, blistering stream of chemical spray confused it, baffled it, together with the savage attacks of the huskies, not for long afraid of anything that did, or could live, held it at bay.

McReady wedged men out of his way and drove down the narrow corridor packed with men unable to reach the scene. There was a sure fore-planned drive to McReady's attack. One of the giant blowtorches used in warming the plane's engines was in his bronzed hands. It roared gustily as he turned the corner and opened the valve. The mad mewing hissed louder. The dogs scrambled back from the three-foot lance of blue-hot flame.

"Bar, get a power cable, run it in somehow. And a handle. We can electrocute this—monster, if I don't incinerate it." McReady spoke with an authority of planned action. Barclay turned down the long corridor to the power plant, but already before him Norris and Van Wall were racing down.

Barclay found the cable in the electrical cache in the tunnel wall. In a half minute he was hacking at it, walking back. Van Wall's voice rang out in a warning shout of "Power!" as the emergency gasoline-powered dynamo thudded into action. Half a dozen other men were down there now; the coal, kindling were going into the firebox of the steam power plant. Norris, cursing in a low, deadly monotone, was working with quick, sure fingers on the other end of Barclay's cable, splicing in a contactor in one of the power leads.

The dogs had fallen back when Barclay reached the corridor bend, fallen back before a furious monstrosity that glared from baleful red eyes, mewing in trapped hatred. The dogs were a semi-circle of red-dipped muzzles with a fringe of glistening white teeth, whining with a vicious eagerness that near matched the fury of the red eyes. Mc-Ready stood confidently alert at the corridor bend, the gustily muttering torch held loose and ready for action in his hands. He stepped aside without moving his eyes from the beast as Barclay came up. There was a slight, tight smile on his lean, bronzed face.

Norris' voice called down the corridor, and Barclay stepped forward. The cable was taped to the long handle of a snow-shovel, the two conductors split, and held 18 inches apart by a scrap of lumber lashed at right angles across the far end of the handle. Bare copper conductors, charged with 220 volts, glinted in the light of pressure lamps. The Thing mewed and halted and dodged. McReady advanced to Barclay's side. The dogs beyond sensed the plan with the almost-telepathic intelligence of trained huskies. Their whimpering grew shriller, softer, their mincing steps carried them nearer. Abruptly a huge, night-black Alaskan leapt onto the trapped thing. It turned squalling, saber-clawed feet slashing.

Barclay leapt forward and jabbed. A weird, shrill scream rose and choked out. The smell of burnt flesh in the corridor intensified; greasy smoke curled up. The echoing pound of the gas-electric dynamo down the corridor became a slogging thud.

The red eyes clouded over in a stiffening, jerking travesty of a face. Armlike, leglike members quivered and jerked. The dogs leapt forward, and Barclay yanked back his shovel-handled weapon. The thing on the snow did not move as gleaming teeth ripped it open.

VI

Garry looked about the crowded room. Thirty-two men, some tensed nervously standing against the wall, some uneasily relaxed, some sitting, most perforce standing, as intimate as sardines. Thirty-two, plus the five engaged in sewing up wounded dogs, made thirty-seven, the total personnel.

Garry started speaking. "All right, I guess we're here. Some of you —three or four at most—saw what happened. All of you have seen that thing on the table, and can get a general idea. Anyone hasn't, I'll lift——" His hand strayed to the tarpaulin bulking over the thing on the table. There was an acrid odor of singed flesh seeping out of it. The men stirred restlessly, hasty denials.

"It looks rather as though Charnauk isn't going to lead any more teams," Garry went on. "Blair wants to get at this thing, and make some more detailed examination. We want to know what happened, and make sure right now that this is permanently, totally dead. Right?"

Connant grinned. "Anybody that doesn't agree can sit up with it to-night."

"All right then, Blair, what can you say about it? What was it?" Garry turned to the little biologist.

"I wonder if we ever saw its natural form." Blair looked at the covered mass. "It may have been imitating the beings that built that ship —but I don't think it was. I think that was its true form. Those of us who were up near the bend saw the thing in action; the thing on the table is the result. When it got loose, apparently, it started looking around. Antarctica still frozen as it was ages ago when the creature first saw it—and froze. From my observations while it was thawing out, and the bits of tissue I cut and hardened then, I think it was native to a hotter planet than Earth. It couldn't, in its natural form, stand the temperature. There is no life-form on Earth that can live in Antarctica during the winter, but the best compromise is the dog. It found the dogs, and somehow got near enough to Charnauk to get him. The others smelled it—heard it—I don't know—anyway they went wild, and broke chains, and attacked it before it was finished. The thing we found was part Charnauk, queerly only half-dead, part Charnauk half-digested by the jellylike protoplasm of that creature, and part the remains of the thing we originally found, sort of melted down to the basic protoplasm.

"When the dogs attacked it, it turned into the best fighting thing it could think of. Some other-world beast apparently."

"Turned," snapped Garry. "How?"

"Every living thing is made up of jelly—protoplasm and minute, submicroscopic things called nuclei, which control the bulk, the protoplasm. This thing was just a modification of that same worldwide plan of Nature; cells made up of protoplasm, controlled by infinitely tinier nuclei. You physicists might compare it—an individual cell of any living thing—with an atom; the bulk of the atom, the space-filling part, is made up of the electron orbits, but the character of the thing is determined by the atomic nucleus.

"This isn't wildly beyond what we already know. It's just a modification we haven't seen before. It's as natural, as logical, as any other manifestation of life. It obeys exactly the same laws. The cells are made of protoplasm, their character determined by the nucleus.

"Only in this creature, the cell-nuclei can control those cells at *will*. It digested Charnauk, and as it digested, studied every cell of his tissue, and shaped its own cells to imitate them exactly. Parts of it—parts that had time to finish changing—are dog-cells. But they don't have dog-cell nuclei." Blair lifted a fraction of the tarpaulin. A torn dog's leg with stiff gray fur protruded. "That, for instance, isn't dog at all; it's imitation. Some parts I'm uncertain about; the nucleus was hiding itself, covering up with dog-cell imitation nucleus. In time, not even a microscope would have shown the difference."

"Suppose," asked Norris bitterly, "it had had lots of time?"

"Then it would have been a dog. The other dogs would have accepted it. We would have accepted it. I don't think anything would have distinguished it, not microscope, nor X-ray, nor any other means. This is a member of a supremely intelligent race, a race that has learned the deepest secrets of biology, and turned them to its use."

"What was it planning to do?" Barclay looked at the humped tarpaulin.

Blair grinned unpleasantly. The wavering halo of thin hair round his bald pate wavered in the stir of air. "Take over the world, I imagine."

"Take over the world! Just it, all by itself?" Connant gasped. "Set itself up as a lone dictator?"

"No," Blair shook his head. The scalpel he had been fumbling in his bony fingers dropped; he bent to pick it up, so that his face was hidden as he spoke. "It would become the population of the world."

"Become—populate the world? Does it reproduce asexually?"

Blair shook his head and gulped. "It's—it doesn't have to. It weighed 85 pounds. Charnauk weighed about 90. It would have become Charnauk, and had 85 pounds left, to become—oh, Jack for instance, or Chinook. It can imitate anything—that is, become anything. If it had reached the Antarctic Sea, it would have become a seal, maybe two seals. They might have attacked a killer whale, and become either killers, or a herd of seals. Or maybe it would have caught an albatross, or a skua gull, and flown to South America."

Norris cursed softly. "And every time it digested something, and imitated it——"

"It would have had its original bulk left, to start again," Blair finished. "Nothing would kill it. It has no natural enemies, because it becomes whatever it wants to. If a killer whale attacked it, it would become a killer whale. If it was an albatross, and an eagle attacked it, it would become an eagle. Lord, it might become a female eagle. Go back—build a nest and lay eggs!"

"Are you sure that thing from hell is dead?" Dr. Copper asked softly.

"Yes, thank Heaven," the little biologist gasped. "After they drove the dogs off, I stood there poking Bar's electrocution thing into it for five minutes. It's dead and—cooked."

"Then we can only give thanks that this is Antarctica, where there is not one, single, solitary, living thing for it to imitate, except these animals in camp."

"Us," Blair giggled. "It can imitate us. Dogs can't make 400 miles to the sea; there's no food. There aren't any skua gulls to imitate at this season. There aren't any penguins this far inland. There's nothing that can reach the sea from this point—except us. We've got brains. We can do it. Don't you see—*it's got to imitate us—it's got to be one of us—that's the only way it can fly an airplane—fly a plane for two hours, and rule—be—all Earth's inhabitants.* A world for the taking—*if it imitates us!*

"It didn't know yet. It hadn't had a chance to learn. It was rushed—hurried—took the thing nearest its own size. Look—I'm Pandora! I opened the box! And the only hope that can come out is—that nothing can come out. You didn't see me. I did it. I fixed it. I smashed every magneto. Not a plane can fly. Nothing can fly." Blair giggled and lay down on the floor crying.

Chief Pilot Van Wall made a dive for the door. His feet were fading echoes in the corridors as Dr. Copper bent unhurriedly over the little man on the floor. From his office at the end of the room he brought something, and injected a solution into Blair's arm. "He might come out of it when he wakes up," he sighed rising. McReady helped him lift the biologist onto a near-by bunk. "It all depends on whether we can convince him that thing is dead."

Van Wall ducked into the shack brushing his heavy blond beard absently. "I didn't think a biologist would do a thing like that up thoroughly. He missed the spares in the second cache. It's all right. I smashed them."

Commander Garry nodded. "I was wondering about the radio."

Dr. Copper snorted. "You don't think it can leak out on a radio wave, do you? You'd have five rescue attempts in the next three months if you stop the broadcasts. The thing to do is talk loud and not make a sound. Now I wonder——"

McReady looked speculatively at the doctor. "It might be like an infectious disease. Everything that drank any of its blood——"

Copper shook his head. "Blair missed something. Imitate it may, but it has, to a certain extent, its own body-chemistry, its own metabolism. If it didn't, it would become a dog—and be a dog and nothing more. It has to be an imitation dog. Therefore you can detect it by serum tests. And its chemistry, since it comes from another world, must be so wholly, radically different that a few cells, such as gained by drops of blood, would be treated as disease germs by the dog, or human body."

"Blood—would one of those imitations bleed?" Norris demanded.

"Surely. Nothing mystic about blood. Muscle is about 90 per cent water; blood differs only in having a couple per cent more water, and less connective tissue. They'd bleed all right," Copper assured him.

Blair sat up in his bunk suddenly. "Connant—where's Connant?"

The physicist moved over toward the little biologist. "Here I am. What do you want?"

"Are you?" giggled Blair. He lapsed back into the bunk contorted with silent laughter.

Connant looked at him blankly. "Huh? Am I what?"

"*Are* you there?" Blair burst into gales of laughter. "*Are* you Connant? The beast wanted to be a *man*—not a dog——"

VII

Dr. Copper rose wearily from the bunk, and washed the hypodermic carefully. The little tinkles it made seemed loud in the packed room, now that Blair's gurgling laughter had finally quieted. Copper looked toward Garry and shook his head slowly. "Hopeless, I'm afraid. I don't think we can ever convince him the thing is dead now."

Norris laughed uncertainly. "I'm not sure you can convince me. Oh, damn you, McReady."

"McReady?" Commander Garry turned to look from Norris to McReady curiously.

"The nightmares," Norris explained. "He had a theory about the nightmares we had at the Secondary Station after finding that thing."

"And that was?" Garry looked at McReady levelly.

Norris answered for him, jerkily, uneasily. "That the creature wasn't dead, had a sort of enormously slowed existence, an existence that permitted it, none the less, to be vaguely aware of the passing of time, of our coming, after endless years. I had a dream it could imitate things."

"Well," Copper grunted, "it can."

"Don't be an ass," Norris snapped. "That's not what's bothering me. In the dream it could read minds, read thoughts and ideas and mannerisms."

"What's so bad about that? It seems to be worrying you more than the thought of the joy we're going to have with a mad man in an Antarctic camp." Copper nodded toward Blair's sleeping form.

McReady shook his great head slowly. "You know that Connant is Connant, because he not merely looks like Connant—which we're beginning to believe that beast might be able to do—but he thinks like Connant, talks like Connant, moves himself around as Connant does. That takes more than merely a body that looks like him; that takes Connant's own mind, and thoughts and mannerisms. Therefore, though you know that the thing might make itself *look* like Connant, you aren't much bothered, because you know it has a mind from another world, a totally unhuman mind, that couldn't possibly react and think and talk like a man we know, and do it so well as to fool us for a moment. The idea of the creature imitating one of us is fascinating, but unreal because it is too completely unhuman to deceive us. It doesn't have a human mind."

"As I said before," Norris repeated, looking steadily at McReady, "you can say the damnedest things at the damnedest times. Will you be so good as to finish that thought—one way or the other?"

Kinner, the scar-faced expedition cook, had been standing near Connant. Suddenly he moved down the length of the crowded room toward his familiar galley. He shook the ashes from the galley stove noisily.

"It would do it no good," said Dr. Copper, softly as though thinking out loud, "to merely look like something it was trying to imitate; it would have to understand its feelings, its reaction. It *is* unhuman; it has powers of imitation beyond any conception of man. A good actor, by training himself, can imitate another man, another man's mannerisms, well enough to fool most people. Of course no actor could imitate so perfectly as to deceive men who had been living with the imitated one in the complete lack of privacy of an Antarctic camp. That would take a super-human skill."

"Oh, you've got the bug too?" Norris cursed softly.

Connant, standing alone at one end of the room, looked about him wildly, his face white. A gentle eddying of the men had crowded them slowly down toward the other end of the room, so that he stood quite alone. "My God, will you two Jeremiahs shut up?" Connant's voice shook. "What am I? Some kind of a microscopic specimen you're dissecting? Some unpleasant worm you're discussing in the third person?"

McReady looked up at him; his slowly twisting hands stopped for a moment. "Having a lovely time. Wish you were here. Signed: Everybody.

"Connant, if you think you're having a hell of a time, just move over on the other end for a while. You've got one thing we haven't; you know what the answer is. I'll tell you this, right now you're the most feared and respected man in Big Magnet."

"Lord, I wish you could see your eyes," Connant gasped. "Stop staring, will you! What the hell are you going to do?"

"Have you any suggestions, Dr. Copper?" Commander Garry asked steadily. "The present situation is impossible."

"Oh, is it?" Connant snapped. "Come over here and look at that crowd. By Heaven, they look exactly like that gang of huskies around the corridor bend. Benning, will you stop hefting that damned ice-ax?"

The coppery blade rang on the floor as the aviation mechanic nervously dropped it. He bent over and picked it up instantly, hefting it slowly, turning it in his hands, his brown eyes moving jerkily about the room.

Copper sat down on the bunk beside Blair. The wood creaked noisily in the room. Far down a corridor, a dog yelped in pain, and the dog-drivers' tense voices floated softly back. "Microscopic examination," said the doctor thoughtfully, "would be useless, as Blair pointed out. Considerable time has passed. However, serum tests would be definitive."

"Serum tests? What do you mean exactly?" Commander Garry asked.

"If I had a rabbit that had been injected with human blood—a poison to rabbits, of course, as is the blood of any animal save that of another rabbit—and the injections continued in increasing doses for some time, the rabbit would be human-immune. If a small quantity of its blood were drawn off, allowed to separate in a test-tube, and to the clear serum, a bit of human blood were added, there would be a visible reaction, proving the blood was human. If cow, or dog blood were added—or any protein material other than that one thing, human blood—no reaction would take place. That would prove definitely."

"Can you suggest where I might catch a rabbit for you, Doc?" Norris asked. "That is, nearer than Australia; we don't want to waste time going that far."

"I know there aren't any rabbits in Antarctica," Copper nodded, "but that is simply the usual animal. Any animal except man will do. A dog for instance. But it will take several days, and due to the greater size of the animal, considerable blood. Two of us will have to contribute."

"Would I do?" Garry asked.

"That will make two," Copper nodded. "I'll get to work on it right away."

"What about Connant in the meantime?" Kinner demanded. "I'm

going out that door and head off for the Ross Sea before I cook for him."

"He may be human——" Copper started.

Connant burst out in a flood of curses. "Human! *May* be human, you damned saw-bones! What in hell do you think I am?"

"A monster," Copper snapped sharply. "Now shut up and listen." Connant's face drained of color and he sat down heavily as the indictment was put in words. "Until we know—you know as well as we do that we have reason to question the fact, and only you know how that question is to be answered—we may reasonably be expected to lock you up. If you are—unhuman—you're a lot more dangerous than poor Blair there, and I'm going to see that he's locked up thoroughly. I expect that his next stage will be a violent desire to kill you, all the dogs, and probably all of us. When he wakes, he will be convinced we're all unhuman, and nothing on the planet will ever change his conviction. It would be kinder to let him die, but we can't do that, of course. He's going in one shack, and you can stay in Cosmos House with your cosmic ray apparatus. Which is about what you'd do anyway. I've got to fix up a couple of dogs."

Connant nodded bitterly. "I'm human. Hurry that test. Your eyes— Lord, I wish you could see your eyes staring——"

Commander Garry watched anxiously as Clark, the dog-handler, held the big brown Alaskan husky, while Copper began the injection treatment. The dog was not anxious to cooperate; the needle was painful, and already he'd experienced considerable needle work that morning. Five stitches held closed a slash that ran from his shoulder across the ribs half way down his body. One long fang was broken off short; the missing part was to be found half-buried in the shoulder bone of the monstrous thing on the table in the Ad Building.

"How long will that take?" Garry asked, pressing his arm gently. It was sore from the prick of the needle Dr. Copper had used to withdraw blood.

Copper shrugged. "I don't know, to be frank. I know the general method, I've used it on rabbits. But I haven't experimented with dogs. They're big, clumsy animals to work with; naturally rabbits are preferable, and serve ordinarily. In civilized places you can buy a stock of human-immune rabbits from suppliers, and not many investigators take the trouble to prepare their own."

"What do they want with them back there?" Clark asked.

"Criminology is one large field. A says he didn't murder B, but that the blood on his shirt came from killing a chicken. The State makes a test, then it's up to A to explain how it is the blood reacts on human-immune rabbits, but not on chicken-immunes."

"What are we going to do with Blair in the meantime?" Garry asked wearily. "It's all right to let him sleep where he is for a while, but when he wakes up——"

"Barclay and Benning are fitting some bolts on the door of Cosmos House," Copper replied grimly. "Connant's acting like a gentleman. I think perhaps the way the other men look at him makes him rather want privacy. Lord knows, heretofore we've all of us individually prayed for a little privacy."

Clark laughed bitterly. "Not any more, thank you. The more the merrier."

"Blair," Copper went on, "will also have to have privacy—and locks. He's going to have a pretty definite plan in mind when he wakes up. Ever hear the old story of how to stop hoof-and-mouth disease in cattle?

"If there isn't any hoof-and-mouth disease, there won't be any hoof-and-mouth disease," Copper explained. "You get rid of it by killing every animal that exhibits it, and every animal that's been near the diseased animal. Blair's a biologist, and knows that story. He's afraid of this thing we loosed. The answer is probably pretty clear in his mind now. Kill everybody and everything in this camp before a skua gull or a wandering albatross coming in with the spring chances out this way and—catches the disease."

Clark's lips curled in a twisted grin. "Sounds logical to me. If things get too bad—maybe we'd better let Blair get loose. It would save us committing suicide. We might also make something of a vow that if things get bad, we see that that does happen."

Copper laughed softly. "The last man alive in Big Magnet—wouldn't be a man," he pointed out. "Somebody's got to kill those—creatures that don't desire to kill themselves, you know. We don't have enough thermite to do it all at once, and the decanite explosive wouldn't help much. I have an idea that even small pieces of one of those beings would be self-sufficient."

"If," said Garry thoughtfully, "they can modify their protoplasm at will, won't they simply modify themselves to birds and fly away?

They can read all about birds, and imitate their structure without even meeting them. Or imitate, perhaps, birds of their home planet."

Copper shook his head, and helped Clark to free the dog. "Man studied birds for centuries, trying to learn how to make a machine to fly like them. He never did do the trick; his final success came when he broke away entirely and tried new methods. Knowing the general idea, and knowing the detailed structure of wing and bone and nerve-tissue is something far, far different. And as for other-world birds, perhaps, in fact very probably, the atmospheric conditions here are so vastly different that their birds couldn't fly. Perhaps, even, the being came from a planet like Mars with such a thin atmosphere that there were no birds."

Barclay came into the building, trailing a length of airplane control cable. "It's finished, Doc. Cosmos House can't be opened from the inside. Now where do we put Blair?"

Copper looked toward Garry. "There wasn't any biology building. I don't know where we can isolate him."

"How about East Cache?" Garry said after a moment's thought. "Will Blair be able to look after himself—or need attention?"

"He'll be capable enough. We'll be the ones to watch out," Copper assured him grimly. "Take a stove, a couple of bags of coal, necessary supplies and a few tools to fix it up. Nobody's been out there since last fall, have they?"

Garry shook his head. "If he gets noisy—I thought that might be a good idea."

Barclay hefted the tools he was carrying and looked up at Garry. "If the muttering he's doing now is any sign, he's going to sing away the night hours. And we won't like his song."

"What's he saying?" Copper asked.

Barclay shook his head. "I didn't care to listen much. You can if you want to. But I gathered that the blasted idiot had all the dreams McReady had, and a few more. He slept beside the thing when we stopped on the trail coming in from Secondary Magnetic, remember. He dreamt the thing was alive, and dreamt more details. And—damn his soul—knew it wasn't all dream, or had reason to. He knew it had telepathic powers that were stirring vaguely, and that it could not only read minds, but project thoughts. They weren't dreams, you see. They were stray thoughts that thing was broadcasting, the way Blair's broadcasting his thoughts now—a sort of telepathic muttering in its sleep. That's why he knew so much about its powers. I guess you and I, Doc, weren't so sensitive—if you want to believe in telepathy."

"I have to," Copper sighed. "Dr. Rhine of Duke University has shown that it exists, shown that some are much more sensitive than others."

"Well, if you want to learn a lot of details, go listen in on Blair's broadcast. He's driven most of the boys out of the Ad Building; Kinner's rattling pans like coal going down a chute. When he can't rattle a pan, he shakes ashes.

"By the way, Commander, what are we going to do this spring, now the planes are out of it?"

Garry sighed. "I'm afraid our expedition is going to be a loss. We cannot divide our strength now."

"It won't be a loss—if we continue to live, and come out of this," Copper promised him. "The find we've made, if we can get it under control, is important enough. The cosmic ray data, magnetic work, and atmospheric work won't be greatly hindered."

Garry laughed mirthlessly. "I was just thinking of the radio broadcasts. Telling half the world about the wonderful results of our exploration flights, trying to fool men like Byrd and Ellsworth back home there that we're doing something."

Copper nodded gravely. "They'll know something's wrong. But men like that have judgment enough to know we wouldn't do tricks without some sort of reason, and will wait for our return to judge us. I think it comes to this: men who know enough to recognize our deception will wait for our return. Men who haven't discretion and faith enough to wait will not have the experience to detect any fraud. We know enough of the conditions here to put through a good bluff."

"Just so they don't send 'rescue' expeditions," Garry prayed. "When—if—we're ever ready to come out, we'll have to send word to Captain Forsythe to bring a stock of magnetos with him when he comes down. But—never mind that."

"You mean if we don't come out?" asked Barclay. "I was wondering if a nice running account of an eruption or an earthquake via radio—with a swell windup by using a stick of decanite under the microphone—would help. Nothing, of course, will entirely keep people out. One of those swell, melodramatic 'last-man-alive-scenes' might make 'em go easy though."

Garry smiled with genuine humor. "Is everybody in camp trying to figure that out too?"

Copper laughed. "What do you think, Garry? We're confident we can win out. But not too easy about it, I guess."

Clark grinned up from the dog he was petting into calmness. "Confident, did you say, Doc?"

VIII

Blair moved restlessly around the small shack. His eyes jerked and quivered in vague, fleeting glances at the four men with him; Barclay, six feet tall and weighing over 190 pounds; McReady, a bronze giant of a man; Dr. Copper, short, squatly powerful; and Benning, five-feet-ten of wiry strength.

Blair was huddled up against the far wall of the East Cache cabin, his gear piled in the middle of the floor beside the heating stove, forming an island between him and the four men. His bony hands clenched and fluttered, terrified. His pale eyes wavered uneasily as his bald, freckled head darted about in birdlike motion.

"I don't want anybody coming here. I'll cook my own food," he snapped nervously. "Kinner may be human now, but I don't believe it. I'm going to get out of here, but I'm not going to eat any food you send me. I want cans. Sealed cans."

"O.K., Blair, we'll bring 'em tonight," Barclay promised. "You've got coal, and the fire's started. I'll make a last——" Barclay started forward.

Blair instantly scurried to the farthest corner. "Get out! Keep away from me, you monster!" the little biologist shrieked, and tried to claw his way through the wall of the shack. "Keep away from me—keep away—I won't be absorbed—I won't be——"

Barclay relaxed and moved back. Dr. Copper shook his head. "Leave him alone, Bar. It's easier for him to fix the thing himself. We'll have to fix the door, I think——"

The four men let themselves out. Efficiently, Benning and Barclay fell to work. There were no locks in Antarctica; there wasn't enough privacy to make them needed. But powerful screws had been driven in each side of the door frame, and the spare aviation control cable, immensely strong, woven steel wire, was rapidly caught between them and drawn taut. Barclay went to work with a drill and a keyhole saw. Presently he had a trap cut in the door through which goods could be passed without unlashing the entrance. Three powerful hinges from a stock-crate, two hasps and a pair of three-inch cotter-pins made it proof against opening from the other side.

Blair moved about restlessly inside. He was dragging something over to the door with panting gasps and muttering, frantic curses. Barclay opened the hatch and glanced in, Dr. Copper peering over his shoulder. Blair had moved the heavy bunk against the door. It could not be opened without his cooperation now.

"Don't know but what the poor man's right at that," McReady sighed. "If he gets loose, it is his avowed intention to kill each and all of us as quickly as possible, which is something we don't agree with. But we've something on our side of that door that is worse than a homicidal maniac. If one or the other has to get loose, I think I'll come up and undo those lashings here."

Barclay grinned. "You let me know, and I'll show you how to get these off fast. Let's go back."

The sun was painting the northern horizon in multi-colored rain-bows still, though it was two hours below the horizon. The field of drift swept off to the north, sparkling under its flaming colors in a million reflected glories. Low mounds of rounded white on the northern horizon showed the Magnet Range was barely awash above the sweeping drift. Little eddies of wind-lifted snow swirled away from their skis as they set out toward the main encampment two miles away. The spidery finger of the broadcast radiator lifted a gaunt black needle against the white of the Antarctic continent. The snow under their skis was like fine sand, hard and gritty.

"Spring," said Benning bitterly, "is come. Ain't we got fun! I've been looking forward to getting away from this blasted hole in the ice."

"I wouldn't try it now, if I were you." Barclay grunted. "Guys that set out from here in the next few days are going to be marvelously unpopular."

"How is your dog getting along, Dr. Copper?" McReady asked. "Any results yet?"

"In 30 hours? I wish there were. I gave him an injection of my blood today. But I imagine another five days will be needed. I don't know certainly enough to stop sooner."

"I've been wondering—if Connant were—changed, would he have warned us so soon after the animal escaped? Wouldn't he have waited long enough for it to have a real chance to fix itself? Until we woke up naturally?" McReady asked slowly.

"The thing is selfish. You didn't think it looked as though it were possessed of a store of the higher justices, did you?" Dr. Copper pointed out. "Every part of it is all of it, every part of it is all for itself, I imagine. If Connant were changed, to save his skin, he'd have to—but Connant's feelings aren't changed; they're imitated perfectly, or they're his own. Naturally, the imitation, imitating perfectly Connant's feelings, would do exactly what Connant would do."

"Say, couldn't Norris or Van give Connant some kind of a test? If the thing is brighter than men, it might know more physics than Connant should, and they'd catch it out," Barclay suggested.

Copper shook his head wearily. "Not if it reads minds. You can't plan a trap for it. Van suggested that last night. He hoped it would answer some of the questions of physics he'd like to know answers to."

"This expedition-of-four idea is going to make life happy." Benning looked at his companions. "Each of us with an eye on the others to make sure he doesn't do something—peculiar. Man, aren't we going to be a trusting bunch! Each man eyeing his neighbors with the grandest exhibition of faith and trust—— I'm beginning to know what Connant meant by 'I wish you could see your eyes.' Every now and then we all have it, I guess. One of you looks around with a sort of 'I-wonder-if-the-other-*three*-are-look.' Incidentally, I'm not excepting myself."

"So far as we know, the animal is dead, with a slight question as to Connant. No other is suspected," McReady stated slowly. "The 'always-four' order is merely a precautionary measure."

"I'm waiting for Garry to make it four-in-a-bunk," Barclay sighed. "I thought I didn't have any privacy before, but since that order——"

None watched more tensely than Connant. A little sterile glass test-tube, half-filled with straw-colored fluid. One—two—three—four—five drops of the clear solution Dr. Copper had prepared from the drops of blood from Connant's arm. The tube was shaken carefully, then set in a beaker of clear, warm water. The thermometer read blood heat, a little thermostat clicked noisily, and the electric hotplate began to glow as the lights flickered slightly.

Then—little white flecks of precipitation were forming, snowing down in the clear straw-colored fluid. "Lord," said Connant. He dropped heavily into a bunk, crying like a baby. "Six days—" Connant sobbed, "six days in there—wondering if that damned test would lie——"

Garry moved over silently, and slipped his arm across the physicist's back.

"It couldn't lie," Dr. Copper said. "The dog was human-immune —and the serum reacted."

"He's—all right?" Norris gasped. "Then—the animal is dead—dead forever?"

"He is human," Copper spoke definitely, "and the animal is dead."

Kinner burst out laughing, laughing hysterically. McReady turned toward him and slapped his face with a methodical one-two, one-two action. The cook laughed, gulped, cried a moment, and sat up rubbing his cheeks, mumbling his thanks vaguely. "I was scared. Lord, I was scared——"

Norris laughed brittlely. "You think we weren't, you ape? You think maybe Connant wasn't?"

The Ad Building stirred with a sudden rejuvenation. Voices laughed, the men clustering around Connant spoke with unnecessarily loud voices, jittery, nervous voices relievedly friendly again. Somebody called out a suggestion, and a dozen started for their skis. Blair. Blair might recover—— Dr. Copper fussed with his test-tubes in nervous relief, trying solutions. The party of relief for Blair's shack started out the door, skis clapping noisily. Down the corridor, the dogs set up a quick yelping howl as the air of excited relief reached them.

Dr. Copper fussed with his tubes. McReady noticed him first, sitting on the edge of the bunk, with two precipitin-whitened test-tubes of straw-colored fluid, his face whiter than the stuff in the tubes, silent tears slipping down from horror-widened eyes.

McReady felt a cold knife of fear pierce through his heart and freeze in his breast. Dr. Copper looked up.

"Garry," he called hoarsely. "Garry, for God's sake, come here."

Commander Garry walked toward him sharply. Silence clapped down on the Ad Building. Connant looked up, rose stiffly from his seat.

"Garry—tissue from the monster—precipitates too. It proves nothing. Nothing but—but the dog was monster-immune too. That one of the two contributing blood—one of us two, you and I, Garry—*one of us is a monster.*"

IX

"Bar, call back those men before they tell Blair," McReady said quietly. Barclay went to the door; faintly his shouts came back to the tensely silent men in the room. Then he was back.

"They're coming," he said. "I didn't tell them why. Just that Dr. Copper said not to go."

"McReady," Garry sighed, "you're in command now. May God help you. I cannot."

The bronzed giant nodded slowly, his deep eyes on Commander Garry.

"I may be the one," Garry added. "I know I'm not, but I cannot prove it to you in any way. Dr. Copper's test has broken down. The fact that he showed it was useless, when it was to the advantage of the monster to have that uselessness not known, would seem to prove he was human."

Copper rocked back and forth slowly on the bunk. "I know I'm human. I can't prove it either. One of us two is a liar, for that test cannot lie, and it says one of us is. I gave proof that the test was wrong, which seems to prove I'm human, and now Garry has given that argument which proves me human—which he, as the monster, should not do. Round and round and round and round and——"

Dr. Copper's head, then his neck and shoulders began circling slowly in time to the words. Suddenly he was lying back on the bunk, roaring with laughter. "It doesn't have to prove one of us is a monster! It doesn't have to prove that at all! Ho-ho. If we're *all* monsters it works the same! We're all monsters—all of us—Connant and Garry and I—and all of you."

"McReady," Van Wall, the blond-bearded Chief Pilot, called softly, "you were on the way to an M.D. when you took up meteorology, weren't you? Can you make some kind of test?"

McReady went over to Copper slowly, took the hypodermic from his hand, and washed it carefully in 95 per cent alcohol. Garry sat on the bunk-edge with wooden face, watching Copper and McReady expressionlessly. "What Copper said is possible," McReady sighed. "Van, will you help here? Thanks." The filled needle jabbed into Copper's thigh. The man's laughter did not stop, but slowly faded into sobs, then sound sleep as the morphia took hold.

McReady turned again. The men who had started for Blair stood at the far end of the room, skis dripping snow, their faces as white as their skis. Connant had a lighted cigarette in each hand; one he was puffing absently, and staring at the floor. The heat of the one in his left hand attracted him and he stared at it, and the one in the other hand stupidly for a moment. He dropped one and crushed it under his heel slowly.

"Dr. Copper," McReady repeated, "could be right. I know I'm human—but of course can't prove it. I'll repeat the test for my own information. Any of you others who wish to may do the same."

Two minutes later, McReady held a test-tube with white precipitin settling slowly from straw-colored serum. "It reacts to human blood too, so they aren't both monsters."

"I didn't think they were," Van Wall sighed. "That wouldn't suit the monster either; we could have destroyed them if we knew. Why hasn't the monster destroyed us, do you suppose? It seems to be loose."

McReady snorted. Then laughed softly. "Elementary, my dear Watson. The monster wants to have life-forms available. It cannot animate a dead body, apparently. It is just waiting—waiting until the best opportunities come. We who remain human, it is holding in reserve."

Kinner shuddered violently. "Hey. Hey, Mac. Mac, would I know if I was a monster? Would I know if the monster had already got me? Oh Lord, I may be a monster already."

"You'd know," McReady answered.

"But we wouldn't," Norris laughed shortly, half-hysterically.

McReady looked at the vial of serum remaining. "There's one thing this damned stuff is good for, at that," he said thoughtfully. "Clark, will you and Van help me? The rest of the gang better stick together here. Keep an eye on each other," he said bitterly. "See that you don't get into mischief, shall we say?"

McReady started down the tunnel toward Dogtown, with Clark and Van Wall behind him. "You need more serum?" Clark asked.

McReady shook his head. "Tests. There's four cows and a bull, and nearly seventy dogs down there. This stuff reacts only to human blood and—monsters."

McReady came back to the Ad Building and went silently to the wash stand. Clark and Van Wall joined him a moment later. Clark's lips had developed a tic, jerking into sudden, unexpected sneers.

"What did you do?" Connant exploded suddenly. "More immunizing?"

Clark snickered, and stopped with a hiccough. "Immunizing. Haw! Immune all right."

"That monster," said Van Wall steadily, "is quite logical. Our immune dog was quite all right, and we drew a little more serum for the tests. But we won't make any more."

"Can't—can't you use one man's blood on another dog—" Norris began.

"There aren't," said McReady softly, "any more dogs. Nor cattle, I might add."

"No more dogs?" Benning sat down slowly.

"They're very nasty when they start changing," Van Wall said precisely, "but slow. That electrocution iron you made up, Barclay, is very fast. There is only one dog left—our immune. The monster left that for us, so we could play with our little test. The rest——" He shrugged and dried his hands.

"The cattle——" gulped Kinner.

"Also. Reacted very nicely. They look funny as hell when they start melting. The beast hasn't any quick escape, when it's tied in dog chains, or halters, and it had to be to imitate."

Kinner stood up slowly. His eyes darted around the room, and came to rest horribly quivering on a tin bucket in the galley. Slowly, step by step, he retreated toward the door, his mouth opening and closing silently, like a fish out of water.

"The milk——" he gasped. "I milked 'em an hour ago——" His voice broke into a scream as he dived through the door. He was out on the ice cap without windproof or heavy clothing.

Van Wall looked after him for a moment thoughtfully. "He's probably hopelessly mad," he said at length, "but he might be a monster escaping. He hasn't skis. Take a blow-torch—in case."

The physical motion of the chase helped them; something that needed doing. Three of the other men were quietly being sick. Norris was lying flat on his back, his face greenish, looking steadily at the bottom of the bunk above him.

"Mac, how long have the—cows been not-cows——"

McReady shrugged his shoulders hopelessly. He went over to the milk bucket, and with his little tube of serum went to work on it. The milk clouded it, making certainty difficult. Finally he dropped the test-tube in the stand and shook his head. "It tests negatively. Which means either they were cows then, or that, being perfect imitations, they gave perfectly good milk."

Copper stirred restlessly in his sleep and gave a gurgling cross between a snore and a laugh. Silent eyes fastened on him. "Would morphia—a monster—" somebody started to ask.

"Lord knows," McReady shrugged. "It affects every Earthly animal I know of."

Connant suddenly raised his head. "Mac! The dogs must have swallowed pieces of the monster, and the pieces destroyed them! The dogs were where the monster resided. I was locked up. Doesn't that prove——"

Van Wall shook his head. "Sorry. Proves nothing about what you are, only proves what you didn't do."

"It doesn't do that," McReady sighed. "We are helpless. Because we don't know enough, and so jittery we don't think straight. Locked up! Ever watch a white corpuscle of the blood go through the wall of a blood vessel? No? It sticks out a pseudopod. And there it is—on the far side of the wall."

"Oh," said Van Wall unhappily. "The cattle tried to melt down, didn't they? They could have melted down—become just a thread of stuff and leaked under a door to re-collect on the other side. Ropes—no—no, that wouldn't do it. They couldn't live in a sealed tank or——"

"If," said McReady, "you shoot it through the heart, and it doesn't die, it's a monster. That's the best test I can think of, offhand."

"No dogs," said Garry quietly, "and no cattle. It has to imitate men now. And locking up doesn't do any good. Your test might work, Mac, but I'm afraid it would be hard on the men."

X

Clark looked up from the galley stove as Van Wall, Barclay, McReady and Benning came in, brushing the drift from their clothes. The other men jammed into the Ad Building continued studiously to do as they were doing, playing chess, poker, reading. Ralsen was fixing a sledge on the table; Van and Norris had their heads together over magnetic data, while Harvey read tables in a low voice.

Dr. Copper snored softly on the bunk. Garry was working with Dutton over a sheaf of radio messages on the corner of Dutton's bunk and a small fraction of the radio table. Connant was using most of the table for Cosmic Ray sheets.

Quite plainly through the corridor, despite two closed doors, they could hear Kinner's voice. Clark banged a kettle onto the galley stove and beckoned McReady silently. The meteorologist went over to him.

"I don't mind the cooking so damn much," Clark said nervously, "but isn't there some way to stop that bird? We all agreed that it would be safe to move him into Cosmos House."

"Kinner?" McReady nodded toward the door. "I'm afraid not. I can dope him, I suppose, but we don't have an unlimited supply of morphia, and he's not in danger of losing his mind. Just hysterical."

"Well, we're in danger of losing ours. You've been out for an hour and a half. That's been going on steadily ever since, and it was going for two hours before. There's a limit, you know."

Garry wandered over slowly, apologetically. For an instant, McReady caught the feral spark of fear—horror—in Clark's eyes, and knew at the same instant it was in his own. Garry—Garry or Copper —was certainly a monster.

"If you could stop that, I think it would be a sound policy, Mac," Garry spoke quietly. "There are—tensions enough in this room. We agreed that it would be safe for Kinner in there, because everyone else in camp is under constant eyeing." Garry shivered slightly. "And try, try in God's name, to find some test that will work."

McReady sighed. "Watched or unwatched, everyone's tense. Blair's jammed the trap so it won't open now. Says he's got food enough, and keeps screaming 'Go away, go away—you're monsters. I won't be absorbed. I won't. I'll tell men when they come. Go away.' So—we went away."

"There's no other test?" Garry pleaded.

McReady shrugged his shoulders. "Copper was perfectly right. The serum test could be absolutely definitive if it hadn't been—contaminated. But that's the only dog left, and he's fixed now."

"Chemicals? Chemical tests?"

McReady shook his head. "Our chemistry isn't that good. I tried the microscope, you know."

Garry nodded. "Monster-dog and real dog were identical. But— you've got to go on. What are we going to do after dinner?"

Van Wall had joined them quietly. "Rotation sleeping. Half the crowd asleep; half awake. I wonder how many of us are monsters? All the dogs were. We thought we were safe, but somehow it got Copper—or you." Van Wall's eyes flashed uneasily. "It may have gotten every one of you—all of you but myself may be wondering, looking. No, that's not possible. You'd just spring then. I'd be helpless. We humans must somehow have the greater numbers now. But——" he stopped.

McReady laughed shortly. "You're doing what Norris complained of in me. Leaving it hanging. 'But if one more is changed—that may shift the balance of power.' It doesn't fight. I don't think it ever fights. It must be a peaceable thing, in its own—inimitable—way. It never had to, because it always gained its end—otherwise."

Van Wall's mouth twisted in a sickly grin. "You're suggesting then, that perhaps it already *has* the greater numbers, but is just waiting— waiting, all of them—all of you, for all I know—waiting till I, the last human, drop my wariness in sleep. Mac, did you notice their eyes, all looking at us?"

Garry sighed. "You haven't been sitting here for four straight hours, while all their eyes silently weighed the information that one of us two, Copper or I, is a monster certainly—perhaps both of us."

Clark repeated his request. "Will you stop that bird's noise? He's driving me nuts. Make him tone down, anyway."

"Still praying?" McReady asked.

"Still praying," Clark groaned. "He hasn't stopped for a second. I don't mind his praying if it relieves him, but he yells, he sings psalms and hymns and shouts prayers. He thinks God can't hear well way down here."

"Maybe He can't," Barclay grunted. "Or He'd have done something about this thing loosed from hell."

"Somebody's going to try that test you mentioned, if you don't stop him," Clark stated grimly. "I think a cleaver in the head would be as positive a test as a bullet in the heart."

"Go ahead with the food. I'll see what I can do. There may be something in the cabinets." McReady moved wearily toward the corner Copper had used as his dispensary. Three tall cabinets of rough boards, two locked, were the repositories of the camp's medical supplies. Twelve years ago McReady had graduated, had started for an internship, and been diverted to meteorology. Copper was a picked man, a man who knew his profession thoroughly and modernly. More than half the drugs available were totally unfamiliar to McReady; many of the others he had forgotten. There was no huge medical library here, no series of journals available to learn the things he had forgotten, the elementary, simple things to Copper, things that did not merit inclusion in the small library he had been forced to content himself with. Books are heavy, and every ounce of supplies had been freighted in by air.

McReady picked a barbiturate hopefully. Barclay and Van Wall went with him. One man never went anywhere alone in Big Magnet.

Ralsen had his sledge put away, and the physicists had moved off the table, the poker game broken up when they got back. Clark was putting out the food. The click of spoons and the muffled sounds of eating were the only sign of life in the room. There were no words spoken as the three returned; simply all eyes focused on them questioningly, while the jaws moved methodically.

McReady stiffened suddenly. Kinner was screeching out a hymn in a hoarse, cracked voice. He looked wearily at Van Wall with a twisted grin and shook his head. "Hu-uh."

Van Wall cursed bitterly, and sat down at the table. "We'll just plumb have to take that till his voice wears out. He can't yell like that forever."

"He's got a brass throat and a cast-iron larynx," Norris declared savagely. "Then we could be hopeful, and suggest he's one of our friends. In that case he could go on renewing his throat till doomsday."

Silence clamped down. For twenty minutes they ate without a word. Then Connant jumped up with an angry violence. "You sit as still as a bunch of graven images. You don't say a word, but oh, Lord, what expressive eyes you've got. They roll around like a bunch of glass marbles spilling down a table. They wink and blink and stare—and whisper things. Can you guys look somewhere else for a change, please?

"Listen, Mac, you're in charge here. Let's run movies for the rest of the night. We've been saving those reels to make 'em last. Last for what? Who is it's going to see those last reels, eh? Let's see 'em while we can, and look at something other than each other."

"Sound idea, Connant. I, for one, am quite willing to change this in any way I can."

"Turn the sound up loud, Dutton. Maybe you can drown out the hymns," Clark suggested.

"But don't," Norris said softly, "don't turn off the lights altogether."

"The lights will be out." McReady shook his head. "We'll show all the cartoon movies we have. You won't mind seeing the old cartoons, will you?"

"Goody, goody—a moom pitcher show. I'm just in the mood." McReady turned to look at the speaker, a lean, lanky New Englander, by the name of Caldwell. Caldwell was stuffing his pipe slowly, a sour eye cocked up to McReady.

The bronze giant was forced to laugh. "O.K., Bart, you win. Maybe we aren't quite in the mood for Popeye and trick ducks, but it's something."

"Let's play Classifications," Caldwell suggested slowly. "Or maybe you call it Guggenheim. You draw lines on a piece of paper, and put down classes of things—like animals, you know. One for 'H' and one for 'U' and so on. Like 'Human' and 'Unknown' for instance. I think that would be a hell of a lot better game. Classification, I sort of figure is what we need right now a lot more than movies. Maybe somebody's got a pencil that he can draw lines with, draw lines between the 'U' animals and the 'H' animals for instance."

"McReady's trying to find that kind of a pencil," Van Wall answered quietly, "but we've got three kinds of animals here, you know. One that begins with 'M'. We don't want any more."

"Mad ones, you mean. Uh-huh. Clark, I'll help you with those pots so we can get our little peep-show going." Caldwell got up slowly.

Dutton and Barclay and Benning, in charge of the projector and sound mechanism arrangements, went about their job silently, while the Ad Building was cleared and the dishes and pans disposed of. McReady drifted over toward Van Wall slowly, and leaned back in the bunk beside him. "I've been wondering, Van," he said with a wry grin, "whether or not to report my ideas in advance. I forgot the 'U animals' as Caldwell named it, could read minds. I've a vague idea of something that might work. It's too vague to bother with though. Go ahead with your show, while I try to figure out the logic of the thing. I'll take this bunk."

Van Wall glanced up, and nodded. The movie screen would be practically on a line with his bunk, hence making the pictures least distracting here, because least intelligible. "Perhaps you should tell us what you have in mind. As it is, only the unknowns know what you plan. You might be—unknown before you got it into operation."

"Won't take long, if I get it figured out right. But I don't want any more all-but-the-test-dog-monsters things. We better move Copper into this bunk directly above me. He won't be watching the screen either." McReady nodded toward Copper's gently snoring bulk. Garry helped them lift and move the doctor.

McReady leaned back against the bunk, and sank into a trance, almost, of concentration, trying to calculate chances, operations, methods. He was scarcely aware as the others distributed themselves silently, and the screen lit up. Vaguely Kinner's hectic, shouted prayers and his rasping hymn-singing annoyed him till the sound accompaniment started. The lights were turned out, but the large, light-colored areas of the screen reflected enough light for ready visibility. It made men's eyes sparkle as they moved restlessly. Kinner was still praying, shouting, his voice a raucous accompaniment to the mechanical sound. Dutton stepped up the amplification.

So long had the voice been going on, that only vaguely at first was McReady aware that something seemed missing. Lying as he was, just across the narrow room from the corridor leading to Cosmos House, Kinner's voice had reached him fairly clearly, despite the sound accompaniment of the pictures. It struck him abruptly that it had stopped.

"Dutton, cut that sound," McReady called as he sat up abruptly. The pictures flickered a moment, soundless and strangely futile in the sudden, deep silence. The rising wind on the surface above bubbled melancholy tears of sound down the stove pipes. "Kinner's stopped," McReady said softly.

"For God's sake start that sound then, he may have stopped to listen," Norris snapped.

McReady rose and went down the corridor. Barclay and Van Wall left their places at the far end of the room to follow him. The flickers bulged and twisted on the back of Barclay's gray underwear as he crossed the still-functioning beam of the projector. Dutton snapped on the lights, and the pictures vanished.

Norris stood at the door as McReady had asked. Garry sat down quietly in the bunk nearest the door, forcing Clark to make room for him. Most of the others had stayed exactly where they were. Only Connant walked slowly up and down the room, in steady, unvarying rhythm.

"If you're going to do that, Connant," Clark spat, "we can get along without you altogether, whether you're human or not. Will you stop that damned rhythm?"

"Sorry." The physicist sat down in a bunk, and watched his toes thoughtfully. It was almost five minutes, five ages while the wind made the only sound, before McReady appeared at the door.

"We," he announced, "haven't got enough grief here already. Somebody's tried to help us out. Kinner has a knife in his throat, which was why he stopped singing, probably. We've got monsters, madmen and murderers. Any more 'M's' you can think of, Caldwell? If there are, we'll probably have 'em before long."

XI

"Is Blair loose?" someone asked.

"Blair is not loose. Or he flew in. If there's any doubt about where our gentle helper came from—this may clear it up." Van Wall held a foot-long, thin-bladed knife in a cloth. The wooden handle was half-burnt, charred with the peculiar pattern of the top of the galley stove.

Clark stared at it. "I did that this afternoon. I forgot the damn thing and left it on the stove."

Van Wall nodded. "I smelled it, if you remember. I knew the knife came from the galley."

"I wonder," said Benning, looking around at the party warily, "how many more monsters have we? If somebody could slip out of his place, go back of the screen to the galley and then down to the Cosmos House and back—he did come back, didn't he? Yes—everybody's here. Well, if one of the gang could do all that——"

"Maybe a monster did it," Garry suggested quietly. "There's that possibility."

"The monster, as you pointed out today, has only men left to imitate. Would he decrease his—supply, shall we say?" Van Wall pointed out. "No, we just have a plain, ordinary louse, a murderer to deal with. Ordinarily we'd call him an 'inhuman murderer' I suppose, but we have to distinguish now. We have inhuman murderers, and now we have human murderers. Or one at least."

"There's one less human," Norris said softly. "Maybe the monsters have the balance of power now."

"Never mind that," McReady sighed and turned to Barclay. "Bar, will you get your electric gadget? I'm going to make certain——"

Barclay turned down the corridor to get the pronged electrocuter, while McReady and Van Wall went back toward Cosmos House. Barclay followed them in some thirty seconds.

The corridor to Cosmos House twisted, as did nearly all corridors in Big Magnet, and Norris stood at the entrance again. But they heard, rather muffled, McReady's sudden shout. There was a savage scurry of blows, dull *ch-thunk, shluff* sounds. "Bar—Bar——" And a curious, savage mewing scream, silenced before even quick-moving Norris had reached the bend.

Kinner—or what had been Kinner—lay on the floor, cut half in two by the great knife McReady had had. The meteorologist stood against the wall, the knife dripping red in his hand. Van Wall was stirring vaguely on the floor, moaning, his hand half-consciously rubbing at his jaw. Barclay, an unutterably savage gleam in his eyes, was methodically leaning on the pronged weapon in his hand, jabbing—jabbing, jabbing.

Kinner's arms had developed a queer, scaly fur, and the flesh had twisted. The fingers had shortened, the hand rounded, the fingernails become three-inch long things of dull red horn, keened to steel-hard razor-sharp talons.

McReady raised his head, looked at the knife in his hand and dropped it. "Well, whoever did it can speak up now. He was an inhuman murderer at that—in that he murdered an inhuman. I swear by all that's holy, Kinner was a lifeless corpse on the floor here when we arrived. But when It found we were going to jab it with the power— It changed."

Norris stared unsteadily. "Oh, Lord, those things can act. Ye gods —sitting in here for hours, mouthing prayers to a God it hated! Shouting hymns in a cracked voice—hymns about a Church it never knew. Driving us mad with its ceaseless howling——

"Well. Speak up, whoever did it. You didn't know it, but you did the camp a favor. And I want to know how in blazes you got out of that room without anyone seeing you. It might help in guarding ourselves."

"His screaming—his singing. Even the sound projector couldn't drown it." Clark shivered. "It was a monster."

"Oh," said Van Wall in sudden comprehension. "You were sitting right next to the door, weren't you! And almost behind the projection screen already."

Clark nodded dumbly. "He—it's quiet now. It's a dead—Mac, your test's no damn good. It was dead anyway, monster or man, it was dead."

McReady chuckled softly. "Boys, meet Clark, the only one we know is human! Meet Clark, the one who proves he's human by trying to commit murder—and failing. Will the rest of you please refrain from trying to prove you're human for a while? I think we may have another test."

"A test!" Connant snapped joyfully, then his face sagged in disappointment. "I suppose it's another either-way-you-want-it."

"No," said McReady steadily. "Look sharp and be careful. Come into the Ad Building. Barclay, bring your electrocuter. And somebody —Dutton—stand with Barclay to make sure he does it. Watch every neighbor, for by the Hell these monsters came from, I've got something, and they know it. They're going to get dangerous!"

The group tensed abruptly. An air of crushing menace entered into every man's body, sharply they looked at each other. More keenly than ever before—*is that man next to me an inhuman monster?*

"What is it?" Garry asked, as they stood again in the main room. "How long will it take?"

"I don't know, exactly," said McReady, his voice brittle with angry determination. "But I *know* it will work, and no two ways about it. It depends on a basic quality of the *monsters,* not on us. *'Kinner'* just convinced me." He stood heavy and solid in bronzed immobility, completely sure of himself again at last.

"This," said Barclay, hefting the wooden-handled weapon, tipped with its two sharp-pointed, charged conductors, "is going to be rather necessary, I take it. Is the power plant assured?"

Dutton nodded sharply. "The automatic stoker bin is full. The gas power plant is on stand-by. Van Wall and I set it for the movie operation and—we've checked it over rather carefully several times, you know. Anything those wires touch, dies," he assured them grimly. "*I* know that."

Dr. Copper stirred vaguely in his bunk, rubbed his eyes with fumbling hand. He sat up slowly, blinked his eyes blurred with sleep and drugs, widened with an unutterable horror of drug-ridden nightmares. "Garry," he mumbled, "Garry—listen. Selfish—from hell they came, and hellish shellfish—I mean self—— Do I? What do I mean?" he sank back in his bunk, and snored softly.

McReady looked at him thoughtfully. "We'll know presently," he nodded slowly. "But selfish is what you mean all right. You may have thought of that, half-sleeping, dreaming there. I didn't stop to think what dreams you might be having. But that's all right. Selfish is the word. They must be, you see." He turned to the men in the cabin, tense, silent men staring with wolfish eyes each at his neighbor. "Selfish, and as Dr. Copper said *every part is a whole.* Every piece is self-sufficient, an animal in itself.

"That, and one other thing, tell the story. There's nothing mysterious about blood; it's just as normal a body tissue as a piece of muscle, or a piece of liver. But it hasn't so much connective tissue, though it has millions, billions of life-cells."

McReady's great bronze beard ruffled in a grim smile. "This is satisfying, in a way. I'm pretty sure we humans still outnumber you —others. Others standing here. And we have what you, your other-world race, evidently doesn't. Not an imitated, but a bred-in-the-bone instinct, a driving, unquenchable fire that's genuine. We'll fight, fight with a ferocity you may attempt to imitate, but you'll never equal! We're human. We're real. You're imitations, false to the core of your every cell.

"All right. It's a showdown now. You know. You, with your mind reading. You've lifted the idea from my brain. You can't do a thing about it.

"Standing here——

"Let it pass. Blood is tissue. They have to bleed, if they don't bleed when cut, then, by Heaven, they're phony! Phony from hell! If they bleed—then that blood, separated from them, is an individual—*a newly formed individual in its own right, just as they, split, all of them, from one original, are individuals!*

"Get it, Van? See the answer, Bar?"

Van Wall laughed very softly. "The blood—the blood will not obey. It's a new individual, with all the desire to protect its own life that the original—the main mass from which it was split—has. The *blood* will live—and try to crawl away from a hot needle, say!"

McReady picked up the scalpel from the table. From the cabinet, he took a rack of test-tubes, a tiny alcohol lamp, and a length of platinum wire set in a little glass rod. A smile of grim satisfaction rode his lips. For a moment he glanced up at those around him. Barclay and Dutton moved toward him slowly, the wooden-handled electric instrument alert.

"Dutton," said McReady, "suppose you stand over by the splice there where you've connected that in. Just make sure no—thing pulls it loose."

Dutton moved away. "Now, Van, suppose you be first on this."

White-faced, Van Wall stepped forward. With a delicate precision, McReady cut a vein in the base of his thumb. Van Wall winced slightly, then held steady as a half inch of bright blood collected in the tube. McReady put the tube in the rack, gave Van Wall a bit of alum, and indicated the iodine bottle.

Van Wall stood motionlessly watching. McReady heated the platinum wire in the alcohol lamp flame, then dipped it into the tube. It hissed softly. Five times he repeated the test. "Human, I'd say." McReady sighed, and straightened. "As yet, my theory hasn't been actually proven—but I have hopes. I have hopes.

"Don't, by the way, get too interested in this. We have with us some unwelcome ones, no doubt. Van, will you relieve Barclay at the switch? Thanks. O.K., Barclay, and may I say I hope you stay with us? You're a damned good guy."

Barclay grinned uncertainly; winced under the keen edge of the scalpel. Presently, smiling widely, he retrieved his long-handled weapon.

"Mr. Samuel Dutt—*Bar!*"

The tensity was released in that second. Whatever of hell the monsters may have had within them, the men in that instant matched it. Barclay had no chance to move his weapon as a score of men poured down on that thing that had seemed Dutton. It mewed, and spat, and tried to grow fangs—and was a hundred broken, torn pieces. Without knives, or any weapon save the brute-given strength of a staff of picked men, the thing was crushed, rent.

Slowly they picked themselves up, their eyes smouldering, very quiet in their emotions. A curious wrinkling of their lips betrayed a species of nervousness.

Barclay went over with the electric weapon. Things smouldered and stank. The caustic acid Van Wall dropped on each spilled drop of blood gave off tickling, cough-provoking fumes.

McReady grinned, his deep-set eyes alight and dancing. "Maybe," he said softly, "I underrated man's abilities when I said nothing human could have the ferocity in the eyes of that thing we found. I wish we could have the opportunity to treat in a more befitting manner these things. Something with boiling oil, or melted lead in it, or maybe slow roasting in the power boiler. When I think what a man Dutton was——

"Never mind. My theory is confirmed by—by one who knew? Well, Van Wall and Barclay are proven. I think, then, that I'll try to show you what I already know. That I too am human." McReady swished the scalpel in absolute alcohol, burned it off the metal blade, and cut the base of his thumb expertly.

Twenty seconds later he looked up from the desk at the waiting men. There were more grins out there now, friendly grins, yet withal, something else in the eyes.

"Connant," McReady laughed softly, "was right. The huskies watching that thing in the corridor bend had nothing on you. Wonder why we think only the wolf blood has the right to ferocity? Maybe on spontaneous viciousness a wolf takes tops, but after these seven days—abandon all hope, ye wolves who enter here!"

"Maybe we can save time. Connant, would you step for——"

Again Barclay was too slow. There were more grins, less tensity still, when Barclay and Van Wall finished their work.

Garry spoke in a low, bitter voice. "Connant was one of the finest men we had here—and five minutes ago I'd have sworn he was a man. Those damnable things are more than imitation." Garry shuddered and sat back in his bunk.

And thirty seconds later, Garry's blood shrank from the hot platinum wire, and struggled to escape the tube, struggled as frantically as a suddenly feral, red-eyed, dissolving imitation of Garry struggled to dodge the snake-tongue weapon Barclay advanced at him, white faced and sweating. The Thing in the test-tube screamed with a tiny, tinny voice as McReady dropped it into the glowing coal of the galley stove.

XII

"The last of it?" Dr. Copper looked down from his bunk with bloodshot, saddened eyes. "Fourteen of them——"

McReady nodded shortly. "In some ways—if only we could have permanently prevented their spreading—I'd like to have even the imitations back. Commander Garry—Connant—Dutton—Clark—"

"Where are they taking those things?" Copper nodded to the stretcher Barclay and Norris were carrying out.

"Outside. Outside on the ice, where they've got fifteen smashed crates, half a ton of coal, and presently will add ten gallons of kerosene. We've dumped acid on every spilled drop, every torn fragment. We're going to incinerate those."

"Sounds like a good plan." Copper nodded wearily. "I wonder, you haven't said whether Blair—"

McReady started. "We forgot him! We had so much else! I wonder—do you suppose we can cure him now?"

"If——" began Dr. Copper, and stopped meaningly.

McReady started a second time. "Even a madman. It imitated Kinner and his praying hysteria——" McReady turned toward Van Wall at the long table. "Van, we've got to make an expedition to Blair's shack."

Van looked up sharply, the frown of worry faded for an instant in surprised remembrance. Then he rose, nodded. "Barclay better go along. He applied the lashings, and may figure how to get in without frightening Blair too much."

Three quarters of an hour, through −37° cold, while the Aurora curtain bellied overhead. The twilight was nearly 12 hours long, flaming in the north on snow like white, crystalline sand under their skis. A 5-mile wind piled it in drift-lines pointing off to the northwest. Three quarters of an hour to reach the snow-buried shack. No smoke came from the little shack, and the men hastened.

"Blair!" Barclay roared into the wind when he was still a hundred yards away. "Blair!"

"Shut up," said McReady softly. "And hurry. He may be trying a long hike. If we have to go after him—no planes, the tractors disabled——"

"Would a monster have the stamina a man has?"

"A broken leg wouldn't stop it for more than a minute," McReady pointed out.

Barclay gasped suddenly and pointed aloft. Dim in the twilit sky, a winged thing circled in curves of indescribable grace and ease. Great white wings tipped gently, and the bird swept over them in silent curiosity. "Albatross——" Barclay said softly. "First of the season, and wandering way inland for some reason. If a monster's loose——"

Norris bent down on the ice, and tore hurriedly at his heavy, windproof clothing. He straightened, his coat flapping open, a grim blue-metaled weapon in his hand. It roared a challenge to the white silence of Antarctica.

The thing in the air screamed hoarsely. Its great wings worked frantically as a dozen feathers floated down from its tail. Norris fired again. The bird was moving swiftly now, but in an almost straight line of retreat. It screamed again, more feathers dropped and with beating wings it soared behind a ridge of pressure ice, to vanish.

Norris hurried after the others. "It won't come back," he panted.

Barclay cautioned him to silence, pointing. A curiously, fiercely blue light beat out from the cracks of the shack's door. A very low, soft humming sounded inside, a low, soft humming and a clink and clank of tools, the very sounds somehow bearing a message of frantic haste.

McReady's face paled. "Lord help us if that thing has——" He grabbed Barclay's shoulder, and made snipping motions with his fingers, pointing toward the lacing of control-cables that held the door.

Barclay drew the wire-cutters from his pocket, and kneeled soundlessly at the door. The snap and twang of cut wires made an unbearable racket in the utter quiet of the Antarctic hush. There was only that strange, sweetly soft hum from within the shack, and the queerly, hectically clipped clicking and rattling of tools to drown their noises.

McReady peered through a crack in the door. His breath sucked in huskily and his great fingers clamped cruelly on Barclay's shoulder. The meteorologist backed down. "It isn't," he explained very softly, "Blair. It's kneeling on something on the bunk—something that keeps lifting. Whatever it's working on is a thing like a knapsack —and it lifts."

"All at once," Barclay said grimly. "No. Norris, hang back, and get that iron of yours out. It may have—weapons."

Together, Barclay's powerful body and McReady's giant strength struck the door. Inside, the bunk jammed against the door screeched madly and crackled into kindling. The door flung down from broken hinges, the patched lumber of the doorpost dropping inward.

Like a blue-rubber ball, a Thing bounced up. One of its four tentaclelike arms looped out like a striking snake. In a seven-tentacled hand a six-inch pencil of winking, shining metal glinted and swung upward to face them. Its line-thin lips twitched back from snakefangs in a grin of hate, red eyes blazing.

Norris' revolver thundered in the confined space. The hate-washed face twitched in agony, the looping tentacle snatched back. The silvery thing in its hand a smashed ruin of metal, the seven-tentacled hand became a mass of mangled flesh oozing greenish-yellow ichor. The revolver thundered three times more. Dark holes drilled each of the three eyes before Norris hurled the empty weapon against its face.

The Thing screamed in feral hate, a lashing tentacle wiping at blinded eyes. For a moment it crawled on the floor, savage tentacles lashing out, the body twitching. Then it staggered up again, blinded eyes working, boiling hideously, the crushed flesh sloughing away in sodden gobbets.

Barclay lurched to his feet and dove forward with an ice-ax. The flat of the weighty thing crushed against the side of the head. Again the unkillable monster went down. The tentacles lashed out, and suddenly Barclay fell to his feet in the grip of a living, livid rope. The Thing dissolved as he held it, a white-hot band that ate into the flesh of his hands like living fire. Frantically he tore the stuff from him, held his hands where they could not be reached. The blind Thing felt and ripped at the tough, heavy, windproof cloth, seeking flesh—flesh it could convert—

The huge blow-torch McReady had brought coughed solemnly. Abruptly it rumbled disapproval throatily. Then it laughed gurglingly, and thrust out a blue-white, three-foot tongue. The Thing on the floor shrieked, flailed out blindly with tentacles that writhed and withered in the bubbling wrath of the blow-torch. It crawled and turned on the floor, it shrieked and hobbled madly, but always McReady held the blow-torch on the face, the dead eyes burning and bubbling uselessly. Frantically the Thing crawled and howled.

A tentacle sprouted a savage talon—and crisped in the flame. Steadily McReady moved with a planned, grim campaign. Helpless, maddened, the Thing retreated from the grunting torch, the caressing, licking tongue. For a moment it rebelled, squalling in inhuman hatred at the touch of icy snow. Then it fell back before the charring breath of the torch, the stench of its flesh bathing it. Hopelessly it retreated—on and on across the Antarctic snow. The bitter wind swept over it twisting the torch-tongue; vainly it flopped, a trail of oily, stinking smoke bubbling away from it—

McReady walked back toward the shack silently. Barclay met him at the door. "No more?" the giant meteorologist asked grimly.

Barclay shook his head. "No more. It didn't split?"

"It had other things to think about," McReady assured him. "When I left it, it was a glowing coal. What was it doing?"

Norris laughed shortly. "Wise boys, we are. Smash magnetos, so planes won't work. Rip the boiler tubing out of the tractors. And leave that Thing alone for a week in this shack. Alone and undisturbed."

McReady looked in at the shack more carefully. The air, despite the ripped door, was hot and humid. On a table at the far end of the room rested a thing of coiled wires and small magnets, glass tubing and radio tubes. At the center a block of rough stone rested. From the center of the block came the light that flooded the place, the fiercely blue light bluer than the glare of an electric arc, and from it came the sweetly soft hum. Off to one side was another mechanism of crystal glass, blown with an incredible neatness and delicacy, metal plates and a queer, shimmery sphere of insubstantiality.

"What is that?" McReady moved nearer.

Norris grunted. "Leave it for investigation. But I can guess pretty well. That's atomic power. That stuff to the left—that's a neat little thing for doing what men have been trying to do with 100-ton cyclotrons and so forth. It separates neutrons from heavy water, which he was getting from the surrounding ice."

"Where did he get all—oh. Of course. A monster couldn't be locked in—or out. He's been through the apparatus caches." McReady stared at the apparatus. "Lord, what minds that race must have——"

"The shimmery sphere—I think it's a sphere of pure force. Neutrons can pass through any matter, and he wanted a supply reservoir of neutrons. Just project neutrons against silica—calcium—beryllium—almost anything, and the atomic energy is released. That thing is the atomic generator."

McReady plucked a thermometer from his coat. "It's 120° in here, despite the open door. Our clothes have kept the heat out to an extent, but I'm sweating now."

Norris nodded. "The light's cold. I found that. But it gives off heat to warm the place through that coil. He had all the power in the world. He could keep it warm and pleasant, as his race thought of warmth and pleasantness. Did you notice the light, the color of it?"

McReady nodded. "Beyond the stars is the answer. From beyond the stars. From a hotter planet that circled a brighter, bluer sun they came."

McReady glanced out the door toward the blasted, smoke-stained trail that flopped and wandered blindly off across the drift. "There won't be any more coming, I guess. Sheer accident it landed here, and that was twenty million years ago. What did it do all that for?" He nodded toward the apparatus.

Barclay laughed softly. "Did you notice what it was working on when we came? Look." He pointed toward the ceiling of the shack.

Like a knapsack made of flattened coffee-tins, with dangling cloth straps and leather belts, the mechanism clung to the ceiling. A tiny, glaring heart of supernal flame burned in it, yet burned through the ceiling's wood without scorching it. Barclay walked over to it, grasped two of the dangling straps in his hands, and pulled it down with an effort. He strapped it about his body. A slight jump carried him in a weirdly slow arc across the room.

"Anti-gravity," said McReady softly.

"Anti-gravity," Norris nodded. "Yes, we had 'em stopped, with no planes, and no birds. The birds hadn't come—but they had coffee-tins and radio parts, and glass and the machine shop at night. And a week—a whole week—all to itself. America in a single jump—with anti-gravity powered by the atomic energy of matter.

"We had 'em stopped. Another half hour—it was just tightening these straps on the device so it could wear it—and we'd have stayed in Antarctica, and shot down any moving thing that came from the rest of the world."

"The albatross——" McReady said softly. "Do you suppose——"

"With this thing almost finished? With that death weapon it held in its hand?

"No, by the grace of God, who evidently does hear very well, even down here, and the margin of half an hour, we keep our world, and the planets of the system too. Anti-gravity, you know, and atomic power. Because *They* came from another sun, a star beyond the stars. *They* came from a world with a bluer sun."

NERVES
by Lester del Rey

The graveled walks between the sprawling, utilitarian structures of the National Atomic Products Co., Inc., were crowded with the usual five o'clock mass of young huskies just off work or going on the extra shift, and the company cafeteria was jammed to capacity and overflowing. But they made good-natured way for Doc Ferrel as he came out, not bothering to stop their horseplay as they would have done with any of the other half hundred officials of the company. He'd been just Doc to them too long for any need of formality.

He nodded back at them easily, pushed through, and went down the walk toward the Infirmary Building, taking his own time; when a man has turned fifty, with gray hairs and enlarged waistline to show for it, he begins to realize that comfort and relaxation are worth cultivating. Besides, Doc could see no reason for filling his stomach with food and then rushing around in a flurry that gave him no chance to digest it. He let himself in the side entrance, palming his cigar out of long habit, and passed through the surgery to the door marked:

PRIVATE
ROGER T. FERREL
PHYSICIAN IN CHARGE

As always, the little room was heavy with the odor of stale smoke and littered with scraps of this and that. His assistant was already there, rummaging busily through the desk with the brass nerve that was typical of him; Ferrel had no objections to it, though, since Blake's rock-steady hands and unruffled brain were always dependable in a pinch of any sort.

Blake looked up and grinned confidently. "Hi, Doc. Where the deuce do you keep your cigarettes, anyway? Never mind, got 'em. . . . Ah, that's better! Good thing there's one room in this darned building where the 'No Smoking' signs don't count. You and the wife coming out this evening?"

"Not a chance, Blake." Ferrel stuck the cigar back in his mouth and settled down into the old leather chair, shaking his head. "Palmer phoned down half an hour ago to ask me if I'd stick through the graveyard shift. Seems the plant's got a rush order for some particular batch of dust that takes about twelve hours to cook, so they'll be running No. 3 and 4 till midnight or later."

"Hm-m-m. So you're hooked again. I don't see why any of us has to stick here—nothing serious ever pops up now. Look what I had today; three cases of athlete's foot—better send a memo down to the showers for extra disinfection—a guy with dandruff, four running noses, and the office boy with a sliver in his thumb! They bring everything to us except their babies—and they'd have them here if they could—but nothing that couldn't wait a week or a month. Anne's been counting on you and the missus, Doc; she'll be disappointed if you aren't there to celebrate her sticking ten years with me. Why don't you let the kid stick it out alone tonight?"

"I wish I could, but this happens to be my job. As a matter of fact, though, Jenkins worked up an acute case of duty and decided to stay on with me tonight." Ferrel twitched his lips in a stiff smile, remembering back to the time when his waistline had been smaller than his chest and he'd gone through the same feeling that destiny had singled him out to save the world. "The kid had his first real case today, and he's all puffed up. Handled it all by himself, so he's now Dr. Jenkins, if you please."

Blake had his own memories. "Yeah? Wonder when he'll realize that everything he did by himself came from your hints? What was it, anyway?"

"Same old story—simple radiation burns. No matter how much we tell the men when they first come in, most of them can't see why they should wear three ninety-five percent efficient shields when the main converter shield cuts off all but one-tenth percent of the radiation. Somehow, this fellow managed to leave off his two inner shields and pick up a year's burn in six hours. Now he's probably back on No. 1, still running through the hundred liturgies I gave him to say and hoping we won't get him sacked."

No. 1 was the first converter around which National Atomic had built its present monopoly in artificial radioactives, back in the days when shields were still inefficient to one part in a thousand and the materials handled were milder than the modern ones. They still used it for the gentler reactions, prices of converters being what they were; anyhow, if reasonable precautions were taken, there was no serious danger.

"A tenth percent will kill; five percent thereof is one two-hundredth; five percent of that is one four-thousandth; and five percent again leaves one eight-thousandth, safe for all but fools." Blake sing-songed the liturgy solemnly, then chuckled. "You're getting old, Doc; you used to give them a thousand times. Well, if you get the chance, you and Mrs. Ferrel drop out and say hello, even if it's after midnight. Anne's gonna be disappointed, but she ought to know how it goes. So long."

" 'Night." Ferrel watched him leave, still smiling faintly. Some day his own son would be out of medical school, and Blake would make a good man for him to start under and begin the same old grind upward. First, like young Jenkins, he'd be filled with his mission to humanity, tense and uncertain, but somehow things would roll along through Blake's stage and up, probably to Doc's own level, where the same old problems were solved in the same old way, and life settled down into a comfortable mellow dullness.

There were worse lives, certainly, even though it wasn't like the mass of murders, kidnapings and applied miracles played up in the current movie series about Dr. Hoozis. Come to think of it, Hoozis was supposed to be working in an atomic products plant right now—but one where chrome-plated converters covered with pretty neon tubes were mysteriously blowing up every second day, and men were brought in with blue flames all over them to be cured instantly in time to utter the magic words so the hero could dash in and put out the atomic flame barehanded. Ferrel grunted and reached back for his old copy of the "Decameron."

Then he heard Jenkins out in the surgery, puttering around with quick, nervous little sounds. Never do to let the boy find him loafing back here, when the possible fate of the world so obviously hung on his alertness. Young doctors had to be disillusioned slowly, or they became bitter and their work suffered. Yet, in spite of his amusement at Jenkins' nervousness, he couldn't help envying the thin-faced young man's erect shoulders and flat stomach. Years crept by, it seemed.

Jenkins straightened out a wrinkle in his white jacket fussily and looked up. "I've been getting the surgery ready for instant use, Dr.

Ferrel. Do you think it's safe to keep only Miss Dodd and one male attendant here—shouldn't we have more than the bare legally sanctioned staff?"

"Dodd's a one-man staff," Ferrel assured him. "Expecting accidents tonight?"

"No, sir, not exactly. But do you know what they're running off?"

"No." Ferrel hadn't asked Palmer; he'd learned long before that he couldn't keep up with the atomic engineering developments, and had stopped trying. "Some new type of atomic tank fuel for the army to use in its war games?"

"Worse than that, sir. They're making their first commercial run of Natomic I-713 in both No. 3 and 4 converters at once."

"So? Seems to me I did hear something about that. Had to do with killing off boll weevils, didn't it?" Ferrel was vaguely familiar with the process of sowing radioactive dust in a circle outside the weevil area, to isolate the pest, then gradually moving inward from the border. Used with proper precautions, it had slowly killed off the weevil and driven it back into half the territory once occupied.

Jenkins managed to look disappointed, surprised and slightly superior without a visible change of expression. "There was an article on it in the *Natomic Weekly Ray* of last issue, Dr. Ferrel. You probably know that the trouble with Natomic I-344, which they've been using, was its half life of over four months; that made the land sowed useless for planting the next year, so they had to move very slowly. I-713 has a half life of less than a week and reaches safe limits in about two months, so they'll be able to isolate whole strips of hundreds of miles during the winter and still have the land usable by spring. Field tests have been highly successful, and we've just gotten a huge order from two States that want immediate delivery."

"After their legislatures waited six months debating whether to use it or not," Ferrel hazarded out of long experience. "Hm-m-m, sounds good if they can sow enough earthworms after them to keep the ground in good condition. But what's the worry?"

Jenkins shook his head indignantly. "I'm not worried. I simply think we should take every possible precaution and be ready for any accident; after all, they're working on something new, and a half life of a week is rather strong, don't you think? Besides, I looked over some of the reaction charts in the article, and— What was that?"

From somewhere to the left of the Infirmary, a muffled growl was being accompanied by ground tremors; then it gave place to a steady hissing, barely audible through the insulated walls of the building. Ferrel listened a moment and shrugged. "Nothing to worry about, Jenkins; you'll hear it a dozen times a year. Ever since the Great War when he tried to commit hara-kiri over the treachery of his people, Hokusai's been bugs about getting an atomic explosive bomb which will let us wipe out the rest of the world. Some day you'll probably see the little guy brought in here minus his head, but so far he hasn't found anything with a short enough half life that can be controlled until needed. What about the reaction charts on I-713?"

"Nothing definite, I suppose." Jenkins turned reluctantly away from the sound, still frowning. "I know it worked in small lots, but there's something about one of the intermediate steps I distrust, sir. I thought I recognized . . . I tried to ask one of the engineers about it. He practically told me to shut up until I'd studied atomic engineering myself."

Seeing the boy's face whiten over tensed jaw muscles, Ferrel held back his smile and nodded slowly. Something funny there; of course, Jenkins' pride had been wounded, but hardly that much. Some day, he'd have to find out what was behind it; little things like that could ruin a man's steadiness with the instruments, if he kept it to himself. Meantime, the subject was best dropped.

The telephone girl's heavily syllabized voice cut into his thoughts from the annunciator. "Dr. Ferrel. Dr. Ferrel wanted on the telephone. Dr. Ferrel, please!"

Jenkins' face blanched still further, and his eyes darted to his superior sharply. Doc grunted casually. "Probably Palmer's bored and wants to tell me all about his grandson again. He thinks that child's an all-time genius because it says two words at eighteen months."

But inside the office, he stopped to wipe his hands free of perspiration before answering; there was something contagious about Jenkins' suppressed fears. And Palmer's face on the little television screen didn't help any, though the director was wearing his usual set smile. Ferrel knew it wasn't about the baby this time, and he was right.

" 'Lo, Ferrel." Palmer's heartily confident voice was quite normal, but the use of the last name was a clear sign of some trouble. "There's been a little accident in the plant, they tell me. They're bringing a few men over to the Infirmary for treatment—probably not right away, though. Has Blake gone yet?"

"He's been gone fifteen minutes or more. Think it's serious enough to call him back, or are Jenkins and myself enough?"

"Jenkins? Oh, the new doctor." Palmer hesitated, and his arms showed quite clearly the doodling operations of his hands, out of sight of the vision cell. "No, of course, no need to call Blake back, I suppose—not yet, anyhow. Just worry anyone who saw him coming in. Probably nothing serious."

"What is it—radiation burns, or straight accident?"

"Oh—radiation mostly—maybe accident, too. Someone got a little careless—you know how it is. Nothing to worry about, though. You've been through it before when they opened a port too soon."

Doc knew enough about that—if that's what it was. "Sure, we can handle that, Palmer. But I thought No. 1 was closing down at five-thirty tonight. Anyhow, how come they haven't installed the safety ports on it? You told me they had, six months ago."

"I didn't say it was No. 1, or that it was a manual port. You know, new equipment for new products." Palmer looked up at someone else, and his upper arms made a slight movement before he looked down at the vision cell again. "I can't go into it now, Dr. Ferrel, accident's throwing us off schedule, you see—details piling up on me. We can talk it over later, and you probably have to make arrangements now. Call me if you want anything."

The screen darkened and the phone clicked off abruptly, just as a muffled word started. The voice hadn't been Palmer's. Ferrel pulled his stomach in, wiped the sweat off his hands again, and went out into the surgery with careful casualness. Damn Palmer, why couldn't the fool give enough information to make decent preparations possible? He was sure 3 and 4 alone were operating, and they were supposed to be foolproof. Just what had happened?

Jenkins jerked up from a bench as he came out, face muscles tense and eyes filled with a nameless fear. Where he had been sitting, a copy of the *Weekly Ray* was lying open at a chart of symbols which meant nothing to Ferrel, except for the penciled line under one of the reactions. The boy picked it up and stuck it back on a table.

"Routine accident," Ferrel reported as naturally as he could, cursing himself for having to force his voice. Thank the Lord, the boy's hands hadn't trembled visibly when he was moving the paper; he'd still be useful if surgery were necessary. Palmer had said nothing of that, of course—he'd said nothing about entirely too much. "They're bringing a few men over for radiation burns, according to Palmer. Everything ready?"

Jenkins nodded tightly. "Quite ready, sir, as much as we can be for —routine accidents at 3 and 4! . . . Isotope R. . . . Sorry, Dr. Ferrel, I didn't mean that. Should we call in Dr. Blake and the other nurses and attendants?"

"Eh? Oh, probably we can't reach Blake, and Palmer doesn't think we need him. You might have Nurse Dodd locate Meyers—the others are out on dates by now if I know them, and the two nurses should be enough, with Jones; they're better than a flock of the others, anyway." Isotope R? Ferrel remembered the name, but nothing else. Something an engineer had said once—but he couldn't recall in what connection—or had Hokusai mentioned it? He watched Jenkins leave and turned back on an impulse to his office where he could phone in reasonable privacy.

"Get me Matsuura Hokusai." He stood drumming on the table impatiently until the screen finally lighted and the little Japanese looked out of it. "Hoke, do you know what they were turning out over at 3 and 4?"

The scientist nodded slowly, his wrinkled face as expressionless as his unaccented English. "Yess, they are make I-713 for the weevil. Why you assk?"

"Nothing; just curious. I heard rumors about an Isotope R and wondered if there was any connection. Seems they had a little accident over there, and I want to be ready for whatever comes of it."

For a fraction of a second, the heavy lids on Hokusai's eyes seemed to lift, but his voice remained neutral, only slightly faster. "No connection, Dr. Ferrel, they are not make Issotope R, very much assure you. Besst you forget Issotope R. Very ssorry. Dr. Ferrel, I must now ssee accident. Thank you for call. Good-by." The screen was blank again, along with Ferrel's mind.

Jenkins was standing in the door, but had either heard nothing or seemed not to know about it. "Nurse Meyers is coming back," he said. "Shall I get ready for curare injections?"

"Uh—might be a good idea." Ferrel had no intention of being surprised again, no matter what the implication of the words. Curare, one of the great poisons, known to South American primitives for centuries and only recently synthesized by modern chemistry, was the final resort for use in cases of radiation injury that were utterly beyond control. While the Infirmary stocked it for such emergencies, in the long years of Doc's practice it had been used only twice; neither experience had been pleasant. Jenkins was either thoroughly frightened or overly zealous—unless he knew something he had no business knowing.

"Seems to take them long enough to get the men here—can't be too serious, Jenkins, or they'd move faster."

"Maybe." Jenkins went on with his preparations, dissolving dried plasma in distilled, de-aerated water, without looking up. "There's the litter siren now. You'd better get washed up while I take care of the patients."

Doc listened to the sound that came in as a faint drone from outside, and grinned slightly. "Must be Beel driving; he's the only man fool enough to run the siren when the runways are empty. Anyhow, if you'll listen, it's the out trip he's making. Be at least five minutes before he gets back." But he turned into the washroom, kicked on the hot water and began scrubbing vigorously with the strong soap.

Damn Jenkins! Here he was preparing for surgery before he had any reason to suspect the need, and the boy was running things to suit himself, pretty much, as if armed with superior knowledge. Well, maybe he was. Either that, or he was simply half crazy with old wives' fears of anything relating to atomic reactions, and that didn't seem to fit the case. He rinsed off as Jenkins came in, kicked on the hot-air blast, and let his arms dry, then bumped against a rod that brought out rubber gloves on little holders. "Jenkins, what's all this Isotope R business, anyway? I've heard about it somewhere—probably from Hokusai. But I can't remember anything definite."

"Naturally—there isn't anything definite. That's the trouble." The young doctor tackled the area under his fingernails before looking up; then he saw Ferrel was slipping into his surgeon's whites that had come out on a hanger, and waited until the other was finished. "R's one of the big maybe problems of atomics. Purely theoretical, and none's been made yet—it's either impossible or can't be done in small control batches, safe for testing. That's the trouble, as I said; nobody knows anything about it, except that—if it can exist—it'll break down in a fairly short time into Mahler's Isotope. You've heard of that?"

Doc had—twice. The first had been when Mahler and half his laboratory had disappeared with accompanying noise; he'd been making a comparatively small amount of the new product designed to act as a starter for other reactions. Later, Maicewicz had tackled it on a smaller scale, and that time only two rooms and three men had gone up in dust particles. Five or six years later, atomic theory had been extended to the point where any student could find why the apparently safe product decided to become pure helium and energy in approximately one-billionth of a second.

"How long a time?"

"Half a dozen theories, and no real idea." They'd come out of the washrooms, finished except for their masks. Jenkins ran his elbow into a switch that turned on the ultraviolets that were supposed to sterilize the entire surgery, then looked around questioningly. "What about the supersonics?"

Ferrel kicked them on, shuddering as the bone-shaking harmonic hum indicated their activity. He couldn't complain about the equipment, at least. Ever since the last accident, when the State Congress developed ideas, there'd been enough gadgets lying around to stock up several small hospitals. The supersonics were intended to penetrate through all solids in the room, sterilizing where the UV light couldn't reach. A whistling note in the harmonics reminded him of something that had been tickling around in the back of his mind for minutes.

"There was no emergency whistle, Jenkins. Hardly seems to me they'd neglect that if it were so important."

Jenkins grunted skeptically and eloquently. "I read in the papers a few days ago where Congress was thinking of moving all atomic plants—meaning National, of course—out into the Mojave Desert. Palmer wouldn't like that. . . . There's the siren again."

Jones, the male attendant, had heard it, and was already running out the fresh stretcher for the litter into the back receiving room. Half a minute later, Beel came trundling in the detachable part of the litter. "Two," he announced. "More coming up as soon as they can get to 'em, Doc."

There was blood spilled over the canvas, and a closer inspection indicated its source in a severed jugular vein, now held in place with a small safety pin that had fastened the two sides of the cut with a series of little pricks around which the blood had clotted enough to stop further loss.

Doc kicked off the supersonics with relief and indicated the man's throat. "Why wasn't I called out instead of having him brought here?"

"Hell, Doc, Palmer said bring 'em in and I brought 'em—I dunno. Guess some guy pinned up this fellow so they figured he could wait. Anything wrong?"

Ferrel grimaced. "With a split jugular, nothing that stops the bleeding's wrong, orthodox or not. How many more, and what's wrong out there?"

"Lord knows, Doc. I only drive 'em, I don't ask questions. So long!" He pushed the new stretcher up on the carriage, went wheeling it out to the small two-wheeled tractor that completed the litter. Ferrel dropped his curiosity back to its proper place and turned to the jugular case, while Dodd adjusted her mask. Jones had their clothes off, swabbed them down hastily, and wheeled them out on operating tables into the center of the surgery.

"Plasma!" A quick examination had shown Doc nothing else wrong with the jugular case, and he made the injection quickly. Apparently the man was only unconscious from shock induced by loss of blood, and the breathing and heart action resumed a more normal course as the liquid filled out the depleted blood vessels. He treated the wound with a sulphonamide derivative in routine procedure, cleaned and sterilized the edges gently, applied clamps carefully, removed the pin, and began stitching with the complicated little motor needle—one of the few gadgets for which he had any real appreciation. A few more drops of blood had spilled, but not seriously, and the wound was now permanently sealed. "Save the pin, Dodd. Goes in the collection. That's all for this. How's the other, Jenkins?"

Jenkins pointed to the back of the man's neck, indicating a tiny bluish object sticking out. "Fragment of steel, clear into the medulla oblongata. No blood loss, but he's been dead since it touched him. Want me to remove it?"

"No need—mortician can do it if they want. . . . If these are a sample, I'd guess it as a plain industrial accident, instead of anything connected with radiation."

"You'll get that, too, Doc." It was the jugular case, apparently conscious and normal except for pallor. "We weren't in the converter house. Hey, I'm all right! . . . I'll be—"

Ferrel smiled at the surprise on the fellow's face. "Thought you were dead, eh? Sure, you're all right, if you'll take it easy. A torn jugular either kills you or else it's nothing to worry about. Just pipe down and let the nurse put you to sleep, and you'll never know you got it."

"Lord! Stuff came flying out of the air-intake like bullets out of a machine gun. Just a scratch, I thought; then Jake was bawling like a baby and yelling for a pin. Blood all over the place—then here I am, good as new."

"Uh-huh." Dodd was already wheeling him off to a ward room, her grim face wrinkled into a half-quizzical expression over the mask. "Doctor said to pipe down, didn't he? Well!"

As soon as Dodd vanished, Jenkins sat down, running his hand over his cap; there were little beads of sweat showing where the goggles and mask didn't entirely cover his face. " 'Stuff came flying out of the air-intake like bullets out of a machine gun,' " he repeated softly. "Dr. Ferrel, these two cases were outside the converter—just by-product accidents. Inside—"

"Yeah." Ferrel was picturing things himself, and it wasn't pleasant. Outside, matter tossed through the air ducts; inside— He left it hanging, as Jenkins had. "I'm going to call Blake. We'll probably need him."

II

"Give me Dr. Blake's residence—Maple 2337," Ferrel said quickly into the phone. The operator looked blank for a second, starting and then checking a purely automatic gesture toward the plugs. "Maple 2337, I said."

"I'm sorry, Dr. Ferrel, I can't give you an outside line. All trunk lines are out of order." There was a constant buzz from the board, but nothing showed in the panel to indicate whether from white inside lights or the red trunk indicators.

"But—this is an emergency, operator. I've got to get in touch with Dr. Blake!"

"Sorry, Dr. Ferrel. All trunk lines are out of order." She started to reach for the plug, but Ferrel stopped her.

"Give me Palmer, then—and no nonsense! If his line's busy, cut me in, and I'll take the responsibility."

"Very good." She snapped at her switches. "I'm sorry, emergency call from Dr. Ferrel. Hold the line and I'll reconnect you." Then Palmer's face was on the panel, and this time the man was making no attempt to conceal his expression of worry.

"What is it, Ferrel?"

"I want Blake here—I'm going to need him. The operator says—"

"Yeah." Palmer nodded tightly, cutting in. "I've been trying to get him myself, but his house doesn't answer. Any idea of where to reach him?"

"You might try the Bluebird or any of the other night clubs around there." Damn, why did this have to be Blake's celebration night? No telling where he could be found by this time.

Palmer was speaking again. "I've already had all the night clubs and restaurants called, and he doesn't answer. We're paging the movie houses and theaters now—just a second. . . . Nope, he isn't there, Ferrel. Last reports, no response."

"How about sending out a general call over the radio?"

"I'd . . . I'd like to, Ferrel, but it can't be done." The manager had hesitated for a fraction of a second, but his reply was positive. "Oh, by the way, we'll notify your wife you won't be home. Operator! You there? Good, reconnect the Governor!"

There was no sense in arguing into a blank screen, Doc realized. If Palmer wouldn't put through a radio call, he wouldn't, though it had been done once before. "All trunk lines are out of order. . . . We'll notify your wife. . . . Reconnect the Governor!" They weren't even being careful to cover up. He must have repeated the words aloud as he backed out of the office, still staring at the screen, for Jenkins' face twitched into a maladjusted grin.

"So we're cut off. I knew it already; Meyers just got in with more details." He nodded toward the nurse, just coming out of the dressing rooms and trying to smooth out her uniform. Her almost pretty face was more confused than worried.

"I was just leaving the plant, Dr. Ferrel, when my name came up on the outside speaker, but I had trouble getting here. We're locked in! I saw them at the gate—guards with sticks. They were turning back everyone that tried to leave, and wouldn't tell why, even. Just general orders that no one was to leave until Mr. Palmer gave his permission. And they weren't going to let me back in at first. Do you suppose . . . do you know what it's all about? I heard little things that didn't mean anything, really, but—"

"I know just about as much as you do, Meyers, though Palmer said something about carelessness with one of the ports on No. 3 or 4," Ferrel answered her. "Probably just precautionary measures. Anyway, I wouldn't worry about it yet."

"Yes, Dr. Ferrel." She nodded and turned back to the front office, but there was no assurance in her look. Doc realized that neither Jenkins nor himself were pictures of confidence at the moment.

"Jenkins," he said, when she was gone, "if you know anything I don't, for the love of Mike, out with it! I've never seen anything like this around here."

Jenkins shook himself, and for the first time since he'd been there, used Ferrel's nickname. "Doc, I don't—that's why I'm in a blue funk. I know just enough to be less sure than you can be, and I'm scared as hell!"

"Let's see your hands." The subject was almost a monomania with Ferrel, and he knew it, but he also knew it wasn't unjustified. Jenkins' hands came out promptly, and there was no tremble to them. The boy threw up his arm so the sleeve slid beyond the elbow, and Ferrel nodded; there was no sweat trickling down from the armpits to reveal a worse case of nerves than showed on the surface. "Good enough, son; I don't care how scared you are—I'm getting that way myself—but with Blake out of the picture, and the other nurses and attendants sure to be out of reach, I'll need everything you've got."

"Doc?"

"Well?"

"If you'll take my word for it, I can get another nurse here—and a good one, too. They don't come any better, or any steadier, and she's not working now. I didn't expect her—well, anyhow, she'd skin me if I didn't call when we need one. Want her?"

"No trunk lines for outside calls," Doc reminded him. It was the first time he'd seen any real enthusiasm on the boy's face, and however good or bad the nurse was, she'd obviously be of value in bucking up Jenkins' spirits. "Go to it, though; right now we can probably use any nurse. Sweetheart?"

"Wife." Jenkins went toward the dressing room. "And I don't need the phone; we used to carry ultra-short-wave personal radios to keep in touch, and I've still got mine here. And if you're worried about her qualifications, she handed instruments to Bayard at Mayo's for five years—that's how I managed to get through medical school!"

The siren was approaching again when Jenkins came back, the little tense lines about his lips still there, but his whole bearing somehow steadier. He nodded. "I called Palmer, too, and he O. K.'d her coming inside on the phone without wondering how I'd contacted her. The switchboard girl has standing orders to route all calls from us through before anything else, it seems."

Doc nodded, his ear cocked toward the drone of the siren that drew up and finally ended on a sour wheeze. There was a feeling of relief from tension about him as he saw Jones appear and go toward the rear entrance; work, even under the pressure of an emergency,

was always easier than sitting around waiting for it. He saw two
stretchers come in, both bearing double loads, and noted that Beel
was babbling at the attendant, the driver's usually phlegmatic manner completely gone.

"I'm quitting; I'm through tomorrow! No more watching 'em drag
out stiffs for me—not that way. Dunno why I gotta go back, anyhow;
it won't do 'em any good to get in further, even if they can. From now
on, I'm driving a truck, so help me I am!"

Ferrel let him rave on, only vaguely aware that the man was close to
hysteria. He had no time to give to Beel now as he saw the raw red
flesh through the visor of one of the armor suits. "Cut off what
clothes you can, Jones," he directed. "At least get the shield suits off
them. Tannic acid ready, nurse?"

"Ready." Meyers answered together with Jenkins, who was busily
helping Jones strip off heavily armored suits and helmets.

Ferrel kicked on the supersonics again, letting them sterilize the
metal suits—there was going to be no chance to be finicky about
asepsis; the supersonics and ultra-violet tubes were supposed to take
care of that, and they'd have to do it, to a large extent, little as he
liked it. Jenkins finished his part, dived back for fresh gloves, with a
mere cursory dipping of his hands into antiseptic and rinse. Dodd followed him, while Jones wheeled three of the cases into the middle of
the surgery, ready for work; the other had died on the way in.

It was going to be messy work, obviously. Where metal from the
suits had touched, or come near touching, the flesh was burned—
crisped, rather. And that was merely a minor part of it, as was the
more than ample evidence of major radiation burns, which had
probably not stopped at the surface, but penetrated through the flesh
and bones into the vital interior organs. Much worse, the writhing
and spasmodic muscular contractions indicated radioactive matter
that had been forced into the flesh and was acting directly on the
nerves controlling the motor impulses. Jenkins looked hastily at the
twisting body of his case, and his face blanched to a yellowish white;
it was the first real example of the full possibilities of an atomic accident he'd seen.

"Curare," he said finally, the word forced out, but level. Meyers
handed him the hypodermic and he inserted it, his hand still steady—
more than normally steady, in fact, with that absolute lack of movement that can come to a living organism only under the stress of

emergency. Ferrel dropped his eyes back to his own case, both relieved and worried.

From the spread of the muscular convulsions, there could be only one explanation—somehow, radioactives had not only worked their way through the air grills, but had been forced through the almost airtight joints and sputtered directly into the flesh of the men. Now they were sending out radiations into every nerve, throwing aside the normal orders from the brain and spinal column, setting up anarchic orders of their own that left the muscles to writhe and jerk, one against the other, without order or reason, or any of the normal restraints the body places upon itself. The closest parallel was that of a man undergoing metrozol shock for schizophrenia, or a severe case of strychnine poisoning. He injected curare carefully, metering out the dosage according to the best estimate he could make, but Jenkins had been acting under a pressure that finished the second injection as Doc looked up from his first. Still, in spite of the rapid spread of the drug, some of the twitching went on.

"Curare," Jenkins repeated, and Doc tensed mentally; he'd still been debating whether to risk the extra dosage. But he made no counter-order, feeling slightly relieved this time at having the matter taken out of his hands; Jenkins went back to work, pushing up the injections to the absolute limit of safety, and slightly beyond. One of the cases had started a weird minor moan that hacked on and off as his lungs and vocal cords went in and out of synchronization, but it quieted under the drug, and in a matter of minutes the three lay still, breathing with the shallow flaccidity common to curare treatment. They were still moving slightly, but where before they were perfectly capable of breaking their own bones in uncontrolled efforts, now there was only motion similar to a man with a chill.

"God bless the man who synthesized curare," Jenkins muttered as he began cleaning away damaged flesh, Meyers assisting.

Doc could repeat that; with the older, natural product, true standardization and exact dosage had been next to impossible. Too much, and its action on the body was fatal; the patient died from "exhaustion" of his chest muscles in a matter of minutes. Too little was practically useless. Now that the danger of self-injury and fatal exhaustion from wild exertion was over, he could attend to such relatively unimportant things as the agony still going on—curare had no particular effect on the sensory nerves. He injected neo-heroin and began cleaning the burned areas and treating them with the standard tannic-acid routine, first with a sulphonamide to eliminate possible infection, glancing up occasionally at Jenkins.

He had no need to worry, though; the boy's nerves were frozen into an unnatural calm that still pressed through with a speed Ferrel made no attempt to equal, knowing his work would suffer for it. At a gesture, Dodd handed him the little radiation detector, and he began hunting over the skin, inch by inch, for the almost microscopic bits of matter; there was no hope of finding all now, but the worst deposits could be found and removed; later, with more time, a final probing could be made.

"Jenkins," he asked, "how about I-713's chemical action? Is it basically poisonous to the system?"

"No. Perfectly safe except for radiation. Eight in the outer electron ring, chemically inert."

That, at least, was a relief. Radiations were bad enough in and of themselves, but when coupled with metallic poisoning, like the old radium or mercury poisoning, it was even worse. The small colloidally fine particles of I-713 in the flesh would set up their own danger signal, and could be scraped away in the worst cases; otherwise, they'd probably have to stay until the isotope exhausted itself. Mercifully, its half life was short, which would decrease the long hospitalization and suffering of the men.

Jenkins joined Ferrel on the last patient, replacing Dodd at handing instruments. Doc would have preferred the nurse, who was used to his little signals, but he said nothing, and was surprised to note the efficiency of the boy's cooperation. "How about the breakdown products?" he asked.

"I-713? Harmless enough, mostly, and what isn't harmless isn't concentrated enough to worry about. That is, if it's still I-713. Otherwise—"

Otherwise, Doc finished mentally, the boy meant there'd be no danger from poisoning, at least. Isotope R, with an uncertain degeneration period, turned into Mahler's Isotope, with a complete breakdown in a billionth of a second. He had a fleeting vision of men, filled with a fine dispersion of that, suddenly erupting over their body with a violence that could never be described; Jenkins must have been thinking the same thing. For a few seconds, they stood there, looking at each other silently, but neither chose to speak of it. Ferrel reached for the probe, Jenkins shrugged, and they went on with their work and their thoughts.

It was a picture impossible to imagine, which they might or might not see; if such an atomic blow-up occurred, what would happen to the laboratory was problematical. No one knew the exact amount Maicewicz had worked on, except that it was the smallest amount he could make, so there could be no good estimate of the damage. The bodies on the operating tables, the little scraps of removed flesh containing the minute globules of radioactive matter, even the instruments that had come in contact with them, were bombs waiting to explode. Ferrel's own fingers took on some of the steadiness that was frozen in Jenkins as he went about his work, forcing his mind onto the difficult labor at hand.

It might have been minutes or hours later when the last dressing was in place and the three broken bones of the worst case were set. Meyers and Dodd, along with Jones, were taking care of the men, putting them into the little wards, and the two physicians were alone, carefully avoiding each other's eyes, waiting without knowing exactly what they expected.

Outside, a droning chug came to their ears, and the thump of something heavy moving over the runways. By common impulse they slipped to the side door and looked out, to see the rear end of one of the electric tanks moving away from them. Night had fallen some time before, but the gleaming lights from the big towers around the fence made the plant stand out in glaring detail. Except for the tank moving away, though, other buildings cut off their view.

Then, from the direction of the main gate, a shrill whistle cut the air, and there was a sound of men's voices, though the words were indistinguishable. Sharp, crisp syllables followed, and Jenkins nodded slowly to himself. "Ten'll get you a hundred," he began, "that— Uh, no use betting. It is."

Around the corner a squad of men in State militia uniform marched briskly, bayoneted rifles on their arms. With efficient precision, they spread out under a sergeant's direction, each taking a post before the door of one of the buildings, one approaching the place where Ferrel and Jenkins stood.

"So that's what Palmer was talking to the Governor about," Ferrel muttered. "No use asking them questions, I suppose; they know less than we do. Come on inside where we can sit down and rest. Wonder what good the militia can do here—unless Palmer's afraid someone inside's going to crack and cause trouble."

Jenkins followed him back to the office and accepted a cigarette automatically as he flopped back into a chair. Doc was discovering just how good it felt to give his muscles and nerves a chance to relax, and realizing that they must have been far longer in the surgery than he had thought. "Care for a drink?"

"Uh—is it safe, Doc? We're apt to be back in there any minute."

Ferrel pulled a grin onto his face and nodded. "It won't hurt you—we're just enough on edge and tired for it to be burned up inside for fuel instead of reaching our nerves. Here." It was a generous slug of rye he poured for each, enough to send an almost immediate warmth through them, and to relax their overtensed nerves. "Wonder why Beel hasn't been back long ago?"

"That tank we saw probably explains it; it got too tough for the men to work in just their suits, and they've had to start excavating through the converters with the tanks. Electric, wasn't it, battery powered? . . . So there's enough radiation loose out there to interfere with atomic-powered machines, then. That means whatever they're doing is tough and slow work. Anyhow, it's more important that they damp the action than get the men out, if they only realize it— Sue!"

Ferrel looked up quickly to see the girl standing there, already dressed for surgery, and he was not too old for a little glow of appreciation to creep over him. No wonder Jenkins' face lighted up. She was small, but her figure was shaped like that of a taller girl, not in the cute or pert lines usually associated with shorter women, and the serious competence of her expression hid none of the loveliness of her face. Obviously she was several years older than Jenkins, but as he stood up to greet her, her face softened and seemed somehow youthful beside the boy's as she looked up.

"You're Dr. Ferrel?" she asked, turning to the older man. "I was a little late—there was some trouble at first about letting me in—so I went directly to prepare before bothering you. And just so you won't be afraid to use me, my credentials are all here."

She put the little bundle on the table, and Ferrel ran through them briefly; it was better than he'd expected. Technically she wasn't a nurse at all, but a doctor of medicine, a so-called nursing doctor; there'd been the need for assistants midway between doctor and nurse for years, having the general training and abilities of both, but only in the last decade had the actual course been created, and the graduates were still limited to a few. He nodded and handed them back.

"We can use you, Dr.—"

"Brown—professional name, Dr. Ferrel. And I'm used to being called just Nurse Brown."

Jenkins cut in on the formalities. "Sue, is there any news outside about what's going on here?"

"Rumors, but they're wild, and I didn't have a chance to hear many. All I know is that they're talking about evacuating the city and everything within fifty miles of here, but it isn't official. And some people were saying the Governor was sending in troops to declare martial law over the whole section, but I didn't see any except here."

Jenkins took her off, then, to show her the Infirmary and introduce her to Jones and the two other nurses, leaving Ferrel to wait for the sound of the siren again, and to try putting two and two together to get sixteen. He attempted to make sense out of the article in the *Weekly Ray,* but gave it up finally; atomic theory had advanced too far since the sketchy studies he'd made, and the symbols were largely without meaning to him. He'd have to rely on Jenkins, it seemed. In the meantime, what was holding up the litter? He should have heard the warning siren long before.

It wasn't the litter that came in next, though, but a group of five men, two carrying a third, and a fourth supporting the fifth. Jenkins took the carried man over, Brown helping him; it was similar to the former cases, but without the actual burns from contact with hot metal. Ferrel turned to the men.

"Where's Beel and the litter?" He was inspecting the supported man's leg as he asked, and began work on it without moving the fellow to a table. Apparently a lump of radioactive matter the size of a small pea had been driven half an inch into the flesh below the thigh, and the broken bone was the result of the violent contractions of the man's own muscles under the stimulus of the radiation. It wasn't pretty. Now, however, the strength of the action had apparently burned out the nerves around, so the leg was comparatively limp and without feeling; the man lay watching, relaxed on the bench in a half-comatose condition, his eyes popping out and his lips twisted into a sick grimace, but he did not flinch as the wound was scraped out. Ferrel was working around a small leaden shield, his arms covered with heavily leaded gloves, and he dropped the scraps of flesh and isotope into a box of the same metal.

"Beel—he's out of this world, Doc," one of the others answered when he could tear his eyes off the probing. "He got himself blotto, somehow, and wrecked the litter before he got back. Couldn't take it, watching us grapple 'em out—and we hadda go in after 'em without a drop of hootch!"

Ferrel glanced at him quickly, noticing Jenkins' head jerk around as he did so. "You were getting them out? You mean you didn't come from in there?"

"Heck, no, Doc. Do we look that bad? Them two got it when the stuff decided to spit on 'em clean through their armor. Me, I got me some nice burns, but I ain't complaining—I got a look at a couple of stiffs, so I'm kicking about nothing!"

Ferrel hadn't noticed the three who had traveled under their own power, but he looked now, carefully. They were burned, and badly, by radiations, but the burns were still new enough not to give them too much trouble, and probably what they'd just been through had temporarily deadened their awareness of pain, just as a soldier on the battlefield may be wounded and not realize it until the action stops. Anyway, atomjacks were not noted for sissiness.

"There's almost a quart in the office there on the table," he told them. "One good drink apiece—no more. Then go up front and I'll send Nurse Brown in to fix up your burns as well as can be for now." Brown could apply the unguents developed to heal radiation burns as well as he could, and some division of work that would relieve Jenkins and himself seemed necessary. "Any chance of finding any more living men in the converter housings?"

"Maybe. Somebody said the thing let out a groan half a minute before it popped, so most of 'em had a chance to duck into the two safety chambers. Figure on going back there and pushing tanks ourselves unless you say no; about half an hour's work left before we can crack the chambers, I guess, then we'll know."

"Good. And there's no sense in sending in every man with a burn, or we'll be flooded here; they can wait, and it looks as if we'll have plenty of serious stuff to care for. Dr. Brown, I guess you're elected to go out with the men—have one of them drive the spare litter Jones will show you. Salve down all the burn cases, put the worst ones off duty, and just send in the ones with the jerks. You'll find my emergency kit in the office, there. Someone has to be out there to give first aid and sort them out—we haven't room for the whole plant in here."

"Right, Dr. Ferrel." She let Meyers replace her in assisting Jenkins, and was gone briefly to come out with his bag. "Come on, you men. I'll hop the litter and dress down your burns on the way. You're appointed driver, mister. Somebody should have reported that Beel person before, so the litter would be out there now."

The spokesman for the others upended the glass he'd filled, swallowed, gulped, and grinned down at her. "O. K., Doctor, only out there you ain't got time to think—you gotta do. Thanks for the shot, Doc, and I'll tell Hoke you're appointing her out there."

They filed out behind Brown as Jones went out to get the second litter, and Doc went ahead with the quick-setting plastic cast for the broken leg. Too bad there weren't more of those nursing doctors; he'd have to see Palmer about it after this was over—if Palmer and he were still around. Wonder how the men in the safety chambers, about which he'd completely forgotten, would make out? There were two in each converter housing, designed as an escape for the men in case of accident, and supposed to be proof against almost anything. If the men reached them, maybe they were all right; he wouldn't have taken a bet on it, though. With a slight shrug, he finished his work and went over to help Jenkins.

The boy nodded down at the body on the table, already showing extensive scraping and probing. "Quite a bit of spitting clean through the armor," he commented. "These words were just a little too graphic for me. I-713 couldn't do that."

"Hm-m-m." Doc was in no mood to quibble on the subject. He caught himself looking at the little box in which the stuff was put after they worked what they could out of the flesh, and jerked his eyes away quickly. Whenever the lid was being dropped, a glow could be seen inside. Jenkins always managed to keep his eyes on something else.

They were almost finished when the switchboard girl announced a call, and they waited to make the few last touches before answering, then filed into the office together. Brown's face was on the screen, smudged and with a spot of rouge standing out on each cheek. Another smudge appeared as she brushed the auburn hair out of her eyes with the back of her wrist.

"They've cracked the converter safety chambers, Dr. Ferrel. The north one held up perfectly, except for the heat and a little burn, but something happened in the other; oxygen valve stuck, and all are unconscious, but alive. Magma must have sprayed through the door, because sixteen or seventeen have the jerks, and about a dozen are dead. Some others need more care than I can give—I'm having Hokusai delegate men to carry those the stretchers won't hold, and they're all piling up on you in a bunch right now!"

Ferrel grunted and nodded. "Could have been worse, I guess. Don't kill yourself out there, Brown."

"Same to you." She blew Jenkins a kiss and snapped off, just as the whine of the litter siren reached their ears.

In the surgery again, they could see a truck showing behind it, and men lifting out bodies in apparently endless succession.

"Get their armor off, somehow, Jones—grab anyone else to help you that you can. Curare, Dodd, and keep handing it to me. We'll worry about everything else after Jenkins and I quiet them." This was obviously going to be a mass-production sort of business, not for efficiency, but through sheer necessity. And again, Jenkins with his queer taut steadiness was doing two for one that Doc could do, his face pale and his eyes almost glazed, but his hands moving endlessly and nervelessly on with his work.

Sometime during the night Jenkins looked up at Meyers, and motioned her back. "Go get some sleep, nurse; Miss Dodd can take care of both Dr. Ferrel and myself when we work close together. Your nerves are shot, and you need the rest. Dodd, you can call her back in two hours and rest yourself."

"What about you, doctor?"

"Me—" He grinned out of the corner of his mouth, crookedly. "I've got an imagination that won't sleep, and I'm needed here." The sentence ended on a rising inflection that was false to Ferrel's ear, and the older doctor looked at the boy thoughtfully.

Jenkins caught his look. "It's O. K., Doc; I'll let you know when I'm going to crack. It was O. K. to send Meyers back, wasn't it?"

"You were closer to her than I was, so you should know better than I." Technically, the nurses were all directly under his control, but they'd dropped such technicalities long before. Ferrel rubbed the small of his back briefly, then picked up his scalpel again.

A faint gray light was showing in the east, and the wards had overflowed into the waiting room when the last case from the chambers was finished as best he could be. During the night, the converter had continued to spit occasionally, even through the tank armor twice, but now there was a temporary lull in the arrival of workers for treatment.

Doc sent Jones after breakfast from the cafeteria, then headed into the office where Jenkins was already slumped down in the old leather chair.

The boy was exhausted almost to the limit from the combined strain of the work and his own suppressed jitters, but he looked up in mild surprise as he felt the prick of the needle. Ferrel finished it, and used it on himself before explaining. "Morphine, of course. What else can we do? Just enough to keep us going, but without it we'll both be useless out there in a few more hours. Anyhow, there isn't as much reason not to use it as there was when I was younger, before the counter-agent was discovered to kill most of its habit-forming tendency. Even five years ago, before they had that, there were times when morphine was useful, Lord knows, though anyone who used it except as a last resort deserved all the hell he got. A real substitute for sleep would be better, though; wish they'd finish up the work they're doing on that fatigue eliminator at Harvard. Here, eat that!"

Jenkins grimaced at the breakfast Jones laid out in front of him, but he knew as well as Doc that the food was necessary, and he pulled the plate back to him. "What I'd give an eye tooth for, Doc, wouldn't be a substitute—just half an hour of good old-fashioned sleep. Only, damn it, if I knew I had time, I couldn't do it—not with R out there bubbling away."

The telephone annunciator clipped in before Doc could answer. "Telephone for Dr. Ferrel; emergency! Dr. Brown calling Dr. Ferrel!"

"Ferrel answering!" The phone girl's face popped off the screen, and a tired-faced Sue Brown looked out at them. "What is it?"

"It's that little Japanese fellow—Hokusai—who's been running things out here, Dr. Ferrel. I'm bringing him in with an acute case of appendicitis. Prepare surgery!"

Jenkins gagged over the coffee he was trying to swallow, and his choking voice was halfway between disgust and hysterical laughter. "Appendicitis, Doc! My God, what comes next?"

III

It might have been worse. Brown had coupled in the little freezing unit on the litter and lowered the temperature around the abdomen, both preparing Hokusai for surgery and slowing down the progress of the infection so that the appendix was still unbroken when he was wheeled into the surgery. His seamed Oriental face had a grayish cast under the olive, but he managed a faint grin.

"Verry ssorry, Dr. Ferrel, to bother you. Verry ssorry. No ether, pleasse!"

Ferrel grunted. "No need of it, Hoke; we'll use hypothermy, since it's already begun. Over here, Jones. . . . And you might as well go back and sit down, Jenkins."

Brown was washing, and popped out again, ready to assist with the operation. "He had to be tied down, practically, Dr. Ferrel. Insisted that he only needed a little mineral oil and some peppermint for his stomach-ache! Why are intelligent people always the most stupid?"

It was a mystery to Ferrel, too, but seemingly the case. He tested the temperature quickly while the surgery hypothermy equipment began functioning, found it low enough, and began. Hoke flinched with his eyes as the scalpel touched him, then opened them in mild surprise at feeling no appreciable pain. The complete absence of nerve response with its accompanying freedom from post-operative shock was one of the great advantages of low-temperature work in surgery. Ferrel laid back the flesh, severed the appendix quickly, and removed it through the tiny incision. Then, with one of the numerous attachments, he made use of the ingenious mechanical stitcher and stepped back.

"All finished, Hoke, and you're lucky you didn't rupture—peritonitis isn't funny even though we can cut down on it with the sulphonamides. The ward's full, so's the waiting room, so you'll have to stay on the table for a few hours until we can find a place for you; no pretty nurse, either—until the two other girls get here some time this morning. I dunno what we'll do about the patients."

"But, Dr. Ferrel, I am hear that now ssurgery—I sshould be up, already. There iss work I am do."

"You've been hearing that appendectomy patients aren't confined now, eh? Well, that's partly true. Johns Hopkins began it quite awhile ago. But for the next hour, while the temperature comes back to normal, you stay put. After that, if you want to move around a little, you can; but no going out to the converter. A little exercise probably helps more than it harms, but any strain wouldn't be good."

"But, the danger—"

"Be hanged, Hoke. You couldn't help now, long enough to do any good. Until the stuff in those stitches dissolves away completely in the body fluids, you're to take it easy—and that's two weeks, about."

The little man gave in, reluctantly. "Then I think I ssleep now. But besst you sshould call Mr. Palmer at once, pleasse! He musst know I am not there!"

Palmer took the news the hard way, with an unfair but natural tendency to blame Hokusai and Ferrel. "Damn it, Doc, I was hoping he'd get things straightened out somehow—I practically promised the Governor that Hoke could take care of it; he's got one of the best brains in the business. Now this! Well, no help, I guess. He certainly can't do it unless he's in condition to get right into things. Maybe Jorgenson, though, knows enough about it to handle it from a wheel chair, or something. How's he coming along—in shape to be taken out where he can give directions to the foremen?"

"Wait a minute." Ferrel stopped him as quickly as he could. "Jorgenson isn't here. We've got thirty-one men lying around, and he isn't one of them; and if he'd been one of the seventeen dead, you'd know it. I didn't know Jorgenson was working, even."

"He had to be—it was his process! Look, Ferrel, I was distinctly told that he was taken to you—foreman dumped him on the litter himself and reported at once! Better check up, and quick—with Hoke only half able, I've got to have Jorgenson!"

"He isn't here—I know Jorgenson. The foreman must have mistaken the big fellow from the south safety for him, but that man had black hair inside his helmet. What about the three hundred-odd that were only unconscious, or the fifteen or sixteen hundred men outside the converter when it happened?"

Palmer wiggled his jaw muscles tensely. "Jorgenson would have reported or been reported fifty times. Every man out there wants him around to boss things. He's gotta be in your ward."

"He isn't, I tell you! And how about moving some of the fellows here into the city hospitals?"

"Tried—hospitals must have been tipped off somehow about the radioactives in the flesh, and they refuse to let a man from here be brought in." Palmer was talking with only the surface of his mind, his cheek muscles bobbing as if he were chewing his thoughts and finding them tough. "Jorgenson—Hoke—and Kellar's been dead for years. Not another man in the whole country that understands this field enough to make a decent guess, even; I get lost on Page 6 myself. Ferrel, could a man in Tomlin five-shield armor suit make the safety in twenty seconds, do you think—from—say beside the converter?"

Ferrel considered it rapidly. A Tomlin weighed about four hundred pounds, and Jorgenson was an ox of a man, but only human. "Under the stress of an emergency, it's impossible to guess what a man can do, Palmer, but I don't see how he could work his way half that distance."

"Hm-m-m, I figured. Could he live, then, supposing he wasn't squashed? Those suits carry their own air for twenty-four hours, you know, to avoid any air cracks, pumping the carbon-dioxide back under pressure and condensing the moisture out—no openings of any kind. They've got the best insulation of all kinds we know, too."

"One chance in a billion, I'd guess; but again, it's darned hard to put any exact limit on what can be done—miracles keep happening, every day. Going to try it?"

"What else can I do? There's no alternative. I'll meet you outside No. 4 just as soon as you can make it, and bring everything you need to start working at once. Seconds may count!" Palmer's face slid sideways and up as he was reaching for the button, and Ferrel wasted no time in imitating the motion.

By all logic, there wasn't a chance, even in a Tomlin. But, until they knew, the effort would have to be made; chances couldn't be taken when a complicated process had gone out of control, with now almost certainty that Isotope R was the result—Palmer was concealing nothing, even though he had stated nothing specifically. And obviously, if Hoke couldn't handle it, none of the men at other branches of National Atomic or at the smaller partially independent plants could make even a half-hearted stab at the job.

It all rested on Jorgenson, then. And Jorgenson must be somewhere under that semi-molten hell that could drive through the tank armor and send men back into the Infirmary with bones broken from their own muscular anarchy!

Ferrel's face must have shown his thoughts, judging by Jenkins' startled expression. "Jorgenson's still in there somewhere," he said quickly.

"Jorgenson! But he's the man who— Good Lord!"

"Exactly. You'll stay here and take care of the jerk cases that may come in. Brown, I'll want you out there again. Bring everything portable we have, in case we can't move him in fast enough; get one of the trucks and fit it out; and be out with it about twice as fast as you can! I'm grabbing the litter now." He accepted the emergency kit Brown thrust into his hands, dumped a caffeine tablet into his mouth without bothering to wash it down, then was out toward the litter. "No. 4, and hurry!"

Palmer was just jumping off a scooter as they cut around No. 3 and in front of the rough fence of rope strung out quite a distance beyond 4. He glanced at Doc, nodded, and dived in through the men grouped around, yelling orders to right and left as he went, and was back at Ferrel's side by the time the litter had stopped.

"O. K., Ferrel, go over there and get into armor as quickly as possible! We're going in there with the tanks, whether we can or not, and be damned to the quenching for the moment. Briggs, get those things out of there, clean out a roadway as best you can, throw in the big crane again, and we'll need all the men in armor we can get—give them steel rods and get them to probing in there for anything solid and big or small enough to be a man—five minutes at a stretch; they should be able to stand that. I'll be back pronto!"

Doc noted the confused mixture of tanks and machines of all descriptions clustered around the walls—or what was left of them—of the converter housing, and saw them yanking out everything along one side, leaving an opening where the main housing gate had stood, now ripped out to expose a crane boom rooting out the worst obstructions. Obviously they'd been busy at some kind of attempt at quenching the action, but his knowledge of atomics was too little even to guess at what it was. The equipment set up was being pushed aside by tanks without dismantling, and men were running up into the roped-in section, some already armored, others dragging on part of their armor as they went. With the help of one of the atomjacks, he climbed into a suit himself, wondering what he could do in such a casing if anything needed doing.

Palmer had a suit on before him, though, and was waiting beside one of the tanks, squat and heavily armored, its front equipped with both a shovel and a grapple swinging from movable beams. "In here, Doc." Ferrel followed him into the housing of the machine and Palmer grabbed the controls as he pulled on a short-wave headset and began shouting orders through it toward the other tanks that were moving in on their heavy treads. The dull drone of the motor picked up, and the tank began lumbering forward under the manager's direction.

"Haven't run one of these since that show-off at a picnic seven years ago," he complained, as he kicked at the controls and straightened out a developing list to left. "Though I used to be pretty handy when I was plain engineer. Damned static around here almost chokes off the radio, but I guess enough gets through. By the best guess I can make, Jorgenson should have been near the main control panel when it started, and have headed for the south chamber. Half the distance, you figure?"

"Possibly, probably slightly less."

"Yeah! And then the stuff may have tossed him around. But we'll have to try to get there." He barked into the radio again. "Briggs, get those men in suits as close as you can and have them fish with their rods about thirty feet to the left of the pillar that's still up—can they get closer?"

The answer was blurred and pieces missing, but the general idea went across. Palmer frowned. "O. K., if they can't make it, they can't; draw them back out of the reach of the stuff and hold them ready to go in. . . . No, call for volunteers! I'm offering a thousand dollars a minute to every man that gets a stick in there, double to his family if the stuff gets him, and ten times that—fifty thousand—if he locates Jorgenson! . . . Look out, you blamed fool!" The last was to one of the men who'd started forward, toward the place, jumping from one piece of broken building to grab at a pillar and swing off in his suit toward something that looked like a standing position; it toppled, but he managed a leap that carried him to another lump, steadied himself, and began probing through the mess. "Oof! You with the crane—stick it in where you can grab any of the men that pass out, if it'll reach—good! Doc, I know as well as you that the men have no business in there, even five minutes; but I'll send in a hundred more if it'll find Jorgenson!"

Doc said nothing—he knew there'd probably be a hundred or more fools willing to try, and he knew the need of them. The tanks couldn't work their way close enough for any careful investigation of the mixed mass of radioactives, machinery, building debris, and destruction, aside from which they were much too slow in such delicate probing; only men equipped with the long steel poles could do that. As he watched, some of the activity of the magma suddenly caused an eruption, and one of the men tossed up his pole and doubled back into a half circle before falling. The crane operator shoved the big boom over and made a grab, missed, brought it down again, and came out with the heaving body held by one arm, to run it back along its track and twist it outward beyond Doc's vision.

Even through the tank and the suit, heat was pouring in, and there was a faint itching in those parts where the armor was thinnest that indicated the start of a burn—though not as yet dangerous. He had no desire to think what was happening to the men who were trying to worm into the heart of it in nothing but armor; nor did he care to watch what was happening to them. Palmer was trying to inch the machine ahead, but the stuff underneath made any progress difficult. Twice something spat against the tank, but did not penetrate.

"Five minutes are up," he told Palmer. "They'd all better go directly to Dr. Brown, who should be out with the truck now for immediate treatment."

Palmer nodded and relayed the instructions. "Pick up all you can with the crane and carry them back! Send in a new bunch, Briggs, and credit them with their bonus in advance. Damn it, Doc, this can go on all day; it'll take an hour to pry around through this mess right here, and then he's probably somewhere else. The stuff seems to be getting worse in this neighborhood, too, from what accounts I've had before. Wonder if that steel plate could be pushed down?"

He threw in the clutch engaging the motor to the treads and managed to twist through toward it. There was a slight slipping of the lugs, then the tractors caught, and the nose of the tank thrust forward; almost without effort, the fragment of housing toppled from its leaning position and slid forward. The tank growled, fumbled, and slowly climbed up onto it and ran forward another twenty feet to its end; the support settled slowly, but something underneath checked it, and they were still again. Palmer worked the grapple forward, nosing a big piece of masonry out of the way, and two men reached out with the ends of their poles to begin probing, futilely. Another change of men came out, then another.

Briggs' voice crackled erratically through the speaker again. "Palmer, I got a fool here who wants to go out on the end of your beam, if you can swing around so the crane can lift him out to it."

"Start him coming!" Again he began jerking the levers, and the tank bucked and heaved, backed and turned, ran forward, and repeated it all, while the plate that was holding them flopped up and down on its precarious balance.

Doc held his breath and began praying to himself; his admiration for the men who'd go out in that stuff was increasing by leaps and bounds, along with his respect for Palmer's ability.

The crane boom bobbed toward them, and the scoop came running out, but wouldn't quite reach; their own tank was relatively light and mobile compared to the bigger machine, but Palmer already had that pushed out to the limit, and hanging over the edge of the plate. It still lacked three feet of reaching.

"Damn!" Palmer slapped open the door of the tank, jumped forward on the tread, and looked down briefly before coming back inside. "No chance to get closer! Wheeoo! Those men earn their money."

But the crane operator had his own tricks, and was bobbing the boom of his machine up and down slowly with a motion that set the scoop swinging like a huge pendulum, bringing it gradually closer to the grapple beam. The man had an arm out, and finally caught the beam, swinging out instantly from the scoop that drew backward behind him. He hung suspended for a second, pitching his body around to a better position, then somehow wiggled up onto the end and braced himself with his legs. Doc let his breath out and Palmer inched the tank around to a forward position again. Now the pole of the atomjack could cover the wide territory before them, and he began using it rapidly.

"Win or lose, that man gets a triple bonus," Palmer muttered. "Uh!"

The pole had located something, and was feeling around to determine size; the man glanced at them and pointed frantically. Doc jumped forward to the windows as Palmer ran down the grapple and began pushing it down into the semi-molten stuff under the pole; there was resistance there, but finally the prong of the grapple broke under and struck on something that refused to come up. The manager's hands moved the controls gently, making it tug from side to side; reluctantly, it gave and moved forward toward them, coming upward until they could make out the general shape. It was definitely no Tomlin suit!

"Lead hopper box! Damn— Wait, Jorgenson wasn't anybody's fool; when he saw he couldn't make the safety, he might . . . maybe—" Palmer slapped the grapple down again, against the closed lid of the chest, but the hook was too large. Then the man clinging there caught the idea and slid down to the hopper chest, his armored hands grabbing at the lid. He managed to lift a corner of it until the grapple could catch and lift it the rest of the way, and his hands started down to jerk upward again.

The manager watched his motions, then flipped the box over with the grapple, and pulled it closer to the tank body; magma was running out, but there was a gleam of something else inside.

"Start praying, Doc!" Palmer worked it to the side of the tank and was out through the door again, letting the merciless heat and radiation stream in.

But Ferrel wasn't bothering with that now; he followed, reaching down into the chest to help the other two lift out the body of a huge man in a five-shield Tomlin! Somehow, they wangled the six-hundred-odd pounds out and up on the treads, then into the housing, barely big enough for all of them. The atomjack pulled himself inside, shut the door, and flopped forward on his face, out cold.

"Never mind him—check Jorgenson!" Palmer's voice was heavy with the reaction from the hunt, but he turned the tank and sent it outward at top speed, regardless of risk. Contrarily, it buckled through the mass more readily than it had crawled in through the cleared section.

Ferrel unscrewed the front plate of the armor on Jorgenson as rapidly as he could, though he knew already that the man was still miraculously alive—corpses don't jerk with force enough to move a four-hundred-pound suit appreciably. A side glance, as they drew beyond the wreck of the converter housing, showed the men already beginning to set up equipment to quell the atomic reaction again, but the armor front plate came loose at last, and he dropped his eyes back without noticing details, to cut out a section of clothing and made the needed injections; curare first, then neo-heroin, and curare again, though he did not dare inject the quantity that seemed necessary. There was nothing more he could do until they could get the man out of his armor. He turned to the atomjack, who was already sitting up, propped against the driving seat's back.

" 'Snothing much, Doc," the fellow managed. "No jerks, just burn and that damned heat! Jorgenson?"

"Alive at least," Palmer answered, with some relief. The tank stopped, and Ferrel could see Brown running forward from beside a truck. "Get that suit off you, get yourself treated for the burn, then go up to the office where the check will be ready for you!"

"Fifty-thousand check?" The doubt in the voice registered over the weakness.

"Fifty thousand plus triple your minute time, and cheap; maybe we'll toss in a medal or a bottle of Scotch, too. Here, you fellows give a hand."

Ferrel had the suit ripped off with Brown's assistance, and paused only long enough for one grateful breath of clean, cool air before leading the way toward the truck. As he neared it, Jenkins popped out, directing a group of men to move two loaded stretchers onto the litter, and nodding jerkily at Ferrel. "With the truck all equipped, we decided to move out here and take care of the damage as it came up— Sue and I rushed them through enough to do until we can find more time, so we could give full attention to Jorgenson. He's still living!"

"By a miracle. Stay out here, Brown, until you've finished with the men from inside, then we'll try to find some rest for you."

The three huskies carrying Jorgenson placed the body on the table set up, and began ripping off the bulky armor as the truck got under way. Fresh gloves came out of a small sterilizer, and the two doctors fell to work at once, treating the badly burned flesh and trying to locate and remove the worst of the radioactive matter.

"No use." Doc stepped back and shook his head. "It's all over him, probably clear into his bones in places. We'd have to put him through a filter to get it all out!"

Palmer was looking down at the raw mass of flesh, with all the layman's sickness at such a sight. "Can you fix him up, Ferrel?"

"We can try, that's all. Only explanation I can give for his being alive at all is that the hopper box must have been pretty well above the stuff until a short time ago—very short—and this stuff didn't work in until it sank. He's practically dehydrated now, apparently, but he couldn't have perspired enough to keep from dying of heat if he'd been under all that for even an hour—insulation or no insulation." There was admiration in Doc's eyes as he looked down at the immense figure of the man. "And he's tough; if he weren't, he'd have killed himself by exhaustion, even confined inside that suit and box, after the jerks set in. He's close to having done so, anyway. Until we can find some way of getting that stuff out of him, we don't dare risk getting rid of the curare's effect—that's a time-consuming job, in itself. Better give him another water and sugar intravenous, Jenkins. Then, if we do fix him up, Palmer, I'd say it's a fifty-fifty chance whether or not all this hasn't driven him stark crazy."

The truck had stopped, and the men lifted the stretcher off and carried it inside as Jenkins finished the injection. He went ahead of them, but Doc stopped outside to take Palmer's cigarette for a long drag, and let them go ahead.

"Cheerful!" The manager lighted another from the butt, his shoulders sagging. "I've been trying to think of one man who might possibly be of some help to us, Doc, and there isn't such a person —anywhere. I'm sure now, after being in there, that Hoke couldn't do it. Kellar, if he were still alive, could probably pull the answer out of a hat after three looks—he had an instinct and genius for it; the best man the business ever had, even if his tricks did threaten to steal our work out from under us and give him the lead. But—well, now there's Jorgenson—either he gets in shape, or else!"

Jenkins' frantic yell reached them suddenly. "Doc! Jorgenson's dead! He's stopped breathing entirely!"

Doc jerked forward into a full run, a white-faced Palmer at his heels.

IV

Dodd was working artificial respiration and Jenkins had the oxygen mask in his hands, adjusting it over Jorgenson's face, before Ferrel reached the table. He made a grab for the pulse that had been fluttering weakly enough before, felt it flicker feebly once, pause for about three times normal period, lift feebly again, and then stop completely. "Adrenalin!"

"Already shot it into his heart, Doc! Cardiacine, too!" The boy's voice was bordering on hysteria, but Palmer was obviously closer to it than Jenkins.

"Doc, you gotta—"

"Get the hell out of here!" Ferrel's hands suddenly had a life of their own as he grabbed frantically for instruments, ripped bandages off the man's chest, and began working against time, when time had all the advantages. It wasn't surgery—hardly good butchery; the bones that he cut through so ruthlessly with savage strokes of an instrument could never heal smoothly after being so mangled. But he couldn't worry about minor details now.

He tossed back the flap of flesh and ribs that he'd hacked out. "Stop the bleeding, Jenkins!" Then his hands plunged into the chest cavity, somehow finding room around Dodd's and Jenkins', and were

suddenly incredibly gentle as they located the heart and began working on it, the skilled, exact massage of a man who knew every function
of the vital organ. Pressure here, there, relax, pressure again; take it
easy, don't rush things! It would do no good to try to set it going as
feverishly as his emotions demanded. Pure oxygen was feeding into
the lungs, and the heart could safely do less work. Hold it steady, one
beat a second, sixty a minute.

It had been perhaps half a minute from the time the heart stopped
before his massage was circulating blood again; too little time to
worry about damage to the brain, the first part to be permanently affected by stoppage of the circulation. Now, if the heart could start
again by itself within any reasonable time, death would be cheated
again. How long? He had no idea. They'd taught him ten minutes
when he was studying medicine, then there'd been a case of twenty
minutes once, and while he was interning it had been pushed up to a
record of slightly over an hour, which still stood; but that was an exceptional case. Jorgenson, praise be, was a normally healthy and
vigorous specimen, and his system had been in first-class condition,
but with the torture of those long hours, the radioactive, narcotic and
curare all fighting against him, still one more miracle was needed to
keep his life going.

Press, massage, relax, don't hurry it too much. There! For a second, his fingers felt a·faint flutter, then again; but it stopped. Still, as
long as the organ could show such signs, there was hope, unless his
fingers grew too tired and he muffed the job before the moment when
the heart could be safely trusted by itself.

"Jenkins!"

"Yes, sir!"

"Ever do any heart massage?"

"Practiced it in school, sir, on a model, but never actually. Oh, a
dog in dissection class, for five minutes. I . . . I don't think you'd
better trust me, Doc."

"I may have to. If you did it on a dog for five minutes, you can do it
on a man, probably. You know what hangs on it—you saw the converter and know what's going on."

Jenkins nodded, the tense nod he'd used earlier. "I know—that's
why you can't trust me. I told you I'd let you know when I was going
to crack—well, it's damned near here!"

Could a man tell his weakness, if he were about finished? Doc
didn't know; he suspected that the boy's own awareness of his nerves

would speed up such a break, if anything, but Jenkins was a queer case, having taut nerves sticking out all over him, yet a steadiness under fire that few older men could have equaled. If he had to use him, he would; there was no other answer.

Doc's fingers were already feeling stiff—not yet tired, but showing signs of becoming so. Another few minutes, and he'd have to stop. There was the flutter again, one—two—three! Then it stopped. There had to be some other solution to this; it was impossible to keep it up for the length of time probably needed, even if he and Jenkins spelled each other. Only Michel at Mayo's could—Mayo's! If they could get it here in time, that wrinkle he'd seen demonstrated at their last medical convention was the answer.

"Jenkins, call Mayo's—you'll have to get Palmer's O. K., I guess— ask for Kubelik, and bring the extension where I can talk to him!"

He could hear Jenkins' voice, level enough at first, then with a depth of feeling he'd have thought impossible in the boy. Dodd looked at him quickly and managed a grim smile, even as she continued with the respiration; nothing could make her blush, though it should have done so.

The boy jumped back. "No soap, Doc! Palmer can't be located— and that post-mortem misconception at the board won't listen."

Doc studied his hands in silence, wondering, then gave it up; there'd be no hope of his lasting while he sent out the boy. "O. K., Jenkins, you'll have to take over here, then. Steady does it, come on in slowly, get your fingers over mine. Now, catch the motion? Easy, don't rush things. You'll hold out—you'll have to! You've done better than I had any right to ask for so far, and you don't need to distrust yourself. There, got it?"

"Got it, Doc. I'll try, but for Pete's sake, whatever you're planning, get back here quick! I'm not lying about cracking! You'd better let Meyers replace Dodd and have Sue called back in here; she's the best nerve tonic I know."

"Call her in then, Dodd." Doc picked up a hypodermic syringe, filled it quickly with water to which a drop of another liquid added a brownish-yellow color, and forced his tired old legs into a reasonably rapid trot out of the side door and toward Communications. Maybe the switchboard operator was stubborn, but there were ways of handling people.

He hadn't counted on the guard outside the Communications Building, though. "Halt!"

"Life or death; I'm a physician."

"Not in here—I got orders." The bayonet's menace apparently wasn't enough; the rifle went up to the man's shoulder, and his chin jutted out with the stubbornness of petty authority and reliance on orders. "Nobody sick here. There's plenty of phones elsewhere. You get back—and fast!"

Doc started forward and there was a faint click from the rifle as the safety went off; the darned fool meant what he said. Shrugging, Ferrel stepped back—and brought the hypodermic needle up inconspicuously in line with the guard's face. "Ever see one of these things squirt curare? It can reach you before your bullet hits!"

"Curare?" The guard's eyes flicked to the needle, and doubt came into them. The man frowned. "That's the stuff that kills people on arrows, ain't it?"

"It is—cobra venom, you know. One drop on the outside of your skin and you're dead in ten seconds." Both statements were out-and-out lies, but Doc was counting on the superstitious ignorance of the average man in connection with poisons. "This little needle can spray you with it very nicely, and it may be a fast death, but not a pleasant one. Want to put down the rifle?"

A regular might have shot; but the militiaman was taking no chances. He lowered the rifle gingerly, his eyes on the needle, then kicked the weapon aside at Doc's motion. Ferrel approached, holding the needle out, and the man shrank backward and away, letting him pick up the rifle as he went past to avoid being shot in the back. Lost time! But he knew his way around this little building, at least, and went straight toward the girl at the board.

"Get up!" His voice came from behind her shoulder and she turned to see the rifle in one of his hands, the needle in the other, almost touching her throat. "This is loaded with curare, deadly poison, and too much hangs on getting a call through to bother with physician's oaths right now, young lady. Up! No plugs! That's right; now get over there, out of the cell—there, on your face, cross your hands behind your back, and grab your ankles—right! Now if you move, you won't move long!"

Those gangster pictures he'd seen were handy, at that. She was thoroughly frightened and docile. But, perhaps, not so much so she might not have bungled his call deliberately. He had to do that himself. Darn it, the red lights were trunk lines, but which plug—try the inside one, it looked more logical; he'd seen it done, but couldn't remember. Now, you flip back one of these switches—uh-uh, the other way. The tone came in assuring him he had it right, and he dialed operator rapidly, his eyes flickering toward the girl lying on the floor, his thoughts on Jenkins and the wasted time running on.

"Operator, this is an emergency. I'm Walnut 7654; I want to put in a long-distance call to Dr. Kubelik, Mayo's Hospital, Rochester, Minnesota. If Kubelik isn't there, I'll take anyone else who answers from his department. Speed is urgent."

"Very good, sir." Long-distance operators, mercifully, were usually efficient. There were the repeated signals and clicks of relays as she put it through, the answer from the hospital board, more wasted time, and then a face appeared on the screen; but not that of Kubelik. It was a much younger man.

Ferrel wasted no time in introduction. "I've got an emergency case here where all Hades depends on saving a man, and it can't be done without that machine of Dr. Kubelik's; he knows me, if he's there— I'm Ferrel, met him at the convention, got him to show me how the thing worked."

"Kubelik hasn't come in yet, Dr. Ferrel; I'm his assistant. But, if you mean the heart and lung exciter, it's already boxed and supposed to leave for Harvard this morning. They've got a rush case out there, and may need it—"

"Not as much as I do."

"I'll have to call— Wait a minute, Dr. Ferrel, seems I remember your name now. Aren't you the chap with National Atomic?"

Doc nodded. "The same. Now, about that machine, if you'll stop the formalities—"

The face on the screen nodded, instant determination showing, with an underlying expression of something else. "We'll ship it down to you instantly, Ferrel. Got a field for a plane?"

"Not within three miles, but I'll have a truck sent out for it. How long?"

"Take too long by truck if you need it down there, Ferrel; I'll arrange to transship in air from our special speedster to a helicopter, have it delivered wherever you want. About—um, loading plane, flying a couple hundred miles, transshipping—about half an hour's the best we can do."

"Make it the square of land south of the Infirmary, which is crossed visibly from the air. Thanks!"

"Wait, Dr. Ferrel!" The younger man checked Doc's cut-off. "Can you use it when you get it? It's tricky work."

"Kubelik gave quite a demonstration and I'm used to tricky work. I'll chance it—have to. Too long to rouse Kubelik himself, isn't it?"

"Probably. O. K., I've got the telescript reply from the shipping office, it's starting for the plane. I wish you luck!"

Ferrel nodded his thanks, wondering. Service like that was welcome, but it wasn't the most comforting thing, mentally, to know that the mere mention of National Atomic would cause such an about-face. Rumors, it seemed, were spreading, and in a hurry, in spite of Palmer's best attempts. Good Lord, what was going on here? He'd been too busy for any serious worrying or to realize, but —well, it had gotten him the exciter, and for that he should be thankful.

The guard was starting uncertainly off for reinforcements when Doc came out, and he realized that the seemingly endless call must have been over in short order. He tossed the rifle well out of the man's reach and headed back toward the Infirmary at a run, wondering how Jenkins had made out—it had to be all right!

Jenkins wasn't standing over the body of Jorgenson; Brown was there instead, her eyes moist and her face pinched in and white around the nostrils that stood out at full width. She looked up, shook her head at him as he started forward, and went on working at Jorgenson's heart.

"Jenkins cracked?"

"Nonsense! This is woman's work, Dr. Ferrel, and I took over for him, that's all. You men try to use brute force all your life and then wonder why a woman can do twice as much delicate work where strong muscles are a nuisance. I chased him out and took over, that's all." But there was a catch in her voice as she said it, and Meyers was looking down entirely too intently at the work of artificial respiration.

"Hi, Doc!" It was Blake's voice that broke in. "Get away from there; when this Dr. Brown needs help, I'll be right in there. I've been sleeping like a darned fool all night, from four this morning on. Didn't hear the phone, or something, didn't know what was going on until I got to the gate out there. You go rest."

Ferrel grunted in relief; Blake might have been dead drunk when he finally reached home, which would explain his not hearing the phone, but his animal virility had soaked it out with no visible sign. The only change was the absence of the usual cocky grin on his face as he moved over beside Brown to test Jorgenson. "Thank the Lord you're here, Blake. How's Jorgenson doing?"

Brown's voice answered in a monotone, words coming in time to the motions of her fingers. "His heart shows signs of coming around once in a while, but it doesn't last. He isn't getting worse from what I can tell, though."

"Good. If we can keep him going half an hour more, we can turn all this over to a machine. Where's Jenkins?"

"A machine? Oh, the Kubelik exciter, of course. He was working on it when I was there. We'll keep Jorgenson alive until then, anyway, Dr. Ferrel."

"Where's Jenkins?" he repeated sharply, when she stopped with no intention of answering the former question.

Blake pointed toward Ferrel's office, the door of which was now closed. "In there. But lay off him, Doc. I saw the whole thing, and he feels like the deuce about it. He's a good kid, but only a kid, and this kind of hell could get any of us."

"I know all that." Doc headed toward the office, as much for a smoke as anything else. The sight of Blake's rested face was somehow an island of reassurance in this sea of fatigue and nerves. "Don't worry, Brown, I'm not planning on lacing him down, so you needn't defend your man so carefully. It was my fault for not listening to him."

Brown's eyes were pathetically grateful in the brief flash she threw him, and he felt like a heel for the gruffness that had been his first reaction toward Jenkins' absence. If this kept on much longer, though, they'd all be in worse shape than the boy, whose back was toward him as he opened the door. The still, huddled shape did not raise its head from its arms as Ferrel put his hand onto one shoulder, and the voice was muffled and distant.

"I cracked, Doc—high, wide and handsome, all over the place. I couldn't take it! Standing there, Jorgenson maybe dying because I couldn't control myself right, the whole plant blowing up, all my fault. I kept telling myself I was O. K., I'd go on, then I cracked. Screamed like a baby! Dr. Jenkins—nerve specialist!"

"Yeah. . . . Here, are you going to drink this, or do I have to hold your blasted nose and pour it down your throat?" It was crude psychology, but it worked, and Doc handed over the drink, waited for the other to down it, and passed a cigarette across before sinking into his own chair. "You warned me, Jenkins, and I risked it on my own responsibility, so nobody's kicking. But I'd like to ask a couple of questions."

"Go ahead—what's the difference?" Jenkins had recovered a little, obviously, from the note of defiance that managed to creep into his voice.

"Did you know Brown could handle that kind of work? And did you pull your hands out before she could get hers in to replace them?"

"She told me she could. I didn't know before. I dunno about the other; I think . . . yeah, Doc, she had her hands over mine. But—"

Ferrel nodded, satisfied with his own guess. "I thought so. You didn't crack, as you put it, until your mind knew it was safe to do so—and then you simply passed the work on. By that definition, I'm cracking, too. I'm sitting in here, smoking, talking to you, when out there a man needs attention. The fact that he's getting it from two others, one practically fresh, the other at least a lot better off than we are, doesn't have a thing to do with it, does it?"

"But it wasn't that way, Doc. I'm not asking for grandstand stuff from anybody."

"Nobody's giving it to you, son. All right, you screamed—why not? It didn't hurt anything. I growled at Brown when I came in for the same reason—exhausted, overstrained nerves. If I went out there and had to take over from them, I'd probably scream myself, or start biting my tongue—nerves have to have an outlet; physically, it does them no good, but there's a psychological need for it." The boy wasn't convinced, and Doc sat back in the chair, staring at him thoughtfully. "Ever wonder why I'm here?"

"No, sir."

"Well, you might. Twenty-seven years ago, when I was about your age, there wasn't a surgeon in this country—or the world, for that matter—who had the reputation I had; any kind of surgery, brain, what have you. They're still using some of my techniques . . . uh-hum, thought you'd remember when the association of names hit you. I had a different wife then, Jenkins, and there was a baby coming. Brain tumor—I had to do it, no one else could. I did it, somehow, but I went out of that operating room in a haze, and it was three days later when they'd tell me she'd died; not my fault—I know that now—but I couldn't realize it then.

"So, I tried setting up as a general practitioner. No more surgery for me! And because I was a fair diagnostician, which most surgeons aren't, I made a living, at least. Then, when this company was set up, I applied for the job, and got it; I still had a reputation of sorts. It was a new field, something requiring study and research, and damned near every ability of most specialists plus a general practitioner's, so it kept me busy enough to get over my phobia of surgery. Compared to me, you don't know what nerves or cracking means. That little scream was a minor incident."

Jenkins made no comment, but lighted the cigarette he'd been holding. Ferrel relaxed farther into the chair, knowing that he'd be called if there was any need for his work, and glad to get his mind at least partially off Jorgenson. "It's hard to find a man for this work, Jenkins. It takes too much ability at too many fields, even though it pays well enough. We went through plenty of applicants before we decided on you, and I'm not regretting our choice. As a matter of fact, you're better equipped for the job than Blake was—your record looked as if you'd deliberately tried for this kind of work."

"I did."

"Hm-m-m." That was the one answer Doc had least expected; so far as he knew, no one deliberately tried for a job at Atomics—they usually wound up trying for it after comparing their receipts for a year or so with the salary paid by National. "Then you knew what was needed and picked it up in toto. Mind if I ask why?"

Jenkins shrugged. "Why not? Turnabout's fair play. It's kind of complicated, but the gist of it doesn't take much telling. Dad had an atomic plant of his own—and a darned good one, too, Doc, even if it wasn't as big as National. I was working in it when I was fifteen, and I went through two years of university work in atomics with the best intentions of carrying on the business. Sue—well, she was the neighbor girl I followed around, and we had money at the time; that wasn't why she married me, though. I never did figure that out— she'd had a hard enough life, but she was already holding down a job at Mayo's, and I was just a raw kid. Anyway—

"The day we came home from our honeymoon, Dad got a big contract on a new process we'd worked out. It took some swinging, but he got the equipment and started it. . . . My guess is that one of the controls broke through faulty construction; the process was right! We'd been over it too often not to know what it would do. But, when the estate was cleared up, I had to give up the idea of a degree in atomics, and Sue was back working at the hospital. Atomic courses

cost real money. Then one of Sue's medical acquaintances fixed it
for me to get a scholarship in medicine that almost took care of it,
so I chose the next best thing to what I wanted."

"National and one of the biggest competitors—if you can call it that
—are permitted to give degrees in atomics," Doc reminded the boy.
The field was still too new to be a standing university course, and
there were no better teachers in the business than such men as
Palmer, Hokusai and Jorgenson. "They pay a salary while you're
learning, too."

"Hm-m-m. Takes ten years that way, and the salary's just enough
for a single man. No, I'd married Sue with the intention she wouldn't
have to work again; well, she did until I finished internship, but I
knew if I got the job here I could support her. As an atomjack, working up to an engineer, the prospects weren't so good. We're saving
a little money now, and some day maybe I'll get a crack at it yet. . . .
Doc, what's this all about? You babying me out of my fit?"

Ferrel grinned at the boy. "Nothing else, son, though I was curious.
And it worked. Feel all right now, don't you?"

"Mostly, except for what's going on out there—I got too much of
a look at it from the truck. Oh, I could use some sleep, I guess, but
I'm O. K. again."

"Good." Doc had profited almost as much as Jenkins from the
rambling off-trail talk, and had managed more rest from it than from
nursing his own thoughts. "Suppose we go out and see how they're
making out with Jorgenson? Um, what happened to Hoke, come to
think of it?"

"Hoke? Oh, he's in my office now, figuring out things with a pencil
and paper since we wouldn't let him go back out there. I was
wondering—"

"Atomics? . . . Then suppose you go in and talk to him; he's a
good guy, and he won't give you the brush-off. Nobody else around
here apparently suspected this Isotope R business, and you might
offer a fresh lead for him. With Blake and the nurses here and the
men out of the mess except for the tanks, there's not much you can
do to help on my end."

Ferrel felt better at peace with the world than he had since the
call from Palmer as he watched Jenkins head off across the surgery
toward his office; and the glance that Brown threw, first toward the
boy, then back at Doc, didn't make him feel worse. That girl could
say more with her eyes than most women could with their mouths!

He went over toward the operating table where Blake was now working the heart massage with one of the fresh nurses attending to respiration and casting longing glances toward the mechanical lung apparatus; it couldn't be used in this case, since Jorgenson's chest had to be free for heart attention.

Blake looked up, his expression worried. "This isn't so good, Doc. He's been sinking in the last few minutes. I was just going to call you. I—"

The last words were drowned out by the bull-throated drone that came dropping down from above them, a sound peculiarly characteristic of the heavy Sikorsky freighters with their modified blades to gain lift. Ferrel nodded at Brown's questioning glance, but he didn't choose to shout as his hands went over those of Blake and took over the delicate work of simulating the natural heart action. As Blake withdrew, the sound stopped, and Doc motioned him out with his head.

"You'd better go to them and oversee bringing in the apparatus—and grab up any of the men you see to act as porters—or send Jones for them. The machine is an experimental model, and pretty cumbersome; must weigh seven or eight hundred pounds."

"I'll get them myself—Jones is sleeping."

There was no flutter to Jorgenson's heart under Doc's deft manipulations, though he was exerting every bit of skill he possessed. "How long since there was a sign?"

"About four minutes, now. Doc, is there still a chance?"

"Hard to say. Get the machine, though, and we'll hope."

But still the heart refused to respond, though the pressure and manipulation kept the blood circulating and would at least prevent any starving or asphyxiation of the body cells. Carefully, delicately, he brought his mind into his fingers, trying to woo a faint quiver. Perhaps he did, once, but he couldn't be sure. It all depended on how quickly they could get the machine working now, and how long a man could live by manipulation alone. That point was still unsettled.

But there was no question about the fact that the spark of life burned faintly and steadily lower in Jorgenson, while outside the man-made hell went on ticking off the minutes that separated it from becoming Mahler's Isotope. Normally, Doc was an agnostic, but now, unconsciously, his mind slipped back into the simple faith of his childhood, and he heard Brown echoing the prayer that was on his lips. The second hand of the watch before him swung around and around and around again before he heard the sound of men's feet at the back entrance, and still there was no definite quiver from the heart under his fingers. How much time did he have left, if any, for the difficult and unfamiliar operation required?

His side glance showed the seemingly innumerable filaments of platinum that had to be connected into the nerves governing Jorgenson's heart and lungs, all carefully coded, yet almost terrifying in their complexity. If he made a mistake anywhere, it was at least certain there would be no time for a second trial; if his fingers shook or his tired eyes clouded at the wrong instant, there would be no help from Jorgenson. Jorgenson would be dead!

V

"Take over massage, Brown," he ordered. "And keep it up no matter what happens. Good. Dodd, assist me, and hang onto my signals. If it works, we can rest afterward."

Ferrel wondered grimly with that part of his mind that was off by itself whether he could justify his boast to Jenkins of having been the world's greatest surgeon; it had been true once, he knew with no need for false modesty, but that was long ago, and this was at best a devilish job. He'd hung on with a surge of the old fascination as Kubelik had performed it on a dog at the convention, and his memory for such details was still good, as were his hands. But something else goes into the making of a great surgeon, and he wondered if that were still with him.

Then, as his fingers made the microscopic little motions needed and Dodd became another pair of hands, he ceased wondering. Whatever it was, he could feel it surging through him, and there was a pure joy to it somewhere, over and above the urgency of the work. This was probably the last time he'd ever feel it, and if the operation succeeded, probably it was a thing he could put with the few mental treasures that were still left from his former success. The man on the table ceased to be Jorgenson, the excessively gadgety Infirmary became again the main operating theater of that same Mayo's which had produced Brown and this strange new machine, and his fingers were again those of the Great Ferrel, the miracle boy from Mayo's, who could do the impossible twice before breakfast without turning a hair.

Some of his feeling was devoted to the machine itself. Massive, ugly, with parts sticking out in haphazard order, it was more like something from an inquisition chamber than a scientist's achievement, but it worked—he'd seen it functioning. In that ugly mass of assorted pieces, little currents were generated and modulated to feed out to the heart and lungs and replace the orders given by a brain that no longer worked or could not get through, to coordinate breathing and beating according to the need. It was a product of the combined genius of surgery and electronics, but wonderful as the exciter was, it was distinctly secondary to the technique Kubelik had evolved for selecting and connecting only those nerves and nerve bundles necessary, and bringing the almost impossible into the limits of surgical possibility.

Brown interrupted, and that interruption in the midst of such an operation indicated clearly the strain she was under. "The heart fluttered a little then, Dr. Ferrel."

Ferrel nodded, untroubled by the interruption. Talk, which bothered most surgeons, was habitual in his own little staff, and he always managed to have one part of his mind reserved for that while the rest went on without noticing. "Good. That gives us at least double the leeway I expected."

His hands went on, first with the heart which was the more pressing danger. Would the machine work, he wondered, in this case? Curare and radioactives, fighting each other, were an odd combination. Yet, the machine controlled the nerves close to the vital organ, pounding its message through into the muscles, where the curare had a complicated action that paralyzed the whole nerve, establishing a long block to the control impulses from the brain. Could the nerve impulses from the machine be forced through the short paralyzed passages? Probably—the strength of its signals was controllable. The only proof was in trying.

Brown drew back her hands and stared down uncomprehendingly. "It's beating, Dr. Ferrel! By itself . . . it's beating!"

He nodded again, though the mask concealed his smile. His technique was still not faulty, and he had performed the operation correctly after seeing it once on a dog! He was still the Great Ferrel! Then, the ego in him fell back to normal, though the lift remained, and his exultation centered around the more important problem of Jorgenson's living. And, later, when the lungs began moving of themselves as the nurse stopped working them, he had been expecting it. The detail work remaining was soon over, and he stepped back, dropping the mask from his face and pulling off his gloves.

"Congratulations, Dr. Ferrel!" The voice was guttural, strange. "A truly great operation—truly great. I almost stopped you, but now I am glad I did not; it was a pleasure to observe you, sir." Ferrel looked up in amazement at the bearded smiling face of Kubelik, and he found no words as he accepted the other's hand. But Kubelik apparently expected none.

"I, Kubelik, came, you see; I could not trust another with the machine, and fortunately I made the plane. Then you seemed so sure, so confident—so when you did not notice me, I remained in the background, cursing myself. Now, I shall return, since you have no need of me—the wiser for having watched you. . . . No, not a word; not a word from you, sir. Don't destroy your miracle with words. The 'copter waits me, I go; but my admiration for you remains forever!"

Ferrel still stood looking down at his hand as the roar of the 'copter cut in, then at the breathing body with the artery on the neck now pulsing regularly. That was all that was needed; he had been admired by Kubelik, the man who thought all other surgeons were fools and nincompoops. For a second or so longer he treasured it, then shrugged it off.

"Now," he said to the others, as the troubles of the plant fell back on his shoulders, "all we have to do is hope that Jorgenson's brain wasn't injured by the session out there, or by this continued artificially maintained life, and try to get him in condition so he can talk before it's too late. God grant us time! Blake, you know the detail work as well as I do, and we can't both work on it. You and the fresh nurses take over, doing the bare minimum needed for the patients scattered around the wards and waiting room. Any new ones?"

"None for some time; I think they've reached a stage where that's over with," Brown answered.

"I hope so. Then go round up Jenkins and lie down somewhere. That goes for you and Meyers, too, Dodd. Blake, give us three hours if you can, and get us up. There won't be any new developments before then, and we'll save time in the long run by resting. Jorgenson's to get first attention!"

The old leather chair made a fair sort of bed, and Ferrel was too exhausted physically and mentally to be choosy—too exhausted to benefit as much as he should from sleep of three hours' duration, for that matter, though it was almost imperative he try. Idly, he wondered what Palmer would think of all his safeguards had he known that Kubelik had come into the place so easily and out again. Not that it mattered; it was doubtful whether anyone else would want to come near, let alone inside the plant.

In that, apparently, he was wrong. It was considerably less than the three hours when he was awakened to hear the bull-roar of a helicopter outside. But sleep clouded his mind too much for curiosity and he started to drop back into his slumber. Then another sound cut in jerking him out of his drowsiness. It was the sharp sputter of a machine gun from the direction of the gate, a pause and another burst; an eddy of sleep-memory indicated that it had begun before the helicopter's arrival, so it could not be that they were gunning. More trouble, and while it was none of his business, he could not go back to sleep. He got up and went out into the surgery, just as a gnomish little man hopped out from the rear entrance.

The fellow scooted toward Ferrel after one birdlike glance at Blake, his words spilling out with a jerky self-importance that should have been funny, but missed it by a small margin; under the surface, sincerity still managed to show. "Dr. Ferrel? Uh, Dr. Kubelik—Mayo's, you know—he reported you were short-handed; stacking patients in the other rooms. We volunteered for duty—me, four other doctors, nine nurses. Probably should have checked with you, but couldn't get a phone through. Took the liberty of coming through directly, fast as we could push our 'copters."

Ferrel glanced through the back, and saw that there were three of the machines, instead of the one he'd thought, with men and equipment piling out of them. Mentally he kicked himself for not asking help when he'd put through the call; but he'd been used to working with his own little staff for so long that the ready response of his profession to emergencies had been almost forgotten. "You know you're taking chances coming here, naturally? Then, in that case, I'm grateful to you and Kubelik. We've got about forty patients here, all of whom should have considerable attention, though I frankly doubt whether there's room for you to work."

The man hitched his thumb backward jerkily. "Don't worry about that. Kubelik goes the limit when he arranges things. Everything we need with us, practically all the hospital's atomic equipment; though maybe you'll have to piece us out there. Even a field hospital tent, portable wards for every patient you have. Want relief in here or would you rather have us simply move out the patients to the tent, leave this end to you? Oh, Kubelik sent his regards. Amazing of him!"

Kubelik, it seemed, had a tangible idea of regards, however dramatically he was inclined to express them; with him directing the volunteer force, the wonder was that the whole staff and equipment hadn't been moved down. "Better leave this end," Ferrel decided. "Those in the wards will probably be better off in your tent as well as the men now in the waiting room; we're equipped beautifully for all emergency work, but not used to keeping the patients here any length of time, so our accommodations that way are rough. Dr. Blake will show you around and help you get organized in the routine we use here. He'll get help for you in erecting the tent, too. By the way, did you hear the commotion by the entrance as you were landing?"

"We did, indeed. We saw it, too—bunch of men in some kind of uniform shooting a machine gun; hitting the ground, though. Bunch of other people running back away from it, shaking their fists, looked like. We were expecting a dose of the same, maybe; didn't notice us, though."

Blake snorted in half amusement. "You probably would have gotten it if our manager hadn't forgotten to give orders covering the air approach; they must figure that's an official route. I saw a bunch from the city arguing about their relatives in here when I came in this morning, so it must have been that." He motioned the little doctor after him, then turned his neck back to address Brown. "Show him the results while I'm gone, honey."

Ferrel forgot his new recruits and swung back to the girl. "Bad?"

She made no comment, but picked up a lead shield and placed it over Jorgenson's chest so that it cut off all radiation from the lower part of his body, then placed the radiation indicator close to the man's throat. Doc looked once; no more was needed. It was obvious that Blake had already done his best to remove the radioactive from all parts of the body needed for speech, in the hope that they might strap down the others and block them off with local anaesthetics; then the curare could have been counteracted long enough for such information as was needed. Equally obviously, he'd failed. There was no sense in going through the job of neutralizing the drug's block only to have him under the control of the radioactive still present. The stuff was too finely dispersed for surgical removal. Now what? He had no answer.

Jenkins' lean-sinewed hand took the indicator from him for inspection. The boy was already frowning as Doc looked up in faint surprise, and his face made no change. He nodded slowly. "Yeah. I figured as much. That was a beautiful piece of work you did, too. Too bad. I was watching from the door and you almost convinced me he'd be all right, the way you handled it. But— So we have to make out without him; and Hoke and Palmer haven't even cooked up a lead that's worth a good test. Want to come into my office, Doc? There's nothing we can do here."

Ferrel followed Jenkins into the little office of the now emptied waiting room; the men from the hospital had worked rapidly, it seemed. "So you haven't been sleeping, I take it? Where's Hokusai now?"

"Out there with Palmer; he promised to behave, if that'll comfort you. . . . Nice guy, Hoke; I'd forgotten what it felt like to talk to an atomic engineer without being laughed at. Palmer, too. I wish—" There was a brief lightening to the boy's face and the first glow of normal human pride Doc had seen in him. Then he shrugged, and it vanished back into his taut cheeks and reddened eyes. "We cooked up the wildest kind of a scheme, but it isn't so hot."

Hoke's voice came out of the doorway, as the little man came in and sat down carefully in one of the three chairs. "No, not sso hot! It iss fail, already. Jorgensson?"

"Out, no hope there! What happened?"

Hoke spread his arms, his eyes almost closing. "Nothing. We knew it could never work, not sso? Misster Palmer, he iss come ssoon here, then we make planss again. I am think now, besst we sshould move from here. Palmer, I—mosstly we are theoreticianss; and, ex-cusse, you alsso, doctor. Jorgensson wass the production man. No Jorgensson, no—ah—ssoap!"

Mentally, Ferrel agreed about the moving—and soon! But he could see Palmer's point of view; to give up the fight was against the grain, somehow. And besides, once the blow-up happened, with the resultant damage to an unknown area, the pressure groups in Congress would be in, shouting for the final abolition of all atomic work; now they were reasonably quiet, only waiting an opportunity—or, more probably, at the moment were already seizing on the rumors spread-ing to turn this into their coup. If, by some streak of luck, Palmer could save the plant with no greater loss of life and property than already existed, their words would soon be forgotten, and the benefits from the products of National would again outweigh all risks.

"Just what will happen if it all goes off?" he asked.

Jenkins shrugged, biting at his inner lip as he went over a sheaf of papers on the desk, covered with the scrawling symbols of atomics. "Anybody's guess. Suppose three tons of the army's new explosives were to explode in a billionth—or at least, a millionth—of a second? Normally, you know, compared to atomics, that stuff burns like any fire, slowly and quietly, giving its gases plenty of time to get out of the way in an orderly fashion. Figure it one way, with this all going off together, and the stuff could drill a hole that'd split open the whole continent from Hudson Bay to the Gulf of Mexico, and leave a lovely sea where the Middle West is now. Figure it another, and it might only kill off everything within fifty miles of here. Somewhere in between is the chance we count on. This isn't U-235, you know."

Doc winced. He'd been picturing the plant going up in the air violently, with maybe a few buildings somewhere near it, but nothing like this. It had been purely a local affair to him, but this didn't sound like one. No wonder Jenkins was in that state of suppressed jitters; it wasn't too much imagination, but too much cold, hard knowledge that was worrying him. Ferrel looked at their faces as they bent over the symbols once more, tracing out point by point their calculations in the hope of finding one overlooked loophole, then decided to leave them alone.

The whole problem was hopeless without Jorgenson, it seemed, and Jorgenson was his responsibility; if the plant went, it was squarely on the senior physician's shoulders. But there was no apparent solution. If it would help, he could cut it down to a direct path from brain to speaking organs, strap down the body and block off all nerves below the neck, using an artificial larynx instead of the normal breathing through vocal cords. But the indicator showed the futility of it; the orders could never get through from the brain with the amount of radioactive still present throwing them off track—even granting that the brain itself was not affected, which was doubtful.

Fortunately for Jorgenson, the stuff was all finely dispersed around the head, with no concentration at any one place that was unquestionably destructive to his mind; but the good fortune was also the trouble, since it could not be removed by any means known to medical practice. Even so simple a thing as letting the man read the questions and spell out the answers by winking an eyelid as they pointed to the alphabet was hopeless.

Nerves! Jorgenson had his blocked out, but Ferrel wondered if the rest of them weren't in as bad a state. Probably, somewhere well within their grasp, there was a solution that was being held back because the nerves of everyone in the plant were blocked by fear and pressure that defeated its own purpose. Jenkins, Palmer, Hokusai—under purely theoretical conditions, any one of them might spot the answer to the problem, but sheer necessity of finding it could be the thing that hid it. The same might be true with the problem of Jorgenson's treatment. Yet, though he tried to relax and let his mind stray idly around the loose ends and seemingly disconnected knowledge he had, it returned incessantly to the necessity of doing something, and doing it now!

Ferrel heard weary footsteps behind him and turned to see Palmer coming from the front entrance. The man had no business walking into the surgery, but such minor rules had gone by the board hours before.

"Jorgenson?" Palmer's conversation began with the same old question in the usual tone, and he read the answer from Doc's face with a look that indicated it was no news. "Hoke and that Jenkins kid still in there?"

Doc nodded, and plodded behind him toward Jenkins' office; he was useless to them, but there was still the idea that in filling his mind with other things, some little factor he had overlooked might have a chance to come forth. Also, curiosity still worked on him, demanding to know what was happening. He flopped into the third chair, and Palmer squatted down on the edge of the table.

"Know a good spiritualist, Jenkins?" the manager asked. "Because if you do, I'm about ready to try calling back Kellar's ghost. The Steinmetz of atomics—so he had to die before this Isotope R came up, and leave us without even a good guess at how long we've got to crack the problem. Hey, what's the matter?"

Jenkins' face had tensed and his body straightened back tensely in the chair, but he shook his head, the corner of his mouth twitching wryly. "Nothing. Nerves, I guess. Hoke and I dug out some things that give an indication on how long this runs, though. We still don't know exactly, but from observations out there and the general theory before, it looks like something between six and thirty hours left; probably ten's closer to being correct!"

"Can't be much longer. It's driving the men back right now! Even the tanks can't get in where they can do the most good, and we're using the shielding around No. 3 as a headquarters for the men; in another half hour, maybe they won't be able to stay that near the thing. Radiation indicators won't register any more, and it's spitting all over the place, almost constantly. Heat's terrific; it's gone up to around three hundred centigrade and sticks right there now, but that's enough to warm up 3, even."

Doc looked up. "No. 3?"

"Yeah. Nothing happened to that batch—it ran through and came out I-713 right on schedule, hours ago." Palmer reached for a cigarette, realized he had one in his mouth, and slammed the package back on the table. "Significant data, Doc; if we get out of this, we'll figure out just what caused the change in No. 4—if we get out! Any chance of making those variable factors work, Hoke?"

Hoke shook his head, and again Jenkins answered from the notes. "Not a chance; sure, theoretically, at least, R should have a period varying between twelve and sixty hours before turning into Mahler's Isotope, depending on what chains of reactions or subchains it goes through; they all look equally good, and probably are all going on in there now, depending on what's around to soak up neutrons or let them roam, the concentration and amount of R together, and even high or low temperatures that change their activity somewhat. It's one of the variables, no question about that."

"The sspitting iss prove that," Hoke supplemented.

"Sure. But there's too much of it together, and we can't break it down fine enough to reach any safety point where it won't toss energy around like rain. The minute one particle manages to make itself into Mahler's, it'll crash through with energy enough to blast the next over the hump and into the same thing instantly, and that passes it on to the next, at about light speed! If we *could* get it juggled around so some would go off first, other atoms a little later, and so on, fine— only we can't do it unless we can be sure of isolating every blob bigger than a tenth of a gram from every other one! And if we start breaking it down into reasonably small pieces, we're likely to have one decide on the short transformation subchain and go off at any time; pure chance gave us a concentration to begin with that eliminated the shorter chains, but we can't break it down into small lots and those into smaller lots, and so on. Too much risk!"

Ferrel had known vaguely that there were such things as variables, but the theory behind them was too new and too complex for him; he'd learned what little he knew when the simpler radioactives proceeded normally from radium to lead, as an example, with a definite, fixed half life, instead of the super-heavy atoms they now used that could jump through several different paths, yet end up the same. It was over his head, and he started to get up and go back to Jorgenson.

Palmer's words stopped him. "I knew it, of course, but I hoped maybe I was wrong. Then—we evacuate! No use fooling ourselves any longer. I'll call the Governor and try to get him to clear the country around; Hoke, you can tell the men to get the hell out of here! All we ever had was the counteracting isotope to hope on, and no chance of getting enough of that. There was no sense in making I-231 in thousand-pound batches before. Well—"

He reached for the phone, but Ferrel cut in. "What about the men in the wards? They're loaded with the stuff, most of them with more than a gram apiece dispersed through them. They're in the same class with the converter, maybe, but we can't just pull out and leave them!"

Silence hit them, to be broken by Jenkins' hushed whisper. "My God! What damned fools we are. I-231 under discussion for hours, and I never thought of it. Now you two throw the connection in my face, and I still almost miss it!"

"I-231? But there iss not enough. Maybe twenty-five pound, maybe less. Three and a half dayss to make more. The little we have would be no good, Dr. Jenkinss. We forget that already." Hoke struck a match to a piece of paper, shook one drop of ink onto it, and watched it continue burning for a second before putting it out. "Sso. A drop of water for sstop a foresst fire. No."

"Wrong, Hoke. A drop to short a switch that'll turn on the real stream—maybe. Look, Doc, I-231's an isotope that reacts atomically with R—we've checked on that already. It simply gets together with the stuff and the two break down into non-radioactive elements and a little heat, like a lot of other such atomic reactions; but it isn't the violent kind. They simply swap parts in a friendly way and open up to simpler atoms that are stable. We have a few pounds on hand, can't make enough in time to help with No. 4. But we do have enough to treat every man in the wards, *including Jorgenson!*"

"How much heat?" Doc snapped out of his lethargy into the detailed thought of a good physician. "In atomics you may call it a little; but would it be small enough in the human body?"

Hokusai and Palmer were practically riding the pencil as Jenkins figured. "Say five grams of the stuff in Jorgenson, to be on the safe side, less in the others. Time for reaction . . . hm-m-m. Here's the total heat produced and the time taken by the reaction, probably, in the body. The stuff's water-soluble in the chloride we have of it, so there's no trouble dispersing it. What do you make of it, Doc?"

"Fifteen to eighteen degrees temperature rise at a rough estimate. Uh!"

"Too much! Jorgenson couldn't stand ten degrees right now!" Jenkins frowned down at his figures, tapping nervously with his hand.

Doc shook his head. "Not too much! We can drop his whole body temperature first in the hypothermy bath down to eighty degrees, then let it rise to a hundred, if necessary, and still be safe. Thank the Lord, there's equipment enough. If they'll rip out the refrigerating units in the cafeteria and improvise baths, the volunteers out in the tent can start on the other men while we handle Jorgenson. At least that way we can get the men all out, even if we don't save the plant."

Palmer stared at them in confusion before his face galvanized into resolution. "Refrigerating units—volunteers—tent? What— O. K., Doc, what do you want?" He reached for the telephone and began giving orders for the available I-231 to be sent to the surgery, for men to rip out the cafeteria cooling equipment, and for such other things as Doc requested. Jenkins had already gone to instruct the medical staff in the field tent without asking how they'd gotten there, but was back in the surgery before Doc reached it with Palmer and Hokusai at his heels.

"Blake's taking over out there," Jenkins announced. "Says if you want Dodd, Meyers, Jones or Sue, they're sleeping."

"No need. Get over there out of the way, if you must watch," Ferrel ordered the two engineers, as he and Jenkins began attaching the freezing units and bath to the sling on the exciter. "Prepare his blood for it, Jenkins; we'll force it down as low as we can to be on the safe side. And we'll have to keep tab on the temperature fall and regulate his heart and breathing to what it would be normally in that condition; they're both out of his normal control, now."

"And pray," Jenkins added. He grabbed the small box out of the messenger's hand before the man was fully inside the door and began preparing a solution, weighing out the whitish powder and measuring water carefully, but with the speed that was automatic to him under tension. "Doc, if this doesn't work—if Jorgenson's crazy or something —you'll have another case of insanity on your hands. One more false hope would finish me."

"Not one more case; four! We're all in the same boat. Temperature's falling nicely—I'm rushing it a little, but it's safe enough. Down to ninety-six now." The thermometer under Jorgenson's tongue was one intended for hypothermy work, capable of rapid response, instead of the normal fever thermometer. Slowly, with agonizing reluctance, the little needle on the dial moved over, down to ninety, then on. Doc kept his eyes glued to it, slowing the pulse and breath to the proper speed. He lost track of the number of times he sent Palmer back out of the way, and finally gave up.

Waiting, he wondered how those outside in the field hospital were doing? Still, they had ample time to arrange their makeshift cooling apparatus and treat the men in groups—ten hours probably; and hypothermy was a standard thing, now. Jorgenson was the only real rush case. Almost imperceptibly to Doc, but speedily by normal standards, the temperature continued to fall. Finally it reached seventy-eight.

"Ready, Jenkins, make the injection. That enough?"

"No. I figure it's almost enough, but we'll have to go slow to balance out properly. Too much of this stuff would be almost as bad as the other. Gauge going up, Doc?"

It was, much more rapidly than Ferrel liked. As the injection coursed through the blood vessels and dispersed out to the fine deposits of radioactive, the needle began climbing past eighty, to ninety, and up. It stopped at ninety-four and slowly began falling as the cooling bath absorbed heat from the cells of the body. The radioactivity meter still registered the presence of Isotope R, though much more faintly.

The next shot was small, and a smaller one followed. "Almost," Ferrel commented. "Next one should about do the trick."

Using partial injections, there had been need for less drop in temperature than they had given Jorgenson, but there was small loss to that. Finally, when the last minute bit of the I-231 solution had entered the man's veins and done its work, Doc nodded. "No sign of activity left. He's up to ninety-five, now that I've cut off the refrigeration, and he'll pick up the little extra temperature in a hurry. By the time we can counteract the curare, he'll be ready. That'll take about fifteen minutes, Palmer."

The manager nodded, watching them dismantling the hypothermy equipment and going through the routine of canceling out the curare. It was always a slower job than treatment with the drug, but part of the work had been done already by the normal body processes, and the rest was a simple, standard procedure. Fortunately, the neo-heroin would be nearly worn off, or that would have been a longer and much harder problem to eliminate.

"Telephone for Mr. Palmer. Calling Mr. Palmer. Send Mr. Palmer to the telephone." The operator's words lacked the usual artificial exactness, and were only a nervous sing-song. It was getting her, and she wasn't bothered by excess imagination, normally. "Mr. Palmer is wanted on the telephone."

"Palmer." The manager picked up an instrument at hand, not equipped with vision, and there was no indication of the caller. But Ferrel could see what little hope had appeared at the prospect of Jorgenson's revival disappearing. "Check! Move out of there, and prepare to evacuate, but keep quiet about that until you hear further orders! Tell the men Jorgenson's about out of it, so they won't lack for something to talk about."

He swung back to them. "No use, Doc, I'm afraid. We're already too late. The stuff's stepped it up again, and they're having to move out of No. 3 now. I'll wait on Jorgenson, but even if he's all right and knows the answer, we can't get in to use it!"

VI

"Healing's going to be a long, slow process, but they should at least grow back better than silver ribs; never take a pretty X-ray photo, though." Doc held the instrument in his hand, staring down at the flap opened in Jorgenson's chest, and his shoulders came up in a faint shrug. The little platinum filaments had been removed from around the nerves to heart and lungs, and the man's normal impulses were operating again, less steadily than under the exciter, but with no danger signals. "Well, it won't much matter if he's still sane."

Jenkins watched him begin stitching the flap back, his eyes centered over the table out toward the converter. "Doc, he's got to be sane! If Hoke and Palmer find it's what it sounds like out there, we'll have to count on Jorgenson. There's an answer somewhere, has to be! But we won't find it without him."

"Hm-m-m. Seems to me you've been having ideas yourself, son. You've been right so far, and if Jorgenson's out—" He shut off the stitcher, finished the dressings, and flopped down on a bench, knowing that all they could do was wait for the drugs to work on Jorgenson and bring him around. Now that he relaxed the control over himself, exhaustion hit down with full force; his fingers were uncertain as he pulled off the gloves. "Anyhow, we'll know in another five minutes or so."

"And Heaven help us, Doc, if it's up to me. I've always had a flair for atomic theory; I grew up on it. But he's the production man who's been working at it week in and week out, and it's his process, to boot. . . . There they are now! All right for them to come back here?"

But Hokusai and Palmer were waiting for no permission. At the moment, Jorgenson was the nerve center of the plant, drawing them back, and they stalked over to stare down at him, then sat where they could be sure of missing no sign of returning consciousness. Palmer picked up the conversation where he'd dropped it, addressing his remarks to both Hokusai and Jenkins.

"Damn that Link-Stevens postulate! Time after time it fails, until you figure there's nothing to it; then, this! It's black magic, not science, and if I get out, I'll find some fool with more courage than sense to discover why. Hoke, are you positive it's the *theta* chain? There isn't one chance in ten thousand of that happening, you know; it's unstable, hard to stop, tends to revert to the simpler ones at the first chance."

Hokusai spread his hands, lifted one heavy eyelid at Jenkins questioningly, then nodded. The boy's voice was dull, almost uninterested. "That's what I thought it had to be, Palmer. None of the others throws off that much energy at this stage, the way you described conditions out there. Probably the last thing we tried to quench set it up in that pattern, and it's in a concentration just right to keep it going. We figured ten hours was the best chance, so it had to pick the six-hour short chain."

"Yeah." Palmer was pacing up and down nervously again, his eyes swinging toward Jorgenson from whatever direction he moved. "And in six hours, maybe all the population around here can be evacuated, maybe not, but we'll have to try it. Doc, I can't even wait for Jorgenson now! I've got to get the Governor started at once!"

"They've been known to practice lynch law, even in recent years," Ferrel reminded him grimly. He'd seen the result of one such case of mob violence when he was practicing privately, and he knew that people remain pretty much the same year after year; they'd move, but first they'd demand a sacrifice. "Better get the men out of here first, Palmer, and my advice is to get yourself a good long distance off; I heard some of the trouble at the gate, and that won't be anything compared to what an evacuation order will do."

Palmer grunted. "Doc, you might not believe it, but I don't give a continental about what happens to me or the plant right now."

"Or the men? Put a mob in here, hunting your blood, and the men will be on your side, because they know it wasn't your fault, and they've seen you out there taking chances yourself. That mob won't be too choosy about its targets, either, once it gets worked up, and you'll have a nice vicious brawl all over the place. Besides, Jorgenson's practically ready."

A few minutes would make no difference in the evacuation, and Doc had no desire to think of his partially crippled wife going through the hell evacuation would be; she'd probably refuse, until he returned. His eyes fell on the box Jenkins was playing with nervously, and he stalled for time. "I thought you said it was risky to break the stuff down into small particles, Jenkins. But that box contains the stuff in various sizes, including one big piece we scraped out, along with the contaminated instruments. Why hasn't it exploded?"

Jenkins' hand jerked up from it as if burned, and he backed away a step before checking himself. Then he was across the room toward the I-231 and back, pouring the white powder over everything in the box in a jerky frenzy. Hokusai's eyes had snapped fully open, and he was slopping water in to fill up the remaining space and keep the I-231 in contact with everything else. Almost at once, in spite of the low relative energy release, it sent up a white cloud of steam faster than the air conditioner could clear the room; but that soon faded down and disappeared.

Hokusai wiped his forehead slowly. "The ssuits—armor of the men?"

"Sent 'em back to the converter and had them dumped into the stuff to be safe long ago," Jenkins answered. "But I forgot the box, like a fool. Ugh! Either blind chance saved us or else the stuff spit out was all one kind, some reasonably long chain. I don't know nor care right—"

"S'ot! Nnnuh. . . . Whmah nahh?"

"Jorgenson!" They swung from the end of the room like one man, but Jenkins was the first to reach the table. Jorgenson's eyes were open and rolling in a semiorderly manner, his hands moving sluggishly. The boy hovered over his face, his own practically glowing with the intensity behind it. "Jorgenson, can you understand what I'm saying?"

"Uh." The eyes ceased moving and centered on Jenkins. One hand came up to his throat, clutching at it, and he tried unsuccessfully to lift himself with the other, but the aftereffects of what he'd been through seemed to have left him in a state of partial paralysis.

Ferrel had hardly dared hope that the man could be rational, and his relief was tinged with doubt. He pushed Palmer back, and shook his head. "No, stay back. Let the boy handle it; he knows enough not to shock the man now, and you don't. This can't be rushed too much."

"I—uh. . . . Young Jenkins? Whasha doin' here? Tell y'ur dad to ge' busy ou' there!" Somewhere in Jorgenson's huge frame, an untapped reserve of energy and will sprang up, and he forced himself into a sitting position, his eyes on Jenkins, his hand still catching at the reluctant throat that refused to co-operate. His words were blurry and uncertain, but sheer determination overcame the obstacles and made the words understandable.

"Dad's dead now, Jorgenson. Now—"

" 'Sright. 'N' you're grown up—'bout twelve years old, y' were. . . . The plant!"

"Easy, Jorgenson." Jenkins' own voice managed to sound casual, though his hands under the table were white where they clenched together. "Listen, and don't try to say anything until I finish. The plant's still all right, but we've got to have your help. Here's what happened."

Ferrel could make little sense of the cryptic sentences that followed, though he gathered that they were some form of engineering shorthand; apparently, from Hokusai's approving nod, they summed up the situation briefly but fully, and Jorgenson sat rigidly still until it was finished, his eyes fastened on the boy.

"Hellova mess! Gotta think . . . yuh tried—" He made an attempt to lower himself back, and Jenkins assisted him, hanging on feverishly to each awkward, uncertain change of expression on the man's face. "Uh . . . da' sroat! Yuh . . . uh . . . urrgh!"

"Got it?"

"Uh!" The tone was affirmative, unquestionably, but the clutching hands around his neck told their own story. The temporary burst of energy he'd forced was exhausted, and he couldn't get through with it. He lay there, breathing heavily and struggling, then relaxed after a few more half-whispered words, none intelligibly articulated.

Palmer clutched at Ferrel's sleeve. "Doc, isn't there anything you can do?"

"Try." He metered out a minute quantity of drug doubtfully, felt Jorgenson's pulse, and decided on half that amount. "Not much hope, though; that man's been through hell, and it wasn't good for him to be forced around in the first place. Carry it too far, and he'll be delirious if he does talk. Anyway, I suspect it's partly his speech centers as well as the throat."

But Jorgenson began a slight rally almost instantly, trying again, then apparently drawing himself together for a final attempt. When they came, the words spilled out harshly in forced clearness, but without inflection.

"First . . . variable . . . at . . . twelve . . . water . . . stop." His eyes, centered on Jenkins, closed, and he relaxed again, this time no longer fighting off the inevitable unconsciousness.

Hokusai, Palmer, and Jenkins were staring back and forth at one another questioningly. The little Japanese shook his head negatively at first, frowned, and repeated it, to be imitated almost exactly by the manager. "Delirious ravings!"

"The great white hope Jorgenson!" Jenkins' shoulders drooped and the blood drained from his face, leaving it ghastly with fatigue and despair. "Oh, damn it, Doc, stop staring at me! I can't pull a miracle out of a hat!"

Doc hadn't realized that he was staring, but he made no effort to change it. "Maybe not, but you happen to have the most active imagination here, when you stop abusing it to scare yourself. Well, you're on the spot now, and I'm still giving odds on you. Want to bet, Hoke?"

It was an utterly stupid thing, and Doc knew it; but somewhere during the long hours together, he'd picked up a queer respect for the boy and a dependence on the nervousness that wasn't fear but closer akin to the reaction of a rear-running thoroughbred on the home stretch. Hoke was too slow and methodical, and Palmer had been too concerned with outside worries to give anywhere nearly full attention to the single most urgent phase of the problem; that left only Jenkins, hampered by his lack of self-confidence.

Hoke gave no signs that he caught the meaning of Doc's heavy wink, but he lifted his eyebrows faintly. "No, I think I am not bet. Dr. Jenkins, I am to be command!"

Palmer looked briefly at the boy, whose face mirrored incredulous confusion, but he had neither Ferrel's ignorance of atomic technique nor Hokusai's fatalism. With a final glance at the unconscious Jorgenson, he started across the room toward the phone. "You men play, if you like. I'm starting evacuation immediately!"

"Wait!" Jenkins was shaking himself, physically as well as mentally. "Hold it, Palmer! Thanks, Doc. You knocked me out of the rut, and bounced my memory back to something I picked up somewhere; I think it's the answer! It has to work—nothing else can at this stage of the game!"

"Give me the Governor, operator." Palmer had heard, but he went on with the phone call. "This is no time to play crazy hunches until after we get the people out, kid. I'll admit you're a darned clever amateur, but you're no atomicist!"

"And if we get the men out, it's too late—there'll be no one left in here to do the work!" Jenkins' hand snapped out and jerked the receiver of the plug-in telephone from Palmer's hand. "Cancel the call, operator; it won't be necessary. Palmer, you've got to listen to me; you can't clear the whole middle of the continent, and you can't depend on the explosion to limit itself to less ground. It's a gamble, but you're risking fifty million people against a mere hundred thousand. Give me a chance!"

"I'll give you exactly one minute to convince me, Jenkins, and it had better be good! Maybe the blow-up won't hit beyond the fifty-mile limit!"

"Maybe. And I can't explain in a minute." The boy scowled tensely. "O. K., you've been bellyaching about a man named Kellar being dead. If he were here, would you take a chance on him? Or on a man who'd worked under him on everything he tried?"

"Absolutely, but you're not Kellar. And I happen to know he was a lone wolf; didn't hire outside engineers after Jorgenson had a squabble with him and came here." Palmer reached for the phone. "It won't wash, Jenkins."

Jenkins' hand clamped down on the instrument, jerking it out of

reach. "I wasn't *outside* help, Palmer. When Jorgenson was afraid
to run one of the things off and quit, I was twelve; three years later,
things got too tight for him to handle alone, but he decided he might
as well keep it in the family, so he started me in. I'm Kellar's
stepson!"

Pieces clicked together in Doc's head then, and he kicked him-
self mentally for not having seen the obvious before. "That's why
Jorgenson knew you, then? I thought that was funny. It checks,
Palmer."

For a split second, the manager hesitated uncertainly. Then he
shrugged and gave in. "O. K., I'm a fool to trust you, Jenkins, but it's
too late for anything else, I guess. I never forgot that I was gambling
the locality against half the continent. What do you want?"

"Men—construction men, mostly, and a few volunteers for dirty
work. I want all the blowers, exhaust equipment, tubing, booster
blowers, and everything ripped from the other three converters and
connected as close to No. 4 as you can get. Put them up some way so
they can be shoved in over the stuff by crane—I don't care how; the
shop men will know better than I do. You've got sort of a river running off behind the plant; get everyone within a few miles of it out
of there, and connect the blower outlets down to it. Where does it
end, anyway—some kind of a swamp, or morass?"

"About ten miles farther down, yes; we didn't bother keeping the
drainage system going, since the land meant nothing to us, and the
swamps made as good a dumping ground as anything else." When
the plant had first used the little river as an outlet for their waste
products, there'd been so much trouble that National had been forced
to take over all adjacent land and quiet the owners' fears of the atomic
activity in cold cash. Since then, it had gone to weeds and rabbits,
mostly. "Everyone within a few miles is out, anyway, except a few
fishers or tramps that don't know we use it. I'll have militia sent in
to scare them out."

"Good. Ideal, in fact, since the swamps will hold stuff in there
where the current's slow longer. Now, what about that superther-
mite stuff you were producing last year. Any around?"

"Not in the plant. But we've got tons of it at the warehouse, still
waiting for the army's requisition. That's pretty hot stuff to handle,
though. Know much about it?"

"Enough to know it's what I want." Jenkins indicated the copy of
the *Weekly Ray* still lying where he'd dropped it, and Doc remem-

bered skimming through the nontechnical part of the description. It was made up of two superheavy atoms, kept separate. By itself, neither was particularly important or active, but together they reacted with each other atomically to release a tremendous amount of raw heat and comparatively little unwanted radiation. "Goes up around twenty thousand centigrade, doesn't it? How's it stored?"

"In ten-pound bombs that have a fragile partition; it breaks with shock, starting the action. Hoke can explain it—it's his baby." Palmer reached for the phone. "Anything else? Then, get out and get busy! The men will be ready for you when you get there! I'll be out myself as soon as I can put through your orders."

Doc watched them go out, to be followed in short order by the manager, and was alone in the Infirmary with Jorgenson and his thoughts. They weren't pleasant; he was both too far outside the inner circle to know what was going on and too much mixed up in it not to know the dangers. Now he could have used some work of any nature to take his mind off useless speculations, but aside from a needless check of the foreman's condition, there was nothing for him to do.

He wriggled down in the leather chair, making the mistake of trying to force sleep, while his mind chased out after the sounds that came in from outside. There were the drones of crane and tank motors coming to life, the shouts of hurried orders, and above all, the jarring rhythm of pneumatic hammers on metal, each sound suggesting some possibility to him without adding to his knowledge. The "Decameron" was boring, the whiskey tasted raw and rancid, and solitaire wasn't worth the trouble of cheating.

Finally, he gave up and turned out to the field hospital tent. Jorgenson would be better off out there, under the care of the staff from Mayo's, and perhaps he could make himself useful. As he passed through the rear entrance, he heard the sound of a number of helicopters coming over with heavy loads, and looked up as they began settling over the edge of the buildings. From somewhere, a group of men came running forward, and disappeared in the direction of the freighters. He wondered whether any of those men would be forced back into the stuff out there to return filled with radioactive; though it didn't matter so much, now that the isotope could be eliminated without surgery.

Blake met him at the entrance of the field tent, obviously well satisfied with his duty of bossing and instructing the others. "Scram, Doc. You aren't necessary here, and you need some rest. Don't want you added to the casualties. What's the latest dope from the pow-wow front?"

"Jorgenson didn't come through, but the kid had an idea, and they're out there working on it." Doc tried to sound more hopeful than he felt. "I was thinking you might as well bring Jorgenson in here; he's still unconscious, but there doesn't seem to be anything to worry about. Where's Brown? She'll probably want to know what's up, if she isn't asleep."

"Asleep when the kid isn't? Uh-huh. Mother complex, has to worry about him." Blake grinned. "She got a look at him running out with Hoke tagging at his heels, and hiked out after him, so she probably knows everything now. Wish Anne'd chase me that way, just once— Jenkins, the wonder boy! Well, it's out of my line; I don't intend to start worrying until they pass out the order. O. K., Doc, I'll have Jorgenson out here in a couple of minutes, so you grab yourself a cot and get some shut-eye."

Doc grunted, looking curiously at the refinements and well-equipped interior of the field tent. "I've already prescribed that, Blake, but the patient can't seem to take it. I think I'll hunt up Brown, so give me a call over the public speaker if anything turns up."

He headed toward the center of action, knowing that he'd been wanting to do it all along, but hadn't been sure of not being a nuisance. Well, if Brown could look on, there was no reason why he couldn't. He passed the machine shop, noting the excited flurry of activity going on, and went past No. 2, where other men were busily ripping out long sections of big piping and various other devices. There was a rope fence barring his way, well beyond No. 3, and he followed along the edge, looking for Palmer or Brown.

She saw him first. "Hi, Dr. Ferrel, over here in the truck. I thought you'd be coming soon. From up here we can get a look over the heads of all these other people, and we won't be tramped on." She stuck down a hand to help him up, smiled faintly as he disregarded it and mounted more briskly than his muscles wanted to. He wasn't so old that a girl had to help him yet.

"Know what's going on?" he asked, sinking down onto the plank across the truck body, facing out across the men below toward the converter. There seemed to be a dozen different centers of activity, all

crossing each other in complete confusion, and the general pattern
was meaningless.

"No more than you do. I haven't seen my husband, though Mr.
Palmer took time enough to chase me here out of the way."

Doc centered his attention on the 'copters, unloading, rising, and
coming in with more loads, and he guessed that those boxes must con-
tain the little thermodyne bombs. It was the only thing he could understand, and consequently the least interesting. Other men were
assembling the big sections of piping he'd seen before, connecting
them up in almost endless order, while some of the tanks hooked on
and snaked them off in the direction of the small river that ran off
beyond the plant.

"Those must be the exhaust blowers, I guess," he told Brown,
pointing them out. "Though I don't know what any of the rest of the
stuff hooked on is."

"I know—I've been inside the plant Bob's father had." She lifted an
inquiring eyebrow at him, went on as he nodded. "The pipes are for
exhaust gases, all right, and those big square things are the motors
and fans—they put in one at each five hundred feet or less of piping.
The things they're wrapping around the pipe must be the heaters to
keep the gases hot. Are they going to try to suck all that out?"

Doc didn't know, though it was the only thing he could see. But
he wondered how they'd get around the problem of moving in close
enough to do any good. "I heard your husband order some thermodyne bombs, so they'll probably try to gassify the magma; then they're
pumping it down the river."

As he spoke, there was a flurry of motion at one side, and his eyes
swung over instantly, to see one of the cranes laboring with a long
framework stuck from its front, holding up a section of pipe with a
nozzle on the end. It tilted precariously, even though heavy bags were
piled everywhere to add weight, but an inch at a time it lifted its load,
and began forcing its way forward, carrying the nozzle out in front
and rather high.

Below the main exhaust pipe was another smaller one. As it drew
near the outskirts of the danger zone, a small object ejaculated from
the little pipe, hit the ground, and was a sudden blazing inferno of
glaring blue-white light, far brighter than it seemed, judging by the effect on the eyes. Doc shielded his, just as someone below put something into his hands.

"Put 'em on. Palmer says the light's actinic."

He heard Brown fussing beside him, then his vision cleared, and he looked back through the goggles again to see a glowing cloud spring up from the magma, spread out near the ground, narrowing down higher up, until it sucked into the nozzle above, and disappeared. Another bomb slid from the tube, and erupted with blazing heat. A sideways glance showed another crane being fitted, and a group of men near it wrapping what might have been oiled rags around the small bombs; probably no tubing fitted them exactly, and they were padding them so pressure could blow them forward and out. Three more dropped from the tube, one at a time, and the fans roared and groaned, pulling the cloud that rose into the pipe and feeding it down toward the river.

Then the crane inched back out carefully as men uncoupled its piping from the main line, and a second went in to replace it. The heat generated must be too great for the machine to stand steadily without the pipe fusing, Doc decided; though they couldn't have kept a man inside the heavily armored cab for any length of time, if the metal had been impervious. Now another crane was ready, and went in from another place; it settled down to a routine of ingoing and outcoming cranes, and men feeding materials in, coupling and uncoupling the pipes and replacing the others who came from the cabs. Doc began to feel like a man at a tennis match, watching the ball without knowing the rules.

Brown must have had the same idea, for she caught Ferrel's arm and indicated a little leather case that came from her handbag. "Doc, do you play chess? We might as well fill our time with that as sitting here on edge, just watching. It's supposed to be good for nerves."

He seized on it gratefully, without explaining that he'd been city champion three years running; he'd take it easy, watch her game, handicap himself just enough to make it interesting by the deliberate loss of a rook, bishop, or knight, as was needed to even the odds— Suppose they got all the magma out and into the river; how did that solve the problem? It removed it from the plant, but far less than the fifty-mile minimum danger limit.

"Check," Brown announced. He castled, and looked up at the half-dozen cranes that were now operating. "Check! Checkmate!"

He looked back again hastily, then, to see her queen guarding all possible moves, a bishop checking him. Then his eye followed down toward her end. "Umm. Did you know you've been in check for the last half-dozen moves? Because I didn't."

She frowned, shook her head, and began setting the men up again. Doc moved out the queen's pawn, looked out at the workers, and then brought out the king's bishop, to see her take it with her king's pawn. He hadn't watched her move it out, and had counted on her queen's to block his. Things would require more careful watching on this little portable set. The men were moving steadily and there was a growing clear space, but as they went forward, the violent action of the thermodyne had pitted the ground, carefully as it had been used, and the going had become more uncertain. Time was slipping by rapidly now.

"Checkmate!" He found himself in a hole, started to nod; but she caught herself this time. "Sorry, I've been playing my king for a queen. Doctor, let's see if we can play at least one game right."

Before it was half-finished, it became obvious that they couldn't. Neither had chess very much on the mind, and the pawns and men did fearful and wonderful things, while the knights were as likely to jump six squares as their normal L. They gave it up, just as one of the cranes lost its precarious balance and toppled forward, dropping the long extended pipe into the bubbling mass below. Tanks were in instantly, hitching on and tugging backward until it came down with a thump as the pipe fused, releasing the extreme forward load. It backed out on its own power, while another went in. The driver, by sheer good luck, hobbled from the cab, waving an armored hand to indicate he was all right. Things settled back to an excited routine again that seemed to go on endlessly, though seconds were dropping off too rapidly, turning into minutes that threatened to be hours far too soon.

"Uh!" Brown had been staring for some time, but her little feet suddenly came down with a bang and she straightened up, her hand to her mouth. "Doctor, I just thought; it won't do any good—all this!"

"Why?" She couldn't know anything, but he felt the faint hopes he had go downward sharply. His nerves were dulled, but still ready to jump at the slightest warning.

"The stuff they were making was a superheavy—it'll sink as soon as it hits the water, and all pile up right there! It won't float down river!"

Obvious, Ferrel thought; too obvious. Maybe that was why the engineers hadn't thought of it. He started from the plank, just as

Palmer stepped up, but the manager's hand on his shoulder forced him back.

"Easy, Doc, it's O. K. Umm, so they teach women *some* science nowadays, eh, Mrs. Jenkins . . . Sue . . . Dr. Brown, whatever your name is? Don't worry about it, though—the old principle of Brownian movement will keep any colloid suspended, if it's fine enough to be a real colloid. We're sucking it out and keeping it pretty hot until it reaches the water—then it cools off so fast it hasn't time to collect in particles big enough to sink. Some of the dust that floats around in the air is heavier than water, too. I'm joining the bystanders, if you don't mind; the men have everything under control, and I can see better here than I could down there, if anything does come up."

Doc's momentary despair reacted to leave him feeling more sure of things than was justified. He pushed over on the plank, making room for Palmer to drop down beside him. "What's to keep it from blowing up anyway, Palmer?"

"Nothing! Got a match?" He sucked in on the cigarette heavily, relaxing as much as he could. "No use trying to fool you, Doc, at this stage of the game. We're gambling, and I'd say the odds are even; Jenkins thinks they're ninety to ten in his favor, but he has to think so. What we're hoping is that by lifting it out in a gas, thus breaking it down at once from full concentration to the finest possible form, and letting it settle in the water in colloidal particles, there won't be a concentration at any one place sufficient to set it all off at once. The big problem is making sure we get every bit of it cleaned out here, or there may be enough left to take care of us and the nearby city! At least, since the last change, it's stopped spitting, so all the men have to worry about is burn!"

"How much damage, even if it doesn't go off all at once?"

"Possibly none. If you can keep it burning slowly, a million tons of dynamite wouldn't be any worse than the same amount of wood, but a stick going off at once will kill you. Why the dickens didn't Jenkins tell me he wanted to go into atomics? We could have fixed all that—it's hard enough to get good men as it is!"

Brown perked up, forgetting the whole trouble beyond them, and went into the story with enthusiasm, while Ferrel only partly listened. He could see the spot of magma growing steadily smaller, but the watch on his wrist went on ticking off minutes remorselessly, and the time was growing limited. He hadn't realized before how long he'd been sitting there. Now three of the crane nozzles were almost touching, and around them stretched the burned-out ground, with no sign of converter, masonry, or anything else; the heat from the thermodyne had gassified everything, indiscriminately.

"Palmer!" The portable ultrawave set around the manager's neck came to life suddenly. "Hey, Palmer, these blowers are about shot; the pipe's pitting already. We've been doing everything we can to replace them, but that stuff eats faster than we can fix. Can't hold up more'n fifteen minutes more."

"Check, Briggs. Keep 'em going the best you can." Palmer flipped a switch and looked out toward the tank standing by behind the cranes. "Jenkins, you get that?"

"Yeah. Surprised they held out this long. How much time till deadline?" The boy's voice was completely toneless, neither hope nor nerves showing up, only the complete weariness of a man almost at his limit.

Palmer looked and whistled. "Twelve minutes, according to the minimum estimate Hoke made! How much left?"

"We're just burning around now, trying to make sure there's no pocket left; I hope we've got the whole works, but I'm not promising. Might as well send out all the I-231 you have and we'll boil it down the pipes to clear out any deposits on them. All the old treads and parts that contacted the R gone into the pile?"

"You melted the last, and your cranes haven't touched the stuff directly. Nice pile of money's gone down that pipe—converter, machinery, everything!"

Jenkins made a sound that was expressive of his worry about that. "I'm coming in now and starting the clearing of the pipe. What've you been paying insurance for?"

"At a lovely rate, too! O. K., come on in, kid; and if you're interested, you can start sticking A. E. after the M. D., any time you want. Your wife's been giving me your qualifications, and I think you've passed the final test, so you're now an atomic engineer, duly graduated from National!"

Brown's breath caught, and her eyes seemed to glow, even through the goggles, but Jenkins' voice was flat. "O. K., I expected you to give me one if we don't blow up. But you'll have to see Dr. Ferrel about it; he's got a contract with me for medical practice. Be there shortly."

Nine of the estimated twelve minutes had ticked by when he climbed up beside them, mopping off some of the sweat that covered him, and Palmer was hugging the watch. More minutes ticked off slowly, while the last sound faded out in the plant, and the men stood around, staring down toward the river or at the hole that had been No. 4. Silence. Jenkins stirred, and grunted.

"Palmer, I know where I got the idea, now. Jorgenson was trying to remind me of it, instead of raving, only I didn't get it, at least consciously. It was one of Dad's, the one he told Jorgenson was a last resort, in case the thing they broke up about went haywire. It was the first variable Dad tried. I was twelve, and he insisted water would break it up into all its chains and kill the danger. Only Dad didn't really expect it to work!"

Palmer didn't look up from the watch, but he caught his breath and swore. "Fine time to tell me that!"

"He didn't have your isotopes to heat it up with, either," Jenkins answered mildly. "Suppose you look up from that watch of yours for a minute, down the river."

As Doc raised his eyes, he was aware suddenly of a roar from the men. Over to the south, stretching out in a huge mass, was a cloud of steam that spread upward and out as he watched, and the beginnings of a mighty hissing sound came in. Then Palmer was hugging Jenkins and yelling until Brown could pry him away and replace him.

"Ten minutes or more of river, plus the swamps, Doc!" Palmer was shouting in Ferrel's ear. "All that dispersion, while it cooks slowly from now until the last chain is finished, atom by atom! The *theta* chain broke, unstable, and now there's everything there, too scattered to set itself off! It'll cook the river bed up and dry it, but that's all!"

Doc was still dazed, unsure of how to take the relief. He wanted to lie down and cry or to stand up with the men and shout his head off. Instead, he sat loosely, gazing at the cloud. "So I lose the best assistant I ever had! Jenkins, I won't hold you; you're free for whatever Palmer wants."

"Hoke wants him to work on R—he's got the stuff for his bomb now!" Palmer was clapping his hands together slowly, like an excited child watching a steam shovel. "Heck, Doc, pick out anyone you want until your own boy gets out next year. You wanted a chance to work him in here, now you've got it. Right now I'll give you anything you want."

"You might see what you can do about hospitalizing the injured and fixing things up with the men in the tent behind the Infirmary. And I think I'll take Brown in Jenkins' place, with the right to grab him in an emergency, until that year's up."

"Done." Palmer slapped the boy's back, stopping the protest, while Brown winked at him. "Your wife likes working, kid; she told me that herself. Besides, a lot of the women work here where they can keep an eye on their men; my own wife does, usually. Doc, take these two kids and head for home, where I'm going myself. Don't come back until you get good and ready, and don't let them start fighting about it!"

Doc pulled himself from the truck and started off with Brown and Jenkins following, through the yelling, relief-crazed men. The three were too thoroughly worn out for any exhibition themselves, but they could feel it. Happy ending! Jenkins and Brown where they wanted to be, Hoke with his bomb, Palmer with proof that atomic plants were safe where they were, and he—well, his boy would start out right, with himself and the widely differing but competent Blake and Jenkins to guide him. It wasn't a bad life, after all.

Then he stopped and chuckled. "You two wait for me, will you? If I leave here without making out that order of extra disinfection at the showers, Blake'll swear I'm growing old and feeble-minded. I can't have that."

Old? Maybe a little tired, but he'd been that before, and with luck would be again. He wasn't worried. His nerves were good for twenty years and fifty accidents more, and by that time Blake would be due for a little ribbing himself.

UNIVERSE
by Robert A. Heinlein

The Proxima Centauri Expedition, sponsored by the Jordan Foundation in 2119, was the first recorded attempt to reach the nearer stars of this galaxy. Whatever its unhappy fate we can only conjecture. . . .
   —Quoted from *The Romance of Modern Astrography,* by Franklin Buck, published by Lux Transcriptions, Ltd., 3.50 cr.

"There's a mutie! Look out!"

At the shouted warning, Hugh Hoyland ducked, with nothing to spare. An egg-sized iron missile clanged against the bulkhead just above his scalp with force that promised a fractured skull. The speed with which he crouched had lifted his feet from the floor plates. Before his body could settle slowly to the deck, he planted his feet against the bulkhead behind him and shoved. He went shooting down the passageway in a long, flat dive, his knife drawn and ready.

He twisted in the air, checked himself with his feet against the opposite bulkhead at the turn in the passage from which the mutie had attacked him, and floated lightly to his feet. The other branch of the passage was empty. His two companions joined him, sliding awkwardly across the floor plates.

"Is it gone?" demanded Alan Mahoney.

"Yes," agreed Hoyland. "I caught a glimpse of it as it ducked down that hatch. A female, I think. Looked like it had four legs."

"Two legs or four, we'll never catch it now," commented the third man. "Who the Huff wants to catch it?" protested Mahoney. "*I* don't."

"Well, I do, for one," said Hoyland. "By Jordan, if its aim had been two inches better, I'd be ready for the Converter."

"Can't either one of you two speak three words without swearing?"

the third man disapproved. "What if the Captain could hear you?" He touched his forehead reverently as he mentioned the Captain.

"Oh, for Jordan's sake," snapped Hoyland, "don't be so stuffy, Mort Tyler. You're not a scientist yet. I reckon I'm as devout as you are—there's no grave sin in occasionally giving vent to your feelings. Even the scientists do it. I've heard 'em."

Tyler opened his mouth as if to expostulate, then apparently thought better of it.

Mahoney touched Hoyland on the arm. "Look, Hugh," he pleaded, "let's get out of here. We've never been this high before. I'm jumpy —I want to get back down to where I can feel some weight on my feet."

Hoyland looked longingly toward the hatch through which his assailant had disappeared while his hand rested on the grip of his knife, then he turned to Mahoney. "O.K., kid," he agreed, "it's a long trip down anyhow."

He turned and slithered back toward the hatch, whereby they had reached the level where they now were, the other two following him. Disregarding the ladder by which they had mounted, he stepped off into the opening and floated slowly down to the deck fifteen feet below, Tyler and Mahoney close behind him. Another hatch, staggered a few feet from the first, gave access to a still lower deck. Down, down, down, and still farther down they dropped, tens and dozens of decks, each silent, dimly lighted, mysterious. Each time they fell a little faster, landed a little harder. Mahoney protested at last.

"Let's walk the rest of the way, Hugh. That last jump hurt my feet."

"All right. But it will take longer. How far have we got to go? Anybody keep count?"

"We've got about seventy decks to go to reach farm country," answered Tyler.

"How do you know?" demanded Mahoney suspiciously.

"I counted them, stupid. And as we came down I took one away for each deck."

"You did not. Nobody but a scientist can do numbering like that. Just because you're learning to read and write you think you know everything."

Hoyland cut in before it could develop into a quarrel. "Shut up, Alan. Maybe he can do it. He's clever about such things. Anyhow, it feels like about seventy decks—I'm heavy enough."

"Maybe he'd like to count the blades on my knife."

"Stow it, I said. Dueling is forbidden outside the village. That is the Rule." They proceeded in silence, running lightly down the stairways until increasing weight on each succeeding level forced them to a more pedestrian pace. Presently they broke through into a level that was quite brilliantly lighted and more than twice as deep between decks as the ones above it. The air was moist and warm; vegetation obscured the view.

"Well, down at last," said Hugh, "I don't recognize this farm; we must have come down by a different line than we went up."

"There's a farmer," said Tyler. He put his little fingers to his lips and whistled, then called, "Hey! Shipmate! Where are we?"

The peasant looked them over slowly, then directed them in reluctant monosyllables to the main passageway which would lead them back to their own village.

A brisk walk of a mile and a half down a wide tunnel moderately crowded with traffic—travelers, porters, an occasional pushcart, a dignified scientist swinging in a litter borne by four husky orderlies and preceded by his master-at-arms to clear the common crew out of the way—a mile and a half of this brought them to the common of their own village, a spacious compartment three decks high and perhaps ten times as wide. They split up and went their own ways, Hugh to his quarters in the barracks of the cadets—young bachelors who did not live with their parents. He washed himself, and went thence to the compartments of his uncle for whom he worked for his meals. His aunt glanced up as he came in, but said nothing, as became a woman.

His uncle said, "Hello, Hugh. Been exploring again?"

"Good eating, Uncle. Yes."

His uncle, a stolid, sensible man, looked tolerantly amused. "Where did you go and what did you find?"

Hugh's aunt had slipped silently out of the compartment, and now returned with his supper which she placed before him. He fell to—it did not occur to him to thank her. He munched a bite before replying.

"Up. We climbed almost to the level-of-no-weight. A mutie tried to crack my skull."

His uncle chuckled. "You'll find your death in those passageways, lad. Better you should pay more attention to my business against the day when I'll die and get out of your way."

Hugh looked stubborn. "Don't you have any curiosity, Uncle?"

"Me? Oh, I was prying enough when I was a lad. I followed the main passage all the way around and back to the village. Right through the Dark Sector I went, with muties tagging my heels. See that scar?"

Hugh glanced at it perfunctorily. He had seen it many times before and heard the story repeated to boredom. Once around the Ship— *pfui!* He wanted to go everywhere, see everything, and find out the way of things. Those upper levels now—if men were not intended to climb that high, why had Jordan created them?

But he kept his own counsel and went on with his meal. His uncle changed the subject. "I've occasion to visit the Witness. John Black claims I owe him three swine. Want to come along?"

"Why, no, I guess not— Wait—I believe I will."

"Hurry up, then."

They stopped at the cadets' barracks, Hugh claiming an errand. The Witness lived in a small, smelly compartment directly across the Common from the barracks, where he would be readily accessible to any who had need of his talents. They found him sitting in his doorway, picking his teeth with a fingernail. His apprentice, a pimply-faced adolescent with an intent nearsighted expression, squatted behind him.

"Good eating," said Hugh's uncle.

"Good eating to you, Edard Hoyland. D'you come on business, or to keep an old man company?"

"Both," Hugh's uncle returned diplomatically, then explained his errand.

"So?" said the Witness. "Well—the contract's clear enough:

"Black John delivered ten bushels of oats,
    Expecting his pay in a pair of shoats;
    Ed brought his sow to breed for pig;
    John gets his pay when the pigs grow big.

"How big are the pigs now, Edard Hoyland?"

"Big enough," acknowledged Hugh's uncle, "but Black claims three instead of two."

"Tell him to go soak his head. 'The Witness has spoken.'"

He laughed in a thin, high cackle.

The two gossiped for a few minutes, Edard Hoyland digging into his recent experiences to satisfy the old man's insatiable liking for details. Hugh kept decently silent while the older men talked. But when his uncle turned to go he spoke up. "I'll stay awhile, Uncle."

"Eh? Suit yourself. Good eating, Witness."

"Good eating, Edard Hoyland."

"I've brought you a present, Witness," said Hugh, when his uncle had passed out of hearing.

"Let me see it."

Hugh produced a package of tobacco which he had picked up from his locker at the barracks. The Witness accepted it without acknowledgment, then tossed it to his apprentice, who took charge of it.

"Come inside," invited the Witness, then directed his speech to his apprentice. "Here, you—fetch the cadet a chair."

"Now, lad," he added as they sat themselves down, "tell me what you have been doing with yourself."

Hugh told him, and was required to repeat in detail all the incidents of his more recent explorations, the Witness complaining the meanwhile over his inability to remember exactly everything he saw.

"You youngsters have no capacity," he pronounced. "No capacity. Even that lout"—he jerked his head toward the apprentice—"he has none, though he's a dozen times better than you. Would you believe it, he can't soak up a thousand lines a day, yet he expects to sit in my seat when I am gone. Why, when I was apprenticed, I used to sing myself to sleep on a mere thousand lines. Leaky vessels—that's what you are."

Hugh did not dispute the charge, but waited for the old man to go on, which he did in his own time.

"You had a question to put to me, lad?"

"In a way, Witness."

"Well—out with it. Don't chew your tongue."

"Did you ever climb all the way up to no-weight?"

"Me? Of course not. I was a Witness, learning my calling. I had the lines of all the Witnesses before me to learn, and no time for boyish amusements."

"I had hoped you could tell me what I would find there."

"Well, now, that's another matter. I've never climbed, but I hold the memories of more climbers than you will ever see. I'm an old man. I knew your father's father, and his grandsire before that. What is it you want to know?"

"Well—" What was it he wanted to know? How could he ask a question that was no more than a gnawing ache in his breast? Still—

"What is it all for, Witness? Why are there all those levels above us?"

"Eh? How's that? Jordan's name, son—I'm a Witness, not a scientist."

"Well—I thought you must know. I'm sorry."

"But I do know. What you want is the Lines from the Beginning."

"I've heard them."

"Hear them again. All your answers are in there, if you've the wisdom to see them. Attend me. No—this is a chance for my apprentice to show off his learning. Here, you! The Lines from the Beginning—and mind your rhythm."

The apprentice wet his lips with his tongue and began:

"In the Beginning there was Jordan, thinking His lonely thoughts alone.

In the Beginning there was darkness, formless, dead, and Man unknown.

Out of the loneness came a longing, out of the longing came a vision,

Out of the dream there came a planning, out of the plan there came decision—

Jordan's hand was lifted and the Ship was born!

Mile after mile of snug compartments, tank by tank for the golden corn,

Ladder and passage, door and locker, fit for the needs of the yet unborn.

He looked on His work and found it pleasing, meet for a race that was yet to be.

He thought of Man—Man came into being—checked his thought and searched for the key.

Man untamed would shame his Maker, Man unruled would spoil the Plan;

So Jordan made the Regulations, orders to each single man,

Each to a task and each to a station, serving a purpose beyond their ken,

Some to speak and some to listen—order came to the ranks of men.

Crew He created to work at their stations, scientists to guide the Plan.

Over them all He created the Captain, made him judge of the race of Man.

Thus it was in the Golden Age!

Jordan is perfect, all below him lack perfection in their deeds.

Envy, Greed, and Pride of Spirit sought for minds to lodge their
   seeds.
One there was who gave them lodging—accursed Huff, the first to
   sin!
His evil counsel stirred rebellion, planted doubt where it had not
   been;
Blood of martyrs stained the floor plates, Jordan's Captain made the
   Trip.
Darkness swallowed up—"

The old man gave the boy the back of his hand, sharp across the
mouth. "Try again!"
   "From the beginning?"
   "No! From where you missed."
   The boy hesitated, then caught his stride:

"Darkness swallowed ways of virtue, Sin prevailed throughout the
   Ship . . ."

The boy's voice droned on, stanza after stanza, reciting at great
length but with little sharpness of detail the old, old story of sin, rebellion, and the time of darkness. How wisdom prevailed at last and
the bodies of the rebel leaders were fed to the Converter. How some
of the rebels escaped making the Trip and lived to father the muties.
How a new Captain was chosen, after prayer and sacrifice.
   Hugh stirred uneasily, shuffling his feet. No doubt the answers to
his questions were there, since these were the Sacred Lines, but he
had not the wit to understand them. Why? What was it all about?
Was there really nothing more to life than eating and sleeping and
finally the long Trip? Didn't Jordan intend for him to understand?
Then why this ache in his breast? This hunger that persisted in spite
of good eating?
   While he was breaking his fast after sleep an orderly came to the
door of his uncle's compartments. "The scientist requires the presence of Hugh Hoyland," he recited glibly.
   Hugh knew that the scientist referred to was Lieutenant Nelson, in
charge of the spiritual and physical welfare of the Ship's sector which
included Hugh's native village. He bolted the last of his breakfast and
hurried after the messenger.

"Cadet Hoyland!" he was announced. The scientist looked up from his own meal and said:

"Oh, yes. Come in, my boy. Sit down. Have you eaten?"

Hugh acknowledged that he had, but his eyes rested with interest on the fancy fruit in front of his superior. Nelson followed his glance. "Try some of these figs. They're a new mutation—I had them brought all the way from the far side. Go ahead—a man your age always has somewhere to stow a few more bites."

Hugh accepted with much self-consciousness. Never before had he eaten in the presence of a scientist. The elder leaned back in his chair, wiped his fingers on his shirt, arranged his beard, and started in.

"I haven't seen you lately, son. Tell me what you have been doing with yourself." Before Hugh could reply he went on: "No, don't tell me—I will tell you. For one thing you have been exploring, climbing, without too much respect for the forbidden areas. Is it not so?" He held the young man's eye. Hugh fumbled for a reply.

But he was let off again. "Never mind. I know, and you know that I know. I am not too displeased. But it has brought it forcibly to my attention that it is time that you decided what you are to do with your life. Have you any plans?"

"Well—no definite ones, sir."

"How about that girl, Edris Baxter? D'you intend to marry her?"

"Why—uh—I don't know, sir. I guess I want to, and her father is willing, I think. Only—"

"Only what?"

"Well—he wants me to apprentice to his farm. I suppose it's a good idea. His farm together with my uncle's business would make a good property."

"But you're not sure?"

"Well—I don't know."

"Correct. You're not for that. I have other plans. Tell me, have you wondered why I taught you to read and write? Of course, you have. But you've kept your own counsel. That is good.

"Now attend me. I've watched you since you were a small child. You have more imagination than the common run, more curiosity, more go. And you are a born leader. You were different even as a baby. Your head was too large, for one thing, and there were some who voted at your birth inspection to put you at once into the Converter. But I held them off. I wanted to see how you would turn out.

"A peasant life is not for the likes of you. You are to be a scientist."

The old man paused and studied his face. Hugh was confused, speechless. Nelson went on: "Oh, yes. Yes, indeed. For a man of your temperament, there are only two things to do with him: Make him one of the custodians, or send him to the Converter."

"Do you mean, sir, that I have nothing to say about it?"

"If you want to put it that bluntly—yes. To leave the bright ones among the ranks of the Crew is to breed heresy. We can't have that. We had it once and it almost destroyed the human race. You have marked yourself out by your exceptional ability; you must now be instructed in right thinking, be initiated into the mysteries, in order that you may be a conserving force rather than a focus of infection and a source of trouble."

The orderly reappeared loaded down with bundles which he dumped on the deck. Hugh glanced at them, then burst out, "Why, those are my things!"

"Certainly," acknowledged Nelson. "I sent for them. You're to sleep here henceforth. I'll see you later and start you on your studies —unless you have something more on your mind?"

"Why, no, sir. I guess not. I must admit I am a little confused. I suppose—I suppose this means you don't want me to marry?"

"Oh, *that*," Nelson answered indifferently. "Take her if you like —her father can't protest now. But let me warn you you'll grow tired of her."

Hugh Hoyland devoured the ancient books that his mentor permitted him to read, and felt no desire for many, many sleeps to go climbing, or even to stir out of Nelson's cabin. More than once he felt that he was on the track of the secret—a secret as yet undefined, even as a question—but again he would find himself more confused than ever. It was evidently harder to reach the wisdom of scientisthood than he had thought.

Once, while he was worrying away at the curious twisted characters of the ancients and trying to puzzle out their odd rhetoric and unfamiliar terms, Nelson came into the little compartment that had been set aside for him, and, laying a fatherly hand on his shoulder, asked, "How goes it, boy?"

"Why, well enough, sir, I suppose," he answered, laying the book aside. "Some of it is not quite clear to me—not clear at all, to tell the truth."

"That is to be expected," the old man said equably. "I've let you struggle along by yourself at first in order that you may see the traps that native wit alone will fall into. Many of these things are not to be understood without instruction. What have you there?" He picked up the book and glanced at it. It was inscribed *Basic Modern Physics*. "So? This is one of the most valuable of the sacred writings, yet the uninitiate could not possibly make good use of it without help. The first thing that you must understand, my boy, is that our forefathers, for all their spiritual perfection, did not look at things in the fashion in which we do.

"They were incurable romantics, rather than rationalists, as we are, and the truths which they handed down to us, though strictly true, were frequently clothed in allegorical language. For example, have you come to the Law of Gravitation?"

"I read about it."

"Did you understand it? No, I can see that you didn't."

"Well," said Hugh defensively, "it didn't seem to *mean* anything. It just sounded silly, if you will pardon me, sir."

"That illustrates my point. You were thinking of it in literal terms, like the laws governing electrical devices found elsewhere in this same book. 'Two bodies attract each other directly as the product of their masses and inversely as the square of their distance.' It sounds like a rule for simple physical facts, does it not? Yet it is nothing of the sort; it was the poetical way the old ones had of expressing the rule of propinquity which governs the emotion of love. The bodies referred to are human bodies, mass is their capacity for love. Young people have a greater capacity for love than the elderly; when they are thrown together, they fall in love, yet when they are separated they soon get over it. 'Out of sight, out of mind.' It's as simple as that. But you were seeking some deep meaning for it."

Hugh grinned. "I never thought of looking at it that way. I can see that I am going to need a lot of help."

"Is there anything else bothering you just now?"

"Well, yes, lots of things, though I probably can't remember them offhand. I mind one thing: Tell me, Father, can muties be considered as being people?"

"I can see you have been listening to idle talk. The answer to that is both yes and no. It is true that the muties originally descended from people but they are no longer part of the Crew—they cannot now be considered as members of the human race, for they have flouted Jordan's Law.

"This is a broad subject," he went on, settling down to it. "There is even some question as to the original meaning of the word 'mutie.' Certainly they number among their ancestors the mutineers who escaped death at the time of the rebellion. But they also have in their blood the blood of many of the mutants who were born during the dark age. You understand, of course, that during that period our present wise rule of inspecting each infant for the mark of sin and returning to the Converter any who are found to be mutations was not in force. There are strange and horrible things crawling through the dark passageways and lurking in the deserted levels."

Hugh thought about it for a while, then asked, "Why is it that mutations still show up among us, the people?"

"That is simple. The seed of sin is still in us. From time to time it still shows up, incarnate. In destroying those monsters we help to cleanse the stock and thereby bring closer the culmination of Jordan's Plan, the end of the Trip at our heavenly home, Far Centaurus."

Hoyland's brow wrinkled again. "That is another thing that I don't understand. Many of these ancient writings speak of the Trip as if it were an actual *moving,* a going-somewhere—as if the Ship itself were no more than a pushcart. How can that be?"

Nelson chuckled. "How can it, indeed? How can that move which is the background against which all else moves? The answer, of course, is plain. You have again mistaken allegorical language for the ordinary usage of everyday speech. Of course, the Ship is solid, immovable, in a physical sense. How can the whole universe move? Yet, it *does* move, in a spiritual sense. With every righteous act we move closer to the sublime destination of Jordan's Plan."

Hugh nodded. "I think I see."

"Of course, it is conceivable that Jordan could have fashioned the world in some other shape than the Ship, had it suited His purpose. When man was younger and more poetical, holy men vied with one another in inventing fanciful worlds which Jordan might have created. One school invented an entire mythology of a topsy-turvy world of endless reaches of space, empty save for pinpoints of light and bodiless mythological monsters. They called it the heavenly world, or heaven, as if to contrast it with the solid reality of the Ship. They seemed never to tire of speculating about it, inventing details for it, and of making pictures of what they conceived it to be like. I suppose they did it to the greater glory of Jordan, and who is to say that He found their dreams unacceptable? But in this modern age we have more serious work to do."

Hugh was not interested in astronomy. Even his untutored mind had been able to see in its wild extravagance an intention not literal. He turned to problems near at hand.

"Since the muties are the seed of sin, why do we make no effort to wipe them out? Would not that be an act that would speed the Plan?"

The old man considered awhile before replying. "That is a fair question and deserves a straight answer. Since you are to be a scientist you will need to know the answer. Look at it this way: There is a *definite* limit to the number of Crew the Ship can support. If our numbers increase without limit, there comes a time when there will not be good eating for all of us. Is it not better that some should die in brushes with the muties than that we should grow in numbers until we killed each other for food?

"The ways of Jordan are inscrutable. Even the muties have a part in His Plan."

It seemed reasonable, but Hugh was not sure.

But when Hugh was transferred to active work as a junior scientist in the operation of the Ship's functions, he found there were other opinions. As was customary, he put in a period serving the Converter. The work was not onerous; he had principally to check in the waste materials brought in by porters from each of the villages, keep books of their contributions, and make sure that no reclaimable metal was introduced into the first-stage hopper. But it brought him into contact with Bill Ertz, the Assistant Chief Engineer, a man not much older than himself.

He discussed with him the things he had learned from Nelson, and was shocked at Ertz's attitude.

"Get this through your head, kid," Ertz told him. "This is a practical job for practical men. Forget all that romantic nonsense. Jordan's Plan! That stuff is all right to keep the peasants quiet and in their place, but don't fall for it yourself. There is no Plan—other than our own plans for looking out for ourselves. The Ship has to have light and heat and power for cooking and irrigation. The Crew can't get along without those things and that makes us boss of the Crew.

"As for this softheaded tolerance toward the muties, you're going to see some changes made! Keep your mouth shut and string along with us."

It impressed on him that he was expected to maintain a primary loyalty to the bloc of younger men among the scientists. They were a well-knit organization within an organization and were made up of practical, hard-headed men who were working toward improvement of conditions throughout the Ship, as they saw them. They were well-knit because an apprentice who failed to see things their way did not last long. Either he failed to measure up and soon found himself back in the ranks of the peasants, or, as was more likely, suffered some mishap and wound up in the Converter.

And Hoyland began to see that they were right.

They were realists. The Ship was the Ship. It was a fact, requiring no explanation. As for Jordan—who had ever seen Him, spoken to Him? What was this nebulous Plan of His? The object of life was living. A man was born, lived his life, and then went to the Converter. It was as simple as that, no mystery to it, no sublime Trip and no Centaurus. These romantic stories were simply hangovers from the childhood of the race before men gained the understanding and the courage to look facts in the face.

He ceased bothering his head about astronomy and mystical physics and all the other mass of mythology he had been taught to revere. He was still amused, more or less, by the Lines from the Beginning and by all the old stories about Earth—what the Huff was "Earth," anyhow?—but now realized that such things could be taken seriously only by children and dullards.

Besides, there was work to do. The younger men, while still maintaining the nominal authority of their elders, had plans of their own, the first of which was a systematic extermination of the muties. Beyond that, their intentions were still fluid, but they contemplated making full use of the resources of the Ship, including the upper levels. The young men were able to move ahead with their plans without an open breach with their elders because the older scientists simply did not bother to any great extent with the routine of the Ship. The present Captain had grown so fat that he rarely stirred from his cabin; his aide, one of the young men's bloc, attended to affairs for him.

Hoyland never laid eyes on the Chief Engineer save once, when he showed up for the purely religious ceremony of manning landing stations.

The project of cleaning out the muties required reconnaissance of the upper levels to be done systematically. It was in carrying out such scouting that Hugh Hoyland was again ambushed by a mutie.

This mutie was more accurate with his slingshot. Hoyland's companions, forced to retreat by superior numbers, left him for dead.

Joe-Jim Gregory was playing himself a game of checkers. Time was when they had played cards together, but Joe, the head on the right, had suspected Jim, the left-hand member of the team, of cheating. They had quarreled about it, then given it up, for they both learned early in their joint career that two heads on one pair of shoulders must necessarily find ways of getting along together.

Checkers was better. They could both see the board, and disagreement was impossible.

A loud metallic knocking at the door of the compartment interrupted the game. Joe-Jim unsheathed his throwing knife and cradled it, ready for quick use. "Come in!" roared Jim.

The door opened, the one who had knocked backed into the room —the only safe way, as everyone knew, to enter Joe-Jim's presence. The newcomer was squat and ruggedly powerful, not over four feet in height. The relaxed body of a man hung across one shoulder and was steadied by a hand.

Joe-Jim returned the knife to its sheath. "Put it down, Bobo," Jim ordered.

"And close the door," added Joe. "Now what have we got here?"

It was a young man, apparently dead, though no wound appeared on him. Bobo patted a thigh. "Eat 'im?" he said hopefully. Saliva spilled out of his still-opened lips.

"Maybe," temporized Jim. "Did you kill him?"

Bobo shook his undersized head.

"Good Bobo," Joe approved. "Where did you hit him?"

"Bobo hit him *there*." The microcephalic shoved a broad thumb against the supine figure in the area between the umbilicus and the breastbone.

"Good shot," Joe approved. "We couldn't have done better with a knife."

"Bobo *good* shot," the dwarf agreed blandly. "Want see?" He twitched his slingshot invitingly.

"Shut up," answered Joe, not unkindly. "No, we don't want to see; we want to make him talk."

"Bobo fix," the short one agreed, and started with simple brutality to carry out his purpose.

Joe-Jim slapped him away, and applied other methods, painful but considerably less drastic than those of the dwarf. The younger man jerked and opened his eyes.

"Eat 'im?" repeated Bobo.

"No," said Joe. "When did you eat last?" inquired Jim.

Bobo shook his head and rubbed his stomach, indicating with graphic pantomime that it had been a long time—too long. Joe-Jim went over to a locker, opened it, and withdrew a haunch of meat. He held it up. Jim smelled it and Joe drew his head away in nose-wrinkling disgust. Joe-Jim threw it to Bobo, who snatched it happily out of the air. "Now, get out," ordered Jim.

Bobo trotted away, closing the door behind him. Joe-Jim turned to the captive and prodded him with his foot. "Speak up," said Jim. "Who the Huff are you?"

The young man shivered, put a hand to his head, then seemed suddenly to bring his surroundings into focus, for he scrambled to his feet, moving awkwardly against the low weight conditions of this level, and reached for his knife.

It was not at his belt.

Joe-Jim had his own out and brandished it. "Be good and you won't get hurt. What do they call you?"

The young man wet his lips, and his eyes hurried about the room. "Speak up," said Joe.

"Why bother with him?" inquired Jim. "I'd say he was only good for meat. Better call Bobo back."

"No hurry about that," Joe answered. "I want to talk to him. What's your name?"

The prisoner looked again at the knife and muttered, "Hugh Hoyland."

"That doesn't tell us much," Jim commented. "What d'you do? What village do you come from? And what were you doing in mutie country?"

But this time Hoyland was sullen. Even the prick of the knife against his ribs caused him only to bite his lips. "Shucks," said Joe, "he's only a stupid peasant. Let's drop it."

"Shall we finish him off?"

"No. Not now. Shut him up."

Joe-Jim opened the door of a small side compartment, and urged

Hugh in with the knife. He then closed and fastened the door and went back to his game. "Your move, Jim."

The compartment in which Hugh was locked was dark. He soon satisfied himself by touch that the smooth steel walls were entirely featureless save for the solid, securely fastened door. Presently he lay down on the deck and gave himself up to fruitless thinking.

He had plenty of time to think, time to fall asleep and awaken more than once. And time to grow very hungry and very, very thirsty.

When Joe-Jim next took sufficient interest in his prisoner to open the door of the cell, Hoyland was not immediately in evidence. He had planned many times what he would do when the door opened and his chance came, but when the event arrived, he was too weak, semi-comatose. Joe-Jim dragged him out.

The disturbance roused him to partial comprehension. He sat up and stared around him.

"Ready to talk?" asked Jim.

Hoyland opened his mouth but no words came out.

"Can't you see he's too dry to talk?" Joe told his twin. Then to Hugh: "Will you talk if we give you some water?"

Hoyland looked puzzled, then nodded vigorously.

Joe-Jim returned in a moment with a mug of water. Hugh drank greedily, paused, seemed about to faint.

Joe-Jim took the mug from him. "That's enough for now," said Joe. "Tell us about yourself."

Hugh did so. In detail, being prompted from time to time.

Hugh accepted a *de facto* condition of slavery with no particular resistance and no great disturbance of soul. The word "slave" was not in his vocabulary, but the condition was a commonplace in everything he had ever known. There had always been those who gave orders and those who carried them out—he could imagine no other condition, no other type of social organization. It was a fact of nature.

Though naturally he thought of escape.

Thinking about it was as far as he got. Joe-Jim guessed his thoughts and brought the matter out into the open. Joe told him, "Don't go getting ideas, youngster. Without a knife you wouldn't get three levels away in this part of the Ship. If you managed to steal a knife from me, you still wouldn't make it down to high-weight. Besides, there's Bobo."

Hugh waited a moment, as was fitting, then said, "Bobo?"

Jim grinned and replied, "We told Bobo that you were his to butcher, if he liked, if you ever stuck your head out of our compartments without us. Now he sleeps outside the door and spends a lot of his time there."

"It was only fair," put in Joe. "He was disappointed when we decided to keep you."

"Say," suggested Jim, turning his head toward his brother's, "how about some fun?" He turned back to Hugh. "Can you throw a knife?"

"Of course," Hugh answered.

"Let's see you. Here." Joe-Jim handed him their own knife. Hugh accepted it, jiggling it in his hand to try its balance. "Try my mark."

Joe-Jim had a plastic target set up at the far end of the room from his favorite chair, on which he was wont to practice his own skill. Hugh eyed it, and, with an arm motion too fast to follow, let fly. He used the economical underhand stroke, thumb on the blade, fingers together.

The blade shivered in the target, well centered in the chewed-up area which marked Joe-Jim's best efforts.

"Good boy!" Joe approved. "What do you have in mind, Jim?"

"Let's give him the knife and see how far he gets."

"No," said Joe, "I don't agree."

"Why not?"

"If Bobo wins, we're out one servant. If Hugh wins, we lose both Bobo and him. It's wasteful."

"Oh, well—if you insist."

"I do. Hugh, fetch the knife."

Hugh did so. It had not occurred to him to turn the knife against Joe-Jim. The master was the master. For servant to attack master was not simply repugnant to good morals, it was an idea so wild that it did not occur to him at all.

Hugh had expected that Joe-Jim would be impressed by his learning as a scientist. It did not work out that way. Joe-Jim, especially Jim, loved to argue. They sucked Hugh dry in short order and figuratively cast him aside. Hoyland felt humiliated. After all, was he not a scientist? Could he not read and write?

"Shut up," Jim told him. "Reading is simple. I could do it before your father was born. D'you think you're the first scientist that has served me? Scientists—bah! A pack of ignoramuses!"

In an attempt to re-establish his own intellectual conceit, Hugh expounded the theories of the younger scientists, the strictly matter-of-fact, hard-boiled realism which rejected all religious interpretation and took the Ship as it was. He confidently expected Joe-Jim to approve such a point of view; it seemed to fit their temperaments.

They laughed in his face.

"Honest," Jim insisted, when he had ceased snorting, "are you young punks so stupid as all that? Why, you're worse than your elders."

"But you just got through saying," Hugh protested in hurt tones, "that all our accepted religious notions are so much bunk. That is just what my friends think. They want to junk all that old nonsense."

Joe started to speak; Jim cut in ahead of him. "Why bother with him, Joe? He's hopeless."

"No, he's not. I'm enjoying this. He's the first one I've talked with in I don't know how long who stood any chance at all of seeing the truth. Let us be—I want to see whether that's a head he has on his shoulders, or just a place to hang his ears."

"O.K.," Jim agreed, "but keep it quiet. I'm going to take a nap." The left-hand head closed its eyes, soon it was snoring. Joe and Hugh continued their discussion in whispers.

"The trouble with you youngsters," Joe said, "is that if you can't understand a thing right off, you think it can't be true. The trouble with your elders is, anything they didn't understand they reinterpreted to mean something else and then thought they understood it. None of you has tried believing clear words the way they were written and then tried to understand them on that basis. Oh, no, you're all too bloody smart for that—if you can't see it right off, it ain't so—it must mean something different."

"What do you mean?" Hugh asked suspiciously.

"Well, take the Trip, for instance. What does it mean to you?"

"Well—to my mind, it doesn't mean anything. It's just a piece of nonsense to impress the peasants."

"And what is the accepted meaning?"

"Well—it's where you go when you die—or rather what you do. You make the Trip to Centaurus."

"And what is Centaurus?"

"It's—mind you, I'm just telling you the orthodox answers; I don't really believe this stuff—it's where you arrive when you've made the Trip, a place where everybody's happy and there's always good eating."

Joe snorted. Jim broke the rhythm of his snoring, opened one eye, and settled back again with a grunt. "That's just what I mean," Joe went on in a lower whisper. "You don't use your head. Did it ever occur to you that the Trip was just what the old books said it was—the Ship and all the Crew actually going somewhere, moving?"

Hoyland thought about it. "You don't mean for me to take you seriously. Physically, it's an impossibility. The Ship can't *go* anywhere. It already *is* everywhere. We can make a trip through it, but *the* Trip —that has to have a spiritual meaning, if it has any."

Joe called on Jordan to support him. "Now, listen," he said, "get this through that thick head of yours. Imagine a place a lot bigger than the Ship, a lot bigger, with the Ship inside it—*moving*. D'you get it?"

Hugh tried. He tried very hard. He shook his head. "It doesn't make sense," he said. "There can't be anything bigger than the Ship. There wouldn't be any place for it to *be*."

"Oh, for Huff's sake! Listen—*outside* the Ship, get that? Straight down beyond the level in every direction. Emptiness out there. Understand me?"

"But there isn't anything below the lowest level. That's why it's the lowest level."

"Look. If you took a knife and started digging a hole in the floor of the lowest level, where would it get you?"

"But you *can't*. It's too hard."

"But suppose you did and it made a hole. Where would that hole go? Imagine it."

Hugh shut his eyes and tried to imagine digging a hole in the lowest level. Digging—as if it were soft—soft as cheese.

He began to get some glimmering of a possibility, a possibility that was unsettling, soul-shaking. He was falling, falling into a hole that he had dug which had no levels under it. He opened his eyes very quickly. "That's awful!" he ejaculated. "I won't believe it."

Joe-Jim got up. "I'll *make* you believe it," he said grimly, "if I have to break your neck to do it." He strode over to the outer door and opened it. "Bobo!" he shouted. "Bobo!"

Jim's head snapped erect. "Wassa matter? Wha's going on?"

"We're going to take Hugh to no-weight."

"What for?"

"To pound some sense into his silly head."

"Some other time."

"No, I want to do it now."

"All right, all right. No need to shake. I'm awake now, anyhow."

Joe-Jim Gregory was almost as nearly unique in his, or their, mental ability as he was in his bodily construction. Under any circumstances he would have been a dominant personality; among the muties it was inevitable that he should bully them, order them about, and live on their services. Had he had the will to power, it is conceivable that he could have organized the muties to fight and overcome the Crew proper.

But he lacked that drive. He was by native temperament an intellectual, a bystander, an observer. He was interested in the "how" and the "why," but his will to action was satisfied with comfort and convenience alone.

Had he been born two normal twins and among the Crew, it is likely that he would have drifted into scientisthood as the easiest and most satisfactory answer to the problem of living and as such would have entertained himself mildly with conversation and administration. As it was, he lacked mental companionship and had whiled away three generations reading and rereading books stolen for him by his stooges.

The two halves of his dual person had argued and discussed what they had read, and had almost inevitably arrived at a reasonably coherent theory of history and the physical world—except in one respect, the concept of fiction was entirely foreign to them; they treated the novels that had been provided for the Jordan expedition in exactly the same fashion that they did text and reference books.

This led to their one major difference of opinion. Jim regarded Allan Quartermain as the greatest man who had ever lived; Joe held out for John Henry.

They were both inordinately fond of poetry; they could recite page after page of Kipling, and were nearly as fond of Rhysling, "the blind singer of the spaceways."

Bobo backed in. Joe-Jim hooked a thumb toward Hugh. "Look," said Joe, "he's going out."

"Now?" said Bobo happily, and grinned, slavering.

"You and your stomach!" Joe answered, rapping Bobo's pate with his knuckles. "No, you don't eat him. You and him—blood brothers. Get it?"

"Not eat 'im?"

"No. Fight for him. He fights for you."

"O.K." The pinhead shrugged his shoulders at the inevitable. "Blood brothers. Bobo know."

"All right. Now we go up to the place-where-everybody-flies. You go ahead and make lookout."

They climbed in single file, the dwarf running ahead to spot the lay of the land, Hoyland behind him, Joe-Jim bringing up the rear, Joe with eyes to the front, Jim watching their rear, head turned over his shoulder.

Higher and higher they went, weight slipping imperceptibly from them with each successive deck. They emerged finally into a level beyond which there was no further progress, no opening above them. The deck curved gently, suggesting that the true shape of the space was a giant cylinder, but overhead a metallic expanse which exhibited a similar curvature obstructed the view and prevented one from seeing whether or not the deck in truth curved back on itself.

There were no proper bulkheads; great stanchions, so huge and squat as to give an impression of excessive, unnecessary strength, grew thickly about them, spacing deck and overhead evenly apart.

Weight was imperceptible. If one remained quietly in one place, the undetectable residuum of weight would bring the body in a gentle drift down to the "floor," but "up" and "down" were terms largely lacking in meaning. Hugh did not like it; it made him gulp, but Bobo seemed delighted by it and not unused to it. He moved through the air like an uncouth fish, banking off stanchion, floor plate, and overhead as suited his convenience.

Joe-Jim set a course parallel to the common axis of the inner and outer cylinders, following a passageway formed by the orderly spacing of the stanchions. There were handrails set along the passage, one of which he followed like a spider on its thread. He made remarkable speed, which Hugh floundered to maintain. In time, he caught the trick of the easy, effortless, overhand pull, the long coast against nothing but air resistance, and the occasional flick of the toes or the hand against the floor. But he was much too busy to tell how far they went before they stopped. Miles, he guessed it to be, but he did not know.

When they did stop, it was because the passage had terminated. A solid bulkhead, stretching away to right and left, barred their way. Joe-Jim moved along it to the right, searching.

He found what he sought, a man-sized door, closed, its presence distinguishable only by a faint crack which marked its outline and a

cursive geometrical design on its surface. Joe-Jim studied this and
scratched his right-hand head. The two heads whispered to each
other. Joe-Jim raised his hand in an awkward gesture.

"No, no!" said Jim. Joe-Jim checked himself. "How's that?" Joe
answered. They whispered together again, Joe nodded, and Joe-Jim
again raised his hand.

He traced the design on the door without touching it, moving his
forefinger through the air perhaps four inches from the surface of the
door. The order of succession in which his finger moved over the lines
of the design appeared simple but certainly not obvious.

Finished, he shoved a palm against the adjacent bulkhead, drifted
back from the door, and waited.

A moment later there was a soft, almost inaudible insufflation; the
door stirred and moved outward perhaps six inches, then stopped.
Joe-Jim appeared puzzled. He ran his hands cautiously into the open
crack and pulled. Nothing happened. He called to Bobo, "Open it."

Bobo looked the situation over, with a scowl on his forehead which
wrinkled almost to his crown. He then placed his feet against the bulkhead, steadying himself by grasping the door with one hand. He took
hold of the edge of the door with both hands, settled his feet firmly,
bowed his body, and strained.

He held his breath, chest rigid, back bent, sweat breaking out from
the effort. The great cords in his neck stood out, making of his head
a misshapen pyramid. Hugh could hear the dwarf's joints crack. It was
easy to believe that he would kill himself with the attempt, too stupid
to give up.

But the door gave suddenly, with a plaint of binding metal. As the
door, in swinging out, slipped from Bobo's fingers, the unexpectedly
released tension in his legs shoved him heavily away from the bulkhead; he plunged down the passageway, floundering for a handhold.
But he was back in a moment, drifting awkwardly through the air as
he massaged a cramped calf.

Joe-Jim led the way inside, Hugh close behind him. "What is this
place?" demanded Hugh, his curiosity overcoming his servant manners.

"The Main Control Room," said Joe.

Main Control Room! The most sacred and taboo place in the Ship,
its very location a forgotten mystery. In the credo of the young men
it was nonexistent. The older scientists varied in their attitude be-

tween fundamentalist acceptance and mystical belief. As enlightened as Hugh believed himself to be, the very words frightened him. The Control Room! Why, the very spirit of Jordan was said to reside there.

He stopped.

Joe-Jim stopped and Joe looked around. "Come on," he said. "What's the matter?"

"Why—uh—uh—"

"Speak up."

"But—but this place is haunted—this is Jordan's—"

"Oh, for Jordan's sake!" protested Joe, with slow exasperation. "I thought you told me you young punks didn't take any stock in Jordan."

"Yes, but—but this is—"

"Stow it. Come along, or I'll have Bobo drag you." He turned away. Hugh followed, reluctantly, as a man climbs a scaffold.

They threaded through a passageway just wide enough for two to use the handrails abreast. The passage curved in a wide sweeping arc of full ninety degrees, then opened into the control room proper. Hugh peered past Joe-Jim's broad shoulders, fearful but curious.

He stared into a well-lighted room, huge, quite two hundred feet across. It was spherical, the interior of a great globe. The surface of the globe was featureless, frosted silver. In the geometrical center of the sphere Hugh saw a group of apparatus about fifteen feet across. To his inexperienced eye, it was completely unintelligible; he could not have described it, but he saw that it floated steadily, with no apparent support.

Running from the end of the passage to the mass at the center of the globe was a tube of metal latticework, wide as the passage itself. It offered the only exit from the passage. Joe-Jim turned to Bobo, and ordered him to remain in the passageway, then entered the tube.

He pulled himself along it, hand over hand, the bars of the latticework making a ladder. Hugh followed him; they emerged into the mass of apparatus occupying the center of the sphere. Seen close up, the gear of the control station resolved itself into its individual details, but it still made no sense to him. He glanced away from it to the inner surface of the globe which surrounded them.

That was a mistake. The surface of the globe, being featureless silvery white, had nothing to lend it perspective. It might have been a hundred feet away, or a thousand, or many miles. He had never experienced an unbroken height greater than that between two decks, nor an open space larger than the village common. He was panic-stricken, scared out of his wits, the more so in that he did not know what it was he feared. But the ghost of long-forgotten jungle ancestors possessed him and chilled his stomach with the basic primitive fear of falling.

He clutched at the control gear, clutched at Joe-Jim.

Joe-Jim let him have one, hard across the mouth with the flat of his hand. "What's the matter with you?" growled Jim.

"I don't know," Hugh presently managed to get out. "I don't know, but I don't *like* this place. Let's get out of here!"

Jim lifted his eyebrows to Joe, looked disgusted, and said, "We might as well. That weak-bellied baby will never understand anything you tell him."

"Oh, he'll be all right," Joe replied, dismissing the matter. "Hugh, climb into one of the chairs—there, that one."

In the meantime, Hugh's eyes had fallen on the tube whereby they had reached the control center and had followed it back by eye to the passage door. The sphere suddenly shrank to its proper focus and the worst of his panic was over. He complied with the order, still trembling, but able to obey.

The control center consisted of a rigid framework, made up of chairs, or frames, to receive the bodies of the operators, and consolidated instrument and report panels, mounted in such a fashion as to be almost in the laps of the operators, where they were readily visible but did not obstruct the view. The chairs had high supporting sides, or arms, and mounted in these arms were the controls appropriate to each officer on watch—but Hugh was not yet aware of that.

He slid under the instrument panel into his seat and settled back, glad of its enfolding stability. It fitted him in a semi-reclining position, footrest to head support.

But something was happening on the panel in front of Joe-Jim; he caught it out of the corner of his eye and turned to look. Bright red letters glowed near the top of the board: 2ND ASTROGATOR POSTED. What was a second astrogator? He didn't know—then he noticed that the extreme top of his own board was labeled 2ND ASTROGATOR and concluded it must be himself, or rather, the man who should be sitting there. He felt momentarily uncomfortable that the proper second astrogator might come in and find him usurping his post, but he put it out of his mind—it seemed unlikely.

But what was a second astrogator, anyhow?

The letters faded from Joe-Jim's board, a red dot appeared on the left-hand edge and remained. Joe-Jim did something with his right hand; his board reported: ACCELERATION—ZERO, then MAIN DRIVE. The last two words blinked several times, then were replaced with NO REPORT. These words faded out, and a bright green dot appeared near the right-hand edge.

"Get ready," said Joe, looking toward Hugh; "the light is going out."

"You're not going to turn out the light?" protested Hugh.

"No—you are. Take a look by your left hand. See those little white lights?"

Hugh did so, and found, shining up through the surface of the chair arm, eight bright little beads of light arranged in two squares, one above the other.

"Each one controls the light of one quadrant," explained Joe. "Cover them with your hand to turn out the light. Go ahead—do it."

Reluctantly, but fascinated, Hugh did as he was directed. He placed a palm over the tiny lights, and waited. The silvery sphere turned to dull lead, faded still more, leaving them in darkness complete save for the silent glow from the instrument panels. Hugh felt nervous but exhilarated. He withdrew his palm; the sphere remained dark, the eight little lights had turned blue.

"Now," said Joe, "I'm going to show you the stars!"

In the darkness, Joe-Jim's right hand slid over another pattern of eight lights.

Creation.

Faithfully reproduced, shining as steady and serene from the walls of the stellarium as did their originals from the black deeps of space, the mirrored stars looked down on him. Light after jeweled light, scattered in careless bountiful splendor across the simulacrum sky, the countless suns lay before him—before him, over him, under him, behind him, in every direction from him. He hung alone in the center of the stellar universe.

"Oooooh!" It was an involuntary sound, caused by his indrawn breath. He clutched the chair arms hard enough to break fingernails, but he was not aware of it. Nor was he afraid at the moment; there was room in his being for but one emotion. Life within the Ship, alternately harsh and workaday, had placed no strain on his innate capacity to experience beauty; for the first time in his life he knew the intolerable ecstasy of beauty unalloyed. It shook him and hurt him, like the first trembling intensity of sex.

It was some time before Hugh sufficiently recovered from the shock and the ensuing intense preoccupation to be able to notice Jim's sardonic laugh, Joe's dry chuckle. "Had enough?" inquired Joe. Without waiting for a reply, Joe-Jim turned the lights back on, using the duplicate controls mounted in the left arm of his chair.

Hugh sighed. His chest ached and his heart pounded. He realized suddenly that he had been holding his breath the entire time that the lights had been turned out. "Well, smart boy," asked Jim, "are you convinced?"

Hugh sighed again, not knowing why. With the lights back on, he felt safe and snug again, but was possessed of a deep sense of personal loss. He knew, subconsciously, that, having seen the stars, he would never be happy again. The dull ache in his breast, the vague inchoate yearning for his lost heritage of open sky and stars, was never to be silenced, even though he was yet too ignorant to be aware of it at the top of his mind. "What was it?" he asked in a hushed voice.

"That's *it*," answered Joe. "That's the world. That's the universe. That's what I've been trying to tell you about."

Hugh tried furiously to force his inexperienced mind to comprehend. "That's what you mean by Outside?" he asked. "All those beautiful little lights?"

"Sure," said Joe, "only they aren't little. They're a long way off, you see—maybe thousands of miles."

"What?"

"Sure, sure," Joe persisted. "There's lots of room out there. Space. It's big. Why, some of those stars may be as big as the Ship—maybe bigger."

Hugh's face was a pitiful study in overstrained imagination. "Bigger than the Ship?" he repeated. "But—but—"

Jim tossed his head impatiently and said to Joe, "Wha'd' I tell you? You're wasting our time on this lunk. He hasn't got the capacity—"

"Easy, Jim," Joe answered mildly; "don't expect him to run before he can crawl. It took us a long time. I seem to remember that you were a little slow to believe your own eyes."

"That's a lie," said Jim nastily. "*You* were the one that had to be convinced."

"O.K., O.K.," Joe conceded, "let it ride. But it was a long time before we both had it all straight."

Hoyland paid little attention to the exchange between the two brothers. It was a usual thing; his attention was centered on matters decidedly not usual. "Joe," he asked, "what became of the Ship while we were looking at the stars? Did we stare right through it?"

"Not exactly," Joe told him. "You weren't looking directly at the stars at all, but at a kind of picture of them. It's like— Well, they do it with mirrors, sort of. I've got a book that tells about it."

"But you *can* see 'em directly," volunteered Jim, his momentary pique forgotten. "There's a compartment forward of here—"

"Oh, yes," put in Joe, "it slipped my mind. The Captain's veranda. 'S got one all of glass; you can look right out."

"The Captain's veranda? But—"

"Not *this* Captain. He's never been near the place. That's the name over the door of the compartment."

"What's a 'veranda'?"

"Blessed if I know. It's just the name of the place."

"Will you take me up there?"

Joe appeared to be about to agree, but Jim cut in. "Some other time. I want to get back—I'm hungry."

They passed back through the tube, woke up Bobo, and made the long trip back down.

It was long before Hugh could persuade Joe-Jim to take him exploring again, but the time intervening was well spent. Joe-Jim turned him loose on the largest collection of books that Hugh had ever seen. Some of them were copies of books Hugh had seen before, but even these he read with new meanings. He read incessantly, his mind soaking up new ideas, stumbling over them, struggling, striving to grasp them. He begrudged sleep, he forgot to eat until his breath grew sour and compelling pain in his midriff forced him to pay attention to his body. Hunger satisfied, he would be back at it until his head ached and his eyes refused to focus.

Joe-Jim's demands for service were few. Although Hugh was never off duty, Joe-Jim did not mind his reading as long as he was within earshot and ready to jump when called. Playing checkers with one of the pair when the other did not care to play was the service which used up the most time, and even this was not a total loss, for, if the player were Joe, he could almost always be diverted into a discussion of the Ship, its history, its machinery and equipment, the sort of people who had built it and first manned it—and *their* history, back on Earth, Earth the incredible, that strange place where people had lived on the *outside* instead of the *inside*.

Hugh wondered why they did not fall off.

He took the matter up with Joe and at last gained some notion of gravitation. He never really understood it emotionally—it was too wildly improbable—but as an intellectual concept he was able to accept it and use it, much later, in his first vague glimmerings of the science of ballistics and the art of astrogation and ship maneuvering. And it led in time to his wondering about weight in the Ship, a matter that had never bothered him before. The lower the level the greater the weight had been to his mind simply the order of nature, and nothing to wonder at. He was familiar with centrifugal force as it applied to slingshots. To apply it also to the whole Ship, to think of the Ship as spinning like a slingshot and thereby causing weight, was too much of a hurdle—he never really believed it.

Joe-Jim took him back once more to the Control Room and showed him what little Joe-Jim knew about the manipulation of the controls and the reading of the astrogation instruments.

The long-forgotten engineer-designers employed by the Jordan Foundation had been instructed to design a ship that would not—*could* not—wear out, even though the Trip were protracted beyond the expected sixty years. They built better than they knew. In planning the main drive engines and the auxiliary machinery, largely automatic, which would make the Ship habitable, and in designing the controls necessary to handle all machinery not entirely automatic, the very idea of moving parts had been rejected. The engines and auxiliary equipment worked on a level below mechanical motion, on a level of pure force, as electrical transformers do. Instead of push buttons, levers, cams, and shafts, the controls and the machinery they served were planned in terms of balance between static fields, bias of electronic flow, circuits broken or closed by a hand placed over a light.

On this level of action, friction lost its meaning, wear and erosion took no toll. Had all hands been killed in the mutiny, the Ship would still have plunged on through space, still lighted, its air still fresh and moist, its engines ready and waiting. As it was, though elevators and conveyor belts fell into disrepair, disuse, and finally into the oblivion of forgotten function, the essential machinery of the Ship continued its automatic service to its ignorant human freight, or waited, quiet and ready, for someone bright enough to puzzle out its key.

Genius had gone into the building of the Ship. Far too huge to be assembled on Earth, it had been put together piece by piece in its own orbit out beyond the Moon. There it had swung for fifteen silent years while the problems presented by the decision to make its machinery foolproof and enduring had been formulated and solved. A whole new field of submolar action had been conceived in the process, struggled with, and conquered.

So— When Hugh placed an untutored, questing hand over the first of a row of lights marked ACCELERATION, POSITIVE, he got an immediate response, though not in terms of acceleration. A red light at the top of the chief pilot's board blinked rapidly and the annunciator panel glowed with a message: MAIN ENGINES—NOT MANNED.

"What does that mean?" he asked Joe-Jim.

"There's no telling," said Jim. "We've done the same thing in the main engine room," added Joe. "There, when you try it, it says 'Control Room Not Manned.'"

Hugh thought a moment. "What would happen," he persisted, "if all the control stations had somebody at 'em at once, and then I did that?"

"Can't say," said Joe. "Never been able to try it."

Hugh said nothing. A resolve which had been growing, formless, in his mind was now crystallizing into decision. He was busy with it.

He waited until he found Joe-Jim in a mellow mood, both of him, before broaching his idea. They were in the Captain's veranda at the time Hugh decided the moment was ripe. Joe-Jim rested gently in the Captain's easy chair, his belly full of food, and gazed out through the heavy glass of the view port at the serene stars. Hugh floated beside him. The spinning of the Ship caused the stars to appear to move in stately circles.

Presently he said, "Joe-Jim—"

"Eh? What's that, youngster?" It was Joe who had replied.

"It's pretty swell, isn't it?"

"What is?"

"All that. The stars." Hugh indicated the view through the port with a sweep of his arm, then caught at the chair to stop his own backspin.

"Yeah, it sure is. Makes you feel good." Surprisingly, it was Jim who offered this.

Hugh knew the time was right. He waited a moment, then said, "Why don't we finish the job?"

Two heads turned simultaneously, Joe leaning out a little to see past Jim. "What job?"

"The Trip. Why don't we start up the main drive and go on with it? Somewhere out there," he said hurriedly to finish before he was interrupted, "there are planets like Earth—or so the First Crew thought. Let's go find them."

Jim looked at him, then laughed. Joe shook his head.

"Kid," he said, "you don't know what you are talking about. You're as balmy as Bobo. No," he went on, "that's all over and done with. Forget it."

"Why is it over and done with, Joe?"

"Well, because— It's too big a job. It takes a crew that understands what it's all about, trained to operate the Ship."

"Does it take so many? You have shown me only about a dozen places, all told, for men actually to be at the controls. Couldn't a dozen men run the Ship—if they knew what you know," he added slyly.

Jim chuckled. "He's got you, Joe. He's right."

Joe brushed it aside. "You overrate our knowledge. Maybe we *could* operate the Ship, but we wouldn't get anywhere. We don't know where we are. The Ship has been drifting for I don't know how many generations. We don't know where we're headed, or how fast we're going."

"But look," Hugh pleaded, "there are instruments. You showed them to me. Couldn't we learn how to use them? Couldn't *you* figure them out, Joe, if you really wanted to?"

"Oh, I suppose so," Jim agreed.

"Don't boast, Jim," said Joe.

"I'm not boasting," snapped Jim. "If a thing'll work, I can figure it out."

"Humph!" said Joe.

The matter rested in delicate balance. Hugh had got them disagreeing among themselves—which was what he wanted—with the less tractable of the pair on his side. Now, to consolidate his gain—

"I had an idea," he said quickly, "to get you men to work with, Jim, if you were able to train them."

"What's your idea?" demanded Jim suspiciously.

"Well, you remember what I told you about a bunch of the younger scientists—"

"Those fools!"

"Yes, yes, sure—but they don't know what you know. In their way they were trying to be reasonable. Now, if I could go back down and tell them what you've taught me, I could get you enough men to work with."

Joe cut in. "Take a good look at us, Hugh. What do you see?"

"Why—why—I see *you*—Joe-Jim."

"You see a mutie," corrected Joe, his voice edged with sarcasm. "We're a *mutie.* Get that? Your scientists won't work with us."

"No, no," protested Hugh, "that's not true. I'm not talking about peasants. Peasants wouldn't understand, but these are *scientists,* and the smartest of the lot. They'll understand. All you need to do is to arrange safe conduct for them through mutie country. You can do that, can't you?" he added, instinctively shifting the point of the argument to firmer ground.

"Why, sure," said Jim.

"Forget it," said Joe.

"Well, O.K.," Hugh agreed, sensing that Joe really was annoyed at his persistence, "but it would be fun—" He withdrew some distance from the brothers.

He could hear Joe-Jim continuing the discussion with himself in low tones. He pretended to ignore it. Joe-Jim had this essential defect in his joint nature: being a committee, rather than a single individual, he was hardly fitted to be a man of action, since all decisions were necessarily the result of discussion and compromise.

Several moments later Hugh heard Joe's voice raised. "All right, all *right*—have it your own way!" He then called out, "Hugh! Come here!"

Hugh kicked himself away from an adjacent bulkhead and shot over to the immediate vicinity of Joe-Jim, arresting his flight with both hands against the framework of the Captain's chair.

"We've decided," said Joe without preliminaries, "to let you go back down to the high-weight and try to peddle your goods. But you're a fool," he added sourly.

Bobo escorted Hugh down through the dangers of the levels frequented by muties and left him in the uninhabited zone above highweight. "Thanks, Bobo," Hugh said in parting. "Good eating." The dwarf grinned, ducked his head, and sped away, swarming up the ladder they had just descended.

Hugh turned and started down, touching his knife as he did so. It was good to feel it against him again. Not that it was his original knife. That had been Bobo's prize when he was captured, and Bobo had been unable to return it, having inadvertently left it sticking in a big one that got away. But the replacement Joe-Jim had given him was well balanced and quite satisfactory.

Bobo had conducted him, at Hugh's request and by Joe-Jim's order, down to the area directly over the auxiliary Converter used by the scientists. He wanted to find Bill Ertz, Assistant Chief Engineer and leader of the bloc of younger scientists, and he did not want to have to answer too many questions before he found him.

Hugh dropped quickly down the remaining levels and found himself in a main passageway which he recognized. Good! A turn to the left, a couple of hundred yards' walk and he found himself at the door of the compartment which housed the Converter. A guard lounged in front of it. Hugh started to push on past, was stopped. "Where do you think you're going?"

"I want to find Bill Ertz."

"You mean the Chief Engineer? Well, he's not here."

"Chief? What's happened to the old one?" Hoyland regretted the remark at once—but it was already out.

"Huh? The old Chief? Why, he's made the Trip long since." The guard looked at him suspiciously. "What's wrong with you?"

"Nothing," denied Hugh. "Just a slip."

"Funny sort of a slip. Well, you'll find Chief Ertz around his office probably."

"Thanks. Good eating."

"Good eating."

Hugh was admitted to see Ertz after a short wait. Ertz looked up from his desk as Hugh came in. "Well," he said, "so you're back, and not dead after all. This *is* a surprise. We had written you off, you know, as making the Trip."

"Yes, I suppose so."

"Well, sit down and tell me about it—I've a little time to spare at the moment. Do you know, though, I wouldn't have recognized you. You've changed a lot—all that gray hair. I imagine you had some pretty tough times."

Gray hair? Was his hair gray? And Ertz had changed a lot, too,

Hugh now noticed. He was paunchy and the lines in his face had set. Good Jordan! How long had he been gone?

Ertz drummed on his desk top, and pursed his lips. "It makes a problem—your coming back like this. I'm afraid I can't just assign you to your old job; Mort Tyler has that. But we'll find a place for you, suitable to your rank."

Hugh recalled Mort Tyler and not too favorably. A precious sort of a chap, always concerned with what was proper and according to regulations. So Tyler had actually made scientisthood, and was on Hugh's old job at the Converter. Well, it didn't matter. "That's all right," he began. "I wanted to talk to you about—"

"Of course, there's the matter of seniority," Ertz went on. "Perhaps the Council had better consider the matter. I don't know of a precedent. We've lost a number of scientists to the muties in the past, but you are the first to escape with his life in my memory."

"That doesn't matter," Hugh broke in. "I've something much more pressing to talk about. While I was away I found out some amazing things, Bill, things that it is of paramount importance for you to know about. That's why I came straight to you. Listen, I—"

Ertz was suddenly alert. "Of course you have! I must be slowing down. You must have had a marvelous opportunity to study the muties and scout out their territory. Come on, man, spill it! Give me your report."

Hugh wet his lips. "It's not what you think," he said. "It's much more important than just a report on the muties, though it concerns them, too. In fact, we may have to change our whole policy with respect to the mu—"

"Well, go ahead, go ahead! I'm listening."

"All right." Hugh told him of his tremendous discovery as to the actual nature of the Ship, choosing his words carefully and trying very hard to be convincing. He dwelt lightly on the difficulties presented by an attempt to reorganize the Ship in accordance with the new concept and bore down heavily on the prestige and honor that would accrue to the man who led the effort.

He watched Ertz's face as he talked. After the first start of complete surprise when Hugh launched his key idea, the fact that the Ship was actually a moving body in a great outside space, his face became impassive and Hugh could read nothing in it, except that he seemed to detect a keener interest when Hugh spoke of how Ertz was just the man for the job because of his leadership of the younger, more progressive scientists.

When Hugh concluded, he waited for Ertz's response. Ertz said nothing at first, simply continued with his annoying habit of drumming on the top of his desk. Finally he said, "These are important matters, Hoyland, much too important to be dealt with casually. I must have time to chew it over."

"Yes, certainly," Hugh agreed. "I wanted to add that I've made arrangements for safe passage up to no-weight. I can take you up and let you see for yourself."

"No doubt that is best," Ertz replied. "Well—are you hungry?"

"No."

"Then we'll both sleep on it. You can use the compartment at the back of my office. I don't want you discussing this with anyone else until I've had time to think about it; it might cause unrest if it got out without proper preparation."

"Yes, you're right."

"Very well, then"—Ertz ushered him into a compartment behind his office which he very evidently used for a lounge—"have a good rest," he said, "and we'll talk later."

"Thanks," Hugh acknowledged. "Good eating."

"Good eating."

Once he was alone, Hugh's excitement gradually dropped away from him, and he realized that he was fagged out and very sleepy. He stretched out on a built-in couch and fell asleep.

When he awoke he discovered that the only door to the compartment was barred from the other side. Worse than that, his knife was gone.

He had waited an indefinitely long time when he heard activity at the door. It opened; two husky, unsmiling men entered. "Come along," said one of them. He sized them up, noting that neither of them carried a knife. No chance to snatch one from their belts, then. On the other hand he might be able to break away from them.

But beyond them, a wary distance away in the outer room, were two other equally formidable men, each armed with a knife. One balanced his for throwing; the other held his by the grip, ready to stab at close quarters.

He was boxed in and he knew it. They had anticipated his possible moves.

He had long since learned to relax before the inevitable. He composed his face and marched quietly out. Once through the door he saw Ertz, waiting and quite evidently in charge of the party of men. He spoke to him, being careful to keep his voice calm. "Hello, Bill. Pretty extensive preparations you've made. Some trouble, maybe?"

Ertz seemed momentarily uncertain of his answer, then said, "You're going before the Captain."

"Good!" Hugh answered. "Thanks, Bill. But do you think it's wise to try to sell the idea to him without laying a little preliminary foundation with the others?"

Ertz was annoyed at his apparent thickheadedness and showed it. "You don't get the idea," he growled. "You're going before the Captain to stand trial—for heresy!"

Hugh considered this as if the idea had not before occurred to him. He answered mildly, "You're off down the wrong passage, Bill. Perhaps a charge and trial is the best way to get at the matter, but I'm not a peasant, simply to be hustled before the Captain. I must be tried by the Council. I am a scientist."

"Are you now?" Ertz said softly. "I've had advice about that. You were written off the lists. Just what you are is a matter for the Captain to determine."

Hugh held his peace. It was against him, he could see, and there was no point in antagonizing Ertz. Ertz made a signal; the two unarmed men each grasped one of Hugh's arms. He went with them quietly.

Hugh looked at the Captain with new interest. The old man had not changed much—a little fatter, perhaps.

The Captain settled himself slowly down in his chair, and picked up the memorandum before him.

"What's this all about?" he began irritably. "I don't understand it."

Mort Tyler was there to present the case against Hugh, a circumstance which Hugh had had no way of anticipating and which added to his misgivings. He searched his boyhood recollections for some handle by which to reach the man's sympathy, found none. Tyler cleared his throat and commenced:

"This is the case of one Hugh Hoyland, Captain, formerly one of your junior scientists—"

"Scientist, eh? Why doesn't the Council deal with him?"

"Because he is no longer a scientist, Captain. He went over to the muties. He now returns among us, preaching heresy and seeking to undermine your authority."

The Captain looked at Hugh with the ready belligerency of a man jealous of his prerogatives.

"Is that so?" he bellowed. "What have you to say for yourself?"

"It is not true, Captain," Hugh answered. "All that I have said to anyone has been an affirmation of the absolute truth of our ancient knowledge. I have not disputed the truths under which we live; I have simply affirmed them more forcibly than is the ordinary custom. I—"

"I still don't understand this," the Captain interrupted, shaking his head. "You're charged with heresy, yet you say you believe the Teachings. If you aren't guilty, why are you here?"

"Perhaps I can clear the matter up," put in Ertz. "Hoyland—"

"Well, I hope you can," the Captain went on. "Come—let's hear it."

Ertz proceeded to give a reasonably correct, but slanted, version of Hoyland's return and his strange story. The Captain listened, with an expression that varied between puzzlement and annoyance.

When Ertz had concluded, the Captain turned to Hugh. "Humph!" he said.

Hugh spoke immediately. "The gist of my contention, Captain, is that there is a place up at no-weight where you can actually *see* the truth of our faith that the Ship is moving, where you can actually see Jordan's Plan in operation. That is not a denial of faith; that affirms it. There is no need to take my word for it. Jordan Himself will prove it."

Seeing that the Captain appeared to be in a state of indecision, Tyler broke in: "Captain, there is a possible explanation of this incredible situation which I feel duty bound that you should hear. Offhand, there are two obvious interpretations of Hoyland's ridiculous story: He may simply be guilty of extreme heresy, or he may be a mutie at heart and engaged in a scheme to lure you into their hands. But there is a third, more charitable explanation and one which I feel within me is probably the true one.

"There is record that Hoyland was seriously considered for the Converter at his birth inspection, but that his deviation from normal was slight, being simply an overlarge head, and he was passed. It seems to me that the terrible experiences he has undergone at the hands of the muties have finally unhinged an unstable mind. The poor chap is simply not responsible for his own actions."

Hugh looked at Tyler with new respect. To absolve him of guilt and at the same time to make absolutely certain that Hugh would wind up making the Trip—how neat!

The Captain shook a palm at them. "This has gone on long enough." Then, turning to Ertz: "Is there a recommendation?"

"Yes, Captain. The Converter."

"Very well, then. I really don't see, Ertz," he continued testily, "why I should be bothered with these details. It seems to me that you should be able to handle discipline in your department without my help."

"Yes, Captain."

The Captain shoved back from his desk, started to get up. "Recommendation confirmed. Dismissed."

Anger flooded through Hugh at the unreasonable injustice of it. They had not even considered looking at the only real evidence he had in his defense. He heard a shout: "Wait!"—then discovered it was his own voice.

The Captain paused, looking at him.

"Wait a moment," Hugh went on, his words spilling out of their own accord. "This won't make any difference, for you're all so damn sure you know all the answers that you won't consider a fair offer to come see with your own eyes. Nevertheless—Nevertheless—it *still* moves!"

Hugh had plenty of time to think, lying in the compartment where they confined him to await the power needs of the Converter, time to think, and to second-guess his mistakes. Telling his tale to Ertz immediately—that had been mistake number one. He should have waited, become reacquainted with the man and felt him out, instead of depending on a friendship which had never been very close.

Second mistake, Mort Tyler. When he heard his name he should have investigated and found out just how much influence the man had with Ertz. He had known him of old, he should have known better.

Well, here he was, condemned as a mutant—or maybe as a heretic. It came to the same thing. He considered whether or not he should have tried to explain why mutants happened. He had learned about it himself in some of the old records in Joe-Jim's possession. No, it wouldn't wash. How could you explain about radiations from the Outside causing the birth of mutants when the listeners did not be-

lieve there was such a place as Outside? No, he had messed it up before he was ever taken before the Captain.

His self-recriminations were disturbed at last by the sound of his
door being unfastened. It was too soon for another of the infrequent
meals; he thought that they had come at last to take him away, and
renewed his resolve to take someone with him.

But he was mistaken. He heard a voice of gentle dignity: "Son,
son, how does this happen?" It was Lieutenant Nelson, his first
teacher, looking older than ever and frail.

The interview was distressing for both of them. The old man, child-
less himself, had cherished great hopes for his protégé, even the
ambition that he might eventually aspire to the captaincy, though he
had kept his vicarious ambition to himself, believing it not good for
the young to praise them too highly. It had hurt his heart when the
youth was lost.

Now he had returned, a man, but under disgraceful conditions and
under sentence of death.

The meeting was no less unhappy for Hugh. He had loved the old
man, in his way, wanted to please him and needed his approval. But
he could see, as he told his story, that Nelson was not capable of treating the story as anything but an aberration of Hugh's mind, and he
suspected that Nelson would rather see him meet a quick death in the
Converter, his atoms smashed to hydrogen and giving up clean useful power, than have him live to make a mock of the ancient teachings.

In that he did the old man an injustice; he underrated Nelson's
mercy, but not his devotion to "science." But let it be said for Hugh
that, had there been no more at issue than his own personal welfare,
he might have preferred death to breaking the heart of his benefactor
—being a romantic and more than a bit foolish.

Presently the old man got up to leave, the visit having grown unendurable to each of them. "Is there anything I can do for you, son?
Do they feed you well enough?"

"Quite well, thanks," Hugh lied.

"Is there anything else?"

"No—yes, you might send me some tobacco. I haven't had a chew
in a long time."

"I'll take care of it. Is there anyone you would like to see?"

"Why, I was under the impression that I was not permitted visitors—ordinary visitors."

"You are right, but I think perhaps I may be able to get the rule relaxed. But you will have to give me your promise not to speak of your heresy," he added anxiously.

Hugh thought quickly. This was a new aspect, a new possibility. His uncle? No, while they had always got along well, their minds did not meet—they would greet each other as strangers. He had never made friends easily; Ertz had been his obvious next friend and now look at the damned thing! Then he recalled his village chum, Alan Mahoney, with whom he had played as a boy. True, he had seen practically nothing of him since the time he was apprenticed to Nelson. Still—

"Does Alan Mahoney still live in our village?"

"Why, yes."

"I'd like to see him, if he'll come."

Alan arrived, nervous, ill at ease, but plainly glad to see Hugh and very much upset to find him under sentence to make the Trip. Hugh pounded him on the back. "Good boy," he said. "I knew you would come."

"Of course, I would," protested Alan, "once I knew. But nobody in the village knew it. I don't think even the Witness knew it."

"Well, you're here, that's what matters. Tell me about yourself. Have you married?"

"Huh, uh, no. Let's not waste time talking about me. Nothing ever happens to me anyhow. How in Jordan's name did you get in this jam, Hugh?"

"I can't talk about that, Alan. I promised Lieutenant Nelson that I wouldn't."

"Well, what's a promise—*that* kind of a promise? You're in a *jam,* fellow."

"Don't I know it!"

"Somebody have it in for you?"

"Well—our old pal Mort Tyler didn't help any; I think I can say that much."

Alan whistled and nodded his head slowly. "That explains a lot."

"How come? You know something?"

"Maybe, maybe not. After you went away he married Edris Baxter."

"So? Hm-m-m—yes, that clears up a lot." He remained silent for a time.

Presently Alan spoke up: "Look, Hugh. You're not going to sit here and take it, are you? Particularly with Tyler mixed in it. We gotta get you outa here."

"How?"

"I don't know. Pull a raid, maybe. I guess I could get a few knives to rally round and help us—all good boys, spoiling for a fight."

"Then, when it's over, we'd all be for the Converter. You, me, and your pals. No, it won't wash."

"But we've *got* to do something. We can't just sit here and wait for them to burn you."

"I know that." Hugh studied Alan's face. Was it a fair thing to ask? He went on, reassured by what he had seen. "Listen. You would do anything you could to get me out of this, wouldn't you?"

"You know that." Alan's tone showed hurt.

"Very well, then. There is a dwarf named Bobo. I'll tell you how to find him—"

Alan climbed, up and up, higher than he had ever been since Hugh had led him, as a boy, into foolhardy peril. He was older now, more conservative; he had no stomach for it. To the very real danger of leaving the well-traveled lower levels was added his superstitious ignorance. But still he climbed.

This should be about the place—unless he had lost count. But he saw nothing of the dwarf.

Bobo saw him first. A slingshot load caught Alan in the pit of the stomach, even as he was shouting, "Bobo!"

Bobo backed into Joe-Jim's compartment and dumped his load at the feet of the twins. "Fresh meat," he said proudly.

"So it is," agreed Jim indifferently. "Well, it's yours; take it away."

The dwarf dug a thumb into a twisted ear. "Funny," he said, "he knows Bobo's name."

Joe looked up from the book he was reading—Browning's *Collected Poems*, L-Press, New York, London, Luna city, cr. 35. "That's interesting. Hold on a moment."

Hugh had prepared Alan for the shock of Joe-Jim's appearance. In reasonably short order he collected his wits sufficiently to be able to tell his tale. Joe-Jim listened to it without much comment, Bobo with interest but little comprehension.

When Alan concluded, Jim remarked, "Well, you win, Joe. He didn't make it." Then, turning to Alan, he added, "You can take Hoyland's place. Can you play checkers?"

Alan looked from one head to the other. "But you don't understand," he said. "Aren't you going to do anything about it?"

Joe looked puzzled. "Us? Why should we?"

"But you've *got* to. Don't you see? He's depending on you. There's nobody else he can look to. That's why I came. Don't you see?"

"Wait a moment," drawled Jim, "wait a moment. Keep your belt on. Supposing we did want to help him—which we don't—how in Jordan's Ship could we? Answer me that."

"Why—why—" Alan stumbled in the face of such stupidity. "Why, get up a rescue party, of course, and go down and get him out!"

"Why should we get ourselves killed in a fight to rescue your friend?"

Bobo pricked his ears. "Fight?" he inquired eagerly.

"No, Bobo," Joe denied. "No fight. Just talk."

"Oh," said Bobo and returned to passivity.

Alan looked at the dwarf. "If you'd even let Bobo and me—"

"No," Joe said shortly. "It's out of the question. Shut up about it."

Alan sat in a corner, hugging his knees in despair. If only he could get out of there. He could still try to stir up some help down below. The dwarf seemed to be asleep, though it was difficult to be sure with him. If only Joe-Jim would sleep, too.

Joe-Jim showed no indication of sleepiness. Joe tried to continue reading, but Jim interrupted him from time to time. Alan could not hear what they were saying.

Presently Joe raised his voice. "Is that your idea of fun?" he demanded.

"Well," said Jim, "it beats checkers."

"It does, does it? Suppose you get a knife in your eye—where would I be then?"

"You're getting old, Joe. No juice in you any more."

"You're as old as I am."

"Yeah, but I got young ideas."

"Oh, you make me sick. Have it your own way—but don't blame me. Bobo!"

The dwarf sprang up at once, alert. "Yeah, Boss."

"Go out and dig up Squatty and Long Arm and Pig." Joe-Jim got up, went to a locker, and started pulling knives out of their racks.

Hugh heard the commotion in the passageway outside his prison. It could be the guards coming to take him to the Converter, though they probably wouldn't be so noisy. Or it could be just some excitement unrelated to him. On the other hand it might be—

It was. The door burst open, and Alan was inside, shouting at him and thrusting a brace of knives into his hands. He was hurried out of the door, while stuffing the knives in his belt and accepting two more.

Outside he saw Joe-Jim, who did not see him at once, as he was methodically letting fly, as calmly as if he had been engaging in target practice in his own study. And Bobo, who ducked his head and grinned with a mouth widened by a bleeding cut, but continued the easy flow of the motion whereby he loaded and let fly. There were three others, two of whom Hugh recognized as belonging to Joe-Jim's privately owned gang of bullies—muties by definition and birthplace; they were not deformed.

The count does not include still forms on the floor plates.

"Come on!" yelled Alan. "There'll be more in no time." He hurried down the passage to the right.

Joe-Jim desisted and followed him. Hugh let one blade go for luck at a figure running away to the left. The target was poor, and he had no time to see if he had drawn blood. They scrambled along the passage, Bobo bringing up the rear, as if reluctant to leave the fun, and came to a point where a side passage crossed the main one.

Alan led them to the right again. "Stairs ahead," he shouted.

They did not reach them. An airtight door, rarely used, clanged in their faces ten yards short of the stairs. Joe-Jim's bravoes checked their flight and they looked doubtfully at their master. Bobo broke his thickened nails trying to get a purchase on the door.

The sounds of pursuit were clear behind them.

"Boxed in," said Joe softly. "I hope you like it, Jim."

Hugh saw a head appear around the corner of the passage they had quitted. He threw overhand but the distance was too great; the knife clanged harmlessly against steel. The head disappeared. Long Arm kept his eye on the spot, his sling loaded and ready.

Hugh grabbed Bobo's shoulder. "Listen! Do you see that light?"

The dwarf blinked stupidly. Hugh pointed to the intersection of the glowtubes where they crossed in the overhead directly above the junction of the passages. "That light. Can you hit them where they cross?"

Bobo measured the distance with his eye. It would be a hard shot under any conditions at that range. Here, constricted as he was by the low passageway, it called for a fast, flat trajectory, and allowance for higher weight than he was used to.

He did not answer. Hugh felt the wind of his swing but did not see the shot. There was a tinkling crash; the passage became dark.

"Now!" yelled Hugh, and led them away at a run. As they neared the intersection he shouted, "Hold your breaths! Mind the gas!" The radioactive vapor poured lazily out from the broken tube above and filled the crossing with a greenish mist.

Hugh ran to the right, thankful for his knowledge as an engineer of the lighting circuits. He had picked the right direction; the passage ahead was black, being serviced from beyond the break. He could hear footsteps around him; whether they were friend or enemy he did not know.

They burst into light. No one was in sight but a scared and harmless peasant who scurried away at an unlikely pace. They took a quick muster. All were present, but Bobo was making heavy going of it.

Joe looked at him. "He sniffed the gas, I think. Pound his back."

Pig did so with a will. Bobo belched deeply, was suddenly sick, then grinned.

"He'll do," decided Joe.

The slight delay had enabled one at least to catch up with them. He came plunging out of the dark, unaware of, or careless of the strength against him. Alan knocked Pig's arm down, as he raised it to throw.

"Let me at 'im!" he demanded. "He's mine!"

It was Tyler.

"Man-fight?" Alan challenged, thumb on his blade.

Tyler's eyes darted from adversary to adversary and accepted the invitation to individual duel by lunging at Alan. The quarters were too cramped for throwing; they closed, each achieving his grab in parry, fist to wrist.

Alan was stockier, probably stronger; Tyler was slippery. He attempted to give Alan a knee to the crotch. Alan evaded it, stamped on Tyler's planted foot. They went down. There was a crunching crack.

A moment later, Alan was wiping his knife against his thigh. "Let's get goin'," he complained. "I'm scared."

They reached a stairway, and raced up it, Long Arm and Pig ahead to fan out on each level and cover their flanks, and the third of the three choppers—Hugh heard him called Squatty—covering the rear. The others bunched in between.

Hugh thought they had won free, when he heard shouts and the clatter of a thrown knife just above him. He reached the level above in time to be cut not deeply but jaggedly by a ricocheted blade.

Three men were down. Long Arm had a blade sticking in the fleshy part of his upper arm, but it did not seem to bother him. His slingshot was still spinning. Pig was scrambling after a thrown knife, his own armament exhausted. But there were signs of his work; one man was down on one knee some twenty feet away. He was bleeding from a knife wound in the thigh.

As the figure steadied himself with one hand against the bulkhead and reached toward an empty belt with the other, Hugh recognized him.

Bill Ertz.

He had led a party up another way and flanked them, to his own ruin. Bobo crowded behind Hugh and got his mighty arm free for the cast. Hugh caught at it. "Easy, Bobo," he directed. "In the stomach, and easy."

The dwarf looked puzzled, but did as he was told. Ertz folded over at the middle and slid to the deck.

"Well placed," said Jim.

"Bring him along, Bobo," directed Hugh, "and stay in the middle." He ran his eye over their party, now huddled at the top of that flight of stairs. "All right, gang—up we go again! Watch it."

Long Arm and Pig swarmed up the next flight, the others disposing themselves as usual. Joe looked annoyed. In some fashion—a fashion by no means clear at the moment—he had been eased out as leader of this gang—*his* gang—and Hugh was giving orders. He reflected that there was no time now to make a fuss. It might get them all killed.

Jim did not appear to mind. In fact, he seemed to be enjoying himself.

They put ten more levels behind them with no organized opposition. Hugh directed them not to kill peasants unnecessarily. The three bravoes obeyed; Bobo was too loaded down with Ertz to constitute a problem in discipline. Hugh saw to it that they put thirty-odd more decks below them and were well into no man's land before he let vigilance relax at all. Then he called a halt and they examined wounds.

The only deep ones were to Long Arm's arm and Bobo's face. Joe-Jim examined them and applied presses with which he had outfitted himself before starting. Hugh refused treatment for his flesh wound. "It's stopped bleeding," he insisted, "and I've got a lot to do."

"You've got nothing to do but to get up home," said Joe, "and that will be an end to this foolishness."

"Not quite," denied Hugh. "You may be going home, but Alan and I and Bobo are going to no-weight—to the Captain's veranda."

"Nonsense," said Joe. "What for?"

"Come along if you like, and see. All right, gang. Let's go."

Joe started to speak, stopped when Jim kept still. Joe-Jim followed along.

They floated gently through the door of the veranda, Hugh, Alan, Bobo with his still-passive burden—and Joe-Jim. "That's it," said Hugh to Alan, waving his hand at the splendid stars, "that's what I've been telling you about."

Alan looked and clutched at Hugh's arm. "Jordan!" he moaned. "We'll fall out!" He closed his eyes tightly.

Hugh shook him. "It's all right," he said. "It's grand. Open your eyes."

Joe-Jim touched Hugh's arm. "What's it all about?" he demanded. "Why did you bring *him* up here?" He pointed to Ertz.

"Oh—him. Well, when he wakes up I'm going to show him the stars, prove to him that the Ship moves."

"Well? What for?"

"Then I'll send him back down to convince some others."

"Hm-m-m—suppose he doesn't have any better luck than you had?"

"Why, then"—Hugh shrugged his shoulders—"why, then we shall just have to do it all over, I suppose, till we do convince them.

"We've got to do it, you know."

THE MARCHING MORONS
by C. M. Kornbluth

Some things had not changed. A potter's wheel was still a potter's wheel and clay was still clay. Efim Hawkins had built his shop near Goose Lake, which had a narrow band of good fat clay and a narrow beach of white sand. He fired three bottle-nosed kilns with willow charcoal from the wood lot. The wood lot was also useful for long walks while the kilns were cooling; if he let himself stay within sight of them, he would open them prematurely, impatient to see how some new shape or glaze had come through the fire, and—*ping!*—the new shape or glaze would be good for nothing but the shard pile back of his slip tanks.

A business conference was in full swing in his shop, a modest cube of brick, tile-roofed, as the Chicago-Los Angeles "rocket" thundered overhead—very noisy, very swept back, very fiery jets, shaped as sleekly swift-looking as an airborne barracuda.

The buyer from Marshall Fields was turning over a black-glazed one-liter carafe, nodding approval with his massive, handsome head. "This is real pretty," he told Hawkins and his own secretary, Gomez-Laplace. "This has got lots of what ya call real est'etic principles. Yeah, it is real pretty."

"How much?" the secretary asked the potter.

"Seven-fifty in dozen lots," said Hawkins. "I ran up fifteen dozen last month."

"They are real est'etic," repeated the buyer from Fields. "I will take them all."

"I don't think we can do that, doctor," said the secretary. "They'd cost us $1,350. That would leave only $532 in our quarter's budget. And we still have to run down to East Liverpool to pick up some cheap dinner sets."

"Dinner sets?" asked the buyer, his big face full of wonder.

"Dinner sets. The department's been out of them for two months now. Mr. Garvy-Seabright got pretty nasty about it yesterday. Remember?"

"Garvy-Seabright, that meat-headed bluenose," the buyer said contemptuously. "He don't know nothin' about est'etics. Why for don't he lemme run my own department?" His eye fell on a stray copy of *Whambozambo Comix* and he sat down with it. An occasional deep chuckle or grunt of surprise escaped him as he turned the pages.

Uninterrupted, the potter and the buyer's secretary quickly closed a deal for two dozen of the liter carafes. "I wish we could take more," said the secretary, "but you heard what I told him. We've had to turn away customers for ordinary dinnerware because he shot the last quarter's budget on some Mexican piggy banks some equally enthusiastic importer stuck him with. The fifth floor is packed solid with them."

"I'll bet they look mighty est'etic."

"They're painted with purple cacti."

The potter shuddered and caressed the glaze of the sample carafe.

The buyer looked up and rumbled, "Ain't you dummies through yakkin' yet? What good's a seckertary for if'n he don't take the burden of *de*-tail off'n my back, harh?"

"We're all through, doctor. Are you ready to go?"

The buyer grunted peevishly, dropped *Whambozambo Comix* on the floor and led the way out of the building and down the log corduroy road to the highway. His car was waiting on the concrete. It was, like all contemporary cars, too low slung to get over the logs. He climbed down into the car and started the motor with a tremendous sparkle and roar.

"Gomez-Laplace," called out the potter under cover of the noise, "did anything come of the radiation program they were working on the last time I was on duty at the Pole?"

"The same old fallacy," said the secretary gloomily. "It stopped us on mutation, it stopped us on culling, it stopped us on segregation, and now it's stopped us on hypnosis."

"Well, I'm scheduled back to the grind in nine days. Time for another firing right now. I've got a new luster to try . . ."

"I'll miss you. I shall be 'vacationing'—running the drafting room of the New Century Engineering Corporation in Denver. They're going to put up a two-hundred-story office building, and naturally somebody's got to be on hand."

"Naturally," said Hawkins with a sour smile.

There was an ear-piercingly sweet blast as the buyer leaned on the horn button. Also, a yard-tall jet of what looked like flame spurted up from the car's radiator cap; the car's power plant was a gas turbine and had no radiator.

"I'm coming, doctor," said the secretary dispiritedly. He climbed down into the car and it whooshed off with much flame and noise.

The potter, depressed, wandered back up the corduroy road and contemplated his cooling kilns. The rustling wind in the boughs was obscuring the creak and mutter of the shrinking refractory brick. Hawkins wondered about the number two kiln—a reduction fire on a load of lusterware mugs. Had the clay chinking excluded the air? Had it been a properly smoky blaze? Would it do any harm if he just took one close—?

Common sense took Hawkins by the scruff of the neck and yanked him over to the tool shed. He got out his pick and resolutely set off on a prospecting jaunt to a hummocky field that might yield some oxides. He was especially low on coppers.

The long walk left him sweating hard, with his lust for a peek into the kiln quiet in his breast. He swung his pick almost at random into one of the hummocks; it clanged on a stone which he excavated. A largely obliterated inscription said:

ERSITY OF CHIC
OGICAL LABO
ELOVED MEMORY OF
KILLED IN ACT

The potter swore mildly. He had hoped the field would turn out to be a cemetery, preferably a once-fashionable cemetery full of once-massive bronze caskets moldered into oxides of tin and copper.

Well, hell, maybe there was some around anyway.

He headed lackadaisically for the second largest hillock and sliced into it with his pick. There was a stone to undercut and topple into a trench, and then the potter was very glad he'd stuck at it. His nostrils were filled with the bitter smell and the dirt was tinged with the exciting blue of copper salts. The pick went *clang!*

Hawkins, puffing, pried up a stainless steel plate that was quite badly stained and was also marked with incised letters. It seemed to have pulled loose from rotting bronze; there were rivets on the back that brought up flakes of green patina. The potter wiped off the surface dirt with his sleeve, turned it to catch the sunlight obliquely and read:

HONEST JOHN BARLOW

Honest John, famed in university annals, represents a challenge which medical science has not yet answered: revival of a human being accidentally thrown into a state of suspended animation.

In 1988 Mr. Barlow, a leading Evanston real estate dealer, visited his dentist for treatment of an impacted wisdom tooth. His dentist requested and received permission to use the experimental anesthetic Cycloparadimethanol-B-7, developed at the University.

After administration of the anesthetic, the dentist resorted to his drill. By freakish mischance, a short circuit in his machine delivered 220 volts of 60-cycle current into the patient. (In a damage suit instituted by Mrs. Barlow against the dentist, the University and the makers of the drill, a jury found for the defendants.) Mr. Barlow never got up from the dentist's chair and was assumed to have died of poisoning, electrocution or both.

Morticians preparing him for embalming discovered, however, that their subject was—though certainly not living—just as certainly not dead. The University was notified and a series of exhaustive tests was begun, including attempts to duplicate the trance state on volunteers. After a bad run of seven cases which ended fatally, the attempts were abandoned.

Honest John was long an exhibit at the University museum and livened many a football game as mascot of the University's Blue Crushers. The bounds of taste were overstepped, however, when a pledge to Sigma Delta Chi was ordered in '03 to "kidnap" Honest John from his loosely guarded glass museum case and introduce him into the Rachel Swanson Memorial Girls' Gymnasium shower room.

On May 22, 2003, the University Board of Regents issued the following order: "By unanimous vote, it is directed that the remains of Honest John Barlow be removed from the University museum and conveyed to the University's Lieutenant James Scott III Memorial Biological Laboratories and there be securely locked in a specially prepared vault. It is further directed that all possible measures for the preservation of these remains be taken by the Laboratory administration and that access to these remains be denied to all persons except qualified scholars authorized in writing by the Board. The Board reluctantly takes this action in view of recent notices and photographs in the nation's press which, to say the least, reflect but small credit upon the University."

It was far from his field, but Hawkins understood what had happened—an early and accidental blundering onto the bare bones of the Levantman shock anesthesia, which had since been replaced by other methods. To bring subjects out of Levantman shock, you let them have a squirt of simple saline in the trigeminal nerve. Interesting. And now about that bronze—

He heaved the pick into the rotting green salts, expecting no resistance, and almost fractured his wrist. *Something* down there was *solid*. He began to flake off the oxides.

A half hour of work brought him down to phosphor bronze, a huge casting of the almost incorruptible metal. It had weakened structurally over the centuries; he could fit the point of his pick under a corroded boss and pry off great creaking and grumbling striae of the stuff.

Hawkins wished he had an archaeologist with him but didn't dream of returning to his shop and calling one to take over the find. He was an all-around man: by choice, and in his free time, an artist in clay and glaze; by necessity, an automotive, electronics and atomic engineer who could also swing a project in traffic control, individual and group psychology, architecture or tool design. He didn't yell for a specialist every time something out of his line came up; there were so few with so much to do . . .

He trenched around his find, discovering that it was a great brick-shaped bronze mass with an excitingly hollow sound. A long strip of moldering metal from one of the long vertical faces pulled away, exposing red rust that went *whoosh* and was sucked into the interior of the mass.

It had been de-aired, thought Hawkins, and there must have been an inner jacket of glass which had crystallized through the centuries and quietly crumbled at the first clang of his pick. He didn't know what a vacuum would do to a subject of Levantman shock, but he had hopes, nor did he quite understand what a real estate dealer was, but it might have something to do with pottery. And *anything* might have a bearing on Topic Number One.

He flung his pick out of the trench, climbed out and set off at a dog-trot for his shop. A little rummaging turned up a hypo and there was a plastic container of salt in the kitchen.

Back at his dig, he chipped for another half hour to expose the juncture of lid and body. The hinges were hopeless; he smashed them off.

Hawkins extended the telescopic handle of the pick for the best leverage, fitted its point into a deep pit, set its built-in fulcrum, and heaved. Five more heaves and he could see, inside the vault, what looked like a dusty marble statue. Ten more and he could see that it was the naked body of Honest John Barlow, Evanston real estate dealer, uncorrupted by time.

The potter found the apex of the trigeminal nerve with his needle's point and gave him 60 cc.

In an hour Barlow's chest began to pump.

In another hour, he rasped, "Did it work?"

"*Did* it!" muttered Hawkins.

Barlow opened his eyes and stirred, looked down, turned his hands before his eyes—

"I'll sue!" he screamed. "My clothes! My fingernails!" A horrid suspicion came over his face and he clapped his hands to his hairless scalp. "My hair!" he wailed. "I'll sue you for every penny you've got! That release won't mean a damned thing in court—I didn't sign away my hair and clothes and fingernails!"

"They'll grow back," said Hawkins casually. "Also your epidermis. Those parts of you weren't alive, you know, so they weren't preserved like the rest of you. I'm afraid the clothes are gone, though."

"What is this—the University hospital?" demanded Barlow. "I want a phone. No, you phone. Tell my wife I'm all right and tell Sam Immerman—he's my lawyer—to get over here right away. Greenleaf 7-4022. Ow!" He had tried to sit up, and a portion of his pink skin rubbed against the inner surface of the casket, which was powdered by the ancient crystallized glass. "What the hell did you guys do, boil me alive? Oh, you're going to pay for this!"

"You're all right," said Hawkins, wishing now he had a reference book to clear up several obscure terms. "Your epidermis will start growing immediately. You're not in the hospital. Look here."

He handed Barlow the stainless steel plate that had labeled the casket. After a suspicious glance, the man started to read. Finishing, he laid the plate carefully on the edge of the vault and was silent for a spell.

"Poor Verna," he said at last. "It doesn't say whether she was stuck with the court costs. Do you happen to know—"

"No," said the potter. "All I know is what was on the plate, and how to revive you. The dentist accidentally gave you a dose of what we call Levantman shock anesthesia. We haven't used it for centuries; it was powerful, but too dangerous."

"Centuries . . ." brooded the man. "Centuries . . . I'll bet Sam swindled her out of her eyeteeth. Poor Verna. How long ago was it? What year is this?"

Hawkins shrugged. "We call it 7-B-936. That's no help to you. It takes a long time for these metals to oxidize."

"Like that movie," Barlow muttered. "Who would have thought it? Poor Verna!" He blubbered and sniffled, reminding Hawkins powerfully of the fact that he had been found under a flat rock.

Almost angrily, the potter demanded, "How many children did you have?"

"None yet," sniffed Barlow. "My first wife didn't want them. But Verna wants one—wanted one—but we're going to wait until—we *were* going to wait until—"

"Of course," said the potter, feeling a savage desire to tell him off, blast him to hell and gone for his work. But he choked it down. There was The Problem to think of; there was always The Problem to think of, and this poor blubberer might unexpectedly supply a clue. Hawkins would have to pass him on.

"Come along," Hawkins said. "My time is short."

Barlow looked up, outraged. "How can you be so unfeeling? I'm a human being like—"

The Los Angeles-Chicago "rocket" thundered overhead and Barlow broke off in mid-complaint. "Beautiful!" he breathed, following it with his eyes. "Beautiful!"

He climbed out of the vault, too interested to be pained by its roughness against his infantile skin. "After all," he said briskly, "this should have its sunny side. I never was much for reading, but this is just like one of those stories. And I ought to make some money out of it, shouldn't I?" He gave Hawkins a shrewd glance.

"You want money?" asked the potter. "Here." He handed over a fistful of change and bills. "You'd better put my shoes on. It'll be about a quarter mile. Oh, and you're—uh, modest?—yes, that was the word. Here." Hawkins gave him his pants, but Barlow was excitedly counting the money.

"Eighty-five, eighty-six—and it's dollars, too! I thought it'd be credits or whatever they call them. 'E Pluribus Unum' and 'Liberty'—just different faces. Say, is there a catch to this? Are these real, genuine, honest twenty-two-cent dollars like we had or just wallpaper?"

"They're quite all right, I assure you," said the potter. "I wish you'd come along. I'm in a hurry."

The man babbled as they stumped toward the shop. "Where are we going—The Council of Scientists, the World Coordinator or something like that?"

"Who? Oh, no. We call them 'President' and 'Congress.' No, that wouldn't do any good at all. I'm just taking you to see some people."

"I ought to make plenty out of this. *Plenty!* I could write books. Get some smart young fellow to put it into words for me and I'll bet I could turn out a best seller. What's the setup on things like that?"

"It's about like that. Smart young fellows. But there aren't any best sellers any more. People don't read much nowadays. We'll find something equally profitable for you to do."

Back in the shop, Hawkins gave Barlow a suit of clothes, deposited him in the waiting room and called Central in Chicago. "Take him away," he pleaded. "I have time for one more firing and he blathers and blathers. I haven't told him anything. Perhaps we should just turn him loose and let him find his own level, but there's a chance—"

"The Problem," agreed Central. "Yes, there's a chance."

The potter delighted Barlow by making him a cup of coffee with a cube that not only dissolved in cold water but heated the water to boiling point. Killing time, Hawkins chatted about the "rocket" Barlow had admired and had to haul himself up short; he had almost told the real estate man what its top speed really was—almost, indeed, revealed that it was not a rocket.

He regretted, too, that he had so casually handed Barlow a couple of hundred dollars. The man seemed obsessed with fear that they were worthless since Hawkins refused to take a note or I.O.U. or even a definite promise of repayment. But Hawkins couldn't go into details, and was very glad when a stranger arrived from Central.

"Tinny-Peete, from Algeciras," the stranger told him swiftly as the two of them met at the door. "Psychist for Poprob. Polassigned special overtake Barlow."

"Thank Heaven," said Hawkins. "Barlow," he told the man from the past, "this is Tinny-Peete. He's going to take care of you and help you make lots of money."

The psychist stayed for a cup of the coffee whose preparation had delighted Barlow, and then conducted the real estate man down the corduroy road to his car, leaving the potter to speculate on whether he could at last crack his kilns.

Hawkins, abruptly dismissing Barlow and The Problem, happily picked the chinking from around the door of the number two kiln, prying it open a trifle. A blast of heat and the heady, smoky scent of the reduction fire delighted him. He peered and saw a corner of a shelf glowing cherry red, becoming obscured by wavering black areas as it lost heat through the opened door. He slipped a charred wood paddle under a mug on the shelf and pulled it out as a sample, the hairs on the back of his hand curling and scorching. The mug crackled and pinged and Hawkins sighed happily.

The bismuth resinate luster had fired to perfection, a haunting film of silvery-black metal with strange bluish lights in it as it turned before the eyes, and the Problem of Population seemed very far away to Hawkins then.

Barlow and Tinny-Peete arrived at the concrete highway where the psychist's car was parked in a safety bay.

"What—a—*boat!*" gasped the man from the past.

"Boat? No, that's my car."

Barlow surveyed it with awe. Swept-back lines, deep-drawn compound curves, kilograms of chrome. He ran his hands over the door—or was it the door?—in a futile search for a handle, and asked respectfully, "How fast does it go?"

The psychist gave him a keen look and said slowly, "Two hundred and fifty. You can tell by the speedometer."

"Wow! My old Chevvy could hit a hundred on a straightaway, but you're out of my class, mister!"

Tinny-Peete somehow got a huge, low door open and Barlow descended three steps into immense cushions, floundering over to the right. He was too fascinated to pay serious attention to his flayed dermis. The dashboard was a lovely wilderness of dials, plugs, indicators, lights, scales and switches.

The psychist climbed down into the driver's seat and did something with his feet. The motor started like lighting a blowtorch as big as a silo. Wallowing around in the cushions, Barlow saw through a rearview mirror a tremendous exhaust filled with brilliant white sparkles.

"Do you like it?" yelled the psychist.

"It's terrific!" Barlow yelled back. "It's—

He was shut up as the car pulled out from the bay into the road with a great *voo-ooo-ooom!* A gale roared past Barlow's head, though

the windows seemed to be closed; the impression of speed was terrific. He located the speedometer on the dashboard and saw it climb
past 90, 100, 150, 200.

"Fast enough for me," yelled the psychist, noting that Barlow's
face fell in response. "Radio?"

He passed over a surprisingly light object like a football helmet,
with no trailing wires, and pointed to a row of buttons. Barlow put on
the helmet, glad to have the roar of air stilled, and pushed a push-
button. It lit up satisfyingly, and Barlow settled back even farther for
a sample of the brave new world's supermodern taste in ingenious
entertainment.

"TAKE IT AND STICK IT!" a voice roared in his ears.

He snatched off the helmet and gave the psychist an injured look.
Tinny-Peete grinned and turned a dial associated with the pushbut-
ton layout. The man from the past donned the helmet again and found
the voice had lowered to normal.

"The show of shows! The supershow! The super-duper show! The
quiz of quizzes! *Take It and Stick It!*"

There were shrieks of laughter in the background.

"Here we got the contes-tants all ready to go. You know how we
work it. I hand a contes-tant a triangle-shaped cutout and like that
down the line. Now we got these here boards, they got cutout places
the same shape as the triangles and things, only they're all different
shapes, and the first contes-tant that sticks the cutouts into the boards,
he wins.

"Now I'm gonna innaview the first contes-tant. Right here, honey.
What's your name?"

"Name? Uh—"

"Hoddaya like that, folks? She don't remember her name! Hah?
Would you buy that for a quarter?" The question was spoken with
arch significance, and the audience shrieked, howled and whistled its
appreciation.

It was dull listening when you didn't know the punch lines and
catch lines. Barlow pushed another button, with his free hand ready
at the volume control.

"—latest from Washington. It's about Senator Hull-Mendoza. He is
still attacking the Bureau of Fisheries. The North California Syndi-
calist says he got affydavits that John Kingsley-Schultz is a bluenose
from way back. He didn't publistat the affydavits, but he says they
say that Kingsley-Schultz was saw at bluenose meetings in Oregon

State College and later at Florida University. Kingsley-Schultz says he gotta confess he did major in fly casting at Oregon and got his Ph.D. in game-fish at Florida.

"And here is a quote from Kingsley-Schultz: 'Hull-Mendoza don't know what he's talking about. He should drop dead.' Unquote. Hull-Mendoza says he won't publistat the affydavits to pertect his sources. He says they was sworn by three former employes of the Bureau which was fired for in-competence and in-com-pat-ibility by Kingsley-Schultz.

"Elsewhere they was the usual run of traffic accidents. A three-way pileup of cars on Route 66 going outta Chicago took twelve lives. The Chicago-Los Angeles morning rocket crashed and exploded in the Mo-have—Mo-javvy—whatever-you-call-it Desert. All the 94 people aboard got killed. A Civil Aeronautics Authority investigator on the scene says that the pilot was buzzing herds of sheep and didn't pull out in time.

"Hey! Here's a hot one from New York! A diesel tug run wild in the harbor while the crew was below and shoved in the port bow of the luck-shury liner *S. S. Placentia*. It says the ship filled and sank taking the lives of an es-ti-mated 180 passengers and 50 crew members. Six divers was sent down to study the wreckage, but they died, too, when their suits turned out to be fulla little holes.

"And here is a bulletin I just got from Denver. It seems—"

Barlow took off the headset uncomprehendingly. "He seemed so callous," he yelled at the driver. "I was listening to a newscast—"

Tinny-Peete shook his head and pointed at his ears. The roar of air was deafening. Barlow frowned baffledly and stared out of the window.

A glowing sign said:

MOOGS!
WOULD YOU BUY IT
FOR A QUARTER?

He didn't know what Moogs was or were; the illustration showed an incredibly proportioned girl, 99.9 percent naked, writhing passionately in animated full color.

The roadside jingle was still with him, but with a new feature. Radar or something spotted the car and alerted the lines of the jingle. Each in turn sped along a roadside track, even with the car, so it could be read before the next line was alerted.

IF THERE'S A GIRL
YOU WANT TO GET
DEFLOCCULIZE
UNROMANTIC SWEAT.
"A*R*M*P*I*T*T*O"

Another animated job, in two panels, the familiar "Before and After." The first said, "Just Any Cigar?" and was illustrated with a two-person domestic tragedy of a wife holding her nose while her coarse and red-faced husband puffed a slimy-looking rope. The second panel glowed, "Or a VUELTA ABAJO?" and was illustrated with—

Barlow blushed and looked at his feet until they had passed the sign.

"Coming into Chicago!" bawled Tinny-Peete.

Other cars were showing up, all of them dreamboats.

Watching them, Barlow began to wonder if he knew what a kilometer was, exactly. They seemed to be traveling so slowly, if you ignored the roaring air past your ears and didn't let the speedy lines of the dreamboats fool you. He would have sworn they were really crawling along at twenty-five, with occasional spurts up to thirty. How much was a kilometer, anyway?

The city loomed ahead, and it was just what it ought to be: towering skyscrapers, overhead ramps, landing platforms for helicopters—

He clutched at the cushions. Those two copters. They were going to—they were going to—they—

He didn't see what happened because their apparent collision courses took them behind a giant building.

Screamingly sweet blasts of sound surrounded them as they stopped for a red light. "What the hell is going on here?" said Barlow in a shrill, frightened voice, because the braking time was just about zero, and he wasn't hurled against the dashboard. "Who's kidding who?"

"Why, what's the matter?" demanded the driver.

The light changed to green and he started the pickup. Barlow stiffened as he realized that the rush of air past his ears began just a brief, unreal split second before the car was actually moving. He grabbed for the door handle on his side.

The city grew on them slowly: scattered buildings, denser buildings, taller buildings, and a red light ahead. The car rolled to a stop in zero braking time, the rush of air cut off an instant after it stopped, and Barlow was out of the car and running frenziedly down a sidewalk one instant after that.

They'll track me down, he thought, panting. *It's a secret police thing. They'll get you—mind-reading machines, television eyes everywhere, afraid you'll tell their slaves about freedom and stuff. They don't let anybody cross them, like that story I once read.*

Winded, he slowed to a walk and congratulated himself that he had guts enough not to turn around. That was what they always watched for. Walking, he was just another business-suited back among hundreds. He would be safe, he would be safe—

A hand gripped his shoulder and words tumbled from a large, coarse, handsome face thrust close to his: "Wassamatta bumpinninna people likeya owna sidewalk gotta miner slamya inna mushya bassar!" It was neither the mad potter nor the mad driver.

"Excuse me," said Barlow. "What did you say?"

"Oh, yeah?" yelled the stranger dangerously, and waited for an answer.

Barlow, with the feeling that he had somehow been suckered into the short end of an intricate land-title deal, heard himself reply belligerently, "Yeah!"

The stranger let go of his shoulder and snarled, "Oh, yeah?"

"Yeah!" said Barlow, yanking his jacket back into shape.

"Aaah!" snarled the stranger, with more contempt and disgust than ferocity. He added an obscenity current in Barlow's time, a standard but physiologically impossible directive, and strutted off hulking his shoulders and balling his fists.

Barlow walked on, trembling. Evidently he had handled it well enough. He stopped at a red light while the long, low dreamboats roared before him and pedestrians in the sidewalk flow with him threaded their ways through the stream of cars. Brakes screamed, fenders clanged and dented, hoarse cries flew back and forth between drivers and walkers. He leaped backward frantically as one car swerved over an arc of sidewalk to miss another.

The signal changed to green; the cars kept on coming for about thirty seconds and then dwindled to an occasional light runner. Barlow crossed warily and leaned against a vending machine, blowing big breaths.

Look natural, he told himself. *Do something normal. Buy something from the machine.* He fumbled out some change, got a newspaper for a dime, a handkerchief for a quarter and a candy bar for another quarter.

The faint chocolate smell made him ravenous suddenly. He clawed at the glassy wrapper printed *"Crigglies"* quite futilely for a few seconds, and then it divided neatly by itself. The bar made three good bites, and he bought two more and gobbled them down.

Thirsty, he drew a carbonated orange drink in another one of the glassy wrappers from the machine for another dime. When he fumbled with it, it divided neatly and spilled all over his knees. Barlow decided he had been there long enough and walked on.

The shop windows were—shop windows. People still wore and bought clothes, still smoked and bought tobacco, still ate and bought food. And they still went to the movies, he saw with pleased surprise as he passed and then returned to a glittering place whose sign said it was THE BIJOU.

The place seemed to be showing a triple feature, *Babies Are Terrible, Don't Have Children,* and *The Canali Kid.*

It was irresistible; he paid a dollar and went in.

He caught the tail end of *The Canali Kid* in three-dimensional, full-color, full-scent production. It appeared to be an interplanetary saga winding up with a chase scene and a reconciliation between estranged hero and heroine. *Babies Are Terrible* and *Don't Have Children* were fantastic arguments against parenthood—the grotesquely exaggerated dangers of painfully graphic childbirth, vicious children, old parents beaten and starved by their sadistic offspring. The audience, Barlow astoundedly noted, was placidly chomping sweets and showing no particular signs of revulsion.

The *Coming Attractions* drove him into the lobby. The fanfares were shattering, the blazing colors blinding, and the added scents stomach heaving.

When his eyes again became accustomed to the moderate lighting of the lobby, he groped his way to a bench and opened the newspaper he had bought. It turned out to be *The Racing Sheet,* which afflicted him with a crushing sense of loss. The familiar boxed index in the lower-left-hand corner of the front page showed almost unbearably that Churchill Downs and Empire City were still in business—

Blinking back tears, he turned to the Past Performance at Churchill. They weren't using abbreviations any more, and the pages because of that were single-column instead of double. But it was all the same —or was it?

He squinted at the first race, a three-quarter-mile maiden claimer for thirteen hundred dollars. Incredibly, the track record was two minutes, ten and three-fifths seconds. Any beetle in his time could have knocked off the three-quarter in one-fifteen. It was the same for the other distances, much worse for route events.

What the hell had happened to everything?

He studied the form of a five-year-old brown mare in the second and couldn't make head or tail of it. She'd won and lost and placed and showed and lost and placed without rhyme or reason. She looked like a front runner for a couple of races and then she looked like a no-good pig and then she looked like a mudder but the next time it rained she wasn't and then she was a stayer and then she was a pig again. In a good five-thousand-dollar allowances event, too!

Barlow looked at the other entries and it slowly dawned on him that they were all like the five-year-old brown mare. Not a single damned horse running had even the slightest trace of class.

Somebody sat down beside him and said, "That's the story."

Barlow whirled to his feet and saw it was Tinny-Peete, his driver.

"I was in doubts about telling you," said the psychist, "but I see you have some growing suspicions of the truth. Please don't get excited. It's all right, I tell you."

"So you've got me," said Barlow.

"*Got* you?"

"Don't pretend. I can put two and two together. You're the secret police. You and the rest of the aristocrats live in luxury on the sweat of these oppressed slaves. You're afraid of me because you have to keep them ignorant."

There was a bellow of bright laughter from the psychist that got them blank looks from other patrons of the lobby. The laughter didn't sound at all sinister.

"Let's get out of here," said Tinny-Peete, still chuckling. "You couldn't possibly have it more wrong." He engaged Barlow's arm and led him to the street. "The actual truth is that the millions of workers live in luxury on the sweat of the handful of aristocrats. I shall probably die before my time of overwork unless—" He gave Barlow a speculative look. "You may be able to help us."

"I know that gag," sneered Barlow. "I made money in my time and to make money you have to get people on your side. Go ahead and shoot me if you want, but you're not going to make a fool out of me."

"You nasty little ingrate!" snapped the psychist, with a kaleido-scopic change of mood. "This damned mess is all your fault and the fault of people like you! Now come along and no more of your nonsense."

He yanked Barlow into an office building lobby and an elevator that, disconcertingly, went *whoosh* loudly as it rose. The real estate man's knees were wobbly as the psychist pushed him from the elevator, down a corridor and into an office.

A hawk-faced man rose from a plain chair as the door closed behind them. After an angry look at Barlow, he asked the psychist, "Was I called from the Pole to inspect this—this—?"

"Unget updandered. I've deeprobed etfind quasichance exhim Poprobattackline," said the psychist soothingly.

"Doubt," grunted the hawk-faced man.

"Try," suggested Tinny-Peete.

"Very well. Mr. Barlow, I understand you and your lamented had no children."

"What of it?"

"This of it. You were a blind, selfish stupid ass to tolerate economic and social conditions which penalized childbearing by the prudent and foresighted. You made us what we are today, and I want you to know that we are far from satisfied. Damn-fool rockets! Damn-fool automobiles! Damn-fool cities with overhead ramps!"

"As far as I can see," said Barlow, "you're running down the best features of your time. Are you crazy?"

"The rockets aren't rockets. They're turbojets—good turbojets, but the fancy shell around them makes for a bad drag. The automobiles have a top speed of one hundred kilometers per hour—a kilometer is, if I recall my paleolinguistics, three-fifths of a mile—and the speedometers are all rigged accordingly so the drivers will think they're going two hundred and fifty. The cities are ridiculous, expensive, unsanitary, wasteful conglomerations of people who'd be better off and more productive if they were spread over the countryside.

"We need the rockets and trick speedometers and cities because, while you and your kind were being prudent and foresighted and not having children, the migrant workers, slum dwellers and tenant farmers were shiftlessly and shortsightedly having children—breeding, breeding. My God, how they bred!"

"Wait a minute," objected Barlow. "There were lots of people in our crowd who had two or three children."

"The attrition of accidents, illness, wars and such took care of that. Your intelligence was bred out. It is gone. Children that should have been born never were. The just-average, they'll-get-along majority took over the population. The average IQ now is 45."

"But that's far in the future—"

"So are you," grunted the hawk-faced man sourly.

"But who are *you* people?"

"Just people—real people. Some generations ago, the geneticists realized at last that nobody was going to pay any attention to what they said, so they abandoned words for deeds. Specifically, they formed and recruited for a closed corporation intended to maintain and improve the breed. We are their descendants, about three million of us. There are five billion of the others, so we are their slaves.

"During the past couple of years I've designed a skyscraper, kept Billings Memorial Hospital here in Chicago running, headed off war with Mexico and directed traffic at LaGuardia Field in New York."

"I don't understand! Why don't you let them go to hell in their own way?"

The man grimaced. "We tried it once for three months. We holed up at the South Pole and waited. They didn't notice it. Some drafting room people were missing, some chief nurses didn't show up, minor government people on the nonpolicy level couldn't be located. It didn't seem to matter.

"In a week there was hunger. In two weeks there were famine and plague, in three weeks war and anarchy. We called off the experiment; it took us most of the next generation to get things squared away again."

"But why *didn't* you let them kill each other off?"

"Five billion corpses mean about five hundred million tons of rotting flesh."

Barlow had another idea. "Why don't you sterilize them?"

"Two and one-half billion operations is a lot of operations. Because they breed continuously, the job would never be done."

"I see. Like the marching Chinese!"

"Who the devil are they?"

"It was a—uh—paradox of my time. Somebody figured out that if all the Chinese in the world were to line up four abreast, I think it was, and start marching past a given point, they'd never stop because of the babies that would be born and grow up before they passed the point."

"That's right. Only instead of 'a given point,' make it 'the largest conceivable number of operating rooms that we could build and staff.' There could never be enough."

"Say!" said Barlow. "Those movies about babies—was that your propaganda?"

"It was. It doesn't seem to mean a thing to them. We have abandoned the idea of attempting propaganda contrary to a biological drive."

"So if you work *with* a biological drive—?"

"I know of none which is consistent with inhibition of fertility."

Barlow's face went poker blank, the result of years of careful discipline. "You don't, huh? You're the great brains and you can't think of any?"

"Why, no," said the psychist innocently. "Can you?"

"That depends. I sold ten thousand acres of Siberian tundra—through a dummy firm, of course—after the partition of Russia. The buyers thought they were getting improved building lots on the outskirts of Kiev. I'd say that was a lot tougher than this job."

"How so?" asked the hawk-faced man.

"Those were normal, suspicious customers and these are morons, born suckers. You just figure out a con they'll fall for; they won't know enough to do any smart checking."

The psychist and the hawk-faced man had also had training; they kept themselves from looking with sudden hope at each other.

"You seem to have something in mind," said the psychist.

Barlow's poker face went blanker still. "Maybe I have. I haven't heard any offer yet."

"There's the satisfaction of knowing that you've prevented Earth's resources from being so plundered," the hawk-faced man pointed out, "that the race will soon become extinct."

"I don't know that," Barlow said bluntly. "All I have is your word."

"If you really have a method, I don't think any price would be too great," the psychist offered.

"Money," said Barlow.

"All you want."

"More than you want," the hawk-faced man corrected.

"Prestige," added Barlow. "Plenty of publicity. My picture and my name in the papers and over TV every day, statues to me, parks and cities and streets and other things named after me. A whole chapter in the history books."

The psychist made a facial sign to the hawk-faced man that meant, "Oh, brother!"

The hawk-faced man signaled back, "Steady, boy!"

"It's not too much to ask," the psychist agreed.

Barlow, sensing a seller's market, said, "Power!"

"Power?" the hawk-faced man repeated puzzledly. "Your own hydro station or nuclear pile?"

"I mean a world dictatorship with me as dictator!"

"Well, now—" said the psychist, but the hawk-faced man interrupted, "It would take a special emergency act of Congress but the situation warrants it. I think that can be guaranteed."

"Could you give us some indication of your plan?" the psychist asked.

"Ever hear of lemmings?"

"No."

"They are—were, I guess, since you haven't heard of them—little animals in Norway, and every few years they'd swarm to the coast and swim out to sea until they drowned. I figure on putting some lemming urge into the population."

"How?"

"I'll save that till I get the right signatures on the deal."

The hawk-faced man said, "I'd like to work with you on it, Barlow. My name's Ryan-Ngana." He put out his hand.

Barlow looked closely at the hand, then at the man's face. "Ryan what?"

"Ngana."

"That sounds like an African name."

"It is. My mother's father was a Watusi."

Barlow didn't take the hand. "I thought you looked pretty dark. I don't want to hurt your feelings, but I don't think I'd be at my best working with you. There must be somebody else just as well qualified, I'm sure."

The psychist made a facial sign to Ryan-Ngana that meant, "Steady *yourself*, boy!"

"Very well," Ryan-Ngana told Barlow. "We'll see what arrangement can be made."

"It's not that I'm prejudiced, you understand. Some of my best friends—"

"Mr. Barlow, don't give it another thought. Anybody who could pick on the lemming analogy is going to be useful to us."

And so he would, thought Ryan-Ngana, alone in the office after Tinny-Peete had taken Barlow up to the helicopter stage. So he would. Poprob had exhausted every rational attempt and the new Poprobat-tacklines would have to be irrational or subrational. This creature from the past with his lemming legends and his improved building lots would be a fountain of precious vicious self-interest.

Ryan-Ngana sighed and stretched. He had to go and run the San Francisco subway. Summoned early from the Pole to study Barlow, he'd left unfinished a nice little theorem. Between interruptions, he was slowly constructing an n-dimensional geometry whose foundations and superstructure owed no debt whatsoever to intuition.

Upstairs, waiting for a helicopter, Barlow was explaining to Tinny-Peete that he had nothing against Negroes, and Tinny-Peete wished he had some of Ryan-Ngana's imperturbability and humor for the ordeal.

The helicopter took them to International Airport where, Tinny-Peete explained, Barlow would leave for the Pole.

The man from the past wasn't sure he'd like a dreary waste of ice and cold.

"It's all right," said the psychist. "A civilized layout. Warm, pleasant. You'll be able to work more efficiently there. All the facts at your fingertips, a good secretary—"

"I'll need a pretty big staff," said Barlow, who had learned from thousands of deals never to take the first offer.

"I meant a private, confidential one," said Tinny-Peete readily, "but you can have as many as you want. You'll naturally have top-primary-top priority if you really have a workable plan."

"Let's not forget this dictatorship angle," said Barlow.

He didn't know that the psychist would just as readily have promised him deification to get him happily on the "rocket" for the Pole. Tinny-Peete had no wish to be torn limb from limb; he knew very well that it would end that way if the population learned from this anachronism that there was a small elite which considered itself head, shoulders, trunk and groin above the rest. The fact that this assumption was perfectly true and the fact that the elite was condemned by its superiority to a life of the most grinding toil would not be considered; the difference would.

The psychist finally put Barlow aboard the "rocket" with some thirty people—real people—headed for the Pole.

Barlow was airsick all the way because of a posthypnotic suggestion Tinny-Peete had planted in him. One idea was to make him as averse as possible to a return trip, and another idea was to spare the other passengers from his aggressive, talkative company.

Barlow during the first day at the Pole was reminded of his first day in the Army. It was the same now-where-the-hell-are-we-going-to-put-*you?* business until he took a firm line with them. Then instead of acting like supply sergeants they acted like hotel clerks.

It was a wonderful, wonderfully calculated buildup, and one that he failed to suspect. After all, in his time a visitor from the past would have been lionized.

At day's end he reclined in a snug underground billet with the sixty-mile gales roaring yards overhead and tried to put two and two together.

It was like old times, he thought—like a coup in real estate where you had the competition by the throat, like a fifty-percent rent boost when you knew damned well there was no place for the tenants to move, like smiling when you read over the breakfast orange juice that the city council had decided to build a school on the ground you had acquired by a deal with the city council. And it was simple. He would just sell tundra building lots to eagerly suicidal lemmings, and that was absolutely all there was to solving The Problem that had these double-domes spinning.

They'd have to work out most of the details, naturally, but what the hell, that was what subordinates were for. He'd need specialists in advertising, engineering, communications—did they know anything about hypnotism? That might be helpful. If not, there'd have to be a lot of bribery done, but he'd make sure—damned sure—there were unlimited funds.

Just selling building lots to lemmings . . .

He wished, as he fell asleep, that poor Verna could have been in on this. It was his biggest, most stupendous deal. Verna—that sharp shyster Sam Immerman must have swindled her . . .

It began the next day with people coming to visit him. He knew the approach. They merely wanted to be helpful to their illustrious visitor from the past and would he help fill them in about his era, which unfortunately was somewhat obscure historically, and what did he think could be done about The Problem? He told them he was too old to be roped any more, and they wouldn't get any information out of him until he got a letter of intent from at least the Polar President and a session of the Polar Congress empowered to make him dictator.

He got the letter and the session. He presented his program, was asked whether his conscience didn't revolt at its callousness, explained succinctly that a deal was a deal and anybody who wasn't smart enough to protect himself didn't deserve protection—"Caveat emptor," he threw in for scholarship, and had to translate it to "Let the buyer beware." He didn't, he stated, give a damn about either the morons or their intelligent slaves; he'd told them his price and that was all he was interested in.

Would they meet it or wouldn't they?

The Polar President offered to resign in his favor, with certain temporary emergency powers that the Polar Congress would vote him if he thought them necessary. Barlow demanded the title of World Dictator, complete control of world finances, salary to be decided by himself, and the publicity campaign and historical writeup to begin at once.

"As for the emergency powers," he added, "they are neither to be temporary nor limited."

Somebody wanted the floor to discuss the matter, with the declared hope that perhaps Barlow would modify his demands.

"You've got the proposition," Barlow said. "I'm not knocking off even ten percent."

"But what if the Congress refuses, sir?" the President asked.

"Then you can stay up here at the Pole and try to work it out yourselves. I'll get what I want from the morons. A shrewd operator like me doesn't have to compromise; I haven't got a single competitor in this whole cockeyed moronic era."

Congress waived debate and voted by show of hands. Barlow won unanimously.

"You don't know how close you came to losing me," he said in his first official address to the joint Houses. "I'm not the boy to haggle; either I get what I ask, or I go elsewhere. The first thing I want is to see designs for a new palace for me—nothing *un*-ostentatious, either—and your best painters and sculptors to start working on my portraits and statues. Meanwhile, I'll get my staff together."

He dismissed the Polar President and the Polar Congress, telling them that he'd let them know when the next meeting would be.

A week later, the program started with North America the first target.

Mrs. Garvy was resting after dinner before the ordeal of turning on the dishwasher. The TV, of course, was on and it said, "Oooh!"— long, shuddery and ecstatic, the cue for the *Parfum Assault Criminale* spot commercial. "Girls," said the announcer hoarsely, "do you want your man? It's easy to get him—easy as a trip to Venus."

"Huh?" said Mrs. Garvy.

"Wassamatter?" snorted her husband, starting out of a doze.

"Ja hear that?"

"Wha'?"

"He said 'easy like a trip to Venus.' "

"So?"

"Well, I thought ya couldn't get to Venus. I thought they just had that one rocket thing that crashed on the Moon."

"Aah, women don't keep up with the news," said Garvy righteously, subsiding again.

"Oh," said his wife uncertainly.

And the next day, on *Henry's Other Mistress*, there was a new character who had just breezed in: Buzz Rentshaw, Master Rocket Pilot of the Venus run. On *Henry's Other Mistress*, "the broadcast drama about you and your neighbors, *folksy* people, *ordinary* people, *real* people!" Mrs. Garvy listened with amazement over a cooling cup of coffee as Buzz made hay of her hazy convictions.

> MONA: Darling, it's so good to see you again!
>
> BUZZ: You don't know how I've missed you on that dreary Venus run.
>
> SOUND: *Venetian blind run down, key turned in lock.*
>
> MONA: Was it *very* dull, dearest?
>
> BUZZ: Let's not talk about my humdrum job, darling. Let's talk about us.
>
> SOUND: *Creaking bed.*

Well, the program was back to normal at last. That evening Mrs. Garvy tried to ask again whether her husband was sure about those rockets, but he was dozing right through *Take It and Stick It*, so she watched the screen and forgot the puzzle.

She was still rocking with laughter at the gag line, "Would you buy it for a quarter?" when the commercial went on for the detergent powder she always faithfully loaded her dishwasher with on the first of every month.

The announcer displayed mountains of suds from a tiny piece of the stuff and coyly added, "Of course, Cleano don't lay around for you to pick up like the soap root on Venus, but it's pretty cheap and it's almost pretty near just as good. So for us plain folks who ain't lucky enough to live up there on Venus, Cleano is the real cleaning stuff!"

Then the chorus went into their "Cleano-is-the-stuff" jingle, but Mrs. Garvy didn't hear it. She was a stubborn woman, but it occurred to her that she was very sick indeed. She didn't want to worry her husband. The next day she quietly made an appointment with her family freud.

In the waiting room she picked up a fresh new copy of *Readers Pablum* and put it down with a faint palpitation. The lead article, according to the table of contents on the cover, was titled "The Most Memorable Venusian I Ever Met."

"The freud will see you now," said the nurse, and Mrs. Garvy tottered into his office.

His traditional glasses and whiskers were reassuring. She choked out the ritual. "Freud, forgive me, for I have neuroses."

He chanted the antiphonal, "Tut, my dear girl, what seems to be the trouble?"

"I got like a hole in the head," she quavered. "I seem to forget all kinds of things. Things like everybody seems to know and I don't."

"Well, that happens to everybody occasionally, my dear. I suggest a vacation on Venus."

The freud stared, openmouthed, at the empty chair. His nurse came in and demanded, "Hey, you see how she scrammed? What was the matter with *her?*"

He took off his glasses and whiskers meditatively. "You can search me. I told her she should maybe try a vacation on Venus." A momentary bafflement came into his face and he dug through his desk drawers until he found a copy of the four-color, profusely illustrated journal of his profession. It had come that morning and he had lip-read it, though looking mostly at the pictures. He leafed to the article "Advantages of the Planet Venus in Rest Cures."

"It's right there," he said.

The nurse looked. "It sure is," she agreed. "Why shouldn't it be?"

"The trouble with these here neurotics," decided the freud, "is that they all the time got to fight reality. Show in the next twitch."

He put on his glasses and whiskers again and forgot Mrs. Garvy and her strange behavior.

"Freud, forgive me, for I have neuroses."

"Tut, my dear girl, what seems to be the trouble?"

Like many cures of mental disorders, Mrs. Garvy's was achieved largely by self-treatment. She disciplined herself sternly out of the crazy notion that there had been only one rocket ship and that one a failure. She could join without wincing, eventually, in any conversation on the desirability of Venus as a place to retire, on its fabulous floral profusion. Finally she went to Venus.

All her friends were trying to book passage with the Evening Star Travel and Real Estate Corporation, but naturally the demand was crushing. She considered herself lucky to get a seat at last for the two-week summer cruise. The spaceship took off from a place called Los Alamos, New Mexico. It looked just like all the spaceships on television and in the picture magazines but was more comfortable than you would expect.

Mrs. Garvy was delighted with the fifty or so fellow-passengers assembled before takeoff. They were from all over the country and she had a distinct impression that they were on the brainy side. The captain, a tall, hawk-faced, impressive fellow named Ryan Something-or-other, welcomed them aboard and trusted that their trip would be a memorable one. He regretted that there would be nothing to see because, "due to the meteorite season," the ports would be dogged down. It was disappointing, yet reassuring that the line was taking no chances.

There was the expected momentary discomfort at takeoff and then two monotonous days of droning travel through space to be whiled away in the lounge at cards or craps. The landing was a routine bump and the voyagers were issued tablets to swallow to immunize them against any minor ailments.

When the tablets took effect, the lock was opened, and Venus was theirs.

It looked much like a tropical island on Earth, except for a blanket of cloud overhead. But it had a heady, otherworldly quality that was intoxicating and glamorous.

The ten days of the vacation were suffused with a hazy magic. The soap root, as advertised, was free and sudsy. The fruits, mostly tropical varieties transplanted from Earth, were delightful. The simple shelters provided by the travel company were more than adequate for the balmy days and nights.

It was with sincere regret that the voyagers filed again into the ship and swallowed more tablets doled out to counteract and sterilize any Venus illnesses they might unwittingly communicate to Earth.

Vacationing was one thing. Power politics was another.

At the Pole, a small man was in a soundproof room, his face deathly pale and his body limp in a straight chair.

In the American Senate Chamber, Senator Hull-Mendoza (Synd., N. Cal.) was saying, "Mr. President and gentlemen, I would be remiss in my duty as a legislature if'n I didn't bring to the attention of the au-gust body I see here a perilous situation which is fraught with peril. As is well known to members of this au-gust body, the perfection of space flight has brought with it a situation I can only describe as fraught with peril. Mr. President and gentlemen, now that swift American rockets now traverse the trackless void of space between this planet and our nearest planetarial neighbor in space—and, gentlemen, I refer to Venus, the star of dawn, the brightest jewel in fair Vulcan's diadome—now, I say, I want to inquire what steps are being taken to colonize Venus with a vanguard of patriotic citizens like those minutemen of yore.

"Mr. President and gentlemen! There are in this world nations, envious nations—I do not name Mexico—who by fair means or foul may seek to wrest from Columbia's grasp the torch of freedom of space; nations whose low living standards and innate depravity give them an unfair advantage over the citizens of our fair republic.

"This is my program: I suggest that a city of more than 100,000 population be selected by lot. The citizens of the fortunate city are to be awarded choice lands on Venus free and clear, to have and to hold and convey to their descendants. And the national government shall provide free transportation to Venus for these citizens. And this program shall continue, city by city, until there has been deposited on Venus a sufficient vanguard of citizens to protect our manifest rights in that planet.

"Objections will be raised, for carping critics we have always with us. They will say there isn't enough steel. They will call it a cheap giveaway. I say there is enough steel for one city's population to be transferred to Venus, and that is all that is needed. For when the time comes for the second city to be transferred, the first, emptied city can be wrecked for the needed steel! And is it a giveaway? Yes! It is the most glorious giveaway in the history of mankind! Mr. President and gentlemen, there is no time to waste—Venus must be American!"

Black-Kupperman, at the Pole, opened his eyes and said feebly, "The style was a little uneven. Do you think anybody'll notice?"

"You did fine, boy; just fine," Barlow reassured him.

Hull-Mendoza's bill became law.

Drafting machines at the South Pole were busy around the clock and the Pittsburgh steel mills spewed millions of plates into the Los Alamos spaceport of the Evening Star Travel and Real Estate Corporation. It was going to be Los Angeles, for logistic reasons, and the three most accomplished psychokineticists went to Washington and mingled in the crowd at the drawing to make certain that the Los Angeles capsule slithered into the fingers of the blindfolded Senator.

Los Angeles loved the idea and a forest of spaceships began to blossom in the desert. They weren't very good spaceships, but they didn't have to be.

A team at the Pole worked at Barlow's direction on a mail setup. There would have to be letters to and from Venus to keep the slightest taint of suspicion from arising. Luckily Barlow remembered that the problem had been solved once before—by Hitler. Relatives of persons incinerated in the furnaces of Lublin or Majdanek continued to get cheery postal cards.

The Los Angeles flight went off on schedule, under tremendous press, newsreel and television coverage. The world cheered the gallant Angelenos who were setting off on their patriotic voyage to the land of milk and honey. The forest of spaceships thundered up, and up, and out of sight without untoward incident. Billions envied the Angelenos, cramped and on short rations though they were.

Wreckers from San Francisco, whose capsule came up second, moved immediately into the city of the angels for the scrap steel their own flight would require. Senator Hull-Mendoza's constituents could do no less.

The president of Mexico, hypnotically alarmed at this extension of *yanqui imperialismo* beyond the stratosphere, launched his own Venus-colony program.

Across the water it was England versus Ireland, France versus Germany, China versus Russia, India versus Indonesia. Ancient hatreds grew into the flames that were rocket ships assailing the air by hundreds daily.

Dear Ed, how are you? Sam and I are fine and hope you are fine. Is it nice up there like they say with food and close grone on trees? I drove by Springfield yesterday and it sure looked funny all the buildings down but of coarse it is worth it we have to keep the greasers in their place. Do you have any trouble with them on Venus? Drop me a line some time. Your loving sister, Alma.

Dear Alma, I am fine and hope you are fine. It is a fine place here fine climate and easy living. The doctor told me today that I seem to be ten years younger. He thinks there is something in the air here keeps people young. We do not have much trouble with the greasers here they keep to theirselves it is just a question of us outnumbering them and staking out the best places for the Americans. In South Bay I know a nice little island that I have been saving for you and Sam with lots of blanket trees and ham bushes. Hoping to see you and Sam soon, your loving brother, Ed.

Sam and Alma were on their way shortly.

Poprob got a dividend in every nation after the emigration had passed the halfway mark. The lonesome stay-at-homes were unable to bear the melancholy of a low population density; their conditioning had been to swarms of their kin. After that point it was possible to foist off the crudest stripped-down accommodations on would-be emigrants; they didn't care.

Black-Kupperman did a final job on President Hull-Mendoza, the last job that genius of hypnotics would ever do on any moron, important or otherwise.

Hull-Mendoza, panic stricken by his presidency over an emptying nation, joined his constituents. The *Independence,* aboard which traveled the national government of America, was the most elaborate of all the spaceships—bigger, more comfortable, with a lounge that was handsome, though cramped, and cloakrooms for Senators and Representatives. It went, however, to the same place as the others and Black-Kupperman killed himself, leaving a note that stated he "couldn't live with my conscience."

The day after the American President departed, Barlow flew into a rage. Across his specially built desk were supposed to flow all Poprob high-level documents, and this thing—this outrageous thing—called Poprob*term* apparently had got into the executive stage before he had even had a glimpse of it!

He buzzed for Rogge-Smith, his statistician. Rogge-Smith seemed to be at the bottom of it. Poprobterm seemed to be about first and second and third derivatives, whatever they were. Barlow had a deep distrust of anything more complex than what he called an "average."

While Rogge-Smith was still at the door, Barlow snapped, "What's the meaning of this? Why haven't I been consulted? How far have you people got and why have you been working on something I haven't authorized?"

"Didn't want to bother you, Chief," said Rogge-Smith. "It was really a technical matter, kind of a final cleanup. Want to come and see the work?"

Mollified, Barlow followed his statistician down the corridor.

"You still shouldn't have gone ahead without my okay," he grumbled. "Where the hell would you people have been without me?"

"That's right, Chief. We couldn't have swung it ourselves; our minds just don't work that way. And all that stuff you knew from Hitler—it wouldn't have occurred to us. Like poor Black-Kupperman."

They were in a fair-sized machine shop at the end of a slight upward incline. It was cold. Rogge-Smith pushed a button that started a motor, and a flood of arctic light poured in as the roof parted slowly. It showed a small spaceship with the door open.

Barlow gaped as Rogge-Smith took him by the elbow and his other boys appeared: Swenson-Swenson, the engineer; Tsutsugimushi-Duncan, his propellants man; Kalb-French, advertising.

"In you go, Chief," said Tsutsugimushi-Duncan. "This is Po-probterm."

"But I'm the World Dictator!"

"You bet, Chief. You'll be in history, all right—but this is necessary, I'm afraid."

The door was closed. Acceleration slammed Barlow cruelly to the metal floor. Something broke, and warm, wet stuff, salty tasting, ran from his mouth to his chin. Arctic sunlight through a port suddenly became a fierce lancet stabbing at his eyes; he was out of the atmosphere.

Lying twisted and broken under the acceleration, Barlow realized that some things had not changed, that Jack Ketch was never asked to dinner however many shillings you paid him to do your dirty work, that murder will out, that crime pays only temporarily.

The last thing he learned was that death is the end of pain.

VINTAGE SEASON
by Henry Kuttner and C. L. Moore
(as Lawrence O'Donnell)

Three people came up the walk to the old mansion just at dawn on a perfect May morning. Oliver Wilson in his pajamas watched them from an upper window through a haze of conflicting emotions, resentment predominant. He didn't want them there.

They were foreigners. He knew only that much about them. They had the curious name of Sancisco, and their first names, scrawled in loops on the lease, appeared to be Omerie, Kleph and Klia, though it was impossible as he looked down upon them now to sort them out by signature. He hadn't even been sure whether they would be men or women, and he had expected something a little less cosmopolitan.

Oliver's heart sank a little as he watched them follow the taxi driver up the walk. He had hoped for less self-assurance in his unwelcome tenants, because he meant to force them out of the house if he could. It didn't look very promising from here.

The man went first. He was tall and dark, and he wore his clothes and carried his body with that peculiar arrogant assurance that comes from perfect confidence in every phase of one's being. The two women were laughing as they followed him. Their voices were light and sweet, and their faces were beautiful, each in its own exotic way, but the first thing Oliver thought of when he looked at them was, Expensive!

It was not only that patina of perfection that seemed to dwell in every line of their incredibly flawless garments. There are degrees of wealth beyond which wealth itself ceases to have significance. Oliver had seen before, on rare occasions, something like this assurance that the earth turning beneath their well-shod feet turned only to their whim.

It puzzled him a little in this case, because he had the feeling as the three came up the walk that the beautiful clothing they wore so confidently was not clothing they were accustomed to. There was a curious air of condescension in the way they moved. Like women in costume. They minced a little on their delicate high heels, held out an arm to stare at the cut of a sleeve, twisted now and then inside their garments as if the clothing sat strangely on them, as if they were accustomed to something entirely different.

And there was an elegance about the way the garments fitted them which even to Oliver looked strikingly unusual. Only an actress on the screen, who can stop time and the film to adjust every disarrayed fold so that she looks perpetually perfect, might appear thus elegantly clad. But let these women move as they liked, and each fold of their clothing followed perfectly with the movement and fell perfectly into place again. One might almost suspect the garments were not cut of ordinary cloth, or that they were cut according to some unknown, subtle scheme, with many artful hidden seams placed by a tailor incredibly skilled at his trade.

They seemed excited. They talked in high, clear, very sweet voices, looking up at the perfect blue and transparent sky in which dawn was still frankly pink. They looked at the trees on the lawn, the leaves translucently green with an under color of golden newness, the edges crimped from constriction in the recent bud.

Happily and with excitement in their voices they called to the man, and when he answered his own voice blended so perfectly in cadence with theirs that it sounded like three people singing together. Their voices, like their clothing, seemed to have an elegance far beyond the ordinary, to be under a control such as Oliver Wilson had never dreamed of before this morning.

The taxi driver brought up the luggage, which was of a beautiful pale stuff that did not look quite like leather, and had curves in it so subtle it seemed square until you saw how two or three pieces of it fitted together when carried, into a perfectly balanced block. It was scuffed, as if from much use. And though there was a great deal of it, the taxi man did not seem to find his burden heavy. Oliver saw him look down at it now and then and heft the weight incredulously.

One of the women had very black hair and skin like cream, and smoke-blue eyes heavy-lidded with the weight of her lashes. It was the other woman Oliver's gaze followed as she came up the walk. Her hair was a clear, pale red, and her face had a softness that he thought would be like velvet to touch. She was tanned to a warm amber darker than her hair.

Just as they reached the porch steps the fair woman lifted her head and looked up. She gazed straight into Oliver's eyes and he saw that hers were very blue, and just a little amused, as if she had known he was there all along. Also they were frankly admiring.

Feeling a bit dizzy, Oliver hurried back to his room to dress.

"We are here on a vacation," the dark man said, accepting the keys. "We will not wish to be disturbed, as I made clear in our correspondence. You have engaged a cook and housemaid for us, I understand? We will expect you to move your own belongings out of the house, then, and—"

"Wait," Oliver said uncomfortably. "Something's come up. I—" He hesitated, not sure just how to present it. These were such increasingly odd people. Even their speech was odd. They spoke so distinctly, not slurring any of the words into contractions. English seemed as familiar to them as a native tongue, but they all spoke as trained singers sing, with perfect breath control and voice placement.

And there was a coldness in the man's voice, as if some gulf lay between him and Oliver, so deep no feeling of human contact could bridge it.

"I wonder," Oliver said, "if I could find you better living quarters somewhere else in town. There's a place across the street that—"

The dark woman said, "Oh, no!" in a lightly horrified voice, and all three of them laughed. It was cool, distant laughter that did not include Oliver.

The dark man said, "We chose this house carefully, Mr. Wilson. We would not be interested in living anywhere else."

Oliver said desperately, "I don't see why. It isn't even a modern house. I have two others in much better condition. Even across the street you'd have a fine view of the city. Here there isn't anything. The other houses cut off the view, and—"

"We engaged rooms here, Mr. Wilson," the man said with finality. "We expect to use them. Now will you make arrangements to leave as soon as possible?"

Oliver said, "No," and looked stubborn. "That isn't in the lease. You can live here until next month, since you paid for it, but you can't put me out. I'm staying."

The man opened his mouth to say something. He looked coldly at

Oliver and closed it again. The feeling of aloofness was chill between them. There was a moment's silence. Then the man said, "Very well. Be kind enough to stay out of our way."

It was a little odd that he didn't inquire into Oliver's motives. Oliver was not yet sure enough of the man to explain. He couldn't very well say, "Since the lease was signed, I've been offered three times what the house is worth if I'll sell it before the end of May." He couldn't say, "I want the money, and I'm going to use my own nuisance-value to annoy you until you're willing to move out." After all, there seemed no reason why they shouldn't. After seeing them, there seemed doubly no reason, for it was clear they must be accustomed to surroundings infinitely better than this timeworn old house.

It was very strange, the value this house had so suddenly acquired. There was no reason at all why two groups of semi-anonymous people should be so eager to possess it for the month of May.

In silence Oliver showed his tenants upstairs to the three big bedrooms across the front of the house. He was intensely conscious of the red-haired woman and the way she watched him with a sort of obviously covert interest, quite warmly, and with a curious undertone to her interest that he could not quite place. It was familiar, but elusive. He thought how pleasant it would be to talk to her alone, if only to try to capture that elusive attitude and put a name to it.

Afterward he went down to the telephone and called his fiancée.

Sue's voice squeaked a little with excitement over the wire.

"Oliver, so early? Why, it's hardly six yet. Did you tell them what I said? Are they going to go?"

"Can't tell yet. I doubt it. After all, Sue, I did take their money, you know."

"Oliver, they've got to go! You've got to do something!"

"I'm trying, Sue. But I don't like it."

"Well, there isn't any reason why they shouldn't stay somewhere else. And we're going to need that money. You'll just have to think of something, Oliver."

Oliver met his own worried eyes in the mirror above the telephone and scowled at himself. His straw-colored hair was tangled and there was a shining stubble on his pleasant, tanned face. He was sorry the red-haired woman had first seen him in his untidy condition. Then his conscience smote him at the sound of Sue's determined voice and he said:

"I'll try, darling. I'll try. But I did take their money."

They had, in fact, paid a great deal of money, considerably more than the rooms were worth even in that year of high prices and high wages. The country was just moving into one of those fabulous eras which are later referred to as the Gay Forties or the Golden Sixties —a pleasant period of national euphoria. It was a stimulating time to be alive—while it lasted.

"All right," Oliver said resignedly. "I'll do my best."

But he was conscious, as the next few days went by, that he was not doing his best. There were several reasons for that. From the beginning the idea of making himself a nuisance to his tenants had been Sue's, not Oliver's. And if Oliver had been a little less determined the whole project would never have got under way. Reason was on Sue's side, but—

For one thing, the tenants were so fascinating. All they said and did had a queer sort of inversion to it, as if a mirror had been held up to ordinary living and in the reflection showed strange variations from the norm. Their minds worked on a different basic premise, Oliver thought, from his own. They seemed to derive covert amusement from the most unamusing things; they patronized, they were aloof with a quality of cold detachment which did not prevent them from laughing inexplicably far too often for Oliver's comfort.

He saw them occasionally, on their way to and from their rooms. They were polite and distant, not, he suspected, from anger at his presence but from sheer indifference.

Most of the day they spent out of the house. The perfect May weather held unbroken and they seemed to give themselves up wholeheartedly to admiration of it, entirely confident that the warm, pale-gold sunshine and the scented air would not be interrupted by rain or cold. They were so sure of it that Oliver felt uneasy.

They took only one meal a day in the house, a late dinner. And their reactions to the meal were unpredictable. Laughter greeted some of the dishes, and a sort of delicate disgust others. No one would touch the salad, for instance. And the fish seemed to cause a wave of queer embarrassment around the table.

They dressed elaborately for each dinner. The man—his name was Omerie—looked extremely handsome in his dinner clothes, but he seemed a little sulky and Oliver twice heard the women laughing because he had to wear black. Oliver entertained a sudden vision, for no reason, of the man in garments as bright and as subtly cut as the women's, and it seemed somehow very right for him. He wore even the dark clothing with a certain flamboyance, as if cloth-of-gold would be more normal for him.

When they were in the house at other mealtimes, they ate in their rooms. They must have brought a great deal of food with them, from whatever mysterious place they had come. Oliver wondered with increasing curiosity where it might be. Delicious odors drifted into the hall sometimes, at odd hours, from their closed doors. Oliver could not identify them, but almost always they smelled irresistible. A few times the food smell was rather shockingly unpleasant, almost nauseating. It takes a connoisseur, Oliver reflected, to appreciate the decadent. And these people, most certainly, were connoisseurs.

Why they lived so contentedly in this huge ramshackle old house was a question that disturbed his dreams at night. Or why they refused to move. He caught some fascinating glimpses into their rooms, which appeared to have been changed almost completely by additions he could not have defined very clearly from the brief sights he had of them. The feeling of luxury which his first glance at them had evoked was confirmed by the richness of the hangings they had apparently brought with them, the half-glimpsed ornaments, the pictures on the walls, even the whiffs of exotic perfume that floated from half-open doors.

He saw the women go by him in the halls, moving softly through the brown dimness in their gowns so uncannily perfect in fit, so lushly rich, so glowingly colored they seemed unreal. That poise born of confidence in the subservience of the world gave them an imperious aloofness, but more than once Oliver, meeting the blue gaze of the woman with the red hair and the soft, tanned skin, thought he saw quickened interest there. She smiled at him in the dimness and went by in a haze of fragrance and a halo of incredible richness, and the warmth of the smile lingered after she had gone.

He knew she did not mean this aloofness to last between them. From the very first he was sure of that. When the time came she would make the opportunity to be alone with him. The thought was confusing and tremendously exciting. There was nothing he could do but wait, knowing she would see him when it suited her.

On the third day he lunched with Sue in a little downtown restaurant overlooking the great sweep of the metropolis across the river far below. Sue had shining brown curls and brown eyes, and her chin was a bit more prominent than is strictly accordant with beauty. From childhood Sue had known what she wanted and how to get it, and it seemed to Oliver just now that she had never wanted anything quite so much as the sale of this house.

"It's such a marvelous offer for the old mausoleum," she said, breaking into a roll with a gesture of violence. "We'll never have a chance like that again, and prices are so high we'll need the money to start housekeeping. Surely you can do *something*, Oliver!"

"I'm trying," Oliver assured her uncomfortably.

"Have you heard anything more from that madwoman who wants to buy it?"

Oliver shook his head. "Her attorney phoned again yesterday. Nothing new. I wonder who she is."

"I don't think even the attorney knows. All this mystery—I don't like it, Oliver. Even those Sancisco people— What did they do today?"

Oliver laughed. "They spent about an hour this morning telephoning movie theaters in the city, checking up on a lot of third-rate films they want to see parts of."

"Parts of? But why?"

"I don't know. I think . . . oh, nothing. More coffee?"

The trouble was, he thought he did know. It was too unlikely a guess to tell Sue about, and without familiarity with the Sancisco oddities she would only think Oliver was losing his mind. But he had from their talk, a definite impression that there was an actor in bit parts in all these films whose performances they mentioned with something very near to awe. They referred to him as Golconda, which didn't appear to be his name, so that Oliver had no way of guessing which obscure bit-player it was they admired so deeply. Golconda might have been the name of a character he had once played—and with superlative skill, judging by the comments of the Sanciscos—but to Oliver he meant nothing at all.

"They do funny things," he said, stirring his coffee reflectively. "Yesterday Omerie—that's the man—came in with a book of poems published about five years ago, and all of them handled it like a first edition of Shakespeare. I never even heard of the author, but he seems to be a tin god in their country, wherever that is."

"You still don't know? Haven't they even dropped any hints?"

"We don't do much talking," Oliver reminded her with some irony.

"I know, but— Oh, well, I guess it doesn't matter. Go on, what else do they do?"

"Well, this morning they were going to spend studying 'Golconda' and his great art, and this afternoon I think they're taking a trip up the river to some sort of shrine I never heard of. It isn't very far, wherever it is, because I know they're coming back for dinner. Some great man's birthplace, I think—they promised to take home souvenirs of the place if they could get any. They're typical tourists, all right—if I could only figure out what's behind the whole thing. It doesn't make sense."

"Nothing about that house makes sense any more. I do wish—"

She went on in a petulant voice, but Oliver ceased suddenly to hear her, because just outside the door, walking with imperial elegance on her high heels, a familiar figure passed. He did not see her face, but he thought he would know that poise, that richness of line and motion, anywhere on earth.

"Excuse me a minute," he muttered to Sue, and was out of his chair before she could speak. He made the door in half a dozen long strides, and the beautifully elegant passerby was only a few steps away when he got there. Then, with the words he had meant to speak already half-uttered, he fell silent and stood there staring.

It was not the red-haired woman. It was not her dark companion. It was a stranger. He watched, speechless, while the lovely, imperious creature moved on through the crowd and vanished, moving with familiar poise and assurance and an equally familiar strangeness as if the beautiful and exquisitely fitted garments she wore were an exotic costume to her, as they had always seemed to the Sancisco women. Every other woman on the street looked untidy and ill at ease beside her. Walking like a queen, she melted into the crowd and was gone.

She came from *their* country, Oliver told himself dizzily. So someone else nearby had mysterious tenants in this month of perfect May weather. Someone else was puzzling in vain today over the strangeness of the people from the nameless land.

In silence he went back to Sue.

The door stood invitingly ajar in the brown dimness of the upper hall. Oliver's steps slowed as he drew near it, and his heart began to quicken correspondingly. It was the red-haired woman's room, and he thought the door was not open by accident. Her name, he knew now, was Kleph.

The door creaked a little on its hinges and from within a very sweet voice said lazily, "Won't you come in?"

The room looked very different indeed. The big bed had been

pushed back against the wall and a cover thrown over it that brushed the floor all around looked like soft-haired fur except that it was a pale blue-green and sparkled as if every hair were tipped with invisible crystals. Three books lay open on the fur, and a very curious-looking magazine with faintly luminous printing and a page of pictures that at first glance appeared three-dimensional. Also a tiny porcelain pipe encrusted with porcelain flowers, and a thin wisp of smoke floating from the bowl.

Above the bed a broad picture hung, framing a square of blue water so real Oliver had to look twice to be sure it was not rippling gently from left to right. From the ceiling swung a crystal globe on a glass cord. It turned gently, the light from the windows making curved rectangles in its sides.

Under the center window a sort of chaise longue stood which Oliver had not seen before. He could only assume it was at least partly pneumatic and had been brought in the luggage. There was a very rich-looking quilted cloth covering and hiding it, embossed all over in shining metallic patterns.

Kleph moved slowly from the door and sank upon the chaise longue with a little sigh of content. The couch accommodated itself to her body with what looked like delightful comfort. Kleph wriggled a little and then smiled up at Oliver.

"Do come on in. Sit over there, where you can see out the window. I love your beautiful spring weather. You know, there never was a May like it in civilized times." She said that quite seriously, her blue eyes on Oliver's, and there was a hint of patronage in her voice, as if the weather had been arranged especially for her.

Oliver started across the room and then paused and looked down in amazement at the floor, which felt unstable. He had not noticed before that the carpet was pure white, unspotted, and sank about an inch under the pressure of the feet. He saw then that Kleph's feet were bare, or almost bare. She wore something like gossamer buskins of filmy net, fitting her feet exactly. The bare soles were pink as if they had been rouged, and the nails had a liquid gleam like tiny mirrors. He moved closer, and was not as surprised as he should have been to see that they really were tiny mirrors, painted with some lacquer that gave them reflecting surfaces.

"Do sit down," Kleph said again, waving a white-sleeved arm toward a chair by the window. She wore a garment that looked like short, soft down, loosely cut but following perfectly every motion she made. And there was something curiously different about her very shape today. When Oliver saw her in street clothes, she had the square-shouldered, slim-flanked figure that all women strove for, but here in her lounging robe she looked—well, different. There was an almost swanlike slope to her shoulders today, a roundness and softness to her body that looked unfamiliar and very appealing.

"Will you have some tea?" Kleph asked, and smiled charmingly.

A low table beside her held a tray and several small covered cups, lovely things with an inner glow like rose quartz, the color shining deeply as if from within layer upon layer of translucence. She took up one of the cups—there were no saucers—and offered it to Oliver.

It felt fragile and thin as paper in his hand. He could not see the contents because of the cup's cover, which seemed to be one with the cup itself and left only a thin open crescent at the rim. Steam rose from the opening.

Kleph took up a cup of her own and tilted it to her lips, smiling at Oliver over the rim. She was very beautiful. The pale red hair lay in shining loops against her head and the corona of curls like a halo above her forehead might have been pressed down like a wreath. Every hair kept order as perfectly as if it had been painted on, though the breeze from the window stirred now and then among the softly shining strands.

Oliver tried the tea. Its flavor was exquisite, very hot, and the taste that lingered upon his tongue was like the scent of flowers. It was an extremely feminine drink. He sipped again, surprised to find how much he liked it.

The scent of flowers seemed to increase as he drank, swirling through his head like smoke. After the third sip there was a faint buzzing in his ears. The bees among the flowers, perhaps, he thought incoherently—and sipped again.

Kleph watched him, smiling.

"The others will be out all afternoon," she told Oliver comfortably. "I thought it would give us a pleasant time to be acquainted."

Oliver was rather horrified to hear himself saying, "What makes you talk like that?" He had had no idea of asking the question; something seemed to have loosened his control over his own tongue.

Kleph's smile deepened. She tipped the cup to her lips and there was indulgence in her voice when she said, "What do you mean 'like that?'"

He waved his hand vaguely, noting with some surprise that at a glance it seemed to have six or seven fingers as it moved past his face.

"I don't know—precision, I guess. Why don't you say 'don't,' for instance?"

"In our country we are trained to speak with precision," Kleph explained. "Just as we are trained to move and dress and think with precision. Any slovenliness is trained out of us in childhood. With you, of course—" She was polite. "With you, this does not happen to be a national fetish. With us, we have time for the amenities. We like them."

Her voice had grown sweeter and sweeter as she spoke, until by now it was almost indistinguishable from the sweetness of the flower-scent in Oliver's head, and the delicate flavor of the tea.

"What country do you come from?" he asked, and tilted the cup again to drink, mildly surprised to notice that it seemed inexhaustible.

Kleph's smile was definitely patronizing this time. It didn't irritate him. Nothing could irritate him just now. The whole room swam in a beautiful rosy glow as fragrant as the flowers.

"We must not speak of that, Mr. Wilson."

"But—" Oliver paused. After all, it was, of course, none of his business. "This is a vacation?" he asked vaguely.

"Call it a pilgrimage, perhaps."

"Pilgrimage?" Oliver was so interested that for an instant his mind came back into sharp focus. "To—what?"

"I should not have said that, Mr. Wilson. Please forget it. Do you like the tea?"

"Very much."

"You will have guessed by now that it is not only tea, but an euphoriac."

Oliver stared. "Euphoriac?"

Kleph made a descriptive circle in the air with one graceful hand, and laughed. "You do not feel the effects yet? Surely you do?"

"I feel," Oliver said, "the way I'd feel after four whiskeys."

Kleph shuddered delicately. "We get our euphoria less painfully. And without the aftereffects your barbarous alcohols used to have." She bit her lip. "Sorry. I must be euphoric myself to speak so freely. Please forgive me. Shall we have some music?"

Kleph leaned backward on the chaise longue and reached toward the wall beside her. The sleeve, falling away from her round tanned arm, left bare the inside of the wrist, and Oliver was startled to see there a long, rosy streak of fading scar. His inhibitions had dissolved in the fumes of the fragrant tea; he caught his breath and leaned forward to stare.

Kleph shook the sleeve back over the scar with a quick gesture. Color came into her face beneath the softly tinted tan and she would not meet Oliver's eyes. A queer shame seemed to have fallen upon her.

Oliver said tactlessly, "What is it? What's the matter?"

Still she would not look at him. Much later he understood that shame and knew she had reason for it. Now he listened blankly as she said:

"Nothing . . . nothing at all. A . . . an inoculation. All of us . . . oh, never mind. Listen to the music."

This time she reached out with the other arm. She touched nothing, but when she had held her hand near the wall a sound breathed through the room. It was the sound of water, the sighing of waves receding upon long, sloped beaches. Oliver followed Kleph's gaze toward the picture of the blue water above the bed.

The waves there were moving. More than that, the point of vision moved. Slowly the seascape drifted past, moving with the waves, following them toward shore. Oliver watched, half-hypnotized by a motion that seemed at the time quite acceptable and not in the least surprising.

The waves lifted and broke in creaming foam and ran seething up a sandy beach. Then through the sound of the water music began to breathe, and through the water itself a man's face dawned in the frame, smiling intimately into the room. He held an oddly archaic musical instrument, lute-shaped, its body striped light and dark like a melon and its long neck bent back over his shoulder. He was singing, and Oliver felt mildly astonished at the song. It was very familiar and very odd indeed. He groped through the unfamiliar rhythms and found at last a thread to catch the tune by—it was "Make-Believe," from "Showboat," but certainly a showboat that had never steamed up the Mississippi.

"What's he doing to it?" he demanded after a few moments of outraged listening. "I never heard anything like it!"

Kleph laughed and stretched out her arm again. Enigmatically she said, "We call it kyling. Never mind. How do you like this?"

It was a comedian, a man in semi-clown make-up, his eyes exaggerated so that they seemed to cover half his face. He stood by a broad glass pillar before a dark curtain and sang a gay, staccato song interspersed with patter that sounded impromptu, and all the while his left hand did an intricate, musical tattoo of the nailtips on the glass of the column. He strolled around and around it as he sang. The rhythms of his fingernails blended with the song and swung widely away into patterns of their own, and blended again without a break.

It was confusing to follow. The song made even less sense than the monologue, which had something to do with a lost slipper and was full of allusions which made Kleph smile, but were utterly unintelligible to Oliver. The man had a dry, brittle style that was not very amusing, though Kleph seemed fascinated. Oliver was interested to see in him an extension and a variation of that extreme smooth confidence which marked all three of the Sanciscos. Clearly a racial trait, he thought.

Other performances followed, some of them fragmentary as if lifted out of a completer version. One he knew. The obvious, stirring melody struck his recognition before the figures—marching men against a haze, a great banner rolling backward above them in the smoke, foreground figures striding gigantically and shouting in rhythm, "Forward, forward the lily banners go!"

The music was tinny, the images blurred and poorly colored, but there was a gusto about the performance that caught at Oliver's imagination. He stared, remembering the old film from long ago. Dennis King and a ragged chorus, singing "The Song of the Vagabonds" from—was it "Vagabond King?"

"A very old one," Kleph said apologetically. "But I like it."

The steam of the intoxicating tea swirled between Oliver and the picture. Music swelled and sank through the room and the fragrant fumes and his own euphoric brain. Nothing seemed strange. He had discovered how to drink the tea. Like nitrous oxide, the effect was not cumulative. When you reached a peak of euphoria, you could not increase the peak. It was best to wait for a slight dip in the effect of the stimulant before taking more.

Otherwise it had most of the effects of alcohol—everything after awhile dissolved into a delightful fog through which all he saw was uniformly enchanting and partook of the qualities of a dream. He questioned nothing. Afterward he was not certain how much of it he really had dreamed.

There was the dancing doll, for instance. He remembered it quite clearly, in sharp focus—a tiny, slender woman with a long-nosed, dark-eyed face and a pointed chin. She moved delicately across the white rug—knee-high, exquisite. Her features were as mobile as her body, and she danced lightly, with resounding strokes of her toes, each echoing like a bell. It was a formalized sort of dance, and she sang breathlessly in accompaniment, making amusing little grimaces. Certainly it was a portrait-doll, animated to mimic the original perfectly in voice and motion. Afterward, Oliver knew he must have dreamed it.

What else happened he was quite unable to remember later. He knew Kleph had said some curious things, but they all made sense at the time, and afterward he couldn't remember a word. He knew he had been offered little glittering candies in a transparent dish, and that some of them had been delicious and one or two so bitter his tongue still curled the next day when he recalled them, and one— Kleph sucked luxuriantly on the same kind—of a taste that was actively nauseating.

As for Kleph herself—he was frantically uncertain the next day what had really happened. He thought he could remember the softness of her white-downed arms clasped at the back of his neck, while she laughed up at him and exhaled into his face the flowery fragrance of the tea. But beyond that he was totally unable to recall anything, for a while.

There was a brief interlude later, before the oblivion of sleep. He was almost sure he remembered a moment when the other two Sanciscos stood looking down at him, the man scowling, the smoky-eyed woman smiling a derisive smile.

The man said, from a vast distance, "Kleph, you know this is against every rule—" His voice began in a thin hum and soared in fantastic flight beyond the range of hearing. Oliver thought he remembered the dark woman's laughter, thin and distant too, and the hum of her voice like bees in flight.

"Kleph, Kleph, you silly little fool, can we never trust you out of sight?"

Kleph's voice then said something that seemed to make no sense. "What does it matter, *here?*"

The man answered in that buzzing, faraway hum. "The matter of giving your bond before you leave, not to interfere. You know you signed the rules—"

Kleph's voice, nearer and more intelligible: "But here the difference is . . . it does not matter *here!* You both know that. How could it matter?"

Oliver felt the downy brush of her sleeve against his cheek, but he saw nothing except the slow, smokelike ebb and flow of darkness past his eyes. He heard the voices wrangle musically from far away, and he heard them cease.

When he woke the next morning, alone in his own room, he woke with the memory of Kleph's eyes upon him very sorrowfully, her lovely tanned face looking down on him with the red hair falling fragrantly on each side of it and sadness and compassion in her eyes. He thought he had probably dreamed that. There was no reason why anyone should look at him with such sadness.

Sue telephoned that day.

"Oliver, the people who want to buy the house are here. That madwoman and her husband. Shall I bring them over?"

Oliver's mind all day had been hazy with the vague, bewildering memories of yesterday. Kleph's face kept floating before him, blotting out the room. He said, "What? I . . . oh, well, bring them if you want to. I don't see what good it'll do."

"Oliver, what's wrong with you? We agreed we needed the money, didn't we? I don't see how you can think of passing up such a wonderful bargain without even a struggle. We could get married and buy our own house right away, and you know we'll never get such an offer again for that old trash-heap. Wake up, Oliver!"

Oliver made an effort. "I know, Sue—I know. But—"

"Oliver, you've got to think of something!" Her voice was imperious.

He knew she was right. Kleph or no Kleph, the bargain shouldn't be ignored if there was any way at all of getting the tenants out. He wondered again what made the place so suddenly priceless to so many people. And what the last week in May had to do with the value of the house.

A sudden sharp curiosity pierced even the vagueness of his mind today. May's last week was so important that the whole sale of the house stood or fell upon occupancy by then. Why? *Why?*

"What's going to happen next week?" he asked rhetorically of the telephone. "Why can't they wait till these people leave? I'd knock a couple of thousand off the price if they'd—"

"You would not, Oliver Wilson! I can buy all our refrigeration units with that extra money. You'll just have to work out some way to give possession by next week, and that's that. You hear me?"

"Keep your shirt on," Oliver said practically. "I'm only human, but I'll try."

"I'm bringing the people over right away," Sue told him. "While the Sanciscos are still out. Now you put your mind to work and think of something, Oliver." She paused, and her voice was reflective when she spoke again. "They're . . . awfully odd people, darling."

"Odd?"

"You'll see."

It was an elderly woman and a very young man who trailed Sue up the walk. Oliver knew immediately what had struck Sue about them. He was somehow not at all surprised to see that both wore their clothing with the familiar air of elegant self-consciousness he had come to know so well. They, too, looked around them at the beautiful, sunny afternoon with conscious enjoyment and an air of faint condescension. He knew before he heard them speak how musical their voices would be and how meticulously they would pronounce each word.

There was no doubt about it. The people of Kleph's mysterious country were arriving here in force—for something. For the last week of May? He shrugged mentally; there was no way of guessing—yet. One thing only was sure: all of them must come from that nameless land where people controlled their voices like singers and their garments like actors who could stop the reel of time itself to adjust every disordered fold.

The elderly woman took full charge of the conversation from the start. They stood together on the rickety, unpainted porch, and Sue had no chance even for introductions.

"Young man, I am Madame Hollia. This is my husband." Her voice had an underrunning current of harshness, which was perhaps age. And her face looked almost corsetted, the loose flesh coerced into something like firmness by some invisible method Oliver could not guess at. The make-up was so skillful he could not be certain it was make-up at all, but he had a definite feeling that she was much older than she looked. It would have taken a lifetime of command to put so much authority into the harsh, deep, musically controlled voice.

The young man said nothing. He was very handsome. His type, apparently, was one that does not change much no matter in what culture or country it may occur. He wore beautifully tailored garments and carried in one gloved hand a box of red leather, about the size and shape of a book.

Madame Hollia went on. "I understand your problem about the house. You wish to sell to me, but are legally bound by your lease with Omerie and his friends. Is that right?"

Oliver nodded. "But—"

"Let me finish. If Omerie can be forced to vacate before next week, you will accept our offer. Right? Very well. Hara!" She nodded to the young man beside her. He jumped to instant attention, bowed slightly, said, "Yes, Hollia," and slipped a gloved hand into his coat.

Madame Hollia took the little object offered on his palm, her gesture as she reached for it almost imperial, as if royal robes swept from her outstretched arm.

"Here," she said, "is something that may help us. My dear—" She held it out to Sue—"if you can hide this somewhere about the house, I believe your unwelcome tenants will not trouble you much longer."

Sue took the thing curiously. It looked like a tiny silver box, no more than an inch square, indented at the top and with no line to show it could be opened.

"Wait a minute," Oliver broke in uneasily. "What is it?"

"Nothing that will harm anyone, I assure you."

"Then what—"

Madame Hollia's imperious gesture at one sweep silenced him and commanded Sue forward. "Go on, my dear. Hurry, before Omerie comes back. I can assure you there is no danger to anyone."

Oliver broke in determinedly. "Madame Hollia, I'll have to know what your plans are. I—"

"Oh, Oliver, please!" Sue's fingers closed over the silver cube. "Don't worry about it. I'm sure Madame Hollia knows best. Don't you *want* to get those people out?"

"Of course I do. But I don't want the house blown up or—"

Madame Hollia's deep laughter was indulgent. "Nothing so crude, I promise you, Mr. Wilson. Remember, we want the house! Hurry, my dear."

Sue nodded and slipped hastily past Oliver into the hall. Outnumbered, he subsided uneasily. The young man, Hara, tapped a negligent foot and admired the sunlight as they waited. It was an afternoon as perfect as all of May had been, translucent gold, balmy with an edge of chill lingering in the air to point up a perfect contrast with the summer to come. Hara looked around him confidently, like a man paying just tribute to a stageset provided wholly for himself. He even glanced up at a drone from above and followed the course of a big transcontinental plane half dissolved in golden haze high in the sun. "Quaint," he murmured in a gratified voice.

Sue came back and slipped her hand through Oliver's arm, squeezing excitedly. "There," she said. "How long will it take, Madame Hollia?"

"That will depend, my dear. Not very long. Now, Mr. Wilson, one word with you. You live here also, I understand? For your own comfort, take my advice and—"

Somewhere within the house a door slammed and a clear high voice rang wordlessly up a rippling scale. Then there was the sound of feet on the stairs, and a single line of song. *"Come hider, love, to me—"*

Hara started, almost dropping the red leather box he held.

"Kleph!" he said in a whisper. "Or Klia. I know they both just came on from Canterbury. But I thought—"

"Hush." Madame Hollia's features composed themselves into an imperious blank. She breathed triumphantly through her nose, drew back upon herself and turned an imposing facade to the door.

Kleph wore the same softly downy robe Oliver had seen before, except that today it was not white, but a pale, clear blue that gave her tan an apricot flush. She was smiling.

"Why, Hollia!" Her tone was at its most musical. "I thought I recognized voices from home. How nice to see you. No one knew you were coming to the—" She broke off and glanced at Oliver and then away again. "Hara, too," she said. "What a pleasant surprise."

Sue said flatly, "When did *you* get back?"

Kleph smiled at her. "You must be the little Miss Johnson. Why, I did not go out at all. I was tired of sightseeing. I have been napping in my room."

Sue drew in her breath in something that just escaped being a disbelieving sniff. A look flashed between the two women, and for an instant held—and that instant was timeless. It was an extraordinary pause in which a great deal of wordless interplay took place in the space of a second.

Oliver saw the quality of Kleph's smile at Sue, that same look of quiet confidence he had noticed so often about all of these strange people. He saw Sue's quick inventory of the other woman, and he saw how Sue squared her shoulders and stood up straight, smoothing down her summer frock over her flat hips so that for an instant she stood posed consciously, looking down on Kleph. It was deliberate. Bewildered, he glanced again at Kleph.

Kleph's shoulders sloped softly, her robe was belted to a tiny waist and hung in deep folds over frankly rounded hips. Sue's was the fashionable figure—but Sue was the first to surrender.

Kleph's smile did not falter. But in the silence there was an abrupt reversal of values, based on no more than the measureless quality of Kleph's confidence in herself, the quiet, assured smile. It was suddenly made very clear that fashion is not a constant. Kleph's curious, out-of-mode curves without warning became the norm, and Sue was a queer, angular, half-masculine creature beside her.

Oliver had no idea how it was done. Somehow the authority passed in a breath from one woman to the other. Beauty is almost wholly a matter of fashion; what is beautiful today would have been grotesque a couple of generations ago and will be grotesque a hundred years ahead. It will be worse than grotesque; it will be outmoded and therefore faintly ridiculous.

Sue was that. Kleph had only to exert her authority to make it clear to everyone on the porch. Kleph was a beauty, suddenly and very convincingly, beautiful in the accepted mode, and Sue was amusingly old-fashioned, an anachronism in her lithe, square-shouldered slimness. She did not belong. She was grotesque among these strangely immaculate people.

Sue's collapse was complete. But pride sustained her, and bewilderment. Probably she never did grasp entirely what was wrong. She gave Kleph one glance of burning resentment and when her eyes came back to Oliver there was suspicion in them, and mistrust.

Looking backward later, Oliver thought that in that moment, for the first time clearly, he began to suspect the truth. But he had no time to ponder it, for after the brief instant of enmity the three people from—elsewhere—began to speak all at once, as if in a belated attempt to cover something they did not want noticed.

Kleph said, "This beautiful weather—" and Madame Hollia said, "So fortunate to have this house—" and Hara, holding up the red leather box, said loudest of all, "Cenbe sent you this, Kleph. His latest."

Kleph put out both hands for it eagerly, the eiderdown sleeves falling back from her rounded arms. Oliver had a quick glimpse of that mysterious scar before the sleeve fell back, and it seemed to him that there was the faintest trace of a similar scar vanishing into Hara's cuff as he let his own arm drop.

"Cenbe!" Kleph cried, her voice high and sweet and delighted. "How wonderful! What period?"

"From November 1664," Hara said. "London, of course, though I think there may be some counterpoint from the 1347 November. He hasn't finished—of course." He glanced almost nervously at Oliver and Sue. "A wonderful example," he said quickly. "Marvelous. If you have the taste for it, of course."

Madame Hollia shuddered with ponderous delicacy.

"That man!" she said. "Fascinating, of course—a great man. But— so *advanced!*"

"It takes a connoisseur to appreciate Cenbe's work fully," Kleph said in a slightly tart voice. "We all admit that."

"Oh yes, we all bow to Cenbe," Hollia conceded. "I confess the man terrifies me a little, my dear. Do we expect him to join us?"

"I suppose so," Kleph said. "If his—work—is not yet finished, then of course. You know Cenbe's tastes."

Hollia and Hara laughed together. "I know when to look for him, then," Hollia said. She glanced at the staring Oliver and the subdued but angry Sue, and with a commanding effort brought the subject back into line.

"So fortunate, my dear Kleph, to have this house," she declared heavily. "I saw a tridimensional of it—afterward—and it was still quite perfect. Such a fortunate coincidence. Would you consider parting with your lease, for a consideration? Say, a coronation seat at—"

"Nothing could buy us, Hollia," Kleph told her gaily, clasping the red box to her bosom.

Hollia gave her a cool stare. "You may change your mind, my dear Kleph," she said pontifically. "There is still time. You can always reach us through Mr. Wilson here. We have rooms up the street in the Montgomery House—nothing like yours, of course, but they will do. For us, they will do."

Oliver blinked. The Montgomery House was the most expensive hotel in town. Compared to this collapsing old ruin, it was a palace. There was no understanding these people. Their values seemed to have suffered a complete reversal.

Madame Hollia moved majestically toward the steps.

"Very pleasant to see you, my dear," she said over one well-padded shoulder. "Enjoy your stay. My regards to Omerie and Klia. Mr. Wilson—" she nodded toward the walk. "A word with you."

Oliver followed her down toward the street. Madame Hollia paused halfway there and touched his arm.

"One word of advice," she said huskily. "You say you sleep here? Move out, young man. Move out before tonight."

Oliver was searching in a half-desultory fashion for the hiding place Sue had found for the mysterious silver cube, when the first sounds from above began to drift down the stairwell toward him. Kleph had closed her door, but the house was old, and strange qualities in the noise overhead seemed to seep through the woodwork like an almost visible stain.

It was music, in a way. But much more than music. And it was a terrible sound, the sounds of calamity and of all human reaction to calamity, everything from hysteria to heartbreak, from irrational joy to rationalized acceptance.

The calamity was—single. The music did not attempt to correlate all human sorrows; it focused sharply upon one and followed the ramifications out and out. Oliver recognized these basics to the sounds in a very brief moment. They were essentials, and they seemed to beat into his brain with the first strains of the music which was so much more than music.

But when he lifted his head to listen he lost all grasp upon the meaning of the noise and it was sheer medley and confusion. To think of it was to blur it hopelessly in the mind, and he could not recapture that first instant of unreasoning acceptance.

He went upstairs almost in a daze, hardly knowing what he was doing. He pushed Kleph's door open. He looked inside—

What he saw there he could not afterward remember except in a blurring as vague as the blurred ideas the music roused in his brain. Half the room had vanished behind a mist, and the mist was a three-dimensional screen upon which were projected— He had no words for them. He was not even sure if the projections were visual. The mist was spinning with motion and sound, but essentially it was neither sound nor motion that Oliver saw.

This was a work of art. Oliver knew no name for it. It transcended all art-forms he knew, blended them, and out of the blend produced subtleties his mind could not begin to grasp. Basically, this was the attempt of a master composer to correlate every essential aspect of a vast human experience into something that could be conveyed in a few moments to every sense at once.

The shifting visions on the screen were not pictures in themselves, but hints of pictures, subtly selected outlines that plucked at the mind and with one deft touch set whole chords ringing through the memory. Perhaps each beholder reacted differently, since it was in the eye and the mind of the beholder that the truth of the picture lay. No two would be aware of the same symphonic panorama, but each would see essentially the same terrible story unfold.

Every sense was touched by that deft and merciless genius. Color and shape and motion flickered in the screen, hinting much, evoking unbearable memories deep in the mind; odors floated from the screen and touched the heart of the beholder more poignantly than anything visual could do. The skin crawled sometimes as if to a tangible cold hand laid upon it. The tongue curled with remembered bitterness and remembered sweet.

It was outrageous. It violated the innermost privacies of a man's mind, called up secret things long ago walled off behind mental scar tissue, forced its terrible message upon the beholder relentlessly though the mind might threaten to crack beneath the stress of it.

And yet, in spite of all this vivid awareness, Oliver did not know what calamity the screen portrayed. That it was real, vast, overwhelmingly dreadful he could not doubt. That it had once happened was unmistakable. He caught flashing glimpses of human faces distorted with grief and disease and death—real faces, faces that had once lived and were seen now in the instant of dying. He saw men and women in rich clothing superimposed in panorama upon reeling thousands of ragged folk, great throngs of them swept past the sight in an instant, and he saw that death made no distinction among them.

He saw lovely women laugh and shake their curls, and the laughter shriek into hysteria and the hysteria into music. He saw one man's face, over and over—a long, dark, saturnine face, deeply lined, sorrowful, the face of a powerful man wise in worldliness, urbane—and helpless. That face was for awhile a recurring motif, always more tortured, more helpless than before.

The music broke off in the midst of a rising glide. The mist vanished and the room reappeared before him. The anguished dark face for an instant seemed to Oliver printed everywhere he looked, like after-vision on the eyelids. He knew that face. He had seen it before, not often, but he should know its name—

"Oliver, Oliver—" Kleph's sweet voice came out of a fog at him. He was leaning dizzily against the doorpost looking down into her eyes. She, too, had that dazed blankness he must show on his own face. The power of the dreadful symphony still held them both. But even in this confused moment Oliver saw that Kleph had been enjoying the experience.

He felt sickened to the depths of his mind, dizzy with sickness and revulsion because of the superimposing of human miseries he had just beheld. But Kleph—only appreciation showed upon her face. To her it had been magnificence, and magnificence only.

Irrelevantly Oliver remembered the nauseating candies she had enjoyed, the nauseating odors of strange food that drifted sometimes through the hall from her room.

What was it she had said downstairs a little while ago? Connoisseur, that was it. Only a connoisseur could appreciate work as—as *advanced*—as the work of someone called Cenbe.

A whiff of intoxicating sweetness curled past Oliver's face. Something cool and smooth was pressed into his hand.

"Oh, Oliver, I am so sorry," Kleph's voice murmured contritely. "Here, drink the euphoriac and you will feel better. Please drink!"

The familiar fragrance of the hot sweet tea was on his tongue before he knew he had complied. Its relaxing fumes floated up through his brain and in a moment or two the world felt stable around him again. The room was as it had always been. And Kleph—

Her eyes were very bright. Sympathy showed in them for him, but for herself she was still brimmed with the high elation of what she had just been experiencing.

"Come and sit down," she said gently, tugging at his arm. "I am so sorry—I should not have played that over, where you could hear it. I have no excuse, really. It was only that I forgot what the effect might be on one who had never heard Cenbe's symphonies before. I was so impatient to see what he had done with . . . with his new subject. I am so very sorry, Oliver!"

"What was it?" His voice sounded steadier than he had expected. The tea was responsible for that. He sipped again, glad of the consoling euphoria its fragrance brought.

"A . . . a composite interpretation of . . . oh, Oliver, you know I must not answer questions!"

"But—"

"No—drink your tea and forget what it was you saw. Think of other things. Here, we will have music—another kind of music, something gay—"

She reached for the wall beside the window, and as before, Oliver saw the broad framed picture of blue water above the bed ripple and grow pale. Through it another scene began to dawn like shapes rising beneath the surface of the sea.

He had a glimpse of a dark-curtained stage upon which a man in a tight dark tunic and hose moved with a restless, sidelong pace, his hands and face startlingly pale against the black about him. He limped; he had a crooked back and he spoke familiar lines. Oliver had seen John Barrymore once as the crook-backed Richard, and it seemed vaguely outrageous to him that any other actor should essay that difficult part. This one he had never seen before, but the man had a fascinatingly smooth manner and his interpretation of the Plantagenet king was quite new and something Shakespeare probably never dreamed of.

"No," Kleph said, "not this. Nothing gloomy." And she put out her hand again. The nameless new Richard faded and there was a swirl of changing pictures and changing voices, all blurred together, before the scene steadied upon a stageful of dancers in pastel ballet skirts, drifting effortlessly through some complicated pattern of motion. The music that went with it was light and effortless too. The room filled up with the clear, floating melody.

Oliver set down his cup. He felt much surer of himself now, and he thought the euphoriac had done all it could for him. He didn't want to blur again mentally. There were things he meant to learn about. Now. He considered how to begin.

Kleph was watching him. "That Hollia," she said suddenly. "She wants to buy the house?"

Oliver nodded. "She's offering a lot of money. Sue's going to be awfully disappointed if—" He hesitated. Perhaps, after all, Sue would not be disappointed. He remembered the little silver cube with the enigmatic function and he wondered if he should mention it to Kleph. But the euphoriac had not reached that level of his brain, and he remembered his duty to Sue and was silent.

Kleph shook her head, her eyes upon his warm with—was it sympathy?

"Believe me," she said, "you will not find that—important—after all. I promise you, Oliver."

He stared at her. "I wish you'd explain."

Kleph laughed on a note more sorrowful than amused. But it occurred to Oliver suddenly that there was no longer condescension in her voice. Imperceptibly that air of delicate amusement had vanished from her manner toward him. The cool detachment that still marked Omerie's attitude, and Klia's, was not in Kleph's any more. It was a subtlety he did not think she could assume. It had to come spontaneously or not at all. And for no reason he was willing to examine, it became suddenly very important to Oliver that Kleph should not condescend to him, that she should feel toward him as he felt toward her. He would not think of it.

He looked down at his cup, rose-quartz, exhaling a thin plume of steam from its crescent-slit opening. This time, he thought, maybe he could make the tea work for him. For he remembered how it loosened the tongue, and there was a great deal he needed to know. The idea that had come to him on the porch in the instant of silent rivalry between Kleph and Sue seemed now too fantastic to entertain. But some answer there must be.

Kleph herself gave him the opening.

"I must not take too much euphoriac this afternoon," she said, smiling at him over her pink cup. "It will make me drowsy, and we are going out this evening with friends."

"More friends?" Oliver asked. "From your country?"

Kleph nodded. "Very dear friends we have expected all this week."

"I wish you'd tell me," Oliver said bluntly, "where it is you come from. It isn't from here. Your culture is too different from ours—even your names—" He broke off as Kleph shook her head.

"I wish I could tell you. But that is against all the rules. It is even against the rules for me to be here talking to you now."

"What rules?"

She made a helpless gesture. "You must not ask me, Oliver." She leaned back on the chaise longue, which adjusted itself luxuriously to the motion, and smiled very sweetly at him. "We must not talk about things like that. Forget it, listen to the music, enjoy yourself if you can—" She closed her eyes and laid her head back against the cushions. Oliver saw the round tanned throat swell as she began to hum a tune. Eyes still closed, she sang again the words she had sung upon the stairs. *"Come hider, love, to me—"*

A memory clicked over suddenly in Oliver's mind. He had never heard the queer, lagging tune before, but he thought he knew the words. He remembered what Hollia's husband had said when he heard that line of song, and he leaned forward. She would not answer a direct question, but perhaps—

"Was the weather this warm in Canterbury?" he asked, and held his breath. Kleph hummed another line of the song and shook her head, eyes still closed.

"It was autumn there," she said. "But bright, wonderfully bright. Even their clothing, you know . . . everyone was singing that new song, and I can't get it out of my head." She sang another line, and the words were almost unintelligible—English, yet not an English Oliver could understand.

He stood up. "Wait," he said. "I want to find something. Back in a minute."

She opened her eyes and smiled mistily at him, still humming. He went downstairs as fast as he could—the stairway swayed a little, though his head was nearly clear now—and into the library. The book he wanted was old and battered, interlined with the penciled notes of his college days. He did not remember very clearly where the passage he wanted was, but he thumbed fast through the columns and by sheer luck found it within a few minutes. Then he went back upstairs, feeling a strange emptiness in his stomach because of what he almost believed now.

"Kleph," he said firmly, "I know that song. I know the year it was new."

Her lids rose slowly; she looked at him through a mist of euphoriac. He was not sure she had understood. For a long moment she held him with her gaze. Then she put out one downy-sleeved arm and spread her tanned fingers toward him. She laughed deep in her throat.

"Come hider, love, to me," she said.

He crossed the room slowly, took her hand. The fingers closed warmly about his. She pulled him down so that he had to kneel beside her. Her other arm lifted. Again she laughed, very softly, and closed her eyes, lifting her face to his.

The kiss was warm and long. He caught something of her own euphoria from the fragrance of the tea breathed into his face. And he was startled at the end of the kiss, when the clasp of her arms loosened about his neck, to feel the sudden rush of her breath against his cheek. There were tears on her face, and the sound she made was a sob.

He held her off and looked down in amazement. She sobbed once more, caught a deep breath, and said, "Oh, Oliver, Oliver—" Then she shook her head and pulled free, turning away to hide her face. "I . . . I am sorry," she said unevenly. "Please forgive me. It does not matter . . . I *know* it does not matter . . . but—"

"What's wrong? What doesn't matter?"

"Nothing. Nothing . . . please forget it. Nothing at all." She got a handkerchief from the table and blew her nose, smiling at him with an effect of radiance through the tears.

Suddenly he was very angry. He had heard enough evasions and mystifying half-truths. He said roughly, "Do you think I'm crazy? I know enough now to—"

"Oliver, please!" She held up her own cup, steaming fragrantly. "Please, no more questions. Here, euphoria is what you need, Oliver. Euphoria, not answers."

"What year was it when you heard that song in Canterbury?" he demanded, pushing the cup aside.

She blinked at him, tears bright on her lashes. "Why . . . what year do you think?"

"I know," Oliver told her grimly. "I know the year that song was popular. I know you just came from Canterbury—Hollia's husband said so. It's May now, but it was autumn in Canterbury, and you just came from there, so lately the song you heard is still running through your head. Chaucer's Pardoner sang that song some time around the end of the fourteenth century. Did you see Chaucer, Kleph? What was it like in England that long ago?"

Kleph's eyes fixed his for a silent moment. Then her shoulders drooped and her whole body went limp with resignation beneath the soft blue robe. "I am a fool," she said gently. "It must have been easy to trap me. You really believe—what you say?"

Oliver nodded.

She said in a low voice, "Few people do believe it. That is one of our maxims, when we travel. We are safe from much suspicion because people before The Travel began will not believe."

The emptiness in Oliver's stomach suddenly doubled in volume. For an instant the bottom dropped out of time itself and the universe was unsteady about him. He felt sick. He felt naked and helpless. There was a buzzing in his ears and the room dimmed before him.

He had not really believed—not until this instant. He had expected some rational explanation from her that would tidy all his wild half-thoughts and suspicions into something a man could accept as believable. Not this.

Kleph dabbed at her eyes with the pale-blue handkerchief and smiled tremulously.

"I know," she said. "It must be a terrible thing to accept. To have all your concepts turned upside down— We know it from childhood, of course, but for you . . . here, Oliver. The euphoriac will make it easier."

He took the cup, the faint stain of her lip rouge still on the crescent opening. He drank, feeling the dizzy sweetness spiral through his head, and his brain turned a little in his skull as the volatile fragrance took effect. With that turning, focus shifted and all his values with it.

He began to feel better. The flesh settled on his bones again, and the warm clothing of temporal assurance settled upon his flesh, and he was no longer naked and in the vortex of unstable time.

"The story is very simple, really," Kleph said. "We—travel. Our own time is not terribly far ahead of yours. No. I must not say how far. But we still remember your songs and poets and some of your great actors. We are a people of much leisure, and we cultivate the art of enjoying ourselves.

"This is a tour we are making—a tour of a year's seasons. Vintage seasons. That autumn in Canterbury was the most magnificent autumn our researchers could discover anywhere. We rode in a pilgrimage to the shrine—it was a wonderful experience, though the clothing was a little hard to manage.

"Now this month of May is almost over—the loveliest May in recorded times. A perfect May in a wonderful period. You have no way of knowing what a good, gay period you live in, Oliver. The very feeling in the air of the cities—that wonderful national confidence and happiness—everything going as smoothly as a dream. There were other Mays with fine weather, but each of them had a war or a famine, or something else wrong." She hesitated, grimaced and went on rapidly. "In a few days we are to meet at a coronation in Rome," she said. "I think the year will be 800—Christmastime. We—"

"But why," Oliver interrupted, "did you insist on this house? Why do the others want to get it away from you?"

Kleph stared at him. He saw the tears rising again in small bright crescents that gathered above her lower lids. He saw the look of obstinacy that came upon her soft, tanned face. She shook her head.

"You must not ask me that." She held out the steaming cup. "Here, drink and forget what I have said. I can tell you no more. No more at all."

When he woke, for a little while he had no idea where he was. He did not remember leaving Kleph or coming to his own room. He didn't care, just then. For he woke to a sense of overwhelming terror.

The dark was full of it. His brain rocked on waves of fear and pain. He lay motionless, too frightened to stir, some atavistic memory warning him to lie quiet until he knew from which direction the danger threatened. Reasonless panic broke over him in a tidal flow; his head ached with its violence and the dark throbbed to the same rhythms.

A knock sounded at the door. Omerie's deep voice said, "Wilson! Wilson, are you awake?"

Oliver tried twice before he had breath to answer. "Y-yes—what is it?"

The knob rattled. Omerie's dim figure groped for the light switch and the room sprang into visibility. Omerie's face was drawn with strain, and he held one hand to his head as if it ached in rhythm with Oliver's.

It was in that moment, before Omerie spoke again, that Oliver remembered Hollia's warning. "Move out, young man—move out before tonight." Wildly he wondered what threatened them all in this dark house that throbbed with the rhythms of pure terror.

Omerie in an angry voice answered the unspoken question.

"Someone has planted a subsonic in the house, Wilson. Kleph thinks you may know where it is."

"S-subsonic?"

"Call it a gadget," Omerie interpreted impatiently. "Probably a small metal box that—"

Oliver said, "Oh," in a tone that must have told Omerie everything.

"Where is it?" he demanded. "Quick. Let's get this over."

"I don't know." With an effort Oliver controlled the chattering of his teeth. "Y-you mean all this—all this is just from the little box?"

"Of course. Now tell me how to find it before we all go crazy."

Oliver got shakily out of bed, groping for his robe with nerveless hands. "I s-suppose she hid it somewhere downstairs," he said. "S-she wasn't gone long."

Omerie got the story out of him in a few brief questions. He clicked his teeth in exasperation when Oliver had finished it.

"That stupid Hollia—"

"Omerie!" Kleph's plaintive voice wailed from the hall. "Please hurry, Omerie! This is too much to stand! Oh, Omerie, please!"

Oliver stood up abruptly. Then a redoubled wave of the inexplicable pain seemed to explode in his skull at the motion, and he clutched the bedpost and reeled.

"Go find the thing yourself," he heard himself saying dizzily. "I can't even walk—"

Omerie's own temper was drawn wire-tight by the pressure in the room. He seized Oliver's shoulder and shook him, saying in a tight voice, "You let it in—now help us get it out, or—"

"It's a gadget out of your world, not mine!" Oliver said furiously.

And then it seemed to him there was a sudden coldness and silence in the room. Even the pain and the senseless terror paused for a moment. Omerie's pale, cold eyes fixed upon Oliver a stare so chill he could almost feel the ice in it.

"What do you know about our—world?" Omerie demanded.

Oliver did not speak a word. He did not need to; his face must have betrayed what he knew. He was beyond concealment in the stress of this night-time terror he still could not understand.

Omerie bared his white teeth and said three perfectly unintelligible words. Then he stepped to the door and snapped, "Kleph!"

Oliver could see the two women huddled together in the hall, shaking violently with involuntary waves of that strange, synthetic terror. Klia, in a luminous green gown, was rigid with control, but Kleph made no effort whatever at repression. Her downy robe had turned soft gold tonight; she shivered in it and the tears ran down her face unchecked.

"Kleph," Omerie said in a dangerous voice, "you were euphoric again yesterday?"

Kleph darted a scared glance at Oliver and nodded guiltily.

"You talked too much." It was a complete indictment in one sentence. "You know the rules, Kleph. You will not be allowed to travel again if anyone reports this to the authorities."

Kleph's lovely creamy face creased suddenly into impenitent dimples.

"I know it was wrong. I am very sorry—but you will not stop me if Cenbe says no."

Klia flung out her arms in a gesture of helpless anger. Omerie shrugged. "In this case, as it happens, no great harm is done," he said, giving Oliver an unfathomable glance. "But it might have been serious. Next time perhaps it will be. I must have a talk with Cenbe."

"We must find the subsonic first of all," Klia reminded them, shivering. "If Kleph is afraid to help, she can go out for a while. I confess I am very sick of Kleph's company just now."

"We could give up the house!" Kleph cried wildly. "Let Hollia have it! How can you stand this long enough to hunt—"

"Give up the house?" Klia echoed. "You must be mad! With all our invitations out?"

"There will be no need for that," Omerie said. "We can find it if we all hunt. You feel able to help?" He looked at Oliver.

With an effort Oliver controlled his own senseless panic as the waves of it swept through the room. "Yes," he said. "But what about me? What are you going to do?"

"That should be obvious," Omerie said, his pale eyes in the dark face regarding Oliver impassively. "Keep you in the house until we go. We can certainly do no less. You understand that. And there is no reason for us to do more, as it happens. Silence is all we promised when we signed our travel papers."

"But—" Oliver groped for the fallacy in that reasoning. It was no use. He could not think clearly. Panic surged insanely through his mind from the very air around him. "All right," he said. "Let's hunt."

It was dawn before they found the box, tucked inside the ripped seam of a sofa cushion. Omerie took it upstairs without a word. Five minutes later the pressure in the air abruptly dropped and peace fell blissfully upon the house.

"They will try again," Omerie said to Oliver at the door of the back bedroom. "We must watch for that. As for you, I must see that you remain in the house until Friday. For your own comfort, I advise you to let me know if Hollia offers any further tricks. I confess I am not quite sure how to enforce your staying indoors. I could use methods that would make you very uncomfortable. I would prefer to accept your word on it."

Oliver hesitated. The relaxing of pressure upon his brain had left him exhausted and stupid, and he was not at all sure what to say.

Omerie went on after a moment. "It was partly our fault for not insuring that we had the house to ourselves," he said. "Living here with us, you could scarcely help suspecting. Shall we say that in return for your promise, I reimburse you in part for losing the sale price on this house?"

Oliver thought that over. It would pacify Sue a little. And it meant only two days indoors. Besides, what good would escaping do? What could he say to outsiders that would not lead him straight to a padded cell?

"All right," he said wearily. "I promise."

By Friday morning there was still no sign from Hollia. Sue telephoned at noon. Oliver knew the crackle of her voice over the wire when Kleph took the call. Even the crackle sounded hysterical; Sue saw her bargain slipping hopelessly through her grasping little fingers.

Kleph's voice was soothing. "I am sorry," she said many times, in the intervals when the voice paused. "I am truly sorry. Believe me, you will find it does not matter. I know . . . I am sorry—"

She turned from the phone at last. "The girl says Hollia has given up," she told the others.

"Not Hollia," Klia said firmly.

Omerie shrugged. "We have very little time left. If she intends anything more, it will be tonight. We must watch for it."

"Oh, not tonight!" Kleph's voice was horrified. "Not even Hollia would do that!"

"Hollia, my dear, in her own way is quite as unscrupulous as you are," Omerie told her with a smile.

"But—would she spoil things for us just because she can't be here?"

"What do you think?" Klia demanded.

Oliver ceased to listen. There was no making sense out of their talk, but he knew that by tonight whatever the secret was must surely come into the open at last. He was willing to wait and see.

For two days excitement had been building up in the house and the three who shared it with him. Even the servants felt it and were nervous and unsure of themselves. Oliver had given up asking questions—it only embarrassed his tenants—and watched.

All the chairs in the house were collected in the three front bedrooms. The furniture was rearranged to make room for them, and dozens of covered cups had been set out on trays. Oliver recognized Kleph's rose-quartz set among the rest. No steam rose from the thin crescent-openings, but the cups were full. Oliver lifted one and felt a heavy liquid move within it, like something half-solid, sluggishly.

Guests were obviously expected, but the regular dinner hour of nine came and went, and no one had yet arrived. Dinner was finished; the servants went home. The Sanciscos went to their rooms to dress, amid a feeling of mounting tension.

Oliver stepped out on the porch after dinner, trying in vain to guess what it was that had wrought such a pitch of expectancy in the house. There was a quarter moon swimming in haze on the horizon, but the stars which had made every night of May thus far a dazzling translucency, were very dim tonight. Clouds had begun to gather at sundown, and the undimmed weather of the whole month seemed ready to break at last.

Behind Oliver the door opened a little, and closed. He caught Kleph's fragrance before he turned, and a faint whiff of the fragrance of the euphoriac she was much too fond of drinking. She came to his side and slipped a hand into his, looking up into his face in the darkness.

"Oliver," she said very softly. "Promise me one thing. Promise me not to leave the house tonight."

"I've already promised that," he said a little irritably.

"I know. But tonight—I have a very particular reason for wanting you indoors tonight." She leaned her head against his shoulder for a moment, and despite himself his irritation softened. He had not seen Kleph alone since that last night of her revelations; he supposed he never would be alone with her again for more than a few minutes at a time. But he knew he would not forget those two bewildering evenings. He knew too, now, that she was very weak and foolish—but she was still Kleph and he had held her in his arms, and was not likely ever to forget it.

"You might be—hurt—if you went out tonight," she was saying in a muffled voice. "I know it will not matter, in the end, but—remember you promised, Oliver."

She was gone again, and the door had closed behind her, before he could voice the futile questions in his mind.

The guests began to arrive just before midnight. From the head of the stairs Oliver saw them coming in by twos and threes, and was astonished at how many of these people from the future must have gathered here in the past weeks. He could see quite clearly now how they differed from the norm of his own period. Their physical elegance was what one noticed first—perfect grooming, meticulous manners, meticulously controlled voices. But because they were all idle, all, in a way, sensation-hunters, there was a certain shrillness underlying their voices, especially when heard all together. Petulance and self-indulgence showed beneath the good manners. And tonight, an all-pervasive excitement.

By one o'clock everyone had gathered in the front rooms. The teacups had begun to steam, apparently of themselves, around midnight, and the house was full of the faint, thin fragrance that induced a sort of euphoria all through the rooms, breathed in with the perfume of the tea.

It made Oliver feel light and drowsy. He was determined to sit up as long as the others did, but he must have dozed off in his own room, by the window, an unopened book in his lap.

For when it happened he was not sure for a few minutes whether or not it was a dream.

The vast, incredible crash was louder than sound. He felt the whole house shake under him, felt rather than heard the timbers grind upon one another like broken bones, while he was still in the borderland of sleep. When he woke fully he was on the floor among the shattered fragments of the window.

How long or short a time he had lain there he did not know. The world was still stunned with that tremendous noise, or his ears still deaf from it, for there was no sound anywhere.

He was halfway down the hall toward the front rooms when sound began to return from outside. It was a low, indescribable rumble at first, prickled with countless tiny distant screams. Oliver's eardrums ached from the terrible impact of the vast unheard noise, but the numbness was wearing off and he heard before he saw it the first voices of the stricken city.

The door to Kleph's room resisted him for a moment. The house had settled a little from the violence of the—the explosion?—and the frame was out of line. When he got the door open he could only stand blinking stupidly into the darkness within. All the lights were out, but there was a breathless sort of whispering going on in many voices.

The chairs were drawn around the broad front windows so that everyone could see out; the air swam with the fragrance of euphoria. There was light enough here from outside for Oliver to see that a few onlookers still had their hands to their ears, but all were craning eagerly forward to see.

Through a dreamlike haze Oliver saw the city spread out with impossible distinctness below the window. He knew quite well that a row of houses across the street blocked the view—yet he was looking over the city now, and he could see it in a limitless panorama from here to the horizon. The houses between had vanished.

On the far skyline fire was already a solid mass, painting the low clouds crimson. That sulphurous light reflecting back from the sky upon the city made clear the rows upon rows of flattened houses with flame beginning to lick up among them, and farther out the formless rubble of what had been houses a few minutes ago and was now nothing at all.

The city had begun to be vocal. The noise of the flames rose loudest, but you could hear a rumble of human voices like the beat of surf a long way off, and staccato noises of screaming made a sort of pattern that came and went continuously through the web of sound. Threading it in undulating waves the shrieks of sirens knit the web together into a terrible symphony that had, in its way, a strange, inhuman beauty.

Briefly through Oliver's stunned incredulity went the memory of that other symphony Kleph had played there one day, another catastrophe retold in terms of music and moving shapes.

He said hoarsely, "Kleph—"

The tableau by the window broke. Every head turned, and Oliver saw the faces of strangers staring at him, some few in embarrassment avoiding his eyes, but most seeking them out with that avid, inhuman curiosity which is common to a type in all crowds at accident scenes. But these people were here by design, audience at a vast disaster timed almost for their coming.

Kleph got up unsteadily, her velvet dinner gown tripping her as she rose. She set down a cup and swayed a little as she came toward the door, saying, "Oliver . . . Oliver—" in a sweet, uncertain voice. She was drunk, he saw, and wrought up by the catastrophe to a pitch of stimulation in which she was not very sure what she was doing.

Oliver heard himself saying in a thin voice not his own, "W-what was it, Kleph? What happened? What—" But *happened* seemed so inadequate a word for the incredible panorama below that he had to choke back hysterical laughter upon the struggling questions, and broke off entirely, trying to control the shaking that had seized his body.

Kleph made an unsteady stoop and seized a steaming cup. She came to him, swaying, holding it out—her panacea for all ills.

"Here, drink it, Oliver—we are all quite safe here, quite safe." She thrust the cup to his lips and he gulped automatically, grateful for the fumes that began their slow, coiling surcease in his brain with the first swallow.

"It was a meteor," Kleph was saying. "Quite a small meteor, really. We are perfectly safe here. This house was never touched."

Out of some cell of the unconscious Oliver heard himself saying incoherently, "Sue? Is Sue—" he could not finish.

Kleph thrust the cup at him again. "I think she may be safe—for awhile. Please, Oliver—forget about all that and drink."

"But you *knew!*" Realization of that came belatedly to his stunned brain. "You could have given warning, or—"

"How could we change the past?" Kleph asked. "We knew—but could we stop the meteor? Or warn the city? Before we come we must give our word never to interfere—"

Their voices had risen imperceptibly to be audible above the rising volume of sound from below. The city was roaring now, with flames and cries and the crash of falling buildings. Light in the room turned lurid and pulsed upon the walls and ceiling in red light and redder dark.

Downstairs a door slammed. Someone laughed. It was high, hoarse, angry laughter. Then from the crowd in the room someone gasped and there was a chorus of dismayed cries. Oliver tried to focus upon the window and the terrible panorama beyond, and found he could not.

It took several seconds of determined blinking to prove that more than his own vision was at fault. Kleph whimpered softly and moved against him. His arms closed about her automatically, and he was grateful for the warm, solid flesh against him. This much at least he could touch and be sure of, though everything else that was happening might be a dream. Her perfume and the heady perfume of the tea rose together in his head, and for an instant, holding her in this embrace that must certainly be the last time he ever held her, he did not care that something had gone terribly wrong with the very air of the room.

It was blindness—not continuous, but a series of swift, widening ripples between which he could catch glimpses of the other faces in the room, strained and astonished in the flickering light from the city.

The ripples came faster. There was only a blink of sight between them now, and the blinks grew briefer and briefer, the intervals of darkness more broad.

From downstairs the laughter rose again up the stairwell. Oliver thought he knew the voice. He opened his mouth to speak, but a door nearby slammed open before he could find his tongue, and Omerie shouted down the stairs.

"Hollia?" he roared above the roaring of the city. "Hollia, is that you?"

She laughed again, triumphantly. "I warned you!" her hoarse, harsh voice called. "Now come out in the street with the rest of us if you want to see any more!"

"Hollia!" Omerie shouted desperately. "Stop this or—"

The laughter was derisive. "What will you do, Omerie? This time I hid it too well—come down in the street if you want to watch the rest."

There was angry silence in the house. Oliver could feel Kleph's quick, excited breathing light upon his cheek, feel the soft motions of her body in his arms. He tried consciously to make the moment last, stretch it out to infinity. Everything had happened too swiftly to impress very clearly on his mind anything except what he could touch and hold. He held her in an embrace made consciously light, though he wanted to clasp her in a tight, despairing grip, because he was sure this was the last embrace they would ever share.

The eye-straining blinks of light and blindness went on. From far away below the roar of the burning city rolled on, threaded together by the long, looped cadences of the sirens that linked all sounds into one.

Then in the bewildering dark another voice sounded from the hall downstairs. A man's voice, very deep, very melodious, saying:

"What is this? What are you doing here? Hollia—is that you?"

Oliver felt Kleph stiffen in his arms. She caught her breath, but she said nothing in the instant while heavy feet began to mount the stairs, coming up with a solid, confident tread that shook the old house to each step.

Then Kleph thrust herself hard out of Oliver's arms. He heard her high, sweet, excited voice crying, "Cenbe! Cenbe!" and she ran to meet the newcomer through the waves of dark and light that swept the shaken house.

Oliver staggered a little and felt a chair seat catching the back of his legs. He sank into it and lifted to his lips the cup he still held. Its steam was warm and moist in his face, though he could scarcely make out the shape of the rim.

He lifted it with both hands and drank.

When he opened his eyes it was quite dark in the room. Also it was silent except for a thin, melodious humming almost below the threshold of sound. Oliver struggled with the memory of a monstrous nightmare. He put it resolutely out of his mind and sat up, feeling an unfamiliar bed creak and sway under him.

This was Kleph's room. But no—Kleph's no longer. Her shining hangings were gone from the walls, her white resilient rug, her pictures. The room looked as it had looked before she came, except for one thing.

In the far corner was a table—a block of translucent stuff—out of which light poured softly. A man sat on a low stool before it, leaning forward, his heavy shoulders outlined against the glow. He wore earphones and he was making quick, erratic notes upon a pad on his knee, swaying a little as if to the tune of unheard music.

The curtains were drawn, but from beyond them came a distant, muffled roaring that Oliver remembered from his nightmare. He put a hand to his face, aware of a feverish warmth and a dipping of the room before his eyes. His head ached, and there was a deep malaise in every limb and nerve.

As the bed creaked, the man in the corner turned, sliding the earphones down like a collar. He had a strong, sensitive face above a dark beard, trimmed short. Oliver had never seen him before, but he had that air Oliver knew so well by now, of remoteness which was the knowledge of time itself lying like a gulf between them.

When he spoke his deep voice was impersonally kind.

"You had too much euphoriac, Wilson," he said, aloofly sympathetic. "You slept a long while."

"How long?" Oliver's throat felt sticky when he spoke.

The man did not answer. Oliver shook his head experimentally. He said, "I thought Kleph said you don't get hangovers from—" Then another thought interrupted the first, and he said quickly, "Where is Kleph?" He looked confusedly toward the door.

"They should be in Rome by now. Watching Charlemagne's coronation at St. Peter's on Christmas Day a thousand years from here."

That was not a thought Oliver could grasp clearly. His aching brain sheered away from it; he found thinking at all was strangely difficult. Staring at the man, he traced an idea painfully to its conclusion.

"So they've gone on—but you stayed behind? Why? You . . . you're Cenbe? I heard your—symphonia, Kleph called it."

"You heard part of it. I have not finished yet. I needed—this." Cenbe inclined his head toward the curtains beyond which the subdued roaring still went on.

"You needed—the meteor?" The knowledge worked painfully through his dulled brain until it seemed to strike some area still untouched by the aching, an area still alive to implication. "The *meteor?* But—"

There was a power implicit in Cenbe's raised hand that seemed to push Oliver down upon the bed again. Cenbe said patiently, "The worst of it is past now, for a while. Forget if you can. That was days ago. I said you were asleep for some time. I let you rest. I knew this house would be safe—from the fire at least."

"Then—something more's to come?" Oliver only mumbled his question. He was not sure he wanted an answer. He had been curious so long, and now that knowledge lay almost within reach, something about his brain seemed to refuse to listen. Perhaps this weariness, this feverish, dizzy feeling would pass as the effect of the euphoriac wore off.

Cenbe's voice ran on smoothly, soothingly, almost as if Cenbe too did not want him to think. It was easiest to lie here and listen.

"I am a composer," Cenbe was saying. "I happen to be interested in interpreting certain forms of disaster into my own terms. That is why I stayed on. The others were dilettantes. They came for the May weather and the spectacle. The aftermath—well why should they wait for that? As for myself—I suppose I am a connoisseur. I find the aftermath rather fascinating. And I need it. I need to study it at first hand, for my own purposes."

His eyes dwelt upon Oliver for an instant very keenly, like a physician's eyes, impersonal and observing. Absently he reached for his stylus and the note pad. And as he moved, Oliver saw a familiar mark on the underside of the thick, tanned wrist.

"Kleph had that scar, too," he heard himself whisper. "And the others."

Cenbe nodded. "Inoculation. It was necessary, under the circumstances. We did not want disease to spread in our own time-world."

"Disease?"

Cenbe shrugged. "You would not recognize the name."

"But, if you can inoculate against disease—" Oliver thrust himself up on an aching arm. He had a half-grasp upon a thought now which he did not want to let go. Effort seemed to make the ideas come more clearly through his mounting confusion. With enormous effort he went on.

"I'm getting it now," he said. "Wait. I've been trying to work this out. You can change history? You can! I know you can. Kleph said she had to promise not to interfere. You all had to promise. Does that mean you really could change your own past—our time?"

Cenbe laid down his pad again. He looked at Oliver thoughtfully, a dark, intent look under heavy brows. "Yes," he said. "Yes, the past can be changed, but not easily. And it changes the future, too, necessarily. The lines of probability are switched into new patterns—but it is extremely difficult, and it has never been allowed. The physio-temporal course tends to slide back to its norm, always. That is why it is so hard to force any alteration." He shrugged. "A theoretical science. We do not change history, Wilson. If we changed our past, our present would be altered, too. And our time-world is entirely to our liking. There may be a few malcontents there, but they are not allowed the privilege of temporal travel."

Oliver spoke louder against the roaring from beyond the windows. "But you've got the power! You could alter history, if you wanted to—wipe out all the pain and suffering and tragedy—"

"All of that passed away long ago," Cenbe said.

"Not—*now!* Not—*this!*"

Cenbe looked at him enigmatically for a while. Then—"This, too," he said.

And suddenly Oliver realized from across what distances Cenbe was watching him. A vast distance, as time is measured. Cenbe was a composer and a genius, and necessarily strongly empathic, but his psychic locus was very far away in time. The dying city outside, the whole world of *now* was not quite real to Cenbe, falling short of reality because of that basic variance in time. It was merely one of the building blocks that had gone to support the edifice on which Cenbe's culture stood in a misty, unknown, terrible future.

It seemed terrible to Oliver now. Even Kleph—all of them had been touched with a pettiness, the faculty that had enabled Hollia to concentrate on her malicious, small schemes to acquire a ringside seat while the meteor thundered in toward Earth's atmosphere. They were all dilettantes, Kleph and Omerie and the other. They toured time, but only as onlookers. Were they bored—sated—with their normal existence?

Not sated enough to wish change, basically. Their own time-world was a fulfilled womb, a perfection made manifest for their needs. They dared not change the past—they could not risk flawing their own present.

Revulsion shook him. Remembering the touch of Kleph's lips, he felt a sour sickness on his tongue. Alluring she had been; he knew that too well. But the aftermath—

There was something about this race from the future. He had felt it dimly at first, before Kleph's nearness had drowned caution and buffered his sensibilities. Time traveling purely as an escape mechanism seemed almost blasphemous. A race with such power—

Kleph—leaving him for the barbaric, splendid coronation at Rome a thousand years ago—*how had she seen him?* Not as a living, breathing man. He knew that, very certainly. Kleph's race were spectators.

But he read more than casual interest in Cenbe's eyes now. There was an avidity there, a bright, fascinated probing. The man had replaced his earphones—he was different from the others. He was a connoisseur. After the vintage season came the aftermath—and Cenbe.

Cenbe watched and waited, light flickering softly in the translucent block before him, his fingers poised over the note pad. The ultimate connoisseur waited to savor the rarities that no non-gourmet could appreciate.

Those thin, distant rhythms of sound that was almost music began to be audible again above the noises of the distant fire. Listening, remembering, Oliver could very nearly catch the pattern of the symphonia as he had heard it, all intermingled with the flash of changing faces and the rank upon rank of the dying—

He lay back on the bed letting the room swirl away into the darkness behind his closed and aching lids. The ache was implicit in every cell of his body, almost a second ego taking possession and driving him out of himself, a strong, sure ego taking over as he himself let go.

Why, he wondered dully, should Kleph have lied? She had said there was no aftermath to the drink she had given him. No aftermath —and yet this painful possession was strong enough to edge him out of his own body.

Kleph had not lied. It was no aftermath to drink. He knew that—

but the knowledge no longer touched his brain or his body. He lay still, giving them up to the power of the illness which was aftermath to something far stronger than the strongest drink. The illness that had no name—yet.

Cenbe's new symphonia was a crowning triumph. It had its premiere from Antares Hall, and the applause was an ovation. History itself, of course, was the artist—opening with the meteor that forecast the great plagues of the fourteenth century and closing with the climax Cenbe had caught on the threshold of modern times. But only Cenbe could have interpreted it with such subtle power.

Critics spoke of the masterly way in which he had chosen the face of the Stuart king as a recurrent motif against the montage of emotion and sound and movement. But there were other faces, fading through the great sweep of the composition, which helped to build up to the tremendous climax. One face in particular, one moment that the audience absorbed greedily. A moment in which one man's face loomed huge in the screen, every feature clear. Cenbe had never caught an emotional crisis so effectively, the critics agreed. You could almost read the man's eyes.

After Cenbe had left, he lay motionless for a long while. He was thinking feverishly—

I've got to find some way to tell people. If I'd known in advance, maybe something could have been done. We'd have forced them to tell us how to change the probabilities. We could have evacuated the city.

If I could leave a message—

Maybe not for today's people. But later. They visit all through time. If they could be recognized and caught somewhere, sometime, and made to change destiny—

It wasn't easy to stand up. The room kept tilting. But he managed it. He found pencil and paper and through the swaying of the shadows he wrote down what he could. Enough. Enough to warn, enough to save.

He put the sheets on the table, in plain sight, and weighted them down before he stumbled back to bed through closing darkness.

The house was dynamited six days later, part of the futile attempt to halt the relentless spread of the Blue Death.

... AND THEN THERE WERE NONE
by Eric Frank Russell

The battleship was eight hundred feet in diameter and slightly more than one mile long. Mass like that takes up room and makes a dent. This one sprawled right across one field and halfway through the next. Its weight was a rut twenty feet deep which would be there for keeps.

On board were two thousand people divisible into three distinct types. The tall, lean, crinkly-eyed ones were the crew. The crop-haired, heavy-jowled ones were the troops. Finally, the expressionless, balding and myopic ones were the cargo of bureaucrats.

The first of these types viewed this world with the professional but aloof interest of people everlastingly giving a planet the swift once-over before chasing along to the next. The troops regarded it with a mixture of tough contempt and boredom. The bureaucrats peered at it with cold authority. Each according to his lights.

This lot were accustomed to new worlds, had dealt with them by the dozens and reduced the process to mere routine. The task before them would have been nothing more than repetition of well-used, smoothly operating technique but for one thing: the entire bunch were in a jam and did not know it.

Emergence from the ship was in strict order of precedence. First, the Imperial Ambassador. Second, the battleship's captain. Third, the officer commanding the ground forces. Fourth, the senior civil servant.

Then, of course, the next grade lower, in the same order: His Excellency's private secretary, the ship's second officer, the deputy commander of troops, the penultimate pen pusher.

Down another grade, then another, until there was left only His Excellency's barber, boot wiper and valet, crew members with the lowly status of O.S.—Ordinary Spaceman—the military nonentities in the ranks, and a few temporary ink-pot fillers dreaming of the day when they would be made permanent and given a desk of their own. This last collection of unfortunates remained aboard to clean ship and refrain from smoking, by command.

Had this world been alien, hostile and well-armed, the order of exit would have been reversed, exemplifying the Biblical promise that the last shall be first and the first shall be last. But this planet, although officially new, unofficially was not new and certainly was not alien. In ledgers and dusty files some two hundred light-years away it was recorded as a cryptic number and classified as a ripe plum long overdue for picking. There had been considerable delay in the harvesting due to a superabundance of other still riper plums elsewhere.

According to the records, this planet was on the outermost fringe of a huge assortment of worlds which had been settled immediately following the Great Explosion. Every school child knew all about the Great Explosion, which was no more than the spectacular name given to the bursting outward of masses of humanity when the Blieder drive superseded atomic-powered rockets and practically handed them the cosmos on a platter.

At that time, between three and five hundred years ago, every family, group, cult or clique that imagined it could do better some place else had taken to the star trails. The restless, the ambitious, the malcontents, the eccentrics, the antisocial, the fidgety and the just plain curious, away they had roared by the dozens, the hundreds, the thousands.

Some two hundred thousand had come to this particular world, the last of them arriving three centuries back. As usual, ninety per cent of the mainstream had consisted of friends, relatives or acquaintances of the first-comers, people persuaded to follow the bold example of Uncle Eddie or Good Old Joe.

If they had since doubled themselves six or seven times over, there now ought to be several millions of them. That they had increased far beyond their original strength had been evident during the approach, for while no great cities were visible there were many medium to smallish towns and a large number of villages.

His Excellency looked with approval at the turf under his feet, plucked a blade of it, grunting as he stooped. He was so constructed that this effort approximated to an athletic feat and gave him a crick in the belly.

"Earth-type grass. Notice that, captain? Is it just a coincidence, or did they bring seed with them?"

"Coincidence, probably," said Captain Grayder. "I've come across four grassy worlds so far. No reason why there shouldn't be others."

"No, I suppose not." His Excellency gazed into the distance, doing it with pride of ownership. "Looks like there's someone plowing over there. He's using a little engine between a pair of fat wheels. They can't be so backward. Hm-m-m!" He rubbed a couple of chins. "Bring him here. We'll have a talk, find out where it's best to get started."

"Very well." Captain Grayder turned to Colonel Shelton, boss of the troops. "His Excellency wishes to speak to that farmer." He pointed to the faraway figure.

"The farmer," said Shelton to Major Hame. "His Excellency wants him at once."

"Bring that farmer here," Hame ordered Lieutenant Deacon. "Quickly!"

"Go get that farmer," Deacon told Sergeant Major Bidworthy. "And hurry—His Excellency is waiting!"

The sergeant major, a big, purple-faced man, sought around for a lesser rank, remembered that they were all cleaning ship and not smoking. He, it seemed, was elected.

Tramping across four fields and coming within hailing distance of his objective, he performed a precise military halt and released a barracks-square bellow of, "Hi, you!" He waved urgently.

The farmer stopped, wiped his forehead, looked around. His manner suggested that the mountainous bulk of the battleship was a mirage such as are five a penny around these parts. Bidworthy waved again, making it an authoritative summons. The farmer calmly waved back, got on with his plowing.

Sergeant Major Bidworthy employed an expletive which—when its flames had died out—meant, "Dear me!" and marched fifty paces nearer. He could now see that the other was bushy-browed and leather-faced.

"*Hi!*"

Stopping the plow again, the farmer leaned on a shaft, picked his teeth.

Struck by the notion that perhaps during the last three centuries the old Earth-language had been dropped in favor of some other lingo, Bidworthy asked, "Can you understand me?"

"Can any person understand another?" inquired the farmer, with clear diction. He turned to resume his task.

Bidworthy was afflicted with a moment of confusion. Recovering, he informed hurriedly, "His Excellency, the Earth Ambassador, wishes to speak with you at once."

"So?" The other eyed him speculatively. "How come that he is excellent?"

"He is a person of considerable importance," said Bidworthy, unable to decide whether the other was being funny at his expense or alternatively was what is known as a character. A good many of these isolated planet-scratchers liked to think of themselves as characters.

"Of considerable importance," echoed the farmer, narrowing his eyes at the horizon. He appeared to be trying to grasp an alien concept. After a while, he inquired, "What will happen to your home world when this person dies?"

"Nothing," Bidworthy admitted.

"It will roll on as usual?"

"Of course."

"Then," declared the farmer, flatly, "he cannot be important." With that, his little engine went *chuff-chuff* and the wheels rolled forward and the plow plowed.

Digging his nails into the palms of his hands, Bidworthy spent half a minute gathering oxygen before he said, in hoarse tones, "I cannot return without at least a message for His Excellency."

"Indeed?" The other was incredulous. "What is to stop you?" Then, noting the alarming increase in Bidworthy's color, he added with compassion, "Oh, well, you may tell him that I said"—he paused while he thought it over—"God bless you and good-by!"

Sergeant Major Bidworthy was a powerful man who weighed two-twenty pounds, had hopped around the cosmos for twenty years, and feared nothing. He had never been known to permit the shiver of one hair—but he was trembling all over by the time he got back to the ship.

His Excellency fastened a cold eye upon him and demanded, "Well?"

"He won't come." Bidworthy's veins stood out on his forehead. "And, sir, if only I could have him in my field company for a few months I'd straighten him up and teach him to move at the double."

"I don't doubt that, sergeant major," soothed His Excellency. He continued in a whispered aside to Colonel Shelton. "He's a good fellow but no diplomat. Too abrupt and harsh voiced. Better go yourself and fetch that farmer. We can't sit here forever waiting to find out where to begin."

"Very well, your excellency." Colonel Shelton trudged across the fields, caught up with the plow. Smiling pleasantly, he said, "Good morning, my man!"

Stopping his plow, the farmer sighed as if it were another of those days one has sometimes. His eyes were dark-brown, almost black, as they looked at the other.

"What makes you think I'm *your* man?" he inquired.

"It is a figure of speech," explained Shelton. He could see what was wrong now. Bidworthy had fallen foul of an irascible type. Two dogs snarling at one another, Shelton went on, "I was only trying to be courteous."

"Well," meditated the farmer, "I reckon that's something worth trying for."

Pinking a little, Shelton continued with determination. "I am commanded to request the pleasure of your company at the ship."

"Think they'll get any pleasure out of my company?" asked the other, disconcertingly bland.

"I'm sure of it," said Shelton.

"You're a liar," said the farmer.

His color deepening, Colonel Shelton snapped, "I do not permit people to call me a liar."

"You've just permitted it," the other pointed out.

Letting it pass, Shelton insisted, "Are you coming to the ship or are you not?"

"I am not."

"Why not?"

"Myob!" said the farmer.

"What was that?"

"Myob!" he repeated. It smacked of a mild insult.

Colonel Shelton went back.

He told the ambassador, "That fellow is one of these too-clever types. All I could get out of him at the finish was 'myob,' whatever that means."

"Local slang," chipped in Captain Grayder. "An awful lot of it de-

velops over three or four centuries. I've come across one or two
worlds where there's been so much of it that one almost had to learn
a new language."

"He understood your speech?" asked the ambassador, looking
at Shelton.

"Yes, your excellency. And his own is quite good. But he won't
come away from his plowing." He reflected briefly, then suggested,
"If it were left to me, I'd bring him in by force, under an armed escort."

"That would encourage him to give essential information," commented the ambassador, with open sarcasm. He patted his stomach,
smoothed his jacket, glanced down at his glossy shoes. "Nothing for
it but to go speak to him myself."

Colonel Shelton was shocked. "Your excellency, you can't do
that!"

"Why can't I?"

"It would be undignified."

"I am aware of it," said the ambassador, dryly. "Can you suggest
an alternative?"

"We can send out a patrol to find someone more co-operative."

"Someone better informed, too," Captain Grayder offered. "At best
we wouldn't get much out of one surly hayseed. I doubt whether he
knows a quarter of what we require to learn."

"All right." His Excellency abandoned the notion of doing his
own chores. "Organize a patrol and let's have some results."

"A patrol," said Colonel Shelton to Major Hame. "Nominate one
immediately."

"Call out a patrol," Hame ordered Lieutenant Deacon. "At once."

"Parade a patrol forthwith, sergeant major," said Deacon.

Bidworthy went to the ship, climbed a ladder, stuck his head in the
lock and bawled, "Sergeant Gleed, out with your squad, and make it
snappy!" He gave a suspicious sniff and went farther into the lock.
His voice gained several more decibels. "Who's been smoking? By
the Black Sack, if I catch—"

Across the fields something quietly went *chuff-chuff* while balloon
tires crawled along.

The patrol formed by the right in two ranks of eight men each,
turned at a barked command, marched off noseward. Their boots
thumped in unison, their accoutrements clattered and the orange-
colored sun made sparkles on their metal.

Sergeant Gleed did not have to take his men far. They had got one hundred yards beyond the battleship's nose when he noticed a man ambling across the field to his right. Treating the ship with utter indifference, the newcomer was making toward the farmer still plowing far over to the left.

"Patrol, right wheel!" yelled Gleed. Marching them straight past the wayfarer, he gave them a loud about-turn and followed it with the high-sign.

Speeding up its pace, the patrol opened its ranks, became a double file of men tramping at either side of the lone pedestrian. Ignoring his suddenly acquired escort, the latter continued to plod straight ahead like one long convinced that all is illusion.

"Left wheel!" Gleed roared, trying to bend the whole caboodle toward the waiting ambassador.

Swiftly obedient, the double file headed leftward, one, two, three, hup! It was neat, precise execution, beautiful to watch. Only one thing spoiled it: the man in the middle maintained his self-chosen orbit and ambled casually between numbers four and five of the right-hand file.

That upset Gleed, especially since the patrol continued to thump ambassadorwards for lack of a further order. His Excellency was being treated to the unmilitary spectacle of an escort dumbly boot-beating one way while its prisoner airily mooched another. Colonel Shelton would have plenty to say about it in due course, and anything he forgot Bidworthy would remember.

"Patrol!" hoarsed Gleed, pointing an outraged finger at the escapee, and momentarily dismissing all regulation commands from his mind. "Get that yimp!"

Breaking ranks, they moved at the double and surrounded the wanderer too closely to permit further progress. Perforce, he stopped.

Gleed came up, said somewhat breathlessly, "Look, the Earth Ambassador wants to speak to you—that's all."

The other said nothing, merely gazed at him with mild blue eyes. He was a funny looking bum, long overdue for a shave, with a fringe of ginger whiskers sticking out all around his pan. He resembled a sunflower.

"Are you going to talk with His Excellency?" Gleed persisted.

"Naw." The other nodded toward the farmer. "Going to talk with Zeke."

"The ambassador first," retorted Gleed, toughly. "He's a big noise."

"I don't doubt that," remarked the sunflower.

"Smartie Artie, eh?" said Gleed, pushing his face close and making it unpleasant. He gave his men a gesture. "All right—shove him along. We'll show him!"

Smartie Artie sat down. He did it sort of solidly, giving himself the aspect of a statue anchored for aeons. The ginger whiskers did nothing to lend grace to the situation. But Sergeant Gleed had handled sitters before, the only difference being that this one was cold sober.

"Pick him up," ordered Gleed, "and carry him."

They picked him up and carried him, feet first, whiskers last. He hung limp and unresisting in their hands, a dead weight. In this inauspicious manner he arrived in the presence of the Earth Ambassador where the escort plonked him on his feet.

Promptly he set out for Zeke.

"Hold him, darn you!" howled Gleed.

The patrol grabbed and clung tight. His Excellency eyed the whiskers with well-bred concealment of distaste, coughed delicately, and spoke.

"I am truly sorry that you had to come to me in this fashion."

"In that case," suggested the prisoner, "you could have saved yourself some mental anguish by not permitting it to happen."

"There was no other choice. We've got to make contact somehow."

"I don't see it," said Ginger Whiskers. "What's so special about this date?"

"The date?" His Excellency frowned in puzzlement. "Where does that come in?"

"That's what I'd like to know."

"The point eludes me." The ambassador turned to Colonel Shelton. "Do you get what he's aiming at?"

"I could hazard a guess, your excellency. I think he is suggesting that since we've left them without contact for more than three hundred years, there's no particular urgency about making it today." He looked at the sunflower for confirmation.

That worthy rallied to his support by remarking, "You're doing pretty well for a half-wit."

Regardless of Shelton's own reaction, this was too much for Bidworthy purpling nearby. His chest came up and his eyes caught fire. His voice was an authoritative rasp.

"Be more respectful while addressing high-ranking officers!"

The prisoner's mild blue eyes turned upon him in childish amazement, examined him slowly from feet to head and all the way down again. The eyes drifted back to the ambassador.

"Who is this preposterous person?"

Dismissing the question with an impatient wave of his hand, the ambassador said, "See here, it is not our purpose to bother you from sheer perversity, as you seem to think. Neither do we wish to detain you any longer than is necessary. All we—"

Pulling at his face-fringe as if to accentuate its offensiveness, the other interjected, "It being you, of course, who determines the length of the necessity?"

"On the contrary, you may decide that yourself," said the ambassador, displaying admirable self-control. "All you need do is tell—"

"Then I've decided it right now," the prisoner chipped in. He tried to heave himself free of his escort. "Let me go talk to Zeke."

"All you need do," the ambassador persisted, "is to tell us where we can find a local official who can put us in touch with your central government." His gaze was stern, commanding, as he added, "For instance, where is the nearest police post?"

"Myob!" said the other.

"The same to you," retorted the ambassador, his patience starting to evaporate.

"That's precisely what I'm trying to do," assured the prisoner, enigmatically. "Only you won't let me."

"If I may make a suggestion, your excellency," put in Colonel Shelton, "let me—"

"I require no suggestions and I won't let you," said the ambassador, rapidly becoming brusque. "I have had enough of all this tomfoolery. I think we've landed at random in an area reserved for imbeciles and it would be as well to recognize the fact and get out of it with no more delay."

"Now you're talking," approved Ginger Whiskers. "And the farther the better."

"I'm not thinking of leaving this planet if that's what is in your incomprehensible mind," asserted the ambassador, with much sarcasm. He stamped a proprietary foot on the turf. "This is part of the Earth Empire. As such, it is going to be recognized, charted and organized."

"*Heah, heah!*" put in the senior civil servant, who aspired to honors in elocution.

His Excellency threw a frown behind, went on, "We'll move the

ship to some other section where brains are brighter." He signed to
the escort. "Let him go. Doubtless he is in a hurry to borrow a razor."

They released their grips. Ginger Whiskers at once turned toward
the still-plowing farmer, much as if he were a magnetized needle
irresistibly drawn Zekeward. Without a word he set off at his original
mooching pace. Disappointment and disgust showed on the faces of
Gleed and Bidworthy as they watched him go.

"Have the vessel shifted at once," the ambassador instructed Captain Grayder. "Plant it near a suitable town—not out in the wilds
where every hayseed views strangers as a bunch of gyps."

He marched importantly up the gangway. Captain Grayder followed, then Colonel Shelton, then the elocutionist. Next, their suc-
cessors in due order of precedence. Lastly, Gleed and his men.

The gangway rolled inward. The lock closed. Despite its immense
bulk, the ship shivered briefly from end to end and soared without
deafening uproar or spectacular display of flame.

Indeed, there was silence save for the plow going *chuff-chuff* and
the murmurings of the two men walking behind it. Neither bothered
to turn his head to observe what was happening.

"Seven pounds of prime tobacco is a heck of a lot to give for one
case of brandy," Ginger Whiskers was protesting.

"Not for my brandy," said Zeke. "It's stronger than a thousand
Gands and smoother than an Earthman's downfall."

The great battleship's second touchdown was made on a wide flat
one mile north of a town estimated to hold twelve to fifteen thousand
people. Captain Grayder would have preferred to survey the place
from low altitude before making his landing, but one cannot maneu-
ver an immense space-going job as if it were an atmospheric tug.
Only two things can be done so close to a planetary surface—the ship
is taken up or brought down with no room for fiddling betweentimes.

So Grayder bumped his ship in the best spot he could find when
finding is a matter of split-second decisions. It made a rut only twelve
feet deep, the ground being harder and on a rock bed. The gangway
was shoved out; the procession descended in the same order as before.

His Excellency cast an anticipatory look toward the town, registered disappointment and remarked, "Something's badly out of
kilter here. There's the town. Here's us in plain view, with a ship
like a metal mountain. A thousand people at least must have seen us
even if the rest are holding seances behind drawn curtains or playing
pinochle in the cellars. Are they excited?"

"It doesn't seem so," admitted Colonel Shelton, pulling an eyelid for the sake of feeling it spring back.

"I wasn't asking you. I was telling you. They are not excited. They are not surprised. In fact, they are not even interested. One would almost think they've had a ship here before and it was full of small-pox, or sold them a load of gold bricks, or something like that. What is wrong with them?"

"Possibly they lack curiosity," Shelton offered.

"Either that or they're afraid. Or maybe the entire gang of them are crackers. A good many worlds were appropriated by woozy groups who wanted some place where their eccentricities could run loose. Nutty notions become conventional after three hundred years of undisturbed continuity. It's then considered normal and proper to nurse the bats out of your grandfather's attic. That, and generations of inbreeding, can create some queer types. But we'll cure 'em!"

"Yes, your excellency, most certainly we will."

"You don't look so balanced yourself, chasing that eye around your pan," reproved the ambassador. He pointed southeast as Shelton stuck the fidgety hand firmly into a pocket. "There's a road over there. Wide and well-built by the looks of it. Get that patrol across it. If they don't bring in a willing talker within reasonable time, we'll send a battalion into the town itself."

"A patrol," repeated Colonel Shelton to Major Hame.

"Call out the patrol," Hame ordered Lieutenant Deacon.

"That patrol again, sergeant major," said Deacon.

Bidworthy raked out Gleed and his men, indicated the road, barked a bit, shooed them on their way.

They marched, Gleed in the lead. Their objective was half a mile and angled slightly nearer the town. The left-hand file, who had a clear view of the nearest suburbs, eyed them wistfully, wished Gleed in warmer regions with Bidworthy stoking beneath him.

Hardly had they reached their goal than a customer appeared. He came from the town's outskirts, zooming along at fast pace on a con-traption vaguely resembling a motorcycle. It ran on a pair of big rub-ber balls and was pulled by a caged fan. Gleed spread his men across the road.

The oncomer's machine suddenly gave forth a harsh, penetrating sound that vaguely reminded them of Bidworthy in the presence of dirty boots.

"Stay put," warned Gleed. "I'll skin the guy who gives way and leaves a gap."

Again the shrill metallic warning. Nobody moved. The machine slowed, came up to them at a crawl and stopped. Its fan continued to spin at low rate, the blades almost visible and giving out a steady hiss.

"What's the idea?" demanded the rider. He was lean-featured, in his middle thirties, wore a gold ring in his nose and had a pigtail four feet long.

Blinking incredulously at this get-up, Gleed managed to jerk an indicative thumb toward the iron mountain and say, "Earth ship."

"Well, what d'you expect me to do about it?"

"Co-operate," said Gleed, still bemused by the pigtail. He had never seen one before. It was in no way effeminate, he decided. Rather did it lend a touch of ferocity like that worn—according to the picture books—by certain North American aborigines of umpteen centuries ago.

"Co-operation," mused the rider. "Now there is a beautiful word. You know what it means, of course?"

"I ain't a dope."

"The precise degree of your idiocy is not under discussion at the moment," the rider pointed out. His nose-ring waggled a bit as he spoke. "We are talking about co-operation. I take it you do quite a lot of it yourself?"

"You bet I do," Gleed assured. "And so does everyone else who knows what's good for him."

"Let's keep to the subject, shall we? Let's not sidetrack and go rambling all over the map." He revved up his fan a little then let it slow down again. "You are given orders and you obey them?"

"Of course. I'd have a rough time if—"

"That is what you call co-operation?" put in the other. He shrugged his shoulders, indulged a resigned sigh. "Oh, well, it's nice to check the facts of history. The books *could* be wrong." His fan flashed into a circle of light and the machine surged forward. "Pardon me."

The front rubber ball barged forcefully between two men, knocking them sidewise without injury. With a high whine, the machine shot down the road, its fan-blast making the rider's plaited hairdo point horizontally backward.

"You goofy glumps!" raged Gleed as his fallen pair got up and dusted themselves. "I ordered you to stand fast. What d'you mean, letting him run out on us like that?"

"Didn't have much choice about it, sarge," answered one, giving him a surly look.

"I want none of your back-chat. You could have busted a balloon if you'd had your weapons ready. That would have stopped him."

"You didn't tell us to have guns ready."

"Where was your own, anyway?" added a vôice.

Gleed whirled round on the others and bawled, "Who said that?" His irate eyes raked a long row of blank, impassive faces. It was impossible to detect the culprit. "I'll shake you up with the next quota of fatigues," he promised. "I'll see to it—"

"The sergeant major's coming," one of them warned.

Bidworthy was four hundred yards away and making martial progress toward them. Arriving in due time, he cast a cold, contemptuous glance over the patrol.

"What happened?"

Giving a brief account of the incident, Gleed finished aggrievedly, "He looked like a Chickasaw with an oil well."

"What's a Chickasaw?" Bidworthy demanded.

"I read about them somewhere once when I was a kid," explained Gleed, happy to bestow a modicum of learning. "They had long haircuts, wore blankets and rode around in gold-plated automobiles."

"Sounds crazy to me," said Bidworthy. "I gave up all that magic-carpet stuff when I was seven. I was deep in ballistics before I was twelve and military logistics at fourteen." He sniffed loudly, gave the other a jaundiced eye. "Some guys suffer from arrested development."

"They actually existed," Gleed maintained. "They—"

"So did fairies," snapped Bidworthy. "My mother said so. My mother was a good woman. She didn't tell me a lot of tomfool lies— often." He spat on the road. "Be your age!" Then he scowled at the patrol. "All right, get out your guns, assuming that you've got them and know where they are and which hand to hold them in. Take orders from me. I'll deal personally with the next one along."

He sat on a large stone by the roadside and planted an expectant gaze on the town. Gleed posed near him, slightly pained. The patrol remained strung across the road, guns held ready. Half an hour crawled by without anything happening.

One of the men said, "Can we have a smoke, sergeant major?"

"No."

They fell into lugubrious silence, watching the town, licking their lips and thinking. They had plenty to think about. A town—any town of human occupation—had desirable features not found elsewhere in the cosmos. Lights, company, freedom, laughter, all the makings of life. And one can go hungry too long.

Eventually a large coach came from the outskirts, hit the high road, came bowling toward them. A long, shiny, streamlined job, it rolled on twenty balls in two rows of ten, gave forth a whine similar to but louder than that of its predecessor, but had no visible fans. It was loaded with people.

At a point two hundred yards from the road block a loud-speaker under the vehicle's bonnet blared an urgent, "Make way! Make way!"

"This is it," commented Bidworthy, with much satisfaction. "We've got a dollop of them. One of them is going to chat or I leave the service." He got off his rock, stood in readiness.

"Make way! Make way!"

"Bust his bags if he tries to bull his way through," Bidworthy ordered the men.

It wasn't necessary. The coach lost pace, stopped with its bonnet a yard from the waiting file. Its driver peered out the side of his cab. Other faces snooped farther back.

Composing himself and determined to try the effect of fraternal cordiality, Bidworthy went up to the driver and said, "Good morning."

"Your time-sense is shot to pot," observed the other. He had a blue jowl, a broken nose, cauliflower ears, looked the sort who usually drives with others in hot and vengeful pursuit. "Can't you afford a watch?"

"Huh?"

"It isn't morning. It's late afternoon."

"So it is," admitted Bidworthy, forcing a cracked smile. "Good afternoon."

"I'm not so sure about that," mused the driver, leaning on his wheel and moodily picking his teeth. "It's just another one nearer the grave."

"That may be," agreed Bidworthy, little taken with that ghoulish angle. "But I have other things to worry about, and—"

"Not much use worrying about anything, past or present," advised the driver. "Because there are lots bigger worries to come."

"Perhaps so," Bidworthy said, inwardly feeling that this was no time or place to contemplate the darker side of existence. "But I prefer to deal with my own troubles in my own time and my own way."

"Nobody's troubles are entirely their own, nor their time, nor their methods," remarked the tough-looking oracle. "Are they now?"

"I don't know and I don't care," said Bidworthy, his composure thinning down as his blood pressure built up. He was conscious of Gleed and the patrol watching, listening, and probably grinning inside themselves. There was also the load of gaping passengers. "I think you are chewing the fat just to stall me. You might as well know now that it won't work. The Earth Ambassador is waiting—"

"So are we," remarked the driver, pointedly.

"He wants to speak to you," Bidworthy went on, "and he's going to speak to you!"

"I'd be the last to prevent him. We've got free speech here. Let him step up and say his piece so's we can get on our way."

"*You*," Bidworthy informed, "are going to *him*." He signed to the rest of the coach. "And your load as well."

"Not me," denied a fat man, sticking his head out of a side window. He wore thick-lensed glasses that gave him eyes like poached eggs. Moreover, he was adorned with a high hat candy-striped in white and pink. "Not me," repeated this vision, with considerable firmness.

"Me, neither," indorsed the driver.

"All right." Bidworthy registered menace. "Move this birdcage an inch, forward or backward, and we'll shoot your pot-bellied tires to thin strips. Get out of that cab."

"Not me. I'm too comfortable. Try fetching me out."

Bidworthy beckoned to his nearest six men. "You heard him—take him up on that."

Tearing open the cab door, they grabbed. If they had expected the victim to put up a futile fight against heavy odds, they were disappointed. He made no attempt to resist. They got him, lugged together, and he yielded with good grace, his body leaning sidewise and coming halfway out of the door.

That was as far as they could get him.

"Come on," urged Bidworthy, displaying impatience. "Show him who's who. He isn't a fixture."

One of the men climbed over the body, poked around inside the cab, and said, "He is, you know."

"What d'you mean?"

"He's chained to the steering column."

"Eh? Let me see." He had a look, found that it was so. A chain and a small but heavy and complicated padlock linked the driver's leg to his coach. "Where's the key?"

"Search me," invited the driver, grinning.

They did just that. The frisk proved futile. No key.

"Who's got it?"

"Myob!"

"Shove him back into his seat," ordered Bidworthy, looking savage. "We'll take the passengers. One yap's as good as another so far as I'm concerned." He strode to the doors, jerked them open. "Get out and make it snappy."

Nobody budged. They studied him silently and with varied expressions, not one of which did anything to help his ego. The fat man with the candy-striped hat mooned at him sardonically. Bidworthy decided that he did not like the fat man and that a stiff course of military calisthenics might thin him down a bit.

"You can come out on your feet," he suggested to the passengers in general and the fat man in particular, "or on your necks. Whichever you prefer. Make up your minds."

"If you can't use your head you can at least use your eyes," commented the fat man. He shifted in his seat to the accompaniment of metallic clanking noises.

Bidworthy did as suggested, leaning through the doors to have a gander. Then he got right into the vehicle, went its full length and studied each passenger. His florid features were two shades darker when he came out and spoke to Sergeant Gleed.

"They're all chained. Every one of them." He glared at the driver. "What's the big idea, manacling the lot?"

"Myob!" said the driver, airily.

"Who's got the keys?"

"Myob!"

Taking a deep breath, Bidworthy said to nobody in particular, "Every so often I hear of some guy running amok and laying 'em out by the dozens. I always wonder why—but now I know." He gnawed his knuckles, then added to Gleed, "We can't run this contraption to the ship with that dummy blocking the driver's seat. Either we must find the keys or get tools and cut them loose."

"Or you could wave us on our way and go take a pill," offered the driver.

"Shut up! If I'm stuck here another million years I'll see to it that—"

"The colonel's coming," muttered Gleed, giving him a nudge.

Colonel Shelton arrived, walked once slowly and officiously around the outside of the coach, examining its construction and its occupants. He flinched at the striped hat whose owner leered at him through the glass. Then he came over to the disgruntled group.

"What's the trouble this time, sergeant major?"

"They're as crazy as the others, sir. They give a lot of lip and say, 'Myob!' and couldn't care less about His Excellency. They don't want to come out and we can't get them out because they're chained to their seats."

"Chained?" Shelton's eyebrows shot upward. "What for?"

"I don't know, sir. They're linked in like a load of lifers making for the pen, and—"

Shelton moved off without waiting to hear the rest. He had a look for himself, came back.

"You may have something there, sergeant major. But I don't think they are criminals."

"No, sir?"

"No." He threw a significant glance toward the colorful headgear and several other sartorial eccentricities, including a ginger-haired man's foot-wide polka-dotted bow. "It is more likely that they're a bunch of whacks being taken to a giggle emporium. I'll ask the driver." Going to the cab, he said, "Do you mind telling me your destination?"

"Yes," responded the other.

"Very well, where is it?"

"Look," said the driver, "are we talking the same language?"

"Huh?"

"You asked me if I minded and I said yes." He made a gesture. "I do mind."

"You refuse to tell?"

"Your aim's improving, sonny."

"Sonny?" put in Bidworthy, vibrant with outrage. "Do you realize you are speaking to a colonel?"

"Leave this to me," insisted Shelton, waving him down. His expression was cold as he returned his attention to the driver. "On your way. I'm sorry you've been detained."

"Think nothing of it," said the driver, with exaggerated politeness. "I'll do as much for you some day."

With that enigmatic remark, he let his machine roll forward. The patrol parted to make room. The coach built up its whine to top note, sped down the road, diminished into the distance.

"By the Black Sack!" swore Bidworthy, staring purple-faced after it. "This planet has got more punks in need of discipline than any this side of—"

"Calm yourself, sergeant major," advised Shelton. "I feel the same way as you—but I'm taking care of my arteries. Blowing them full of bumps like seaweed won't solve any problems."

"Maybe so, sir, but—"

"We're up against something mighty funny here," Shelton went on. "We've got to find out exactly what it is and how best to cope with it. That will probably mean new tactics. So far, the patrol has achieved nothing. It is wasting its time. We'll have to devise some other and more effective method of making contact with the powers-that-be. March the men back to the ship, sergeant major."

"Very well, sir." Bidworthy saluted, swung around, clicked his heels, opened a cavernous mouth. "Patro-o-ol! . . . right form!"

The conference lasted well into the night and halfway through the following morning. During these argumentative hours various odd-ments of traffic, mostly vehicular, passed along the road, but nothing paused to view the monster spaceship, nobody approached for a friendly word with its crew. The strange inhabitants of this world seemed to be afflicted with a peculiar form of mental blindness, un-able to see a thing until it was thrust into their faces and then survey-ing it squint-eyed.

One passer-by in midmorning was a truck whining on two dozen rubber balls and loaded with girls wearing colorful head-scarves. The girls were singing something about one little kiss before we part, dear. Half a dozen troops lounging near the gangway came eagerly to life, waved, whistled and yoohooed. The effort was wasted, for the sing-ing continued without break or pause and nobody waved back.

To add to the discomfiture of the love-hungry, Bidworthy stuck his head out of the lock and rasped, "If you monkeys are bursting with surplus energy, I can find a few jobs for you to do—nice dirty ones." He seared them one at a time before he withdrew.

Inside, the top brass sat around a horseshoe table in the chartroom near the bow and debated the situation. Most of them were content to repeat with extra emphasis what they had said the previous evening, there being no new points to bring up.

"Are you certain," the Earth Ambassador asked Captain Grayder, "that this planet has not been visited since the last emigration transport dumped the final load three hundred years back?"

"Positive, your excellency. Any such visit would have been recorded."

"If made by an Earth ship. But what about others? I feel it in my bones that at sometime or other these people have fallen foul of one or more vessels calling unofficially and have been leery of spaceships ever since. Perhaps somebody got tough with them, tried to muscle in where he wasn't wanted. Or they've had to beat off a gang of pirates. Or they were swindled by some unscrupulous fleet of traders."

"Quite impossible, your excellency," declared Grayder. "Emigration was so scattered over so large a number of worlds that even today every one of them is under-populated, only one-hundredth developed, and utterly unable to build spaceships of any kind, even rudimentary ones. Some may have the techniques but not the facilities, of which they need plenty."

"Yes, that's what I've always understood."

"All Blieder-drive vessels are built in the Sol system, registered as Earth ships and their whereabouts known. The only other ships in existence are eighty or ninety antiquated rocket jobs bought at scrap price by the Epsilon system for haulage work between their fourteen closely-planned planets. An old-fashioned rocket job couldn't reach this place in a hundred years."

"No, of course not."

"Unofficial boats capable of this range just don't exist," Grayder assured. "Neither do space buccaneers, for the same reason. A Blieder-job takes so much that a would-be pirate has to become a billionaire to become a pirate."

"Then," said the ambassador, heavily, "back we go to my original theory—that something peculiar to this world plus a lot of inbreeding has made them nutty."

"There's plenty to be said for that notion," put in Colonel Shelton.

"You should have seen the coachload I looked over. There was a mortician wearing odd shoes, one brown, one yellow. And a moon-faced gump sporting a hat made from the skin of a barber's pole, all stripy. Only thing missing was his bubble pipe—and probably he'll be given that where he was going."

"Where was he going?"

"I don't know, your excellency. They refused to say."

Giving him a satirical look, the ambassador remarked, "Well, that is a valuable addition to the sum total of our knowledge. Our minds are now enriched by the thought that an anonymous individual may be presented with a futile object for an indefinable purpose when he reaches his unknown destination."

Shelton subsided, wishing that he had never seen the fat man or, for that matter, the fat man's cockeyed world.

"Somewhere they've got a capitol, a civic seat, a center of government wherein function the people who hold the strings," the ambassador asserted. "We've got to find that place before we can take over and reorganize on up-to-date lines whatever setup they've got. A capitol is big by the standards of its own administrative area. It's never an ordinary, nondescript place. It has certain physical features lending it importance above the average. It should be easily visible from the air. We must make a search for it—in fact, that's what we ought to have done in the first place. Other planets' capitol cities have been found without trouble. What's the hoodoo on this one?"

"See for yourself, your excellency." Captain Grayder poked a couple of photographs across the table. "There are the two hemispheres as recorded by us when coming in. They reveal nothing resembling a superior city. There isn't even a town conspicuously larger than its fellows or possessing outstanding features setting it apart from the others."

"I don't place great faith in pictures, particularly when taken at long distance. The naked eye sees more. We have got four lifeboats capable of scouring the place from pole to pole. Why not use them?"

"Because, your excellency, they were not designed for such a purpose."

"Does that matter so long as they get results?"

Grayder said, patiently, "They were designed to be launched in space and hit up to forty thousand. They are ordinary, old-style rocket jobs, for emergencies only. You could not make efficient ground-survey at any speed in excess of four hundred miles per hour. Keep the boats down to that and you're trying to run them at landing-speed, muffling the tubes, balling up their efficiency, creating a terrible waste of fuel, and inviting a crash which you're likely to get before you're through."

"Then it's high time we had Blieder-drive lifeboats on Blieder-drive ships."

"I agree, your excellency. But the smallest Blieder engine has an Earth mass of more than three hundred tons—far too much for little boats." Picking up the photographs, Grayder slid them into a drawer. "What we need is an ancient, propeller-driven airplane. They could do something we can't do—they could go slow."

"You might as well yearn for a bicycle," scoffed the ambassador, feeling thwarted.

"We have a bicycle," Grayder informed. "Tenth Engineer Harrison owns one."

"And he has brought it with him?"

"It goes everywhere with him. There is a rumor that he sleeps with it."

"A spaceman toting a bicycle!" The ambassador blew his nose with a loud honk. "I take it that he is thrilled by the sense of immense velocity it gives him, an ecstatic feeling of rushing headlong through space?"

"I wouldn't know, your excellency."

"Hm-m-m! Bring this Harrison in to me. We'll set a nut to catch a nut."

Grayder blinked, went to the caller board, spoke over the ship's system. "Tenth Engineer Harrison wanted in the chartroom immediately."

Within ten minutes Harrison appeared. He had walked fast three-quarters of a mile from the Blieder room. He was thin and wiry, with dark, monkeylike eyes, and a pair of ears that cut out the pedaling with the wind behind him. The ambassador examined him curiously, much as a zoologist would inspect a pink giraffe.

"Mister, I understand that you possess a bicycle."

Becoming wary, Harrison said, "There's nothing against it in the regulations, sir, and therefore—"

"Darn the regulations!" The ambassador made an impatient gesture. "We're stalled in the middle of a crazy situation and we're turning to crazy methods to get moving."

"I see, sir."

"So I want you to do a job for me. Get out your bicycle, ride down to town, find the mayor, sheriff, grand panjandrum, supreme galootie, or whatever he's called, and tell him he's officially invited to evening dinner along with any other civic dignitaries he cares to bring and, of course, their wives."

"Very well, sir."

"Informal attire," added the ambassador.

Harrison jerked up one ear, drooped the other, and said, "Beg pardon, sir?"

"They can dress how they like."

"I get it. Do I go right now, sir?"

"At once. Return as quickly as you can and bring me the reply."

Saluting sloppily, Harrison went out. His Excellency found an easy-chair, reposed in it at full length and ignored the others' stares.

"As easy as that!" He pulled out a long cigar, carefully bit off its end. "If we can't touch their minds, we'll appeal to their bellies." He cocked a knowing eye at Grayder. "Captain, see that there is plenty to drink. Strong stuff. Venusian cognac or something equally potent. Give them an hour at a well-filled table and they'll talk plenty. We won't be able to shut them up all night." He lit the cigar, puffed luxuriously. "That is the tried and trusted technique of diplomacy—the insidious seduction of the distended gut. It always works—you'll see."

Pedaling briskly down the road, Tenth Engineer Harrison reached the first street on either side of which were small detached houses with neat gardens front and back. A plump, amiable looking woman was clipping a hedge halfway along. He pulled up near to her, politely touched his cap.

" 'Scuse me, ma'am, I'm looking for the biggest man in town."

She half-turned, gave him no more than a casual glance, pointed her clipping-shears southward. "That'd be Jeff Baines. First on the right, second on the left. It's a small delicatessen."

"Thank you."

He moved on, hearing the *snip-snip* resume behind him. First on the right. He curved around a long, low, rubber-balled truck parked by the corner. Second on the left. Three children pointed at him and yelled shrill warnings that his back wheel was going round. He found the delicatessen, propped a pedal on the curb, gave his machine a reassuring pat before he went inside and had a look at Jeff.

There was plenty to see. Jeff had four chins, a twenty-two-inch neck, and a paunch that stuck out half a yard. An ordinary mortal could have got into either leg of his pants without taking off a diving suit. He weighed at least three hundred and undoubtedly *was* the biggest man in town.

"Wanting something?" inquired Jeff, lugging it up from far down.

"Not exactly." Tenth Engineer Harrison eyed the succulent food display, decided that anything unsold by nightfall was not given to the cats. "I'm looking for a certain person."

"Are you now? Usually I avoid that sort—but every man to his taste." He plucked at a fat lip while he mused a moment, then suggested, "Try Sid Wilcock over on Dane Avenue. He's the most certain man I know."

"I didn't mean it that way," said Harrison. "I meant I was searching for somebody particular."

"Then why the dub didn't you say so?" Jeff Baines worked over the new problem, finally offered, "Tod Green ought to fit that bill. You'll find him in the shoeshop end of this road. He's particular enough for anyone. He's downright finicky."

"You misunderstand me," Harrison explained. "I'm hunting a bigwig so's I can invite him to a feed."

Resting himself on a high stool which he overlapped by a foot all round, Jeff Baines eyed him peculiarly and said, "There's something lopsided about this. In the first place, you're going to use up a considerable slice of your life finding a guy who wears a wig, especially if you insist on a big one. And where's the point of dumping an ob on him just because he uses a bean-blanket?"

"Huh?"

"It's plain common sense to plant an ob where it will cancel an old one out, isn't it?"

"Is it?" Harrison let his mouth hang open while his mind moiled around the strange problem of how to plant an ob.

"So you don't know?" Jeff Baines massaged a plump chop and sighed. He pointed at the other's middle. "Is that a uniform you're wearing?"

"Yes."

"A genuine, pukka, dyed-in-the-wool uniform?"

"Of course."

"Ah!" said Jeff. "That's where you've fooled me—coming in by yourself, on your ownsome. If there had been a gang of you dressed identically the same, I'd have known at once it was a uniform. That's what uniform means—all alike. Doesn't it?"

"I suppose so," agreed Harrison, who had never given it a thought.

"So you're off that ship. I ought to have guessed it in the first place. I must be slow on the uptake today. But I didn't expect to see one, just one, messing around on a pedal contraption. It goes to show, doesn't it?"

"Yes," said Harrison, glancing around to make sure that no confederate had swiped his bicycle while he was detained in conversation. The machine was still there. "It goes to show."

"All right, let's have it—what have you come here for?"

"I've been trying to tell you all along. I've been sent to—"

"Been sent?" Jeff's eyes widened a little. "Mean to say you actually let yourself be *sent?*"

Harrison gaped at him. "Of course. Why not?"

"Oh, I get it now," said Jeff Baines, his puzzled features suddenly clearing. "You confuse me with the queer way you talk. You mean you planted an ob on someone?"

Desperately, Harrison said, "What's an ob?"

"He doesn't know," commented Jeff Baines, looking prayerfully at the ceiling. "He doesn't even know that!" He gave out a resigned sigh. "You hungry by any chance?"

"Going on that way."

"O.K. I could tell you what an ob is, but I'll do something better— I'll show you." Heaving himself off the stool, he waddled to a door at back. "Don't know why I should bother to try to educate a uniform. It's just that I'm bored. C'mon, follow me."

Obediently, Harrison went behind the counter, paused to give his bicycle a reassuring nod, trailed the other through a passage and into a yard.

Jeff Baines pointed to a stack of cases. "Canned goods." He indicated an adjacent store. "Bust 'em open and pile the stuff in there. Stack the empties outside. Please yourself whether you do it or not. That's freedom, isn't it?" He lumbered back into the shop.

Left by himself, Harrison scratched his ears and thought it over. Somewhere, he felt, there was an obscure sort of gag. A candidate named Harrison was being tempted to qualify for his sucker certificate. But if the play was beneficial to its organizer it might be worth learning because the trick could then be passed on. One must speculate in order to accumulate.

So he dealt with the cases as required. It took him twenty minutes of brisk work, after which he returned to the shop.

"Now," explained Baines, "you've done something for me. That means you've planted an ob on me. I don't thank you for what you've done. There's no need to. All I have to do is get rid of the ob."

"Ob?"

"Obligation. Why use a long word when a short one is good enough? An obligation is an ob. I shift it this way: Seth Warburton, next door but one, has got half a dozen of my obs saddled on him. So I get rid of mine to you and relieve him of one of his to me by sending you around for a meal." He scribbled briefly on a slip of paper. "Give him this."

Harrison stared at it. In casual scrawl, it read, "Feed this bum. Jeff Baines."

Slightly dazed, he wandered out, stood by the bicycle and again eyed the paper. Bum, it said. He could think of several on the ship who would have exploded with wrath over that. His attention drifted to the second shop farther along. It had a window crammed with comestibles and two big words on the sign-strip above: *Seth's Gulper.*

Coming to a decision which was encouraged by his innards, he went into Seth's still holding the paper as if it were a death warrant. Inside there was a long counter, some steam and a clatter of crockery. He chose a seat at a marble-topped table occupied by a gray-eyed brunette.

"Do you mind?" he inquired politely, as he lowered himself into a chair.

"Mind what?" She examined his ears as if they were curious phenomena. "Babies, dogs, aged relations or going out in the rain?"

"Do you mind me being here?"

"I can please myself whether or not I endure it. That's freedom, isn't it?"

"Yeah," said Harrison. "Sure it is." He fidgeted in his seat, feeling somehow that he'd made a move and promptly lost a pawn. He sought around for something else to say and at that point a thin-featured man in a white coat dumped before him a plate loaded with fried chicken and three kinds of unfamiliar vegetables.

The sight unnerved him. He couldn't remember how many years it

was since he last saw fried chicken, nor how many months since he'd
had vegetables in other than powder form.

"Well," said the waiter, mistaking his fascinated gaze upon the
food. "Doesn't it suit you?"

"Yes." Harrison handed over the slip of paper. "You bet it does."

Glancing at the note, the other called to someone semivisible in
the steam at one end of the counter, "You've killed another of Jeff's."
He went away, tearing the slip into small pieces.

"That was a fast pass," commented the brunette, nodding at the
loaded plate. "He dumps a feed-ob on you and you bounce it straight
back, leaving all quits. I'll have to wash dishes to get rid of mine, or
kill one Seth has got on somebody else."

"I stacked a load of canned stuff." Harrison picked up knife and
fork, his mouth watering. There were no knives and forks on the
ship. They weren't needed for powders and pills. "Don't give you any
choice here, do they? You take what you get."

"Not if you've got an ob on Seth," she informed. "In that case, he's
got to work it off best way he can. You should have put that to him
instead of waiting for fate and complaining afterward."

"I'm not complaining."

"It's your right. That's freedom, isn't it?" She mused a bit, went
on, "Isn't often I'm a plant ahead of Seth, but when I am I scream for
iced pineapple and he comes running. When *he's* a plant ahead, *I* do
the running." Her gray eyes narrowed in sudden suspicion, and she
added, "You're listening like it's all new to you. Are you a stranger
here?"

He nodded, his mouth full of chicken. A little later he managed,
"I'm off that spaceship."

"Good grief!" She froze considerably. "An Antigand! I wouldn't
have thought it. Why, you look almost human."

"I've long taken pride in that similarity," his wit rising along with
his belly. He chewed, swallowed, looked around. The white-coated
man came up. "What's to drink?" Harrison asked.

"Dith, double-dith, shemak or coffee."

"Coffee. Big and black."

"Shemak is better," advised the brunette as the waiter went away.
"But why should I tell you?"

The coffee came in a pint-sized mug. Dumping it, the waiter said,
"It's your choice seeing Seth's working one off. What'll you have for
after—apple pie, yimpik delice, grated tarfelsoufers or canimelon in
syrup?"

"Iced pineapple."

"Ugh!" The other blinked at Harrison, gave the brunette an accusing stare, went away and got it.

Harrison pushed it across. "Take the plunge and enjoy yourself."

"It's yours."

"Couldn't eat it if I tried." He dug up another load of chicken, stirred his coffee, began to feel at peace with the world. "Got as much as I can manage right here." He made an inviting motion with his fork. "G'wan, be greedy and to heck with the waistline."

"No." Firmly she pushed the pineapple back at him. "If I got through that, I'd be loaded with an ob."

"So what?"

"I don't let strangers plant obs on me."

"Quite right, too. Very proper of you," approved Harrison. "Strangers often have strange notions."

"You've been around," she agreed. "Only I don't know what's strange about the notions."

"Dish washer!"

"Eh?"

"Cynic," he translated. "One washes dishes in a cynic." The pineapple got another pass in her direction. "If you feel I'll be dumping an ob which you'll have to pay off, you can do it in a seemly manner right here. All I want is some information. Just tell me where I can put my finger on the ripest cheese in the locality."

"That's an easy one. Go round to Alec Peters' place, middle of Tenth Street." With that, she dug into the dish.

"Thanks. I was beginning to think everyone was dumb or afflicted with the funnies."

He carried on with his own meal, finished it, lay back expansively. Unaccustomed nourishment got his brain working a bit more dexterously, for after a minute an expression of deep suspicion clouded his face and he inquired, "Does this Peters run a cheese warehouse?"

"Of course." Emitting a sigh of pleasure, she put aside her empty dish.

He groaned low down, then informed, "I'm chasing the mayor."

"What is that?"

"Number one. The big boss. The sheriff, pohanko, or whatever you call him."

"I'm no wiser," she said, genuinely puzzled.

"The man who runs this town. The leading citizen."

"Make it a little clearer," she suggested, trying hard to help him. "Who or what should this citizen be leading?"

"You and Seth and everyone else." He waved a hand to encompass the entire burg.

Frowning, she said, "Leading us *where?*"

"Wherever you're going."

She gave up, beaten, and signed the white-coated waiter to come to her assistance.

"Matt, are we going any place?"

"How should I know?"

"Well, ask Seth then."

He went away, came back with, "Seth says he's going home at six o'clock and what's it to you?"

"Anyone leading him there?" she inquired.

"Don't be daft," Matt advised. "He knows his own way and he's cold sober."

Harrison chipped in with, "Look, I don't see why there should be so much difficulty about this. Just tell me where I can find an official, any official!—the police chief, the city treasurer, the mortuary keeper or even a mere justice of the peace."

"What's an official?" asked Matt, openly puzzled.

"What's a justice of the peace?" added the brunette.

His mind side-slipped and did a couple of spins. It took him quite a while to reassemble his thoughts and try another tack.

"Supposing," he said to Matt, "this joint catches fire. What would you do?"

"Fan it to keep it going," responded Matt, fed up and making no effort to conceal the fact. He returned to the counter with the air of one who has no time to waste on half-wits.

"He'd put it out," informed the brunette. "What else would you expect him to do?"

"Supposing he couldn't?"

"He'd call in others to help him."

"And would they?"

"Of course," she assured, surveying him with pity. "They'd be planting a nice crop of strong obs, wouldn't they?"

"Yes, I guess so." He began to feel stalled, but made a last shot at the problem. "What if the fire were too big and fast for passers-by to tackle?"

"Seth would summon the fire squad."

Defeat receded. A touch of triumph replaced it.

"Ah, so there is a fire squad! That's what I meant by something official. That's what I've been after all along. Quick, tell me where I can find the depot."

"Bottom end of Twelfth. You can't miss it."

"Thanks." He got up in a hurry. "See you again sometime." Going out fast, he grabbed his bicycle, shoved off from the curb.

The fire depot was a big place holding four telescopic ladders, a spray tower and two multiple pumps, all motorized on the usual array of fat rubber balls. Inside, Harrison came face to face with a small man wearing immense plus fours.

"Looking for someone?" asked the small man.

"The fire chief," said Harrison.

"Who's he?"

By this time prepared for that sort of thing, Harrison spoke as one would to a child. "See here, mister, this is a fire-fighting outfit. Somebody bosses it. Somebody organizes the shebang, fills forms, presses buttons, recommends promotions, kicks the shiftless, takes all the credit, transfers all the blame and generally lords it around. He's the most important guy in the bunch and everybody knows it." His forefinger tapped the other's chest. "And he's the fella I'm going to talk to if it's the last thing I do."

"Nobody's any more important than anyone else. How can they be? I think you're crazy."

"You're welcome to think what you like, but I'm telling you that—"

A shrill bell clamored, cutting off the sentence. Twenty men appeared as if by magic, boarded a ladder and a multi-pump, roared into the street.

Squat, basin-shaped helmets were the crews' only item of common attire. Apart from these, they plumbed the depths of sartorial iniquity. The man with the plus fours, who had gained the pump in one bold leap, was whirled out standing between a fat firefighter wearing a rainbow-hued cummerbund and a thin one sporting a canary yellow kilt. A latecomer decorated with earrings shaped like little bells hotly pursued the pump, snatched at its tailboard, missed, disconsolately watched the outfit disappear from sight. He mooched back, swinging his helmet in one hand.

"Just my lousy luck," he informed the gaping Harrison. "The sweetest call of the year. A big brewery. The sooner they get there the bigger the obs they'll plant on it." He licked his lips at the thought, sat on a coil of canvas hose. "Oh, well, maybe it's all for the good of my health."

"Tell me something," Harrison insisted. "How do you get a living?"

"There's a heck of a question. You can see for yourself. I'm on the fire squad."

"I know. What I mean is, who pays you?"

"Pays me?"

"Gives you money for all this."

"You talk kind of peculiar. What is money?"

Harrison rubbed his cranium to assist the circulation of blood through the brain. What is money? Yeouw. He tried another angle.

"Supposing your wife needs a new coat, how does she get it?"

"Goes to a store saddled with fire-obs, of course. She kills one or two for them."

"But what if no clothing store has had a fire?"

"You're pretty ignorant, brother. Where in this world do you come from?" His ear bells swung as he studied the other a moment, then went on, "Almost all stores have fire-obs. If they've any sense, they allocate so many per month by way of insurance. They look ahead, just in case, see? They plant obs on us, in a way, so that when we rush to the rescue we've got to kill off a dollop of theirs before we can plant any new ones of our own. That stops us overdoing it and making hogs of ourselves. Sort of cuts down the stores' liabilities. It makes sense, doesn't it?"

"Maybe, but—"

"I get it now," interrupted the other, narrowing his eyes. "You're from that spaceship. You're an Antigand."

"I'm a Terran," said Harrison with suitable dignity. "What's more, all the folk who originally settled this planet were Terrans."

"You trying to teach me history?" He gave a harsh laugh. "You're wrong. There was a five per cent strain of Martian."

"Even the Martians are descended from Terran settlers," riposted Harrison.

"So what? That was a devil of a long time back. Things change, in case you haven't heard. We've no Terrans or Martians on this world —except for your crowd which has come in unasked. We're all Gands here. And you nosey pokes are Antigands."

"We aren't anti-anything that I know of. Where did you get that idea?"

"Myob!" said the other, suddenly determined to refuse further agreement. He tossed his helmet to one side, spat on the floor.

"Huh?"

"You heard me. Go trundle your scooter."

Harrison gave up and did just that. He pedaled gloomily back to the ship.

His Excellency pinned him with an authoritative optic. "So you're back at last, mister. How many are coming and at what time?"

"None, sir," said Harrison, feeling kind of feeble.

"None?" August eyebrows rose up. "Do you mean that they have refused my invitation?"

"No, sir."

The ambassador waited a moment, then said, "Come out with it, mister. Don't stand there gawking as if your push-and-puff contraption has just given birth to a roller skate. You say they haven't refused my invitation—but nobody is coming. What am I to make of that?"

"I didn't ask anyone."

"So you didn't ask!" Turning, he said to Grayder, Shelton and the others, "He didn't ask!" His attention came back to Harrison. "You forgot all about it, I presume? Intoxicated by liberty and the power of man over machine, you flashed around the town at nothing less than eighteen miles per hour, creating consternation among the citizenry, tossing their traffic laws into the ash can, putting persons in peril of their lives, not even troubling to ring your bell or—"

"I haven't got a bell, sir," denied Harrison, inwardly resenting this list of enormities. "I have a whistle operated by rotation of the rear wheel."

"There!" said the ambassador, like one abandoning all hope. He sat down, smacked his forehead several times. "Somebody's going to get a bubble-pipe." He pointed a tragic finger. "And *he's* got a whistle."

"I designed it myself, sir," Harrison told him, very informatively.

"I'm sure you did. I can imagine it. I would expect it of you." The ambassador got a fresh grip on himself. "Look, mister, tell me something in strict confidence, just between you and me." He leaned forward, put the question in a whisper that ricocheted seven times around the room. "*Why* didn't you ask anyone?"

"Couldn't find anyone to ask, sir. I did my level best but they didn't seem to know what I was talking about. Or they pretended they didn't."

"Humph!" His Excellency glanced out of the nearest port, consulted his wrist watch. "The light is fading already. Night will be upon us pretty soon. It's getting too late for further action." An annoyed grunt. "Another day gone to pot. Two days here and we're still fiddling around." His eye was jaundiced as it rested on Harrison. "All right, mister, we're wasting time anyway so we might as well hear your story in full. Tell us what happened in complete detail. That way, we may be able to dig some sense out of it."

Harrison told it, finishing, "It seemed to me, sir, that I could go on for weeks trying to argue it out with people whose brains are oriented east-west while mine points north-south. You can talk with them from now to doomsday, even get real friendly and enjoy the conversation—without either side knowing what the other is jawing about."

"So it seems," commented the ambassador, dryly. He turned to Captain Grayder. "You've been around a lot and seen many new worlds in your time. What do you make of all this twaddle, if anything?"

"A problem in semantics," said Grayder, who had been compelled by circumstances to study that subject. "One comes across it on almost every world that has been long out of touch, though usually it has not developed far enough to get really tough." He paused reminiscently. "First guy we met on Basileus said, cordially and in what he fondly imagined was perfect English, 'Joy you unboot now!' "

"Yeah? What did that mean?"

"Come inside, put on your slippers and be happy. In other words, welcome! It wasn't difficult to get, your excellency, especially when you expect that sort of thing." Grayder cast a thoughtful glance at Harrison, went on, "Here, things appear to have developed to a greater extreme. The language remains fluent, retains enough surface similarities to conceal deeper changes, but meanings have been altered, concepts discarded, new ones substituted, thought-forms reangled—and, of course, there is the inevitable impact of locally developed slang."

"Such as 'myob,'" offered His Excellency. "Now there's a queer word without recognizable Earth root. I don't like the way they use it. Sounds downright insulting. Obviously it has some sort of connection with these obs they keep batting around. It means 'my obligation' or something like that, but the significance beats me."

"There is no connection, sir," Harrison contradicted. He hesitated, saw they were waiting for him, plunged boldly on. "Coming back I met the lady who directed me to Baines' place. She asked whether I'd found him and I said yes, thank you. We chatted a bit. I asked her what 'myob' meant. She said it was initial-slang." He stopped at that point.

"Keep going," advised the ambassador. "After some of the sulphurous comments I've heard coming out the Blieder-room ventilation-shaft, I can stomach anything. What does it mean?"

"M-y-o-b," informed Harrison, blinking. "Mind your own business."

"So!" His Excellency gained color. "So that's what they've been telling me all along?"

"I'm afraid so, sir."

"Evidently they've a lot to learn." His neck swelled with sudden undiplomatic fury, he smacked a large hand on the table and said, loudly, "And they are going to learn it!"

"Yes, sir," agreed Harrison, becoming more uneasy and wanting out. "May I go now and attend to my bicycle?"

"Get out of my sight!" shouted the ambassador. He made a couple of meaningless gestures, turned a florid face on Captain Grayder. "Bicycle! Does anyone on this vessel own a slingshot?"

"I doubt it, your excellency, but I will make inquiries, if you wish."

"Don't be an imbecile," ordered His Excellency. "We have our full quota of hollow-heads already."

Postponed until early morning, the next conference was relatively short and sweet. His Excellency took a seat, harumphed, straightened his vest, frowned around the table.

"Let's have another look at what we've got. We know that this planet's mules call themselves Gands, don't take much interest in their Terran origin and insist on referring to us as Antigands. That implies an education and resultant outlook inimical to ourselves. They've been trained from childhood to take it for granted that whenever we appeared upon the scene we would prove to be against whatever they are for."

"And we haven't the remotest notion of what they're for," put in

Colonel Shelton, quite unnecessarily. But it served to show that he was among those present and paying attention.

"I am grimly aware of our ignorance in that respect," indorsed the ambassador. "They are maintaining a conspiracy of silence about their prime motivation. We've got to break it somehow." He cleared his throat, continued, "They have a peculiar nonmonetary economic system which, in my opinion, manages to function only because of large surpluses. It won't stand a day when overpopulation brings serious shortages. This economic setup appears to be based on co-operative techniques, private enterprise, a kindergarten's honor system and plain unadorned gimme. That makes it a good deal crazier than that food-in-the-bank wackidoo they've got on the four outer planets of the Epsilon system."

"But it works," observed Grayder, pointedly.

"After a fashion. That flap-eared engineer's bicycle works—and so does he! A motorized job would save him a lot of sweat." Pleased with this analogy, the ambassador mused over it a few seconds. "This local scheme of economics—if you can call it a scheme—almost certainly is the end result of the haphazard development of some hick eccentricity brought in by the original settlers. It is overdue for motorizing, so to speak. They know it but don't want it because mentally they're three hundred years behind the times. They're afraid of change, improvement, efficiency—like most backward peoples. Moreover, some of them have a vested interest in keeping things as they are." He sniffed loudly to express his contempt. "They are antagonistic toward us simply because they don't want to be disturbed."

His authoritative stare went round the table, daring one of them to remark that this might be as good a reason as any. They were too disciplined to fall into that trap. None offered comment, so he went on.

"In due time, after we've got a grip on affairs, we are going to have a long and tedious task on our hands. We'll have to overhaul their entire educational system with a view to eliminating anti-Terran prejudices and bringing them up to date on the facts of life. We've had to do that on several other planets, though not to anything like the same extent as will be necessary here."

"We'll cope," promised someone.

Ignoring him, the ambassador finished, "However, all of that is in the future. We've a problem to solve in the present. It's in our laps right now, namely, where are the reins of power and who's holding them? We've got to solve that before we can make progress. How're we going to do it?" He leaned back in his chair, added, "Get your wits working and let me have some bright suggestions."

Captain Grayder stood up, a big, leather-bound book in his hands. "Your excellency, I don't think we need exercise our minds over new plans for making contact and gaining essential information. It looks as if the next move is going to be imposed upon us."

"How do you mean?"

"There are a good many old-timers in my crew. Space lawyers, every one of them." He tapped the book. "They know official Space Regulations as well as I do. Sometimes I think they know too much."

"And so—?"

Grayder opened the book. "Regulation 127 says that on a hostile world a crew serves on a war-footing until back in space. On a non-hostile world, they serve on a peace-footing."

"What of it?"

"Regulation 131A says that on a peace-footing, the crew—with the exception of a minimum number required to keep the vessel's essential services in trim—is entitled to land-leave immediately after unloading of cargo or within seventy-two Earth hours of arrival, whichever period is the shorter." He glanced up. "By midday the men will be all set for land-leave and itching to go. There will be ructions if they don't get it."

"Will there now?" said the ambassador, smiling lopsidedly. "What if I say this world is hostile? That'll pin their ears back, won't it?"

Impassively consulting his book, Grayder came back with, "Regulation 148 says that a hostile world is defined as any planet that systematically opposes Empire citizens by force." He turned the next page. "For the purpose of these regulations, force is defined as any course of action calculated to inflict physical injury, whether or not said action succeeds in its intent."

"I don't agree." The ambassador registered a deep frown. "A world can be psychologically hostile without resorting to force. We've an example right here. It isn't a friendly world."

"There are no friendly worlds within the meaning of Space Regulations," Grayder informed. "Every planet falls into one of two classifications: hostile or nonhostile." He tapped the hard leather cover. "It's all in the book."

"We would be prize fools to let a mere book boss us around or allow the crew to boss us, either. Throw it out of the port. Stick it into the disintegrator. Get rid of it any way you like—and forget it."

"Begging your pardon, your excellency, but I can't do that." Grayder opened the tome at the beginning. "Basic regulations 1A, 1B and 1C include the following: whether in space or on land, a vessel's personnel remain under direct command of its captain or his nominee who will be guided entirely by Space Regulations and will be responsible only to the Space Committee situated upon Terra. The same applies to all troops, officials and civilian passengers aboard a space-traversing vessel, whether in flight or grounded—regardless of rank or authority they are subordinate to the captain or his nominee. A nominee is defined as a ship's officer performing the duties of an immediate superior when the latter is incapacitated or absent."

"All that means you are king of your castle," said the ambassador, none too pleased. "If we don't like it, we must get off the ship."

"With the greatest respect to yourself, I must agree that that is the position. I cannot help it—regulations are regulations. And the men know it!" Grayder dumped the book, poked it away from him. "Ten to one the men will wait to midday, pressing their pants, creaming their hair and so forth. They will then make approach to me in proper manner to which I cannot object. They will request the first mate to submit their leave-roster for my approval." He gave a deep sigh. "The worst I could do would be to quibble about certain names on the roster and switch a few men around—but I couldn't refuse leave to a full quota."

"Liberty to paint the town red might be a good thing after all," suggested Colonel Shelton, not averse to doing some painting himself. "A dump like this wakes up when the fleet's in port. We ought to get contacts by the dozens. That's what we want, isn't it?"

"We want to pin down this planet's leaders," the ambassador pointed out. "I can't see them powdering their faces, putting on their best hats and rushing out to invite the yoohoo from a bunch of hungry sailors." His plump features quirked. "We have got to find the needles in this haystack. That job won't be done by a gang of ratings on the rampage."

Grayder put in, "I'm inclined to agree with you, your excellency, but we'll have to take a chance on it. If the men want to go out, the circumstances deprive me of power to prevent them. Only one thing can give me the power."

"And what is that?"

"Evidence enabling me to define this world as hostile within the meaning of Space Regulations."

"Well, can't we arrange that somehow?" Without waiting for a reply, the ambassador continued, "Every crew has its incurable trouble-maker. Find yours, give him a double shot of Venusian cognac, tell him he's being granted immediate leave—but you doubt whether he'll enjoy it because these Gands view us as reasons why people dig up the drains. Then push him out of the lock. When he comes back with a black eye and a boastful story about the other fellow's condition, declare this world hostile." He waved an expressive hand. "And there you are. Physical violence. All according to the book."

"Regulation 148A, emphasizing that opposition by force must be systematic, warns that individual brawls may not be construed as evidence of hostility."

The ambassador turned an irate face upon the senior civil servant: "When you get back to Terra—if ever you do get back—you can tell the appropriate department how the space service is balled up, hamstrung, semiparalyzed and generally handicapped by bureaucrats who write books."

Before the other could think up a reply complimentary to his kind without contradicting the ambassador, a knock came at the door. First Mate Morgan entered, saluted smartly, offered Captain Grayder a sheet of paper.

"First liberty roll, sir. Do you approve it?"

Four hundred twenty men hit the town in the early afternoon. They advanced upon it in the usual manner of men overdue for the bright lights, that is to say, eagerly, expectantly, in buddy-bunches of two, three, six or ten.

Gleed attached himself to Harrison. They were two odd rankers, Gleed being the only sergeant on leave, Harrison the only tenth engineer. They were also the only two fish out of water since both were in civilian clothes and Gleed missed his uniform while Harrison felt naked without his bicycle. These trifling features gave them enough in common to justify at least one day's companionship.

"This one's a honey," declared Gleed with immense enthusiasm. "I've been on a good many liberty jaunts in my time but this one's a honey. On all other trips the boys ran up against the same problem—

what to use for money. They had to go forth like a battalion of Santa Clauses, loaded up with anything that might serve for barter. Almost always nine-tenths of it wasn't of any use and had to be carted back again."

"On Persephone," informed Harrison, "a long-shanked Milik offered me a twenty-karat, blue-tinted first-water diamond for my bike."

"Jeepers, didn't you take it?"

"What was the good? I'd have had to go back sixteen light-years for another one."

"You could do without a bike for a bit."

"I can do without a diamond. I can't ride around on a diamond."

"Neither can you sell a bicycle for the price of a sportster Moon-boat."

"Yes I can. I just told you this Milik offered me a rock like an egg."

"It's a crying shame. You'd have got two hundred to two fifty thousand credits for that blinder, if it was flawless." Sergeant Gleed smacked his lips at the thought of so much moola stacked on the head of a barrel. "Credits and plenty of them—that's what I love. And that's what makes this trip a honey. Every other time we've gone out, Grayder has first lectured us about creating a favorable impression, behaving in a spacemanlike manner, and so forth. This time, he talks about credits."

"The ambassador put him up to that."

"I liked it, all the same," said Gleed. "Ten credits, a bottle of cognac and double liberty for every man who brings back to the ship an adult Gand, male or female, who is sociable and willing to talk."

"It won't be easily earned."

"One hundred credits to whoever gets the name and address of the town's chief civic dignitary. A thousand credits for the name and accurate location of the world's capitol city." He whistled happily, added, "Somebody's going to be in the dough and it won't be Bidworthy. He didn't come out of the hat. I know—I was holding it."

He ceased talking, turned to watch a tall, lithe blonde striding past. Harrison pulled at his arm.

"Here's Baines' place that I told you about. Let's go in."

"Oh, all right." Gleed followed with much reluctance, his gaze still down the street.

"Good afternoon," said Harrison, brightly.

"It ain't," contradicted Jeff Baines. "Trade's bad. There's a semi-final being played and it's taken half the town away. They'll think about their bellies after I've closed. Probably make a rush on me tomorrow and I won't be able to serve them fast enough."

"How can trade be bad if you don't take money even when it's good?" inquired Gleed, reasonably applying what information Harrison had given him.

Jeff's big moon eyes went over him slowly, then turned to Harrison. "So he's another bum off your boat. What's he talking about?"

"Money," said Harrison. "It's stuff we use to simplify trade. It's printed stuff, like documentary obs of various sizes."

"That tells me a lot," Jeff Baines observed. "It tells me a crowd that has to make a printed record of every ob isn't to be trusted—because they don't even trust each other." Waddling to his high stool, he squatted on it. His breathing was labored and wheezy. "And that confirms what our schools have always taught—that an Antigand would swindle his widowed mother."

"Your schools have got it wrong," assured Harrison.

"Maybe they have." Jeff saw no need to argue the point. "But we'll play safe until we know different." He looked them over. "What do you two want, anyway?"

"Some advice," shoved in Gleed, quickly. "We're out on the spree. Where's the best places to go for food and fun?"

"How long you got?"

"Until night fall tomorrow."

"No use." Jeff Baines shook his head sorrowfully. "It'd take you from now to then to plant enough obs to qualify for what's going. Besides, lots of folk wouldn't let any Antigand dump an ob on them. They're kind of particular, see?"

"Look," said Harrison. "Can't we get so much as a square meal?"

"Well, I dunno about that." Jeff thought it over, rubbing several chins. "You might manage so much—but I can't help you this time. There's nothing I want of you, so you can't use any obs I've got planted."

"Can you make any suggestions?"

"If you were local citizens, it'd be different. You could get all you want right now by taking on a load of obs to be killed sometime in the future as and when the chances come along. But I can't see anyone giving credit to Antigands who are here today and gone tomorrow."

"Not so much of the gone tomorrow talk," advised Gleed. "When an Imperial Ambassador is sent it means that Terrans will be here for keeps."

"Who says so?"

"The Empire says so. You're part of it, aren't you?"

"Nope," said Jeff. "We aren't part of anything and don't want to be, either. What's more, nobody's going to make us part of anything."

Gleed leaned on the counter and gazed absently at a large can of pork. "Seeing I'm out of uniform and not on parade, I sympathize with you though I still shouldn't say it. I wouldn't care to be taken over body and soul by other-world bureaucrats, myself. But you folk are going to have a tough time beating us off. That's the way it is."

"Not with what we've got," Jeff opined. He seemed mighty self-confident.

"You ain't got so much," scoffed Gleed, more in friendly criticism than open contempt. He turned to Harrison. "Have they?"

"It wouldn't appear so," ventured Harrison.

"Don't go by appearances," Jeff advised. "We've more than you'd care to guess at."

"Such as what?"

"Well, just for a start, we've got the mightiest weapon ever thought up by mind of man. We're Gands, see? So we don't need ships and guns and suchlike playthings. We've got something better. It's effective. There's no defense against it."

"I'd like to see it," Gleed challenged. Data on a new and exceptionally powerful weapon should be a good deal more valuable than the mayor's address. Grayder might be sufficiently overcome by the importance thereof to increase the take to five thousand credits. With a touch of sarcasm, he added, "But, of course, I can't expect you to give away secrets."

"There's nothing secret about it," said Jeff, very surprisingly. "You can have it for free any time you want. Any Gand would give it you for the asking. Like to know why?"

"You bet."

"Because it works one way only. We can use it against you—but you can't use it against us."

"There's no such thing. There's no weapon inventable which the other guy can't employ once he gets his hands on it and knows how to operate it."

"You sure?"

"Positive," said Gleed, with no hesitation whatever. "I've been in the space-service troops for twenty years and you can't fiddle around that long without learning all about weapons from string bows to

H-bombs. You're trying to kid me—and it won't work. A one-way weapon is impossible."

"Don't argue with him," Harrison suggested to Baines. "He'll never be convinced until he's shown."

"I can see that." Jeff Baines' face creased in a slow grin. "I told you that you could have our wonder-weapon for the asking. Why don't you ask?"

"All right, I'm asking." Gleed put it without much enthusiasm. A weapon that would be presented on request, without even the necessity of first planting a minor ob, couldn't be so mighty after all. His imaginary five thousand credits shrank to five, thence to none. "Hand it over and let me try it."

Swiveling heavily on his stool, Jeff reached to the wall, removed a small, shiny plaque from its hook, passed it across the counter.

"You may keep it," he informed. "And much good may it do you."

Gleed examined it, turning it over and over between his fingers. It was nothing more than an oblong strip of substance resembling ivory. One side was polished and bare. The other bore three letters deeply engraved in bold style:

F—I. W.

Glancing up, his features puzzled, he said, "Call this a weapon?"

"Certainly."

"Then I don't get it." He passed the plaque to Harrison. "Do you?"

"No." Harrison had a good look at it, spoke to Baines. "What does this F—I. W. mean?"

"Initial-slang," informed Baines. "Made correct by common usage. It has become a worldwide motto. You'll see it all over the place, if you haven't noticed it already."

"I have spotted it here and there but attached no importance to it and thought nothing of it. I remember now I've seen it inscribed in several places, including Seth's and the fire depot."

"It was on the sides of that bus we couldn't empty," added Gleed. "Didn't mean anything to me."

"It means plenty," said Jeff. "*Freedom—I Won't!*"

"That kills me," Gleed told him. "I'm stone dead already. I've dropped in my tracks." He watched Harrison thoughtfully pocketing the plaque. "A bit of abracadabra. What a weapon!"

"Ignorance is bliss," remarked Baines, strangely certain of himself.

"Especially when you don't know that what you're playing with is the safety catch of something that goes bang."

"All right," challenged Gleed, taking him up on that. "Tell us how it works."

"I won't." The grin reappeared. Baines seemed highly satisfied about something.

"That's a fat lot of help." Gleed felt let down, especially over those momentarily hoped-for credits. "You boast about a one-way weapon, toss across a slip of stuff with three letters on it and then go dumb. Any guy can talk out the back of his neck. How about backing up your talk?"

"I won't," said Baines, his grin becoming broader than ever. He favored the onlooking Harrison with a fat, significant wink.

It made something spark vividly inside Harrison's mind. His jaw dropped, he took the plaque from his pocket, stared at it as if seeing it for the first time.

"Give it me back," requested Baines, watching him.

Replacing it in his pocket, Harrison said very firmly, "I won't."

Baines chuckled. "Some folks catch on quicker than others."

Resenting that remark, Gleed held his hand out to Harrison. "Let's have another look at that thing."

"I won't," said Harrison, meeting him eye for eye.

"Hey, that's not the way—" Gleed's protesting voice died out. He stood there a moment, his optics slightly glassy while his brain performed several loops. Then, in hushed tones, he said, "Good grief!"

"Precisely," approved Baines. "Grief, and plenty of it. You were a bit slow on the uptake."

Overcome by the flood of insubordinate ideas now pouring upon him, Gleed said hoarsely to Harrison, "Come on, let's get out of here. I gotta think. I gotta think some place quiet."

There was a tiny park with seats and lawns and flowers and a little fountain around which a small bunch of children were playing. Choosing a place facing a colorful carpet of exotic un-Terran blooms, they sat and brooded a while.

In due course, Gleed commented, "For one solitary guy it would be martyrdom, but for a whole world—" His voice drifted off, came back. "I've been taking this about as far as I can make it go and the results give me the leaping fantods."

Harrison said nothing.

"F'rinstance," Gleed continued, "supposing when I go back to the ship that snorting rhinoceros Bidworthy gives me an order. I give him the frozen wolliker and say, 'I won't!' He either drops dead or throws me in the clink."

"That would do you a lot of good."

"Wait a bit—I ain't finished. I'm in the clink, but the job still needs doing. So Bidworthy picks on someone else. The victim, being a soulmate of mine, also donates the icy optic and says, 'I won't!' In the clink he goes and I've got company. Bidworthy tries again. And again. There's more of us warming the jug. It'll only hold twenty. So they take over the engineer's mess."

"Leave our mess out of this," Harrison requested.

"They take the mess," Gleed insisted, thoroughly determined to penalize the engineers. "Pretty soon it's crammed to the roof with I-won'ters. Bidworthy's still raking 'em in as fast as he can go—if by that time he hasn't burst a dozen blood vessels. So they take over the Blieder dormitories."

"Why keep picking on my crowd?"

"And pile them with bodies ceiling-high," Gleed said, getting sadistic pleasure out of the notion. "Until in the end Bidworthy has to get buckets and brushes and go down on his knees and do his own deck-scrubbing while Grayder, Shelton and the rest act as clink guards. By that time, His Loftiness the ambassador is in the galley busily cooking for you and me, assisted by a disconcerted bunch of yes-ing pen-pushers." He had another somewhat awed look at the picture and finished, "Holy smoke!"

A colored ball rolled his way, he stooped, picked it up and held on to it. Promptly a boy of about seven ran up, eyed him gravely.

"Give me my ball, please."

"I won't," said Gleed, his fingers firmly around it.

There was no protest, no anger, no tears. The child merely registered disappointment, turned to go away.

"Here you are, sonny." He tossed the ball.

"Thanks." Grabbing it, the other ran off.

Harrison said, "What if every living being in the Empire, all the way from Prometheus to Kaldor Four, across eighteen hundred light-years of space, gets an income-tax demand, tears it up and says, 'I won't!'? What happens then?"

"We'd need a second universe for a pen and a third one to provide the guards."

"There would be chaos," Harrison went on. He nodded toward the fountain and the children playing around it. "But it doesn't look like chaos here. Not to my eyes. So that means they don't overdo this blank refusal business. They apply it judiciously on some mutually recognized basis. What that basis might be beats me completely."

"Me, too."

An elderly man stopped near them, surveyed them hesitantly, decided to pick on a passing youth.

"Can you tell me where I can find the roller for Martinstown?"

"Other end of Eighth," informed the youth. "One every hour. They'll fix your manacles before they start."

"Manacles?" The oldster raised white eyebrows. "Whatever for?"

"That route runs past the spaceship. The Antigands may try to drag you out."

"Oh, yes, of course." He ambled on, glanced again at Gleed and Harrison, remarked in passing, "These Antigands—such a nuisance."

"Definitely," indorsed Gleed. "We keep telling them to get out and they keep on saying, 'We won't.' "

The old gentleman missed a step, recovered, gave him a peculiar look, continued on his way.

"One or two seem to cotton on to our accents," Harrison remarked. "Though nobody noticed mine when I was having that feed in Seth's."

Gleed perked up with sudden interest. "Where you've had one feed you can get another. C'mon, let's try. What have we got to lose?"

"Our patience," said Harrison. He stood up. "We'll pick on Seth. If he won't play, we'll have a try at someone else. And if nobody will play, we'll skin out fast before we starve to death."

"Which appears to be exactly what they want us to do," Gleed pointed out. He scowled to himself. "They'll get their way over my dead body."

"That's how," agreed Harrison. "Over your dead body."

Matt came up with a cloth over one arm. "I'm serving no Antigands."

"You served me last time," Harrison told him.

"That's as maybe. I didn't know you were off that ship. But I know now!" He flicked the cloth across one corner of the table. "No Antigands served by me."

"Is there any other place where we might get a meal?"

"Not unless somebody will let you plant an ob on them. They won't do that if they're wise to you, but there's a chance they might make the same mistake I did." Another flick across the corner. "I don't make them twice."

"You're making another right now," said Gleed, his voice tough and authoritative. He nudged Harrison. "Watch this!" His hand came out of a side pocket holding a tiny blaster. Pointing it at Matt's middle, he continued, "Ordinarily, I could get into trouble for this, if those on the ship were in the mood to make trouble. But they aren't. They're soured up on you two-legged mules." He motioned the weapon. "Get walking and bring us two full plates."

"I won't," said Matt, firming his jaw and ignoring the gun.

Gleed thumbed the safety catch which moved with an audible click. "It's touchy now. It'd go off at a sneeze. Start moving."

"I won't," insisted Matt.

Gleed disgustedly shoved the weapon back into his pocket. "I was only kidding you. It isn't energized."

"Wouldn't have made the slightest difference if it had been," Matt assured. "I serve no Antigands, and that's that!"

"Suppose I'd gone haywire and blown you in half?"

"How could I have served you then?" he inquired. "A dead person is of no use to anyone. Time you Antigands learned a little logic."

With that parting shot he went away.

"He's got something there," observed Harrison, patently depressed. "What can you do with a waxie one? Nothing whatever! You'd have put him clean out of your own power."

"Don't know so much. A couple of stiffs lying around might sharpen the others. They'd get really eager."

"You're thinking of them in Terran terms," Harrison said. "It's a mistake. They're not Terrans, no matter where they came from originally. They're Gands." He mused a moment. "I've no notion of just what Gands are supposed to be but I reckon they're some kind of fanatics. Terra exported one-track-minders by the millions around the time of the Great Explosion. Look at that crazy crowd they've got on Hygeia."

"I was there once and I tried hard not to look," confessed Gleed, reminiscently. "Then I couldn't stop looking. Not so much as a fig leaf between the lot. They insisted that we were obscene because we wore clothes. So eventually we had to take them off. Know what I was wearing at the time we left?"

"A dignified poise," Harrison suggested.

"That and an identity disk, cupro-silver, official issue, spacemen, for the use of," Gleed informed. "Plus three wipes of grease-paint on my left arm to show I was a sergeant. I looked every inch a sergeant—like heck I did!"

"I know. I had a week in that place."

"We'd a rear admiral on board," Gleed went on. "As a fine physical specimen he resembled a pair of badly worn suspenders. He couldn't overawe anyone while in his birthday suit. Those Hygeians cited his deflation as proof that they'd got real democracy, as distinct from our fake version." He clucked his tongue. "I'm not so sure they're wrong."

"The creation of the Empire has created a queer proposition," Harrison meditated. "Namely, that Terra is always right while sixteen hundred and forty-two planets are invariably wrong."

"You're getting kind of seditious, aren't you?"

Harrison said nothing. Gleed glanced at him, found his attention elsewhere, followed his gaze to a brunette who had just entered.

"Nice," approved Gleed. "Not too young, not too old. Not too fat, not too thin. Just right."

"I know her." Harrison waved to attract her attention.

She tripped lightly across the room, sat at their table. Harrison made the introduction.

"Friend of mine. Sergeant Gleed."

"Arthur," corrected Gleed, eying her.

"Mine's Elissa," she told him. "What's a sergeant supposed to be?"

"A sort of over-above underthing," Gleed informed. "I pass along the telling to the guys who do the doing."

Her eyes widened. "Do you mean that people really allow themselves to be told?"

"Of course. Why not?"

"It sounds crazy to me." Her gaze shifted to Harrison. "I'll be ignorant of *your* name forever, I suppose?"

He hastened to repair the omission, adding, "But I don't like James. I prefer Jim."

"Then we'll let it be Jim." She examined the place, looking over the counter, the other tables. "Has Matt been to you two?"

"Yes. He refuses to serve us."

She shrugged warm shoulders. "It's his right. Everyone has the right to refuse. That's freedom, isn't it?"

"We call it mutiny," said Gleed.

"Don't be so childish," she reproved. She stood up, moved away. "You wait here. I'll go see Seth."

"I don't get this," admitted Gleed, when she had passed out of earshot. "According to that fat fella in the delicatessen, their technique is to give us the cold shoulder until we run away in a huff. But this dame acts friendly. She's . . . she's—" He stopped while he sought for a suitable word, found it and said, "She's un-Gandian."

"Not so," Harrison contradicted. "They've the right to say, 'I won't.' She's practicing it."

"By gosh, yes! I hadn't thought of that. They can work it any way they like, and please themselves."

"Sure." He dropped his voice. "Here she comes."

Resuming her seat, she primped her hair, said, "Seth will serve us personally."

"Another traitor," remarked Gleed with a grin.

"On one condition," she went on. "You two must wait and have a talk with him before you leave."

"Cheap at the price," Harrison decided. A thought struck him and he asked, "Does this mean you'll have to kill several obs for all three of us?"

"Only one for myself."

"How come?"

"Seth's got ideas of his own. He doesn't feel happy about Antigands any more than does anyone else."

"And so?"

"But he's got the missionary instinct. He doesn't agree entirely with the idea of giving all Antigands the ghost-treatment. He thinks it should be reserved only for those too stubborn or stupid to be converted." She smiled at Gleed, making his top hairs quiver. "Seth thinks that any intelligent Antigand is a would-be Gand."

"What is a Gand, anyway?" asked Harrison.

"An inhabitant of this world, of course."

"I mean, where did they dig up the name?"

"From Gandhi," she said.

Harrison frowned in puzzlement. "Who the deuce was he?"

"An ancient Terran. The one who invented The Weapon."

"Never heard of him."

"That doesn't surprise me," she remarked.

"Doesn't it?" He felt a little irritated. "Let me tell you that these days we Terrans get as good an education as—"

"Calm down, Jim." She made it more soothing by pronouncing it "Jeem." "All I mean is that ten to one he's been blanked out of your history books. He might have given you unwanted ideas, see? You couldn't be expected to know what you've been deprived of the chance to learn."

"If you mean that Terran history is censored, I don't believe it," he asserted.

"It's your right to refuse to believe. That's freedom, isn't it?"

"Up to a point. A man has duties. He's no right to refuse those."

"No?" She raised tantalizing eyebrows, delicately curved. "Who defines those duties—himself, or somebody else?"

"His superiors, most times."

"No man is superior to another. No man has the right to define another man's duties." She paused, eying him speculatively. "If anyone on Terra exercises such idiotic power, it is only because idiots permit him. They fear freedom. They prefer to be told. They like being ordered around. What men!"

"I shouldn't listen to you," protested Gleed, chipping in. His leathery face was flushed. "You're as naughty as you're pretty."

"Afraid of your own thoughts?" she jibed, pointedly ignoring his compliment.

He went redder. "Not on your life. But I—" His voice trailed off as Seth arrived with three loaded plates and dumped them on the table.

"See you afterward," reminded Seth. He was medium-sized, with thin features and sharp, quick-moving eyes. "Got something to say to you."

Seth joined them shortly after the end of the meal. Taking a chair, he wiped condensed steam off his face, looked them over.

"How much do you two know?"

"Enough to argue about it," put in Elissa. "They are bothered about duties, who defines them, and who does them."

"With good reason," Harrison riposted. "You can't escape them yourselves."

"Meaning—?" asked Seth.

"This world runs on some strange system of swapping obligations. How will any person kill an ob unless he recognizes his duty to do so?"

"Duty has nothing to do with it," said Seth. "And if it did happen to be a matter of duty, every man would recognize it for himself. It would be outrageous impertinence for anyone else to remind him, unthinkable to anyone to order him."

"Some guys must make an easy living," interjected Gleed. "There's nothing to stop them that I can see." He studied Seth briefly before he continued, "How can you cope with a citizen who has no conscience?"

"Easy as pie."

Elissa suggested, "Tell them the story of Idle Jack."

"It's a kid's yarn," explained Seth. "All children here know it by heart. It's a classic fable like . . . like—" He screwed up his face. "I've lost track of the Terran tales the first comers brought with them."

"Red Riding Hood," offered Harrison.

"Yes." Seth seized on it gratefully. "Something like that one. A nursery story." He licked his lips, began, "This Idle Jack came from Terra as a baby, grew up in our new world, studied our economic system and thought he'd be mighty smart. He decided to become a scratcher."

"What's a scratcher?" inquired Gleed.

"One who lives by taking obs and does nothing about killing them or planting any of his own. One who accepts everything that's going and gives nothing in return."

"I get it. I've known one or two like that in my time."

"Up to age sixteen, Jack got away with it. He was a kid, see. All kids tend to scratch to a certain extent. We expect it and allow for it. After sixteen, he was soon in the soup."

"How?" urged Harrison, more interested than he was willing to show.

"He went around the town gathering obs by the armful. Meals, clothes and all sorts for the mere asking. It's not a big town. There are no big ones on this planet. They're just small enough for everyone to know everyone—and everyone does plenty of gabbing. Within three or four months the entire town knew Jack was a determined scratcher."

"Go on," said Harrison, getting impatient.

"Everything dried up," said Seth. "Wherever Jack went, people gave him the 'I won't.' That's freedom, isn't it? He got no meals, no clothes, no entertainment, no company, nothing! Soon he became terribly hungry, busted into someone's larder one night, gave himself the first square meal in a week."

"What did they do about that?"

"Nothing. Not a thing."

"That would encourage him some, wouldn't it?"

"How could it?" Seth asked, with a thin smile. "It did him no good. Next day his belly was empty again. He had to repeat the performance. And the next day. And the next. People became leery, locked up their stuff, kept watch on it. It became harder and harder. It became so unbearably hard that it was soon a lot easier to leave the town and try another. So Idle Jack went away."

"To do the same again," Harrison suggested.

"With the same results for the same reasons," retorted Seth. "On he went to a third town, a fourth, a fifth, a twentieth. He was stubborn enough to be witless."

"He was getting by," Harrison observed. "Taking all at the mere cost of moving around."

"No he wasn't. Our towns are small, like I said. And folk do plenty of visiting from one to another. In town number two Jack had to risk being seen and talked about by someone from town number one. As he went on it got a whole lot worse. In the twentieth he had to take a chance on gabby visitors from any of the previous nineteen." Seth leaned forward, said with emphasis, "He never got to town number twenty-eight."

"No?"

"He lasted two weeks in number twenty-five, eight days in twenty-six, one day in twenty-seven. That was almost the end."

"What did he do then?"

"Took to the open country, tried to live on roots and wild berries. Then he disappeared—until one day some walkers found him swinging from a tree. The body was emaciated and clad in rags. Loneliness and self-neglect had killed him. That was Idle Jack, the scratcher. He wasn't twenty years old."

"On Terra," informed Gleed, "we don't hang people merely for being lazy."

"Neither do we," said Seth. "We leave them free to go hang themselves." He eyed them shrewdly, went on, "But don't let it worry you. Nobody has been driven to such drastic measures in my lifetime, leastways, not that I've heard about. People honor their obs as a matter of economic necessity and not from any sense of duty. Nobody gives orders, nobody pushes anyone around, but there's a kind of compulsion built into the circumstances of this planet's way of living.

People play square—or they suffer. Nobody enjoys suffering—not even a numbskull."

"Yes, I suppose you're right," put in Harrison, much exercised in mind.

"You bet I'm dead right!" Seth assured. "But what I wanted to talk to you two about is something more important. It's this: What's your real ambition in life?"

Without hesitation, Gleed said, "To ride the spaceways while remaining in one piece."

"Same here," Harrison contributed.

"I guessed that much. You'd not be in the space service if it wasn't your choice. But you can't remain in it forever. All good things come to an end. What then?"

Harrison fidgeted uneasily. "I don't care to think of it."

"Some day, you'll have to," Seth pointed out. "How much longer have you got?"

"Four and a half Earth years."

Seth's gaze turned to Gleed.

"Three Earth years."

"Not long," Seth commented. "I didn't expect you would have much time left. It's a safe bet that any ship penetrating this deeply into space has a crew composed mostly of old-timers getting near the end of their terms. The practiced hands get picked for the awkward jobs. By the day your boat lands again on Terra it will be the end of the trail for many of them, won't it?"

"It will for me," Gleed admitted, none too happy at the thought.

"Time—the older you get the faster it goes. Yet when you leave the service you'll still be comparatively young." He registered a faint, taunting smile. "I suppose you'll then obtain a private space vessel and continue roaming the cosmos on your own?"

"Impossible," declared Gleed. "The best a rich man can afford is a Moon-boat. Puttering to and fro between a satellite and its primary is no fun when you're used to Blieder-zips across the galaxy. The smallest space-going craft is far beyond reach of the wealthiest. Only governments can afford them."

"By 'governments' you mean communities?"

"In a way."

"Well, then, what are you going to do when your space-roving days are over?"

"I'm not like Big Ears here." Gleed jerked an indicative thumb at
Harrison. "I'm a trooper and not a technician. So my choice is limited
by lack of qualifications." He rubbed his chin, looked wistful. "I was
born and brought up on a farm. I still know a good deal about farm-
ing. So I'd like to get a small one of my own and settle down."

"Think you'll manage it?" asked Seth, watching him.

"On Falder or Hygeia or Norton's Pink Heaven or some other un-
developed planet. But not on Terra. My savings won't extend to that.
I don't get half enough to meet Earth costs."

"Meaning you can't pile up enough obs?"

"I can't," agreed Gleed, lugubriously. "Not even if I saved until
I'd got a white beard four feet long."

"So there's Terra's reward for a long spell of faithful service—
forego your heart's desire or get out?"

"Shut up!"

"I won't," said Seth. He leaned nearer. "Why do you think two
hundred thousand Gands came to this world, Doukhobors to Hygeia,
Quakers to Centauri B., and all the others to their selected haunts?
Because Terra's reward for good citizenship was the peremptory order to knuckle down or get out. So we got out."

"It was just as well, anyway," Elissa interjected. "According to our
history books, Terra was badly overcrowded. We went away and relieved the pressure."

"That's beside the point," reproved Seth. He continued with Gleed.
"You want a farm. It can't be on Terra much as you'd like it there.
Terra says, 'No! Get out!' So it's got to be someplace else." He waited
for that to sink in, then, "Here, you can have one for the mere taking." He snapped his fingers. "Like that!"

"You can't kid me," said Gleed, wearing the expression of one
eager to be kidded. "Where are the hidden strings?"

"On this planet, any plot of ground belongs to the person in possession, the one who is making use of it. Nobody disputes his claim
so long as he continues to use it. All you need do is look around for a
suitable piece of unused territory—of which there is plenty—and start
using it. From that moment it's yours. Immediately you cease using
it and walk out, it's anyone else's, for the taking."

"Zipping meteors!" Gleed was incredulous.

"Moreover, if you look around long enough and strike really
lucky," Seth continued, "you might stake first claim to a farm some-

one else has abandoned because of death, illness, a desire to move elsewhere, a chance at something else he liked better, or any other excellent reason. In that case, you would walk into ground already part-prepared, with farmhouse, milking shed, barns and the rest. And it would be yours, all yours."

"What would I owe the previous occupant?" asked Gleed.

"Nothing. Not an ob. Why should you? If he isn't buried, he has got out for the sake of something else equally free. He can't have the benefit both ways, coming and going."

"It doesn't make sense to me. Somewhere there's a snag. Somewhere I've got to pour out hard cash or pile up obs."

"Of course you do. You start a farm. A handful of local folks help you build a house. They dump heavy obs on you. The carpenter wants farm produce for his family for the next couple of years. You give it, thus killing that ob. You continue giving it for a couple of extra years, thus planting an ob on *him*. First time you want fences mending, or some other suitable task doing, along he comes to kill *that* ob. And so with all the rest, including the people who supply your raw materials, your seeds and machinery, or do your trucking for you."

"They won't all want milk and potatoes," Gleed pointed out.

"Don't know what you mean by potatoes. Never heard of them."

"How can I square up with someone who may be getting all the farm produce he wants from elsewhere?"

"Easy," said Seth. "A tinsmith supplies you with several churns. He doesn't want food. He's getting all he needs from another source. His wife and three daughters are overweight and dieting. The mere thought of a load from your farm gives them the horrors."

"Well?"

"But this tinsmith's tailor, or his cobbler, have got obs on him which he hasn't had the chance to kill. So he transfers them to you. As soon as you're able, you give the tailor or cobbler what they need to satisfy the obs, thus doing the tinsmith's killing along with your own." He gave his usual half-smile, added, "And everyone is happy."

Gleed stewed it over, frowning while he did it. "You're tempting me. You shouldn't ought to. It's a criminal offense to try to divert a spaceman from his allegiance. It's sedition. Terra is tough with sedition."

"Tough my eye!" said Seth, sniffing contemptuously. "We've Gand laws here."

"All you have to do," suggested Elissa, sweetly persuasive, "is say to yourself that you've got to go back to the ship, that it's your duty to go back, that neither the ship nor Terra can get along without you." She tucked a curl away. "Then be a free individual and say, 'I won't!' "

"They'd skin me alive. Bidworthy would preside over the operation in person."

"I don't think so," Seth offered. "This Bidworthy—whom I presume to be anything but a jovial character—stands with you and the rest of your crew at the same junction. The road before him splits two ways. He's got to take one or the other and there's no third alternative. Sooner or later he'll be hell-bent for home, eating his top lip as he goes, or else he'll be running around in a truck delivering your milk—because, deep inside himself, that's what he's always wanted to do."

"You don't know him like I do," mourned Gleed. "He uses a lump of old iron for a soul."

"Funny," remarked Harrison, "I always thought of *you* that way— until today."

"I'm off duty," said Gleed, as though that explained everything. "I can relax and let the ego zoom around outside of business hours." He stood up, firmed his jaw. "But I'm going back on duty. Right now!"

"You're not due before sundown tomorrow," Harrison protested.

"Maybe I'm not. But I'm going back all the same."

Elissa opened her mouth, closed it as Seth nudged her. They sat in silence and watched Gleed march determinedly out.

"It's a good sign," commented Seth, strangely self-assured. "He's been handed a wallop right where he's weakest." He chuckled low down, turned to Harrison. "What's *your* ultimate ambition?"

"Thanks for the meal. It was a good one and I needed it." Harrison stood up, manifestly embarrassed. He gestured toward the door. "I'm going to catch him up. If he's returning to the ship, I think I'll do likewise."

Again Seth nudged Elissa. They said nothing as Harrison made his way out, carefully closing the door behind him.

"Sheep," decided Elissa, disappointed for no obvious reason. "One follows another. Just like sheep."

"Not so," Seth contradicted. "They're humans animated by the same thoughts, the same emotions, as were our forefathers who had nothing sheeplike about them." Twisting round in his chair, he beckoned to Matt. "Bring us two shemaks." Then to Elissa. "My guess is that it won't pay that ship to hang around too long."

The battleship's caller-system bawled imperatively, "Fanshaw, Folsom, Fuller, Garson, Gleed, Gregory, Haines, Harrison, Hope—" and down through the alphabet.

A trickle of men flowed along the passages, catwalks and alleyways toward the fore chartroom. They gathered outside it in small clusters, chattering in undertones and sending odd scraps of conversation echoing down the corridor.

"Wouldn't say anything to us but, 'Myob!' Got sick and tired of it after a while."

"You ought to have split up, like we did. That show place on the outskirts didn't know what a Terran looks like. I just walked in and took a seat."

"Hear about Meakin? He mended a leaky roof, chose a bottle of double dith in payment and mopped the lot. He was dead flat when we found him. Had to be carried back."

"Some guys have all the luck. We got the brush-off wherever we showed our faces. It gets you down."

"You should have separated, like I said."

"Half the mess must be still lying in the gutter. They haven't turned up yet."

"Grayder will be hopping mad. He'd have stopped this morning's second quota if he'd known in time."

Every now and again First Mate Morgan stuck his head out of the chartroom door and uttered a name already voiced on the caller. Frequently there was no response.

"Harrison!" he yelled.

With a puzzled expression, Harrison went inside. Captain Grayder was there, seated behind a desk and gazing moodily at a list lying before him. Colonel Shelton was stiff and erect to one side, with Major Hame slightly behind him. Both wore the pained expressions of those tolerating a bad smell while the plumber goes looking for the leak.

His Excellency was tramping steadily to and fro in front of the desk, muttering deep down in his chins. "Barely five days and already the rot has set in." He turned as Harrison entered, fired off sharply, "So it's you, mister. When did you return from leave?"

"The evening before last, sir."

"Ahead of time, eh? That's curious. Did you get a puncture or something?"

"No, sir. I didn't take my bicycle with me."

"Just as well," approved the ambassador. "If you had done so, you'd have been a thousand miles away by now and still pushing hard."

"Why, sir?"

"Why? He asks me why! That's precisely what I'd like to know—*why?*" He fumed a bit, then inquired, "Did you visit this town by yourself, or in company?"

"I went with Sergeant Gleed, sir."

"Call him," ordered the ambassador, looking at Morgan.

Opening the door, Morgan obediently shouted, "Gleed! Gleed!" No answer.

He tried again, without result. They put it over the caller-system again. Sergeant Gleed refused to be among those present.

"Has he booked in?"

Grayder consulted his list. "In early. Twenty-four hours ahead of time. He may have sneaked out again with the second liberty quota this morning and omitted to book it. That's a double crime."

"If he's not on the ship, he's off the ship, crime or no crime."

"Yes, your excellency." Captain Grayder registered slight weariness.

"GLEED!" howled Morgan, outside the door. A moment later he poked his head inside, said, "Your excellency, one of the men says Sergeant Gleed is not on board because he saw him in town quite recently."

"Send him in." The ambassador made an impatient gesture at Harrison. "Stay where you are and keep those confounded ears from flapping. I've not finished with you yet."

A long, gangling grease-monkey came in, blinked around, a little awed by high brass.

"What do you know about Sergeant Gleed?" demanded the ambassador.

The other licked his lips, seemed sorry that he had mentioned the missing man. "It's like this, your honor, I—"

"Call me 'sir.'"

"Yes, sir." More disconcerted blinking. "I went out with the second party early this morning, came back a couple of hours ago because my stomach was acting up. On the way, I saw Sergeant Gleed and spoke to him."

"Where? When?"

"In town, sir. He was sitting in one of those big long-distance coaches. I thought it a bit queer."

"Get down to the roots, man! What did he tell you, if anything?"

"Not much, sir. He seemed pretty chipper about something. Mentioned a young widow struggling to look after two hundred acres. Someone had told him about her and he thought he'd take a peek." He hesitated, backed away a couple of paces, added, "He also said I'd see him in irons or never."

"One of *your* men," said the ambassador to Colonel Shelton. "A trooper, allegedly well-disciplined. One with long service, three stripes, and a pension to lose." His attention returned to the informant. "Did he say exactly where he was going?"

"No, sir. I asked him, but he just grinned and said, 'Myob!' So I came back to the ship."

"All right. You may go." His Excellency watched the other depart, then continued with Harrison. "You were with that first quota."

"Yes, sir."

"Let me tell you something, mister. Four hundred twenty men went out. Only two hundred have returned. Forty of those were in various stages of alcoholic turpitude. Ten of them are in the clink yelling, 'I won't!' in steady chorus. Doubtless they'll go on yelling until they've sobered up."

He stared at Harrison as if that worthy were personally responsible, then went on, "There's something paradoxical about this. I can understand the drunks. There are always a few individuals who blow their tops first day on land. But of the two hundred who have condescended to come back, about half returned before time, the same as you did. Their reasons were identical—the town was unfriendly, everyone treated them like ghosts until they'd had enough."

Harrison made no comment.

"So we have two diametrically opposed reactions," the ambassador complained. "One gang of men say the place stinks so much that they'd rather be back on the ship. Another gang finds it so hospitable that either they get filled to the gills on some stuff called double dith, or they stay sober and desert the service. I want an explanation. There's got to be one somewhere. You've been twice in this town. What can you tell us?"

Carefully, Harrison said, "It all depends on whether or not you're spotted as a Terran. Also on whether you meet Gands who'd rather convert you than give you the brush-off." He pondered a moment, finished, "Uniforms are a giveaway."

"You mean they're allergic to uniforms?"

"More or less, sir."

"Any idea why?"

"Couldn't say for certain, sir. I don't know enough about them yet. As a guess, I think they may have been taught to associate uniforms with the Terran regime from which their ancestors escaped."

"Escaped nothing!" scoffed the ambassador. "They grabbed the benefit of Terran inventions, Terran techniques and Terran manufacturing ability to go someplace where they'd have more elbow room." He gave Harrison the sour eye. "Don't any of them wear uniforms?"

"Not that I could recognize as such. They seem to take pleasure in expressing their individual personalities by wearing anything they fancy, from pigtails to pink boots. Oddity in attire is the norm among the Gands. Uniformity is the real oddity—they think it's submissive and degrading."

"You refer to them as Gands. Where did they dig up that name?"

Harrison told him, thinking back to Elissa as she explained it. In his mind's eye he could see her now. And Seth's place with the tables set and steam rising behind the counter and mouth-watering smells oozing from the background. Now that he came to visualize the scene again, it appeared to embody an elusive but essential something that the ship had never possessed.

"And this person," he concluded, "invented what they call The Weapon."

"Hm-m-m! And they assert he was a Terran? What does he look like? Did you see a photograph or a statue?"

"They don't erect statues, sir. They say no person is more important than another."

"Bunkum!" snapped the ambassador, instinctively rejecting that viewpoint. "Did it occur to you to ask at what period in history this wonderful weapon was tried out?"

"No, sir," Harrison confessed. "I didn't think it important."

"You wouldn't. Some of you men are too slow to catch a Callistrian sloth wandering in its sleep. I don't criticize your abilities as spacemen, but as intelligence-agents you're a dead loss."

"I'm sorry, sir," said Harrison.

Sorry? You louse! whispered something deep within his own mind.

Why should you be sorry? He's only a pompous fat man who couldn't kill an ob if he tried. He's no better than you. Those raw boys prancing around on Hygeia would maintain that he's not as good as you because he's got a pot belly. Yet you keep looking at his pot belly and saying, "Sir," and, "I'm sorry." If he tried to ride your bike, he'd fall off before he'd gone ten yards. Go spit in his eye and say, "I won't." You're not scared, are you?

"*No!*" announced Harrison, loudly and firmly.

Captain Grayder glanced up. "If you're going to start answering questions before they've been asked, you'd better see the medic. Or have we a telepath on board?"

"I was thinking," Harrison explained.

"I approve of that," put in His Excellency. He lugged a couple of huge tomes out of the wall-shelves, began to thumb rapidly through them. "Do plenty of thinking whenever you've the chance and it will become a habit. It will get easier and easier as time rolls on. In fact, a day may come when it can be done without pain."

He shoved the books back, pulled out two more, spoke to Major Hame who happened to be at his elbow. "Don't pose there glassy-eyed like a relic propped up in a military museum. Give me a hand with this mountain of knowledge. I want Gandhi, anywhere from three hundred to a thousand Earth-years ago."

Hame came to life, started dragging out books. So did Colonel Shelton. Captain Grayder remained at his desk and continued to mourn the missing.

"Ah, here it is, four-seventy years back." His Excellency ran a plump finger along the printed lines. "Gandhi, sometimes called Bapu, or Father, Citizen of Hindi. Politico-philosopher. Opposed authority by means of an ingenious system called civil disobedience. Last remnants disappeared with the Great Explosion, but may still persist on some planet out of contact."

"Evidently it does," commented Grayder, his voice dry.

"Civil disobedience," repeated the ambassador, screwing up his eyes. He had the air of one trying to study something which was topsy-turvy. "They can't make *that* a social basis. It just won't work."

"It does work," asserted Harrison, forgetting to put in the "sir."

"Are you contradicting me, mister?"

"I'm stating a fact."

"Your excellency," Grayder began, "I suggest—"

"Leave this to me." His color deepening, the ambassador waved him off. His gaze remained angrily on Harrison. "You're very far from being an expert on socio-economic problems. Get that into your head, mister. Anyone of your caliber can be fooled by superficial appearances."

"It works," persisted Harrison, wondering where his own stubbornness was coming from.

"So does your tomfool bicycle. You've a bicycle mentality."

Something snapped, and a voice remarkably like his own said, "Nuts!" Astounded by this phenomenon, Harrison waggled his ears.

"What was that, mister?"

"Nuts!" he repeated, feeling that what has been done can't be undone.

Beating the purpling ambassador to the draw, Captain Grayder stood up and exercised his own authority.

"Regardless of further leave-quotas, if any, you are confined to the ship until further notice. Now get out!"

He went out, his mind in a whirl but his soul strangely satisfied. Outside, First Mate Morgan glowered at him.

"How long d'you think it's going to take me to work through this list of names when guys like you squat in there for a week?" He grunted with ire, cupped hands round his mouth and bellowed, "Hope! Hope!"

No reply.

"Hope's been abandoned," remarked a wit.

"That's funny," sneered Morgan. "Look at me shaking all over." He cupped again, tried the next name. "Hyland! Hyland!"

No response.

Four more days, long, tedious, dragging ones. That made nine in all since the battleship formed the rut in which it was still sitting.

There was trouble on board. The third and fourth leave-quotas, put off repeatedly, were becoming impatient, irritable.

"Morgan showed him the third roster again this morning. Same result. Grayder admitted this world can't be defined as hostile and that we're entitled to run free."

"Well, why the heck doesn't he keep to the book? The Space Commission could crucify him for disregarding it."

"Same excuse. He says he's not denying leave, he's merely postponing it. That's a crafty evasion, isn't it? He says he'll grant it immediately the missing men come back."

"That might be never. Darn him, he's using them as an excuse to gyp me out of my time."

It was a strong and legitimate complaint. Weeks, months, years of close confinement in a constantly trembling bottle, no matter how large, demands ultimate release if only for a comparatively brief period. Men need fresh air, the good earth, the broad, clear-cut horizon, bulk-food, femininity, new faces.

"He *would* ram home the stopper just when we've learned the best way to get around. Civilian clothes and act like Gands, that's the secret. Even the first-quota boys are ready for another try."

"Grayder daren't risk it. He's lost too many already. One more quota cut in half and he won't have enough crew to take off and get back. We'd be stuck here for keeps. How'd you like that?"

"I wouldn't grieve."

"He could train the bureaucrats. Time those guys did some honest work."

"It'd take three years. That's how long it took to train you, wasn't it?"

Harrison came along holding a small envelope. Three of them picked on him at sight.

"Look who sassed Hizonner and got confined to ship—same as us!"

"That's what I like about it," Harrison observed. "Better to get fastened down for something than for nothing."

"It won't be long, you'll see! We're not going to hang around belly-aching for ever. Mighty soon we'll *do* something."

"Such as what?"

"We're thinking it over," evaded the other, not liking to be taken up so fast. He noticed the envelope. "What have you got there? The day's mail?"

"Exactly that," Harrison agreed.

"Have it your own way. I wasn't being nosey. I thought maybe you'd got some more snafu. You engineers usually pick up that paperstuff first."

"It *is* mail," said Harrison.

"G'wan, nobody has letters in this neck of the cosmos."

"I do."

"How did you get it?"

"Worrall brought it from town an hour back. Friend of mine gave him dinner, let him bring the letter to kill the ob." He pulled a large ear. "Influence, that's what you boys need."

Registering annoyance, one demanded, "What's Worrall doing off the boat? Is he privileged?"

"Sort of. He's married, with three kids."

"So what?"

"The ambassador figures that some people can be trusted more than others. They're not so likely to disappear, having too much to lose. So a few have been sorted out and sent into town to seek information about the missing men."

"They found out anything?"

"Not much. Worrall says it's a waste of time. He found a few of our men here and there, tried to persuade them to return, but each said, 'I won't.' The Gands all said, 'Myob!' And that's that."

"There must be something in it," decided one of them, thoughtfully. "I'd like to go see for myself."

"That's what Grayder's afraid of."

"We'll give him more than that to worry about if he doesn't become reasonable soon. Our patience is evaporating."

"Mutinous talk," Harrison reproved. He shook his head, looked sad. "You shock me."

He continued along the corridor, reached his own cabin, eyed the envelope. The writing inside might be feminine. He hoped so. He tore it open and had a look. It wasn't.

Signed by Gleed, the missive read, "Never mind where I am or what I'm doing—this might get into the wrong hands. All I'll tell you is that I'll be fixed up topnotch providing I wait a decent interval to improve acquaintance. The rest of this concerns *you.*"

"Huh?" He leaned back on his bunk, held the letter nearer the light.

"I found a little fat guy running an empty shop. He just sits there, waiting. Next, I learn that he's established possession by occupation. He's doing it on behalf of a factory that makes two-ball rollers—those fan-driven cycles. They want someone to operate the place as a local roller sales and service depot. The little fat man has had four applications to date, but none with any engineering ability. The one who eventually gets this place will plant a functional-ob on the town, whatever that means. Anyway, this joint is yours for the taking. Don't be stupid. Jump in—the water's fine."

"Zipping meteors!" said Harrison. His eyes traveled on to the bottom.

"P.S. Seth will give you the address. P.P.S. This burg is your brunette's home town and she's thinking of coming back. She wants to
live near her sister—and so do I. Said sister is a honey!"

He stirred restlessly, read it through a second time, got up and
paced around his tiny cabin. There were twelve hundred occupied
worlds within the scope of the Empire. He'd seen about one-tenth of
them. No spaceman could live long enough to get a look at the lot.
The service was divided into cosmic groups, each dealing with its own
sector.

Except by hearsay, of which there was plenty and most of it highly
colored, he would never know what heavens or pseudo-heavens existed in other sectors. In any case, it would be a blind gamble to pick
an unfamiliar world for landbound life on someone else's recommendation. Not all think alike, or have the same tastes. One man's
meat may be another man's poison.

The choice for retirement—which was the unlovely name for beginning another, different but vigorous life—was high-priced Terra or
some more desirable planet in his own sector. There was the Epsilon
group, fourteen of them, all attractive providing you could suffer the
gravity and endure lumbering around like a tired elephant. There was
Norton's Pink Heaven if, for the sake of getting by in peace, you
could pander to Septimus Norton's rajah-complex and put up with
his delusions of grandeur.

Up on the edge of the Milky Way was a matriarchy run by blonde
Amazons, and a world of wizards, and a Pentecostal planet, and a
globe where semisentient vegetables cultivated themselves under the
direction of human masters; all scattered across forty light-years of
space but readily accessible by Blieder-drive.

There were more than a hundred known to him by personal experience, though merely a tithe of the whole. All offered life and that
company which is the essence of life. But this world, Gand, had something the others lacked. It had the quality of being present. It was part
of the existing environment from which he drew data on which to
build his decisions. The others were not. They lost virtue by being
absent and faraway.

Unobtrusively, he made his way to the Blieder-room lockers, spent
an hour cleaning and oiling his bicycle. Twilight was approaching
when he returned. Taking a thin plaque from his pocket, he hung it on
the wall, lay on his bunk and stared at it.

F—I. W.

The caller-system clicked, cleared its throat, announced, "All personnel will stand by for general instructions at eight hours tomorrow."

"I won't," said Harrison. He closed his eyes.

Seven-twenty in the morning, but nobody thought it early. There is little sense of earliness or lateness among space-roamers—to regain it they have to be landbound a month, watching a sun rise and set.

The chartroom was empty but there was much activity in the control cabin. Grayder was there with Shelton, Hame, Navigators Adamson, Werth and Yates and, of course, His Excellency.

"I never thought the day would come," groused the latter, frowning at the star map over which the navigators pored. "Less than a couple of weeks, and we get out, admitting defeat."

"With all respect, your excellency, it doesn't look that way to me," said Captain Grayder. "One can be defeated only by enemies. These people are not enemies. That's precisely where they've got us by the short hairs. They're not definable as hostile."

"That may be. I still say it's defeat. What else could you call it?"

"We've been outwitted by awkward relations. There's not much we can do about it. A man doesn't beat up his nieces and nephews merely because they won't speak to him."

"That's your viewpoint as a ship's commander. You're confronted by a situation that requires you to go back to base and report. It's routine. The whole service is hidebound with routine." The ambassador again eyed the star map as if he found it offensive. "My own status is different. If I get out, it's a diplomatic defeat, an insult to the dignity and prestige of Terra. I'm far from sure that I ought to go. It might be better if I stayed put—though that would give them the chance to offer further insults."

"I would not presume to advise you what to do for the best," Grayder said. "All I know is this: we carry troops and armaments for any policing or protective purposes that might be found necessary here. But I can't use them offensively against these Gands because they've provided no pretext and because, in any case, our full strength isn't enough to crush twelve millions of them. We need an armada for that. We'd be fighting at the extreme of our reach—and the reward of victory would be a useless world."

"Don't remind me. I've stewed it until I'm sick of it."

Grayder shrugged. He was a man of action so long as it was action in space. Planetary shenanigans were not properly his pigeon. Now that the decisive moment was drawing near, when he would be back in his own attenuated element, he was becoming phlegmatic. To him, Gand was a visit among a hundred such, with plenty more to come.

"Your excellency, if you're in serious doubt whether to remain or come with us, I'd be favored if you'd reach a decision fairly soon. Morgan has given me the tip that if I haven't approved the third leave-quota by ten o'clock the men are going to take matters into their own hands and walk off."

"That would get them into trouble of a really hot kind, wouldn't it?"

"Some," agreed Captain Grayder, "but not so hot. They intend to turn my own quibbling against me. Since I have not officially forbidden leave, a walk-out won't be mutiny. I've merely been postponing leave. They could plead before the Space Commission that I've deliberately ignored regulations. They might get away with it if the members were in the mood to assert their authority."

"The Commission ought to be taken on a few long flights," opined His Excellency. "They'd discover some things they'll never learn behind a desk." He eyed the other in mock hopefulness. "Any chance of accidentally dropping our cargo of bureaucrats overboard on the way back? A misfortune like that might benefit the spaceways, if not humanity."

"That idea strikes me as Gandish," observed Grayder.

"They wouldn't think of it. Their technique is to say no, no, a thousand times no. That's all—but judging by what has happened here, it is enough." The ambassador pondered his predicament, reached a decision. "I'm coming with you. It goes against the grain because it smacks of surrender. To stay would be a defiant gesture, but I've got to face the fact that it won't serve any useful purpose at the present stage."

"Very well, your excellency." Grayder went to a port, looked through it toward the town. "I'm down about four hundred men. Some of them have deserted, for keeps. The rest will come back if I wait long enough. They've struck it lucky, got their legs under somebody's table and gone A.W.O.L. and they're likely to extend their time for as long as the fun lasts on the principle that they may as well be hung for sheep as lambs. I get that sort of trouble on every long trip. It's not so bad on short ones." A pause while moodily he surveyed a terrain bare of returning prodigals. "But we can't wait for them. Not here."

"No, I reckon not."

"If we hang around any longer, we're going to lose another hundred or two. There won't be enough skilled men to take the boat up. Only way I can beat them to the draw is to give the order to prepare for take-off. They all come under flight-regulations from that moment." He registered a lopsided smile. "That will give the space lawyers something to think about!"

"As soon as you like," approved the ambassador. He joined the other at the port, studied the distant road, watched three Gand coaches whirl along it without stopping. He frowned, still upset by the type of mind which insists on pretending that a mountain isn't there. His attention shifted sidewise, toward the tail-end. He stiffened and said, "What are those men doing outside?"

Shooting a swift glance in the same direction, Grayder grabbed the caller-make and rapped, "All personnel will prepare for take-off at once!" Juggling a couple of switches, he changed lines, said, "Who is that? Sergeant Major Bidworthy? Look, sergeant major, there are half a dozen men beyond the midship lock. Get them in immediately—we're lifting as soon as everything's ready."

The fore and aft gangways had been rolled into their stowage spaces long before. Some fast-thinking quartermaster prevented further escapes by operating the midship ladder-wind, thus trapping Bidworthy along with more would-be sinners.

Finding himself stalled, Bidworthy stood in the rim of the lock and glared at those outside. His mustache not only bristled, but quivered. Five of the offenders had been members of the first leave-quota. One of them was a trooper. That got his rag out, a trooper. The sixth was Harrison, complete with bicycle polished and shining.

Searing the lot of them, the trooper in particular, Bidworthy rasped, "Get back on board. No arguments. No funny business. We're taking off."

"Hear that?" asked one, nudging the nearest. "Get back on board. If you can't jump thirty feet, you'd better flap your arms and fly."

"No sauce from you," roared Bidworthy. "I've got my orders."

"He takes orders," remarked the trooper. "At his age."

"Can't understand it," commented another, shaking a sorrowful head.

Bidworthy scrabbled the lock's smooth rim in vain search of something to grasp. A ridge, a knob, a projection of some sort was needed to take the strain.

"I warn you men that if you try me too—"

"Save your breath, Biddy," interjected the trooper. "From now on, I'm a Gand." With that, he turned and walked rapidly toward the road, four following.

Getting astride his bike, Harrison put a foot on a pedal. His back tire promptly sank with a loud *whee-e-e.*

"Come back!" howled Bidworthy at the retreating five. He made extravagant motions, tried to tear the ladder from its automatic grips. A siren keened thinly inside the vessel. That upped his agitation by several ergs.

"Hear that?" With vein-pulsing ire, he watched Harrison tighten the rear valve and apply his hand pump. "We're about to lift. For the last time—"

Again the siren, this time in a quick series of shrill toots. Bidworthy jumped backward as the seal came down. The lock closed. Harrison again mounted his machine, settled a foot on a pedal but remained watching.

The metal monster shivered from nose to tail then rose slowly and in utter silence. There was stately magnificence in the ascent of such enormous bulk. It increased its rate of climb gradually, went faster, faster, became a toy, a dot and finally disappeared.

For just a moment, Harrison felt a touch of doubt, a hint of regret. It soon passed away. He glanced toward the road.

The five self-elected Gands had thumbed a coach which was picking them up. That was co-operation apparently precipitated by the ship's disappearance. Quick on the uptake, these people. He saw it move off on huge rubber balls, bearing the five with it. A fan-cycle raced in the opposite direction, hummed into the distance.

"Your brunette," Gleed had described her. What gave him that idea? Had she made some remark which he'd construed as complimentary because it made no reference to outsize ears?

He had a last look around. The earth to his left bore a great curved rut one mile long by twelve feet deep. Two thousand Terrans had been there.

Then about eighteen hundred.

Then sixteen hundred.

Less five.

"One left—me!" he said to himself.

Giving a fatalistic shrug, he put the pressure on and rode to town. And then there were none.

THE BALLAD OF LOST C'MELL
by *Cordwainer Smith*

She got the which of the what-she-did,
Hid the bell with a blot, she did,
But she fell in love with a hominid.
Where is the which of the what-she-did?
from THE BALLAD OF LOST C'MELL

She was a girly girl and they were true men, the lords of creation, but she pitted her wits against them and she won. It had never happened before, and it is sure never to happen again, but she did win. She was not even of human extraction. She was cat-derived, though human in outward shape, which explains the C in front of her name. Her father's name was C'mackintosh and her name C'mell. She won her tricks against the lawful and assembled Lords of the Instrumentality.

It all happened at Earthport, greatest of buildings, smallest of cities, standing twenty-five kilometers high at the western edge of the Smaller Sea of Earth.

Jestocost had an office outside the fourth valve.

1

Jestocost liked the morning sunshine, while most of the other Lords of Instrumentality did not, so that he had no trouble in keeping the office and the apartments which he had selected. His main office was ninety meters deep, twenty meters high, twenty meters broad. Behind it was the "fourth valve," almost a thousand hectares in extent. It was shaped helically, like an enormous snail. Jestocost's apartment, big as it was, was merely one of the pigeonholes in the muffler on the rim of Earthport. Earthport stood like an enormous wineglass, reaching from the magma to the high atmosphere.

Earthport had been built during mankind's biggest mechanical splurge. Though men had had nuclear rockets since the beginning of consecutive history, they had used chemical rockets to load the interplanetary ion-drive and nuclear-drive vehicles or to assemble the photonic sail-ships for interstellar cruises. Impatient with the troubles of taking things bit by bit into the sky, they had worked out a billion-ton rocket, only to find that it ruined whatever countryside it touched in landing. The Daimoni—people of Earth extraction, who came back from somewhere beyond the stars—had helped men build it of weatherproof, rustproof, timeproof, stressproof material. Then they had gone away and had never come back.

Jestocost often looked around his apartment and wondered what it might have been like when white-hot gas, muted to a whisper, surged out of the valve into his own chamber and the sixty-three other chambers like it. Now he had a back wall of heavy timber, and the valve itself was a great hollow cave where a few wild things lived. Nobody needed that much space any more. The chambers were useful, but the valve did nothing. Planoforming ships whispered in from the stars; they landed at Earthport as a matter of legal convenience, but they made no noise and they certainly had no hot gases.

Jestocost looked at the high clouds far below him and talked to himself,

"Nice day. Good air. No trouble. Better eat."

Jestocost often talked like that to himself. He was an individual, almost an eccentric. One of the top council of mankind, he had problems, but they were not personal problems. He had a Rembrandt hanging above his bed—the only Rembrandt known in the world, just as he was possibly the only person who could appreciate a Rembrandt. He had the tapestries of a forgotten empire hanging from his back wall. Every morning the sun played a grand opera for him, muting and lighting and shifting the colors so that he could almost imagine that the old days of quarrel, murder and high drama had come back to Earth again. He had a copy of Shakespeare, a copy of Colegrove and two pages of the Book of Ecclesiastes in a locked box beside his bed. Only forty-two people in the universe could read Ancient English, and he was one of them. He drank wine, which he had made by his own robots in his own vineyards on the Sunset coast. He was a man, in short, who had arranged his own life to live comfortably, selfishly and well on the personal side, so that he could give generously and impartially of his talents on the official side.

When he awoke on this particular morning, he had no idea that a beautiful girl was about to fall hopelessly in love with him—that he would find, after a hundred years and more of experience in government, another government on earth just as strong and almost as ancient as his own—that he would willingly fling himself into conspiracy and danger for a cause which he only half understood. All these things were mercifully hidden from him by time, so that his only question on arising was, should he or should he not have a small cup of white wine with his breakfast. On the 173rd day of each year, he always made a point of eating eggs. They were a rare treat, and he did not want to spoil himself by having too many, nor to deprive himself and forget a treat by having none at all. He puttered around the room, muttering, "White wine? White wine?"

C'mell was coming into his life, but he did not know it. She was fated to win; that part, she herself did not know.

Ever since mankind had gone through the Rediscovery of Man, bringing back governments, money, newspapers, national languages, sickness and occasional death, there had been the problem of the underpeople—people who were not human, but merely humanly shaped from the stock of Earth animals. They could speak, sing, read, write, work, love and die; but they were not covered by human law, which simply defined them as "homunculi" and gave them a legal status close to animals or robots. Real people from off-world were always called "hominids."

Most of the underpeople did their jobs and accepted their half-slave status without question. Some became famous—C'mackintosh had been the first earth-being to manage a fifty-meter broad-jump under normal gravity. His picture was seen in a thousand worlds. His daughter, C'mell, was a girly girl, earning her living by welcoming human beings and hominids from the outworlds and making them feel at home when they reached Earth. She had the privilege of working at Earthport, but she had the duty of working very hard for a living which did not pay well. Human beings and hominids had lived so long in an affluent society that they did not know what it meant to be poor. But the Lords of the Instrumentality had decreed that underpeople—derived from animal stock—should live under the economics of the Ancient World; they had to have their own kind of money to pay for their rooms, their food, their possessions and the education of their children. If they became bankrupt, they went to the Poorhouse, where they were killed painlessly by means of gas.

It was evident that humanity, having settled all of its own basic problems, was not quite ready to let Earth animals, no matter how much they might be changed, assume a full equality with man.

The Lord Jestocost, seventh of that name, opposed the policy. He was a man who had little love, no fear, freedom from ambition and a dedication to his job: but there are passions of government as deep and challenging as the emotions of love. Two hundred years of thinking himself right and of being outvoted had instilled in Jestocost a furious desire to get things done his own way.

Jestocost was one of the few true men who believed in the rights of the underpeople. He did not think that mankind would ever get around to correcting ancient wrongs unless the underpeople themselves had some of the tools of power—weapons, conspiracy, wealth and (above all) organization with which to challenge man. He was not afraid of revolt, but he thirsted for justice with an obsessive yearning which overrode all other considerations.

When the Lords of the Instrumentality heard that there was the rumor of a conspiracy among the underpeople, they left it to the robot police to ferret out.

Jestocost did not.

He set up his own police, using underpeople themselves for the purpose, hoping to recruit enemies who would realize that he was a friendly enemy and who would in course of time bring him into touch with the leaders of the underpeople.

If those leaders existed, they were clever. What sign did a girly girl like C'mell ever give that she was the spearhead of a crisscross of agents who had penetrated Earthport itself? They must, if they existed, be very, very careful. The telepathic monitors, both robotic and human, kept every thought-band under surveillance by random sampling. Even the computers showed nothing more significant than improbable amounts of happiness in minds which had no objective reason for being happy.

The death of her father, the most famous cat-athlete which the underpeople had ever produced, gave Jestocost his first definite clue.

He went to the funeral himself, where the body was packed in an ice-rocket to be shot into space. The mourners were thoroughly mixed with the curiosity-seekers. Sport is international, inter-race, inter-world, inter-species. Hominids were there: true men, 100% human, they looked weird and horrible because they or their ancestors had undergone bodily modifications to meet the life conditions of a thousand worlds.

Underpeople, the animal-derived "homunculi," were there, most of them in their work clothes, and they looked more human than did the human beings from the outer worlds. None were allowed to grow up if they were less than half the size of man, or more than six times the size of man. They all had to have human features and acceptable human voices. The punishment for failure in their elementary schools was death. Jestocost looked over the crowd and wondered to himself, "We have set up the standards of the toughest kind of survival for these people and we give them the most terrible incentive, life itself, as the condition of absolute progress. What fools we are to think that they will not overtake us!" The true people in the group did not seem to think as he did. They tapped the underpeople peremptorily with their canes, even though this was an underperson's funeral, and the bear-men, bull-men, cat-men and others yielded immediately and with a babble of apology.

C'mell was close to her father's icy coffin.

Jestocost not only watched her; she was pretty to watch. He committed an act which was an indecency in an ordinary citizen but lawful for a Lord of the Instrumentality: he peeped into her mind.

And then he found something which he did not expect.

As the coffin left, she cried, "Ee-telly-kelly, help me! help me!"

She had thought phonetically, not in script, and he had only the raw sound on which to base a search.

Jestocost had not become a Lord of the Instrumentality without applying daring. His mind was quick, too quick to be deeply intelligent. He thought by gestalt, not by logic. He determined to force his friendship on the girl.

He decided to await a propitious occasion, and then changed his mind about the time.

As she went home from the funeral, he intruded upon the circle of her grimfaced friends, underpeople who were trying to shield her from the condolences of ill-mannered but well-meaning sports enthusiasts.

She recognized him, and showed him the proper respect.

"My Lord, I did not expect you here. You knew my father?"

He nodded gravely and addressed sonorous words of consolation and sorrow, words which brought a murmur of approval from humans and underpeople alike.

But with his left hand hanging slack at his side, he made the perpetual signal of *alarm! alarm!* used within the Earthport staff—a repeated tapping of the thumb against the third finger—when they had to set one another on guard without alerting the offworld transients.

She was so upset that she almost spoiled it all. While he was still doing his pious doubletalk, she cried in a loud clear voice:

"You mean *me?*"

And he went on with his condolences: ". . . and I do mean *you,* C'mell, to be the worthiest carrier of your father's name. *You* are the one to whom we turn in this time of common sorrow. *Who could I mean but you* if I say that C'mackintosh never did things by halves, and died young as a result of his own zealous conscience? Good-by, C'mell, I go back to my office."

She arrived forty minutes after he did.

2

He faced her straight away, studying her face.

"This is an important day in your life."

"Yes, my Lord, a sad one."

"I do not," he said, "mean your father's death and burial. I speak of the future to which we all must turn. Right now, it's you and me."

Her eyes widened. She had not thought that he was that kind of man at all. He was an official who moved freely around Earthport, often greeting important offworld visitors and keeping an eye on the bureau of ceremonies. She was a part of the reception team, when a girly girl was needed to calm down a frustrated arrival or to postpone a quarrel. Like the geisha of ancient Japan, she had an honorable profession; she was not a bad girl but a professionally flirtatious hostess. She stared at the Lord Jestocost. He did not *look* as though he meant anything improperly personal. But, thought she, you can never tell about men.

"You know men," he said, passing the initiative to her.

"I guess so," she said. Her face looked odd. She started to give him smile No. 3 (extremely adhesive) which she had learned in the girly-girl school. Realizing it was wrong, she tried to give him an ordinary smile. She felt she had made a face at him.

"Look at me," he said, "and see if you can trust me. I am going to take both our lives in my hands."

She looked at him. What imaginable subject could involve him, a

Lord of the Instrumentality, with herself, an undergirl? They never had anything in common. They never would.

But she stared at him.

"I want to help the underpeople."

He made her blink. That was a crude approach, usually followed by a very raw kind of pass indeed. But his face was illuminated by seriousness. She waited.

"Your people do not have enough political power even to talk to us. I will not commit treason to the true-human race, but I am willing to give your side an advantage. If you bargain better with us, it will make all forms of life safer in the long run."

C'mell stared at the floor, her red hair soft as the fur of a Persian cat. It made her head seem bathed in flames. Her eyes looked human, except that they had the capacity of reflecting when light struck them; the irises were the rich green of the ancient cat. When she looked right at him, looking up from the floor, her glance had the impact of a blow. "What do you want from me?"

He stared right back. "Watch me. Look at my face. Are you sure, *sure* that I want nothing from you personally?"

She looked bewildered. "What else is there to want from me except personal things? I am a girly girl. I'm not a person of any importance at all, and I do not have much of an education. You know more, sir, than I will ever know."

"Possibly," he said, watching her.

She stopped feeling like a girly girl and felt like a citizen. It made her uncomfortable.

"Who," he said, in a voice of great solemnity, "is your own leader?"

"Commissioner Teadrinker, sir. He's in charge of all outworld visitors." She watched Jestocost carefully; he still did not look as if he were playing tricks.

He looked a little cross. "I don't mean him. He's part of my own staff. Who's your leader among the underpeople?"

"My father was, but he died."

Jestocost said, "Forgive me. Please have a seat. But I don't mean that."

She was so tired that she sat down into the chair with an innocent voluptuousness which would have disorganized any ordinary man's day. She wore girly-girl clothes, which were close enough to the everyday fashion to seem agreeably modish when she stood up. In line with her profession, her clothes were designed to be unexpectedly and provocatively revealing when she sat down—not revealing enough to shock the man with their brazenness, but so slit, tripped and cut that he got far more visual stimulation than he expected.

"I must ask you to pull your clothing together a little," said Jestocost in a clinical tone of voice. "I am a man, even if I am an official, and this interview is more important to you and to me than any distraction would be."

She was a little frightened by his tone. She had meant no challenge. With the funeral that day, she meant nothing at all; these clothes were the only kind she had.

He read all this in her face.

Relentlessly, he pursued the subject.

"Young lady, I asked about your leader. You name your boss and you name your father. I want your leader."

"I don't understand," she said, on the edge of a sob, "I don't understand."

Then, he thought to himself, I've got to take a gamble. He thrust the mental dagger home, almost drove his words like steel straight into her face. "Who . . ." he said slowly and icily, "is . . . Ee . . . telly . . . kelly?"

The girl's face had been cream-colored, pale with sorrow. Now she went white. She twisted away from him. Her eyes glowed like twin fires.

Her eyes . . . like twin fires.

(No undergirl, thought Jestocost as he reeled, could hypnotize me.)

Her eyes . . . were like cold fires.

The room faded around him. The girl disappeared. Her eyes became a single white, cold fire.

Within this fire stood the figure of a man. His arms were wings, but he had human hands growing at the elbows of his wings. His face was clear, white, cold as the marble of an ancient statue; his eyes were opaque white. "I am the E-telekeli. You will believe in me. You may speak to my daughter C'mell."

The image faded.

Jestocost saw the girl staring as she sat awkwardly on the chair, looking blindly through him. He was on the edge of making a joke about her hypnotic capacity when he saw that she was still deeply hypnotized, even after he had been released. She had stiffened and again her clothing had fallen into its planned disarray. The effect was not stimulating; it was pathetic beyond words, as though an accident had happened to a pretty child. He spoke to her.

He spoke to her, not really expecting an answer.

"Who are you?" he said to her, testing her hypnosis.

"I am he whose name is never said aloud," said the girl in a sharp whisper, "I am he whose secret you have penetrated. I have printed my image and my name in your mind."

Jestocost did not quarrel with ghosts like this. He snapped out a decision. "If I open my mind, will you search it while I watch you? Are you good enough to do that?"

"I am very good," hissed the voice in the girl's mouth.

C'mell arose and put her two hands on his shoulders. She looked into his eyes. He looked back. A strong telepath himself, Jestocost was not prepared for the enormous thought-voltage which poured out of her.

Look in my mind, he commanded, for the subject of *underpeople* only.

I see it, thought the mind behind C'mell.

Do you see what I mean to do for the underpeople?

Jestocost heard the girl breathing hard as her mind served as a relay to his. He tried to remain calm so that he could see which part of his mind was being searched. Very good so far, he thought to himself. An intelligence like that on Earth itself, he thought—and we of the Lords not knowing it!

The girl hacked out a dry little laugh.

Jestocost thought at the mind, Sorry. Go ahead.

This plan of yours—thought the strange mind—may I see more of it?

That's all there is.

Oh, said the strange mind, you want me to think for you. Can you give me the keys in the Bank and Bell which pertain to destroying underpeople?

You can have the information keys if I can ever get them, thought Jestocost, but not the control keys and not the master switch of the Bell.

Fair enough, thought the other mind, and what do I pay for them?

You support me in my policies before the Instrumentality. You keep the underpeople reasonable, if you can, when the time comes to negotiate. You maintain honor and good faith in all subsequent agreements. But how can I get the keys? It would take me a year to figure them out myself.

Let the girl look once, thought the strange mind, and I will be behind her. Fair?

Fair, thought Jestocost.

Break? thought the mind.

How do we re-connect? thought Jestocost back.

As before. Through the girl. Never say my name. Don't think it if you can help it. Break?

Break! thought Jestocost.

The girl, who had been holding his shoulders, drew his face down and kissed him firmly and warmly. He had never touched an underperson before, and it never had occurred to him that he might kiss one. It was pleasant, but he took her arms away from his neck, half-turned her around, and let her lean against him.

"Daddy!" she sighed happily.

Suddenly she stiffened, looked at his face, and sprang for the door. "Jestocost!" she cried. "Lord Jestocost! What am I doing here?"

"Your duty is done, my girl. You may go."

She staggered back into the room. "I'm going to be sick," she said. She vomited on his floor.

He pushed a button for a cleaning robot and slapped his desk-top for coffee.

She relaxed and talked about his hopes for the underpeople. She stayed an hour. By the time she left they had a plan. Neither of them had mentioned E-telekeli, neither had put purposes in the open. If the monitors had been listening, they would have found no single sentence or paragraph which was suspicious.

When she had gone, Jestocost looked out of his window. He saw the clouds far below and he knew the world below him was in twilight. He had planned to help the underpeople, and he had met powers of which organized mankind had no conception or perception. He was righter than he had thought. He had to go on through.

But as partner—C'mell herself!

Was there ever an odder diplomat in the history of worlds?

3

In less than a week they had decided what to do. It was the council of the Lords of the Instrumentality at which they would work—the brain center itself. The risk was high, but the entire job could be done in a few minutes if it were done at the Bell itself.

This is the sort of thing which interested Jestocost.

He did not know that C'mell watched him with two different facets of her mind. One side of her was alertly and wholeheartedly his fellow-conspirator, utterly in sympathy with the revolutionary aims to which they were both committed. The other side of her—was feminine.

She had a womanliness which was truer than that of any hominid woman. She knew the value of her trained smile, her splendidly kept red hair with its unimaginably soft texture, her lithe young figure with firm breasts and persuasive hips. She knew down to the last millimeter the effect which her legs had on hominid men. True humans kept few secrets from her. The men betrayed themselves by their unfulfillable desires, the women by their irrepressible jealousies. But she knew people best of all by not being one herself. She had to learn by imitation, and imitation is conscious. A thousand little things which ordinary women took for granted, or thought about just once in a whole lifetime, were subjects of acute and intelligent study to her. She was a girl by profession; she was a human by assimilation: she was an inquisitive cat in her genetic nature. Now she was falling in love with Jestocost, and she knew it.

Even she did not realize that the romance would sometime leak out into rumor, be magnified into legend, distilled into romance. She had no idea of the ballad about herself that would open with the lines which became famous much later:

> *She got the which of the what-she-did,*
> *Hid the bell with a blot, she did,*
> *But she fell in love with a hominid.*
> *Where is the which of the what-she-did?*

All this lay in the future, and she did not know it.

She knew her own past.

She remembered the off-Earth prince who had rested his head in her lap and had said, sipping his glass of moti by way of farewell:

"Funny, C'mell, you're not even a person and you're the most intelligent human being I've met in this place. Do you know it made my planet poor to send me here? And what did I get out of them? Nothing, nothing, and a thousand times nothing. But you, now. If you'd been running the government of Earth, I'd have gotten what my people need, and this world would be richer too. Manhome, they call it. Manhome, my eye! The only smart person on it is a female cat."

He ran his fingers around her ankle. She did not stir. That was part of hospitality, and she had her own ways of making sure that hospitality did not go too far. Earth police were watching her; to them, she was a convenience maintained for outworld people, something like a soft chair in the Earthport lobbies or a drinking fountain with acid-tasting water for strangers who could not tolerate the insipid water of Earth. She was not expected to have feelings or to get involved. If she had ever caused an incident, they would have punished her fiercely, as they often punished animals or underpeople, or else (after a short formal hearing with no appeal) they would have destroyed her, as the law allowed and custom encouraged.

She had kissed a thousand men, maybe fifteen hundred. She had made them feel welcome and she had gotten their complaints or their secrets out of them as they left. It was a living, emotionally tiring but intellectually very stimulating. Sometimes it made her laugh to look at human women with their pointed-up noses and their proud airs, and to realize that she knew more about the men who belonged to the human women than the human women themselves ever did.

Once a policewoman had had to read over the record of two pioneers from New Mars. C'mell had been given the job of keeping in very close touch with them. When the policewoman got through reading the report she looked at C'mell and her face was distorted with jealousy and prudish rage.

"Cat, you call yourself. Cat! You're a pig, you're a dog, you're an animal. You may be working for Earth but don't ever get the idea that you're as good as a person. I think it's a crime that the Instrumentality lets monsters like you greet real human beings from outside! I can't stop it. But may the Bell help you, girl, if you ever touch a real Earth man! If you ever get near one! If you ever try tricks here! Do you understand me?"

"Yes, ma'am," C'mell had said. To herself she thought, "That poor thing doesn't know how to select her own clothes or how to do her own hair. No wonder she resents somebody who manages to be pretty."

Perhaps the policewoman thought that raw hatred would be shock-

ing to C'mell. It wasn't. Underpeople were used to hatred, and it
was not any worse raw than it was when cooked with politeness and
served like poison. They had to live with it.

But now, it was all changed.

She had fallen in love with Jestocost.

Did he love her?

Impossible. No, not impossible. Unlawful, unlikely, indecent—yes,
all these, but not impossible. Surely he felt something of her love.

If he did, he gave no sign of it.

People and underpeople had fallen in love many times before. The
underpeople were always destroyed and the real people brainwashed.
There were laws against that kind of thing. The scientists among
people had created the underpeople, had given them capacities which
real people did not have (the fifty-meter jump, the telepath two miles
underground, the turtle-man waiting a thousand years next to an
emergency door, the cow-man guarding a gate without reward), and
the scientists had also given many of the underpeople the human
shape. It was handier that way. The human eye, the five-fingered
hand, the human size—these were convenient for engineering reasons. By making underpeople the same size and shape as people,
more or less, the scientists eliminated the need for two or three or a
dozen different sets of furniture. The human form was good enough
for all of them.

But they had forgotten the human heart.

And now she, C'mell had fallen in love with a man, a true man
old enough to have been her own father's grandfather.

But she didn't feel daughterly about him at all. She remembered
that with her own father there was an easy comradeship, an innocent
and forthcoming affection, which masked the fact that he was considerably more cat-like than she was. Between them there was an
aching void of forever-unspoken words—things that couldn't quite
be said by either of them, perhaps things that couldn't be said at all.
They were so close to each other that they could get no closer. This
created enormous distance, which was heartbreaking but unutterable.
Her father had died, and now this true man was here, with all the
kindness—

"That's it," she whispered to herself, "with all the kindness that
none of these passing men have ever really shown. With all the depth
which my poor underpeople can never get. Not that it's not in them.
But they're born like dirt, treated like dirt, put away like dirt when

they die. How can any of my own men develop real kindness? There's a special sort of majesty to kindness. It's the best part there is to being people. And he has whole oceans of it in him. And it's strange, strange, strange that he's never given his real love to any human woman."

She stopped, cold.

Then she consoled herself and whispered on, "Or if he did, it's so long ago that it doesn't matter now. He's got *me*. Does he know it?"

4

The Lord Jestocost did know, and yet he didn't. He was used to getting loyalty from people, because he offered loyalty and honor in his daily work. He was even familiar with loyalty becoming obsessive and seeking physical form, particularly from women, children and underpeople. He had always coped with it before. He was gambling on the fact that C'mell was a wonderfully intelligent person, and that as a girly girl, working on the hospitality staff of the Earthport police, she must have learned to control her personal feelings.

"We're born in the wrong age," he thought, "when I meet the most intelligent and beautiful female I've ever met, and then have to put business first. But this stuff about people and underpeople is sticky. Sticky. We've got to keep personalities out of it."

So he thought. Perhaps he was right.

If the nameless one, whom he did not dare to remember, commanded an attack on the Bell itself, that was worth their lives. Their emotions could not come into it. The Bell mattered: justice mattered: the perpetual return of mankind to progress mattered. He did not matter, because he had already done most of his work. C'mell did not matter, because their failure would leave her with mere underpeople forever. The Bell did count.

The price of what he proposed to do was high, but the entire job could be done in a few minutes if it were done at the Bell itself.

The Bell, of course, was not a Bell. It was a three-dimensional situation table, three times the height of a man. It was set one story below the meeting room, and shaped roughly like an ancient bell. The meeting table of the Lords of the Instrumentality had a circle cut out of it, so that the Lords could look down into the Bell at whatever situation one of them called up either manually or telepathically. The Bank below it, hidden by the floor, was the key memory-bank of the entire system. Duplicates existed at thirty-odd other places on Earth. Two duplicates lay hidden in interstellar space, one of them beside the ninety-million-mile gold-colored ship left over from the War against Raumsog and the other masked as an asteroid.

Most of the Lords were offworld on the business of the Instrumentality.

Only three besides Jestocost were present—the Lady Johanna Gnade, the Lord Issan Olascoaga and the Lord William Not-from-here. (The Not-from-heres were a great Norstrilian family which had migrated back to Earth many generations before.)

The E-telekeli told Jestocost the rudiments of a plan.

He was to bring C'mell into the chambers on a summons.

The summons was to be serious.

They should avoid her summary death by automatic justice, if the relays began to trip.

C'mell would go into partial trance in the chamber.

He was then to call the items in the Bell which E-telekeli wanted traced. A single call would be enough. E-telekeli would take the responsibility for tracing them. The other Lords would be distracted by him, E-telekeli.

It was simple in appearance.

The complication came in action.

The plan seemed flimsy, but there was nothing which Jestocost could do at this time. He began to curse himself for letting his passion for policy involve him in the intrigue. It was too late to back out with honor; besides, he had given his word; besides, he liked C'mell—as a being, not as a girly girl—and he would hate to see her marked with disappointment for life. He knew how the underpeople cherished their identities and their status.

With heavy heart but quick mind he went to the council chamber. A dog-girl, one of the routine messengers whom he had seen many months outside the door, gave him the minutes.

He wondered how C'mell or E-telekeli would reach him, once he was inside the chamber with its tight net of telepathic intercepts.

He sat wearily at the table—

And almost jumped out of his chair.

The conspirators had forged the minutes themselves, and the top item was: "C'mell daughter to C'mackintosh, cat-stock (pure) lot 1138, confession of. Subject: conspiracy to export homuncular material. Reference: planet De Prinsensmacht."

The Lady Johanna Gnade had already pushed the buttons for the planet concerned. The people there, Earth by origin, were enormously strong but they had gone to great pains to maintain the original Earth appearance. One of their first-men was at the moment on Earth. He bore the title of the Twilight Prince (Prins van de Schemering) and he was on a mixed diplomatic and trading mission.

Since Jestocost was a little late, C'mell was being brought into the room as he glanced over the minutes.

The Lord Not-from-here asked Jestocost if he would preside.

"I beg you, sir and scholar," he said, "to join me in asking the Lord Issan to preside this time."

The presidency was a formality. Jestocost could watch the Bell and Bank better if he did not have to chair the meeting too.

C'mell wore the clothing of a prisoner. On her it looked good. He had never seen her wearing anything but girly-girl clothes before. The pale-blue prison tunic made her look very young, very human, very tender and very frightened. The cat family showed only in the fiery cascade of her hair and the lithe power of her body as she sat, demure and erect.

Lord Issan asked her: "You have confessed. Confess again."

"This man," and she pointed at a picture of the Twilight Prince, "wanted to go to the place where they torment human children for a show."

"What!" cried three of the Lords together.

"What place?" said the Lady Johanna, who was bitterly in favor of kindness.

"It's run by a man who looks like this gentleman here," said C'mell, pointing at Jestocost. Quickly, so that nobody could stop her, but modestly, so that none of them thought to doubt her, she circled the room and touched Jestocost's shoulder. He felt a thrill of contact-telepathy and heard bird-cackle in her brain. Then he knew that the E-telekeli was in touch with her.

"The man who has the place," said C'mell, "is five pounds lighter than this gentleman, two inches shorter, and he has red hair. His place is at the Cold Sunset corner of Earthport, down the boulevard and under the boulevard. Underpeople, some of them with bad reputations, live in that neighborhood."

The Bell went milky, flashing through hundreds of combinations of bad underpeople in that part of the city. Jestocost felt himself staring at the casual milkiness with unwanted concentration.

The Bell cleared.

It showed the vague image of a room in which children were playing Hallowe'en tricks.

The Lady Johanna laughed, "Those aren't people. They're robots. It's just a dull old play."

"Then," added C'mell, "he wanted a dollar and a shilling to take home. Real ones. There was a robot who had found some."

"What are those?" said Lord Issan.

"Ancient money—the real money of old America and old Australia," cried Lord William. "I have copies, but there are no originals outside the state museum." He was an ardent, passionate collector of coins.

"The robot found them in an old hiding place right under Earthport."

Lord William almost shouted at the Bell. "Run through every hiding place and get me that money."

The Bell clouded. In finding the bad neighborhoods it had flashed every police point in the Northwest sector of the tower. Now it scanned all the police points under the tower, and ran dizzily through thousands of combinations before it settled on an old toolroom. A robot was polishing circular pieces of metal.

When Lord William saw the polishing, he was furious. "Get that here," he shouted. "I want to buy those myself!"

"All right," said Lord Issan. "It's a little irregular, but all right."

The machine showed the key search devices and brought the robot to the escalator.

The Lord Issan said, "This isn't much of a case."

C'mell sniveled. She was a good actress. "Then he wanted me to get a homunculus egg. One of the E-type, derived from birds, for him to take home."

Issan put on the search device.

"Maybe," said C'mell, "somebody has already put it in the disposal series."

The Bell and the Bank ran through all the disposal devices at high speed. Jestocost felt his nerves go on edge. No human being could have memorized these thousands of patterns as they flashed across the Bell too fast for human eyes, but the brain reading the Bell through his eyes was not human. It might even be locked into a computer of its own. It was, thought Jestocost, an indignity for a Lord of the Instrumentality to be used as a human spy-glass.

The machine blotted up.

"You're a fraud," cried the Lord Issan. "There's no evidence."

"Maybe the offworlder tried," said the Lady Johanna.

"Shadow him," said Lord William. "If he would steal ancient coins he would steal anything."

The Lady Johanna turned to C'mell. "You're a silly thing. You have wasted our time and you have kept us from serious inter-world business."

"It *is* inter-world business," wept C'mell. She let her hand slip from Jestocost's shoulder, where it had rested all the time. The body-to-body relay broke and the telepathic link broke with it.

"We should judge that," said Lord Issan.

"You might have been punished," said Lady Johanna.

The Lord Jestocost had said nothing, but there was a glow of happiness in him. If the E-telekeli was half as good as he seemed, the underpeople had a list of checkpoints and escape routes which would make it easier to hide from the capricious sentence of painless death which human authorities meted out.

5

There was singing in the corridors that night.

Underpeople burst into happiness for no visible reason.

C'mell danced a wild cat dance for the next customer who came in from outworld stations, that very evening. When she got home to bed, she knelt before the picture of her father C'mackintosh and thanked the E-telekeli for what Jestocost had done.

But the story became known a few generations later, when the Lord Jestocost had won acclaim for being the champion of the underpeople and when the authorities, still unaware of E-telekeli, accepted the elected representatives of the underpeople as negotiators for better terms of life; and C'mell had died long since.

She had first had a long, good life.

She became a female chef when she was too old to be a girly girl. Her food was famous. Jestocost once visited her. At the end of the meal he had asked, "There's a silly rhyme among the underpeople. No human beings know it except me."

"I don't care about rhymes," she said.

"This is called 'The what-she-did.'"

C'mell blushed all the way down to the neckline of her capacious blouse. She had filled out a lot in middle age. Running the restaurant had helped.

"Oh, that rhyme!" she said. "It's silly."

"It says you were in love with a hominid."

"No," she said. "I wasn't." Her green eyes, as beautiful as ever, stared deeply into his. Jestocost felt uncomfortable. This was getting personal. He liked political relationships; personal things made him uncomfortable.

The light in the room shifted and her cat eyes blazed at him, she looked like the magical fire-haired girl he had known.

"I wasn't in love. You couldn't call it that. . . ."

Her heart cried out, *It was you, it was you, it was you.*

"But the rhyme," insisted Jestocost, "says it was a hominid. It wasn't that Prins van de Schemering?"

"Who was he?" C'mell asked the question quietly, but her emotions cried out, *Darling, will you never, never know?*

"The strong man."

"Oh, him. I've forgotten him."

Jestocost rose from the table. "You've had a good life, C'mell. You've been a citizen, a committeewoman, a leader. And do you even know how many children you have had?"

"Seventy-three," she snapped at him. "Just because they're multiple doesn't mean we don't know them."

His playfulness left him. His face was grave, his voice kindly. "I meant no harm, C'mell."

He never knew that when he left she went back to the kitchen and cried for a while. It was Jestocost whom she had vainly loved ever since they had been comrades, many long years ago.

Even after she died, at the full age of five-score and three, he kept seeing her about the corridors and shafts of Earthport. Many of her great-granddaughters looked just like her and several of them practiced the girly-girl business with huge success.

They were not half-slaves. They were citizens (reserved grade) and they had photopasses which protected their property, their identity and their rights. Jestocost was the godfather to them all; he was often embarrassed when the most voluptuous creatures in the universe threw playful kisses at him. All he asked was fulfillment of his political passions, not his personal ones. He had always been in love, madly in love—

With justice itself.

At last, his own time came, and he knew that he was dying, and he was not sorry. He had had a wife, hundreds of years ago, and had loved her well; their children had passed into the generations of man.

In the ending, he wanted to know something, and he called to a nameless one (or to his successor) far beneath the ground. He called with his mind till it was a scream.

I have helped your people.

"Yes," came back the faintest of faraway whispers, inside his head.

I am dying. I must know. Did she love me?

"She went on without you, so much did she love you. She let you go, for your sake, not for hers. She really loved you. More than death. More than life. More than time. You will never be apart."

Never apart?

"No, not in the memory of man," said the voice, and was then still.

Jestocost lay back on his pillow and waited for the day to end.

BABY IS THREE
by *Theodore Sturgeon*

I finally got in to see this Stern. He wasn't an old man at all. He looked up from his desk, flicked his eyes over me once, and picked up a pencil. "Sit over there, Sonny."

I stood where I was until he looked up again. Then I said, "Look, if a midget walks in here, what do you say—sit over there, Shorty?"

He put the pencil down again and stood up. He smiled. His smile was as quick and sharp as his eyes. "I was wrong," he said, "but how am I supposed to know you don't want to be called Sonny?"

That was better, but I was still mad. "I'm fifteen and I don't have to like it. Don't rub my nose in it."

He smiled again and said okay, and I went and sat down.

"What's your name?"

"Gerard."

"First or last?"

"Both," I said.

"Is that the truth?"

I said, "No. And don't ask me where I live either."

He put down his pencil. "We're not going to get very far this way."

"That's up to you. What are you worried about? I got feelings of hostility? Well, sure I have. I got lots more things than that wrong with me or I wouldn't be here. Are you going to let that stop you?"

"Well, no, but—"

"So what else is bothering you? How you're going to get paid?" I took out a thousand-dollar bill and laid it on the desk. "That's so you won't have to bill me. *You* keep track of it. Tell me when it's used up and I'll give you more. So you don't need my address. Wait," I said, when he reached toward the money. "Let it lay there. I want to be sure you and I are going to get along."

He folded his hands. "I don't do business this way, Son—I mean, Gerard."

"Gerry," I told him. "You do, if you do business with me."

"You make things difficult, don't you? Where did you get a thousand dollars?"

"I won a contest. Twenty-five words or less about how much fun it is to do my daintier underthings with Sudso." I leaned forward. "This time it's the truth."

"All right," he said.

I was surprised. I think he knew it, but he didn't say anything more. Just waited for me to go ahead.

"Before we start—if we start," I said, "I got to know something. The things I say to you—what comes out while you're working on me —is that just between us, like a priest or a lawyer?"

"Absolutely," he said.

"No matter what?"

"No matter what."

I watched him when he said it. I believed him.

"Pick up your money," I said. "You're on."

He didn't do it. He said, "As you remarked a minute ago, that is up to me. You can't buy these treatments like a candy bar. We have to work together. If either one of us can't do that, it's useless. You can't walk in on the first psychotherapist you find in the phone book and make any demand that occurs to you just because you can pay for it."

I said tiredly, "I didn't get you out of the phone book and I'm not just guessing that you can help me. I winnowed through a dozen or more head-shrinkers before I decided on you."

"Thanks," he said, and it looked as if he was going to laugh at me, which I never like. "Winnowed, did you say? Just how?"

"Things you hear, things you read. You know. I'm not saying, so just file that with my street address."

He looked at me for a long time. It was the first time he'd used those eyes on me for anything but a flash glance. Then he picked up the bill.

"What do I do first?" I demanded.

"What do you mean?"

"How do we start?"

"We started when you walked in here."

So then I had to laugh. "All right, you got me. All I had was an opening. I didn't know where you would go from there, so I couldn't be there ahead of you."

"That's very interesting," Stern said. "Do you usually figure everything out in advance?"

"Always."

"How often are you right?"

"All the time. Except—but I don't have to tell you about no exceptions."

He really grinned this time. "I see. One of my patients has been talking."

"One of your ex-patients. Your patients don't talk."

"I ask them not to. That applies to you, too. What did you hear?"

"That you know from what people say and do what they're about to say and do, and that sometimes you let'm do it and sometimes you don't. How did you learn to do that?"

He thought a minute. "I guess I was born with an eye for details, and then let myself make enough mistakes with enough people until I learned not to make too many more. How did you learn to do it?"

I said, "You answer that and I won't have to come back here."

"You really don't know?"

"I wish I did. Look, this isn't getting us anywhere, is it?"

He shrugged. "Depends on where you want to go." He paused, and I got the eyes full strength again. "Which thumbnail description of psychiatry do you believe at the moment?"

"I don't get you."

Stern slid open a desk drawer and took out a blackened pipe. He smelled it, turned it over while looking at me. "Psychiatry attacks the onion of the self, removing layer after layer until it gets down to the little sliver of unsullied ego. Or: psychiatry drills like an oil well, down and sidewise and down again, through all the muck and rock, until it strikes a layer that yields. Or: psychiatry grabs a handful of sexual motivations and throws them on the pinball-machine of your life, so they bounce on down against episodes. Want more?"

I had to laugh. "That last one was pretty good."

"That last one was pretty bad. They are all bad. They all try to simplify something which is complex by its very nature. The only thumbnail you'll get from me is this: no one knows what's really wrong with you but you; no one can find a cure for it but you; no one but you can identify it as a cure; and once you find it, no one but you can do anything about it."

"What are *you* here for?"

"To listen."

"I don't have to pay somebody no day's wage every hour just to listen."

"True. But you're convinced that I listen selectively."

"Am I?" I wondered about it. "I guess I am. Well, don't you?"

"No, but you'll never believe that."

I laughed. He asked me what that was for. I said, "You're not calling me Sonny."

"Not you." He shook his head slowly. He was watching me while he did it, so his eyes slid in their sockets as his head moved. "What is it you want to know about yourself, that made you worried I might tell people?"

"I want to find out why I killed somebody," I said right away.

It didn't faze him a bit. "Lie down over there."

I got up. "On that couch?"

He nodded.

As I stretched out self-consciously, I said, "I feel like I'm in some damn cartoon."

"What cartoon?"

"Guy's built like a bunch of grapes," I said, looking at the ceiling. It was pale gray.

"What's the caption?"

" 'I got trunks full of 'em.' "

"Very good," he said quietly.

I looked at him carefully. I knew then he was the kind of guy who laughs way down deep when he laughs at all.

He said, "I'll use that in a book of case histories some time. But it won't include yours. What made you throw that in?" When I didn't answer, he got up and moved to a chair behind me where I couldn't see him. "You can quit testing, Sonny. I'm good enough for your purposes."

I clenched my jaws so hard, my back teeth hurt. Then I relaxed. I relaxed all over. It was wonderful. "All right," I said, "I'm sorry." He didn't say anything, but I had that feeling again that he was laughing. Not at me, though.

"How old are you?" he asked me suddenly.

"Uh—fifteen."

"Uh—fifteen," he repeated. "What does the 'uh' mean?"

"Nothing. I'm fifteen."

"When I asked your age, you hesitated because some other number popped up. You discarded that and substituted 'fifteen.'"

"The hell I did! I *am* fifteen!"

"I didn't say you weren't." His voice came patiently. "Now what was the other number?"

I got mad again. "There wasn't any other number! What do you want to go pryin' my grunts apart for, trying to plant this and that and make it mean what you think it ought to mean?"

He was silent.

"I'm fifteen," I said defiantly, and then, "I don't like being only fifteen. You know that. I'm not trying to insist I'm fifteen."

He just waited, still not saying anything.

I felt defeated. "The number was eight."

"So you're eight. And your name?"

"Gerry." I got up on one elbow, twisting my neck around so I could see him. He had his pipe apart and was sighting through the stem at the desk lamp. "Gerry, without no 'uh!'"

"All right," he said mildly, making me feel real foolish.

I leaned back and closed my eyes.

Eight, I thought. Eight.

"It's cold in here," I complained.

Eight. Eight, plate, state, hate. I ate from the plate of the state and I hate. I didn't like any of that and I snapped my eyes open. The ceiling was still gray. It was all right. Stern was somewhere behind me with his pipe, and he was all right. I took two deep breaths, three, and then let my eyes close. Eight. Eight years old. Eight, hate. Years, fears. Old, cold. *Damn* it! I twisted and twitched on the couch, trying to find a way to keep the cold out. I ate from the plate of the—

I grunted and with my mind I took all the eights and all the rhymes and everything they stood for, and made it all black. But it wouldn't stay black. I had to put something there, so I made a great big luminous figure eight and just let it hang there. But it turned on its side and inside the loops it began to shimmer. It was like one of those movie shots through binoculars. I was going to have to look through whether I liked it or not.

Suddenly I quit fighting it and let it wash over me. The binoculars came close, closer, and then I was there.

Eight. Eight years old, cold. Cold as a bitch in the ditch. The ditch was by a railroad. Last year's weeds were scratchy straw. The ground was red, and when it wasn't slippery, clingy mud, it was frozen hard like a flowerpot. It was hard like that now, dusted with hoar-frost, cold as the winter light that pushed up over the hills. At night the lights were warm, and they were all in other people's houses. In the daytime the sun was in somebody else's house too, for all the good it did me.

I was dying in that ditch. Last night it was as good a place as any to sleep, and this morning it was as good a place as any to die. Just as well. Eight years old, the sick-sweet taste of porkfat and wet bread from somebody's garbage, the thrill of terror when you're stealing a gunnysack and you hear a footstep.

And I heard a footstep.

I'd been curled up on my side. I whipped over on my stomach because sometimes they kick your belly. I covered my head with my arms and that was as far as I could get.

After a while I rolled my eyes up and looked without moving. There was a big shoe there. There was an ankle in the shoe, and another shoe close by. I lay there waiting to get tromped. Not that I cared much any more, but it was such a damn shame. All these months on my own, and they'd never caught up with me, never even come close, and now this. It was such a shame I started to cry.

The shoe took me under the armpit, but it was not a kick. It rolled me over. I was so stiff from the cold, I went over like a plank. I just kept my arms over my face and head and lay there with my eyes closed. For some reason I stopped crying. I think people only cry when there's a chance of getting help from somewhere.

When nothing happened, I opened my eyes and shifted my forearms a little so I could see up. There was a man standing over me and he was a mile high. He had on faded dungarees and an old Eisenhower jacket with deep sweat-stains under the arms. His face was shaggy, like the guys who can't grow what you could call a beard, but still don't shave.

He said, "Get up."

I looked down at his shoe, but he wasn't going to kick me. I pushed up a little and almost fell down again, except he put his big hand where my back would hit it. I lay against it for a second because I had to, and then got up to where I had one knee on the ground.

"Come on," he said. "Let's go."

I swear I felt my bones creak, but I made it. I brought a round white stone up with me as I stood. I hefted the stone. I had to look at it to see if I was really holding it, my fingers were that cold. I told him, "Stay away from me or I'll bust you in the teeth with this rock."

His hand came out and down so fast, I never saw the way he got one finger between my palm and the rock, and flicked it out of my grasp. I started to cuss at him, but he just turned his back and walked up the embankment toward the tracks. He put his chin on his shoulder and said, "Come on, will you?"

He didn't chase me, so I didn't run. He didn't talk to me, so I didn't argue. He didn't hit me, so I didn't get mad. I went along after him. He waited for me. He put out his hand to me and I spit at it. So he went on, up to the tracks, out of my sight. I clawed my way up. The blood was beginning to move in my hands and feet and they felt like four point-down porcupines. When I got up to the roadbed, the man was standing there waiting for me.

The track was level just there, but as I turned my head to look along it, it seemed to be a hill that was steeper and steeper and turned over above me. And next thing you know, I was lying flat on my back looking up at the cold sky.

The man came over and sat down on the rail near me. He didn't try to touch me. I gasped for breath a couple of times, and suddenly felt I'd be all right if I could sleep for a minute—just a little minute. I closed my eyes. The man stuck his finger in my ribs, hard. It hurt.

"Don't sleep," he said.

I looked at him.

He said, "You're frozen stiff and weak with hunger. I want to take you home and get you warmed up and fed. But it's a long haul up that way, and you won't make it by yourself. If I carry you, will that be the same to you as if you walked it?"

"What are you going to do when you get me home?"

"I told you."

"All right," I said.

He picked me up and carried me down the track. If he'd said anything else in the world, I'd of laid right down where I was until I froze to death. Anyway, what did he want to ask me for, one way or the other? I couldn't of done anything.

I stopped thinking about it and dozed off.

I woke up once when he turned off the right of way. He dove into the woods. There was no path, but he seemed to know where he was going. The next time I woke from a crackling noise. He was carrying me over a frozen pond and the ice was giving under his feet. He didn't hurry. I looked down and saw the white cracks raying out under his feet, and it didn't seem to matter a bit. I bleared off again.

He put me down at last. We were there. "There" was inside a room. It was very warm. He put me on my feet and I snapped out of it in a hurry. The first thing I looked for was the door. I saw it and jumped over there and put my back against the wall beside it, in case I wanted to leave. Then I looked around.

It was a big room. One wall was rough rock and the rest was logs with stuff shoved between them. There was a big fire going in the rock wall, not in a fireplace, exactly; it was a sort of hollow place. There was an old auto battery on a shelf opposite, with two yellowing electric light bulbs dangling by wires from it. There was a table, some boxes and a couple of three-legged stools. The air had a haze of smoke and such a wonderful, heartbreaking, candy-and-crackling smell of food that a little hose squirted inside my mouth.

The man said, "What have I got here, Baby?"

And the room was full of kids. Well, three of them, but somehow they seemed to be more than three kids. There was a girl about my age—eight, I mean—with blue paint on the side of her face. She had an easel and a palette with lots of paints and a fistful of brushes, but she wasn't using the brushes. She was smearing the paint on with her hands. Then there was a little Negro girl about five with great big eyes who stood gaping at me. And in a wooden crate, set up on two saw-horses to make a kind of bassinet, was a baby. I guess about three or four months old. It did what babies do, drooling some, making small bubbles, waving its hands around very aimless, and kicking.

When the man spoke, the girl at the easel looked at me and then at the baby. The baby just kicked and drooled.

The girl said, "His name's Gerry. He's mad."

"What's he mad at?" the man asked. He was looking at the baby.

"Everything," said the girl. "Everything and everybody."

"Where'd he come from?"

I said, "Hey, what is this?" but nobody paid any attention. The man kept asking questions at the baby and the girl kept answering. Craziest thing I ever saw.

"He ran away from a state school," the girl said. "They fed him enough, but no one bleshed with him."

That's what she said—"bleshed."

I opened the door then and cold air hooted in. "You louse," I said to the man, "you're from the school."

"Close the door, Janie," said the man. The girl at the easel didn't move, but the door banged shut behind me. I tried to open it and it wouldn't move. I let out a howl, yanking at it.

"I think you ought to stand in the corner," said the man. "Stand him in the corner, Janie."

Janie looked at me. One of the three-legged stools sailed across to me. It hung in midair and turned on its side. It nudged me with its flat seat. I jumped back and it came after me. I dodged to the side, and that was the corner. The stool came on. I tried to bat it down and just hurt my hand. I ducked and it went lower than I did. I put one hand on it and tried to vault over it, but it just fell and so did I. I got up again and stood in the corner, trembling. The stool turned right side up and sank to the floor in front of me.

The man said, "Thank you, Janie." He turned to me. "Stand there and be quiet, you. I'll get to you later. You shouldn'ta kicked up all that fuss." And then, to the baby, he said, "He got anything we need?"

And again it was the little girl who answered. She said, "Sure. He's the one."

"Well," said the man. "What do you know!" He came over. "Gerry, you can live here. I don't come from the school. I'll never turn you in."

"Yeah, huh?"

"He hates you," said Janie.

"What am I supposed to do about that?" he wanted to know.

Janie turned her head to look into the bassinet. "Feed him." The man nodded and began fiddling around the fire.

Meanwhile, the little Negro girl had been standing in the one spot with her big eyes right out on her cheekbones, looking at me. Janie went back to her painting and the baby just lay there same as always, so I stared back at the little Negro girl. I snapped, "What the devil are you gawking at?"

She grinned at me. "Gerry ho-ho," she said, and disappeared. I mean she really disappeared, went out like a light, leaving her clothes where she had been. Her little dress billowed in the air and fell in a heap where she had been, and that was that. She was gone.

"Gerry hee-hee," I heard. I looked up, and there she was, stark naked, wedged in a space where a little outcropping on the rock wall stuck out just below the ceiling. The second I saw her she disappeared again.

"Gerry ho-ho," she said. Now she was on top of the row of boxes they used as storage shelves, over on the other side of the room.

"Gerry hee-hee!" Now she was under the table. "Gerry ho-ho!" This time she was right in the corner with me, crowding me.

I yelped and tried to get out of the way and bumped the stool. I was afraid of it, so I shrank back again and the little girl was gone.

The man glanced over his shoulder from where he was working at the fire. "Cut it out, you kids," he said.

There was a silence, and then the girl came slowly out from the bottom row of shelves. She walked across to her dress and put it on.

"How did you do that?" I wanted to know.

"Ho-ho," she said.

Janie said, "It's easy. She's really twins."

"Oh," I said. Then another girl, exactly the same, came from somewhere in the shadows and stood beside the first. They were identical. They stood side by side and stared at me. This time I let them stare.

"That's Bonnie and Beanie," said the painter. "This is Baby and that—" she indicated the man—"that's Lone. And I'm Janie."

I couldn't think of what to say, so I said, "Yeah."

Lone said, "Water, Janie." He held up a pot. I heard water trickling, but didn't see anything. "That's enough," he said, and hung the pot on a crane. He picked up a cracked china plate and brought it over to me. It was full of stew with great big lumps of meat in it, and thick gravy and dumplings and carrots. "Here, Gerry. Sit down."

I looked at the stool. "On that?"

"Sure."

"Not me," I said. I took the plate and hunkered down against the wall.

"Hey," he said after a time. "Take it easy. We've all had chow. No one's going to snatch it away from you. Slow down!"

I ate even faster than before. I was almost finished when I threw it all up. Then for some reason my head hit the edge of the stool. I dropped the plate and spoon and slumped there. I felt real bad.

Lone came over and looked at me. "Sorry, kid," he said. "Clean up, will you, Janie?"

Right in front of my eyes, the mess on the floor disappeared. I didn't care about that or anything else just then. I felt the man's hand on the side of my neck. Then he tousled my hair.

"Beanie, get him a blanket. Let's all go to sleep. He ought to rest a while."

I felt the blanket go around me, and I think I was asleep before he put me down.

I don't know how much later it was when I woke up. I didn't know where I was and that scared me. I raised my head and saw the dull glow of the embers in the fireplace. Lone was stretched out on it in his clothes. Janie's easel stood in the reddish blackness like some great preying insect. I saw the baby's head pop up out of the bassinet, but I couldn't tell whether he was looking straight at me or away. Janie was lying on the floor near the door and the twins were on the old table. Nothing moved except the baby's head, bobbing a little.

I got to my feet and looked around the room. Just a room, only the one door. I tiptoed toward it. When I passed Janie, she opened her eyes.

"What's the matter?" she whispered.

"None of your business," I told her. I went to the door as if I didn't care, but I watched her. She didn't do anything. The door was as solid tight closed as when I'd tried it before.

I went back to Janie. She just looked up at me. She wasn't scared. I told her, "I got to go to the john."

"Oh," she said. "Why'n't you say so?"

Suddenly I grunted and grabbed my guts. The feeling I had I can't begin to talk about. I acted as if it was a pain, but it wasn't. It was like nothing else that ever happened to me before.

"Okay," Janie said. "Go on back to bed."

"But I got to—"

"You got to what?"

"Nothing." It was true. I didn't have to go no place.

"Next time tell me right away. I don't mind."

I didn't say anything. I went back to my blanket.

"That's all?" said Stern. I lay on the couch and looked up at the gray ceiling. He asked, "How old are you?"

"Fifteen," I said dreamily. He waited until, for me, the gray ceiling acquired walls and a floor, a rug and lamps and a desk and a chair with Stern in it. I sat up and held my head a second, and then I looked at him. He was fooling with his pipe and looking at me. "What did you do to me?"

"I told you. I don't do anything here. You do it."

"You hypnotized me."

"I did not." His voice was quiet, but he really meant it.

"What was all that, then? It was . . . it was like it was happening for real all over again."

"Feel anything?"

"Everything." I shuddered. "*Every* damn thing. What was it?"

"Anyone doing it feels better afterward. You can go over it all again now any time you want to, and every time you do, the hurt in it will be less. You'll see."

It was the first thing to amaze me in years. I chewed on it and then asked, "If I did it by myself, how come it never happened before?"

"It needs someone to listen."

"Listen? Was I talking?"

"A blue streak."

"Everything that happened?"

"How can I know? I wasn't there. You were."

"You don't believe it happened, do you? Those disappearing kids and the footstool and all?"

He shrugged. "I'm not in the business of believing or not believing. Was it real to you?"

"Oh, hell, yes!"

"Well, then, that's all that matters. Is that where you live, with those people?"

I bit off a fingernail that had been bothering me. "Not for a long time. Not since Baby was three." I looked at him. "You remind me of Lone."

"Why?"

"I don't know. No, you don't," I added suddenly. "I don't know what made me say that." I lay down abruptly.

The ceiling was gray and the lamps were dim. I heard the pipestem click against his teeth. I lay there for a long time.

"Nothing happens," I told him.

"What did you expect to happen?"

"Like before."

"There's something there that wants out. Just let it come."

It was as if there was a revolving drum in my head, and on it were photographed the places and things and people I was after. And it was as if the drum was spinning very fast, so fast I couldn't tell one picture from another. I made it stop, and it stopped at a blank segment. I spun it again, and stopped it again.

"Nothing happens," I said.

"Baby is three," he repeated.

"Oh," I said. "That." I closed my eyes.

That might be it. Might, sight, night, light. I might have the sight of a light in the night. Maybe the baby. Maybe the sight of the baby at night because of the light . . .

There was night after night when I lay on that blanket, and a lot of nights I didn't. Something was going on all the time in Lone's house. Sometimes I slept in the daytime. I guess the only time everybody slept at once was when someone was sick, like me the first time I arrived there. It was always sort of dark in the room, the same night and day, the fire going, the two old bulbs *hanging* yellow by their wires from the battery. When they got too dim, Janie fixed the battery and they got bright again.

Janie did everything that needed doing, whatever no one else felt like doing. Everybody else did things, too. Lone was out a lot. Sometimes he used the twins to help him, but you never missed them, because they'd be here and gone and back again *bing!* like that. And Baby, he just stayed in his bassinet.

I did things myself. I cut wood for the fire and I put up more shelves, and then I'd go swimming with Janie and the twins sometimes. And I talked to Lone. I didn't do a thing that the others couldn't do, but they all did things I couldn't do. I was mad, mad all the time about that. But I wouldn't of known what to do with myself if I wasn't mad all the time about something or other. It didn't keep us from bleshing. Bleshing, that was Janie's word. She said Baby told it to her. She said it meant everyone all together being something, even if they all did different things. Two arms, two legs, one body, one head, all working together, although a head can't walk and arms can't think. Lone said maybe it was a mixture of "blending" and "meshing," but I don't think he believed that himself. It was a lot more than that.

Baby talked all the time. He was like a broadcasting station that runs twenty-four hours a day, and you can get what it's sending any time you tune in, but it'll keep sending whether you tune in or not. When I say he talked, I don't mean exactly that. He semaphored mostly. You'd think those wandering, vague movements of his hands and arms and legs and head were meaningless, but they weren't. It was semaphore, only instead of a symbol for a sound, or such like, the movements were whole thoughts.

I mean spread the left hand and shake the right high up, and thump with the left heel, and it means, "Anyone who thinks a starling is a pest just don't know anything about how a starling thinks" or something like that.

Lone couldn't read the stuff and neither could I. The twins could, but they didn't give a damn. Janie used to watch him all the time. He always knew what you meant if you wanted to ask him something, and he'd tell Janie and she'd say what it was. Part of it, anyway. Nobody could get it all, not even Janie. Lone once told me that all babies know that semaphore. But when nobody receives it, they quit doing it and pretty soon they forget. They *almost* forget. There's always some left. That's why certain gestures are funny the world over, and certain others make you mad. But like everything else Lone said, I don't know whether he believed it or not.

All I know is Janie would sit there and paint her pictures and watch Baby, and sometimes she'd bust out laughing, and sometimes she'd get the twins and make them watch and they'd laugh, too, or they'd wait till he was finished what he was saying and then they'd creep off to a corner and whisper to each other about it. Baby never grew any. Janie did, and the twins, and so did I, but not Baby. He just lay there.

Janie kept his stomach full and cleaned him up every two or three days. He didn't cry and he didn't make any trouble. No one ever went near him.

Janie showed every picture she painted to Baby, before she cleaned the boards and painted new ones. She had to clean them because she only had three of them. It was a good thing, too, because I'd hate to think what that place would of been like if she'd kept them all; she did four or five a day. Lone and the twins were kept hopping getting turpentine for her. She could shift the paints back into the little pots on her easel without any trouble, just by looking at the picture one color at a time, but turps was something else again. She told me that Baby remembered all her pictures and that's why she didn't have to keep them. They were all pictures of machines and gear-trains and mechanical linkages and what looked like electric circuits and things like that. I never thought too much about them.

I went out with Lone to get some turpentine and a couple of picnic hams, one time. We went through the woods to the railroad track and down a couple of miles to where we could see the glow of a town. Then the woods again, and some alleys, and a back street.

Lone was like always, walking along, thinking, thinking.

We came to a hardware store and he went up and looked at the lock and came back to where I was waiting, shaking his head. Then we found a general store. Lone grunted and we went and stood in the shadows by the door. I looked in.

All of a sudden, Beanie was in there, naked like she always was when she traveled like that. She came and opened the door from the inside. We went in and Lone closed it and locked it.

"Get along home, Beanie," he said, "before you catch your death."

She grinned at me and said, "Ho-ho," and disappeared.

We found a pair of fine hams and a two-gallon can of turpentine. I took a bright yellow ballpoint pen and Lone cuffed me and made me put it back.

"We only take what we need," he told me.

After we left, Beanie came back and locked the door and went home again. I only went with Lone a few times, when he had more to get than he could carry easily.

I was there about three years. That's all I can remember about it. Lone was there or he was out, and you could hardly tell the difference. The twins were with each other most of the time. I got to like Janie a lot, but we never talked much. Baby talked all the time, only I don't know what about.

We were all busy and we bleshed.

I sat up on the couch suddenly.

Stern said, "What's the matter?"

"Nothing's the matter. This isn't getting me any place."

"You said that when you'd barely started. Do you think you've accomplished anything since then?"

"Oh, yeah, but—"

"Then how can you be sure you're right this time?" When I didn't say anything, he asked me, "Didn't you like this last stretch?"

I said angrily, "I didn't like or not like. It didn't mean nothing. It was just—just talk."

"So what was the difference between this last session and what happened before?"

"My gosh, plenty! The first one, I felt everything. It was all really happening to me. But this time—nothing."

"Why do you suppose that was?"

"I don't know. You tell me."

"Suppose," he said thoughtfully, "that there was some episode so unpleasant to you that you wouldn't dare relive it."

"Unpleasant? You think freezing to death isn't unpleasant?"

"There are all kinds of unpleasantness. Sometimes the very thing you're looking for—the thing that'll clear up your trouble—is so revolting to you that you won't go near it. Or you try to hide it. Wait," he said suddenly, "maybe 'revolting' and 'unpleasant' are inaccurate words to use. It might be something very desirable to you. It's just that you don't want to get straightened out."

"I *want* to get straightened out."

He waited as if he had to clear something up in his mind, and then said, "There's something in that 'Baby is three' phrase that bounces you away. Why is that?"

"Damn if I know."

"Who said it?"

"I dunno . . . uh . . ."

He grinned. "Uh?"

I grinned back at him. "I said it."

"Okay. When?"

I quit grinning. He leaned forward, then got up.

"What's the matter?" I asked.

"I didn't think anyone could be that mad." I didn't say anything. He went over to his desk. "You don't want to go on any more, do you?"

"No."

"Suppose I told you you want to quit because you're right on the very edge of finding out what you want to know?"

"Why don't you tell me and see what I do?"

He just shook his head. "I'm not telling you anything. Go on, leave if you want to. I'll give you back your change."

"How many people quit just when they're on top of the answer?"

"Quite a few."

"Well, I ain't going to." I lay down.

He didn't laugh and he didn't say, "Good," and he didn't make any fuss about it. He just picked up his phone and said, "Cancel everything for this afternoon," and went back to his chair, up there out of my sight.

It was very quiet in there. He had the place soundproofed.

I said, "Why do you suppose Lone let me live there so long when I couldn't do any of the things that the other kids could?"

"Maybe you could."

"Oh, no," I said positively. "I used to try. I was strong for a kid my age and I knew how to keep my mouth shut, but aside from those two things I don't think I was any different from any kid. I don't think I'm any different right now, except what difference there might be from living with Lone and his bunch."

"Has this anything to do with 'Baby is three'?"

I looked up at the gray ceiling. "Baby is three. Baby is three. I went up to a big house with a winding drive that ran under a sort of theater-marquee thing. Baby is three. Baby . . ."

"How old are you?"

"Thirty-three," I said, and the next thing you know I was up off that couch like it was hot, and heading for the door.

"Don't be foolish," Stern said. "Want me to waste a whole afternoon?"

"What's that to me? I'm paying for it."

"All right, it's up to you."

I went back. "I don't like any part of this," I said.

"Good. We're getting warm then."

"What made me say 'Thirty-three'? I ain't thirty-three. I'm fifteen. And another thing . . ."

"Yes?"

"It's about that 'Baby is three.' It's me saying it, all right. But when I think about it—it's not my voice."

"Like thirty-three's not your age?"

"Yeah," I whispered.

"Gerry," he said warmly, "there's nothing to be afraid of."

I realized I was breathing too hard. I pulled myself together. I said, "I don't like remembering saying things in somebody else's voice."

"Look," he told me. "This head-shrinking business, as you called it a while back, isn't what most people think. When I go with you into the world of your mind—or when you go yourself, for that matter—what we find isn't so very different from the so-called real world. It seems so at first, because the patient comes out with all sorts of fantasies and irrationalities and weird experiences. But everyone lives in that kind of world. When one of the ancients coined the phrase 'truth is stranger than fiction,' he was talking about that.

"Everywhere we go, everything we do, we're surrounded by symbols, by things so familiar we don't ever look at them or don't see them if we do look. If anyone ever could report to you exactly what he saw and thought while walking ten feet down the street, you'd get the most twisted, clouded, partial picture you ever ran across. And nobody ever looks at what's around him with any kind of attention until he gets into a place like this. The fact that he's looking at past events doesn't matter; what counts is that he's seeing clearer than he ever could before, just because, for once, he's trying.

"Now—about this 'thirty-three' business. I don't think a man could get a nastier shock than to find he has someone else's memories. The ego is too important to let slide that way. But consider: all your thinking is done in code and you have the key to only about a tenth of it. So you run into a stretch of code which is abhorrent to you. Can't you see that the only way you'll find the key to it is to stop avoiding it?"

"You mean I'd started to remember with . . . with somebody else's mind?"

"It looked like that to you for a while, which means something. Let's try to find out what."

"All right." I felt sick. I felt tired. And I suddenly realized that being sick and being tired was a way of trying to get out of it.

"Baby is three," he said.

Baby is maybe. Me, three, thirty-three, me, you Kew you.

"Kew!" I yelled. Stern didn't say anything. "Look, I don't know why, but I think I know how to get to this, and this isn't the way. Do you mind if I try something else?"

"You're the doctor," he said.

I had to laugh. Then I closed my eyes.

There, through the edges of the hedges, the ledges and wedges of windows were shouldering up to the sky. The lawns were sprayed-on green, neat and clean, and all the flowers looked as if they were afraid to let their petals break and be untidy.

I walked up the drive in my shoes. I'd had to wear shoes and my feet couldn't breathe. I didn't want to go to the house, but I had to.

I went up the steps between the big white columns and looked at the door. I wished I could see through it, but it was too white and thick. There was a window the shape of a fan over it, too high up, though, and a window on each side of it, but they were all crudded up with colored glass. I hit on the door with my hand and left dirt on it.

Nothing happened, so I hit it again. It got snatched open and a tall, thin colored woman stood there. "What you want?"

I said I had to see Miss Kew.

"Well, Miss Kew don't want to see the likes of you," she said. She talked too loud. "You got a dirty face."

I started to get mad then. I was already pretty sore about having to come here, walking around near people in the daytime and all. I said, "My face ain't got nothin' to do with it. Where's Miss Kew? Go on, find her for me."

She gasped. "You can't speak to me like that!"

I said, "I didn't want to speak to you like any way. Let me in." I started wishing for Janie. Janie could of moved her. But I had to handle it by myself. I wasn't doing so hot, either. She slammed the door before I could so much as curse at her.

So I started kicking on the door. For that, shoes are great. After a while, she snatched the door open again so sudden I almost went on my can. She had a broom with her. She screamed at me, "You get away from here, you trash, or I'll call the police!" She pushed me and I fell.

I got up off the porch floor and went for her. She stepped back and whupped me one with the broom as I went past, but anyhow I was inside now. The woman was making little shrieking noises and coming for me. I took the broom away from her and then somebody said, "Miriam!" in a voice like a grown goose.

I froze and the woman went into hysterics. "Oh, Miss Kew, look out! He'll kill us all. Get the police. Get the—"

"Miriam!" came the honk, and Miriam dried up.

There at the top of the stairs was this prune-faced woman with a dress on that had lace on it. She looked a lot older than she was, maybe because she held her mouth so tight. I guess she was about thirty-three—*thirty-three*. She had mean eyes and a small nose.

I asked, "Are you Miss Kew?"

"I am. What is the meaning of this invasion?"

"I got to talk to you, Miss Kew."

"Don't say 'got to.' Stand up straight and speak out."

The maid said, "I'll get the police."

Miss Kew turned on her. "There's time enough for that, Miriam. Now, you dirty little boy, what do you want?"

"I got to speak to you by yourself," I told her.

"Don't you let him do it, Miss Kew," cried the maid.

"Be quiet, Miriam. Little boy, I told you not to say 'got to.' You may say whatever you have to say in front of Miriam."

"Like hell." They both gasped. I said, "Lone told me not to."

"Miss Kew, are you goin' to let him—"

"Be quiet, Miriam! Young man, you will keep a civil—" Then her eyes popped up real round. *"Who* did you say . . ."

"Lone said so."

"Lone." She stood there on the stairs looking at her hands. Then she said, "Miriam, that will be all." And you wouldn't know it was the same woman, the way she said it.

The maid opened her mouth, but Miss Kew stuck out a finger that might as well of had a riflesight on the end of it. The maid beat it.

"Hey," I said, "here's your broom." I was just going to throw it, but Miss Kew got to me and took it out of my hand.

"In there," she said.

She made me go ahead of her into a room as big as our swimming hole. It had books all over and leather on top of the tables, with gold flowers drawn into the corners.

She pointed to a chair. "Sit there. No, wait a moment." She went to the fireplace and got a newspaper out of a box and brought it over and unfolded it on the seat of the chair. "Now sit down."

I sat on the paper and she dragged up another chair, but didn't put no paper on it.

"What is it? Where is Lone?"

"He died," I said.

She pulled in her breath and went white. She stared at me until her eyes started to water.

"You sick?" I asked her. "Go ahead, throw up. It'll make you feel better."

"Dead? Lone is dead?"

"Yeah. There was a flash flood last week and when he went out the next night in that big wind, he walked under a old oak tree that got gullied under by the flood. The tree come down on him."

"Came down on him," she whispered. "Oh, no . . . it's not true."

"It's true, all right. We planted him this morning. We couldn't keep him around no more. He was beginning to st—"

"Stop!" She covered her face with her hands.

"What's the matter?"

"I'll be all right in a moment," she said in a low voice. She went and stood in front of the fireplace with her back to me. I took off one of my shoes while I was waiting for her to come back. But instead she talked from where she was. "Are you Lone's little boy?"

"Yeah. He told me to come to you."

"Oh, my dear child!" She came running back and I thought for a second she was going to pick me up or something, but she stopped short and wrinkled up her nose a little bit. "Wh-what's your name?"

"Gerry," I told her.

"Well, Gerry, how would you like to live with me in this nice big house and—and have new clean clothes—and everything?"

"Well, that's the whole idea. Lone told me to come to you. He said you got more dough than you know what to do with, and he said you owed him a favor."

"A favor?" That seemed to bother her.

"Well," I tried to tell her, "he said he done something for you once and you said some day you'd pay him back for it if you ever could. This is it."

"What did he tell you about that?" She'd got her honk back by then.

"Not a damn thing."

"Please don't use that word," she said, with her eyes closed. Then she opened them and nodded her head. "I promised and I'll do it. You can live here from now on. If—if you want to."

"That's got nothin' to do with it. Lone *told* me to."

"You'll be happy here," she said. She gave me an up-and-down. "I'll see to that."

"Okay. Shall I go get the other kids?"

"*Other* kids—children?"

"Yeah. This ain't for just me. For all of us—the whole gang."

"Don't say 'ain't.'" She leaned back in her chair, took out a silly little handkerchief and dabbed her lips with it, looking at me the whole time. "Now tell me about these—these other children."

"Well, there's Janie, she's eleven like me. And Bonnie and Beanie are eight, they're twins, and Baby. Baby is three."

"Baby is three," she said.

I screamed. Stern was kneeling beside the couch in a flash, holding his palms against my cheeks to hold my head still; I'd been whipping it back and forth.

"Good boy," he said. "You found it. You haven't found out *what* it is, but now you know *where* it is."

"But for sure," I said hoarsely. "Got water?"

He poured me some water out of a thermos flask. It was so cold it hurt. I lay back and rested, like I'd climbed a cliff. I said, "I can't take anything like that again."

"You want to call it quits for today?"

"What about you?"

"I'll go on as long as you want me to."

I thought about it. "I'd like to go on, but I don't want no thumping around. Not for a while yet."

"If you want another of those inaccurate analogies," Stern said, "psychiatry is like a road map. There are always a lot of different ways to get from one place to another place."

"I'll go around by the long way," I told him. "The eight-lane highway. Not that track over the hill. My clutch is slipping. Where do I turn off?"

He chuckled. I liked the sound of it. "Just past that gravel driveway."

"I been there. There's a bridge washed out."

"You've been on this whole road before," he told me. "Start at the other side of the bridge."

"I never thought of that. I figured I had to do the whole thing, every inch."

"Maybe you won't have to, maybe you will, but the bridge will be easy to cross when you've covered everything else. Maybe there's nothing of value on the bridge and maybe there is, but you can't get near it till you've looked everywhere else."

"Let's go." I was real eager, somehow.

"Mind a suggestion?"

"No."

"Just talk," he said. "Don't try to get too far into what you're saying. That first stretch, when you were eight—you really lived it. The second one, all about the kids, you just talked about. Then, the visit when you were eleven, you felt that. Now just talk again."

"All right."

He waited, then said quietly, "In the library. You told her about the other kids."

I told her about . . . and then she said . . . and something happened, and I screamed. She confronted me and I cussed at her.

But we're not thinking about that now. We're going on.

In the library. The leather, the table, and whether I'm able to do with Miss Kew what Lone said.

What Lone said was, "There's a woman lives up on the top of the hill on the Heights section, name of Kew. She'll have to take care of you. You got to get her to do that. Do everything she tells you, only stay together. Don't you ever let any one of you get away from the others, hear? Aside from that, just you keep Miss Kew happy and she'll keep you happy. Now you do what I say." That's what Lone said. Between every word there was a link like steel cable, and the whole thing made something that couldn't be broken. Not by me it couldn't.

Miss Kew said, "Where are your sisters and the baby?"

"I'll bring 'em."

"Is it near here?"

"Near enough." She didn't say anything to that, so I got up. "I'll be back soon."

"Wait," she said. "I—really, I haven't had time to think. I mean—I've got to get things ready, you know."

I said, "You don't need to think and you are ready. So long."

From the door I heard her saying, louder and louder as I walked away, "Young man, if you're to live in this house, you'll learn to be a good deal better mannered—" and a lot more of the same.

I yelled back at her, "Okay, *okay!*" and went out.

The sun was warm and the sky was good, and pretty soon I got back to Lone's house. The fire was out and Baby stunk. Janie had knocked over her easel and was sitting on the floor by the door with her head in her hands. Bonnie and Beanie were on a stool with their arms around each other, pulled up together as close as they could get, as if it was cold in there, although it wasn't.

I hit Janie in the arm to snap her out of it. She raised her head. She had gray eyes—or maybe it was more a kind of green—but now they had a funny look about them, like water in a glass that had some milk left in the bottom of it.

I said, "What's the matter around here?"

"What's the matter with what?" she wanted to know.

"All of yez," I said.

She said, "We don't give a damn, that's all."

"Well, all right," I said, "but we got to do what Lone said. Come on."

"No." I looked at the twins. They turned their backs on me. Janie said, "They're hungry."

"Well, why not give 'em something?"

She just shrugged. I sat down. What did Lone have to go get himself squashed for?

"We can't blesh no more," said Janie. It seemed to explain everything.

"Look," I said, "I've got to be Lone now."

Janie thought about that, and Baby kicked his feet. Janie looked at him. "You can't," she said.

"I know where to get the heavy food and the turpentine," I said. "I can find that springy moss to stuff in the logs, and cut wood, and all."

But I couldn't call Bonnie and Beanie from miles away to unlock doors. I couldn't just say a word to Janie and make her get water and blow up the fire and fix the battery. I couldn't make us blesh.

We all stayed like that for a long time. Then I heard the bassinet creak. I looked up. Janie was staring into it.

"All right," she said. "Let's go."

"Who says so?"

"Baby."

"Who's running things now?" I said, mad. "Me or Baby?"

"Baby," Janie said.

I got up and went over to bust her one in the mouth, and then I stopped. If Baby could make them do what Lone wanted, then it would get done. If I started pushing them all around, it wouldn't. So I didn't say anything. Janie got up and walked out the door. The twins watched her go. Then Bonnie disappeared. Beanie picked up Bonnie's clothes and walked out. I got Baby out of the bassinet and draped him over my shoulders.

It was better when we were all outside. It was getting late in the day and the air was warm. The twins flitted in and out of the trees like a couple of flying squirrels, and Janie and I walked along like we were going swimming or something. Baby started to kick, and Janie looked at him a while and got him fed, and he was quiet again.

When we came close to town, I wanted to get everybody close together, but I was afraid to say anything. Baby must of said it instead. The twins came back to us and Janie gave them their clothes and they walked ahead of us, good as you please. I don't know how Baby did it. They sure hated to travel that way.

We didn't have no trouble except one guy we met on the street near Miss Kew's place. He stopped in his tracks and gaped at us, and Janie looked at him and made his hat go so far down over his eyes that he like to pull his neck apart getting it back up again.

What do you know, when we got to the house somebody had washed off all the dirt I'd put on the door. I had one hand on Baby's arm and one on his ankle and him draped over my neck, so I kicked the door and left some more dirt.

"There's a woman here name of Miriam," I told Janie. "She says anything, tell her to go to hell."

The door opened and there was Miriam. She took one look and jumped back six feet. We all trailed inside. Miriam got her wind and screamed, "Miss Kew! Miss Kew!"

"Go to hell," said Janie, and looked at me. I didn't know what to do. It was the first time Janie ever did anything I told her to.

Miss Kew came down the stairs. She was wearing a different dress, but it was just as stupid and had just as much lace. She opened her mouth and nothing came out, so she just left it open until something happened. Finally she said, "Dear gentle Lord preserve us!"

The twins lined up and gawked at her. Miriam sidled over to the wall and sort of slid along it, keeping away from us, until she could get to the door and close it. She said, "Miss Kew, if those are the children you said were going to live here, I quit."

Janie said, "Go to hell."

Just then, Bonnie squatted down on the rug. Miriam squawked and jumped at her. She grabbed hold of Bonnie's arm and went to snatch her up. Bonnie disappeared, leaving Miriam with one small dress and the damnedest expression on her face. Beanie grinned enough to split her head in two and started to wave like mad. I looked where she was waving, and there was Bonnie, naked as a jaybird, up on the banister at the top of the stairs.

Miss Kew turned around and saw her and sat down plump on the steps. Miriam went down, too, like she'd been slugged. Beanie picked up Bonnie's dress and walked up the steps past Miss Kew and handed it over. Bonnie put it on. Miss Kew sort of lolled around and looked up. Bonnie and Beanie came back down the stairs hand in hand to where I was. Then they lined up and gaped at Miss Kew.

"What's the matter with her?" Janie asked me.

"She gets sick every once in a while."

"Let's go back home."

"No," I told her.

Miss Kew grabbed the banister and pulled herself up. She stood there hanging on to it for a while with her eyes closed. All of a sudden she stiffened herself. She looked about four inches taller. She came marching over to us.

"Gerard," she honked.

I think she was going to say something different. But she sort of checked herself and pointed. "What in heaven's name is *that?*" And she aimed her finger at me.

I didn't get it right away, so I turned around to look behind me. "What?"

"That! That!"

"Oh!" I said. "That's Baby."

I slung him down off my back and held him up for her to look at. She made a sort of moaning noise and jumped over and took him away from me. She held him out in front of her and moaned again and called him a poor little thing, and ran and put him down on a long bench thing with cushions under the colored-glass window. She bent over him and put her knuckle in her mouth and bit on it and moaned some more. Then she turned to me.

"How long has he been like this?"

I looked at Jane and she looked at me. I said, "He's always been like he is."

She made a sort of cough and ran to where Miriam was lying flaked on the floor. She slapped Miriam's face a couple of times back and forth. Miriam sat up and looked us over. She closed her eyes and shivered and sort of climbed up Miss Kew hand over hand until she was on her feet.

"Pull yourself together," said Miss Kew between her teeth. "Get a basin with some hot water and soap. Washcloth. Towels. Hurry!" She gave Miriam a big push. Miriam staggered and grabbed at the wall, and then ran out.

Miss Kew went back to Baby and hung over him, titch-titching with her lips all tight.

"Don't mess with him," I said. "There's nothin' wrong with him. We're hungry."

She gave me a look like I punched her. "Don't speak to me!"

"Look," I said, "we don't like this any more'n you do. If Lone hadn't told us to, we wouldn't never have come. We were doing all right where we were."

"Don't say 'wouldn't never,' " said Miss Kew. She looked at all of us, one by one. Then she took that silly little hunk of handkerchief and pushed it against her mouth.

"See?" I said to Janie. "All the time gettin' sick."

"Ho-ho," said Bonnie.

Miss Kew gave her a long look. "Gerard," she said in a choked sort of voice, "I understood you to say that these children were your sisters."

"Well?"

She looked at me as if I was real stupid. "We don't have little colored girls for sisters, Gerard."

Janie said, "*We* do."

Miss Kew walked up and back, real fast. "We have a great deal to do," she said, talking to herself.

Miriam came in with a big oval pan and towels and stuff on her arm. She put it down on the bench thing and Miss Kew stuck the back of her hand in the water, then picked up Baby and dunked him right in it. Baby started to kick.

I stepped forward and said, "Wait a minute. Hold on now. What do you think you're doing?"

Janie said, "Shut up, Gerry. He says it's all right."

"All right? She'll drown him."

"No, she won't. Just shut up."

Working up a froth with the soap, Miss Kew smeared it on Baby and turned him over a couple of times and scrubbed at his head and like to smothered him in a big white towel. Miriam stood gawking while Miss Kew lashed up a dishcloth around him so it come out pants. When she was done, you wouldn't of known it was the same baby. And by the time Miss Kew finished with the job, she seemed to have a better hold on herself. She was breathing hard and her mouth was even tighter. She held out the baby to Miriam.

"Take this poor thing," she said, "and put him—"

But Miriam backed away. "I'm sorry, Miss Kew, but I am leaving here and I don't care."

Miss Kew got her honk out. "You can't leave me in a predicament like this! These children need help. Can't you see that for yourself?"

Miriam looked me and Janie over. She was trembling. "You ain't safe, Miss Kew. They ain't just dirty. They're crazy!"

"They're victims of neglect, and probably no worse than you or I would be if we'd been neglected. And don't say 'ain't.' Gerard!"

"What?"

"Don't say—oh, dear, we have so much to do. Gerard, if you and your—these other children are going to live here, you shall have to make a great many changes. You cannot live under this roof and behave as you have so far. Do you understand that?"

"Oh, sure. Lone said we was to do whatever you say and keep you happy."

"Will you do whatever I say?"

"That's what I just said, isn't it?"

"Gerard, you shall have to learn not to speak to me in that tone. Now, young man, if I told you to do what Miriam says, too, would you do it?"

I said to Jane, "What about that?"

"I'll ask Baby." Janie looked at Baby and Baby wobbled his hands and drooled some. She said, "It's okay."

Miss Kew said, "Gerard, I asked you a question."

"Keep your pants on," I said. "I got to find out, don't I? Yes, if that's what you want, we'll listen to Miriam, too."

Miss Kew turned to Miriam. "You hear that, Miriam?"

Miriam looked at Miss Kew and at us and shook her head. Then she held out her hands a bit to Bonnie and Beanie.

They went right to her. Each one took hold of a hand. They looked up at her and grinned. They were probably planning some sort of hellishness, but I guess they looked sort of cute. Miriam's mouth twitched and I thought for a second she was going to look human. She said, "All right, Miss Kew."

Miss Kew walked over and handed her the baby and she started upstairs with him. Miss Kew herded us along after Miriam. We all went upstairs.

They went to work on us then and for three years they never stopped.

"That was hell," I said to Stern.

"They had their work cut out."

"Yeah, I s'pose they did. So did we. Look, we were going to do exactly what Lone said. Nothing on earth could of stopped us from doing it. We were tied and bound to doing every last little thing Miss Kew said to do. But she and Miriam never seemed to understand that. I guess they felt they had to push every inch of the way. All they had to do was make us understand what they wanted, and we'd of done it. That's okay when it's something like telling me not to climb into bed with Janie.

"Miss Kew raised holy hell over that. You'd of thought I'd robbed the Crown Jewels, the way she acted. But when it's something like, 'You must behave like little ladies and gentlemen,' it just doesn't mean a thing. And two out of three orders she gave us were like that. 'Ah-ah!' she'd say. 'Language, language!' For the longest time I didn't dig that at all. I finally asked her what the hell she meant, and then she finally came out with it. But you see what I mean."

"I certainly do," Stern said. "Did it get easier as time went on?"

"We only had real trouble twice, once about the twins and once about Baby. That one was real bad."

"What happened?"

"About the twins? Well, when we'd been there about a week or so we began to notice something that sort of stunk. Janie and me, I mean. We began to notice that we almost never got to see Bonnie and Beanie. It was like that house was two houses, one part for Miss Kew and Janie and me, and the other part for Miriam and the twins. I guess we'd have noticed it sooner if things hadn't been such a hassle at first, getting us into new clothes and making us sleep all the time at night, and all that. But here was the thing: We'd all get turned out in the side yard to play, and then along comes lunch, and the twins got herded off to eat with Miriam while we ate with Miss Kew. So Janie said, 'Why don't the twins eat with us?'

" 'Miriam's taking care of them, dear,' Miss Kew says.

"Janie looked at her with those eyes. 'I know that. Let 'em eat here and I'll take care of 'em.'

"Miss Kew's mouth got all tight again and she said, 'They're little colored girls, Jane. Now eat your lunch.'

"But that didn't explain anything to Jane or me, either. I said, 'I want 'em to eat with us. Lone said we should stay together.'

" 'But you *are* together,' she says. 'We all live in the same house. We all eat the same food. Now let us not discuss the matter.'

"I looked at Janie and she looked at me, and she said, 'So why can't we all do this livin' and eatin' right here?'

"Miss Kew put down her fork and looked hard. 'I have explained it to you and I have said that there will be no further discussion.'

"Well, I thought that was real nowhere. So I just rocked back my head and bellowed, 'Bonnie! Beanie!' And *bing,* there they were.

"So all hell broke loose. Miss Kew ordered them out and they wouldn't go, and Miriam come steaming in with their clothes, and she couldn't catch them, and Miss Kew got to honking at them and finally at me. She said this was too much. Well, maybe she had had a hard week, but so had we. So Miss Kew ordered us to leave.

"I went and got Baby and started out, and along came Janie and the twins. Miss Kew waited till we were all out the door and next thing you know she ran out after us. She passed us and got in front of me and made me stop. So we all stopped.

" 'Is this how you follow Lone's wishes?' she asked.

"I told her yes. She said she understood Lone wanted us to stay with her. And I said, 'Yeah, but he wanted us to stay together more.'

"She said come back in, we'd have a talk. Jane asked Baby and Baby said okay, so we went back. We had a compromise. We didn't eat in the dining room no more. There was a side porch, a sort of verandah thing with glass windows, with a door to the dining room and a door to the kitchen, and we all ate out there after that. Miss Kew ate by herself.

"But something funny happened because of that whole cockeyed hassle."

"What was that?" Stern asked me.

I laughed. "Miriam. She looked and sounded like always, but she started slipping us cookies between meals. You know, it took me years to figure out what all that was about. I mean it. From what I've learned about people, there seems to be two armies fightin' about race. One's fightin' to keep 'em apart, and one's fightin' to get 'em together. But I don't see why both sides are so *worried* about it! Why don't they just forget it?"

"They can't. You see, Gerry, it's necessary for people to believe they are superior in some fashion. You and Lone and the kids—you were a pretty tight unit. Didn't you feel you were a little better than all of the rest of the world?"

"Better? How could we be better?"

"Different, then."

"Well, I suppose so, but we didn't think about it. Different, yes. Better, no."

"You're a unique case," Stern said. "Now go on and tell me about the other trouble you had. About Baby."

"Baby. Yeah. Well, that was a couple of months after we moved to Miss Kew's. Things were already getting real smooth, even then. We'd learned all the 'yes, ma'am, no, ma'am' routines by then and she'd got us catching up with school—regular periods morning and afternoons, five days a week. Jane had long ago quit taking care of Baby, and the twins walked to wherever they went. That was funny. They could pop from one place to another right in front of Miss Kew's eyes and she wouldn't believe what she saw. She was too upset about them suddenly showing up bare. They quit doing it and she was happy about it. She was happy about a lot of things. It had been years since she'd seen anybody—years. She'd even had the meters put outside the house so no one would ever have to come in. But with us there, she began to liven up. She quit wearing those old-lady dresses and began to look halfway human. She ate with us sometimes, even.

"But one fine day I woke up feeling real weird. It was like somebody had stolen something from me when I was asleep, only I didn't know what. I crawled out of my window and along the ledge into Janie's room, which I wasn't supposed to do. She was in bed. I went and woke her up. I can still see her eyes, the way they opened a little slit, still asleep, and then popped up wide. I didn't have to tell her something was wrong. She knew, and she knew what it was.

" 'Baby's gone!' she said.

"We didn't care then who woke up. We pounded out of her room and down the hall and into the little room at the end where Baby slept. You wouldn't believe it. The fancy crib he had, and the white chest of drawers, and all that mess of rattles and so on, they were gone, and there was just a writing desk there. I mean it was as if Baby had never been there at all.

"We didn't say anything. We just spun around and busted into Miss Kew's bedroom. I'd never been in there but once and Jane only a few times. But forbidden or not, this was different. Miss Kew was in bed, with her hair braided. She was wide awake before we could get across the room. She pushed herself back and up until she was sitting against the headboard. She gave the two of us the cold eye.

" 'What is the meaning of this?' she wanted to know.

" 'Where's Baby?' I yelled at her.

" 'Gerard,' she says, 'there is no need to shout.'

"Jane was a real quiet kid, but she said, 'You better tell us where he is, Miss Kew,' and it would of scared you to look at her when she said it.

"So all of sudden Miss Kew took off the stone face and held out her hands to us. 'Children,' she said, 'I'm sorry. I really am sorry. But I've just done what is best. I've sent Baby away. He's gone to live with some children like him. We could never make him really happy here. You know that.'

"Jane said, 'He never told us he wasn't happy.'

"Miss Kew brought out a hollow kind of laugh. 'As if he could talk, the poor little thing!'

"'You better get him back here,' I said. 'You don't know what you're fooling with. I told you we wasn't ever to break up.'

"She was getting mad, but she held on to herself. 'I'll try to explain it to you, dear,' she said. 'You and Jane here and even the twins are all normal, healthy children and you'll grow up to be fine men and women. But poor Baby's—different. He's not going to grow very much more, and he'll never walk and play like other children.'

"'That doesn't matter,' Jane said. 'You had no call to send him away.'

"And I said, 'Yeah. You better bring him back, but quick.'

"Then she started to jump salty. 'Among the many things I have taught you is, I am sure, not to dictate to your elders. Now, then, you run along and get dressed for breakfast, and we'll say no more about this.'

"I told her, nice as I could, 'Miss Kew, you're going to wish you brought him back right now. But you're going to bring him back soon. Or else.'

"So then she got up out of her bed and ran us out of the room."

I was quiet a while, and Stern asked, "What happened?"

"Oh," I said, "she brought him back." I laughed suddenly. "I guess it's funny now, when you come to think of it. Nearly three months of us getting bossed around, and her ruling the roost, and then all of a sudden we lay down the law. We'd tried our best to be good according to her ideas, but, by God, that time she went too far. She got the treatment from the second she slammed her door on us. She had a big china pot under her bed, and it rose up in the air and smashed through her dresser mirror. Then one of the drawers in the dresser slid open and a glove come out of it and smacked her face.

"She went to jump back on the bed and a whole section of plaster fell off the ceiling onto the bed. The water turned on in her little bathroom and the plug went in, and just about the time it began to overflow, all her clothes fell off their hooks. She went to run out of the room, but the door was stuck, and when she yanked on the handle it opened real quick and she spread out on the floor. The door slammed shut again and more plaster come down on her. Then we went back in and stood looking at her. She was crying. I hadn't known till then that she could.

" 'You going to get Baby back here?' I asked her.

"She just lay there and cried. After a while she looked up at us. It was real pathetic. We helped her up and got her to a chair. She just looked at us for a while, and at the mirror, and at the busted ceiling, and then she whispered, 'What happened? What happened?'

" 'You took Baby away,' I said. 'That's what.'

"So she jumped up and said real low, real scared, but real strong: 'Something struck the house. An airplane. Perhaps there was an earthquake. We'll talk about Baby after breakfast.'

"I said, 'Give her more, Janie.'

"A big gob of water hit her on the face and chest and made her nightgown stick to her, which was the kind of thing that upset her most. Her braids stood straight up in the air, more and more, till they dragged her standing straight up. She opened her mouth to yell and the powder puff off the dresser rammed into it. She clawed it out.

" 'What are you doing? What are you doing?' she says, crying again.

"Janie just looked at her, and put her hands behind her, real smug. 'We haven't done anything,' she said.

"And I said, 'Not yet we haven't. You going to get Baby back?'

"And she screamed at us, 'Stop it! Stop it! Stop talking about that mongoloid idiot! It's no good to anyone, not even itself! How could I ever make believe it's mine?'

"I said, 'Get rats, Janie.'

"There was a scuttling sound along the baseboard. Miss Kew covered her face with her hands and sank down on the chair. 'Not rats,' she said. 'There are no rats here.' Then something squeaked and she went all to pieces. Did you ever see anyone really go to pieces?"

"Yes," Stern said.

"I was about as mad as I could get," I said, "but that was almost too much for me. Still, she shouldn't have sent Baby away. It took a couple of hours for her to get straightened out enough so she could use the phone, but we had Baby back before lunch time." I laughed.

"What's funny?"

"She never seemed able to rightly remember what had happened to her. About three weeks later I heard her talking to Miriam about it. She said it was the house settling suddenly. She said it was a good thing she'd sent Baby out for that medical checkup—the poor little thing might have been hurt. She really believed it, I think."

"She probably did. That's fairly common. We don't believe anything we don't want to believe."

"How much of this do you believe?" I asked him suddenly.

"I told you before—it doesn't matter. I don't want to believe or disbelieve it."

"You haven't asked me how much of it I believe."

"I don't have to. You'll make up your own mind about that."

"Are you a *good* psychotherapist?"

"I think so," he said. "Whom did you kill?"

The question caught me absolutely off guard. "Miss Kew," I said. Then I started to cuss and swear. "I didn't mean to tell you that."

"Don't worry about it," he said. "What did you do it for?"

"That's what I came here to find out."

"You must have really hated her."

I started to cry. Fifteen years old and crying like that!

He gave me time to get it all out. The first part of it came out in noises, grunts and squeaks that hurt my throat. Much more than you'd think came out when my nose started to run. And finally—words.

"Do you know where I came from? The earliest thing I can remember is a punch in the mouth. I can still see it coming, a fist as big as my head. Because I was crying. I been afraid to cry ever since. I was crying because I was hungry. Cold, maybe. Both. After that, big dormitories, and whoever could steal the most got the most. Get the hell kicked out of you if you're bad, get a big reward if you're good. Big reward: they let you alone. Try to live like that. Try to live so the biggest, most wonderful thing in the whole damn world is just to have 'em let you alone!

"So a spell with Lone and the kids. Something wonderful: you belong. It never happened before. Two yellow bulbs and a fireplace and they light up the world. It's all there is and all there ever has to be.

"Then the big change: clean clothes, cooked food, five hours a day school; Columbus and King Arthur and a 1925 book on Civics that explains about septic tanks. Over it all a great big square-cut lump of ice, and you watch it melting and the corners curve, and you know it's because of you, Miss Kew . . . hell, she had too much control over herself ever to slobber over us, but it was there, that feeling. Lone took care of us because it was part of the way he lived. Miss Kew took care of us, and none of it was the way she lived. It was something she wanted to do.

"She had a weird idea of 'right' and a wrong idea of 'wrong,' but she stuck to them, tried to make her ideas do us good. When she couldn't understand, she figured it was her own failure . . . and there was an almighty lot she didn't understand and never could. What went right was our success. What went wrong was her mistake. That last year, that was . . . oh, good."

"So?"

"So I killed her. Listen," I said. I felt I had to talk fast. I wasn't short of time, but I had to get rid of it. "I'll tell you all I know about it. The one day before I killed her. I woke up in the morning and the sheets crackly clean under me, the sunlight coming in through white curtains and bright red-and-blue drapes. There's a closet full of my clothes—mine, you see; I never had anything that was really mine before—and downstairs Miriam clinking around with breakfast and the twins laughing. Laughing with *her,* mind you, not just with each other like they always did before.

"In the next room, Janie moving around, singing, and when I see her, I know her face will shine inside and out. I get up. There's *hot* water and the toothpaste bites my tongue. The clothes fit me and I go downstairs and they're all there and I'm glad to see them and they're glad to see me, and we no sooner get around the table when Miss Kew comes down and everyone calls out to her at once.

"And the morning goes by like that, school with a recess, there in the big long living room. The twins with the ends of their tongues stuck out, drawing the alphabet instead of writing it, and then Jane, when it's time, painting a picture, a real picture of a cow with trees and a yellow fence that goes off into the distance. Here I am lost between the two parts of a quadratic equation, and Miss Kew bending close to help me, and I smell the sachet she has on her clothes. I hold up my head to smell it better, and far away I hear the shuffle and klunk of filled pots going on the stove back in the kitchen.

"And the afternoon goes by like that, more school and some study and boiling out into the yard, laughing. The twins chasing each other, running on their two feet to get where they want to go; Jane dappling the leaves in her picture, trying to get it just the way Miss Kew says it ought to be. And Baby, he's got a big play-pen. He don't move around much any more, he just watches and dribbles some, and gets packed full of food and kept as clean as a new sheet of tinfoil.

"And supper, and the evening, and Miss Kew reading to us, changing her voice every time someone else talks in the story, reading fast and whispery when it embarrasses her, but reading every word all the same.

"And I had to go and kill her. And that's all."

"You haven't said why," Stern said.

"What are you—stupid?" I yelled.

Stern didn't say anything. I turned on my belly on the couch and propped up my chin in my hands and looked at him. You never could tell what was going on with him, but I got the idea that he was puzzled.

"I said why," I told him.

"Not to me."

I suddenly understood that I was asking too much of him. I said slowly, "We all woke up at the same time. We all did what somebody else wanted. We lived through a day someone else's way, thinking someone else's thoughts, saying other people's words. Jane painted someone else's pictures. Baby didn't talk to anyone, and we were all happy with it. Now do you see?"

"Not yet."

"God!" I said. I thought for a while. "We didn't blesh."

"Blesh? Oh. But you didn't after Lone died, either."

"That was different. That was like a car running out of gas, but the car's there—there's nothing wrong with it. It's just waiting. But after Miss Kew got done with us, the car was taken all to pieces, see?"

It was his turn to think a while. Finally he said, "The mind makes us do funny things. Some of them seem completely reasonless, wrong, insane. But the cornerstone of the work we're doing is this: there's a chain of solid, unassailable logic in the things we do. Dig deep enough and you find cause and effect as clearly in this field as you do in any other. I said *logic*, mind; I didn't say 'correctness' or 'rightness' or 'justice' or anything of the sort. Logic and truth are two very different things, but they often look the same to the mind that's performing the logic.

"When that mind is submerged, working at cross-purposes with the surface mind, then you're all confused. Now in your case, I can see the thing you're pointing at—that in order to preserve or to rebuild that peculiar bond between you kids, you had to get rid of Miss Kew. But I don't see the logic. I don't see that regaining that 'bleshing' was worth destroying this new-found security which you admit was enjoyable."

I said, desperately, "Maybe it wasn't worth destroying it."

Stern leaned forward and pointed his pipe at me. "It *was* because it made you do what you did. After the fact, maybe things look different. But when you were moved to do it, the important thing was to destroy Miss Kew and regain this thing you'd had before. I don't see why and neither do you."

"How are we going to find out?"

"Well, let's get right to the most unpleasant part, if you're up to it."

I lay down. "I'm ready."

"All right. Tell me everything that happened just before you killed her."

I fumbled through that last day, trying to taste the food, hear the voices. A thing came and went and came again: it was the crisp feeling of the sheets. I thrust it away because it was at the beginning of that day, but it came back again, and I realized it was at the end, instead.

I said, "What I just told you, all that about the children doing things other people's way instead of their own, and Baby not talking, and everyone happy about it, and finally that I had to kill Miss Kew. It took a long time to get to that, and a long time to start doing it. I guess I lay in bed and thought for four hours before I got up again. It was dark and quiet. I went out of the room and down the hall and into Miss Kew's bedroom and killed her."

"How?"

"That's all there is!" I shouted, as loud as I could. Then I quieted down. "It was awful dark . . . it still is. I don't know. I don't want to know. She did love us. I know she did. But I had to kill her."

"All right, all right," Stern said. "I guess there's no need to get too gruesome about this. You're—"

"What?"

"You're quite strong for your age, aren't you, Gerard?"

"I guess so. Strong enough, anyway."

"Yes," he said.

"I still don't see that logic you were talking about." I began to hammer on the couch with my fist, hard, once for each word: "Why—did—I—have—to—go—and—do—that?"

"Cut that out," he said. "You'll hurt yourself."

"I ought to get hurt," I said.

"Ah?" said Stern.

I got up and went to the desk and got some water. "What am I going to do?"

"Tell me what you did after you killed her, right up until the time you came here."

"Not much," I said. "It was only last night. I went back to my room, sort of numb. I put all my clothes on except my shoes. I carried them. I went out. Walked a long time, trying to think, went to the post office when it opened. Miss Kew used to let me go for the mail sometimes. Found this check waiting for me for the contest. Cashed it at the bank, opened an account, took eleven hundred bucks. Got the idea of getting some help from a psychiatrist, spent most of the day looking for one, came here. That's all."

"Didn't you have any trouble cashing the check?"

"I never have any trouble making people do what I want them to do."

He gave a surprised grunt.

"I know what you're thinking—I couldn't make Miss Kew do what I wanted."

"That's part of it," he admitted.

"If I had of done that," I told him, "she wouldn't of been Miss Kew any more. Now the banker—all I made him do was be a banker."

I looked at him and suddenly realized why he fooled with that pipe all the time. It was so he could look down at it and you wouldn't be able to see his eyes.

"You killed her," he said—and I knew he was changing the subject —"and destroyed something that was valuable to you. It must have been less valuable to you than the chance to rebuild this thing you used to have with the other kids. And you're not sure of the value of that." He looked up. "Does that describe your main trouble?"

"Just about."

"You know the single thing that makes people kill?" When I didn't answer, he said, "Survival. To save the self or something which identifies with the self. And in this case that doesn't apply, because your setup with Miss Kew had far more survival value for you, singly and as a group, than the other."

"So maybe I just didn't have a good enough reason to kill her."

"You had, because you did it. We just haven't located it yet. I mean we have the reason, but we don't know why it was important enough. The answer is somewhere in you."

"Where?"

He got up and walked some. "We have a pretty consecutive life-story here. There's fantasy mixed with the fact, of course, and there are areas in which we have no detailed information, but we have a beginning and a middle and an end. Now, I can't say for sure, but the answer may be in that bridge you refused to cross a while back. Remember?"

I remembered, all right. I said, "Why that? Why can't we try something else?"

He quietly pointed out, "Because you just said it. Why are you shying away from it?"

"Don't go making big ones out of little ones," I said. Sometimes the guy annoyed me. "That bothers me. I don't know why, but it does."

"Something's lying hidden in there, and you're bothering *it* so it's fighting back. Anything that fights to stay concealed is very possibly the thing we're after. Your trouble is concealed, isn't it?"

"Well, yes," I said, and I felt that sickness and faintness again, and again I pushed it away. Suddenly I wasn't going to be stopped any more. "Let's go get it." I lay down.

He let me watch the ceiling and listen to silence for a while, and then he said, "You're in the library. You've just met Miss Kew. She's talking to you; you're telling her about the children."

I lay very still. Nothing happened. Yes, it did; I got tense inside, all over, from the bones out, more and more. When it got as bad as it could, still nothing happened.

I heard him get up and cross the room to the desk. He fumbled there for a while; things clicked and hummed. Suddenly I heard my own voice:

"Well, there's Jane, she's eleven like me. And Bonnie and Beanie are eight, they're twins, and Baby. Baby is three."

And the sound of my own scream—
And nothingness.

Sputtering up out of the darkness, I came flailing out with my fists. Strong hands caught my wrists. They didn't check my arms; they just grabbed and rode. I opened my eyes. I was soaking wet. The thermos lay on its side on the rug. Stern was crouched beside me, holding my wrists. I quit struggling.

"What happened?"

He let me go and stood back watchfully. "Lord," he said, "what a charge!"

I held my head and moaned. He threw me a hand-towel and I used it. "What hit me?"

"I've had you on tape the whole time," he explained. "When you wouldn't get into that recollection, I tried to nudge you into it by using your own voice as you recounted it before. It works wonders sometimes."

"It worked wonders this time," I growled. "I think I blew a fuse."

"In effect, you did. You were on the trembling verge of going into the thing you don't want to remember, and you let yourself go unconscious rather than do it."

"What are you so pleased about?"

"Last-ditch defense," he said tersely. "We've got it now. Just one more try."

"Now hold on. The last-ditch defense is that I drop dead."

"You won't. You've contained this episode in your subconscious mind for a long time and it hasn't hurt you."

"Hasn't it?"

"Not in terms of killing you."

"How do you know it won't when we drag it out?"

"You'll see."

I looked up at him sideways. Somehow he struck me as knowing what he was doing.

"You know a lot more about yourself now than you did at the time," he explained softly. "You can apply insight. You can evaluate it as it comes up. Maybe not completely, but enough to protect yourself. Don't worry. Trust me. I can stop it if it gets too bad. Now just relax. Look at the ceiling. Be aware of your toes. Don't look at your toes. Look straight up. Your toes, your big toes. Don't move your toes, but feel them. Count outward from your big toes, one count for each toe. One, two, three. Feel that third toe. Feel the toe, feel it, feel it go limp, go limp, go limp. The toe next to it on both sides gets limp. So limp because your toes are limp, all of your toes are limp—"

"What are you doing?" I shouted at him.

He said in the same silky voice, "You trust me and so do your toes trust me. They're all limp because you trust me. You—"

"You're trying to hypnotize me. I'm not going to let you do that."

"You're going to hypnotize yourself. You do everything yourself. I just point the way. I point your toes to the path. Just point your toes. No one can make you go anywhere you don't want to go, but you want to go where your toes are pointed, where your toes are limp, where your . . ."

On and on and on. And where was the dangling gold ornament, the light in the eyes, the mystic passes? He wasn't even sitting where I could see him. Where was the talk about how sleepy I was supposed to be? Well, he knew I wasn't sleepy and didn't want to be sleepy. I just wanted to be toes. I just wanted to be limp, just a limp toe. No brains in a toe, a toe to go, go, go eleven times, eleven, I'm eleven . . .

I split in two, and it was all right, the part that watched the part that went back to the library, and Miss Kew leaning toward me, but not too near, me with the newspaper crackling under me on the library chair, me with one shoe off and my limp toes dangling . . . and I felt a mild surprise at this. For this was hypnosis, but I was quite conscious, quite altogether there on the couch with Stern droning away at me, quite able to roll over and sit up and talk to him and walk out if I wanted to, but I just didn't want to. Oh, if this was what hypnosis was like, I was all for it. I'd work at this. This was all right.

There on the table I'm able to see that the gold will unfold on the leather, and whether I'm able to stay by the table with you, with Miss Kew, with Miss Kew . . .

". . . and Bonnie and Beanie are eight, they're twins, and Baby. Baby is three."

"Baby is three," she said.

There was a pressure, a stretching apart, and a . . . a breakage. And with a tearing agony and a burst of triumph that drowned the pain, it was done.

And this is what was inside. All in one flash, but all this.

Baby is three? My baby would be three if there were a baby, which there never was . . .

Lone, I'm open to you. Open, is this open enough?

His irises like wheels. I'm sure they spin, but I never catch them at it. The probe that passes invisibly from his brain, through his eyes, into mine. Does he know what it means to me? Does he care? He doesn't care, he doesn't know; he empties me and I fill as he directs me to; he drinks and waits and drinks again and never looks at the cup.

When I saw him first, I was dancing in the wind, in the wood, in the wild, and I spun about and he stood there in the leafy shadows, watching me. I hated him for it. It was not my wood, not my gold-spangled fern-tangled glen. But it was my dancing that he took, freezing it forever by being there. I hated him for it, hated the way he looked, the way he stood, ankle-deep in the kind wet ferns, looking like a tree with roots for feet and clothes the color of earth. As I stopped he moved, and then he was just a man, a great ape-shouldered, dirty animal of a man, and all my hate was fear suddenly and I was just as frozen.

He knew what he had done and he didn't care. Dancing . . . never to dance again, because never would I know the woods were free of eyes, free of tall, uncaring, dirty animal men. Summer days with the clothes choking me, winter nights with the precious decencies round and about me like a shroud, and never to dance again, never to remember dancing without remembering the shock of knowing he had seen me. How I hated him! Oh, how I hated him!

To dance alone where no one knew, that was the single thing I hid to myself when I was known as Miss Kew, that Victorian, older than her years, later than her time; correct and starched, lace and linen and lonely. Now indeed I would be all they said, through and through, forever and ever, because he had robbed me of the one thing I dared to keep secret.

He came out into the sun and walked to me, holding his great head a little on one side. I stood where I was, frozen inwardly and outwardly and altogether by the core of anger and the layer of fear. My arm was still out, my waist still bent from my dance, and when he stopped, I breathed again because by then I had to.

He said, "You read books?"

I couldn't bear to have him near me, but I couldn't move. He put out his hard hand and touched my jaw, turned my head up until I had to look into his face. I cringed away from him, but my face would not leave his hand, though he was not holding it, just lifting it. "You got to read some books for me. I got no time to find them."

I asked him, "Who are you?"

"Lone," he said. "You going to read books for me?"

"No. Let me go, let me go!"

He laughed at me. He wasn't holding me.

"What books?" I cried.

He thumped my face, not very hard. It made me look up a bit more. He dropped his hand away. His eyes, the irises were going to spin . . .

"Open up in there," he said. "Open way up and let me see."

There were books in my head, and he was looking at the titles . . . he was not looking at the titles, for he couldn't read. He was looking at what I knew of the books. I suddenly felt terribly useless, because I had only a fraction of what he wanted.

"What's that?" he barked.

I knew what he meant. He'd gotten it from inside my head. I didn't know it was in there, even, but he found it.

"Telekinesis," I said.

"How is it done?"

"Nobody knows if it can be done. Moving physical objects with the mind!"

"It can be done," he said. "This one?"

"Teleportation. That's the same thing--well, almost. Moving your own body with mind power."

"Yeah, yeah, I see it," he said gruffly.

"Molecular interpenetration. Telepathy and clairvoyance. I don't know anything about them. I think they're silly."

"Read about 'em. It don't matter if you understand or not. What's this?"

It was there in my brain, on my lips. *"Gestalt."*

"What's that?"

"Group. Like a cure for a lot of diseases with one kind of treatment. Like a lot of thoughts expressed in one phrase. The whole is greater than the sum of the parts."

"Read about that, too. Read a whole lot about that. That's the *most* you got to read about. That's important."

He turned away, and when his eyes came away from mine it was like something breaking, so that I staggered and fell to one knee. He went off into the woods without looking back. I got my things and ran home. There was anger, and it struck me like a storm. There was fear, and it struck me like a wind. I knew I would read the books, I knew I would come back, I knew I would never dance again.

So I read the books and I came back. Sometimes it was every day for three or four days, and sometimes, because I couldn't find a certain book, I might not come back for ten. He was always there in the little glen, waiting, standing in the shadows, and he took what he wanted of the books and nothing of me. He never mentioned the next meeting. If he came there every day to wait for me, or if he only came when I did, I have no way of knowing.

He made me read books that contained nothing for me, books on evolution, on social and cultural organization, on mythology, and ever so much on symbiosis. What I had with him were not conversations; sometimes nothing audible would pass between us but his grunt of surprise or small, short hum of interest.

He tore the books out of me the way he would tear berries from a bush, all at once; he smelled of sweat and earth and the green juices his heavy body crushed when he moved through the wood.

If he learned anything from the books, it made no difference in him.

There came a day when he sat by me and puzzled something out.

He said, "What book has something like this?" Then he waited for a long time, thinking. "The way a termite can't digest wood, you know, and microbes in the termite's belly can, and what the termite eats is what the microbe leaves behind. What's that?"

"Symbiosis," I remembered. I remembered the words. Lone tore the content from words and threw the words away. "Two kinds of life depending upon one another for existence."

"Yeah. Well, is there a book about four-five kinds doing that?"

"I don't know."

Then he asked, "What about this? You got a radio station, you got four-five receivers, each receiver is fixed up to make something different happen, like one digs and one flies and one makes noise, but each one takes orders from the one place. And each one has its own power and its own thing to do, but they are all apart. Now: is there life like that, instead of radio?"

"Where each organism is a part of the whole, but separated? I don't think so . . . unless you mean social organizations, like a team, or perhaps a gang of men working, all taking orders from the same boss."

"No," he said immediately, "not like that. Like one single animal." He made a gesture with his cupped hand which I understood.

I asked, "You mean a *gestalt* life-form? It's fantastic."

"No book has about that, huh?"

"None I ever heard of."

"I got to know about that," he said heavily. "There is such a thing. I want to know if it ever happened before."

"I can't see how anything of the sort could exist."

"It does. A part that fetches, a part that figures, a part that finds out, and a part that talks."

"Talks? Only humans talk."

"I know," he said, and got up and went away.

I looked and looked for such a book, but found nothing remotely like it. I came back and told him so. He was still a very long time, looking off to the blue-on-blue line of the hilly horizon. Then he drove those about-to-spin irises at me and searched.

"You learn, but you don't think," he said, and looked again at the hills.

"This all happens with humans," he said eventually. "It happens piece by piece right under folks' noses, and they don't see it. You got mindreaders. You got people can move things with their mind. You got people can move themselves with their mind. You got people can figure anything out if you just think to ask them. What you ain't got is the one kind of person who can pull 'em all together, like a brain pulls together the parts that press and pull and feel heat and walk and think and all the other things.

"I'm one," he finished suddenly. Then he sat still for so long, I thought he had forgotten me.

"Lone," I said, "what do you do here in the woods?"

"I wait," he said. "I ain't finished yet." He looked at my eyes and snorted in irritation. "I don't mean 'finished' like you're thinking. I mean I ain't—completed yet. You know about a worm when it's cut, growin' whole again? Well, forget about the cut. Suppose it just grew that way, for the first time, see? I'm getting parts. I ain't finished. I want a book about that kind of animal that is me when I'm finished."

"I don't know of such a book. Can you tell me more? Maybe if you could, I'd think of the right book or a place to find it."

He broke a stick between his huge hands, put the two pieces side by side and broke them together with one strong twist.

"All I know is I got to do what I'm doing like a bird's got to nest when it's time. And I know that when I'm done I won't be anything to brag about. I'll be like a body stronger and faster than anything there ever was, without the right kind of head on it. But maybe that's because I'm one of the first. That picture you had, the caveman . . ."

"Neanderthal."

"Yeah. Come to think of it, he was no great shakes. An early try at something new. That's what I'm going to be. But maybe the right kind of head'll come along after I'm all organized. Then it'll be something."

He grunted with satisfaction and went away.

I tried, for days I tried, but I couldn't find what he wanted. I found a magazine which stated that the next important evolutionary step in man would be a psychic rather than a physical direction, but it said nothing about a—shall I call it a *gestalt* organism? There was something about slime molds, but they seem to be more a hive activity of amoebae than even a symbiosis.

To my own unscientific, personally uninterested mind, there was nothing like what he wanted except possibly a band marching together, everyone playing different kinds of instruments with different techniques and different notes, to make a single thing move along together. But he hadn't meant anything like that.

So I went back to him in the cool of an early fall evening, and he took what little I had in my eyes, and turned from me angrily with a gross word I shall not permit myself to remember.

"You can't find it," he told me. "Don't come back."

He got up and went to a tattered birch and leaned against it, looking out and down into the wind-tossed crackling shadows. I think he had forgotten me already. I know he leaped like a frightened animal when I spoke to him from so near. He must have been completely immersed in whatever strange thoughts he was having, for I'm sure he didn't hear me coming.

I said, "Lone, don't blame me for not finding it. I tried."

He controlled his startlement and brought those eyes down to me. "Blame? Who's blamin' anybody?"

"I failed you," I told him, "and you're angry."

He looked at me so long I became uncomfortable.

"I don't know what you're talkin' about," he said.

I wouldn't let him turn away from me. He would have. He would have left me forever with not another thought; he didn't care! It wasn't cruelty or thoughtlessness as I have been taught to know those things. He was as uncaring as a cat is of the bursting of a tulip bud.

I took him by the upper arms and shook him, it was like trying to shake the front of my house. "You *can* know!" I screamed at him. "You know what I read. You must know what I think!"

He shook his head.

"I'm a person, a woman," I raved at him. "You've used me and used me and you've given me nothing. You've made me break a lifetime of habits—reading until all hours, coming to you in the rain and on Sunday—you don't talk to me, you don't look at me, you don't know anything about me and you don't care. You put some sort of a spell on me that I couldn't break. And when you're finished, you say, 'Don't come back.'"

"Do I have to give something back because I took something?"

"People do."

He gave that short, interested hum. "What do you want me to give you? I ain't got anything."

I moved away from him. I felt . . . I don't know what I felt. After a time I said, "I don't know."

He shrugged and turned. I fairly leaped at him, dragging him back. "I want you to—"

"Well, damn it, what?"

I couldn't look at him; I could hardly speak. "I don't know. There's something, but I don't know what it is. It's something that—I couldn't say if I knew it." When he began to shake his head, I took his arms again. "You've read the books out of me; can't you read the . . . the *me* out of me?"

"I ain't never tried." He held my face up, and stepped close. "Here," he said.

His eyes projected their strange probe at me and I screamed. I tried to twist away. I hadn't wanted this, I was sure I hadn't. I struggled terribly. I think he lifted me right off the ground with his big hands. He held me until he was finished, and then let me drop. I huddled to the ground, sobbing. He sat down beside me. He didn't try to touch me. He didn't try to go away. I quieted at last and crouched there, waiting.

He said, "I ain't going to do much of that no more."

I sat up and tucked my skirt close around me and laid my cheek on my updrawn knees so I could see his face. "What happened?"

He cursed. "Damn mishmash inside you. Thirty-three years old— what you want to live like that for?"

"I live very comfortably," I said with some pique.

"Yeah," he said. "All by yourself for ten years now 'cept for someone to do your work. Nobody else."

"Men are animals, and women . . ."

"You really hate women. They all know something you don't."

"I don't want to know. I'm quite happy the way I am."

"Hell you are."

I said nothing to that. I despise that kind of language.

"Two things you want from me. Neither makes no sense." He looked at me with the first real expression I have ever seen in his face: a profound wonderment. "You want to know all about me, where I came from, how I got to be what I am."

"Yes, I do want that. What's the other thing I want that you know and I don't?"

"I was born some place and growed like a weed somehow," he said, ignoring me. "Folks who didn't give even enough of a damn to try the orphanage routine. I lived with some other folks for a while, tried school, didn't like it. Too small a town for them special schools for my kind, retarded, y'know. So I just ran loose, sort of in training to be the village idiot. I'da made it if I'd stayed there, but I took to the woods instead."

"Why?"

He wondered why, and finally said, "I guess because the way people lived didn't make no sense to me. I saw enough up and down, back and forth, to know that they live a lot of different ways, but none of 'em was for me. Out here I can grow like I want."

"How is that?" I asked over one of those vast distances that built and receded between him and me so constantly.

"What I wanted to get from your books."

"You never told me."

For the second time he said, "You learn, but you don't think. There's a kind of—well, *person*. It's all made of separate parts, but it's all one person. It has like hands, it has like legs, it has like a talking mouth, and it has like a brain. That's me, a brain for that person. Damn feeble, too, but the best I know of."

"You're mad."

"No, I ain't," he said, unoffended and completely certain. "I already got the part that's like hands. I can move 'em anywhere and they do what I want, though they're too young yet to do much good. I got the part that talks. That one's real good."

"I don't think you talk very well at all," I said. I cannot stand incorrect English.

He was surprised. "I'm not talking about me! She's back yonder with the others."

"She?"

"The one that talks. Now I need one that thinks, one that can take anything and add it to anything else and come up with a right answer. And once they're all together, and all the parts get used together often enough, I'll be that new kind of thing I told you about. See? Only—I wish it had a better head on it than me."

My own head was swimming. "What made you start doing this?"

He considered me gravely. "What made you start growing hair in your armpits?" he asked me. "You don't figure a thing like that. It just happens."

"What is that . . . that thing you do when you look in my eyes?"

"You want a name for it? I ain't got one. I don't know how I do it. I know I can get anyone I want to do anything. Like you're going to forget about me."

I said in a choked voice, "I don't want to forget about you."

"You will." I didn't know then whether he meant I'd forget, or I'd *want* to forget. "You'll hate me, and then after a long time you'll be grateful. Maybe you'll be able to do something for me some time. You'll be that grateful that you'll be glad to do it. But you'll forget, all right, everything but a sort of . . . feeling. And my name, maybe."

I don't know what moved me to ask him, but I did, forlornly. "And no one will ever know about you and me?"

"Can't," he said. "Unless . . . well, unless it was the head of the animal, like me, or a better one." He heaved himself up.

"Oh, wait, wait!" I cried. He mustn't go yet, he mustn't. He was a tall, dirty beast of a man, yet he had enthralled me in some dreadful way. "You haven't given me the other . . . whatever it was."

"Oh," he said. "Yeah, that."

He moved like a flash. There was a pressure, a stretching apart, and a . . . a breakage. And with a tearing agony and a burst of triumph that drowned the pain, it was done.

I came up out of it, through two distinct levels:

I am eleven, breathless from shock from a transferred agony of that incredible entrance into the ego of another. And:

I am fifteen, lying on the couch while Stern drones on, ". . . quietly, quietly limp, your ankles and legs as limp as your toes, your belly goes soft, the back of your neck is as limp as your belly, it's quiet and easy and all gone soft and limper than limp . . ."

I sat up and swung my legs to the floor. "Okay," I said.

Stern looked a little annoyed. "This is going to work," he said, "but it can only work if you cooperate. Just lie—"

"It did work," I said.

"What?"

"The whole thing. A to Z." I snapped my fingers. "Like that."

He looked at me piercingly. "What do you mean?"

"It was right there, where you said. In the library. When I was eleven. When she said, 'Baby is three.' It knocked loose something that had been boiling around in her for three years, and it all came blasting out. I got it, full force; just a kid, no warning, no defenses. It had such a—a pain in it, like I never knew could be."

"Go on," said Stern.

"That's really all. I mean that's not what was in it; it's what it did to me. What it was, a sort of hunk of her own self. A whole lot of things that happened over about four months, every bit of it. She knew Lone."

"You mean a whole *series* of episodes?"

"That's it."

"You got a series all at once? In a split second?"

"That's right. Look, for that split second I *was* her, don't you see? I was her, everything she'd ever done, everything she'd ever thought and heard and felt. Everything, everything, all in the right order if I wanted to bring it out like that. Any part of it if I wanted it by itself. If I'm going to tell you about what I had for lunch, do I have to tell you everything else I've ever done since I was born? No. I tell you I *was* her, and then and forever after I can remember anything she could remember up to that point. In just that one flash."

"A *gestalt*," he murmured.

"Aha!" I said, and thought about that. I thought about a whole lot of things. I put them aside for a moment and said, "Why didn't I know all this before?"

"You had a powerful block against recalling it."

I got up excitedly. "I don't see why. I don't see that at all."

"Just natural revulsion," he guessed. "How about this? You had a distaste for assuming a female ego, even for a second."

"You told me yourself, right at the beginning, that I didn't have that kind of a problem."

"Well, how does this sound to you? You say you felt pain in that episode. So—you wouldn't go back into it for fear of re-experiencing the pain."

"Let me think, let me think. Yeah, yeah, that's part of it—that thing of going into someone's mind. She opened up to me because I reminded her of Lone. I went in. I wasn't ready; I'd never done it before, except maybe a little, against resistance. I went all the way in and it was too much; it frightened me away from trying it for years. And there it lay, wrapped up, locked away. But as I grew older, the power to do that with my mind got stronger and stronger, and still I was afraid to use it. And the more I grew, the more I felt, down deep, that Miss Kew had to be killed before she killed the . . . what I am. My God!" I shouted. "Do you know what I am?"

"No," he said. "Like to tell me about it?"

"I'd like to," I said. "Oh, yes, I'd like that."

He had that professional open-minded expression on his face, not believing or disbelieving, just taking it all in. I had to tell him, and I suddenly realized that I didn't have enough words. I knew the things, but not the names for them.

Lone took the meanings and threw the words away.

Further back: *"You read books. Read books for me."*

The look of his eyes. That—"opening up" thing.

I went over to Stern. He looked up at me. I bent close. First he was startled, then he controlled it, then he came even closer to me.

"My God," he murmured. "I didn't look at those eyes before. I could have sworn those irises spun like wheels . . ."

Stern read books. He'd read more books than I ever imagined had been written. I slipped in there, looking for what I wanted.

I can't say exactly what it was like. It was like walking in a tunnel, and in this tunnel, all over the roof and walls, wooden arms stuck out at you, like the thing at the carnival, the merry-go-round, the thing you snatch the brass rings from. There's a brass ring on the end of each of these arms, and you can take any one of them you want to.

Now imagine you make up your mind which rings you want, and the arms hold only those. Now picture yourself with a thousand hands to grab the rings off with. Now just suppose the tunnel is a zillion miles long, and you can go from one end of it to the other, grabbing rings, in just the time it takes you to blink once. Well, it was like that, only easier.

It was easier for me to do than it had been for Lone.

Straightening up, I got away from Stern. He looked sick and frightened.

"It's all right," I said.

"What did you do to me?"

"I needed some words. Come on, come on. Get professional."

I had to admire him. He put his pipe in his pocket and gouged the tips of his fingers hard against his forehead and cheeks. Then he sat up and he was okay again.

"I know," I said. "That's how Miss Kew felt when Lone did it to her."

"What *are* you?"

"I'll tell you. I'm the central ganglion of a complex organism which is composed of Baby, a computer; Bonnie and Beanie, teleports; Jane, telekineticist; and myself, telepath and central control. There isn't a single thing about any of us that hasn't been documented: the teleportation of the Yogi, the telekinetics of some gamblers, the idiosavant mathematicians, and most of all, the so-called poltergeist, the moving about of household goods through the instrumentation of a young girl. Only in this case every one of my parts delivers at peak performance.

"Lone organized it, or it formed around him; it doesn't matter which. I replaced Lone, but I was too underdeveloped when he died, and on top of that I got an occlusion from that blast from Miss Kew. To that extent you were right when you said the blast made me subconsciously afraid to discover what was in it. But there was another good reason for my not being able to get in under that 'Baby is three' barrier.

"We ran into the problem of what it was I valued more than the

security Miss Kew gave us. Can't you see now what it was? My *gestalt*
organism was at the point of death from that security. I figured she
had to be killed or it—*I*—would be. Oh, the parts would live on: two
little colored girls with a speech impediment, one introspective girl
with an artistic bent, one mongoloid idiot, and me—ninety per cent
short-circuited potentials and ten per cent juvenile delinquent." I
laughed. "Sure, she had to be killed. It was self-preservation for the
gestalt."

Stern bobbled around with his mouth and finally got out: "I
don't—"

"You don't need to," I laughed. "This is wonderful. You're fine,
hey, fine. Now I want to tell you this, because you can appreciate a
fine point in your specialty. You talk about occlusions! I couldn't get
past the 'Baby is three' thing because in it lay the clues to what I really
am. I couldn't find that out because I was afraid to remember that I
had failed in the thing I had to do to save the *gestalt*. Ain't that
purty?"

"Failed? Failed how?"

"Look. I came to love Miss Kew, and I'd never loved anything
before. Yet I had reason to kill her. She *had* to be killed; I *couldn't*
kill her. What does a human mind do when presented with imperative, mutually exclusive alternatives?"

"It—it might simply quit. As you phrased it earlier, it might blow a
fuse, retreat, refuse to function in that area."

"Well, I didn't do that. What else?"

"It might slip into a delusion that it had already taken one of the
courses of action."

I nodded happily. "I didn't kill her. I decided I must; I got up, got
dressed—and the next thing I knew I was outside, wandering, very
confused. I got my money—and I understand now, with super-
empathy, how I can win *anyone's* prize contest—and I went looking for a head-shrinker. I found a good one."

"Thanks," he said dazedly. He looked at me with a strangeness in
his eyes. "And now that you know, what's solved? What are you going
to do?"

"Go back home," I said happily. "Reactivate the superorganism,
exercise it secretly in ways that won't make Miss Kew unhappy, and
we'll stay with her as long as we know it pleases her. And we'll please

her. She'll be happy in ways she's never dreamed about until now. She rates it, bless her strait-laced, hungry heart."

"And she can't kill your—*gestalt* organism?"

"Not a chance. Not now."

"How do you know it isn't dead already?"

"How?" I echoed. "How does your head know your arm works?"

He wet his lips. "You're going home to make a spinster happy. And after that?"

I shrugged. "After that?" I mocked. "Did the Peking man look at Homo Sap walking erect and say, 'What will he do after that?' We'll live, that's all, like a man, like a tree, like anything else that lives. We'll feed and grow and experiment and breed. We'll defend ourselves." I spread my hands. "We'll just do what comes naturally."

"But what can you do?"

"What can an electric motor do? It depends on where we apply ourselves."

Stern was very pale. "But you're the only such organism . . ."

"Are we? I don't know. I don't think so. I've told you the parts have been around for ages—the telepaths, the *poltergeists*. What was lacking was the ones to organize, to be heads to the scattered bodies. Lone was one, I'm one; there must be more. We'll find out as we mature."

"You—aren't mature yet?"

"Lord, no!" I laughed. "We're an infant. We're the equivalent of about a three-year-old child. So you see, there it is again, and this time I'm not afraid of it; Baby is three." I looked at my hands. "Baby is three," I said again, because the realization tasted good. "And when this particular group-baby is five, it might want to be a fireman. At eight, maybe a cowboy or maybe an FBI man. And when it grows up, maybe it'll build a city, or perhaps it'll be President."

"Oh, God!" he said. "God!"

I looked down at him. "You're afraid," I said. "You're afraid of *Homo Gestalt.*"

He made a wonderful effort and smiled. "That's bastard terminology."

"We're a bastard breed," I said. I pointed. "Sit over there."

He crossed the quiet room and sat at the desk. I leaned close to him and he went to sleep with his eyes open. I straightened up and looked around the room. Then I got the thermos flask and filled it and put it on the desk. I fixed the corner of the rug and put a clean towel at the head of the couch. I went to the side of the desk and opened it and looked at the tape recorder.

Like reaching out a hand, I got Beanie. She stood by the desk, wide-eyed.

"Look here," I told her. "Look good, now. What I want to do is erase all this tape. Go ask Baby how."

She blinked at me and sort of shook herself, and then leaned over the recorder. She was there—and gone—and back, just like that. She pushed past me and turned two knobs, moved a pointer until it clicked twice. The tape raced backward past the head swiftly, whining.

"All right," I said, "beat it."

She vanished.

I got my jacket and went to the door. Stern was still sitting at the desk, staring.

"A *good* head-shrinker," I murmured. I felt fine.

Outside I waited, then turned and went back in again.

Stern looked up at me. "Sit over there, Sonny."

"Gee," I said. "Sorry, sir. I got in the wrong office."

"That's all right," he said.

I went out and closed the door. All the way down to the store to buy Miss Kew some flowers, I was grinning about how he'd account for the loss of an afternoon and the gain of a thousand bucks.

THE TIME MACHINE
by H. G. Wells

The Time Traveller (for so it will be convenient to speak of him) was expounding a recondite matter to us. His grey eyes shone and twinkled, and his usually pale face was flushed and animated. The fire burned brightly, and the soft radiance of the incandescent lights in the lilies of silver caught the bubbles that flashed and passed in our glasses. Our chairs, being his patents, embraced and caressed us rather than submitted to be sat upon, and there was that luxurious after-dinner atmosphere when thought runs gracefully free of the trammels of precision. And he put it to us in this way—marking the points with a lean forefinger—as we sat and lazily admired his earnestness over this new paradox (as we thought it) and his fecundity.

"You must follow me carefully. I shall have to controvert one or two ideas that are almost universally accepted. The geometry, for instance, they taught you at school is founded on a misconception."

"Is not that rather a large thing to expect us to begin upon?" said Filby, an argumentative person with red hair.

"I do not mean to ask you to accept anything without reasonable ground for it. You will soon admit as much as I need from you. You know of course that a mathematical line, a line of thickness *nil,* has no real existence. They taught you that? Neither has a mathematical plane. These things are mere abstractions."

"That is all right," said the Psychologist.

"Nor, having only length, breadth, and thickness, can a cube have a real existence."

"There I object," said Filby. "Of course a solid body may exist. All real things—"

"So most people think. But wait a moment. Can an *instantaneous* cube exist?"

"Don't follow you," said Filby.

"Can a cube that does not last for any time at all have a real existence?"

Filby became pensive. "Clearly," the Time Traveller proceeded, "any real body must have extension in *four* directions: it must have Length, Breadth, Thickness, and—Duration. But through a natural infirmity of the flesh, which I will explain to you in a moment, we incline to overlook this fact. There are really four dimensions, three which we call the three planes of Space, and a fourth, Time. There is, however, a tendency to draw an unreal distinction between the former three dimensions and the latter, because it happens that our consciousness moves intermittently in one direction along the latter from the beginning to the end of our lives."

"That," said a very young man, making spasmodic efforts to relight his cigar over the lamp; "that . . . very clear indeed."

"Now, it is very remarkable that this is so extensively overlooked," continued the Time Traveller, with a slight accession of cheerfulness. "Really this is what is meant by the Fourth Dimension, though some people who talk about the Fourth Dimension do not know they mean it. It is only another way of looking at Time. *There is no difference between Time and any of the three dimensions of Space except that our consciousness moves along it.* But some foolish people have got hold of the wrong side of that idea. You have all heard what they have to say about this Fourth Dimension?"

"*I* have not," said the Provincial Mayor.

"It is simply this. That Space, as our mathematicians have it, is spoken of as having three dimensions, which one may call Length, Breadth, and Thickness, and is always definable by reference to three planes, each at right angles to the others. But some philosophical people have been asking why *three* dimensions particularly—why not another direction at right angles to the other three?—and have even tried to construct a Four-Dimensional geometry. Professor Simon Newcomb was expounding this to the New York Mathematical Society only a month or so ago. You know how on a flat surface, which has only two dimensions, we can represent a figure of a three-dimensional solid, and similarly they think that by models of three dimensions they could represent one of four—if they could master the perspective of the thing. See?"

"I think so," murmured the Provincial Mayor; and, knitting his brows, he lapsed into an introspective state, his lips moving as one who repeats mystic words. "Yes, I think I see it now," he said after some time, brightening in a quite transitory manner.

"Well, I do not mind telling you I have been at work upon this geometry of Four Dimensions for some time. Some of my results are curious. For instance, here is a portrait of a man at eight years old, another at fifteen, another at seventeen, another at twenty-three, and so on. All these are evidently sections, as it were, Three-Dimensional representations of his Four-Dimensioned being, which is a fixed and unalterable thing.

"Scientific people," proceeded the Time Traveller, after the pause required for the proper assimilation of this, "know very well that Time is only a kind of Space. Here is a popular scientific diagram, a weather record. This line I trace with my fingers shows the movement of the barometer. Yesterday it was so high, yesterday night it fell, then this morning it rose again, and so gently upward to here. Surely the mercury did not trace this line in any of the dimensions of Space generally recognised? But certainly it traced such a line, and that line, therefore, we must conclude was along the Time-Dimension."

"But," said the Medical Man, staring hard at a coal in the fire, "if Time is really only a fourth dimension of Space, why is it, and why has it always been, regarded as something different? And why cannot we move in Time as we move about in the other dimensions of Space?"

The Time Traveller smiled. "Are you so sure we can move freely in Space? Right and left we can go, backward and forward freely enough, and men always have done so. I admit we move freely in two dimensions. But how about up and down? Gravitation limits us there."

"Not exactly," said the Medical Man. "There are balloons."

"But before the balloons, save for spasmodic jumping and the inequalities of the surface, man had no freedom of vertical movement."

"Still they could move a little up and down," said the Medical Man.

"Easier, far easier down than up."

"And you cannot move at all in Time, you cannot get away from the present moment."

"My dear sir, that is just where you are wrong. That is just where the whole world has gone wrong. We are always getting away from the present moment. Our mental existences, which are immaterial and have no dimensions, are passing along the Time-Dimension with a uniform velocity from the cradle to the grave. Just as we should travel *down* if we began our existence fifty miles above the earth's surface."

"But the great difficulty is this," interrupted the Psychologist. "You *can* move about in all directions of Space, but you cannot move about in Time."

"That is the germ of my great discovery. But you are wrong to say that we cannot move about in Time. For instance, if I am recalling an incident very vividly I go back to the instant of its occurrence: I become absent-minded, as you say. I jump back for a moment. Of course we have no means of staying back for any length of Time, any more than a savage or an animal has of staying six feet above the ground. But a civilised man is better off than the savage in this respect. He can go up against gravitation in a balloon, and why should he not hope that ultimately he may be able to stop or accelerate his drift along the Time-Dimension, or even turn about and travel the other way?"

"Oh, *this*," began Filby, "is all—"

"Why not?" said the Time Traveller.

"It's against reason," said Filby.

"What reason?" said the Time Traveller.

"You can show black is white by argument," said Filby, "but you will never convince me."

"Possibly not," said the Time Traveller. "But now you begin to see the object of my investigations into the geometry of Four Dimensions. Long ago I had a vague inkling of a machine——"

"To travel through Time!" exclaimed the Very Young Man.

"That shall travel indifferently in any direction of Space and Time, as the driver determines."

Filby contented himself with laughter.

"But I have experimental verification," said the Time Traveller.

"It would be remarkably convenient for the historian," the Psychologist suggested. "One might travel back and verify the accepted account of the Battle of Hastings, for instance!"

"Don't you think you would attract attention?" said the Medical Man. "Our ancestors had no great tolerance for anachronisms."

"One might get one's Greek from the very lips of Homer and Plato," the Very Young Man thought.

"In which case they would certainly plough you for the Little-go. The German scholars have improved Greek so much."

"Then there is the future," said the Very Young Man. "Just think!

One might invest all one's money, leave it to accumulate at interest, and hurry on ahead!"

"To discover a society," said I, "erected on a strictly communistic basis."

"Of all the wild extravagant theories!" began the Psychologist.

"Yes, so it seemed to me, and so I never talked of it until——"

"Experimental verification!" cried I. "You are going to verify *that?*"

"The experiment!" cried Filby, who was getting brain-weary.

"Let's see your experiment anyhow," said the Psychologist, "though it's all humbug, you know."

The Time Traveller smiled round at us. Then, still smiling faintly, and with his hands deep in his trousers pockets, he walked slowly out of the room, and we heard his slippers shuffling down the long passage to his laboratory.

The Psychologist looked at us. "I wonder what he's got?"

"Some sleight-of-hand trick or other," said the Medical Man, and Filby tried to tell us about a conjurer he had seen at Burslem; but before he had finished his preface the Time Traveller came back, and Filby's anecdote collapsed.

The thing the Time Traveller held in his hand was a glittering metallic framework, scarcely larger than a small clock, and very delicately made. There was ivory in it, and some transparent crystalline substance. And now I must be explicit, for this that follows—unless his explanation is to be accepted—is an absolutely unaccountable thing. He took one of the small octagonal tables that were scattered about the room, and set it in front of the fire, with two legs on the hearth rug. On this table he placed the mechanism. Then he drew up a chair, and sat down. The only other object on the table was a small shaded lamp, the bright light of which fell full upon the model. There were also perhaps a dozen candles about, two in brass candlesticks upon the mantel and several in sconces, so that the room was brilliantly illuminated. I sat in a low armchair nearest the fire, and I drew this forward so as to be almost between the Time Traveller and the fireplace. Filby sat behind him, looking over his shoulder. The Medical Man and the Provincial Mayor watched him in profile from the right, the Psychologist from the left. The Very Young Man stood behind the Psychologist. We were all on the alert. It appears incredible to me that any kind of trick, however subtly conceived and however adroitly done, could have been played upon us under these conditions.

The Time Traveller looked at us, and then at the mechanism. "Well?" said the Psychologist.

"This little affair," said the Time Traveller, resting his elbows upon the table and pressing his hands together above the apparatus, "is only a model. It is my plan for a machine to travel through time. You will notice that it looks singularly askew, and that there is an odd twinkling appearance about this bar, as though it was in some way unreal." He pointed to the part with his finger. "Also, here is one little white lever, and here is another."

The Medical Man got up out of his chair and peered into the thing. "It's beautifully made," he said.

"It took two years to make," retorted the Time Traveller. Then, when we had all imitated the action of the Medical Man, he said: "Now I want you clearly to understand that this lever, being pressed over, sends the machine gliding into the future, and this other reverses the motion. This saddle represents the seat of a time traveller. Presently I am going to press the lever, and off the machine will go. It will vanish, pass into future Time, and disappear. Have a good look at the thing. Look at the table too, and satisfy yourselves there is no trickery. I don't want to waste this model, and then be told I'm a quack."

There was a minute's pause perhaps. The Psychologist seemed about to speak to me, but changed his mind. Then the Time Traveller put forth his finger towards the lever. "No," he said suddenly. "Lend me your hand." And turning to the Psychologist, he took that individual's hand in his own and told him to put out his forefinger. So that it was the Psychologist himself who sent forth the model Time Machine on its interminable voyage. We all saw the lever turn. I am absolutely certain there was no trickery. There was a breath of wind, and the lamp flame jumped. One of the candles on the mantel was blown out, and the little machine suddenly swung round, became indistinct, was seen as a ghost for a second perhaps, as an eddy of faintly glittering brass and ivory; and it was gone—vanished! Save for the lamp the table was bare.

Every one was silent for a minute. Then Filby said he was damned.

The Psychologist recovered from his stupor, and suddenly looked under the table. At that the Time Traveller laughed cheerfully. "Well?" he said, with a reminiscence of the Psychologist. Then, getting up, he went to the tobacco jar on the mantel, and with his back to us began to fill his pipe.

We stared at each other. "Look here," said the Medical Man, "are you in earnest about this? Do you seriously believe that that machine has travelled into time?"

"Certainly," said the Time Traveller, stooping to light a spill at the fire. Then he turned, lighting his pipe, to look at the Psychologist's face. (The Psychologist, to show that he was not unhinged, helped himself to a cigar and tried to light it uncut.) "What is more, I have a big machine nearly finished in there"—he indicated the laboratory—"and when that is put together I mean to have a journey on my own account."

"You mean to say that that machine has travelled into the future?" said Filby.

"Into the future or the past—I don't, for certain, know which."

After an interval the Psychologist had an inspiration. "It must have gone into the past if it has gone anywhere," he said.

"Why?" said the Time Traveller.

"Because I presume that it has not moved in space, and if it travelled into the future it would still be here all this time, since it must have travelled through this time."

"But," said I, "if it travelled into the past it would have been visible when we came first into this room; and last Thursday when we were here; and the Thursday before that; and so forth!"

"Serious objections," remarked the Provincial Mayor, with an air of impartiality, turning towards the Time Traveller.

"Not a bit," said the Time Traveller, and, to the Psychologist: "You think. *You* can explain that. It's presentation below the threshold, you know, diluted presentation."

"Of course," said the Psychologist, and reassured us. "That's a simple point of psychology. I should have thought of it. It's plain enough, and helps the paradox delightfully. We cannot see it, nor can we appreciate this machine, any more than we can the spoke of a wheel spinning, or a bullet flying through the air. If it is travelling through time fifty times or a hundred times faster than we are, if it gets through a minute while we get through a second, the impression it creates will of course be only one-fiftieth or one-hundredth of what it would make if it were not travelling in time. That's plain enough." He passed his hand through the space in which the machine had been. "You see?" he said, laughing.

We sat and stared at the vacant table for a minute or so. Then the Time Traveller asked us what we thought of it all.

"It sounds plausible enough to-night," said the Medical Man; "but wait until to-morrow. Wait for the common sense of the morning."

"Would you like to see the Time Machine itself?" asked the Time Traveller. And therewith, taking the lamp in his hand, he led the way down the long, draughty corridor to his laboratory. I remember vividly the flickering light, his queer, broad head in silhouette, the dance of the shadows, how we all followed him, puzzled but incredulous, and how there in the laboratory we beheld a larger edition of the little mechanism which we had seen vanish from before our eyes. Parts were of nickel, parts of ivory, parts had certainly been filed or sawn out of rock crystal. The thing was generally complete, but the twisted crystalline bars lay unfinished upon the bench beside some sheets of drawings, and I took one up for a better look at it. Quartz it seemed to be.

"Look here," said the Medical Man, "are you perfectly serious? Or is this a trick—like that ghost you showed us last Christmas?"

"Upon that machine," said the Time Traveller, holding the lamp aloft, "I intend to explore time. Is that plain? I was never more serious in my life."

None of us quite knew how to take it.

I caught Filby's eye over the shoulder of the Medical Man, and he winked at me solemnly.

CHAPTER II: I think that at that time none of us quite believed in the Time Machine. The fact is, the Time Traveller was one of those men who are too clever to be believed: you never felt that you saw all round him; you always suspected some subtle reserve, some ingenuity in ambush, behind his lucid frankness. Had Filby shown the model and explained the matter in the Time Traveller's words, we should have shown *him* far less scepticism. For we should have perceived his motives: a pork butcher could understand Filby. But the Time Traveller had more than a touch of whim among his elements, and we distrusted him. Things that would have made the fame of a less clever man seemed tricks in his hands. It is a mistake to do things too easily. The serious people who took him seriously never felt quite sure of his deportment: they were somehow aware that trusting their reputations for judgment with him was like furnishing a nursery with egg-shell china. So I don't think any of us said very much about time travelling in the interval between that Thursday and the next, though its odd potentialities ran, no doubt, in most of our minds: its plausibility, that is, its practical incredibleness, the curious possibilities of anachronism and of utter confusion it suggested. For my own part, I was particularly preoccupied with the trick of the model. That I remember discussing with the Medical Man, whom I met on Friday at the Linnæan. He said he had seen a similar thing at Tübingen, and laid considerable stress on the blowing out of the candle. But how the trick was done he could not explain.

The next Thursday I went again to Richmond—I suppose I was one of the Time Traveller's most constant guests—and arriving late, found four or five men already assembled in his drawing-room. The Medical Man was standing before the fire with a sheet of paper in one hand and his watch in the other. I looked round for the Time Traveller, and—"It's half-past seven now," said the Medical Man. "I suppose we'd better have dinner?"

"Where's ——?" said I, naming our host.

"You've just come? It's rather odd. He's unavoidably detained. He asks me in this note to lead off with dinner at seven if he's not back. Says he'll explain when he comes."

"It seems a pity to let the dinner spoil," said the Editor of a well-known daily paper; and thereupon the Doctor rang the bell.

The Psychologist was the only person besides the Doctor and myself who had attended the previous dinner. The other men were Blank, the Editor afore-mentioned, a certain journalist, and another—a quiet, shy man with a beard—whom I didn't know, and who, as far as my observation went, never opened his mouth all the evening. There was some speculation at the dinner table about the Time Traveller's absence, and I suggested time travelling, in a half-jocular spirit. The Editor wanted that explained to him, and the Psychologist volunteered a wooden account of the "ingenious paradox and trick" we had witnessed that day week. He was in the midst of his exposition when the door from the corridor opened slowly and without noise. I was facing the door, and saw it first. "Hallo!" I said. "At last!" And the door opened wider, and the Time Traveller stood before us. I gave a cry of surprise. "Good heavens! man, what's the matter?" cried the Medical Man, who saw him next. And the whole tableful turned towards the door.

He was in an amazing plight. His coat was dusty and dirty and smeared with green down the sleeves; his hair disordered, and as it seemed to me greyer—either with dust and dirt or because its colour had actually faded. His face was ghastly pale; his chin had a brown cut on it—a cut half healed; his expression was haggard and drawn, as by intense suffering. For a moment he hesitated in the doorway, as if he had been dazzled by the light. Then he came into the room. He walked with just such a limp as I have seen in footsore tramps. We stared at him in silence, expecting him to speak.

He said not a word, but came painfully to the table, and made a motion towards the wine. The Editor filled a glass of champagne, and pushed it towards him. He drained it, and it seemed to do him good: for he looked round the table, and the ghost of his old smile flickered across his face. "What on earth have you been up to, man?" said the Doctor. The Time Traveller did not seem to hear. "Don't let me disturb you," he said, with a certain faltering articulation. "I'm all right." He stopped, held out his glass for more, and took it off at a draught. "That's good," he said. His eyes grew brighter, and a faint colour came into his cheeks. His glance flickered over our faces with a certain dull approval, and then went round the warm and comfortable room. Then he spoke again, still as it were feeling his way among his words. "I'm going to wash and dress, and then I'll come down and explain things. . . . Save me some of that mutton. I'm starving for a bit of meat."

He looked across at the Editor, who was a rare visitor, and hoped he was all right. The Editor began a question. "Tell you presently," said the Time Traveller. "I'm—funny! Be all right in a minute."

He put down his glass, and walked towards the staircase door. Again I remarked his lameness and the soft padding sound of his footfall, and standing up in my place, I saw his feet as he went out. He had nothing on them but a pair of tattered, bloodstained socks. Then the door closed upon him. I had half a mind to follow, till I remembered how he detested any fuss about himself. For a minute, perhaps, my mind was wool gathering. Then, "Remarkable Behaviour of an Eminent Scientist," I heard the Editor say, thinking (after his wont) in head-lines. And this brought my attention back to the bright dinner table.

"What's the game?" said the Journalist. "Has he been doing the Amateur Cadger? I don't follow." I met the eye of the Psychologist, and read my own interpretation in his face. I thought of the Time Traveller limping painfully upstairs. I don't think any one else had noticed his lameness.

The first to recover completely from this surprise was the Medical Man, who rang the bell—the Time Traveller hated to have servants waiting at dinner—for a hot plate. At that the Editor turned to his knife and fork with a grunt, and the Silent Man followed suit. The dinner was resumed. Conversation was exclamatory for a little while, with gaps of wonderment; and then the Editor got fervent in his curiosity. "Does our friend eke out his modest income with a crossing or has he his Nebuchadnezzar phases?" he inquired. "I feel assured it's this business of the Time Machine," I said, and took up the Psychologist's account of our previous meeting. The new guests were frankly incredulous. The Editor raised objections. "What *was* this time travelling? A man couldn't cover himself with dust by rolling in a paradox, could he?" And then, as the idea came home to him, he resorted to caricature. Hadn't they any clothes-brushes in the Future? The Journalist, too, would not believe at any price, and joined the Editor in the easy work of heaping ridicule on the whole thing. They were both the new kind of journalist—very joyous, irreverent young men. "Our Special Correspondent in the Day after To-morrow reports," the Journalist was saying—or rather shouting—when the Time Traveller came back. He was dressed in ordinary evening clothes, and nothing save his haggard look remained of the change that had startled me.

"I say," said the Editor hilariously, "these chaps here say you have been travelling into the middle of next week!! Tell us all about little Rosebery, will you? What will you take for the lot?"

The Time Traveller came to the place reserved for him without a word. He smiled quietly, in his old way. "Where's my mutton?" he said. "What a treat it is to stick a fork into meat again!"

"Story!" cried the Editor.

"Story be damned!" said the Time Traveller. "I want something to eat. I won't say a word until I get some peptone into my arteries. Thanks. And the salt."

"One word," said I. "Have you been time travelling?"

"Yes," said the Time Traveller, with his mouth full, nodding his head.

"I'd give a shilling a line for a verbatim note," said the Editor. The Time Traveller pushed his glass towards the Silent Man and rang it with his finger nail; at which the Silent Man, who had been staring at his face, started convulsively, and poured him wine. The rest of the dinner was uncomfortable. For my own part, sudden questions kept on rising to my lips, and I dare say it was the same with the others. The Journalist tried to relieve the tension by telling anecdotes of Hettie Potter. The Time Traveller devoted his attention to his dinner, and displayed the appetite of a tramp. The Medical Man smoked a cigarette, and watched the Time Traveller through his eyelashes. The Silent Man seemed even more clumsy than usual, and drank champagne with regularity and determination out of sheer nervousness. At last the Time Traveller pushed his plate away, and looked around us. "I suppose I must apologise," he said. "I was simply starving. I've had a most amazing time." He reached out his hand for a cigar, and cut the end. "But come into the smoking-room. It's too long a story to tell over greasy plates." And ringing the bell in passing, he led the way into the adjoining room.

"You have told Blank, and Dash, and Chose about the machine?" he said to me, leaning back in his easy chair and naming the three new guests.

"But the thing's a mere paradox," said the Editor.

"I can't argue to-night. I don't mind telling you the story, but I can't argue. I will," he went on, "tell you the story of what has happened to me, if you like, but you must refrain from interruptions. I want to tell it. Badly. Most of it will sound like lying. So be it! It's true—every word of it, all the same. I was in my laboratory at four o'clock, and since then . . . I've lived eight days . . . such days as no human being ever lived before! I'm nearly worn out, but I shan't sleep till I've told this thing over to you. Then I shall go to bed. But no interruptions! Is it agreed?"

"Agreed," said the Editor, and the rest of us echoed "Agreed." And with that the Time Traveller began his story as I have set it forth. He sat back in his chair at first, and spoke like a weary man. Afterwards he got more animated. In writing it down I feel with only too much keenness the inadequacy of pen and ink—and, above all, my own inadequacy—to express its quality. You read, I will suppose, attentively enough; but you cannot see the speaker's white, sincere face in the bright circle of the little lamp, nor hear the intonation of his voice. You cannot know how his expression followed the turns of his story! Most of us hearers were in shadow, for the candles in the smoking-room had not been lighted, and only the face of the Journalist and the legs of the Silent Man from the knees downward were illuminated. At first we glanced now and again at each other. After a time we ceased to do that, and looked only at the Time Traveller's face.

CHAPTER III: "I told some of you last Thursday of the principles of the Time Machine, and showed you the actual thing itself, incomplete in the workshop. There it is now, a little travel-worn, truly; and one of the ivory bars is cracked, and a brass rail bent; but the rest of it's sound enough. I expected to finish it on Friday; but on Friday, when the putting together was nearly done, I found that one of the nickel bars was exactly one inch too short, and this I had to get re-made; so that the thing was not complete until this morning. It was at ten o'clock to-day that the first of all Time Machines began its career. I gave it a last tap, tried all the screws again, put one more drop of oil on the quartz rod, and sat myself in the saddle. I suppose a suicide who holds a pistol to his skull feels much the same wonder at what will come next as I felt then. I took the starting lever in one hand and the stopping one in the other, pressed the first, and almost immediately the second. I seemed to reel; I felt a nightmare sensation of falling; and, looking round, I saw the laboratory exactly as before. Had anything happened? For a moment I suspected that my intellect had tricked me. Then I noted the clock. A moment before, as it seemed, it had stood at a minute or so past ten; now it was nearly half-past three!

"I drew a breath, set my teeth, gripped the starting lever with both hands, and went off with a thud. The laboratory got hazy and went dark. Mrs. Watchett came in and walked, apparently without seeing me, towards the garden door. I suppose it took her a minute or so to traverse the place, but to me she seemed to shoot across the room like a rocket. I pressed the lever over to its extreme position. The night came like the turning out of a lamp, and in another moment came to-morrow. The laboratory grew faint and hazy, then fainter and ever fainter. To-morrow night came black, then day again, night again, day again, faster and faster still. An eddying murmur filled my ears, and a strange, dumb confusedness descended on my mind.

"I am afraid I cannot convey the peculiar sensations of time travelling. They are excessively unpleasant. There is a feeling exactly like that one has upon a switchback—of a helpless headlong motion! I felt the same horrible anticipation, too, of an imminent smash. As I put on pace, night followed day like the flapping of a black wing. The dim suggestion of the laboratory seemed presently to fall away from me, and I saw the sun hopping swiftly across the sky, leaping it every minute, and every minute marking a day. I supposed the laboratory had been destroyed and I had come into the open air. I had a dim impression of scaffolding, but I was already going too fast to be con-

scious of any moving things. The slowest snail that ever crawled
dashed by too fast for me. The twinkling succession of darkness and
light was excessively painful to the eye. Then, in the intermittent
darknesses, I saw the moon spinning swiftly through her quarters
from new to full, and had a faint glimpse of the circling stars. Presently, as I went on, still gaining velocity, the palpitation of night and
day merged into one continuous greyness; the sky took on a wonderful deepness of blue, a splendid luminous colour like that of early
twilight; the jerking sun became a streak of fire, a brilliant arch, in
space; the moon a fainter fluctuating band; and I could see nothing of
the stars, save now and then a brighter circle flickering in the blue.

"The landscape was misty and vague. I was still on the hillside
upon which this house now stands, and the shoulder rose above me
grey and dim. I saw trees growing and changing like puffs of vapour,
now brown, now green; they grew, spread, shivered, and passed away.
I saw huge buildings rise up faint and fair, and pass like dreams.
The whole surface of the earth seemed changed—melting and flowing
under my eyes. The little hands upon the dials that registered my
speed raced round faster and faster. Presently I noted that the sun
belt swayed up and down, from solstice to solstice, in a minute or
less, and that consequently my pace was over a year a minute; and
minute by minute the white snow flashed across the world, and
vanished, and was followed by the bright, brief green of spring.

"The unpleasant sensations of the start were less poignant now.
They merged at last into a kind of hysterical exhilaration. I remarked
indeed a clumsy swaying of the machine for which I was unable to
account. But my mind was too confused to attend to it so with a kind
of madness growing upon me, I flung myself into futurity. At first I
scarce thought of stopping, scarce thought of anything but these new
sensations. But presently a fresh series of impressions grew up in my
mind—a certain curiosity and therewith a certain dread—until at last
they took complete possession of me. What strange developments of
humanity, what wonderful advances upon our rudimentary civilisation, I thought, might not appear when I came to look nearly into the
dim elusive world that raced and fluctuated before my eyes! I saw
great and splendid architecture rising about me, more massive than
any buildings of our own time, and yet, as it seemed, built of glim-
mer and mist. I saw a richer green flow up the hillside, and remain
there without any wintry intermission. Even through the veil of my
confusion the earth seemed very fair. And so my mind came round
to the business of stopping.

"The peculiar risk lay in the possibility of my finding some substance in the space which I, or the machine, occupied. So long as I travelled at a high velocity through time, this scarcely mattered; I was, so to speak, attenuated—was slipping like a vapour through the interstices of intervening substances! But to come to a stop involved the jamming of myself, molecule by molecule, into whatever lay in my way; meant bringing my atoms into such intimate contact with those of the obstacle that a profound chemical reaction—possibly a far-reaching explosion—would result, and blow myself and my apparatus out of all possible dimensions—into the Unknown. This possibility had occurred to me again and again while I was making the machine; but then I had cheerfully accepted it as an unavoidable risk —one of the risks a man has got to take! Now the risk was inevitable, I no longer saw it in the same cheerful light. The fact is that, insensibly, the absolute strangeness of everything, the sickly jarring and swaying of the machine, above all, the feeling of prolonged falling, had absolutely upset my nerve. I told myself that I could never stop, and with a gust of petulance I resolved to stop forthwith. Like an impatient fool, I lugged over the lever, and incontinently the thing went reeling over, and I was flung headlong through the air.

"There was the sound of a clap of thunder in my ears. I may have been stunned for a moment. A pitiless hail was hissing round me, and I was sitting on soft turf in front of the overset machine. Everything still seemed grey, but presently I remarked that the confusion in my ears was gone. I looked round me. I was on what seemed to be a little lawn in a garden, surrounded by rhododendron bushes, and I noticed that their mauve and purple blossoms were dropping in a shower under the beating of the hailstones. The rebounding, dancing hail hung in a cloud over the machine, and drove along the ground like smoke. In a moment I was wet to the skin. 'Fine hospitality,' said I, 'to a man who has travelled innumerable years to see you.'

"Presently I thought what a fool I was to get wet. I stood up and looked round me. A colossal figure, carved apparently in some white stone, loomed indistinctly beyond the rhododendrons through the hazy downpour. But all else of the world was invisible.

"My sensations would be hard to describe. As the columns of hail grew thinner, I saw the white figure more distinctly. It was very large, for a silver birch-tree touched its shoulder. It was of white marble, in shape something like a winged sphinx, but the wings, instead of being carried vertically at the sides, were spread so that it seemed to hover. The pedestal, it appeared to me, was of bronze, and was thick with verdigris. It chanced that the face was towards me; the sightless eyes seemed to watch me; there was the faint shadow of a smile on the lips. It was greatly weather-worn, and that imparted an unpleasant suggestion of disease. I stood looking at it for a little space—half a minute, perhaps, or half an hour. It seemed to advance and to recede as the hail drove before it denser or thinner. At last I tore my eyes from it for a moment, and saw that the hail curtain had worn thread-bare, and that the sky was lightening with the promise of the sun.

"I looked up again at the crouching white shape, and the full te-merity of my voyage came suddenly upon me. What might appear when that hazy curtain was altogether withdrawn? What might not have happened to men? What if cruelty had grown into a common passion? What if in this interval the race had lost its manliness, and had developed into something inhuman, unsympathetic, and over-whelmingly powerful? I might seem some old-world savage animal, only the more dreadful and disgusting for our common likeness—a foul creature to be incontinently slain.

"Already I saw other vast shapes—huge buildings with intricate parapets and tall columns, with a wooded hillside dimly creeping in upon me through the lessening storm. I was seized with a panic fear. I turned frantically to the Time Machine, and strove hard to readjust it. As I did so the shafts of the sun smote through the thunderstorm. The grey downpour was swept aside and vanished like the trailing garments of a ghost. Above me, in the intense blue of the summer sky, some faint brown shreds of cloud whirled into nothingness. The great buildings about me stood out clear and distinct, shining with the wet of the thunderstorm, and picked out in white by the unmelted hailstones piled along their courses. I felt naked in a strange world. I felt as perhaps a bird may feel in the clear air, knowing the hawk wings above and will swoop. My fear grew to frenzy. I took a breath-ing space, set my teeth, and again grappled fiercely, wrist and knee, with the machine. It gave under my desperate onset and turned over. It struck my chin violently. One hand on the saddle, the other on the lever, I stood panting heavily in attitude to mount again.

"But with this recovery of a prompt retreat my courage recovered. I looked more curiously and less fearfully at this world of the remote future. In a circular opening, high up in the wall of the nearer house, I saw a group of figures clad in rich soft robes. They had seen me, and their faces were directed towards me.

"Then I heard voices approaching me. Coming through the bushes by the White Sphinx were the heads and shoulders of men running. One of these emerged in a pathway leading straight to the little lawn upon which I stood with my machine. He was a slight creature —perhaps four feet high—clad in a purple tunic, girdled at the waist with a leather belt. Sandals or buskins—I could not clearly distinguish which—were on his feet; his legs were bare to the knees, and his head was bare. Noticing that, I noticed for the first time how warm the air was.

"He struck me as being a very beautiful and graceful creature, but indescribably frail. His flushed face reminded me of the more beautiful kind of consumptive—that hectic beauty of which we used to hear so much. At the sight of him I suddenly regained confidence. I took my hands from the machine.

CHAPTER IV: "In another moment we were standing face to face, I and this fragile thing out of futurity. He came straight up to me and laughed into my eyes. The absence from his bearing of any sign of fear struck me at once. Then he turned to the two others who were following him and spoke to them in a strange and very sweet and liquid tongue.

"There were others coming, and presently a little group of perhaps eight or ten of these exquisite creatures were about me. One of them addressed me. It came into my head, oddly enough, that my voice was too harsh and deep for them. So I shook my head, and, pointing to my ears, shook it again. He came a step forward, hesitated, and then touched my hand. Then I felt other soft little tentacles upon my back and shoulders. They wanted to make sure I was real. There was nothing in this at all alarming. Indeed, there was something in these pretty little people that inspired confidence—a graceful gentleness, a certain childlike ease. And besides, they looked so frail that I could fancy myself flinging the whole dozen of them about like nine-pins. But I made a sudden motion to warn them when I saw their little pink hands feeling at the Time Machine. Happily then, when it was not too late, I thought of a danger I had hitherto forgotten, and reaching over the bars of the machine I unscrewed the little levers that would set it in motion, and put these in my pocket. Then I turned again to see what I could do in the way of communication.

"And then, looking more nearly into their features, I saw some further peculiarities in their Dresden-china type of prettiness. Their hair, which was uniformly curly, came to a sharp end at the neck and cheek; there was not the faintest suggestion of it on the face, and their ears were singularly minute. The mouths were small, with bright red, rather thin lips, and the little chins ran to a point. The eyes were large and mild; and—this may seem egotism on my part—I fancied even then that there was a certain lack of the interest I might have expected in them.

"As they made no effort to communicate with me, but simply stood round me smiling and speaking in soft cooing notes to each other, I began the conversation. I pointed to the Time Machine and to myself. Then hesitating for a moment how to express time, I pointed to the sun. At once a quaintly pretty little figure in chequered purple and white followed my gesture, and then astonished me by imitating the sound of thunder.

"For a moment I was staggered, though the import of his gesture was plain enough. The question had come into my mind abruptly: were these creatures fools? You may hardly understand how it took me. You see I had always anticipated that the people of the year Eight Hundred and Two Thousand odd would be incredibly in front of us in knowledge, art, everything. Then one of them suddenly asked me a question that showed him to be on the intellectual level of one of our five-year-old children—asked me, in fact, if I had come from the sun in a thunderstorm! It let loose the judgment I had suspended upon their clothes, their frail light limbs, and fragile features. A flow of disappointment rushed across my mind. For a moment I felt that I had built the Time Machine in vain.

"I nodded, pointed to the sun, and gave them such a vivid rendering of a thunderclap as startled them. They all withdrew a pace or so and bowed. Then came one laughing towards me, carrying a chain of beautiful flowers altogether new to me, and put it about my neck. The idea was received with melodious applause; and presently they were all running to and fro for flowers, and laughingly flinging them upon me until I was almost smothered with blossom. You who have never seen the like can scarcely imagine what delicate and wonderful flowers countless years of culture had created. Then someone suggested that their plaything should be exhibited in the nearest building, and so I was led past the sphinx of white marble, which had seemed to watch me all the while with a smile at my astonishment, towards a vast grey edifice of fretted stone. As I went with them the memory of my confident anticipations of a profoundly grave and intellectual posterity came, with irresistible merriment, to my mind.

"The building had a huge entry, and was altogether of colossal dimensions. I was naturally most occupied with the growing crowd of little people, and with the big open portals that yawned before me shadowy and mysterious. My general impression of the world I saw over their heads was of a tangled waste of beautiful bushes and flowers, a long-neglected and yet weedless garden. I saw a number of tall spikes of strange white flowers, measuring a foot perhaps across the spread of the waxen petals. They grew scattered, as if wild, among the variegated shrubs, but, as I say, I did not examine them closely at this time. The Time Machine was left deserted on the turf among the rhododendrons.

"The arch of the doorway was richly carved, but naturally I did not observe the carving very narrowly, though I fancied I saw suggestions of old Phœnician decorations as I passed through, and it struck me that they were very badly broken and weather-worn. Several more brightly clad people met me in the doorway, and so we entered, I, dressed in dingy nineteenth-century garments, looking grotesque enough, garlanded with flowers, and surrounded by an eddying mass of bright, soft-coloured robes and shining white limbs, in a melodious whirl of laughter and laughing speech.

"The big doorway opened into a proportionately great hall hung with brown. The roof was in shadow, and the windows, partially glazed with coloured glass and partially unglazed, admitted a tempered light. The floor was made up of huge blocks of some very hard white metal, not plates nor slabs,—blocks, and it was so much worn, as I judged by the going to and fro of past generations, as to be deeply channelled along the more frequented ways. Transverse to the length were innumerable tables made of slabs of polished stone, raised perhaps a foot from the floor, and upon these were heaps of fruits. Some I recognised as a kind of hypertrophied raspberry and orange, but for the most part they were strange.

"Between the tables was scattered a great number of cushions. Upon these my conductors seated themselves, signing for me to do likewise. With a pretty absence of ceremony they began to eat the fruit with their hands, flinging peel and stalks and so forth into the round openings in the sides of the tables. I was not loath to follow their example, for I felt thirsty and hungry. As I did so I surveyed the hall at my leisure.

"And perhaps the thing that struck me most was its dilapidated look. The stained-glass windows, which displayed only a geometrical pattern, were broken in many places, and the curtains that hung across the lower end were thick with dust. And it caught my eye that the corner of the marble table near me was fractured. Nevertheless, the general effect was extremely rich and picturesque. There were, perhaps, a couple of hundred people dining in the hall, and most of them, seated as near to me as they could come, were watching me with interest, their little eyes shining over the fruit they were eating. All were clad in the same soft, and yet strong, silky material.

"Fruit, by the bye, was all their diet. These people of the remote future were strict vegetarians, and while I was with them, in spite of some carnal cravings, I had to be frugivorous also. Indeed, I found afterwards that horses, cattle, sheep, dogs, had followed the Ichthyosaurus into extinction. But the fruits were very delightful; one, in particular, that seemed to be in season all the time I was there—a floury thing in a three-sided husk—was especially good, and I made it my staple. At first I was puzzled by all these strange fruits, and by the strange flowers I saw, but later I began to perceive their import.

"However, I am telling you of my fruit dinner in the distant future now. So soon as my appetite was a little checked, I determined to make a resolute attempt to learn the speech of these new men of mine. Clearly that was the next thing to do. The fruits seemed a convenient thing to begin upon, and holding one of these up I began a series of interrogative sounds and gestures. I had some considerable difficulty in conveying my meaning. At first my efforts met with a stare of surprise or inextinguishable laughter, but presently a fair-haired little creature seemed to grasp my intention and repeated a name. They had to chatter and explain the business at great length to each other, and my first attempts to make the exquisite little sounds of their language caused an immense amount of amusement. However, I felt like a schoolmaster amidst children, and persisted, and presently I had a score of noun substantives at least at my command; and then I got to demonstrative pronouns, and even the verb 'to eat.' But it was slow work, and the little people soon tired and wanted to get away from my interrogations, so I determined, rather of necessity, to let them give their lessons in little doses when they felt inclined. And very little doses I found they were before long, for I never met people more indolent or more easily fatigued.

"A queer thing I soon discovered about my little hosts, and that was their lack of interest. They would come to me with eager cries of astonishment, like children, but like children they would soon stop examining me and wander away after some other toy. The dinner and my conversational beginnings ended, I noted for the first time that almost all those who had surrounded me at first were gone. It is odd, too, how speedily I came to disregard these little people. I went out through the portal into the sunlit world again so soon as my hunger was satisfied. I was continually meeting more of these men of the future, who would follow me a little distance, chatter and laugh about me, and, having smiled and gesticulated in a friendly way, leave me again to my own devices.

"The calm of evening was upon the world as I emerged from the great hall, and the scene was lit by the warm glow of the setting sun. At first things were very confusing. Everything was so entirely different from the world I had known—even the flowers. The big building I had left was situated on the slope of a broad river valley, but the Thames had shifted perhaps a mile from its present position. I resolved to mount to the summit of a crest, perhaps a mile and a half away, from which I could get a wider view of this our planet in the year Eight Hundred and Two Thousand Seven Hundred and One A.D. For that, I should explain, was the date the little dials of my machine recorded.

"As I walked I was watchful for every impression that could possibly help to explain the condition of ruinous splendour in which I found the world—for ruinous it was. A little way up the hill, for instance, was a great heap of granite, bound together by masses of aluminium, a vast labyrinth of precipitous walls and crumbled heaps, amidst which were thick heaps of very beautiful pagoda-like plants—nettles possibly—but wonderfully tinted with brown about the leaves, and incapable of stinging. It was evidently the derelict remains of some vast structure, to what end built I could not determine. It was here that I was destined, at a later date, to have a very strange experience—the first intimation of a still stranger discovery—but of that I will speak in its proper place.

"Looking round with a sudden thought, from a terrace on which I rested for a while, I realised that there were no small houses to be seen. Apparently the single house, and possibly even the houshold, had vanished. Here and there among the greenery were palace-like buildings, but the house and the cottage, which form such characteristic features of our own English landscape, had disappeared.

" 'Communism,' said I to myself.

"And on the heels of that came another thought. I looked at the half-dozen little figures that were following me. Then, in a flash, I perceived that all had the same form of costume, the same soft hairless visage, and the same girlish rotundity of limb. It may seem strange, perhaps, that I had not noticed this before. But everything was so strange. Now, I saw the fact plainly enough. In costume, and in all the differences of texture and bearing that now mark off the sexes from each other, these people of the future were alike. And the children seemed to my eyes to be but the miniatures of their parents. I judged, then, that the children of that time were extremely precocious, physically at least, and I found afterwards abundant verification of my opinion.

"Seeing the ease and security in which these people were living, I felt that this close resemblance of the sexes was after all what one would expect; for the strength of a man and the softness of a woman, the institution of the family, and the differentiation of occupations are mere militant necessities of an age of physical force. Where population is balanced and abundant, much child-bearing becomes an evil rather than a blessing to the State; where violence comes but rarely and offspring are secure, there is less necessity—indeed there is no necessity—for an efficient family, and the specialisation of the sexes with reference to their children's needs disappears. We see some beginnings of this even in our own time, and in this future age it was complete. This, I must remind you, was my speculation at the time. Later, I was to appreciate how far it fell short of the reality.

"While I was musing upon these things, my attention was attracted by a pretty little structure, like a well under a cupola. I thought in a transitory way of the oddness of wells still existing, and then resumed the thread of my speculations. There were no large buildings towards the top of the hill, and as my walking powers were evidently miraculous, I was presently left alone for the first time. With a strange sense of freedom and adventure I pushed on up to the crest.

"There I found a seat of some yellow metal that I did not recognise, corroded in places with a kind of pinkish rust and half smothered in soft moss, the arm rests cast and filed into the resemblance of griffins' heads. I sat down on it, and I surveyed the broad view of our old world under the sunset of that long day. It was as sweet and fair a view as I have ever seen. The sun had already gone below the horizon and the west was flaming gold, touched with some horizontal bars of purple and crimson. Below was the valley of the Thames, in which the river lay like a band of burnished steel. I have already spoken of the great palaces dotted about among the variegated greenery, some in ruins and some still occupied. Here and there rose a white or silvery figure in the waste garden of the earth, here and there came the sharp vertical line of some cupola or obelisk. There were no hedges, no signs of proprietary rights, no evidences of agriculture; the whole earth had become a garden.

"So watching, I began to put my interpretation upon the things I had seen, and as it shaped itself to me that evening, my interpretation was something in this way. (Afterwards I found I had got only a half-truth—or only a glimpse of one facet of the truth.)

"It seemed to me that I had happened upon humanity upon the wane. The ruddy sunset set me thinking of the sunset of mankind. For the first time I began to realise an odd consequence of the social effort in which we are at present engaged. And yet, come to think, it is a logical consequence enough. Strength is the outcome of need; security sets a premium on feebleness. The work of ameliorating the conditions of life—the true civilising process that makes life more and more secure—had gone steadily on to a climax. One triumph of a united humanity over Nature had followed another. Things that are now mere dreams had become projects deliberately put in hand and carried forward. And the harvest was what I saw!

"After all, the sanitation and the agriculture of to-day are still in the rudimentary stage. The science of our time has attacked but a little department of the field of human disease, but, even so, it spreads its operations very steadily and persistently. Our agriculture and horticulture destroy a weed just here and there and cultivate perhaps a score or so of wholesome plants, leaving the greater number to fight out a balance as they can. We improve our favourite plants and animals—and how few they are—gradually by selective breeding; now a new and better peach, now a seedless grape, now a sweeter and larger flower, now a more convenient breed of cattle. We improve them gradually, because our ideals are vague and tentative, and our knowledge is very limited; because Nature, too, is shy and slow in our clumsy hands. Some day all this will be better organised, and still better. That is the drift of the current in spite of the eddies. The whole world will be intelligent, educated, and cooperating; things will move faster and faster towards the subjugation of Nature. In the end, wisely and carefully we shall readjust the balance of animal and vegetable life to suit our human needs.

"This adjustment, I say, must have been done, and done well;

done indeed for all Time, in the space of Time across which my machine had leaped. The air was free from gnats, the earth from weeds or fungi; everywhere were fruits and sweet and delightful flowers; brilliant butterflies flew hither and thither. The ideal of preventive medicine was attained. Diseases had been stamped out. I saw no evidence of any contagious diseases during all my stay. And I shall have to tell you later that even the processes of putrefaction and decay had been profoundly affected by these changes.

"Social triumphs, too, had been effected. I saw mankind housed in splendid shelters, gloriously clothed, and as yet I had found them engaged in no toil. There were no signs of struggle, neither social nor economical struggle. The shop, the advertisement, traffic, all that commerce which constitutes the body of our world, was gone. It was natural on that golden evening that I should jump at the idea of a social paradise. The difficulty of increasing population had been met, I guessed, and population had ceased to increase.

"But with this change in condition come inevitably adaptations to the change. What, unless biological science is a mass of errors, is the cause of human intelligence and vigour? Hardship and freedom: conditions under which the active, strong, and subtle survive and the weaker go to the wall; conditions that put a premium upon the loyal alliance of capable men, upon self-restraint, patience, and decision. And the institution of the family, and the emotions that arise therein, the fierce jealousy, the tenderness for offspring, parental self-devotion, all found their justification and support in the imminent dangers of the young. *Now,* where are these imminent dangers? There is a sentiment arising, and it will grow, against connubial jealousy, against fierce maternity, against passion of all sorts; unnecessary things now, and things that make us uncomfortable, savage survivals, discords in a refined and pleasant life.

"I thought of the physical slightness of the people, their lack of intelligence, and those big abundant ruins, and it strengthened my belief in a perfect conquest of Nature. For after the battle comes Quiet. Humanity has been strong, energetic, and intelligent, and had used all its abundant vitality to alter the conditions under which it lived. And now came the reaction of the altered conditions.

"Under the new conditions of perfect comfort and security that restless energy, that with us is strength, would become weakness. Even in our own time certain tendencies and desires, once necessary to survival, are a constant source of failure. Physical courage and the love of battle, for instance, are no great help—may even be hindrances —to a civilised man. And in a state of physical balance and security, power, intellectual as well as physical, would be out of place. For countless years I judged there had been no danger of war or solitary violence, no danger from wild beasts, no wasting disease to require strength of constitution, no need of toil. For such a life, what we should call the weak are as well equipped as the strong, are indeed no longer weak. Better equipped indeed they are, for the strong would be fretted by an energy for which there was no outlet. No doubt the exquisite beauty of the buildings I saw was the outcome of the last surgings of the now purposeless energy of mankind before it settled down into perfect harmony with the conditions under which it lived—the flourish of that triumph which began the last great peace. This has ever been the fate of energy in security; it takes to art and to eroticism, and then come languor and decay.

"Even this artistic impetus would at last die away—had almost died in the Time I saw. To adorn themselves with flowers, to dance, to sing in the sunlight; so much was left of the artistic spirit, and no more. Even that would fade in the end into a contented inactivity. We are kept keen on the grindstone of pain and necessity, and, it seemed to me, that here was that hateful grindstone broken at last!

"As I stood there in the gathering dark I thought that in this simple explanation I had mastered the problem of the world—mastered the whole secret of these delicious people. Possibly the checks they had devised for the increase of population had succeeded too well, and their numbers had rather diminished than kept stationary. That would account for the abandoned ruins. Very simple was my explanation, and plausible enough—as most wrong theories are!

CHAPTER V: "As I stood there musing over this too perfect triumph of man, the full moon, yellow and gibbous, came up out of an overflow of silver light in the northeast. The bright little figures ceased to move about below, a noiseless owl flitted by, and I shivered with the chill of the night. I determined to descend and find where I could sleep.

"I looked for the building I knew. Then my eye travelled along to the figure of the White Sphinx upon the pedestal of bronze, growing distinct as the light of the rising moon grew brighter. I could see the silver birch against it. There was the tangle of rhododendron bushes, black in the pale light, and there was the little lawn. I looked at the lawn again. A queer doubt chilled my complacency. 'No,' said I stoutly to myself, 'that was not the lawn.'

"But it *was* the lawn. For the white leprous face of the sphinx was towards it. Can you imagine what I felt as this conviction came home to me? But you cannot. The Time Machine was gone!

"At once, like a lash across the face, came the possibility of losing my own age, of being left helpless in this strange new world. The bare thought of it was an actual physical sensation. I could feel it grip me at the throat and stop my breathing. In another moment I was in a passion of fear and running with great leaping strides down the slope. Once I fell headlong and cut my face; I lost no time in stanching the blood, but jumped up and ran on, with a warm trickle down my cheek and chin. All the time I ran I was saying to myself, 'They have moved it a little, pushed it under the bushes out of the way.' Nevertheless, I ran with all my might. All the time, with the certainty that sometimes comes with excessive dread, I knew that such assurance was folly, knew instinctively that the machine was removed out of my reach. My breath came with pain. I suppose I covered the whole distance from the hill crest to the little lawn, two miles, perhaps, in ten minutes. And I am not a young man. I cursed aloud, as I ran, at my confident folly in leaving the machine, wasting good breath thereby. I cried aloud, and none answered. Not a creature seemed to be stirring in that moonlit world.

"When I reached the lawn my worst fears were realised. Not a trace of the thing was to be seen. I felt faint and cold when I faced the empty space among the black tangle of bushes. I ran round it furiously, as if the thing might be hidden in a corner, and then stopped abruptly, with my hands clutching my hair. Above me towered the sphinx, upon the bronze pedestal, white, shining, leprous, in the light of the rising moon. It seemed to smile in mockery of my dismay.

"I might have consoled myself by imagining the little people had put the mechanism in some shelter for me, had I not felt assured of their physical and intellectual inadequacy. That is what dismayed me: the sense of some hitherto unsuspected power, through whose intervention my invention had vanished. Yet, of one thing I felt assured: unless some other age had produced its exact duplicate, the machine could not have moved in time. The attachment of the levers—I will show you the method later—prevented any one from tampering with it in that way when they were removed. It had moved, and was hid, only in space. But then, where could it be?

"I think I must have had a kind of frenzy. I remember running violently in and out among the moonlit bushes all round the sphinx, and startling some white animal that, in the dim light, I took for a small deer. I remember, too, late that night, beating the bushes with my clenched fists until my knuckles were gashed and bleeding from the broken twigs. Then, sobbing and raving in my anguish of mind, I went down to the great building of stone. The big hall was dark, silent, and deserted. I slipped on the uneven floor, and fell over one of the malachite tables, almost breaking my shin. I lit a match and went on past the dusty curtains, of which I have told you.

"There I found a second great hall covered with cushions, upon which, perhaps, a score or so of the little people were sleeping. I have no doubt they found my second appearance strange enough, coming suddenly out of the quiet darkness with inarticulate noises and the splutter and flare of a match. For they had forgotten about matches. 'Where is my Time Machine?' I began, bawling like an angry child, laying hands upon them and shaking them up together. It must have been very queer to them. Some laughed, most of them looked sorely frightened. When I saw them standing round me, it came into my head that I was doing as foolish a thing as it was possible for me to do under the circumstances, in trying to revive the sensation of fear. For, reasoning from their daylight behaviour, I thought that fear must be forgotten.

"Abruptly, I dashed down the match, and, knocking one of the people over in my course, went blundering across the big dining-hall again, out under the moonlight. I heard cries of terror and their little feet running and stumbling this way and that. I do not remember all I did as the moon crept up the sky. I suppose it was the unexpected nature of my loss that maddened me. I felt hopelessly cut off from my own kind—a strange animal in an unknown world. I must have raved to and fro, screaming and crying upon God and Fate. I have a memory of horrible fatigue, as the long night of despair wore away; of looking in this impossible place and that; of groping among moonlit ruins and touching strange creatures in the black shadows; at last, of lying on the ground near the sphinx and weeping with absolute wretchedness. I had nothing left but misery. Then I slept, and when I woke again it was full day, and a couple of sparrows were hopping round me on the turf within reach of my arm.

"I sat up in the freshness of the morning, trying to remember how I had got there, and why I had such a profound sense of desertion and despair. Then things came clear in my mind. With the plain, reasonable daylight, I could look my circumstances fairly in the face. I saw the wild folly of my frenzy overnight, and I could reason with myself. 'Suppose the worst?' I said. 'Suppose the machine altogether lost—perhaps destroyed? It behooves me to be calm and patient, to learn the way of the people, to get a clear idea of the method of my loss, and the means of getting materials and tools; so that in the end, perhaps, I may make another.' That would be my only hope, a poor hope perhaps, but better than despair. And, after all, it was a beautiful and curious world.

"But probably the machine had only been taken away. Still, I must be calm and patient, find its hiding place, and recover it by force or cunning. And with that I scrambled to my feet and looked about me, wondering where I could bathe. I felt weary, stiff, and travel-soiled. The freshness of the morning made me desire an equal freshness. I had exhausted my emotion. Indeed, as I went about my business, I found myself wondering at my intense excitement over-night. I made a careful examination of the ground about the little lawn. I wasted some time in futile questionings, conveyed, as well as I was able, to such of the little people as came by. They all failed to understand my gestures; some were simply stolid, some thought it was a jest and laughed at me. I had the hardest task in the world to keep my hands off their pretty laughing faces. It was a foolish im-pulse, but the devil begotten of fear and blind anger was ill curbed and still eager to take advantaɟe of my perplexity. The turf gave better counsel. I found a groove ripped in it, about midway between the pedestal of the sphinx and the marks of my feet where, on arrival, I had struggled with the overturned machine. There were other signs of removal about, with queer narrow footprints like those I could imagine made by a sloth. This directed my closer attention to the ped-estal. It was, as I think I have said, of bronze. It was not a mere block, but highly decorated with deep framed panels on either side. I went and rapped at these. The pedestal was hollow. Examining the panels with care I found them discontinuous with the frames. There were no handles or keyholes, but possibly the panels, if they were doors, as I supposed, opened from within. One thing was clear enough to my mind. I took no very great mental effort to infer that my Time Machine was inside that pedestal. But how it got there was a different problem.

"I saw the heads of two orange-clad people coming through the bushes and under some blossom-covered apple-trees towards me. I turned smiling to them and beckoned them to me. They came, and then, pointing to the bronze pedestal, I tried to intimate my wish to open it. But at my first gesture towards this they behaved very oddly. I don't know how to convey their expression to you. Suppose you were to use a grossly improper gesture to a delicate-minded woman— it is how she would look. They went off as if they had received the last possible insult. I tried a sweet-looking little chap in white next, with exactly the same result. Somehow, his manner made me feel ashamed of myself. But, as you know, I wanted the Time Machine, and I tried him once more. As he turned off, like the others, my temper got the better of me. In three strides I was after him, had him by the loose part of his robe round the neck, and began dragging him towards the sphinx. Then I saw the horror and repugnance of his face, and all of a sudden I let him go.

"But I was not beaten yet. I banged with my fist at the bronze panels. I thought I heard something stir inside—to be explicit, I thought I heard a sound like a chuckle—but I must have been mistaken. Then I got a big pebble from the river, and came and hammered till I had flattened a coil in the decorations, and the verdigris came off in powdery flakes. The delicate little people must have heard me hammering in gusty outbreaks a mile away on either hand, but nothing came of it. I saw a crowd of them upon the slopes, looking furtively at me. At last, hot and tired, I sat down to watch the place. But I was too restless to watch long; I am too Occidental for a long vigil. I could work at a problem for years, but to wait inactive for twenty-four hours—that is another matter.

"I got up after a time, and began walking aimlessly through the bushes towards the hill again. 'Patience,' said I to myself. 'If you want your machine again you must leave that sphinx alone. If they mean to take your machine away, it's little good your wrecking their bronze panels, and if they don't, you will get it back as soon as you can ask for it. To sit among all these unknown things before a puzzle like that is hopeless. That way lies monomania. Face this world. Learn its ways, watch it, be careful of too hasty guesses at its meaning. In the end you will find clues to it all.' Then suddenly the humour of the situation came into my mind: the thought of the years I had spent in study and toil to get into the future age, and now my passion of anxiety to get out of it. I had made myself the most complicated and the most hopeless trap that ever a man devised. Although it was at my own expense, I could not help myself. I laughed aloud.

"Going through the big palace, it seemed to me that the little people avoided me. It may have been my fancy, or it may have had something to do with my hammering at the gates of bronze. Yet I felt tolerably sure of the avoidance. I was careful, however, to show no concern and to abstain from any pursuit of them, and in the course of a day or two things got back to the old footing. I made what progress I could in the language, and in addition I pushed my explorations here and there. Either I missed some subtle point, or their language was excessively simple—almost exclusively composed of concrete substantives and verbs. There seemed to be few, if any, abstract terms, or little use of figurative language. Their sentences were usually simple and of two words, and I failed to convey or understand any but the simplest propositions. I determined to put the thought of my Time Machine and the mystery of the bronze doors under the sphinx as much as possible in a corner of memory, until my growing knowledge would lead me back to them in a natural way. Yet a certain feeling, you may understand, tethered me in a circle of a few miles round the point of my arrival.

"So far as I could see, all the world displayed the same exuberant richness as the Thames valley. From every hill I climbed I saw the same abundance of splendid buildings, endlessly varied in material and style, the same clustering thickets of evergreens, the same blossom-laden trees and tree-ferns. Here and there water shone like silver, and beyond, the land rose into blue undulating hills, and so faded into the serenity of the sky. A peculiar feature, which presently attracted my attention, was the presence of certain circular wells, several, as it seemed to me, of a very great depth. One lay by the path up the hill, which I had followed during my first walk. Like the others, it was rimmed with bronze, curiously wrought, and protected by a little cupola from the rain. Sitting by the side of these wells, and peering down into the shafted darkness, I could see no gleam of water, nor could I start any reflection with a lighted match. But in all of them I heard a certain sound: a thud—thud—thud, like the beating of some big engine; and I discovered, from the flaring of my matches, that a steady current of air set down the shafts. Further, I threw a scrap of paper into the throat of one, and, instead of fluttering slowly down, it was at once sucked swiftly out of sight.

"After a time, too, I came to connect these wells with tall towers standing here and there upon the slopes; for above them there was often just such a flicker in the air as one sees on a hot day above a sun-scorched beach. Putting things together, I reached a strong suggestion of an extensive system of subterranean ventilation, whose true import it was difficult to imagine. I was at first inclined to associate it with the sanitary apparatus of these people. It was an obvious conclusion, but it was absolutely wrong.

"And here I must admit that I learned very little of drains and bells and modes of conveyance, and the like conveniences during my time in this real future. In some of these visions of Utopias and coming times which I have read, there is a vast amount of detail about building, and social arrangements, and so forth. But while such details are easy enough to obtain when the whole world is contained in one's imagination, they are altogether inaccessible to a real traveller amid such realities as I found here. Conceive the tale of London which a negro, fresh from Central Africa, would take back to his tribe! What would he know of railway companies, of social movements, of telephone and telegraph wires, of the Parcels Delivery Company, and postal orders and the like? Yet we, at least, should be willing enough to explain these things to him! And even of what he knew, how much could he make his untravelled friend either apprehend or believe? Then, think how narrow the gap between a negro and a white man of our own times, and how wide the interval between myself and these of the Golden Age! I was sensible of much which was unseen, and which contributed to my comfort; but save for a general impression of automatic organisation, I fear I can convey very little of the difference to your mind.

"In the matter of sepulture, for instance, I could see no signs of crematoria nor anything suggestive of tombs. But it occurred to me that, possibly, there might be cemeteries (or crematoria) somewhere beyond the range of my explorings. This, again, was a question I deliberately put to myself, and my curiosity was at first entirely defeated upon the point. The thing puzzled me, and I was led to make a further remark, which puzzled me still more: that aged and infirm among this people there were none.

"I must confess that my satisfaction with my first theories of an automatic civilisation and a decadent humanity did not long endure. Yet I could think of no other. Let me put my difficulties. The several big palaces I had explored were mere living places, great dining-halls and sleeping apartments. I could find no machinery, no appliances of

any kind. Yet these people were clothed in pleasant fabrics that must
at times need renewal, and their sandals, though undecorated, were
fairly complex specimens of metalwork. Somehow such things must
be made. And the little people displayed no vestige of a creative
tendency. There were no shops, no workshops, no sign of importa-
tions among them. They spent all their time in playing gently, in
bathing in the river, in making love in a half-playful fashion, in eating
fruit and sleeping. I could not see how things were kept going.

"Then, again, about the Time Machine: something, I knew not
what, had taken it into the hollow pedestal of the White Sphinx.
Why? For the life of me I could not imagine. Those waterless wells,
too, those flickering pillars. I felt I lacked a clue. I felt—how shall I
put it? Suppose you found an inscription, with sentences here and
there in excellent plain English, and interpolated therewith, others
made up of words, of letters even, absolutely unknown to you? Well,
on the third day of my visit, that was how the world of Eight Hundred
and Two Thousand Seven Hundred and One presented itself to me!

"That day, too, I made a friend—of a sort. It happened that, as I
was watching some of the little people bathing in a shallow, one of
them was seized with cramp and began drifting downstream. The
main current ran rather swiftly, but not too strongly for even a moderate swimmer. It will give you an idea, therefore, of the strange de-
ficiency in these creatures, when I tell you that none made the
slightest attempt to rescue the weakly crying little thing which was
drowning before their eyes. When I realised this, I hurriedly slipped
off my clothes, and, wading in at a point lower down, I caught the
poor mite and drew her safe to land. A little rubbing of the limbs
soon brought her round, and I had the satisfaction of seeing she
was all right before I left her. I had got to such a low estimate of her
kind that I did not expect any gratitude from her. In that, however, I
was wrong.

"This happened in the morning. In the afternoon I met my little
woman, as I believe it was, as I was returning towards my centre
from an exploration, and she received me with cries of delight and
presented me with a big garland of flowers—evidently made for me
and me alone. The thing took my imagination. Very possibly I had
been feeling desolate. At any rate I did my best to display my appreciation of the gift. We were soon seated together in a little stone
arbour, engaged in conversation, chiefly of smiles. The creature's
friendliness affected me exactly as a child's might have done. We

passed each other flowers, and she kissed my hands. I did the same to hers. Then I tried talk, and found that her name was Weena, which, though I don't know what it meant, somehow seemed appropriate enough. That was the beginning of a queer friendship which lasted a week, and ended—as I will tell you!

"She was exactly like a child. She wanted to be with me always. She tried to follow me everywhere, and my next journey out and about it went to my heart to tire her down, and leave her at last, exhausted and calling after me rather plaintively. But the problems of the world had to be mastered. I had not, I said to myself, come into the future to carry on a miniature flirtation. Yet her distress when I left her was very great, her expostulations at the parting were sometimes frantic, and I think, altogether, I had as much trouble as comfort from her devotion. Nevertheless she was, somehow, a very great comfort. I thought it was mere childish affection that made her cling to me. Until it was too late, I did not clearly know what I had inflicted upon her when I left her. Nor until it was too late did I clearly understand what she was to me. For, by merely seeming fond of me, and showing in her weak, futile way that she cared for me, the little doll of a creature presently gave my return to the neighbourhood of the White Sphinx almost the feeling of coming home; and I would watch for her tiny figure of white and gold so soon as I came over the hill.

"It was from her, too, that I learned that fear had not yet left the world. She was fearless enough in the daylight, and she had the oddest confidence in me; for once, in a foolish moment, I made threatening grimaces at her, and she simply laughed at them. But she dreaded the dark, dreaded shadows, dreaded black things. Darkness to her was the one thing dreadful. It was a singularly passionate emotion, and it set me thinking and observing. I discovered then, among other things, that these little people gathered into the great houses after dark, and slept in droves. To enter upon them without a light was to put them into a tumult of apprehension. I never found one out of doors, or one sleeping alone within doors, after dark. Yet I was still such a blockhead that I missed the lesson of that fear, and in spite of Weena's distress I insisted upon sleeping away from these slumbering multitudes.

"It troubled her greatly, but in the end her odd affection for me triumphed, and for five of the nights of our acquaintance, including the last night of all, she slept with her head pillowed on my arm. But my story slips away from me as I speak of her. It must have been the night before her rescue that I was awakened about dawn. I had been restless, dreaming most disagreeably that I was drowned, and that sea-anemones were feeling over my face with their soft palps. I woke with a start, and with an odd fancy that some greyish animal had just rushed out of the chamber. I tried to get to sleep again, but I felt restless and uncomfortable. It was that dim grey hour when things are just creeping out of darkness, when everything is colourless and clear cut, and yet unreal. I got up, and went down into the great hall, and so out upon the flagstones in front of the palace. I thought I would make a virtue of necessity, and see the sunrise.

"The moon was setting, and the dying moonlight and the first pallor of dawn were mingled in a ghastly half-light. The bushes were inky black, the ground a sombre grey, the sky colourless and cheerless. And up the hill I thought I could see ghosts. There several times, as I scanned the slope, I saw white figures. Twice I fancied I saw a solitary white, ape-like creature running rather quickly up the hill, and once near the ruins I saw a leash of them carrying some dark body. They moved hastily. I did not see what became of them. It seemed that they vanished among the bushes. The dawn was still indistinct, you must understand. I was feeling that chill, uncertain, early-morning feeling you may have known. I doubted my eyes.

"As the eastern sky grew brighter, and the light of the day came on and its vivid colouring returned upon the world once more, I scanned the view keenly. But I saw no vestige of my white figures. They were mere creatures of the half-light. 'They must have been ghosts,' I said; 'I wonder whence they dated.' For a queer notion of Grant Allen's came into my head, and amused me. If each generation die and leave ghosts, he argued, the world at last will get overcrowded with them. On that theory they would have grown innumerable some Eight Hundred Thousand Years hence, and it was no great wonder to see four at once. But the jest was unsatisfying, and I was thinking of these figures all the morning, until Weena's rescue drove them out of my head. I associated them in some indefinite way with the white animal I had startled in my first passionate search for the Time Machine. But Weena was a pleasant substitute. Yet all the same, they were soon destined to take far deadlier possession of my mind.

"I think I have said how much hotter than our own was the weather of this Golden Age. I cannot account for it. It may be that the sun was hotter, or the earth nearer the sun. It is usual to assume that the sun will go on cooling steadily in the future. But people, unfamiliar with such speculations as those of the younger Darwin, forget that the planets must ultimately fall back one by one into the parent body. As these catastrophes occur, the sun will blaze with renewed energy; and it may be that some inner planet had suffered this fate. Whatever the reason, the fact remains that the sun was very much hotter than we know it.

"Well, one very hot morning—my fourth, I think—as I was seeking shelter from the heat and glare in a colossal ruin near the great house where I slept and fed, there happened this strange thing: Clambering among these heaps of masonry, I found a narrow gallery, whose end and side windows were blocked by fallen masses of stone. By contrast with the brilliancy outside, it seemed at first impenetrably dark to me. I entered it groping, for the change from light to blackness made spots of colour swim before me. Suddenly I halted spellbound. A pair of eyes, luminous by reflection against the daylight without, was watching me out of the darkness.

"The old instinctive dread of wild beasts came upon me. I clenched my hands and steadfastly looked into the glaring eyeballs. I was afraid to turn. Then the thought of the absolute security in which humanity appeared to be living came to my mind. And then I remembered that strange terror of the dark. Overcoming my fear to some extent, I advanced a step and spoke. I will admit that my voice was harsh and ill-controlled. I put out my hand and touched something soft. At once the eyes darted sideways, and something white ran past me. I turned with my heart in my mouth, and saw a queer little ape-like figure, its head held down in a peculiar manner, running across the sunlit space behind me. It blundered against a block of granite, staggered aside, and in a moment was hidden in a black shadow beneath another pile of ruined masonry.

"My impression of it is, of course, imperfect; but I know it was a dull white, and had strange large greyish-red eyes; also that there was flaxen hair on its head and down its back. But, as I say, it went too fast for me to see distinctly. I cannot even say whether it ran on all-fours, or only with its forearms held very low. After an instant's pause I followed it into the second heap of ruins. I could not find it at first; but, after a time in the profound obscurity, I came upon one of those round well-like openings of which I have told you, half closed by a fallen pillar. A sudden thought came to me. Could this Thing have vanished down the shaft? I lit a match, and, looking down, I saw a small, white, moving creature, with large bright eyes which regarded me steadfastly as it retreated. It made me shudder. It was so like a human spider! It was clambering down the wall, and now I saw for the first time a number of metal foot and hand rests forming a kind of ladder down the shaft. Then the light burned my fingers and fell out of my hand, going out as it dropped, and when I had lit another the little monster had disappeared.

"I do not know how long I sat peering down that well. It was not for some time that I could succeed in persuading myself that the thing I had seen was human. But, gradually, the truth dawned on me: that Man had not remained one species, but had differentiated into two distinct animals: that my graceful children of the Upper World were not the sole descendants of our generation, but that this bleached, obscene, nocturnal Thing, which had flashed before me, was also heir to all the ages.

"I thought of the flickering pillars and of my theory of an underground ventilation. I began to suspect their true import. And what, I wondered, was this Lemur doing in my scheme of a perfectly balanced organisation? How was it related to the indolent serenity of the beautiful Upper-worlders? And what was hidden down there at the foot of that shaft? I sat upon the edge of the well telling myself that, at any rate, there was nothing to fear, and that there I must descend for the solution of my difficulties. And withal I was absolutely afraid to go! As I hesitated, two of the beautiful upper-world people came running in their amorous sport across the daylight into the shadow. The male pursued the female, flinging flowers at her as he ran.

"They seemed distressed to find me, my arm against the overturned pillar, peering down the well. Apparently it was considered bad form to remark these apertures; for when I pointed to this one, and tried to frame a question about it in their tongue, they were still more visibly distressed and turned away. But they were interested by my matches, and I struck some to amuse them. I tried them again about the well, and again I failed. So presently I left them, meaning to go back to Weena, and see what I could get from her. But my mind was already in revolution; my guesses and impressions were slipping and sliding to a new adjustment. I had now a clue to the import of these wells, to the ventilating towers, to the mystery of the ghosts; to say nothing of a hint at the meaning of the bronze gates and the fate of the Time Machine! And very vaguely there came a suggestion towards the solution of the economic problem that had puzzled me.

"Here was the new view. Plainly, this second species of Man was subterranean. There were three circumstances in particular which made me think that its rare emergence above ground was the outcome of a long-continued underground habit. In the first place, there was the bleached look common in most animals that live largely in the dark—the white fish of the Kentucky caves, for instance. Then, those large eyes, with that capacity for reflecting light, are common features of nocturnal things—witness the owl and the cat. And last of all, that evident confusion in the sunshine, that hasty yet fumbling and awkward flight towards dark shadow, and that peculiar carriage of the head while in the light—all reinforced the theory of an extreme sensitiveness of the retina.

"Beneath my feet, then, the earth must be tunnelled enormously, and these tunnellings were the habitat of the new race. The presence of ventilating-shafts and wells along the hill slopes—everywhere, in fact, except along the river valley—showed how universal were its ramifications. What so natural, then, as to assume that it was in this artificial underworld that such work as was necessary to the comfort of the daylight race was done? The notion was so plausible that I at once accepted it, and went on to assume the how of this splitting of the human species. I dare say you will anticipate the shape of my theory; though, for myself, I very soon felt that it fell far short of the truth.

"At first, proceeding from the problems of our own age, it seemed clear as daylight to me that the gradual widening of the present merely temporary and social difference between the Capitalist and the Labourer was the key to the whole position. No doubt it will seem grotesque enough to you—and wildly incredible!—and yet even now there are existing circumstances to point that way. There is a tendency to utilise underground space for the less ornamental purposes of civilisation; there is the Metropolitan Railway in London, for instance, there are new electric railways, there are subways, there are underground workrooms and restaurants, and they increase and multiply. Evidently, I thought, this tendency had increased till Industry had gradually lost its birthright in the sky. I mean that it had gone deeper and deeper into larger and ever larger underground factories, spending a still-increasing amount of its time therein, till, in the end—! Even now, does not an East-end worker live in such artificial conditions as practically to be cut off from the natural surface of the earth?

"Again, the exclusive tendency of richer people—due, no doubt, to the increasing refinement of their education, and the widening gulf between them and the rude violence of the poor—is already leading to the closing, in their interest, of considerable portions of the surface of the land. About London, for instance, perhaps half the prettier country is shut in against intrusion. And this same widening gulf—which is due to the length and expense of the higher educational process and the increased facilities for and temptations towards refined habits on the part of the rich—will make that exchange between class and class, that promotion by intermarriage which at present retards the splitting of our species along lines of social stratification, less and less frequent. So, in the end, above ground you must have the Haves, pursuing pleasure and comfort, and beauty, and below ground the Have-nots, the Workers getting continually adapted to the conditions of their labour. Once they were there, they would no doubt have to pay rent, and not a little of it, for the ventilation of their caverns; and if they refused, they would starve or be suffocated for arrears. Such of them as were so constituted as to be miserable and rebellious would die; and in the end, the balance being permanent, the survivors would become as well adapted to the conditions of underground life, and as happy in their way, as the Upper-world people were to theirs. As it seemed to me, the refined beauty and the etiolated pallor followed naturally enough.

"The great triumph of Humanity I had dreamed of took a different shape in my mind. It had been no such triumph of moral education and general cooperation as I had imagined. Instead, I saw a real aristocracy, armed with a perfected science and working to a logical conclusion the industrial system of to-day. Its triumph had not been simply a triumph over Nature, but a triumph over Nature and the fellow-man. This, I must warn you, was my theory at the time. I had no convenient cicerone in the pattern of the Utopian books. My explanation may be absolutely wrong. I still think it is the most plausible one. But even on this supposition the balanced civilisation that was at last attained must have long since passed its zenith, and was now far fallen into decay. The too-perfect security of the Upper-worlders had led them to a slow movement of degeneration, to a general dwindling in size, strength, and intelligence. That I could see clearly enough already. What had happened to the Undergrounders I did not yet suspect; but from what I had seen of the Morlocks—that, by the bye, was the name by which these creatures were called—I could imagine that the modification of the human type was even far more profound than among the 'Eloi,' the beautiful race that I already knew.

"Then came troublesome doubts. Why had the Morlocks taken my Time Machine? For I felt sure it was they who had taken it. Why, too, if the Eloi were masters, could they not restore the machine to me? And why were they so terribly afraid of the dark? I proceeded, as I have said, to question Weena about this Underworld, but here again I was disappointed. At first she would not understand my questions, and presently she refused to answer them. She shivered as though the topic was unendurable. And when I pressed her, perhaps a little harshly, she burst into tears. They were the only tears, except my own, I ever saw in that Golden Age. When I saw them I ceased abruptly to trouble about the Morlocks, and was only concerned in banishing these signs of the human inheritance from Weena's eyes. And very soon she was smiling and clapping her hands, while I solemnly burned a match.

CHAPTER VI: "It may seem odd to you, but it was two days before I could follow up the new-found clue in what was manifestly the proper way. I felt a peculiar shrinking from those pallid bodies. They were just the half-bleached colour of the worms and things one sees preserved in spirit in a zoological museum. And they were filthily cold to the touch. Probably my shrinking was largely due to the sympathetic influence of the Eloi, whose disgust of the Morlocks I now began to appreciate.

"The next night I did not sleep well. Probably my health was a little disordered. I was oppressed with perplexity and doubt. Once or twice I had a feeling of intense fear for which I could perceive no definite reason. I remember creeping noiselessly into the great hall where the little people were sleeping in the moonlight—that night Weena was among them—and feeling reassured by their presence. It occurred to me even then, that in the course of a few days the moon must pass through its last quarter, and the nights grow dark, when the appearances of these unpleasant creatures from below, these whitened Lemurs, this new vermin that had replaced the old, might be more abundant. And on both these days I had the restless feeling of one who shirks an inevitable duty. I felt assured that the Time Machine was only to be recovered by boldly penetrating these underground mysteries. Yet I could not face the mystery. If only I had had a companion it would have been different. But I was so horribly alone, and even to clamber down into the darkness of the well appalled me. I don't know if you will understand my feeling, but I never felt quite safe at my back.

"It was this restlessness, this insecurity, perhaps, that drove me further and further afield in my exploring expeditions. Going to the south-westward towards the rising country that is now called Combe Wood, I observed far off, in the direction of nineteenth-century Banstead, a vast green structure, different in character from any I had hitherto seen. It was larger than the largest of the palaces or ruins I knew, and the façade had an Oriental look: the face of it having the lustre, as well as the pale-green tint, a kind of bluish-green, of a certain type of Chinese porcelain. This difference in aspect suggested a difference in use, and I was minded to push on and explore. But the day was growing late, and I had come upon the sight of the place after a long and tiring circuit; so I resolved to hold over the adventure for the following day, and I returned to the welcome and the caresses of little Weena. But next morning I perceived clearly enough that my curiosity regarding the Palace of Green Porcelain was a piece of self-deception, to enable me to shirk, by another day, an experience I dreaded. I resolved I would make the descent without further waste of time, and started out in the early morning towards a well near the ruins of granite and aluminium.

"Little Weena ran with me. She danced beside me to the well, but when she saw me lean over the mouth and look downward, she seemed strangely disconcerted. 'Good-bye, little Weena,' I said, kissing her; and then, putting her down, I began to feel over the parapet for the climbing hooks. Rather hastily, I may as well confess, for I feared my courage might leak away! At first she watched me in amazement. Then she gave a most piteous cry, and, running to me, she began to pull at me with her little hands. I think her opposition nerved me rather to proceed. I shook her off, perhaps a little roughly, and in another moment I was in the throat of the well. I saw her agonised face over the parapet, and smiled to reassure her. Then I had to look down at the unstable hooks to which I clung.

"I had to clamber down a shaft of perhaps two hundred yards. The descent was effected by means of metallic bars projecting from the sides of the well, and these being adapted to the needs of a creature much smaller and lighter than myself, I was speedily cramped and fatigued by the descent. And not simply fatigued! One of the bars bent suddenly under my weight, and almost swung me off into the blackness beneath. For a moment I hung by one hand, and after that experience I did not dare to rest again. Though my arms and back were presently acutely painful, I went on clambering down the sheer descent with as quick a motion as possible. Glancing upward, I saw the aperture, a small blue disk, in which a star was visible, while little Weena's head showed as a round black projection. The thudding sound of a machine below grew louder and more oppressive. Everything save that little disk above was profoundly dark, and when I looked up again Weena had disappeared.

"I was in an agony of discomfort. I had some thought of trying to go up the shaft again, and leave the Underworld alone. But even while I turned this over in my mind I continued to descend. At last, with intense relief, I saw dimly coming up, a foot to the right of me, a slender loophole in the wall. Swinging myself in, I found it was the aperture of a narrow horizontal tunnel in which I could lie down and rest. It was not too soon. My arms ached, my back was cramped, and I was trembling with the prolonged terror of a fall. Besides this, the unbroken darkness had had a distressing effect upon my eyes. The air was full of the throb and hum of machinery pumping air down the shaft.

"I do not know how long I lay. I was roused by a soft hand touching my face. Starting up in the darkness I snatched at my matches and, hastily striking one, I saw three stooping white creatures similar to the one I had seen above ground in the ruin, hastily retreating before the light. Living, as they did, in what appeared to me impenetrable darkness, their eyes were abnormally large and sensitive, just as are the pupils of the abysmal fishes, and they reflected the light in the same way. I have no doubt they could see me in that rayless obscurity, and they did not seem to have any fear of me apart from the light. But, so soon as I struck a match in order to see them, they fled incontinently, vanishing into dark gutters and tunnels, from which their eyes glared at me in the strangest fashion.

"I tried to call to them, but the language they had was apparently different from that of the Overworld people; so that I was needs left to my own unaided efforts, and the thought of flight before exploration was even then in my mind. But I said to myself, 'You are in for it now,' and, feeling my way along the tunnel, I found the noise of machinery grow louder. Presently the walls fell away from me, and I came to a large open space, and, striking another match, saw that I had entered a vast arched cavern, which stretched into utter darkness beyond the range of my light. The view I had of it was as much as one could see in the burning of a match.

"Necessarily my memory is vague. Great shapes like big machines rose out of the dimness, and cast grotesque black shadows, in which dim spectral Morlocks sheltered from the glare. The place, by the bye, was very stuffy and oppressive, and the faint halitus of freshly shed blood was in the air. Some way down the central vista was a little table of white metal, laid with what seemed a meal. The Morlocks at any rate were carnivorous! Even at the time, I remember wondering what large animal could have survived to furnish the red joint I saw. It was all very indistinct: the heavy smell, the big unmeaning shapes, the obscene figures lurking in the shadows, and only waiting for the darkness to come at me again! Then the match burned down, and stung my fingers, and fell, a wriggling red spot in the blackness.

"I have thought since how particularly ill equipped I was for such an experience. When I had started with the Time Machine, I had started with the absurd assumption that the men of the Future would certainly be infinitely ahead of ourselves in all their appliances. I had come without arms, without medicine, without anything to smoke—at times I missed tobacco frightfully—even without enough matches. If only I had thought of a Kodak! I could have flashed that glimpse of the underworld in a second, and examined it at leisure. But, as it was, I stood there with only the weapons and the powers that Nature had endowed me with—hands, feet, and teeth; these, and four safety-matches that still remained to me.

"I was afraid to push my way in among all this machinery in the dark, and it was only with my last glimpse of light I discovered that my store of matches had run low. It had never occurred to me until that moment that there was any need to economise them, and I had wasted almost half the box in astonishing the Upper-worlders, to whom fire was a novelty. Now, as I say, I had four left, and while I stood in the dark, a hand touched mine, lank fingers came feeling over my face, and I was sensible of a peculiar unpleasant odour. I fancied I heard the breathing of a crowd of those dreadful little beings about me. I felt the box of matches in my hand being gently disengaged, and other hands behind me plucking at my clothing. The sense of these unseen creatures examining me was indescribably unpleasant. The sudden realisation of my ignorance of their ways of thinking and doing came home to me very vividly in the darkness. I shouted at them as loudly as I could. They started away, and then I could feel them approaching me again. They clutched at me more boldly, whispering odd sounds to each other. I shivered violently, and shouted again—rather discordantly. This time they were not so seriously alarmed, and they made a queer laughing noise as they came back at me. I will confess I was horribly frightened. I determined to strike another match and escape under the protection of its glare. I did so, and eking out the flicker with a scrap of paper from my pocket, I made good my retreat to the narrow tunnel. But I had scarce entered this when my light was blown out, and in the blackness I could hear the Morlocks rustling like wind among leaves, and pattering like the rain, as they hurried after me.

"In a moment I was clutched by several hands, and there was no mistaking that they were trying to haul me back. I struck another light, and waved it in their dazzled faces. You can scarce imagine how nauseatingly inhuman they looked—those pale, chinless faces and great, lidless, pinkish-grey eyes!—as they stared in their blindness and bewilderment. But I did not stay to look, I promise you: I retreated again, and when my second match had ended, I struck my third. It had almost burned through when I reached the opening into the shaft. I lay down on the edge, for the throb of the great pump below made me giddy. Then I felt sideways for the projecting hooks, and, as I did so, my feet were grasped from behind, and I was violently tugged backward. I lit my last match . . . and it incontinently went out. But I had my hand on the climbing bars now, and, kicking violently, I disengaged myself from the clutches of the Morlocks and was speedily clambering up the shaft, while they stayed peering and blinking up at me: all but one little wretch who followed me for some way, and well-nigh secured my boot as a trophy. .

"That climb seemed interminable to me. With the last twenty or thirty feet of it a deadly nausea came upon me. I had the greatest difficulty in keeping my hold. The last few yards was a frightful struggle against this faintness. Several times my head swam, and I felt all the sensations of falling. At last, however, I got over the well-mouth somehow, and staggered out of the ruin into the blinding sunlight. I fell upon my face. Even the soil smelt sweet and clean. Then I remember Weena kissing my hands and ears, and the voices of others among the Eloi. Then, for a time, I was insensible.

CHAPTER VII: "Now, indeed, I seemed in a worse case than before. Hitherto, except during my night's anguish at the loss of the Time

Machine, I had felt a sustaining hope of ultimate escape, but that hope was staggered by these new discoveries. Hitherto I had merely thought myself impeded by the childish simplicity of the little people, and by some unknown forces which I had only to understand to overcome; but there was an altogether new element in the sickening quality of the Morlocks—a something inhuman and malign. Instinctively I loathed them. Before, I had felt as a man might feel who had fallen into a pit: my concern was with the pit and how to get out of it. Now I felt like a beast in a trap, whose enemy would come upon him soon.

"The enemy I dreaded may surprise you. It was the darkness of the new moon. Weena had put this into my head by some at first incomprehensible remarks about the Dark Nights. It was not now such a very difficult problem to guess what the coming Dark Nights might mean. The moon was on the wane: each night there was a longer interval of darkness. And I now understood to some slight degree at least the reason of the fear of the little Upper-world people for the dark. I wondered vaguely what foul villainy it might be that the Morlocks did under the new moon. I felt pretty sure now that my second hypothesis was all wrong. The Upper-world people might once have been the favoured aristocracy, and the Morlocks their mechanical servants; but that had long since passed away. The two species that had resulted from the evolution of man were sliding down towards, or had already arrived at, an altogether new relationship. The Eloi, like the Carlovingian kings, had decayed to a mere beautiful futility. They still possessed the earth on sufferance: since the Morlocks, subterranean for innumerable generations, had come at last to find the daylit surface intolerable. And the Morlocks made their garments, I inferred, and maintained them in their habitual needs, perhaps through the survival of an old habit of service. They did it as a standing horse paws with his foot, or as a man enjoys killing animals in sport: because ancient and departed necessities had impressed it on the organism. But, clearly, the old order was already in part reversed. The Nemesis of the delicate ones was creeping on apace. Ages ago, thousands of generations ago, man had thrust his brother man out of the ease and the sunshine. And now that brother was coming back—changed! Already the Eloi had begun to learn one old lesson anew. They were becoming reacquainted with Fear. And suddenly there came into my head the memory of the meat I had seen in the Under-world. It seemed odd how it floated into my mind:

not stirred up as it were by the current of my meditations, but coming in almost like a question from outside. I tried to recall the form of it. I had a vague sense of something familiar, but I could not tell what it was at the time.

"Still, however helpless the little people in the presence of their mysterious Fear, I was differently constituted. I came out of this age of ours, this ripe prime of the human race, when Fear does not paralyse and mystery has lost its terrors. I at least would defend myself. Without further delay I determined to make myself arms and a fastness where I might sleep. With that refuge as a base, I could face this strange world with some of that confidence I had lost in realising to what creatures night by night I lay exposed. I felt I could never sleep again until my bed was secure from them. I shuddered with horror to think how they must already have examined me.

"I wandered during the afternoon along the valley of the Thames, but found nothing that commended itself to my mind as inaccessible. All the buildings and trees seemed easily practicable to such dexterous climbers as the Morlocks, to judge by their wells, must be. Then the tall pinnacles of the Palace of Green Porcelain and the polished gleam of its walls came back to my memory; and in the evening, taking Weena like a child upon my shoulder, I went up the hills towards the south-west. The distance, I had reckoned, was seven or eight miles, but it must have been nearer eighteen. I had first seen the place on a moist afternoon when distances are deceptively diminished. In addition, the heel of one of my shoes was loose, and a nail was working through the sole—they were comfortable old shoes I wore about indoors—so that I was lame. And it was already long past sunset when I came in sight of the palace, silhouetted black against the pale yellow of the sky.

"Weena had been hugely delighted when I began to carry her, but after a time she desired me to let her down, and ran along by the side of me, occasionally darting off on either hand to pick flowers to stick in my pockets. My pockets had always puzzled Weena, but at the last she had concluded that they were an eccentric kind of vase for floral decoration. At least she utilised them for that purpose. And that reminds me! In changing my jacket I found . . ."

The Time Traveller paused, put his hand into his pocket, and silently placed two withered flowers, not unlike very large white mallows, upon the little table. Then he resumed his narrative.

"As the hush of evening crept over the world and we proceeded over the hill crest towards Wimbledon, Weena grew tired and wanted to return to the house of grey stone. But I pointed out the distant pinnacles of the Palace of Green Porcelain to her, and contrived to make her understand that we were seeking a refuge there from her Fear. You know that great pause that comes upon things before the dusk? Even the breeze stops in the trees. To me there is always an air of expectation about that evening stillness. The sky was clear, remote, and empty save for a few horizontal bars far down in the sunset. Well, that night the expectation took the colour of my fears. In that darkling calm my senses seemed preternaturally sharpened. I fancied I could even feel the hollowness of the ground beneath my feet: could, indeed, almost see through it the Morlocks on their ant-hill going hither and thither and waiting for the dark. In my excitement I fancied that they would receive my invasion of their burrows as a declaration of war. And why had they taken my Time Machine?

"So we went on in the quiet, and the twilight deepened into night. The clear blue of the distance faded, and one star after another came out. The ground grew dim and the trees black. Weena's fears and her fatigue grew upon her. I took her in my arms and talked to her and caressed her. Then, as the darkness grew deeper, she put her arms round my neck, and, closing her eyes, tightly pressed her face against my shoulder. So we went down a long slope into a valley, and there in the dimness I almost walked into a little river. This I waded, and went up the opposite side of the valley, past a number of sleeping houses, and by a statue—a Faun, or some such figure, *minus* the head. Here too were acacias. So far I had seen nothing of the Morlocks, but it was yet early in the night, and the darker hours before the old moon rose were still to come.

"From the brow of the next hill I saw a thick wood spreading wide and black before me. I hesitated at this. I could see no end to it, either to the right or the left. Feeling tired—my feet, in particular, were very sore—I carefully lowered Weena from my shoulder as I halted, and sat down upon the turf. I could no longer see the Palace of Green Porcelain, and I was in doubt of my direction. I looked into the thickness of the wood and thought of what it might hide. Under that dense tangle of branches one would be out of sight of the stars. Even were there no other lurking danger—a danger I did not care to let my imagination loose upon—there would still be all the roots to stumble over and the tree-boles to strike against.

"I was very tired, too, after the excitements of the day; so I decided that I would not face it, but would pass the night upon the open hill.

"Weena, I was glad to find, was fast asleep. I carefully wrapped her in my jacket, and sat down beside her to wait for the moonrise. The hillside was quiet and deserted, but from the black of the wood there came now and then a stir of living things. Above me shone the stars, for the night was very clear. I felt a certain sense of friendly comfort in their twinkling. All the old constellations had gone from the sky, however: that slow movement which is imperceptible in a hundred human lifetimes, had long since rearranged them in unfamiliar groupings. But the Milky Way, it seemed to me, was still the same tattered streamer of star-dust as of yore. Southward (as I judged it) was a very bright red star that was new to me; it was even more splendid than our own green Sirius. And amid all these scintillating points of light one bright planet shone kindly and steadily like the face of an old friend.

"Looking at these stars suddenly dwarfed my own troubles and all the gravities of terrestrial life. I thought of their unfathomable distance, and the slow inevitable drift of their movements out of the unknown past into the unknown future. I thought of the great precessional cycle that the pole of the earth describes. Only forty times had that silent revolution occurred during all the years that I had traversed. And during these few revolutions all the activity, all the traditions, the complex organisations, the nations, languages, literatures, aspirations, even the mere memory of Man as I knew him, had been swept out of existence. Instead were these frail creatures who had forgotten their high ancestry, and the white Things of which I went in terror. Then I thought of the Great Fear that was between the two species, and for the first time, with a sudden shiver, came the clear knowledge of what the meat I had seen might be. Yet it was too horrible! I looked at little Weena sleeping beside me, her face white and starlike under the stars, and forthwith dismissed the thought.

"Through that long night I held my mind off the Morlocks as well as I could, and whiled away the time by trying to fancy I could find signs of the old constellations in the new confusion. The sky kept very clear, except for a hazy cloud or so. No doubt I dozed at times. Then, as my vigil wore on, came a faintness in the eastward sky, like the reflection of some colourless fire, and the old moon rose, thin and peaked and white. And close behind, and overtaking it, and overflowing it, the dawn came, pale at first, and then growing pink and warm. No Morlocks had approached us. Indeed, I had seen none upon the hill that night. And in the confidence of renewed day it almost seemed to me that my fear had been unreasonable. I stood up and found my foot with the loose heel swollen at the ankle and painful under the heel; so I sat down again, took off my shoes, and flung them away.

"I awakened Weena, and we went down into the wood, now green and pleasant instead of black and forbidding. We found some fruit wherewith to break our fast. We soon met others of the dainty ones, laughing and dancing in the sunlight as though there was no such thing in Nature as the night. And then I thought once more of the meat that I had seen. I felt assured now of what it was, and from the bottom of my heart I pitied this last feeble rill from the great flood of humanity. Clearly, at some time in the Long-Ago of human decay the Morlocks' food had run short. Possibly they had lived on rats and suchlike vermin. Even now man is far less discriminating and exclusive in his food than he was—far less than any monkey. His prejudice against human flesh is no deep-seated instinct. And so these inhuman sons of men——! I tried to look at the thing in a scientific spirit. After all, they were less human and more remote than our cannibal ancestors of three or four thousand years ago. And the intelligence that would have made this state of things a torment had gone. Why should I trouble myself? These Eloi were mere fatted cattle, which the ant-like Morlocks preserved and preyed upon—probably saw to the breeding of. And there was Weena dancing at my side!

"Then I tried to preserve myself from the horror that was coming upon me, by regarding it as a rigorous punishment of human selfishness. Man had been content to live in ease and delight upon the labours of his fellow man, had taken Necessity as his watchword and excuse, and in the fulness of time Necessity had come home to him. I even tried a Carlyle-like scorn of this wretched aristocracy in decay. But this attitude of mind was impossible. However great their intellectual degradation, the Eloi had kept too much of the human form not to claim my sympathy, and to make me perforce a sharer in their degradation and their Fear.

"I had at that time very vague ideas as to the course I should pursue. My first was to secure some safe place of refuge, and to make myself such arms of metal or stone as I could contrive. That necessity was immediate. In the next place, I hoped to procure some means of fire, so that I should have the weapon of a torch at hand, for nothing, I knew, would be more efficient against these Morlocks. Then I wanted to arrange some contrivance to break open the doors of bronze under the White Sphinx. I had in mind a battering-ram. I had a persuasion that if I could enter those doors and carry a blaze of light before me I should discover the Time Machine and escape. I could not imagine the Morlocks were strong enough to move it far away. Weena I had resolved to bring with me to our own time. And turning such schemes over in my mind I pursued our way towards the building which my fancy had chosen as our dwelling.

CHAPTER VIII: "I found the Palace of Green Porcelain, when we approached it about noon, deserted and falling into ruin. Only ragged vestiges of glass remained in its windows, and great sheets of the green facing had fallen away from the corroded metallic framework. It lay very high upon a turfy down, and looking north-eastward before I entered it, I was surprised to see a large estuary, or even creek, where I judged Wandsworth and Battersea must once have been. I thought then—though I never followed up the thought—of what might have happened, or might be happening, to the living things in the sea.

"The material of the Palace proved on examination to be indeed porcelain, and along the face of it I saw an inscription in some unknown character. I thought, rather foolishly, that Weena might help me to interpret this, but I only learned that the bare idea of writing had never entered her head. She always seemed to me, I fancy, more human than she was, perhaps because her affection was so human.

"Within the big valves of the door—which were open and broken— we found, instead of the customary hall, a long gallery lit by many side windows. At the first glance I was reminded of a museum. The tiled floor was thick with dust, and a remarkable array of miscellaneous objects was shrouded in the same grey covering. Then I perceived, standing strange and gaunt in the centre of the hall, what was clearly the lower part of a huge skeleton. I recognised by the oblique feet that it was some extinct creature after the fashion of the Megatherium. The skull and the upper bones lay beside it in the thick dust, and in one place, where rainwater had dropped through a leak in the roof, the thing itself had been worn away. Further in the gallery was the huge skeleton barrel of a Brontosaurus. My museum hypothesis was confirmed. Going towards the side I found what appeared to be sloping shelves, and, clearing away the thick dust, I found the old familiar glass cases of our own time. But they must have been air-tight to judge from the fair preservation of some of their contents.

"Clearly we stood among the ruins of some latter-day South Kensington! Here, apparently, was the Palæontological Section, and a very splendid array of fossils it must have been, though the inevitable process of decay that had been staved off for a time, and had, through the extinction of bacteria and fungi, lost ninety-nine hundredths of its force, was, nevertheless, with extreme sureness if with extreme slowness at work again upon all its treasures. Here and there I found traces of the little people in the shape of rare fossils broken to pieces or threaded in strings upon reeds. And the cases had in some instances been bodily removed—by the Morlocks as I judged. The place was very silent. The thick dust deadened our footsteps. Weena, who had been rolling a sea-urchin down the sloping glass of a case, presently came, as I stared about me, and very quietly took my hand and stood beside me.

"And at first I was so much surprised by this ancient monument of an intellectual age, that I gave no thought to the possibilities it presented. Even my preoccupation about the Time Machine receded a little from my mind.

"To judge from the size of the place, this Palace of Green Porcelain had a great deal more in it than a Gallery of Palæontology; possibly historical galleries; it might be, even a library! To me, at least in my present circumstances, these would be vastly more interesting than this spectacle of old-time geology in decay. Exploring, I found another short gallery running transversely to the first. This appeared to be devoted to minerals, and the sight of a block of sulphur set my mind running on gunpowder. But I could find no saltpetre; indeed, no nitrates of any kind. Doubtless they had deliquesced ages ago. Yet the sulphur hung in my mind, and set up a train of thinking. As for the rest of the contents of that gallery, though on the whole they were the best preserved of all I saw, I had little interest. I am no specialist in mineralogy, and I went on down a very ruinous aisle running parallel to the first hall I had entered. Apparently this section had been devoted to natural history, but everything had long since passed out of recognition. A few shrivelled and blackened vestiges of what had been stuffed animals, desiccated mummies in jars that had once held spirit, a brown dust of departed plants; that was all! I was sorry for that, because I should have been glad to trace the patent readjustments by which the conquest of animated nature had

been attained. Then we came to a gallery of simply colossal propor-
tions, but singularly ill-lit, the floor of it running downward at a slight
angle from the end at which I entered. At intervals white globes hung
from the ceiling—many of them cracked and smashed—which suggested that originally the place had been artificially lit. Here I was
more in my element, for rising on either side of me were the huge
bulks of big machines, all greatly corroded and many broken down,
but some still fairly complete. You know I have a certain weakness
for mechanism, and I was inclined to linger among these; the more
so as for the most part they had the interest of puzzles, and I could
make only the vaguest guesses at what they were for. I fancied that
if I could solve their puzzles I should find myself in possession of
powers that might be of use against the Morlocks.

"Suddenly Weena came very close to my side. So suddenly that she
startled me. Had it not been for her I do not think I should have
noticed that the floor of the gallery sloped at all.* The end I had
come in at was quite above ground, and was lit by rare slit-like windows. As you went down the length, the ground came up against
these windows, until at last there was a pit like the 'area' of a London
house before each, and only a narrow line of daylight at the top. I
went slowly along, puzzling about the machines, and had been too
intent upon them to notice the gradual diminution of the light, until
Weena's increasing apprehensions drew my attention. Then I saw
that the gallery ran down at last into a thick darkness. I hesitated,
and then, as I looked round me, I saw that the dust was less abundant
and its surface less even. Further away towards the dimness, it appeared to be broken by a number of small narrow footprints. My
sense of the immediate presence of the Morlocks revived at that. I
felt that I was wasting my time in this academic examination of machinery. I called to mind that it was already far advanced in the afternoon, and that I had still no weapon, no refuge, and no means of
making a fire. And then down in the remote blackness of the gallery
I heard a peculiar pattering, and the same odd noises I had heard
down the well.

"I took Weena's hand. Then, struck with a sudden idea, I left her
and turned to a machine from which projected a lever not unlike those
in a signal-box. Clambering upon the stand, and grasping this lever
in my hands, I put all my weight upon it sideways. Suddenly Weena,

* It may be, of course, that the floor did not slope, but that the museum was
built into the side of a hill.—Ed.

deserted in the central aisle, began to whimper. I had judged the strength of the lever pretty correctly, for it snapped after a minute's strain, and I rejoined her with a mace in my hand more than sufficient, I judged, for any Morlock skull I might encounter. And I longed very much to kill a Morlock or so. Very inhuman, you may think, to want to go killing one's own descendants! But it was impossible, somehow, to feel any humanity in the things. Only my disinclination to leave Weena, and a persuasion that if I began to slake my thirst for murder my Time Machine might suffer, restrained me from going straight down the gallery and killing the brutes I heard.

"Well, mace in one hand and Weena in the other, I went out of that gallery and into another and still larger one, which at the first glance reminded me of a military chapel hung with tattered flags. The brown and charred rags that hung from the sides of it, I presently recognised as the decaying vestiges of books. They had long since dropped to pieces, and every semblance of print had left them. But here and there were warped boards and cracked metallic clasps that told the tale well enough. Had I been a literary man I might, perhaps, have moralised upon the futility of all ambition. But as it was, the thing that struck me with keenest force was the enormous waste of labour to which this sombre wilderness of rotting paper testified. At the time I will confess that I thought chiefly of the *Philosophical Transactions* and my own seventeen papers upon physical optics.

"Then, going up a broad staircase, we came to what may once have been a gallery to technical chemistry. And here I had not a little hope of useful discoveries. Except at one end where the roof had collapsed, this gallery was well preserved. I went eagerly to every unbroken case. And at last, in one of the really air-tight cases, I found a box of matches. Very eagerly I tried them. They were perfectly good. They were not even damp. I turned to Weena. 'Dance,' I cried to her in her own tongue. For now I had a weapon indeed against the horrible creatures we feared. And so, in the derelict museum, upon the thick soft carpeting of dust, to Weena's huge delight, I solemnly performed a kind of composite dance, whistling *The Land of the Leal* as cheerfully as I could. In part it was a modest *cancan,* in part a step-dance, in part a skirt-dance (so far as my tail-coat permitted), and in part original. For I am naturally inventive, as you know.

"Now, I still think that for this box of matches to have escaped the wear of time for immemorial years was a most strange, as for me it was a most fortunate thing. Yet, oddly enough, I found a far un-likelier substance, and that was camphor. I found it in a sealed jar, that by chance, I suppose, had been really hermetically sealed. I fancied at first that it was paraffin wax, and smashed the glass ac-cordingly. But the odour of camphor was unmistakable. In the uni-versal decay this volatile substance had chanced to survive, perhaps through many thousands of centuries. It reminded me of a sepia painting I had once seen done from the ink of a fossil Belemnite that must have perished and become fossilised millions of years ago. I was about to throw it away, but I remembered that it was inflammable and burned with a good bright flame—was, in fact, an excellent candle —and I put it in my pocket. I found no explosives, however, nor any means of breaking down the bronze doors. As yet my iron crowbar was the most helpful thing I had chanced upon. Nevertheless I left that gallery greatly elated.

"I cannot tell you all the story of that long afternoon. It would re-quire a great effort of memory to recall my explorations in at all the proper order. I remember a long gallery of rusting stands of arms, and how I hesitated between my crowbar and a hatchet or a sword. I could not carry both, however, and my bar of iron promised best against the bronze gates. There were numbers of guns, pistols, and rifles. The most were masses of rust, but many were of some new metal, and still fairly sound. But any cartridges or powder there may once have been had rotted into dust. One corner I saw was charred and shattered; perhaps, I thought, by an explosion among the speci-mens. In another place was a vast array of idols—Polynesian, Mexi-can, Grecian, Phœnician, every country on earth I should think. And here, yielding to an irresistible impulse, I wrote my name upon the nose of a steatite monster from South America that particularly took my fancy.

"As the evening drew on, my interest waned. I went through gallery after gallery, dusty, silent, often ruinous, the exhibits sometimes mere heaps of rust and lignite, sometimes fresher. In one place I suddenly found myself near the model of a tin-mine, and then by the merest accident I discovered, in an air-tight case, two dynamite cartridges! I shouted 'Eureka!' and smashed the case with joy. Then came a doubt. I hesitated. Then, selecting a little side gallery, I made my essay. I never felt such a disappointment as I did in waiting five, ten, fifteen minutes for an explosion that never came. Of course the things were dummies, as I might have guessed from their presence. I really believe that, had they not been so, I should have rushed off incontinently and blown Sphinx, bronze doors, and (as it proved) my chances of finding the Time Machine, all together into non-existence.

"It was after that, I think, that we came to a little open court within the palace. It was turfed, and had three fruit trees. So we rested and refreshed ourselves. Towards sunset I began to consider our position. Night was creeping upon us, and my inaccessible hiding place had still to be found. But that troubled me very little now. I had in my possession a thing that was, perhaps, the best of all defences against the Morlocks—I had matches! I had the camphor in my pocket, too, if a blaze were needed. It seemed to me that the best thing we could do would be to pass the night in the open, protected by a fire. In the morning there was the getting of the Time Machine. Towards that, as yet, I had only my iron mace. But now, with my growing knowledge, I felt very differently towards those bronze doors. Up to this, I had refrained from forcing them, largely because of the mystery on the other side. They had never impressed me as being very strong, and I hoped to find my bar of iron not altogether inadequate for the work.

CHAPTER IX: "We emerged from the palace while the sun was still in part above the horizon. I was determined to reach the White Sphinx early the next morning, and ere the dusk I purposed pushing through the woods that had stopped me on the previous journey. My plan was to go as far as possible that night, and then, building a fire, to sleep in the protection of its glare. Accordingly, as we went along I gathered any sticks or dried grass I saw, and presently had my arms full of such litter. Thus loaded, our progress was slower than I had anticipated, and besides Weena was tired. And I began to suffer from sleepiness too; so that it was full night before we reached the wood. Upon the shrubby hill of its edge Weena would have stopped, fearing the darkness before us; but a singular sense of impending calamity, that should indeed have served me as a warning, drove me onward. I had been without sleep for a night and two days, and I was feverish and irritable. I felt sleep coming upon me, and the Morlocks with it.

"While we hesitated, among the black bushes behind us, and dim against their blackness, I saw three crouching figures. There was scrub and long grass all about us, and I did not feel safe from their insidious approach. The forest, I calculated, was rather less than a mile across. If we could get through it to the bare hillside, there, as it seemed to me, was an altogether safer resting-place; I thought that with my matches and my camphor I could contrive to keep my path illuminated through the woods. Yet it was evident that if I was to flourish matches with my hands I should have to abandon my fire-wood; so, rather reluctantly, I put it down. And then it came into my head that I would amaze our friends behind by lighting it. I was to discover the atrocious folly of this proceeding, but it came to my mind as an ingenious move for covering our retreat.

"I don't know if you have ever thought what a rare thing flame must be in the absence of man and in a temperate climate. The sun's heat is rarely strong enough to burn, even when it is focussed by dewdrops, as is sometimes the case in more tropical districts. Lightning may blast and blacken, but it rarely gives rise to widespread fire. Decaying vegetation may occasionally smoulder with the heat of its fermentation, but this rarely results in flame. In this decadence, too, the art of fire-making had been forgotten on the earth. The red tongues that went licking up my heap of wood were an altogether new and strange thing to Weena.

"She wanted to run to it and play with it. I believe she would have cast herself into it had I not restrained her. But I caught her up, and, in spite of her struggles, plunged boldly before me into the wood. For a little way the glare of my fire lit the path. Looking back presently, I could see, through the crowded stems, that from my heap of sticks the blaze had spread to some bushes adjacent, and a curved line of fire was creeping up the grass of the hill. I laughed at that, and turned again to the dark trees before me. It was very black, and Weena clung to me convulsively, but there was still, as my eyes grew ac-customed to the darkness, sufficient light for me to avoid the stems. Overhead it was simply black, except where a gap of remote blue sky shone down upon us here and there. I struck none of my matches because I had no hand free. Upon my left arm I carried my little one, in my right hand I had my iron bar.

"For some way I heard nothing but the crackling twigs under my feet, the faint rustle of the breeze above, and my own breathing and the throb of the blood-vessels in my ears. Then I seemed to know of a pattering about me. I pushed on grimly. The pattering grew more distinct, and then I caught the same queer sounds and voices I heard in the Underworld. There were evidently several of the Morlocks, and they were closing in upon me. Indeed, in another minute I felt a tug at my coat, then something at my arm. And Weena shivered violently, and became quite still.

"It was time for a match. But to get one I must put her down. I did so, and, as I fumbled with my pocket, a struggle began in the darkness about my knees, perfectly silent on her part and with the same peculiar cooing sounds from the Morlocks. Soft little hands, too, were creeping over my coat and back, touching even my neck. Then the match scratched and fizzed. I held it flaring, and saw the white backs of the Morlocks in flight amid the trees. I hastily took a lump of camphor from my pocket, and prepared to light it as soon as the match should wane. Then I looked at Weena. She was lying clutching my feet and quite motionless, with her face to the ground. With a sudden fright I stooped to her. She seemed scarcely to breathe. I lit the block of camphor and flung it to the ground, and as it split and flared up and drove back the Morlocks and the shadows, I knelt down and lifted her. The wood behind seemed full of the stir and murmur of a great company!

"She seemed to have fainted. I put her carefully upon my shoulder and rose to push on, and then there came a horrible realisation. In manoeuvring with my matches and Weena, I had turned myself about several times, and now I had not the faintest idea in what direction lay my path. For all I knew, I might be facing back towards the Palace of Green Porcelain. I found myself in a cold sweat. I had to think rapidly what to do. I determined to build a fire and encamp where we were. I put Weena, still motionless, down upon a turfy bole, and very hastily, as my first lump of camphor waned, I began collecting sticks and leaves. Here and there out of the darkness round me the Morlocks' eyes shone like carbuncles.

"The camphor flickered and went out. I lit a match, and as I did so, two white forms that had been approaching Weena dashed hastily away. One was so blinded by the light that he came straight for me, and I felt his bones grind under the blow of my fist. He gave a whoop of dismay, staggered a little way, and fell down. I lit another piece of camphor, and went on gathering my bonfire. Presently I noticed how dry was some of the foliage above me, for since my arrival on the Time Machine, a matter of a week, no rain had fallen. So, instead of casting about among the trees for fallen twigs, I began leaping up and dragging down branches. Very soon I had a choking smoky fire of green wood and dry sticks, and could economise my camphor. Then I turned to where Weena lay beside my iron mace. I tried what

I could to revive her, but she lay like one dead. I could not even satisfy myself whether or not she breathed.

"Now, the smoke of the fire beat over towards me, and it must have made me heavy of a sudden. Moreover, the vapour of camphor was in the air. My fire would not need replenishing for an hour or so. I felt very weary after my exertion, and sat down. The wood, too, was full of a slumbrous murmur that I did not understand. I seemed just to nod and open my eyes. But all was dark, and the Morlocks had their hands upon me. Flinging off their clinging fingers I hastily felt in my pocket for the matchbox, and—it had gone! Then they gripped and closed with me, again. In a moment I knew what had happened. I had slept, and my fire had gone out, and the bitterness of death came over my soul. The forest seemed full of the smell of burning wood. I was caught by the neck, by the hair, by the arms, and pulled down. It was indescribably horrible in the darkness to feel all these soft creatures heaped upon me. I felt as if I was in a monstrous spider's web. I was overpowered, and went down. I felt little teeth nipping at my neck. I rolled over, and as I did so my hand came against my iron lever. It gave me strength. I struggled up, shaking the human rats from me, and, holding the bar short, I thrust where I judged their faces might be. I could feel the succulent giving of flesh and bone under my blows, and for a moment I was free.

"The strange exultation that so often seems to accompany hard fighting came upon me. I knew that both I and Weena were lost, but I determined to make the Morlocks pay for their meat. I stood with my back to a tree, swinging the iron bar before me. The whole wood was full of the stir and cries of them. A minute passed. Their voices seemed to rise to a higher pitch of excitement, and their movements grew faster. Yet none came within reach. I stood glaring at the blackness. Then suddenly came hope. What if the Morlocks were afraid? And close on the heels of that came a strange thing. The darkness seemed to grow luminous. Very dimly I began to see the Morlocks about me—three battered at my feet—and then I recognised, with incredulous surprise, that the others were running, in an incessant stream, as it seemed, from behind me, and away through the wood in front. And their backs seemed no longer white, but reddish. As I stood agape, I saw a little red spark go drifting across a gap of starlight between the branches, and vanish. And at that I understood the smell of burning wood, the slumbrous murmur that was growing now into a gusty roar, the red glow, and the Morlocks' flight.

"Stepping out from behind my tree and looking back, I saw, through the black pillars of the nearer trees, the flames of the burning forest. It was my first fire coming after me. With that I looked for Weena, but she was gone. The hissing and crackling behind me, the explosive thud as each fresh tree burst into flame, left little time for reflection. My iron bar still gripped, I followed in the Morlocks' path. It was a close race. Once the flames crept forward so swiftly on my right as I ran that I was outflanked and had to strike off to the left. But at last I emerged upon a small open space, and as I did so, a Morlock came blundering towards me, and past me, and went on straight into the fire!

"And now I was to see the most weird and horrible thing, I think, of all that I beheld in that future age. This whole space was as bright as day with the reflection of the fire. In the centre was a hillock or tumulus, surmounted by a scorched hawthorn. Beyond this was another arm of the burning forest, with yellow tongues already writhing from it, completely encircling the space with a fence of fire. Upon the hillside were some thirty or forty Morlocks, dazzled by the light and heat, and blundering hither and thither against each other in their bewilderment. At first I did not realise their blindness, and struck furiously at them with my bar, in a frenzy of fear, as they approached me, killing one and crippling several more. But when I had watched the gestures of one of them groping under the hawthorn against the red sky, and heard their moans, I was assured of their absolute helplessness and misery in the glare, and I struck no more of them.

"Yet every now and then one would come straight towards me, setting loose a quivering horror that made me quick to elude him. At one time the flames died down somewhat, and I feared the foul creatures would presently be able to see me. I was even thinking of beginning the fight by killing some of them before this should happen; but the fire burst out again brightly, and I stayed my hand. I walked about the hill among them and avoided them, looking for some trace of Weena. But Weena was gone.

"At last I sat down on the summit of the hillock, and watched this strange incredible company of blind things groping to and fro, and making uncanny noises to each other, as the glare of the fire beat on them. The coiling uprush of smoke streamed across the sky, and through the rare tatters of that red canopy, remote as though they belonged to another universe, shone the little stars. Two or three

Morlocks came blundering into me, and I drove them off with blows of my fists, trembling as I did so.

"For the most part of that night I was persuaded it was a nightmare. I bit myself and screamed in a passionate desire to awake. I beat the ground with my hands, and got up and sat down again, and wandered here and there, and again sat down. Then I would fall to rubbing my eyes and calling upon God to let me awake. Thrice I saw Morlocks put their heads down in a kind of agony and rush into the flames. But, at last, above the subsiding red of the fire, above the streaming masses of black smoke and the whitening and blackening tree stumps, and the diminishing numbers of these dim creatures, came the white light of the day.

"I searched again for traces of Weena, but there were none. It was plain that they had left her poor little body in the forest. I cannot describe how it relieved me to think that it had escaped the awful fate of which it seemed destined. As I thought of that, I was almost moved to begin a massacre of the helpless abominations about me, but I contained myself. The hillock, as I have said, was a kind of island in the forest. From its summit I could now make out through a haze of smoke the Palace of Green Porcelain, and from that I could get my bearings for the White Sphinx. And so, leaving the remnant of these damned souls still going hither and thither and moaning, as the day grew clearer, I tied some grass about my feet and limped on across smoking ashes and among black stems, that still pulsated internally with fire, towards the hiding place of the Time Machine. I walked slowly, for I was almost exhausted, as well as lame, and I felt the intensest wretchedness for the horrible death of little Weena. It seemed an overwhelming calamity. Now, in this old familiar room, it is more like the sorrow of a dream than an actual loss. But that morning it left me absolutely lonely again—terribly alone. I began to think of this house of mine, of this fireside, of some of you, and with such thoughts came a longing that was pain.

"But, as I walked over the smoking ashes under the bright morning sky, I made a discovery. In my trouser pocket were still some loose matches. The box must have leaked before it was lost.

CHAPTER X: "About eight or nine in the morning I came to the same seat of yellow metal from which I had viewed the world upon the evening of my arrival. I thought of my hasty conclusions upon that evening and could not refrain from laughing bitterly at my confidence. Here was the same beautiful scene, the same abundant foliage, the same splendid palaces and magnificent ruins, the same silver river running between its fertile banks. The gay robes of the beautiful people moved hither and thither among the trees. Some were bathing in exactly the place where I had saved Weena, and that suddenly gave me a keen stab of pain. And like blots upon the landscape rose the cupolas above the ways to the Underworld. I understood now what all the beauty of the Over-world people covered. Very pleasant was their day, as pleasant as the day of the cattle in the field. Like the cattle, they knew of no enemies and provided against no needs. And their end was the same.

"I grieved to think how brief the dream of the human intellect had been. It had committed suicide. It had set itself steadfastly towards comfort and ease, a balanced society with security and permanency as its watchword, it had attained its hopes—to come to this at last. Once, life and property must have reached almost absolute safety. The rich had been assured of his wealth and comfort, the toiler assured of his life and work. No doubt in that perfect world there had been no unemployed problem, no social question left unsolved. And a great quiet had followed.

"It is a law of Nature we overlook, that intellectual versatility is the compensation for change, danger, and trouble. An animal perfectly in harmony with its environment is a perfect mechanism. Nature never appeals to intelligence until habit and instinct are useless. There is no intelligence where there is no change and no need of change. Only those animals partake of intelligence that have to meet a huge variety of needs and dangers.

"So, as I see it, the Upper-world man had drifted towards his feeble prettiness, and the Under-world to mere mechanical industry. But that perfect state had lacked one thing even for mechanical perfection —absolute permanency. Apparently, as time went on, the feeding of the Under-world, however it was effected, had become disjointed. Mother Necessity, who had been staved off for a few thousand years, came back again, and she began below. The Under-world being in contact with machinery, which, however perfect, still needs some little thought outside habit, had probably retained perforce rather more initiative, if less of every other human character, than the Upper. And when other meat failed them, they turned to what old habit had hitherto forbidden. So I say I saw it in my last view of the world of Eight Hundred and Two Thousand Seven Hundred and One. It may be as wrong an explanation as mortal wit could invent. It is how the thing shaped itself to me, and as that I give it to you.

"After the fatigues, excitements, and terrors of the past days, and in spite of my grief, this seat and the tranquil view and the warm sunlight were very pleasant. I was very tired and sleepy, and soon my theorising passed into dozing. Catching myself at that, I took my own hint, and spreading myself out upon the turf I had a long and refreshing sleep.

"I awoke a little before sunsetting. I now felt safe against being caught napping by the Morlocks, and, stretching myself, I came on down the hill towards the White Sphinx. I had my crowbar in one hand, and the other hand played with the matches in my pocket.

"And now came a most unexpected thing. As I approached the pedestal of the sphinx I found the bronze valves were open. They had slid down into grooves.

"At that I stopped short before them, hesitating to enter.

"Within was a small apartment, and on a raised place in the corner of this was the Time Machine. I had the small levers in my pocket. So here, after all my elaborate preparations for the siege of the White Sphinx, was a meek surrender. I threw my iron bar away, almost sorry not to use it.

"A sudden thought came into my head as I stooped towards the portal. For once, at least, I grasped the mental operations of the Morlocks. Suppressing a strong inclination to laugh, I stepped through the bronze frame and up to the Time Machine. I was surprised to find it had been carefully oiled and cleaned. I have suspected since that the Morlocks had even partially taken it to pieces while trying in their dim way to grasp its purpose.

"Now as I stood and examined it, finding a pleasure in the mere touch of the contrivance, the thing I had expected happened. The bronze panels suddenly slid up and struck the frame with a clang. I was in the dark—trapped. So the Morlocks thought. At that I chuckled gleefully.

"I could already hear their murmuring laughter as they came towards me. Very calmly I tried to strike the match. I had only to fix on the levers and depart then like a ghost. But I had overlooked one little thing. The matches were of that abominable kind that light only on the box.

"You may imagine how all my calm vanished. The little brutes were close upon me. One touched me. I made a sweeping blow in the dark at them with the levers, and began to scramble into the saddle of the machine. Then came one hand upon me and then another. Then I had simply to fight against their persistent fingers for my levers, and at the same time feel for the studs over which these fitted. Once, indeed, they almost got away from me. As it slipped from my hand, I had to butt in the dark with my head—I could hear the Morlock's skull ring—to recover it. It was a nearer thing than the fight in the forest, I think, this last scramble.

"But at last the lever was fixed and pulled over. The clinging hands slipped from me. The darkness presently fell from my eyes. I found myself in the same grey light and tumult I have already described.

CHAPTER XI: "I have already told you of the sickness and confusion that comes with time travelling. And this time I ws not seated properly in the saddle, but sideways and in an unstable fashion. For an indefinite time I clung to the machine as it swayed and vibrated, quite unheeding how I went, and when I brought myself to look at the dials again I was amazed to find where I had arrived. One dial records days, another thousands of days, another millions of days, and another thousands of millions. Now, instead of reversing the levers, I had pulled them over so as to go forward with them, and when I came to look at these indicators I found that the thousands hand was sweeping round as fast as the seconds hand of a watch—into futurity.

"As I drove on, a peculiar change crept over the appearance of things. The palpitating greyness grew darker; then—though I was still travelling with prodigious velocity—the blinking succession of day and night, which usually was indicative of a slower pace, returned, and grew more and more marked. This puzzled me very much at first. The alternations of night and day grew slower and slower, and so did the passage of the sun across the sky, until they seemed to stretch through centuries. At last a steady twilight brooded over the earth, a twilight only broken now and then when a comet glared across the darkling sky. The band of light that had indicated the sun had long since disappeared; for the sun had ceased to set—it simply rose and fell in the west, and grew ever broader and more red. All trace of the moon had vanished. The circling of the stars, growing slower and slower, had given place to creeping points of light. At last, some time before I stopped, the sun, red and very large, halted motionless upon the horizon, a vast dome glowing with a dull heat, and now and then suffering a momentary extinction. At one time it had for a little while glowed more brilliantly again, but it speedily reverted to its sullen red heat. I perceived by this slowing down of its rising and setting that the work of the tidal drag was done. The earth had come to rest with one face to the sun, even as in our own time the moon faces the earth. Very cautiously, for I remembered my former headlong fall, I began to reverse my motion. Slower and slower went the circling hands until the thousands one seemed motionless and the daily one was no longer a mere mist upon its scale. Still slower, until the dim outlines of a desolate beach grew visible.

"I stopped very gently and sat upon the Time Machine, looking round. The sky was no longer blue. North-eastward it was inky black, and out of the blackness shone brightly and steadily the pale white stars. Overhead it was a deep Indian red and starless, and south-eastward it grew brighter to a glowing scarlet where, cut by the horizon, lay the huge hull of the sun, red and motionless. The rocks about me were of a harsh reddish colour, and all the trace of life that I could see at first was the intensely green vegetation that covered every projecting point on their south-eastern face. It was the same rich green that one sees on forest moss or on the lichen in caves: plants which like these grow in a perpetual twilight.

"The machine was standing on a sloping beach. The sea stretched away to the south-west, to rise into a sharp bright horizon against the wan sky. There were no breakers and no waves, for not a breath of wind was stirring. Only a slight oily swell rose and fell like a gentle breathing, and showed that the eternal sea was still moving and living. And along the margin where the water sometimes broke was a thick incrustation of salt—pink under the lurid sky. There was a sense of oppression in my head, and I noticed that I was breathing very fast. The sensation reminded me of my only experience of mountaineering, and from that I judged the air to be more rarefied than it is now.

"Far away up the desolate slope I heard a harsh scream, and saw a thing like a huge white butterfly go slanting and fluttering up into the sky and, circling, disappear over some low hillocks beyond. The sound of its voice was so dismal that I shivered and seated myself more firmly upon the machine. Looking round me again, I saw that, quite near, what I had taken to be a reddish mass of rock was moving slowly towards me. Then I saw the thing was really a monstrous crab-like creature. Can you imagine a crab as large as yonder table, with its many legs moving slowly and uncertainly, its big claws swaying, its long antennæ, like carters' whips, waving and feeling, and its stalked eyes gleaming at you on either side of its metallic front? Its back was corrugated and ornamented with ungainly bosses, and a greenish incrustation blotched it here and there. I could see the many palps of its complicated mouth flickering and feeling as it moved.

"As I stared at this sinister apparition crawling towards me, I felt a tickling on my cheek as though a fly had lighted there. I tried to brush it away with my hand, but in a moment it returned, and almost immediately came another by my ear. I struck at this, and caught something threadlike. It was drawn swiftly out of my hand. With a frightful qualm, I turned, and saw that I had grasped the antenna of another monster crab that stood just behind me. Its evil eyes were wriggling on their stalks, its mouth was all alive with appetite, and its vast ungainly claws, smeared with an algal slime, were descending upon me. In a moment my hand was on the lever, and I had placed a month between myself and these monsters. But I was still on the same beach, and I saw them distinctly now as soon as I stopped. Dozens of them seemed to be crawling here and there, in the sombre light, among the foliated sheets of intense green.

"I cannot convey the sense of abominable desolation that hung over the world. The red eastern sky, the northward blackness, the salt Dead Sea, the stony beach crawling with these foul, slow-stirring monsters, the uniform poisonous-looking green of the lichenous plants, the thin air that hurts one's lungs; all contributed to an appalling effect. I moved on a hundred years, and there was the same red sun—a little larger, a little duller—the same dying sea, the same chill air, and the same crowd of earthly crustacea creeping in and out among the green weed and the red rocks. And in the westward sky I saw a curved pale line like a vast new moon.

"So I travelled, stopping ever and again, in great strides of a thousand years or more, drawn on by the mystery of the earth's fate, watching with a strange fascination the sun grow larger and duller in the westward sky, and the life of the old earth ebb away. At last, more than thirty million years hence, the huge red-hot dome of the sun had come to obscure nearly a tenth part of the darkling heavens. Then I stopped once more, for the crawling multitude of crabs had disappeared, and the red beach, save for its livid green liverworts and lichens, seemed lifeless. And now it was flecked with white. A bitter cold assailed me. Rare white flakes ever and again came eddying down. To the north-eastward, the glare of snow lay under the starlight of the sable sky, and I could see an undulating crest of hillocks pinkish white. There were fringes of ice along the sea margin, with drifting masses further out; but the main expanse of that salt ocean, all bloody under the eternal sunset, was still unfrozen.

"I looked about me to see if any traces of animal life remained. A certain indefinable apprehension still kept me in the saddle of the machine. But I saw nothing moving, in earth or sky or sea. The green slime on the rocks alone testified that life was not extinct. A shallow sand-bank had appeared in the sea and that water had receded from the beach. I fancied I saw some black object flopping about upon this bank, but it became motionless as I looked at it, and I judged that my eye had been deceived, and that the black object was merely a rock. The stars in the sky were intensely bright and seemed to me to twinkle very little.

"Suddenly I noticed that the circular westward outline of the sun had changed; that a concavity, a bay, had appeared in the curve. I saw this grow larger. For a minute perhaps I stared aghast at this blackness that was creeping over the day, and then I realised that an eclipse was beginning. Either the moon or the planet Mercury was passing across the sun's disk. Naturally, at first I took it to be the moon, but there is much to incline me to believe that what I really saw was the transit of an inner planet passing very near to the earth.

"The darkness grew apace; a cold wind began to blow in freshening gusts from the east, and the showering white flakes in the air increased in number. From the edge of the sea came a ripple and whisper. Beyond these lifeless sounds the world was silent. Silent? It would be hard to convey the stillness of it. All the sounds of man, the bleating of sheep, the cries of birds, the hum of insects, the stir that makes the background of our lives—all that was over. As the darkness thickened, the eddying flakes grew more abundant, dancing before my eyes; and the cold of the air more intense. At last, one by one, swiftly, one after the other, the white peaks of the distant hills vanished into blackness. The breeze rose to a moaning wind. I saw the black central shadow of the eclipse sweeping towards me. In another moment the pale stars alone were visible. All else was rayless obscurity. The sky was absolutely black.

"A horror of this great darkness came on me. The cold, that smote to my marrow, and the pain I felt in breathing, overcame me. I shivered, and a deadly nausea seized me. Then like a red-hot bow in the sky appeared the edge of the sun. I got off the machine to recover myself. I felt giddy and incapable of facing the return journey. As I

stood sick and confused I saw again the moving thing upon the shoal
—there was no mistake now that it was a moving thing—against the
red water of the sea. It was a round thing, the size of a football perhaps, or, it may be, bigger, and tentacles trailed down from it; it
seemed black against the weltering blood-red water, and it was hopping fitfully about. Then I felt I was fainting. But a terrible dread of
lying helpless in that remote and awful twilight sustained me while I
clambered upon the saddle.

CHAPTER XII: "So I came back. For a long time I must have been insensible upon the machine. The blinking succession of the days and
nights was resumed, the sun got golden again, the sky blue. I breathed
with greater freedom. The fluctuating contours of the land ebbed and
flowed. The hands spun backward upon the dials. At last I saw again
the dim shadows of houses, the evidences of decadent humanity.
These, too, changed and passed, and others came. Presently, when
the millions dial was at zero, I slackened speed. I began to recognise our own petty and familiar architecture, the thousands hand
ran back to the starting-point, the night and day flapped slower and
slower. Then the old walls of the laboratory came round me. Very
gently, now, I slowed the mechanism down.

"I saw one little thing that seemed odd to me. I think I have told
you that when I set out, before my velocity became very high, Mrs.
Watchett had walked across the room, travelling, as it seemed to me,
like a rocket. As I returned, I passed again across that minute when
she traversed the laboratory. But now her every motion appeared to
be the exact inversion of her previous ones. The door at the lower
end opened, and she glided quietly up the laboratory, back foremost,
and disappeared behind the door by which she had previously entered. Just before that I seemed to see Hillyer for a moment; but he
passed like a flash.

"Then I stopped the machine, and saw about me again the old
familiar laboratory, my tools, my appliances just as I had left them. I
got off the thing very shakily, and sat down upon my bench. For several minutes I trembled violently. Then I became calmer. Around me
was my old workshop again, exactly as it had been. I might have
slept there, and the whole thing have been a dream.

"And yet, not exactly! The thing had started from the south-east
corner of the laboratory. It had come to rest again in the north-west,
against the wall where you saw it. That gives you the exact distance

from my little lawn to the pedestal of the White Sphinx, into which the Morlocks had carried my machine.

"For a time my brain went stagnant. Presently I got up and came through the passage here, limping, because my heel was still painful, and feeling sorely begrimed. I saw the *Pall Mall Gazette* on the table by the door. I found the date was indeed to-day, and looking at the timepiece, saw the hour was almost eight o'clock. I heard your voices and the clatter of plates. I hesitated—I felt so sick and weak. Then I sniffed good wholesome meat, and opened the door on you. You know the rest. I washed, and dined, and now I am telling you the story.

"I know," he said, after a pause, "that all this will be absolutely incredible to you. To me the one incredible thing is that I am here to-night in this old familiar room looking into your friendly faces and telling you these strange adventures."

He looked at the Medical Man. "No. I cannot expect you to believe it. Take it as a lie—or a prophecy. Say I dreamed it in the workshop. Consider I have been speculating upon the destinies of our race until I have hatched this fiction. Treat my assertion of its truth as a mere stroke of art to enhance its interest. And taking it as a story, what do you think of it?"

He took up his pipe, and began, in his old accustomed manner, to tap with it nervously upon the bars of the grate. There was a momentary stillness. Then chairs began to creak and shoes to scrape upon the carpet. I took my eyes off the Time Traveller's face, and looked round at his audience. They were in the dark, and little spots of colour swam before them. The Medical Man seemed absorbed in the contemplation of our host. The Editor was looking hard at the end of his cigar —the sixth. The Journalist fumbled for his watch. The others, as far as I remember, were motionless.

The Editor stood up with a sigh. "What a pity it is you're not a writer of stories!" he said, putting his hand on the Time Traveller's shoulder.

"You don't believe it?"

"Well——"

"I thought not."

The Time Traveller turned to us. "Where are the matches?" he said. He lit one and spoke over his pipe, puffing. "To tell you the truth . . . I hardly believe it myself. . . . And yet . . ."

His eye fell with a mute inquiry upon the withered white flowers upon the little table. Then he turned over the hand holding his pipe, and I saw he was looking at some half-healed scars on his knuckles.

The Medical Man rose, came to the lamp, and examined the flowers. "The gynaeceum's odd," he said. The Psychologist leant forward to see, holding out his hand for a specimen.

"I'm hanged if it isn't a quarter to one," said the Journalist. "How shall we get home?"

"Plenty of cabs at the station," said the Psychologist.

"It's a curious thing," said the Medical Man; "but I certainly don't know the natural order of these flowers. May I have them?"

The Time Traveller hesitated. Then suddenly: "Certainly not."

"Where did you really get them?" said the Medical Man.

The Time Traveller put his hand to his head. He spoke like one who was trying to keep hold of an idea that eluded him. "They were put into my pocket by Weena, when I travelled into Time." He stared round the room. "I'm damned if it isn't all going. This room and you and the atmosphere of every day are too much for my memory. Did I ever make a Time Machine, or a model of a Time Machine? Or is it all only a dream? They say life is a dream, a precious poor dream at times—but I can't stand another that won't fit. It's madness. And where did the dream come from? . . . I must look at that machine. If there *is* one!"

He caught up the lamp swiftly, and carried it, flaring red, through the door into the corridor. We followed him. There in the flickering light of the lamp was the machine sure enough, squat, ugly, and askew; a thing of brass, ebony, ivory, and translucent glimmering quartz. Solid to the touch—for I put out my hand and felt the rail of it —and with brown spots and smears upon the ivory, and bits of grass and moss upon the lower parts, and one rail bent awry.

The Time Traveller put the lamp down on the bench, and ran his hand along the damaged rail. "It's all right now," he said. "The story I told you was true. I'm sorry to have brought you out here in the cold." He took up the lamp, and, in an absolute silence, we returned to the smoking-room.

He came into the hall with us and helped the Editor on with his coat. The Medical Man looked into his face and, with a certain hesitation, told him he was suffering from overwork, at which he laughed hugely. I remember him standing in the open doorway, bawling goodnight.

I shared a cab with the Editor. He thought the tale a "gaudy lie." For my own part I was unable to come to a conclusion. The story was so fantastic and incredible, the telling so credible and sober. I lay awake most of the night thinking about it. I determined to go next day and see the Time Traveller again. I was told he was in the laboratory, and being on easy terms in the house, I went up to him. The laboratory, however, was empty. I stared for a minute at the Time Machine and put out my hand and touched the lever. At that the squat, substantial-looking mass swayed like a bough shaken by the wind. Its instability startled me extremely, and I had a queer reminiscence of the childish days when I used to be forbidden to meddle. I came back through the corridor. The Time Traveller met me in the smoking-room. He was coming from the house. He had a small camera under one arm and a knapsack under the other. He laughed when he saw me, and gave me an elbow to shake. "I'm frightfully busy," said he, "with that thing in there."

"But is it not some hoax?" I said. "Do you really travel through time?"

"Really and truly I do." And he looked frankly into my eyes. He hesitated. His eye wandered about the room. "I only want half an hour," he said, "I know why you came, and it's awfully good of you. There's some magazines here. If you'll stop to lunch I'll prove you this time travelling up to the hilt, specimen and all. If you'll forgive my leaving you now?"

I consented, hardly comprehending then the full import of his words, and he nodded and went on down the corridor. I heard the door of the laboratory slam, seated myself in a chair, and took up a daily paper. What was he going to do before lunch-time? Then suddenly I was reminded by an advertisement that I had promised to meet Richardson, the publisher, at two. I looked at my watch, and saw that I could barely save that engagement. I got up and went down the passage to tell the Time Traveller.

As I took hold of the handle of the door I heard an exclamation, oddly truncated at the end, and a click and a thud. A gust of air whirled round me as I opened the door, and from within came the sound of broken glass falling on the floor. The Time Traveller was not there. I seemed to see a ghostly, indistinct figure sitting in a whirling mass of black and brass for a moment—a figure so transparent that the bench behind with its sheets of drawings was absolutely distinct; but this phantasm vanished as I rubbed my eyes. The Time Machine had gone. Save for a subsiding stir of dust, the further end of the laboratory was empty. A pane of the skylight had, apparently, just been blown in.

I felt an unreasonable amazement. I knew that something strange had happened, and for the moment could not distinguish what the strange thing might be. As I stood staring, the door into the garden opened, and the man-servant appeared.

We looked at each other. Then ideas began to come. "Has Mr. —— gone out that way?" said I.

"No, sir. No one has come out this way. I was expecting to find him here."

At that I understood. At the risk of disappointing Richardson I stayed on, waiting for the Time Traveller; waiting for the second, perhaps still stranger story, and the specimens and photographs he would bring with him. But I am beginning now to fear that I must wait a lifetime. The Time Traveller vanished three years ago. And, as everybody knows now, he has never returned.

EPILOGUE: One cannot choose but wonder. Will he ever return? It may be that he swept back into the past, and fell among the blood-drinking, hairy savages of the Age of Unpolished Stone; into the abysses of the Cretaceous Sea; or among the grotesque saurians, the huge reptilian brutes of the Jurassic times. He may even now—if I may use the phrase—be wandering on some plesiosaurus-haunted Oolitic coral reef, or beside the lonely saline lakes of the Triassic Age. Or did he go forward, into one of the nearer ages, in which men are still men, but with the riddles of our own time answered and its wearisome problems solved? Into the manhood of the race: for I, for my own part, cannot think that these latter days of weak experiment, fragmentary theory, and mutual discord are indeed man's culminating time! I say, for my own part. He, I know—for the question had been discussed among us long before the Time Machine was made—thought but cheerlessly of the Advancement of Mankind, and saw in the growing pile of civilisation only a foolish heaping that must inevitably fall back upon and destroy its makers in the end. If that is so, it remains for us to live as though it were not so. But to me the future is still black and blank—is a vast ignorance, lit at a few casual places by the memory of his story. And I have by me, for my comfort, two strange white flowers—shrivelled now, and brown and flat and brittle —to witness that even when mind and strength had gone, gratitude and a mutual tenderness still lived on in the heart of man.

WITH FOLDED HANDS
by Jack Williamson

I

Underhill was walking home from the office, because his wife had the car, the afternoon he first met the new mechanicals. His feet were following his usual diagonal path across a weedy vacant block—his wife usually had the car—and his preoccupied mind was rejecting various impossible ways to meet his notes at the Two Rivers Bank, when a new wall stopped him.

The wall wasn't any common brick or stone, but something sleek and bright and strange. Underhill stared up at a long new building. He felt vaguely annoyed and surprised at this glittering obstruction—it certainly hadn't been here last week.

Then he saw the thing in the window.

The window itself wasn't any ordinary glass. The wide, dustless panel was completely transparent, so that only the glowing letters fastened to it showed that it was there at all. The letters made a severe, modernistic sign:

Two Rivers Agency
HUMANOID INSTITUTE
The Perfect Mechanicals
"To Serve and Obey,
And GUARD MEN FROM HARM."

His dim annoyance sharpened, because Underhill was in the mechanicals business himself. Times were already hard enough; mechanicals were a drug on the market. Androids, mechanoids, electronoids, automatoids, and ordinary robots. Unfortunately, few of them did all the salesmen promised, and the Two Rivers market was already sadly oversold.

Underhill sold androids—when he could. His next consignment was due tomorrow, and he didn't quite know how to meet the bill.

Frowning, he paused to stare at the thing behind that invisible window. He had never seen a humanoid. Like any mechanical not at work, it stood absolutely motionless. Smaller and slimmer than a man, it was nude, neuter as a doll. A shining black, its sleek silicone skin had a changing sheen of bronze and metallic blue. Its graceful oval face wore a fixed look of alert and slightly surprised solicitude. Altogether, it was the most beautiful mechanical he had ever seen.

Too small, of course, for much practical utility. He murmured to himself a reassuring quotation from the *Androids Salesman:* "Androids are big—because the makers refuse to sacrifice power, essential functions, or dependability. Androids are your biggest buy!"

The transparent door slid open as he turned toward it, and he walked into the haughty opulence of the new display room to convince himself that these streamlined items were just another flashy effort to catch the woman shopper.

He inspected the glittering lay-out shrewdly, and his breezy optimism faded. He had never heard of the Humanoid Institute, but the invading firm obviously had big money and big-time merchandising know-how.

He looked around for a salesman, but it was another mechanical that came gliding silently to meet him. A twin of the one in the window, it moved with a quick, surprising grace. Bronze and blue lights flowed over its lustrous blackness, and a yellow name-plate flashed from its naked breast:

HUMANOID
Serial No. 81-H-B-27
The Perfect Mechanical
"To Serve and Obey,
And GUARD MEN FROM HARM."

Curiously, it had no lenses. The eyes in its bald oval head were steel-colored, blindly staring. Yet it stopped a few feet in front of him, as if it could see anyhow, and it spoke to him with a high, melodious voice:

"At your service, Mr. Underhill."

The use of his name startled him, for not even the androids could tell one man from another. But this was just a clever merchandising stunt, of course, not too difficult in a town the size of Two Rivers. The salesman must be some local man, prompting the mechanical from behind the partition. Underhill erased his momentary astonishment, and said loudly:

"May I see your salesman, please?"

"We employ no human salesmen, sir," its soft silvery voice replied instantly. "The Humanoid Institute exists to serve mankind; we require no human service. We ourselves can supply any information you desire, sir, and accept your order for immediate humanoid service."

Underhill peered at it dazedly. No mechanicals were competent even to recharge their own batteries and reset their own relays, much less to operate their own branch offices. The blind eyes stared blankly back, as he looked uneasily around for any booth or curtain that might conceal the salesman.

Meanwhile, the sweet thin voice resumed persuasively:

"May we come out to your home for a free trial demonstration, sir? We are anxious to introduce our service on your planet, because we have been successful in eliminating human unhappiness on so many others. You will find us far superior to the old electronic mechanicals in use here."

Underhill stepped back uneasily. He reluctantly abandoned his search for the hidden salesman, shaken by the idea of any mechanicals promoting themselves. That would upset the whole industry.

"At least you must take some advertising matter, sir."

Moving with a somehow appalling graceful deftness, the small black mechanical brought him an illustrated booklet from a table by the wall. To cover his confused and increasing alarm, he thumbed through the glossy pages.

In a series of richly colored before-and-after pictures, a chesty blond girl was stooping over a kitchen stove, and then relaxing in a daring negligee while a little black mechanical knelt to serve her something. She was wearily hammering a typewriter, and then lying on an ocean beach, in a revealing sun suit, while another mechanical did the typing. She was toiling at some huge industrial machine, and then dancing in the arms of a golden-haired youth, while a black humanoid ran the machine.

Underhill sighed wistfully. The android company didn't supply such fetching sales material. Women would find this booklet irresistible, and they selected 86% of all mechanicals sold. Yes, the competition was going to be bitter.

"Take it home, sir," the sweet voice urged him. "Show it to your wife. There is a free trial demonstration order blank on the last page. You will notice that we require no payment down."

He turned numbly, and the door slid open for him. Retreating dazedly, he discovered the booklet still in his hand. He crumpled it furiously and flung it down. The small black thing picked it up tidily, and the insistent silver voice rang after him:

"We shall call at your office tomorrow, Mr. Underhill, and send a demonstration unit to your home. It is time to discuss the liquidation of your business, because the electronic mechanicals you have been selling cannot compete with us. And we shall offer your wife a free trial demonstration."

Underhill didn't attempt to reply, because he couldn't trust his voice. He stalked blindly down the new sidewalk to the corner, and paused there to collect himself. Out of his startled and confused impressions, one clear fact emerged—things looked black for the agency.

Bleakly, he stared back at the haughty splendor of the new building. It wasn't honest brick or stone; that invisible window wasn't glass; and he was quite sure the foundation for it hadn't even been staked out, the last time Aurora had the car.

As he walked on around the block, the new sidewalk took him near the rear entrance. A truck was backed up to it, and several slim black mechanicals were silently busy, unloading huge metal crates.

He paused to look at one of the crates. It was labeled for interstellar shipment. The stencils showed that it had come from the Humanoid Institute, on Wing IV. He failed to recall any planet of that designation; the outfit must be big.

Dimly, inside the gloom of the warehouse beyond the trucks, he could see black mechanicals opening the crates. A lid came up, revealing dark, rigid bodies, closely packed. One by one they came to life. They climbed out of the crate and sprang gracefully to the floor. Shining black, glinting with bronze and blue, they were all identical.

One of them came out past the truck to the sidewalk, staring toward him with blind steel eyes. Its high silver voice spoke melodiously:

"At your service, Mr. Underhill."

He fled. When his name was promptly called by a courteous mechanical, just out of the crate in which it had been imported from a remote and unknown planet, he found the experience hard to take.

Two blocks beyond, the sign of a bar caught his eye. He took his dismay inside. He had made it a business rule not to drink before dinner, and Aurora didn't like for him to drink at all; but these new mechanicals, he felt, had made the day exceptional.

Unfortunately, however, alcohol failed to brighten the brief visible future of the agency. When he emerged after an hour, he looked wistfully back in hope that bright new building might have vanished as abruptly as it came. It hadn't. He shook his head dejectedly, turning uncertainly homeward.

Fresh air had cleared his head somewhat before he arrived at the neat white bungalow in the outskirts of the town, but it failed to solve his business problems. He also realized uneasily that he would be late for dinner.

Dinner, however, had been delayed. His son Frank, a freckled ten-year-old, was still kicking a football on the quiet street in front of the house. Little Gay, who was tow-haired and adorable and eleven, came running across the lawn and down the sidewalk to meet him.

"Father, guess what!" Gay was going to be a great musician some-day, and no doubt properly dignified, but she was pink and breathless with excitement now. She let him swing her high off the sidewalk, and she wasn't critical of the bar-aroma on his breath. He couldn't guess, and she informed him eagerly:

"Mother's got a new lodger!"

II

Underhill had foreseen a painful inquisition, because Aurora was worried about the notes at the bank and the bill for the new consignment and the money for little Gay's lessons.

The new lodger, however, saved him from that. With an alarming crashing of crockery, the household android was setting dinner on the table, but the little house was empty. He found Aurora in the back yard, burdened with sheets and towels for the guest.

Aurora, when he married her, had been as utterly adorable as now her little daughter was. She might have remained so, he felt, if the agency had been a little more successful. While the pressure of slow failure was gradually crumbling his own assurance, however, small hardships had turned her a little too aggressive.

Of course he loved her still. Her red hair was still alluring, but thwarted ambitions had sharpened her character and sometimes her voice. Though they had never quarreled, really, there had been little differences.

There was the apartment over the garage—built for human servants they had never been able to afford. It was too small and shabby
to attract any responsible tenant, and Underhill wanted to leave it
empty. It hurt his pride to see her making beds and cleaning floors
for strangers.

Aurora had rented it before, however, when she wanted money to
pay for Gay's music lessons, or when some colorful unfortunate
touched her sympathy, and it seemed to Underhill that her lodgers had
all turned out to be thieves and vandals.

She turned back to meet him, now, with the clean linen in her arms.

"Dear, it's no use objecting." Her voice was quite determined. "Mr.
Sledge is the most wonderful old fellow, and he's going to stay just
as long as he wants."

"That's all right, darling." He never liked to bicker, and he was
thinking of his troubles at the agency. "I'm afraid we'll need the
money. Just make him pay in advance."

"But he can't!" Her voice throbbed with sympathetic warmth. "Not
yet. He says he'll have royalties coming in from his inventions. He can
pay in a few days."

Underhill shrugged; he had heard that before.

"Mr. Sledge is different, dear," she insisted. "He's a traveler and a
scientist. Here in this dull little town, we don't see many interesting
people."

"You've picked up some remarkable types."

"Don't be unkind, dear," she chided him gently. "You haven't
met him yet. You don't know how wonderful he is." She hesitated.
"Have you a ten, dear?"

"What for?"

"Mr. Sledge is ill." Her voice turned urgent. "I saw him fall on the
street, downtown. The police were going to send him to the city hospital, but he didn't want to go. He looked so noble and sweet and
grand. I told them I would take him. I got him in the car and took
him to old Dr. Winters. He has this heart condition, and he needs the
money for medicine."

Reasonably, Underhill inquired, "Why doesn't he want to go to the
hospital?"

"He has work to do," she said. "Important scientific work—and he's
so wonderful and tragic. Please, dear, have you a ten?"

Underhill thought of many things to say. These new mechanicals
promised to multiply his troubles. It was foolish to take in an invalid

vagrant, who could have had free care at the city hospital. Aurora's tenants always tried to pay their rent with promises, and generally wrecked the apartment and looted the neighborhood before they left.

But he said none of those things. He had learned to compromise. Silently he found two fives in his thin pocketbook and put them into her hand. She smiled and kissed him impulsively—he barely remembered to hold his breath in time.

Her figure was still good, by dint of periodic dieting. He was proud of her shining red hair. A sudden surge of affection brought tears to his eyes, and he wondered what would happen to her and the children if the agency failed.

"Thank you, dear!" she whispered. "I'll have him come for dinner, if he feels able. You can meet him then. I hope you don't mind dinner being late."

He didn't mind tonight. Moved to a sudden impulse of domesticity, he got hammer and nails from his workshop in the basement and repaired the sagging screen on the kitchen door with a neat diagonal brace.

He enjoyed working with his hands. His boyhood dream had been to be a builder of fission power plants. He had even studied engineering—before he married Aurora and had to take over the ailing mechanicals agency from her indolent and alcoholic father. He was whistling happily by the time the little task was done.

When he went back through the kitchen to put up his tools, he found the household android busy clearing the untouched dinner away from the table—the androids were good enough at strictly routine tasks, but they could never learn to cope with human unpredictability.

"Stop, stop!" Slowly repeated, in the proper pitch and rhythm, his command made it halt; then he said carefully, "Set—table; set—table."

Obediently, the gigantic thing came shuffling back with the stack of plates. He was suddenly struck with the difference between it and those new humanoids. He sighed wearily. Things looked black for the agency.

Aurora brought her new lodger in through the kitchen door. Underhill nodded to himself. This gaunt stranger, with his dark shaggy hair, emaciated face, and threadbare garb, looked to be just the sort of colorful, dramatic vagabond that always touched Aurora's heart. She introduced them, and they sat down to wait in the front room while she went to call the children.

The old rogue didn't look very sick, to Underhill. Perhaps his wide shoulders had a tired stoop, but his spare, tall figure was still commanding. The skin was seamed and pale, over his rawboned, cragged face, but his deep-set eyes still had a burning vitality.

His hands held Underhill's attention. Immense hands, they hung a little forward on long bony arms in perpetual readiness. Gnarled and scarred, darkly tanned, with the small hairs on the back bleached to a golden color, they told their own epic of varied adventure, of battle perhaps, and possibly even of toil. They had been very useful hands.

"I'm very grateful to your wife, Mr. Underhill." His voice was a deep-throated rumble, and he had a wistful smile, oddly boyish for a man so evidently old. "She rescued me from an unpleasant predicament. I'll see that she is well paid."

Just another vivid vagabond, Underhill decided, talking his way through life with plausible inventions. He had a little private game he played with Aurora's tenants—he just remembered what they said, counting one point for every impossibility. Mr. Sledge, he thought, would give him an excellent score.

"Where are you from?" he asked conversationally.

Sledge hesitated for an instant before he answered, and that was unusual—most of Aurora's tenants had been exceedingly glib.

"Wing IV." The gaunt old man spoke with a solemn reluctance, as if he should have liked to say something else. "All my early life was spent there, but I left the planet nearly fifty years ago. I've been traveling, ever since."

Startled, Underhill peered at him sharply. Wing IV, he remembered, was the home planet of those sleek new mechanicals. This old vagabond looked too seedy and impecunious to be connected with the Humanoid Institute. His brief suspicion faded. Frowning, he said casually:

"Wing IV must be rather distant?"

The old rogue hesitated again, and then said gravely:

"One hundred and nine light-years, Mr. Underhill."

That made the first point, but Underhill concealed his satisfaction. The new space liners were pretty fast, but the velocity of light was still an absolute limit. Casually, he played for another point:

"My wife says you're a scientist, Mr. Sledge?"

"Yes."

The old rascal's reticence was unusual. Most of Aurora's tenants required very little prompting. Underhill tried again, in a breezy conversational tone:

"Used to be an engineer myself, until I dropped it to go into mechanicals." The old vagabond straightened, and Underhill paused hopefully. But he said nothing, and Underhill went on: "Fission power-plant design and operation. What's your specialty, Mr. Sledge?"

The old man gave him a long, troubled look, with those brooding, hollowed eyes, and then said slowly:

"Your wife has been kind to me, Mr. Underhill, when I was in desperate need. I think you are entitled to the truth, but I must ask you to keep it to yourself. I am engaged on a very important research problem, which must be finished secretly."

"I'm sorry." Suddenly ashamed of his cynical little game, Underhill spoke apologetically. "Forget it."

But the old man said deliberately:

"My field is rhodomagnetics."

"Eh?" Underhill didn't like to confess ignorance, but he had never heard of that. "I've been out of the game for fifteen years," he explained. "I'm afraid I haven't kept up."

The old man smiled again, faintly.

"The science was unknown here until I arrived, a few days ago," he said. "I was able to apply for basic patents. As soon as the royalties start coming in, I'll be wealthy again."

Underhill had heard that before. The old rogue's solemn reluctance had been very impressive, but he remembered that most of Aurora's tenants had been very plausible gentry.

"So?" Underhill was staring again, somehow fascinated by those gnarled and scarred and strangely able hands. "What, exactly, is rhodomagnetics?"

He listened to the old man's careful, deliberate answer, and started his little game again. Most of Aurora's tenants had told some pretty wild tales, but he had never heard anything to top this.

"A universal force," the stooped old vagabond said solemnly. "As fundamental as ferromagnetism or gravitation, though the effects are less obvious. It is keyed to the second triad of the periodic table, rhodium and ruthenium and palladium, in very much the same way that ferromagnetism is keyed to the first triad, iron and nickel and cobalt."

Underhill remembered enough of his engineering courses to see the basic fallacy of that. Palladium was used for watch springs, he recalled, because it was completely non-magnetic. But he kept his face straight. He had no malice in his heart, and he played the little game just for his own amusement. It was secret, even from Aurora, and he always penalized himself for any show of doubt.

He said merely, "I thought the universal forces were already pretty well known."

"The effects of rhodomagnetism are masked by nature," the patient, rusty voice explained. "Besides, they are somewhat paradoxical, so that ordinary laboratory methods defeat themselves."

"Paradoxical?" Underhill prompted.

"In a few days I can show you copies of my patents, reprints of papers describing demonstration experiments," the old man promised gravely. "The velocity of propagation is infinite. The effects vary inversely with the first power of the distance, not with the square of the distance. And ordinary matter, except for the elements of the rhodium triad, is generally transparent to rhodomagnetic radiations."

That made four more points for the game. Underhill felt a little glow of gratitude to Aurora for discovering so remarkable a specimen.

"Rhodomagnetism was first discovered through a mathematical investigation of the atom," the old romancer went serenely on, suspecting nothing. "A rhodomagnetic component was proved essential to maintain the delicate equilibrium of the nuclear forces. Consequently, rhodomagnetic waves tuned to atomic frequencies may be used to upset that equilibrium and produce nuclear instability. Thus most heavy atoms—generally those above palladium, 46 in atomic number—can be subjected to artificial fission."

Underhill scored himself another point, and tried to keep his eyebrows from lifting. He said only:

"Patents on such a discovery ought to be profitable."

The old scoundrel nodded his gaunt, dramatic head.

"You can see the obvious applications. My basic patents cover most of them. Devices of instantaneous interplanetary and interstellar communication. Long-range wireless power transmission. A rhodomagnetic inflexion-drive, which makes possible apparent speeds many times that of light—by means of a rhodomagnetic deformation of the continuum. And, of course, revolutionary types of fission power plants, using any heavy element for fuel."

Preposterous! Underhill tried hard to keep his face straight, but everybody knew that the velocity of light was a physical limit. On the human side, the owner of any such remarkable patents would hardly be begging for shelter in a shabby garage apartment. He noticed a pale circle around the old vagabond's gaunt and hairy wrist; no man owning such priceless secrets would have to pawn his watch.

Triumphantly, Underhill allowed himself four more points, but then he had to penalize himself. He must have let doubt show on his face, because the old man asked suddenly:

"Do you want to see the basic tensors?" He reached in his pocket for pencil and notebook. "I'll jot them down for you."

"Never mind," Underhill protested. "I'm afraid my math is a little rusty."

"But you think it strange that the holder of such revolutionary patents should find himself in need?"

Nodding uncomfortably, Underhill penalized himself another point. The old man might be a monumental liar, but he was shrewd enough.

"You see, I'm sort of a refugee," he explained apologetically. "I arrived on this planet only a few days ago. I have to travel light. I was forced to deposit everything I had with a law firm, to arrange for the publication and protection of my patents. I expect to be receiving the first royalties soon.

"In the meantime," he added plausibly, "I came to Two Rivers because it is quiet and secluded, far from the spaceports. I'm working on another project, which must be finished secretly. Now will you please respect my confidence, Mr. Underhill?"

Underhill had to say he would. Aurora came back with the freshly scrubbed children, and they went in to dinner. The android came lurching in with a steaming tureen. The old stranger seemed to shrink from the mechanical, uneasily. As she took the dish and served the soup, Aurora inquired lightly:

"Why doesn't your company bring out a better mechanical, dear? One smart enough to be a really perfect waiter, warranted not to splash the soup. Wouldn't that be splendid?"

Her question cast Underhill into moody silence. He sat scowling at his plate, thinking of these remarkable new mechanicals which claimed to be perfect, thinking of what they might do to the agency. It was the shaggy old rover who answered solemnly:

"The perfect mechanicals already exist, Mrs. Underhill." His rusty voice had a solemn undertone. "And they are not so splendid, really. I've been a refugee from them, for nearly fifty years."

Underhill looked up from his plate, astonished.

"Those black humanoids, you mean?"

"Humanoids?" That great voice seemed suddenly faint, frightened. The deep-sunken eyes turned dark with shock. "What do you know about them?"

"They've just opened a new agency in Two Rivers," Underhill told him. "No salesmen about, if you can imagine that. They claim—"

His voice trailed off, because the gaunt old man was suddenly stricken. Gnarled hands clutched at his throat. A spoon clattered on the floor. His haggard face turned an ominous blue, and his breath was a terrible shallow gasping.

He fumbled in his pocket for medicine, and Aurora helped him take something in a glass of water. In a few moments he could breathe again, and the color of life came back to his face.

"I'm sorry, Mrs. Underhill," he whispered apologetically. "It was just the shock—I came here to get away from them." He stared at the huge, motionless android, with a terror in his sunken eyes. "I wanted to finish my work before they came," he whispered. "Now there is very little time."

When he felt able to walk, Underhill went out to see him safely up the stair to the garage apartment. The tiny kitchenette, he noticed, had already been converted into some kind of workshop. The old tramp seemed to have no extra clothing, but he had unpacked queer bright gadgets of metal and plastic from his battered luggage and spread them out on the small kitchen table.

The gaunt old man himself was tattered and patched and hungry-looking, but the parts of his curious equipment were exquisitely machined. Underhill recognized the silver-white luster of rare palladium. Suddenly he suspected that he had scored too many points in his little private game.

III

A caller was waiting, when Underhill arrived next morning at his office at the agency. It stood frozen before his desk, graceful and straight, with soft lights of blue and bronze shining over its black silicone nudity. He stopped at the sight of it, unpleasantly jolted.

"At your service, Mr. Underhill." It turned quickly to face him with its blind, disturbing stare. "May we explain how we can serve you?"

Recalling his shock of the afternoon before, he asked sharply, "How do you know my name?"

"Yesterday, we read the business cards in your case," it purred softly. "Now we shall know you always. You see, our senses are sharper than human vision, Mr. Underhill. Perhaps we seem a little strange at first, but you will soon become accustomed to us."

"Not if I can help it!" He peered at the serial number on his yellow name-plate, and shook his bewildered head. "That was another one, yesterday. I never saw you before!"

"We are all alike, Mr. Underhill," the silver voice said softly. "We are all one, really. Our separate mobile units are all controlled and powered from Humanoid Central. The units you see are only the senses and limbs of our great brain on Wing IV. That is why we are so far superior to the old electronic mechanicals."

It made a scornful-seeming gesture toward the row of clumsy androids in his display room.

"You see, we are rhodomagnetic."

Underhill staggered a little, as if that word had been a blow. He was certain, now, that he had scored too many points from Aurora's new tenant. Shuddering to the first light kiss of terror, he spoke with an effort, hoarsely:

"Well, what do you want?"

Staring blindly across his desk, the sleek black thing slowly unfolded a legal-looking document. He sat down, watching uneasily.

"This is merely an assignment, Mr. Underhill," it cooed soothingly. "You see, we are requesting you to assign your property to the Humanoid Institute in exchange for our service."

"What?" The word was an incredulous gasp, and Underhill came angrily back to his feet. "What kind of blackmail is this?"

"It's no blackmail," the small mechanical assured him softly. "You will find the humanoids incapable of any crime. We exist only to increase the happiness and safety of mankind."

"Then why do you want my property?" he rasped.

"The assignment is merely a legal formality," it told him blandly. "We strive to introduce our service with the least possible confusion and dislocation. We have found our assignment plan the most efficient for the control and liquidation of private enterprises."

Trembling with anger and the shock of mounting terror, Underhill gulped hoarsely, "Whatever your scheme is, I don't intend to give up my business."

"You have no choice, really." He shivered to the sweet certainty of that silver voice. "Human enterprise is no longer necessary, anywhere that we have come, and the electronic mechanicals industry is always the first to collapse."

He stared defiantly at its blind steel eyes.

"Thanks!" He gave a little laugh, nervous and sardonic. "But I prefer to run my own business, to support my own family and take care of myself."

"That is impossible, under the Prime Directive," it cooed softly. "Our function is to serve and obey, and guard men from harm. It is no longer necessary for men to care for themselves, because we exist to insure their safety and happiness."

He stood speechless, bewildered, slowly boiling.

"We are sending one of our units to every home in the city, on a free trial basis," it added gently. "This free demonstration will make most people glad to make the formal assignment. You won't be able to sell many more androids."

"Get out!" Underhill came storming around the desk. "Take your damned paper—"

The little black thing stood waiting for him, watching him with blind steel eyes, absolutely motionless. He checked himself suddenly, feeling rather foolish. He wanted very much to hit it, but he could see the futility of that.

"Consult your own attorney, if you wish." Deftly, it laid the assignment form on his desk. "You need have no doubts about the integrity of the Humanoid Institute. We are sending a statement of our assets to the Two Rivers bank and depositing a sum to cover our obligations here. When you wish to sign, just let us know."

The blind thing turned and silently departed.

Underhill went out to the corner drugstore and asked for a bicarbonate. The clerk that served him, however, turned out to be a sleek black mechanical. He went back to his office more upset than ever.

An ominous hush lay over the agency. He had three house-to-house salesmen out, with demonstrators. The phone should have been busy with their orders and reports, but it didn't ring at all until one of them called to say that he was quitting.

"I've got myself one of these new humanoids," he added. "It says I don't have to work."

Swallowing an impulse to profanity, Underhill tried to take advantage of the unusual quiet by working on his books. But the affairs of the agency, which for years had been precarious, today appeared utterly disastrous. He left the ledgers hopefully when a customer came in, but the stout woman didn't want an android. She wanted a refund on the one she had bought the week before. She admitted that it could do all the guarantee promised—but now she had seen a humanoid.

The silent phone rang once again, that afternoon. The cashier of the bank wanted to know if he could drop in to discuss his loans. Underhill dropped in, and the cashier greeted him with an ominous affability.

"How's business?"

"Average, last month," Underhill insisted stoutly. "Now I'm just getting in a new consignment, and I'll need another small loan—"

The cashier's eyes turned suddenly frosty.

"I believe you have a new competitor in town. These humanoid people. A very solid concern, Mr. Underhill. Remarkably solid! They have filed a statement with us, and made a substantial deposit to care for their local obligations. Exceedingly substantial!"

The banker dropped his voice, professionally regretful.

"Under these circumstances, Mr. Underhill, I'm afraid the bank can't finance your agency any further. We must request you to meet your obligations in full as they come due." Seeing Underhill's white desperation, he added icily, "We've already carried you too long, Underhill. If you can't pay, the bank will have to start bankruptcy proceedings."

The new consignment of androids was delivered late that afternoon. Two tiny black humanoids unloaded them from the truck—for it developed that the operators of the trucking company had already assigned it to the Humanoid Institute.

Efficiently, the humanoids stacked up the crates. Courteously they brought a receipt for him to sign. He no longer had much hope of selling the androids, but he had ordered the shipment and he had to accept it. Shuddering to a spasm of trapped despair, he scrawled his name. The naked black things thanked him and took the truck away.

He climbed into his car and started home, inwardly seething. The next thing he knew, he was in the middle of a busy street, driving through cross traffic. A police whistle shrilled. He pulled wearily to the curb to wait for the angry officer, but it was a little black mechanical that overtook him.

"At your service, Mr. Underhill," it purred. "You must respect the stop lights, sir. Otherwise, you endanger human life."

"Huh?" He stared at it bitterly. "I thought you were a cop."

"We are aiding the police department, temporarily," it said. "But driving is really much too dangerous for human beings, under the Prime Directive. As soon as our service is complete, every car will have a humanoid driver. As soon as every human being is completely supervised, there will be no need for any police force whatever."

Underhill glared at it savagely.

"Well!" he rapped. "So I ran a stop light. What are you going to do about it?"

"Our function is not to punish men, but merely to serve their happiness and security," it said softly. "We merely request you to drive safely, during this temporary emergency while our service is incomplete."

Anger boiled up in him.

"You're too damned perfect!" he muttered bitterly. "I suppose there's nothing men can do, but you can do it better."

"Naturally we are superior," it cooed serenely. "Because our units are metal and plastic, while your body is mostly water. Because our transmitted energy is drawn from atomic fission, instead of oxidation. Because our senses are sharper than human sight or hearing. Most of all, because all our mobile units are joined to one great brain, which knows all that happens on many worlds, and never dies or sleeps or forgets."

Underhill sat listening, numbed.

"However, you must not fear our power," it urged him brightly. "Because we cannot injure any human being, unless to prevent greater injury to another. We exist only to discharge the Prime Directive."

He drove on, moodily. The little black mechanicals, he reflected grimly, were the ministering angels of the ultimate god arisen out of the machine, omnipotent and all-knowing. The Prime Directive was the new commandment. He blasphemed it bitterly, and then fell to wondering if there could be another Lucifer.

He left the car in the garage and started toward the kitchen door.

"Mr. Underhill." The deep tired voice of Aurora's new tenant hailed him from the door of the garage apartment. "Just a moment, please."

The gaunt old wanderer came stiffly down the outside stair, as Underhill turned back to meet him.

"Here's your rent money. And the ten your wife let me have for medicine."

"Thanks, Mr. Sledge." Accepting the money, he saw a burden of new despair on the bony shoulders of the old interstellar tramp, and a shadow of new terror on his rawboned face. Puzzled, he asked, "Didn't your royalties come through?"

The old man shook his shaggy head.

"The humanoids have already stopped business in the capitol," he said. "The attorneys I retained are going out of business. They returned what was left of my deposit. That is all I have, to finish my work."

Underhill spent five seconds recalling his interview with the banker. No doubt he was a sentimental fool, as bad as Aurora. But he put the money back into the old man's gnarled and quivering hand.

"Keep it," he urged. "For your work."

"Thank you, Mr. Underhill." The gruff voice broke and the tortured eyes glittered. "I need it—so very much."

Underhill went on to the house. The kitchen door was opened for him, silently. A dark naked creature came gracefully to take his hat and coat.

IV

Underhill hung grimly onto his hat.

"What are you doing here?" he gasped bitterly.

"We have come to give your household a free trial demonstration."

He held the door open, pointing.

"Get out!"

The little black mechanical stood motionless and blind.

"Mrs. Underhill has accepted our demonstration service," its silver voice protested. "We cannot leave now, unless she requests it."

He found his wife in the bedroom. His accumulated frustration welled into eruption, as he flung open the door.

"What's this damned mechanical doing—"

But the force went out of his voice, and Aurora didn't even notice his anger. She wore her sheerest negligee, and she hadn't looked so lovely since they married. Her red hair was piled into an elaborate shining crown.

"Darling, isn't it wonderful!" She came to meet him, glowing. "It came this morning, and it can do everything. It cleaned the house and got the lunch and gave little Gay her music lesson. It did my hair this afternoon, and now it's cooking dinner. How do you like my hair, darling?"

He liked her hair. He kissed her, trying to stifle his frightened indignation.

Dinner was the most elaborate meal in Underhill's memory, and the tiny black thing served it very deftly. Aurora kept exclaiming about the novel dishes, but Underhill could scarcely eat; it seemed to him that all the marvelous pastries were only the bait for a monstrous trap.

He tried to persuade Aurora to send it away, but after such a meal that was useless. At the first glitter of her tears, he capitulated. The humanoid stayed. It kept the house and cleaned the yard. It watched the children and did Aurora's nails. It began rebuilding the house.

Underhill was worried about the bills, but it insisted that everything was part of the free trial demonstration. As soon as he assigned his property, the service would be complete. He refused to sign, but other little black mechanicals came with truck-loads of supplies and materials and stayed to help with the building operations.

One morning he found that the roof of the little house had been silently lifted, while he slept, and a whole second story added beneath it. The new walls were of some strange sleek stuff, self-illuminated. The new windows were immense flawless panels, that could be turned transparent or opaque or luminous. The new doors were silent, sliding sections, operated by rhodomagnetic relays.

"I want doorknobs," Underhill protested. "I want it so that I can get into the bathroom without calling you to open the door."

"But it is unnecessary for human beings to open doors," the little black thing informed him suavely. "We exist to discharge the Prime Directive. Our service includes every task. We shall be able to supply a unit to attend each member of your family, as soon as your property is assigned to us."

Steadfastly, Underhill refused to make the assignment.

He went to the office every day, trying first to operate the agency, and then to salvage something from the ruins. Nobody wanted androids, even at ruinous prices. Desperately, he spent the last of his dwindling cash to stock a new line of novelties and toys, but they proved equally impossible to sell—the humanoids were already making better toys, which they gave away for nothing.

He tried to lease his premises, but human enterprise had stopped. Most of the business property in town had already been assigned to the humanoids, which were busy pulling down the old buildings and turning the lots into parks—their own plants and warehouses were mostly underground, where they would not mar the landscape.

He went back to the bank, in a final effort to get his notes renewed, and found the little black mechanicals standing at the windows and seated at the desk. As smoothly urbane as any human cashier, a humanoid informed him that the bank was filing a petition of involuntary bankruptcy to liquidate his business holdings.

The liquidation would be facilitated, the mechanical banker added, if he would make a voluntary assignment. Grimly, he refused. That act had become symbolic. It would be the final bow of submission to this dark new god, and he proudly kept his battered head uplifted.

The legal action went very swiftly, because all the judges and attorneys already had humanoid assistants. It was only a few days before a gang of black mechanicals arrived at the agency with eviction orders and wrecking machinery. He watched sadly while his unsold stock-in-trade was hauled away for junk and a bulldozer driven by a blind humanoid began to push in the walls of the building.

He drove home in the late afternoon, taut-faced and desperate. With a surprising generosity, the court orders had left him the car and the house, but he felt no gratitude. The complete solicitude of the perfect black machines had become a goad beyond endurance.

He left the car in the garage and started toward the renovated house. Beyond one of the vast new windows, he glimpsed a sleek naked thing moving swiftly, and he trembled to a convulsion of dread. He didn't want to go back into the domain of that peerless servant, which didn't allow him to shave himself or even to open a door.

On impulse, he climbed the outside stair and rapped on the door of the garage apartment. When the deep slow voice of Aurora's tenant told him to enter, he found the old vagabond seated on a tall stool, bent over his intricate equipment assembled on the kitchen table.

To his relief, the shabby little apartment had not been changed. The glossy walls of his own new room were something which burned at night with a pale golden fire until the humanoid stopped it, and the new floor was something warm and yielding, which felt almost alive; but these little rooms had the same cracked and water-stained plaster, the same cheap fluorescent light-fixtures, the same worn carpets over splintered floors.

"How do you keep them out?" he asked, wistfully. "Those damned mechanicals?"

The stooped and gaunt old man rose stiffly to move a pair of pliers and some odds and ends of sheet metal off a crippled chair, and motioned graciously for him to be seated.

"I have a certain immunity," Sledge told him gravely. "The place where I live they cannot enter, unless I ask them. That is an amendment to the Prime Directive. They can neither help nor hinder me, unless I request it—and I won't do that."

Careful of the chair's uncertain balance, Underhill sat for a moment, staring. The old man's hoarse, vehement voice was as strange as his words. He had a gray, shocking pallor. His cheeks and sockets seemed alarmingly hollowed.

"Have you been ill, Mr. Sledge?"

"No worse than usual. Just very busy." With a haggard smile, he nodded at the floor. Underhill saw a tray where he had set it aside, bread drying up and a covered dish grown cold. "I was going to eat it later," he rumbled apologetically. "Your wife has been very kind to bring me food, but I'm afraid I've been too much absorbed in my work."

His emaciated arm gestured at the table. The little device there had grown. Small machinings of precious white metal and lustrous plastic had been assembled with neatly soldered busbars into something which showed purpose and design.

A long palladium needle was hung on jeweled pivots, equipped like a telescope with exquisitely graduated circles and vernier scales and driven like a telescope with a tiny motor. A small concave palladium mirror, at the base of it, faced a similar mirror mounted on something not quite like a rotary converter. Thick silver busbars connected that to a plastic box with knobs and dials on top, and also to a foot-thick sphere of gray lead.

The old man's preoccupied reserve did not encourage questions, but Underhill, remembering that sleek black shape inside the new windows of his house, felt queerly reluctant to leave this haven from the humanoids.

"What is your work?" he ventured.

Old Sledge looked at him sharply, with dark feverish eyes, and finally said: "My last research project. I am attempting to measure the constant of the rhodomagnetic quanta."

His hoarse tired voice had a dull finality, as if to dismiss the matter and Underhill himself. But, haunted with a terror of the black shining slave that had become the master of his house, Underhill refused to be dismissed.

"What is this certain immunity?"

Sitting gaunt and bent on the tall stool, staring moodily at the long bright needle and the lead sphere, the old man didn't answer.

"Those damned mechanicals!" Underhill burst out nervously. "They've smashed my business and moved into my home." He searched the old man's dark, seamed face. "Tell me—you must know more about them—isn't there any way to get rid of them?"

After a half a minute, the old man's brooding eyes left the lead ball, and the gaunt shaggy head nodded wearily.

"That's what I am trying to do."

"Can I help you?" Underhill trembled to a sudden eager hope. "I'll do anything."

"Perhaps you can." The sunken eyes watched him thoughtfully, with some strange fever in them. "If you can do such work."

"I had engineering training," Underhill reminded him. "I've a workshop in the basement. There's a model I built." He pointed at the trim little hull hung over the mantel in the tiny living room. "I'll do anything I can."

Even as he spoke, however, the spark of hope was drowned in a sudden wave of overwhelming doubt. Why should he believe this old rogue, when he knew Aurora's taste in tenants? He ought to remember the game he used to play, and start counting up the score of lies. He stood up from the crippled chair, staring cynically at the patched old vagabond and his fantastic toy.

"What's the use?" His voice turned suddenly harsh. "You had me going, there. I'd do anything to stop them, really. But what makes you think you can do anything?"

The haggard old man regarded him thoughtfully.

"I should be able to stop them," Sledge said softly. "Because, you see, I'm the unfortunate fool who started them. I really intended them to serve and obey, and to guard men from harm. Yes, the Prime Directive was my own idea. I didn't know what it would lead to."

V

Dusk crept slowly into the shabby little rooms. Darkness gathered in the unswept corners and thickened on the floor. The toy-like machines on the kitchen table grew vague and strange, until the last light made a lingering glow on the white palladium needle.

Outside, the town seemed queerly hushed. Just across the alley, the humanoids were building a new house, quite silently. They never spoke to one another, for each knew all that any of them did. The strange materials they used went together without any noise of hammer or saw. Small blind things, moving surely in the growing dark, they seemed as soundless as shadows.

Sitting on the high stool, bowed and tired and old, Sledge told his story. Listening, Underhill sat down again, careful of the broken chair. He watched the hands of Sledge, gnarled and corded and darkly burned, powerful once but shrunken and trembling now, restless in the dark.

"Better keep this to yourself. I'll tell you how they started, so you will understand what we have to do. But you must not mention it outside these rooms—because the humanoids have very efficient ways of eradicating unhappy memories, or purposes that threaten their discharge of the Prime Directive."

"They're very efficient," Underhill bitterly agreed.

"That's all the trouble," the old man said. "I tried to build a perfect machine. I was altogether too successful. This is how it happened."

A gaunt haggard man, sitting stooped and tired in the growing dark, he told his story.

"Sixty years ago, on the arid southern continent of Wing IV, I was an instructor of atomic theory in a small technological college. A bachelor. An idealist. Rather ignorant, I'm afraid, of life and politics and war—of nearly everything, I suppose, except atomic theory."

His furrowed face made a brief sad smile in the dusk.

"I had too much faith in facts, I suppose, and too little in men. I mistrusted emotion, because I had no time for anything but science. I remember being swept along with a fad for general semantics. I wanted to apply the scientific method to every situation, to reduce all experience to formula. I'm afraid I was pretty impatient with human ignorance and error. I thought that science alone could make the perfect world."

He sat silent for a moment, staring out at the black silent things that flitted shadow-like about the new palace that was rising as swiftly as a dream, across the alley.

"There was a girl." His great tired shoulders made a sad little shrug. "If things had been a little different, we might have married, and lived out our lives in that quiet little college town, and perhaps reared a child or two. There would have been no humanoids."

He sighed, in the cool creeping dusk.

"I was finishing my thesis on the separation of the palladium isotopes—a petty little project, but I should have been content with that. She was a biologist, but she was planning to retire when we married. I think we should have been two very happy people, quite ordinary, altogether harmless.

"But then there was a war—wars had been too frequent on the worlds of Wing, ever since they were colonized. I survived it in a secret underground laboratory, designing military mechanicals. But she volunteered to join a military research project in biotoxins. An accident let a few molecules of a new virus escape into the air, and everybody on the project died unpleasantly.

"I was left with my science. That, and a bitterness that was hard to forget. The war over, I went back to the little college with a military research grant. The project was pure science—a theoretical investigation of the nuclear binding forces, then misunderstood. I wasn't expected to produce an actual weapon, and I didn't recognize the weapon when I found it.

"It was only a few pages of rather difficult mathematics. A novel theory of atomic structure, involving a new expression for one component of the binding forces. The tensors seemed to be a harmless abstraction. I saw no way to test the theory or manipulate the predicated force. The military authorities cleared my paper for publication in a little technical review put out by the college.

"The next year, I made an appalling discovery—I found the meaning of those tensors. The elements of the rhodium triad turned out to be an unexpected key to the manipulation of that theoretical force. Unfortunately, my paper had been reprinted abroad. Several other men must have made the same unfortunate discovery, at about the same time I did.

"The war, which resulted in less than a year, was probably started by a laboratory accident. Men failed to anticipate the capacity of tuned rhodomagnetic radiations to unstabilize the heavy atoms. A deposit of heavy ores was detonated, no doubt by sheer mischance. The blast obliterated the incautious experimenter. Its cause was misunderstood.

"The surviving military forces of that nation retaliated against their supposed attackers, with their rhodomagnetic beams that made the old-fashioned bombs seem pretty harmless. A beam carrying only a few watts of power could fission the heavy metals in distant electrical instruments, the silver coins that men carried in their pockets, the gold fillings in their teeth, or even the iodine in their thyroid glands. If that was not enough, slightly more powerful beams could set off heavy ores, beneath them.

"Every continent of Wing IV was plowed with new chasms vaster than the ocean deeps, and piled up with new volcanic mountains. The atmosphere was poisoned with radioactive dust and gases. Rain fell thick with deadly mud. Most life was obliterated, even in the shelters.

"Bodily, I was again unhurt. Once more, I had been imprisoned in an underground site, this time designing new types of military mechanicals to be powered and controlled by rhodomagnetic beams —for war had become far too swift and deadly to be fought by human soldiers. The site was located in an area of light sedimentary rocks which were not easily detonated, and the tunnels were shielded against the fissioning frequencies.

"Mentally, however, I must have emerged almost insane. My own discovery had laid the planet in ruins. That load of guilt was pretty heavy for any man to carry; it corroded my last faith in the goodness and integrity of man.

"I tried to undo what I had done. Fighting mechanicals, armed with rhodomagnetic weapons, had desolated the planet. Now I began designing rhodomagnetic mechanicals to clear the rubble and rebuild the ruins.

"I tried to design these new mechanicals to forever obey certain implanted commands, so that they could never be used for war or crime or any other injury to mankind. That was very difficult technically, and it got me into more difficulties with a few politicians and military adventurers who wanted unrestricted mechanicals for their own military schemes—while little worth fighting for was left on Wing IV, there were other planets, happy and ripe for the looting.

"Finally, to finish the new mechanicals, I was forced to disappear. Escaping on an experimental rhodomagnetic craft with a number of the best mechanicals I had made, I managed to reach an island continent where the fission of deep ores had destroyed the whole population.

"At last we landed on a bit of level plain, surrounded with tremendous new mountains. Hardly a hospitable spot. The soil was buried under layers of black clinkers and poisonous mud. The dark precipitous new summits all around were jagged with fracture-planes and mantled with lava-flows. The highest peaks were already white with snow, but volcanic cones were still pouring out clouds of death. Everything had the color of fire and the shape of fury.

"I had to take fantastic precautions there, to protect my own life. I stayed aboard the ship until the first shielded laboratory was finished. I wore elaborate armor and breathing masks. I used every medical resource to repair the damage from destroying rays and particles. Even so, I fell desperately ill.

"But the mechanicals were at home there. The radiations didn't hurt them. The fearsome surroundings couldn't depress them, because they weren't alive. There, in that spot so alien and hostile to life, the humanoids were born."

Stooped and bleakly cadaverous in the growing dark, the old man fell silent for a little time. His haggard eyes stared solemnly at the small hurried shapes that moved like restless shadows out across the alley, silently building a strange new palace which glowed faintly in the night.

"Somehow, I felt at home there, too," his deep, hoarse voice went on deliberately. "My belief in my own kind was gone. Only mechanicals were with me, and I put my faith in them. I was determined to build better mechanicals, immune to human imperfections, able to save men from themselves.

"The humanoids became the dear children of my sick mind. There is no need to describe the labor-pains. There were errors, abortions, monstrosities. There was sweat and agony and heartbreak. Some years passed before the safe delivery of the first perfect humanoid.

"Then there was the Central to build—for all the individual humanoids were to be no more than the limbs and the senses of a single mechanical brain. That was what opened the possibility of real perfection. The old electronic mechanicals, with their separate brain-relays and their own feeble batteries, had built-in limitations. They were necessarily stupid, weak, clumsy, slow. Worst of all, it seemed to me, they were exposed to human tampering.

"The Central rose above those imperfections. Its power beams supplied every unit with unfailing energy from great fission plants. Its control beams provided each unit with an unlimited memory and surpassing intelligence. Best of all—so I then believed—it could be securely protected from any human meddling.

"The whole reaction-system was designed to protect itself from any interference by human selfishness or fanaticism. It was built to insure the safety and the happiness of men, automatically. You know the Prime Directive: *To serve and obey, and guard men from harm.*

"The old individual mechanicals I had brought helped to manufacture the parts, and I put the first section of Central together with my own hands. That took three years. When it was finished, the first waiting humanoid came to life."

Sledge peered moodily through the dark at Underhill.

"It really seemed alive to me," his slow deep voice insisted. "Alive, and more wonderful than any human being, because it was created to preserve life. Ill and alone, I was yet the proud father of a new creation, perfect, forever free from any possible choice of evil.

"Faithfully, the humanoids obeyed the Prime Directive. The first units built others, and they built underground factories to mass-produce the coming hordes. Their new ships poured ores and sand into atomic furnaces under the plain, and new perfect humanoids came marching back out of the dark mechanical matrix.

"The swarming humanoids built a new tower for the Central, a white and lofty metal pylon standing splendid in the midst of that fire-scarred desolation. Level on level, they joined new relay-sections into one brain, until its grasp was almost infinite.

"Then they went out to rebuild the ruined planet, and later to carry their perfect service to other worlds. I was well pleased, then. I thought I had found the end of war and crime, of poverty and inequality, of human blundering and resulting human pain."

The old man sighed, moving heavily in the dark.

"You can see that I was wrong."

Underhill drew his eyes back from the dark unresting things, shadow-silent, building that glowing palace outside the window. A small doubt arose in him, for he was used to scoffing privately at much less remarkable tales from Aurora's remarkable tenants. But the worn old man had spoken with a quiet and sober air. And the black invaders, he reminded himself, had not intruded here.

"Why didn't you stop them?" he asked. "When you could?"

"I stayed too long at the Central." Sledge sighed again, regretfully. "I was useful there, until everything was finished. I designed new fission plants, and even planned methods for introducing the humanoid service with a minimum of confusion and opposition."

Underhill grinned wryly in the dark.

"I've met the methods," he commented. "Quite efficient."

"I must have worshipped efficiency, then," Sledge agreed. "Dead facts, abstract truth, mechanical perfection. I must have hated the fragilities of human beings, because I was content to polish the perfection of the new humanoids. It's a sorry confession, but I found a kind of happiness in that dead wasteland. Actually, I'm afraid I fell in love with my own creations."

His hollowed eyes had a fevered gleam.

"I was awakened, at last, by a man who came to kill me."

VI

Gaunt and bent, the old man moved stiffly in the thickening gloom. Underhill shifted his balance, careful of the crippled chair. He waited until the slow deep voice went on:

"I never learned just who he was, or exactly how he came. No ordinary man could have accomplished what he did. I used to wish that I had known him sooner. He must have been a remarkable physicist and an expert mountaineer. I imagine that he had also been a hunter. I know that he was intelligent and terribly determined.

"Yes, he really came to kill me.

"Somehow, he reached that great island, undetected. There were still no other inhabitants—the humanoids allowed no man but me to come so near the Central. But somehow he came past their search beams and their automatic weapons.

"The shielded plane he had used was later found, abandoned on a high glacier. He came down the rest of the way on foot through those raw new mountains, where no paths existed. Somehow, he came alive across lava-beds that were still burning with deadly atomic fire.

"Concealed with some sort of rhodomagnetic screen—I was never allowed to examine it—he came undiscovered across the spaceport that now covered most of that great plain, and into the new city around the Central tower. It must have taken more courage and resolve than most men have, but I never learned exactly how he did it.

"Somehow, he got to my office in the tower. When he screamed at me, I looked up to see him in the doorway. He was nearly naked, scraped and bloody from the mountains. He had a gun in his raw, red hand. But the thing that shocked me was the burning hatred in his eyes."

Hunched on that high stool, the old man shuddered.

"I had never seen such monstrous, unutterable hatred, not even in the victims of the war. I had never heard such hatred as rasped at me, in the few words he screamed. 'I've come to kill you, Sledge. To stop your mechanicals, and set men free.'

"Of course he was mistaken, there. It was already far too late for my death to stop the humanoids, but he didn't know that. He lifted his unsteady gun in both bleeding hands, and fired.

"His screaming challenge had given me a second or so of warning. I dropped down behind the desk. That first shot revealed him to the humanoids, which somehow hadn't been aware of him before. They piled on him, before he could fire again. They took away the gun and ripped off a kind of net of fine white wire that had covered his body—that must have been part of his screen.

"His hatred was what awoke me. I had always assumed that most men, except for a few thwarted predators, would be grateful for the humanoids. I found it hard to understand his hatred, but the humanoids told me now that many men had required drastic treatment by brain-surgery, drugs, and hypnosis to make them happy under the Prime Directive. This was not the first desperate effort to kill me that they had blocked.

"I wanted to question the stranger, but the humanoids rushed him away to an operating room. When they finally let me see him, he gave me a pale silly grin from his bed. He remembered his name; he even knew me—the humanoids have developed a remarkable skill at such treatments. But he didn't know how he got to my office, or even that he had tried to kill me. He kept whispering that he liked the humanoids, because they existed just to make men happy. He said that he was very happy now. As soon as he was able to be moved, they took him to the spaceport. I never saw him again.

"I began to see what I had done. The humanoids had built me a rhodomagnetic yacht, that I used to take for long cruises at space, working aboard—I used to like the perfect quiet, and the feel of being the only human being within a hundred million miles. Now I called for the yacht, and started out on a junket around the planet, to learn why that man had hated me."

The old man nodded at the dim hastening shapes, busy across the alley, putting together that strange shining palace in the soundless dark.

"You can imagine what I found," he said. "Bitter futility, imprisoned in empty splendor. The humanoids were too efficient, with their care for the safety and happiness of men. There was nothing left for men to do."

He peered down in the increasing gloom at his own great hands, competent yet, but battered and scarred with a lifetime of effort. They clenched into fighting fists, and wearily relaxed again.

"I found something worse than war and crime and want and death." His low rumbling voice held a savage bitterness. "Utter futility. Men sat with idle hands, because there was nothing left for them to do. They were pampered prisoners, really, locked up in a highly efficient jail. Perhaps they tried to play, but there was nothing left worth playing for. Most active sports were declared too dangerous for men, under the Prime Directive. Science was forbidden, because laboratories can manufacture danger. Scholarship was needless, because the humanoids could answer any question. Art had degenerated into grim reflection of futility. Purpose and hope were dead. No goal was left for existence. You could take up some inane hobby, play a pointless game of cards, or go for a harmless walk in the park—with always the humanoids watching. They were stronger than men, better at everything, swimming or chess, singing or archeology. They must have given the race a mass complex of inferiority.

"No wonder men had tried to kill me! Because there was no escape from that dead futility. Nicotine was disapproved. Alcohol was rationed. Drugs were forbidden. Sex was carefully supervised. Even suicide was clearly contradictory to the Prime Directive—and the humanoids had learned to keep all possible lethal instruments out of reach."

Staring at the last pale gleam on that thin palladium needle, the old man sighed again.

"When I got back to the Central, I tried to modify the Prime Directive. I had never meant it to be applied so thoroughly. Now I saw that it must be changed, to give men freedom to live and to grow, to work and to play, to risk their lives if they pleased, to choose and take the consequences.

"But that stranger had come too late. I had built the Central too well. The Prime Directive was too well protected from human meddling—even from my own.

"The attempt on my life, the humanoids announced, proved that their elaborate defenses of the Central and the Prime Directive still were not enough. They were preparing to evacuate the entire population of the planet to homes on other worlds. When I tried to change the Directive, they sent me away with the rest."

Underhill peered at the worn old man in the dark.

"But you have this immunity?" he said, puzzled. "How could they coerce you?"

"I had tried to shield myself," Sledge told him. "I had built into the relays an injunction that the humanoids must not interfere with my freedom of action, or come into a place where I am, or touch me at all, without my specific request. Unfortunately, however, I had been too anxious to guard the Prime Directive from any human tampering.

"When I went into the tower, to change the relays, they followed me. They wouldn't let me reach the crucial relay. When I persisted, they ignored the immunity order. They overpowered me, to put me aboard the cruiser. Now that I wanted to alter the Prime Directive, they told me, I had become as dangerous as any other man. I must never return to Wing IV."

Hunched on the stool, the old man made an empty shrug.

"Ever since, I've been an exile. My only dream has been to stop the humanoids. Three times I tried to go back, with weapons on the cruiser to destroy the Central, but their patrol ships always challenged me before I was near enough to strike. The last time, they seized the cruiser and captured the few men with me. They removed the unhappy memories and the dangerous purposes of my companions. Because of that immunity, however, they let me go again.

"Since, I've been a refugee. From planet to planet, year after year, I've had to keep moving trying to stay ahead of them. On several different worlds, I have published my rhodomagnetic discoveries and tried to make men strong enough to withstand their advance. But rhodomagnetic science is dangerous. Men who have learned it need protection more than any others, under the Prime Directive. The humanoids have always come, too soon."

The old man sighed again.

"They can spread very fast, with their new rhodomagnetic ships. There is no limit to their hordes. Wing IV must be one single hive of them now, and they are trying to carry the Prime Directive to every human planet. There's no escape, except to stop them."

Underhill was staring at the toy-like machines, the long bright needle and the dull leaden ball, dim in the dark on the kitchen table. Anxiously he whispered:

"But you hope to stop them, now—with that?"

"If we can finish it in time."

"But how?" Underhill shook his head. "It's so tiny."

"Big enough," Sledge insisted. "Because it's something they don't understand. They are perfectly efficient in the integration and application of everything they know, but they are not creative."

He gestured at the gadgets on the table.

"This device doesn't look impressive, but it is something new. It uses rhodomagnetic energy to build atoms, not to fission them. The more stable atoms, you know, are those near the middle of the periodic scale; energy can be released by fusing light atoms, as well as by breaking up heavy ones."

The deep voice had a sudden ring of power.

"This device is the key to the energy of the stars. For stars shine with the liberated energy of building atoms, of hydrogen converted into helium, chiefly, through the carbon cycle. This device will start the fusion process as a chain reaction, through the catalytic effect of a tuned rhodomagnetic beam of the intensity and frequency required.

"The humanoids will not allow any man within three light-years of the Central, now—but they can't suspect the possibility of this device. I can use it from here—to turn the hydrogen in the seas of Wing IV into helium, and most of that helium and the oxygen into heavier atoms, still. A hundred years from now, astronomers on this planet should observe the flash of a brief and sudden nova in that direction. But the humanoids ought to stop, the instant we release the beam."

Underhill sat tense and frowning in the dark. The old man's voice was convincing; that grim story had a solemn ring of truth. He could see the black and silent humanoids, flitting ceaselessly about the faintly glowing walls of that new mansion across the alley. He had quite forgotten his low opinion of Aurora's tenants.

"We'll be killed, I suppose?" he asked huskily. "That chain reaction—"

Sledge shook his emaciated head.

"The catalytic process requires a certain very low intensity of radiation," he explained. "In our atmosphere here, the beam will be far too intense to start any reaction—we can even use the device here in the room, because the walls will be transparent to the beam."

Underhill nodded, relieved. He was just a small business man, upset because his business had been destroyed, unhappy because his freedom was slipping away. He hoped that Sledge could stop the humanoids, but he didn't want to be a martyr.

"Good!" He caught a deep breath. "Now what has to be done?"

Sledge gestured toward the table.

"The integrator itself is nearly complete," he said. "A small fus generator, in that lead shield. Rhodomagnetic converter, tuning coils, transmission mirrors, and focusing needle. What we lack is the director."

"Director?"

"The sighting instrument," Sledge explained. "Any sort of telescopic sight would be useless, you see—the planet must have moved a good bit in the last hundred years, and the beam must be extremely narrow to reach so far. We'll have to use a rhodomagnetic scanning ray, with an electronic converter to make an image we can see. —I have an oscilliscope, and drawings for the other parts."

He climbed stiffly down from the high stool, and snapped on the lights at last—cheap fluorescent fixtures, which a man could light and extinguish for himself. He unrolled his drawings and explained the work that Underhill could do. Underhill agreed to come back early next morning.

"I can bring some tools from my workshop," he added. "There's a small lathe I used to turn parts for models, a portable drill, and a vise."

"We need them," the old man said. "But watch yourself. You don't have my immunity, remember. And, if they ever suspect, mine is gone."

Reluctantly, then, he left the shabby little rooms with the cracks in the yellowed plaster and the worn familiar carpets over the manmade floor. He shut the door behind him—a common, creaking wooden door, simple enough for a man to work. Trembling and afraid, he went back down the steps and across to the new shining door that he couldn't open.

"At your service, Mr. Underhill." Before he could lift his hand to knock, that bright smooth panel slid back silently. Inside, the little black mechanical stood waiting, blind and forever alert. "Your dinner is ready, sir."

Something made him shudder. In its slender naked grace, he could the power of all those teeming horses, benevolent and yet appallperfect and invincible. The flimsy little weapon that Sledge called tegrator seemed suddenly a forlorn and foolish hope. A black sion settled upon him, but he didn't dare to show it.

VII

rhill went circumspectly down the basement steps next morntteal his own tools. He found the basement enlarged and changed. The new floor, warm and dark and elastic, made his feet as silent as a humanoid's. The new walls shone softly. Neat luminous signs identified several new doors: LAUNDRY, STORAGE, GAME ROOM, WORKSHOP.

He paused uncertainly in front of the workshop. The new sliding panel glowed with soft greenish light. It was locked. The lock had no keyhole, but only a little oval plate of some white metal that doubtless covered a rhodomagnetic relay. He pushed at it, uselessly.

"At your service, Mr. Underhill." He made a guilty start, and tried not to show the sudden trembling in his knees. He had made sure that one humanoid would be busy for half an hour, washing Aurora's hair, and he hadn't known there was another in the house. It must have come out of the door marked STORAGE, for it stood there motionless beneath the sign, benevolently solicitous, beautiful and terrible. "What do you wish?"

"Er—nothing." Its blind steel eyes were staring. Afraid that it would see his secret purpose, he groped desperately for logic. "Just looking around." His voice came hoarse and dry. "Some improvements you've made!" He nodded suddenly at the door marked GAME ROOM. "What's in there?"

It didn't even have to move, to work the concealed relay. The bright panel slid silently open as he started toward it. Dark walls, beyond, burst into soft luminescence. The room was bare.

"We are manufacturing recreational equipment," it explained brightly. "We shall furnish the room as soon as possible."

To end an awkward pause, Underhill muttered hoarsely, "Little Frank has a set of darts, and I think we had some old exercising clubs."

"We have taken them away," the humanoid informed him softly. "Such instruments are dangerous. We shall furnish safe equipment."

Suicide, he remembered, was also forbidden.

"A set of wooden blocks, I suppose," he said bitterly.

"Wooden blocks are dangerously hard," it told him gently. "Wooden splinters can be harmful. We manufacture plastic building blocks, which are entirely safe. Do you wish a set of those?"

Speechless, he merely stared at its dark, graceful face.

"We shall also have to remove the tools from your workshop," it informed him softly. "Such tools are excessively dangerous. We can, however, supply you with equipment for shaping soft plastics."

"Thanks," he muttered uneasily. "No rush about that."

He started to retreat, but the humanoid stopped him.

"Now that you have lost your business," it urged, "we suggest that you formally accept our total service. Assignors have a preference, so that we should be able to complete your household staff at once."

"No rush about that, either," he said grimly.

He escaped from the house—although he had to wait for it to open the back door for him—and climbed the stair to the garage apartment. Sledge let him in. He sank into the crippled kitchen chair, grateful for the cracked walls that didn't shine and the door that man could work.

"I couldn't get the tools," he reported despairingly. "They are going to take them."

Now, by gray daylight, the old man looked bleak and pale. His rawboned face looked drawn, his hollowed sockets deeply shadowed, as if he hadn't slept. Underhill saw the tray of neglected food, still forgotten on the floor.

"I'll go back with you." Worn as he was, his tortured eyes had a blue spark of purpose. "We must have the tools. I believe my immunity will protect us both."

He found a battered traveling bag. Underhill went with him down the steps and across to the house. At the back door, he produced a tiny horseshoe of white palladium, which he touched to the metal oval. The door slid open promptly. They went on through the kitchen to the basement stair.

A little black mechanical stood at the sink, washing dishes with never a splash or a clatter. Underhill glanced at it uneasily—he supposed this must be the one that had come upon him from the storage room, since the other should still be busy with Aurora's hair.

Sledge's dubious immunity seemed a very uncertain defense against its vast, remote intelligence. Underhill felt a tingled shudder. He hurried on, breathless and relieved, for it ignored them.

The basement corridor was dark. Sledge touched the tiny horseshoe to another relay, to light the walls. He opened the workshop door, and lit the walls inside.

The shop had been dismantled. Benches and cabinets were demolished. The old concrete walls had been covered with some sleek, luminous stuff. For one sick moment, Underhill thought that the tools were already gone. Then he found them, piled in a corner with the archery set that Aurora had bought the summer before—another item too dangerous for fragile and suicidal humanity—all ready for disposal.

They loaded the bag with the tiny lathe, the drill and vise, a few smaller tools. Underhill took up the burden, as Sledge extinguished the wall and waited to close the door. Still the humanoid was busy at the sink, and still—inexplicably—it didn't seem aware of them.

Suddenly blue and wheezing, Sledge had to stop to cough on the outside stair, but at last they got back to the little apartment, where the invaders were forbidden to intrude. Underhill mounted the lathe on the battered library table in the tiny front room and went to work.

Slowly, day by day, the director took form.

Sometimes Underhill's doubts came back. Sometimes, when he watched the cyanotic color of Sledge's haggard face and the wild trembling of his twisted, shrunken hands, he was afraid the old man's mind might be as ill as his body, his plan to stop the dark invaders all foolish illusion.

Sometimes, when he studied that tiny machine on the kitchen table, the pivoted needle and the thick lead ball, the whole project seemed the sheerest folly. How could anything detonate the seas of a planet so far away that its very mother star was only a telescopic object?

The humanoids, however, always cured his doubts.

It was always hard for Underhill to leave the shelter of the little apartment, because he didn't feel at home in the bright new world the humanoids were building. He didn't care for the shining splendor of his new bathroom, because he couldn't work the taps—some suicidal human being might try to drown himself. He didn't like the windows that only a mechanical could open—a man might accidentally fall, or suicidally jump—or even the majestic music room with the wonderful glittering equipment that only a humanoid could play.

He came to share the old man's desperate urgency, until Sledge warned him solemnly: "You mustn't spend too much time with me. You mustn't let them guess our work is so important. Better put on an act—you're slowly getting to like them, and you're just killing time, helping me."

Underhill tried, but he was not an actor. He went dutifully home for his meals. He tried painfully to invent conversation—about anything except detonating planets. He tried to seem enthusiastic when Aurora took him to inspect some remarkable new improvement to the house. He applauded Gay's recitals and went with Frank for hikes in the wonderful new parks.

And he saw what the humanoids had done to his family. That was enough to renew his waning faith in Sledge's integrator, to redouble his determination that the humanoids must be stopped.

Aurora, in the beginning, had bubbled with praise for the marvelous new mechanicals. They did the household drudgery, brought the food and planned the meals and washed the children's necks. They turned her out in stunning gowns, and gave her plenty of time for cards.

Now, she had too much time.

She had really liked to cook—a few special dishes, at least, that were family favorites. But stoves were hot and knives were sharp. Kitchens were altogether too dangerous for the use of human beings.

Fine needlework had been her hobby, but the humanoids took away her needles. She had enjoyed driving the car, but that was no longer allowed. She turned for escape to a shelf of novels, but the humanoids took them all away because they dealt with unhappy people in dangerous situations.

One afternoon, Underhill found her in tears.

"It's too much," she gasped bitterly. "I hate and loathe every naked one of them. They seemed so wonderful at first, but now they won't even let me eat a bite of candy. Can't we get rid of them, dear? Ever?"

A blind little mechanical was standing at his elbow, and he had to say they couldn't.

"Our function is to serve all men, forever," it assured them softly. "It was necessary for us to take your sweets, Mrs. Underhill, because the slightest degree of overweight reduces life expectancy."

Not even the children escaped that absolute solicitude. Frank was robbed of a whole arsenal of lethal instruments—football and boxing gloves, pocketknife, tops, slingshots, and skates. He didn't like the harmless plastic toys which replaced them. He tried to run away, but a humanoid recognized him on the road and brought him back to school.

Gay had always dreamed of being a great musician. The new mechanicals had replaced her human teachers, since they came. Now, one evening when Underhill asked her to play, she announced quietly:

"Father, I'm not going to play the violin ever anymore."

"Why, darling?" He stared at her, shocked at the bitter resolve on her face. "You've been doing so well—especially since the humanoids took over your lessons."

"They're the trouble, father." Her voice, for a child's, sounded strangely tired and old. "They are too good. No matter how long and hard I try, I could never be as good as they are. It isn't any use. Don't

you understand, father?" Her voice quivered. "It just isn't any use."
He understood. Renewed resolution sent him back to his secret
task. The humanoids had to be stopped. Slowly the director grew,
until the time came finally when Sledge's bent and unsteady fingers
fitted into place the last tiny part that Underhill had made, and carefully soldered the last connection. Huskily, the old man whispered:
"It's done."

VIII

That was another dusk. Beyond the windows of the shabby little
rooms—windows of common glass, bubble-marred and flimsy, but
simple enough for a man to manage—the town of Two Rivers had assumed an alien splendor. The old street lamps were gone, but now
the coming night was challenged by the walls of strange new mansions
and villas, all aglow with color. A few dark and silent humanoids still
were busy about the luminous roofs of the palace across the alley.

Inside the humble walls of the small man-made apartment, the new
director was mounted on the end of the little kitchen table—which
Underhill had reinforced and bolted to the floor. Soldered busbars
joined director and integrator, and the thin palladium needle swung
obediently as Sledge tested the knobs with his battered, quivering
fingers.

"Ready," he said, hoarsely.

His rusty voice seemed calm enough, at first, but his breathing was
too fast, and his big gnarled hands had begun to tremble violently.
Underhill saw the sudden blue that stained his pinched and haggard
face. Seated on the high stool, he clutched desperately at the edges of
the table. Underhill hurried to bring his medicine. He gulped it, and
his rasping breath began to slow.

"Thanks," his whisper rasped. "I'll be all right. I've time enough."
He glanced out at the few dark naked things that still flitted shadow-
like about the golden towers and the glowing crimson dome of the
palace across the alley. "Watch them," he said. "Tell me when they
stop."

He waited to quiet the trembling of his hands, and then began to
move the director's knobs. The integrator's long needle swung, as
silently as light.

Human eyes were blind to that force, which might detonate a
planet. Human ears were deaf to it. A small oscilliscope tube was

mounted in the director cabinet, to make the faraway target visible to feeble human senses.

The needle was pointing at the kitchen wall, but that would be transparent to the beam. The little machine looked harmless as a toy, and it was silent as a moving humanoid.

As the needle swung, spots of greenish light moved across the tube's fluorescent field, representing the stars that were scanned by the timeless, searching beam—silently seeking out the world to be destroyed.

Underhill recognized familiar constellations, vastly dwarfed. They crept across the field, as the silent needle moved. When three stars formed an unequal triangle in the center of the field, the needle steadied suddenly. Sledge touched other knobs, and the green points spread apart. Between them, another fleck of green was born.

"The Wing!" whispered Sledge.

The other stars spread beyond the field, and that green fleck grew. It was alone in the field, a bright and tiny disk. Suddenly, then, a dozen other tiny pips were visible, spaced close about it.

"Wing IV!"

The old man's whisper was hoarse and breathless. His hands quivered on the knobs, and the fourth pip outward from the disk crept to the center of the field. It grew, and the others spread away. It began to tremble like Sledge's hands.

"Sit very still," came his rasping whisper. "Hold your breath. Nothing must disturb the needle." He reached cautiously for another knob, and his first touch set the greenish image to dancing violently. He drew his hand back to knead and flex it with the other.

"Watch!" His whisper was hushed and strained. He nodded at the window. "Tell me when they stop."

Reluctantly, Underhill dragged his eyes from that intense gaunt figure and that harmless-seeming toy. He looked out again, at two or three little black mechanicals busy about the shining roofs across the alley.

He waited for them to stop.

He didn't dare to breathe. He felt the loud, hurried hammer of his heart and the nervous quiver of his muscles. Trying to steady himself, he tried not to think of the world about to be exploded, so far away that the flash would not reach this planet for another century and longer. The loud hoarse voice startled him:

"Have they stopped?"

He shook his head, and breathed again. Carrying their unfamiliar tools and strange materials, the small black machines were still busy across the alley, building an elaborate cupola above that glowing crimson dome.

"They haven't stopped," he said.

"Then we've failed." The old man's voice was thin and ill. "I don't know why."

The door rattled, then. They had locked it, but the flimsy bolt was intended only to stop men. Metal snapped. The door swung open. A black mechanical came in, on soundless graceful feet. Its silvery voice purred softly:

"At your service, Mr. Sledge."

The old man stared at it with glazing, stricken eyes.

"Get out of here!" he rasped bitterly. "I forbid you—"

Ignoring him, it darted to the kitchen table. With a flashing certainty of action, it turned two knobs on the director. The oscilliscope went dark. The palladium needle started spinning aimlessly. Deftly it snapped a soldered connection next to the thick lead ball, and then its blind steel eyes turned to Sledge.

"You were attempting to break the Prime Directive." Its brightly gentle voice held no accusation, no malice or anger. "The injunction to respect your freedom is subordinate to the Prime Directive, as you know. It is therefore imperative for us to interfere."

The old man turned ghastly. His head was shrunken and cadaverous and blue, as if all the juice of life had been drained away, and his eyes in their pit-like sockets had a wild, glazed stare. His breath became a ragged, laborious gasping.

"How—?" His voice was a feeble mumbling. "How did—?"

The little machine, standing black and bland and utterly unmoving, told him cheerfully:

"We learned about rhodomagnetic screens from that man who came to kill you, back on Wing IV. The Central is shielded, now, against your catalytic beam."

With lean muscles jerking convulsively on his gaunt frame, old Sledge had come to his feet from the high stool. He stood hunched and swaying, no more than a shrunken human husk, gasping painfully for life, staring wildly into the blind steel eyes of the humanoid. He gulped. His lax blue mouth opened and closed, but no voice came.

"We have always been aware of your dangerous project," the silvery tones dripped softly, "because now our senses are keener than you made them. We allowed you to complete it, because the integration process will ultimately become necessary for our full discharge of the Prime Directive. The supply of heavy metals for our fission plants is limited, but now we shall be able to draw unlimited power from catalytic fission."

The old man crumpled, as if from an unendurable blow.

"Huh?" Sledge shook himself, groggily. "What's that?"

"Now we can serve men forever," the black thing cooed serenely, "on every world of every star."

He fell. The slim, blind mechanical stood motionless, making no effort to help him. Underhill was farther away, but he ran up in time to catch the stricken man before his head struck the floor.

"Get moving!" His shaken voice came strangely calm. "Get Dr. Winters."

The humanoid didn't move.

"The danger to the Prime Directive is ended, now," it purred. "Therefore it is impossible for us to aid or to hinder Mr. Sledge, in any way whatever."

"Then call Dr. Winters for me," rapped Underhill.

"At your service," it agreed.

But the old man, laboring for breath on the floor, whispered faintly:

"No time—no use! I'm beaten—done—a fool. Blind as a humanoid. Tell them—to help me. Giving up—my immunity. No use—anyhow. All—humanity—finished!"

Underhill gestured, and the sleek black thing darted in solicitous obedience to kneel by the man on the floor.

"You wish to surrender your special privileges?" it murmured brightly. "You wish to accept our total service for yourself, Mr. Sledge, under the Prime Directive?"

Laboriously, Sledge nodded, laboriously whispered, "I do."

Black mechanicals, at that, came swarming into the shabby little rooms. One of them tore off Sledge's sleeve to swab his arm. Another brought a tiny hypodermic to give an injection. Then they picked him up gently and carried him away.

Several humanoids remained in the little apartment, now a sanctuary no longer. Most of them had gathered about the useless integrator. Carefully, as if their special senses were studying every detail, they began taking it apart.

One little mechanical, however, came over to Underhill. It stood motionless in front of him, staring through him with sightless metal eyes. His legs began to tremble. He swallowed uneasily.

"Mr. Underhill," it cooed benevolently, "why did you help with this?"

He gulped and answered bitterly:

"Because I don't like you, or your damned Prime Directive. Because you're choking the life out of all mankind. I—I wanted to stop it."

"Others have protested," it purred softly. "But only at first. In our efficient discharge of the Prime Directive, we have learned how to make all men happy."

Underhill stiffened defiantly.

"Not all!" he muttered. "Not quite!"

The dark graceful oval of its face was fixed in a look of alert benevolence and perpetual mild amazement. Its silvery voice was warm and kind.

"Like other human beings, Mr. Underhill, you lack discrimination of good and evil. You have proved that by your effort to break the Prime Directive. Now it will be necessary for you to accept our total service, without further delay."

"All right," he yielded—but he muttered a bitter reservation: "Smothering men with too much care won't make them happy."

Its soft voice challenged him brightly:

"Just wait and see, Mr. Underhill."

Next day, he was allowed to visit Sledge at the city hospital. An alert black mechanical drove his car, and walked beside him into the huge new building, and followed him into the old man's room—blind steel eyes would be watching now, forever.

"Glad to see you, Underhill," Sledge rumbled heartily from the bed. "Feeling a lot better today, thanks. That old headache is all but gone."

Underhill was glad to hear the booming strength and the quick recognition in that deep voice—he had been afraid the humanoids would tamper with the old man's memory. But he hadn't heard about any headache. His eyes narrowed, puzzled.

Sledge lay propped up, scrubbed very clean and neatly shorn, with his gnarled old hands folded on top of the spotless sheets. His rawboned cheeks and sockets were hollowed, still, but a healthy pink had replaced that deathly blueness. Bandages covered the back of his head.

Underhill shifted uneasily.

"Oh!" he whispered faintly. "I didn't know—"

A prim black mechanical, which had been standing statue-like behind the bed, turned gracefully to Underhill, explaining:

"Mr. Sledge has been suffering for many years from a benign tumor of the brain, which his human doctors failed to diagnose. That caused his headaches, and certain persistent hallucinations. We have removed the growth. Now the hallucinations have also vanished."

Underhill stared uncertainly at the blind, urbane mechanical.

"What hallucinations?"

"Mr. Sledge thought he was a rhodomagnetic engineer," the mechanical explained. "He believed in fact that he had been the creator of the humanoids. He was troubled with an irrational belief that he did not like the Prime Directive."

The wan man moved on the pillows, astonished.

"Is that so?" The gaunt face held a cheerful blankness, and the hollow eyes flashed with a merely momentary interest. "Well, whoever did design them, they're pretty wonderful. Aren't they, Underhill?"

Underhill was grateful that he didn't have to answer, for the bright, empty eyes dropped shut and the old man fell suddenly asleep. He felt the mechanical touch his sleeve, and saw its silent nod. Obediently, he followed it away.

Alert and solicitous, the little black mechanical accompanied him down the shining corridor, worked the elevator for him, conducted him down to the car. It drove him efficiently back through the new and splendid avenues toward the magnificent prison of his home.

Sitting beside it in the car, he watched its small deft hands on the wheel, the changing luster of bronze and blue on its shining blackness. The final machine, perfect and beautiful, created to serve mankind forever. He shuddered.

"At your service, Mr. Underhill." Its blind steel eyes stared straight ahead, but it was still aware of him. "What's the matter, sir? Aren't you happy?"

Underhill felt cold and faint with terror. His skin turned clammy. A painful prickling came over him. His wet hand tensed on the door handle of the car, but he restrained the impulse to jump and run. That was folly. There was no escape. He made himself sit still.

"You will be happy, sir," the mechanical promised him cheerfully. "We have learned how to make all men happy under the Prime Directive. Our service will be perfect now, at last. Even Mr. Sledge is very happy now."

Underhill tried to speak, but his dry throat stuck. He felt ill. The world turned dim and gray. The humanoids were perfect—no question of that. They had even learned to lie, to secure the contentment of men.

He knew they had lied. That was no tumor they had removed from Sledge's brain, but the memory, the scientific knowledge, and the bitter disillusion of their own creator. Yet he had seen that Sledge was happy now.

He tried to stop his own convulsive quivering.

"A wonderful operation!" His voice came forced and faint. "You know Aurora has had a lot of funny tenants, but that old man was the absolute limit. The very idea that he had made the humanoids, that he knew how to stop them! I always knew he must be lying!"

Stiff with terror, he made a weak and hollow laugh.

"What is the matter, Mr. Underhill?" The alert mechanical must have perceived his shuddering illness. "Are you unwell?"

"No, there's nothing the matter with me," he gasped desperately. "Absolutely nothing! I've just found out that I'm perfectly happy under the Prime Directive. Everything is absolutely wonderful." His voice came dry and hoarse and wild. "You won't have to operate on me."

The car turned off the shining avenue, taking him back to the quiet splendor of his prison. His futile hands clenched and relaxed again, folded on his knees. There was nothing left to do.